KU-199-187

READER'S DIGEST

CONDENSED BOOKS

FIRST EDITION

Published by
THE READER'S DIGEST ASSOCIATION LIMITED
25 Berkeley Square, London W1X 6AB

THE READER'S DIGEST ASSOCIATION SOUTH AFRICA (PTY) LTD.
Nedbank Centre, Strand Street, Cape Town

Typeset in 10 on 12 pt. Highland Lumitype Roman
and printed in Great Britain by Petty & Sons Ltd., of Leeds

Original cover design by Jeffery Matthews A. R. C. A.

For information as to ownership
of copyright in the material in this book see last page

ISBN 0 340 17182 0

READER'S DIGEST CONDENSED BOOKS

FLIGHT INTO DANGER
Arthur Hailey and John Castle

HALIC: THE STORY OF A GREY SEAL
Ewan Clarkson

GREEN DARKNESS
Anya Seton

THE STRANGE FATE OF THE MORRO CASTLE
Gordon Thomas and Max Morgan-Witts

A DAY NO PIGS WOULD DIE
Robert Newton Peck

COLLECTOR'S LIBRARY EDITION

In this volume

FLIGHT INTO DANGER
by Arthur Hailey and John Castle (p.11)

No man knows for certain just how much courage and resourcefulness he is capable of. When George Spencer, salesman, first embarked on an ordinary charter flight from Winnipeg to Vancouver he certainly had no reason to ask such a question of himself. Nobody could be expected to foresee the combination of circumstances that would impel him into a situation perilous beyond his worst nightmares . . . .

Flight into Danger represents Arthur Hailey at his most exciting and authentic. It is the earliest, least-known, yet possibly the best of all his novels.

HALIC: THE STORY OF A GREY SEAL
by Ewan Clarkson (p.109)

Halic was born on a rugged island off the northwest coast of Wales. Separated from his mother at a few weeks old, he learned alone where to find food and how to avoid both his natural enemies and man's fouling of his wide ocean world. His story is not only a timely reminder of the dangers of pollution; it is also the fascinating story of a remarkable animal who must quickly grow wise in the ways of the deep or perish.

GREEN DARKNESS
by Anya Seton (p.165)

Anya Seton is well-loved for her precise and enthralling evocations of times past. Here she tells an eerie tale of illicit love, and the penalties exacted from the lovers through the ruthless machinations of Tudor religious bigotry. Their fate leaves ghostly echoes down the centuries even to the present day, imperilling the happiness of people at first sight uninvolved and innocent.

THE STRANGE FATE OF THE MORRO CASTLE
by Gordon Thomas and Max Morgan-Witts (p.361)

The machinery of fire-fighting at sea is complex and efficient. When, therefore, fire broke out in the luxury cruise liner *Morro Castle* in September, 1934, there should have been safe, orderly procedures and few casualties. Yet 134 people from the *Morro Castle* lost their lives. While the captain lay dead in his cabin, possibly murdered, and in the radio office sat a man with a dangerous criminal record . . . .

A DAY NO PIGS WOULD DIE
by Robert Newton Peck (p.473)

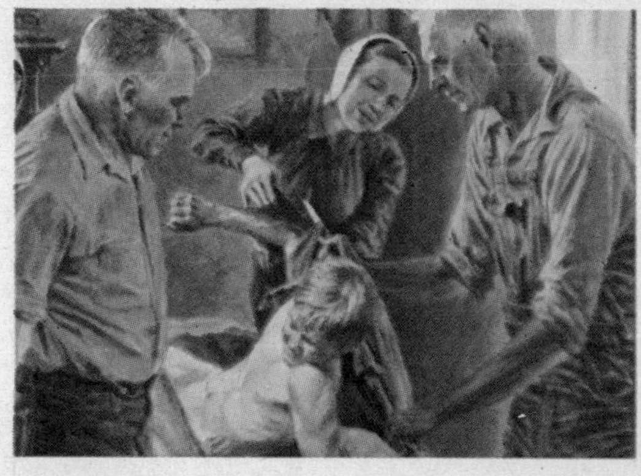

Wealth need not only mean cash in the bank. The poorest folk may be rich in family love. This is a tender childhood story of simple rural life. A boy had duties then, and responsibilities, and joys also. Robert Newton Peck tells of these, and of his journey into manhood, with wit and gentle truthfulness.

FLIGHT INTO DANGER
Arthur Hailey and John Castle

Title page illustration: Christopher Foss

Flight into Danger

A CONDENSATION OF THE BOOK BY

Arthur Hailey & John Castle

Published by Souvenir Press, London

Suddenly, four miles above the earth, the lives of everybody on board the airliner were placed in the hands of three courageous, frightened people:

DOCTOR BAIRD: *"I know nothing about flying. All I know is this. There are people on this plane who will die within a few hours . . ."*

STEWARDESS JANET BENSON: *"I know they use that to talk to the ground, but I don't know which switches you have to set."*

SALESMAN GEORGE SPENCER: *"My name is Spencer. I am a passenger on this airplane. Correction: I was a passenger. I am now the pilot."*

ONE

STEADY RAIN slanting through the harsh glare of its headlights, the taxi swung into the approach to Winnipeg Airport and, braking hard, came to a spring-shuddering stop outside the reception building. Its one passenger leaped out, tossed a couple of dollar bills to the driver, seized an overnight bag and hurried to the swing doors.

Inside, he turned down the collar of his damp topcoat, glanced at the wall clock, then half-ran to the departure desk of Cross-Canada Airlines, deserted now except for a passenger agent checking through a manifest. As the man reached him the agent picked up a small stand microphone on the desk and with measured precision began to speak.

"Flight 98. Flight 98. Direct fleetliner service to Vancouver, with connections for Victoria, Seattle, and Honolulu, will be leaving immediately. All passengers for Flight 98 are asked to proceed to gate four, please."

A group of people rose from the lounge seats and made their way thankfully across the hall. The man in the topcoat opened his mouth to speak but was elbowed aside by an elderly woman. "Young man," she demanded, "is Flight 63 from Montreal in yet?"

"No, madam," said the passenger agent smoothly. "It's running approximately thirty-seven minutes late."

"Oh, dear. I've arranged for my niece to be—"

"Look," said the man in the topcoat urgently, "have you got a seat on Flight 98 for Vancouver?"

The passenger agent shook his head. "Sorry, sir. Not one. With the big game on in Vancouver tomorrow things are chock-full. I doubt if you'll be able to get out of here before tomorrow afternoon."

The man swore softly and dropped his bag to the floor. "Of all the lousy deals. I've got to be in Vancouver by tomorrow noon at the latest."

"Don't be so rude," snapped the anxious old woman. "I was talking. Now, young man, my niece is bringing—"

"Just a moment, madam," cut in the passenger agent. He leaned across the desk and tapped the sleeve of the man with his pencil. "Look, I'm not supposed to tell you this—"

"Well, really!" exploded the old lady.

"But there's a charter flight in from Toronto on its way to the football game. They were a few seats light when they came in. Perhaps you could grab one."

"That's great," exclaimed the man in the topcoat, picking up his bag again. "Where do I ask?"

The agent pointed across the hall. "Right over there. The Maple Leaf Air Charter. But mind, I didn't say a thing."

"This is scandalous!" stormed the old lady. "My niece—"

"Thanks a lot," said the man. He walked briskly over to the charter company desk. The agent there looked up, pencil poised, as the man arrived. "Sir?"

"Have you by any chance a seat on a flight to Vancouver?"

"Vancouver." The pencil checked rapidly down a list. "Yes; just one. Flight's leaving straight away, though."

"That's fine. Can I have that seat, please?"

The agent reached for a ticket book. "Name, sir?"

"George Spencer." It was entered quickly, with the flight details.

"That's sixty-five dollars for the one-way trip, sir. Thank you, glad to be of service. Any bags, sir?"

"Only one. I'll keep it with me."

"Here you are, sir. The ticket is your boarding pass. Go to gate three and ask for Flight 714."

Spencer nodded, turned to give a thumbs-up to the Cross-Canada desk, where the agent grinned in acknowledgment over the old lady's shoulder, and hurried to the departure gate. Outside, as with any busy airport after dark, all seemed to be in confusion but in fact was strictly regulated. A commissionaire directed him across the floodlit apron to a waiting aircraft, a silver dart gleaming in the light of the overhead arc lamps. Already men were preparing to disengage the passenger ramp. Bounding across puddles, Spencer reached them, handed over the detachable half of his ticket, and ran lightly up the steps. He ducked into the aircraft and stood there fighting to regain his breath. He was joined by a stewardess who smiled and made fast the door. As she did, he felt the motors start.

"Out of condition, I guess," he said apologetically.

"Good evening, sir. Pleased to have you aboard. There's a seat for'ard."

Spencer walked to the vacant seat and with some difficulty bundled his coat into an empty spot on the luggage rack, remarking to the neighbouring passenger, "They never seem to make these things big enough." He disposed of his bag under the seat and sank gratefully down on the soft cushions.

"Good evening," came the stewardess's voice over the public address system. "The Maple Leaf Air Charter Company welcomes its new passengers to Flight 714. We hope you will enjoy your flight. Please fasten your seat belts and observe the 'No Smoking' sign. We shall be taking off in a few moments."

As Spencer fumbled with his catch, the man next to him grunted, "That's a pretty sobering sentence," and nodded down to a small notice on the back of the seat in front reading *Your lifebelt is under the seat.*

Spencer laughed. "*I'd* certainly have been sunk if I hadn't caught this bus," he said.

"Oh? Pretty keen fan, eh?"

"Er—no," Spencer said. "I hadn't given the game a thought. I hate to admit it but I'm rushing off to Vancouver to keep a business appointment."

His companion lowered his voice conspiratorially. "I shouldn't say that too loudly. This plane is crammed with fans who are going to Vancouver to root like hell for their boys and to roar damnation at the enemy. They're quite likely to do you harm if you use such a light tone about it."

Spencer chuckled again and leaned out from his seat to look round the crowded cabin. There was evidence in plenty of a noisy but good-natured party of football fans travelling with the one objective of triumphing with their team. To Spencer's immediate right sat a man and his wife, their noses buried in sports magazines. Behind them, four supporters were pouring rye into paper cups and arguing the respective merits of various players; a snatch of their conversation came over to him. "*Haggerty?* Don't give me that. He's not in the same league as the Thunderbolt. Now *there's* a man. . . ." Behind the slightly alcoholic foursome were other team supporters, mostly big, red-faced men, wearing team favours.

Spencer turned to the man beside him. Trained to observe detail, he noted the quiet suit, of good cut but well-crumpled, the lined face and greying hair, the indefinable impression of confidence and authority. Behind him the blue lights of the perimeter track had begun to slide past.

Spencer said conversationally, "I'm on my way to the coast on a sales trip, and a mighty important one."

His companion showed polite interest. "What do you sell?"

"Trucks. The local salesmen don't like me too well because they say I'm the sharpshooter from head office with the special prices. I get called for when a deal involves maybe thirty to a hundred trucks. Selling has its little problems, all right. Still, it's a reasonable living."

Spencer stretched his legs in front of him. "Man, I'm tired. It's been one of those days. First this Winnipeg guy decides he likes a competitor's trucks better than ours. Then, when I've sold him after all and figure I can close the order over supper tonight and be back with my wife and kids tomorrow night, I get a wire telling me to be in Vancouver by lunchtime tomorrow because a big contract is going off the rails there—and fast." Spencer sighed, then said in mock earnestness, "Hey, if you want forty or fifty trucks today I can give you a good discount."

The man beside him laughed. "Sorry, no. They're a bit outside my usual line of work. I'm a doctor. I couldn't afford to buy one truck, let alone forty. Football is the only extravagance I can allow myself. Hence my trip tonight."

Leaning back in his seat, Spencer said, "Glad to have you around, Doctor. If I can't sleep you can prescribe me a sedative."

As he spoke the engines thundered to full power, the whole aircraft vibrating as it strained against the wheel brakes. The doctor put his mouth to Spencer's ear and bellowed, "A sedative would be no good in this racket. I never could understand why they have to make all this noise before take-off."

Spencer nodded, then, when the roar had subsided sufficiently for him to make himself heard without much trouble, he said, "The run-up for the engines is always done before the plane starts its take-off. Each engine has two magnetos, in case one packs in during flight, and in the run-up each of the mags is tested separately. When the pilot has satisfied himself that they are running O.K. he takes off. Airlines have to be fussy, thank goodness."

"You sound as though you knew a lot about it."

"Not really. I flew fighters in the war but I'm rusty now."

The engine roar took on a deeper note and a powerful thrust in the backs of their seats told them the aircraft was gathering speed; almost immediately a slight lurch indicated that they were airborne and the engines settled back to a steady hum. Still climbing, the aircraft banked steeply.

"You may unfasten your seat belts," announced the public address system. "Smoke if you wish."

"Never sorry when that bit's over." The doctor released his belt and accepted a cigarette. "Thanks. By the way, I'm Bruno Baird."

"Glad to know you, Doc. I'm George Spencer of the Fulbright Motor Company."

The two men lapsed into silence. Spencer's thoughts were sombre: he had decided there would have to be a showdown when he got back to head office. Although he had explained the position on the telephone to the local Winnipeg salesman, that order would take some holding onto now. It would have to be a big show in Vancouver to justify this mix-up. It might be a good idea to use this as a lever for a pay rise when he got back. Or better yet, promotion. If he were a manager in the dealer sales division, Mary and he, Bobsie and little Kit, could move up to Parkway Heights. Or pay off the bills—the new boiler, instalments on the car and the hospital charges for Mary's last pregnancy.

Dr. Baird found himself thinking about the small-town surgery he had abandoned for a couple of days. I wonder how Lewis Evans will cope, he thought. Doris would keep him on the right track. Doctors' wives were wonderful like that. Had to be. That was a thing Lewis would have to learn in time: to find the right woman.

The couple in the seats across the aisle were still engrossed in their sports papers. The four fans in the seats behind were starting their third round of rye. Three were of the usual type: beefy, argumentative, out to enjoy themselves, with all the customary restraints cast aside for two memorable days. But the fourth was a short, lean-featured man of lugubrious expression who spoke with a Lancashire accent and rejoiced in the nickname of 'Otpot. "'Ere's t'Lions t'morrer," he called, raising his paper cup. His friends acknowledged the toast solemnly. One of them, his coat lapel displaying a badge which appeared to depict a mangy alley cat in rampant mood but presumably represented the king of beasts himself, remarked, "Never thought we'd make it. Not after having to wait in Toronto with all that fog around. Still, we're only a few hours late and we can always sleep on the plane."

"Not before we eat, though, I hope," said one of the others. "When do they bring round the grub?"

"Should be along soon, I reckon. Everything's been put behind with that delay."

"Never mind. 'Ave a drink while you wait," suggested 'Otpot.

The rest of the fifty-six passengers were reading or talking, all glad to be on the last leg of their journey.

The twinkling blue and yellow lights of the last suburbs of Winnipeg could be seen from the port windows before they were swallowed in cloud as Stewardess Janet Benson prepared for a dinner that should have been served over two hours ago. The mirror over the glassware cabinet reflected the swing of her blond hair from beneath her airline cap and the movements of her trim body as she busied herself efficiently about the galley. Taking napkins and cutlery from the built-in cupboards, Janet hummed contentedly to herself. Waitressing was the least attractive part of a stewardess's duties, and she knew she was in for an exhausting hour, catering to a plane-load of hungry people, but she was filled with the exhilaration she always felt at the beginning of a flight. At twenty-one, Janet was just tasting life and finding it good.

On the flight deck, the only sound was the steady drone of the engines. Both pilots sat still except for an occasional leg or arm movement, their faces faintly illuminated in the glow of light from the myriad dials on the instrument panels. From their headsets came the crackle of conversation between another aircraft and the ground. Round their necks hung small boom microphones.

Captain "Dun" Dunning stretched himself in his seat and blew through the luxuriant growth of his moustache in a mannerism that his crew knew well. He looked older than his thirty-one years. "How are the cylinder-head temperatures on number three engine, Pete?" he asked, his eyes flickering to the first officer.

Pete stirred and glanced at the panel.

"O.K. now, Skip. I had it checked at Winnipeg."

"Good." Dun peered ahead. A thin moon shone bleakly down. Shredded wisps of cotton wool clouds lazily approached, suddenly to whisk by; or occasionally the ship would plunge into a tumble of grey-white cloud. "With a bit of luck it'll be a clear run through," he commented. "The weather report was reasonable for a change. Not often you keep to the original flight plan on this joyride."

"You said it," agreed the first officer. "Come winter, it'll be a very different story."

The aircraft began to bump and roll a little as she hit a succession of thermal currents and for a few minutes the captain concentrated on correcting her trim. Then he remarked, "Are you planning to take in this game in Vancouver?"

Pete hesitated before answering. "I don't know yet," he answered. "I'll see how it works out."

The captain looked sharply at him.

"If you've got your eyes on Janet, you can take them off again.

She's too young to come under the corrupting influence of a Casanova like you."

Few people looked less deserving of this description than the fresh-faced, thoughtful-eyed first officer, still in his twenties. "Go easy, Skipper," he protested, colouring. "I never corrupted anyone in my life."

"Well, don't aim to start with Janet." The captain grinned. "Half the airline personnel of Canada have tried to. Don't make life hard for yourself."

Twelve feet away from them, on the other side of a sliding door, the subject of their conversation was collecting orders for the evening meal, offering a choice between lamb chops or grilled salmon.

George Spencer and Dr. Baird both chose the lamb chops, but many others ordered fish.

Back in the galley, Janet spent the next half-hour preparing and serving meals. When everyone who felt like eating had been served with a main course, she picked up the telephone in the galley and pressed the intercom buzzer.

"Flight deck," came Pete's voice.

"I'm finally serving dinner," said Janet. "What'll it be—lamb chop or grilled salmon?"

"Hold it." She could hear him putting the question to Dunning. "Janet, the skipper says he'll have the lamb—no, he's changed his mind. Is the fish good?"

"Looks O.K. to me," said Janet. "Had no complaints."

"Skipper will take salmon, then. Better make it two. Big helpings, mind. We're growing boys."

"All right—double portions as usual. Two fish coming up."

She quickly arranged two trays and took them forward, balancing them with practised ease. Pete opened the sliding door for her and relieved her of one tray. The captain had completed his switchover to automatic pilot and was now halfway through his routine radio check with Control at Winnipeg.

"Height 16,000," he continued, speaking into the tiny microphone held before his mouth on a slender plastic arm. "Course 285 true. Airspeed 210 knots. Ground speed 174 knots. ETA Vancouver 0505 Pacific Standard. Over."

He switched from transmit to receive and there was a clearly audible crackle from his headset as the acknowledgment came on the air. "Flight 714. This is Winnipeg Control. Roger. Out."

Dun reached for his log sheet, made an entry, then slid his seat back so that he was well clear of the controls but within easy reach if it were necessary for him to take them over again quickly. Pete was starting to eat, a tray resting on his knees.

"Shan't be long, Skip," he said.

"There's no hurry," replied Dun. "I can wait. How is the fish?"

"Not bad," mumbled the first officer, his mouth full. "If there were about four times as much it might be a square meal."

The captain chuckled. "You'd better watch that waistline, Pete." He turned to the stewardess, who was waiting behind the seat. "How are the football fans, Janet?"

Janet shrugged. "Very quiet now. Four of them have been knocking back rye pretty steadily, but there's been no need to speak to them about it. It'll help to keep them quiet. It looks like being a peaceful, easy night—fingers crossed."

Pete raised a quizzical eyebrow. "Uh-huh, young woman. That's the kind of night to watch. I'll bet someone's getting ready to be sick right now."

"Not yet," said Janet lightly. "But you warn me when *you're* going to fly the ship and I'll get the bags ready."

"I'm glad you found out about him," said the captain.

"How's the weather?" asked Janet.

"Let's see. General fog east of the mountains, extending nearly as far as Manitoba. There's nothing to bother us up there, though. It should be a smooth ride all the way to the coast."

"Good. Well, keep Junior here off the controls while I serve coffee, won't you?"

She slipped away before Pete could retort, made her way through the passenger deck taking orders for coffee, and then brought a tray to the pilots. Dun had eaten his dinner, and now drained his coffee with satisfaction. Pete had taken the controls and was intent on the instrument dials as the captain got to his feet.

"Keep her steaming, Pete. I'll just tuck the customers up for the night."

Pete nodded without turning round. "Right, Skipper."

The captain followed Janet out into the passenger section and stopped first at the seats occupied by Spencer and Baird. "Good evening. Everything all right?"

Baird looked up. "Very nice meal. We were ready for it."

"Yes, I'm sorry it was so late."

The doctor waved aside his apology. "You can hardly be blamed if Toronto decides to have a bit of fog." He settled himself back in his seat, "I'm going to get my head down for a doze."

"That goes for me as well." Spencer yawned.

"I hope you have a comfortable night," said Dun. "The stewardess will bring you some rugs." He passed on down the aisle, saying a few words to each of the passengers, describing the flight's future progress and expected weather conditions.

"Well, it's me for dreamland," said Spencer. "One thing, Doctor, at least you won't be getting any calls tonight."

"How long is it?" murmured Baird drowsily, his eyes closed. "A good five hours anyway. Better make the most of it. 'Night."

Now blanketed off by thick cloud into a cold, remote world of her own, the aircraft droned steadily on her course. Sixteen thousand feet beneath her lay the silent prairies of Saskatchewan.

When Dun reached the whisky-drinking quartet, he politely forbade any further consumption of liquor that night. "You know," he told them with a reproving grin, "this sort of thing isn't permitted. Don't let me see any more bottles or you'll have to get out and walk."

"Any objection to cards?" inquired one of the party.

"None at all, if you don't disturb the other passengers."

"Pity the poor captain," said the man from Lancashire. "What's it like—taking a massive job like this through t'night?"

"Routine," said Dun. "Just plain, dull routine."

"Comes to that, every flight is just routine, I s'pose?"

"Well, yes. I guess that's so."

"Until summat happens—eh?"

There was an outburst of chuckles in which Dunning joined before moving on. Only 'Otpot, through the haze of his evening's drinking, looked thoughtful at his own words.

TWO

THE CAPTAIN had almost completed his rounds and was enjoying a few moments' chaffing with a little man who appeared to have travelled with him before. "I know it looks a bit like R.C.A.F.," Dun was saying, fingering his great bush of a moustache apologetically, "but I've had it so long I couldn't part with it now."

"I'll bet it's a wow with the girls," said the little man.

The captain moved on. While he had been speaking his eyes had been fixed on the stewardess, farther along the aisle, who was bending over a woman, the palm of her hand on the passenger's forehead. As he approached, the woman, who slumped rather than sat in her seat, suddenly grimaced. The captain touched the stewardess on the arm.

"Anything wrong, Miss Benson?"

Janet straightened. "The lady is feeling a little under the weather, Captain," she said. "I'll get her some aspirin."

Dun took her place and leaned over the woman and the man beside her. "Sorry to hear that," he said sympathetically. "What seems to be the trouble?"

The woman stared up at him. "I-I don't know," she said in a small voice. "It seemed to hit me all of a sudden. I feel sick and dizzy and—and there's an awful pain . . . down here." She indicated her stomach. "I'm sorry to be a nuisance—I—"

"Now, honey," murmured her companion. "Just lie quietly." He glanced at the captain. "A touch of airsickness, I guess?"

"I expect so, sir," answered Dun. He looked down thoughtfully at the woman, taking in the perspiration beginning to bead on her pallid forehead, the whiteness of her knuckles as she gripped the armrest of the seat. "I'm sorry you don't feel well," he said gently. "Try to relax as much as you can. If it's any comfort, I can tell you that it looks like being a calm trip." He moved aside for Janet.

"Now here we are," said the stewardess, handing down the pills. "Try these." She eased the woman's head forward, to help her take a few sips of water from a glass. "Now let's make you a little more comfortable." She tucked a rug round the woman. "How's that?"

The woman nodded gratefully. "I'll be back in a few minutes to see how you're feeling. And if you need me quickly, just press the bell by the window."

"Thank you, miss," said the husband. "We'll be O.K. in a little while." He looked at his wife with a smile, as if to reassure himself. "Try to rest, dear. It'll pass over."

"I hope so," said Dun. "I know how unpleasant these things can be. I hope you soon feel better, madam."

He passed back down the aisle and waited for Janet in the galley. "Who are they?" he asked when she returned.

"Mr. and Mrs. John Childer. She was all right fifteen minutes ago."

"Let me know if she gets any worse and I'll radio ahead. I don't like the look of her. Could be airsickness or just a bilious attack, I suppose—but it seems to have hit her pretty hard." The captain looked worried. "Have we a doctor on board?"

"No one who's listed as a doctor," replied Janet, "but I could ask around."

Dun shook his head. "Don't disturb them. Most of them are getting down to sleep. Let me know how she is in half an hour. The trouble is," he added as he turned to go, "we've got over four hours' flying before we reach the coast."

Making his way to the flight deck, he stopped for a moment to smile down at the sick woman. She attempted to smile back, but a sudden stab of pain closed her eyes and made her arch back against the seat. For a few seconds Dun stood studying her. Then he continued forward, closed the door of the flight deck behind him, and slid into his seat. He put on his headset and then the boom microphone.

Pete was flying manually. Scattered banks of cloud seemed to rush at the forward windows, envelop them momentarily, and then disappear. "Cumulo-nimbus building up," he commented.

"Rough stuff," Dun said. "I'll take it. We'd better try to climb on top. Ask for 20,000, will you?"

"Right." Pete depressed a stud on his microphone attachment. "This is 714 to Regina," he called.

"Go ahead, 714," crackled a voice.

"We're running into some weather. We'd like clearance for 20,000 feet."

"Stand by 714. I'll ask ATC."

The captain peered into the cloudy turbulence ahead. "Better switch on the seat-belt sign, Pete."

"O.K." Pete reached for the switch on the overhead panel. There was a brief shudder as the plane freed herself from a wall of cloud, only to plunge almost instantly into another.

"Flight 714," came the voice on the radio. "ATC gives clearance for 20,000. Over."

"714," acknowledged Pete. "Thanks and out."

"Let's go," said the captain. The note of the engines took on a deeper intensity as the deck began to tilt and the altimeter needle registered a climb of 500 feet a minute. The window wiper swished rhythmically.

"Shan't be sorry when we're clear of this muck," remarked Pete.

Dun didn't answer, his eyes on the dials in front of him. Neither of the pilots heard the stewardess enter.

"Captain," she said urgently, but keeping her voice well under control. "That woman's worse, and I have another passenger sick now—one of the men."

Dun stretched up an arm and switched on the landing lights. Ahead of them the sharp beams cut into driving rain and snow. He turned off the lights and began to adjust engine and de-icer switches. "I can't come right now, Janet. You'd better see if you can find a doctor. And make sure all the seat belts are fastened. This may get pretty rough. I'll come as soon as I can."

"Yes, Captain."

Emerging from the flight deck, Janet called out in a voice just loud enough to carry to the rows of passengers, "Fasten your seat belts, please. It may be getting a little bumpy." She leaned over the first two passengers to her right. They blinked up at her, half-asleep. "Excuse me," she said casually, "but do either of you gentlemen happen to be a doctor?"

The man nearest her shook his head. "Sorry, no," he grunted. "Is there something wrong?"

"No, nothing serious."

An exclamation of pain snapped her to attention. She hurried along the aisle to where Mrs. Childer lay half-cradled in her husband's arms, with eyes closed, and partially doubled over. Janet knelt down and wiped the sweat from the woman's brow. Childer's face was creased with anxiety.

"What can we do, miss?" he asked her. "What d'you think it is?"

"Keep her warm," said Janet. "I'm going to see if there's a doctor on board. I'll be back straight away."

Janet looked down briefly at the suffering woman and moved on to the next seats, repeating her question in a low voice.

"Is someone ill?" she was asked.

"Just feeling unwell. It sometimes happens, flying."

A hand clutched at her arm. It was one of the whisky quartet, his face yellow and shining.

"Sorry, miss, to trouble you again. I'm feeling like hell. D'you think I could have a glass of water?"

"Yes, of course. I'll get it right away."

"It's my insides," said the sick man. "Feels like they're coming apart." His hands clenched his stomach.

Janet shook Spencer gently by the shoulder. He opened one eye, then both. "I'm very sorry to wake you up, sir," she said, "but is anyone here a doctor?"

Spencer gathered himself. "A doctor? Yes, this gentleman beside me is a doctor."

"Oh, thank goodness," breathed the stewardess. "Would you wake him, please?"

"Sure." Spencer looked up at her as he nudged the recumbent form next to him. "Someone ill? Come on, Doc, wake up." The doctor shook his head and grunted.

"Are you a doctor, sir?" asked Janet anxiously.

He snapped awake. "Yes, I'm Dr. Baird. What's wrong?"

"We have two passengers who are quite sick. Would you take a look at them, please?"

"Yes, certainly." Spencer stood up to let the doctor out.

"I think you'd better see the woman first, Doctor," said Janet, leading the way and calling out quietly, "Fasten your seat belts, please," as she passed along.

Shivers of pain racked Mrs. Childer's body, she breathed heavily, with long, shuddering gasps. Her hair was wet with sweat. Baird knelt and took her wrist.

"This gentleman is a doctor," said Janet.

"Am I glad to see you, Doctor," Childer said fervently.

The woman opened her eyes. "Doctor...."

"Just relax," said Baird, his eyes on his watch. He released her wrist, felt in his jacket and took out a small pocket torch. "Open your eyes wide," he ordered gently and examined each eye in the bright pencil of light. "Any pain?" The woman nodded. "Where? Here? Or here?" As he palpated her abdomen, she stiffened suddenly, choking back a cry. He felt her forehead, then stood up. "Has this lady complained of anything in addition to the pain?"

"My wife's been very sick, throwing up everything." Childer looked helplessly at Janet. "It's all come on so suddenly."

Baird nodded reflectively. He moved away, taking Janet by the arm and speaking very quietly so as not to be overheard by the nearby passengers.

"Have you given her anything?" he inquired.

"Only aspirin and water," replied Janet. "That reminds me. I promised a glass of water to the man who's sick—"

"Wait," said Baird. His sleepiness had vanished. "Where did you learn your nursing?"

Janet coloured at his tone. "Why, at the airline training school."

"Well, it's no use giving aspirin to anyone who is actually vomiting—you'll make 'em worse. Water only."

"I—I'm sorry, Doctor," Janet stammered.

"I think you'd better go to the captain," he said. "Tell him we should land at once. This woman has to be taken to hospital. Ask to have an ambulance waiting."

"Very well, Doctor. While I'm gone, will you take a look at another sick passenger? He's complaining of the same sickness and pains."

Baird looked at her sharply. "Where is he?"

Janet led him forward to where the sick man sat, bent over, retching. Baird crouched down. "I'm a doctor. Will you put your head back, please?" As he made a quick examination, he asked, "What have you had to eat in the last twenty-four hours?"

"Just the usual things," muttered the man, all the strength appearing to have been drained from him. "Breakfast," he said weakly, "bacon and eggs . . . salad for lunch . . . a sandwich at the airport . . . then dinner here." A trickle of saliva ran disregarded down his chin. "It's this pain, Doctor. And my eyes. Can't seem to focus. I keep seeing double."

His companion seemed to find it amusing. "That rye has got a real kick, yes sir!" he exclaimed.

"Be quiet," said Baird. He rose, to find Janet and the captain standing beside him. "Keep him warm—get more blankets round him," he told Janet. The captain motioned him down to the galley. Immediately they were alone, Baird demanded, "How quickly can we land, Captain?"

"That's the trouble," said Dun briefly. "We can't."

Baird stared at him. "Why?"

"It's the weather. I've just checked by radio. There's low cloud and fog right over the prairies. Calgary's shut in completely. We'll have to go through to the coast."

"What about turning back?" Baird asked.

Dun shook his head, his face taut. "That's out, too. Winnipeg closed down with fog shortly after we left. Anyway, it'll be quicker now to go on."

Baird grimaced. "How soon do you expect to land?"

"About five a.m., Pacific Time." Dun saw the doctor glance at his wrist watch, and added, "Three and a half hours from now."

"Then I'll have to do what I can for these people until we arrive at Vancouver. I'll need my bag. Do you think it can be reached? I checked it at Toronto."

"We can try," said the captain. "Let me have your tags."

Baird's long fingers dug into his hip pocket and came out with his wallet. He took out two baggage tickets and handed them to Dun. "There are two bags, Captain," he said. "It's the smaller one I want."

He had barely finished speaking before a violent lurch sent the two men sprawling to the far wall. There was a loud, persistent buzzing. The captain was on his feet first and sprang to the intercom telephone. "Captain here," he rapped out. "What's wrong, Pete?"

The voice of the first officer was struggling and painful. "I'm . . . sick . . . come quickly."

"You'd better come with me," said Dun to the doctor and they hurried out of the galley. As they burst into the flight deck, it was only too apparent that the first officer was very sick: he was slumped in his seat, his face streaming perspiration.

"Get him out of there," directed the captain urgently. Baird and Janet, who had followed the men in, lifted Pete out while Dun slipped into his own seat and took the control column in his hands. "There's a seat at the back of the flight deck, for when we carry a radio operator," he told them. "Put him there."

Pete vomited as they helped him to the vacant seat. Baird loosened his collar and tie and tried to make him comfortable.

"Doctor," called Dun. "What's happening?"

"I'm not sure," said Baird grimly. "But there's a common denominator to these attacks. The most likely thing is food. What did he have for dinner?"

"The first officer had fish." Janet's face began to register alarm. "Fish," she almost whispered.

"Do you remember what the two passengers had?"

"No—I don't think so—"

"Find out, will you, please?"

The stewardess hurried out, her face pale. Baird knelt beside the first officer. "Try to relax," he said quietly. "I'll give you something in a few minutes that'll help the pain. Here." He reached up and pulled down a blanket from a rack. "You'll feel better if you stay warm."

Pete opened his eyes a little and ran his tongue over dry lips. "Are you a doctor?" he asked. Baird nodded. Pete said with a sheepish attempt to smile, "I'm sorry about this. I thought I was going to pass out."

"Don't talk," said Baird. "Try to rest."

Janet returned. "Doctor," she spoke rapidly, hardly able to get the words out quickly enough. "Both passengers had salmon. There are three others complaining of pains now."

"I'll come, but I'll need that bag of mine."

Dun called over his shoulder, "Janet, take these tags and dig out the smaller of the doctor's two bags, will you?" Janet took the tags, and Dun continued, "I'm going to radio Vancouver and report what's happening. Is there anything you want me to add?"

"Yes," said Baird. "Say we have three serious cases of suspected food poisoning and that there seem to be others developing. We suspect that the poisoning could have been caused by fish served on board."

"I remember now," exclaimed Dun. "That food didn't come from our usual caterers. We had to get it from some other outfit because we were so late getting into Winnipeg."

"Doctor, *please*," Janet implored him. "I do wish you'd come and see Mrs. Childer. She seems to have collapsed altogether."

Baird stepped to the door. The lines in his face had deepened, but his eyes were steady as rock.

"See that the passengers are not alarmed," he instructed Janet. "We shall be depending on you a great deal. Now if you'll be good enough to find my bag and bring it to me, I'll attend to Mrs. Childer." He pushed back the door, then stopped her as something occurred to him. "By the way, what did *you* eat for dinner?"

"I had meat."

"Thank heavens for that." Janet smiled and made to go on again, but he gripped her suddenly by the arm. "I suppose the captain had meat, too?"

She looked up at him, as if trying both to remember and to grasp the implications of what he had asked. Then, suddenly, shock and realization flooded into her. She almost fell against him, her eyes dilated with an overpowering fear.

THREE

BRUNO BAIRD regarded the stewardess thoughtfully. Behind the calm reassurance of his blue-grey eyes his mind rapidly assessed the situation. He released the girl's arm.

"Well, we won't jump to conclusions," he said, almost to himself. Then, more briskly, "You find my bag—just as quickly as you can. I'll have another word with the captain."

He retraced his steps forward. They were now in level flight, above the turbulence. Over the pilot's shoulder he could see the cold white brilliance of the moon, converting the carpet of cloud below them into a seemingly limitless landscape of snow with here and there what looked like a pinnacle of ice thrusting through the surrounding billows. The effect was dreamlike.

"Captain," he said, leaning over the empty co-pilot's seat. Dun looked round, his face drawn and colourless in the moon's glow.

"Yes, Doctor. What is it?"

"I presume you ate after the other officer did?"

"Yes, that's so." Dun's eyes narrowed. "About half an hour later. Maybe a little more." The point of the doctor's question suddenly hit him, and he sat upright with a jerk. "Holy smoke, that's right. I had fish too. But I feel O.K."

"Good." Relief showed in Baird's voice. "As soon as I've got my bag I'll give you an emetic. You can't have digested it all yet. Anyway, not everyone who ate fish will be affected. You could be the one to avoid trouble."

"I'd better be," muttered Dun, staring now into the moonlight ahead.

"Is there any way of locking the controls of this airplane?"

"Why yes," said Dun. "There's the automatic pilot. But that wouldn't get us down—"

"I suggest you switch it on just in case. If you do feel ill, yell for me immediately."

The knuckles of Dun's hands gleamed white as he gripped the control column.

"O.K.," he said quietly. "What about Miss Benson, the stewardess?"

"She's all right. She had meat."

"Well, that's something—look, for heaven's sake hurry with that emetic. I can't take any chances, flying this ship."

"Miss Benson is hurrying. Are you absolutely certain that we've no other course but to go on to Vancouver?"

"Certain," answered Dun instantly. "I've checked and double-checked. Thick cloud and ground fog until the other side of the mountains. Calgary, Edmonton—all closed."

The doctor stepped back to leave, but Dun said, "Oh, Doctor . . . glad you're aboard."

Baird left without another word. Dun took a deep breath, experiencing not for the first time in his flying career acute apprehension and awareness of his responsibility for the safety of a huge aircraft and nearly sixty lives. He felt an icy premonition of disaster. In the space of half an hour a normal, routine flight had changed into a nightmare nearly four miles above the earth.

He pushed these thoughts from him in self-disgust, flicked the switches on the automatic pilot panel, waiting until the appropriate indicator light gleamed to show that the next stage of the switching over could be started. Ailerons first, needing a slight adjustment to bring them fully under electrical control; then rudder and elevators were nursed until all the four lights set into the top of the panel had ceased winking and settled down to a steady glow. Satisfied, he took his hands off the wheel and let the aircraft fly itself while he carried out a thorough cockpit check.

To an inexperienced eye, the flight deck would have presented a weird sight. Just as though two invisible men sat in the pilots' seats, the twin control columns moved slightly forward, backward, then forward again. Compensating for the air currents as they gently buffeted the aircraft, the rudder bar moved also.

His check completed, Dun reached for the microphone that hung beside his head, quickly clipped it to his neck and adjusted the padded earphones. Aggressively, he blew at his moustache, puffing it up so that it practically touched his nose. Well, he thought to himself, here goes.

"Hello, Vancouver Control. This is Maple Leaf Charter Flight 714. I have an emergency message. I have an emergency message."

His earphones crackled instantly: "Maple Leaf Charter Flight 714. Come in please."

"Vancouver Control. This is Flight 714. We have three serious cases of suspected food poisoning on board, including the first officer, and possibly others. When we land we shall want ambulances and medical help standing by. We're not sure but we think the poisoning may have been caused by the fish served at dinner. You'd better put a ban on all food coming from the same source. We understand that owing to our late arrival at Winnipeg the food was not supplied by the regular contractor. Is this understood?"

He listened to the acknowledgment, his eyes gazing bleakly at the frozen sea of cloud below and ahead. Vancouver Control sounded as crisp and impersonal as ever but he could guess at the burst of activity his words would have triggered off. Almost wearily, he ended the transmission and leaned back in his seat. He felt strangely heavy and tired, as if lead had begun to flow into his limbs. The instrument dials seemed to recede until they were far away. He was conscious of sweat on his forehead and he shivered in a sudden uncontrollable spasm. Then, angered at the perfidy of his body, he flung all his strength and concentration into re-checking their flight path, their estimated time of arrival, the expected winds over the mountains, the runway plan of Vancouver. . . .

Back in the body of the aircraft, Dr. Baird tucked fresh blankets round the limp form of Mrs. Childer. The woman lay back helplessly, her eyes closed, moaning quietly. The top of her dress was stained and damp. As Baird watched her she was seized with a fresh paroxysm. Her eyes did not open.

Baird spoke to her husband. "Keep her mopped up and as dry as you can. And warm. She must be warm."

Childer reached up and grabbed the doctor by the wrist. "She's pretty bad, isn't she?" His voice was shrill.

Baird looked again at the woman. Her breathing was rapid and shallow.

"Yes," he said, "she is."

"Well, can't you give her something?"

Baird shook his head. "She needs drugs we haven't got."

"But surely even some water—"

"No. She'd gag on it. Your wife is nearly unconscious, Childer. Hold it, now," Baird added hastily as the other man half-rose in alarm. "That's nature's own anaesthetic. Don't worry. She'll be all right. Your job is to watch her and keep her warm."

Baird moved to the next row of seats. A middle-aged man, collar undone and hands clasping his stomach, sat slumped partly out of his seat, his face glistening with sweat. He looked up at the doctor, drawing back his lips in a rictus of pain.

"This is murder," the man mumbled. "I've never felt like this before."

Baird took a pencil from his jacket pocket and held it in front of the man.

"Listen to me," he said. "I want you to take this pencil."

The man tried to grasp the pencil but it slipped through his fingers. Baird's eyes narrowed. He lifted the man into a more comfortable position and tucked a blanket in tightly around him. The stewardess hurried towards him holding a leather bag.

"Good girl," said Baird. "That's the one. Not that I can do much. . . . Where's your p.a. system?"

"I'll show you," said Janet. She led the way aft to the galley and pointed to a small microphone. "How is Mrs. Childer, Doctor?" she asked.

Baird pursed his lips. "She's seriously ill," he said. "And there are others who'll be as bad before long."

"Do you still think it's food poisoning?" Janet's cheeks were very pale.

"Tolerably certain. Staphylococcal, I'd say, though some of the symptoms out there could indicate even worse."

"Are you going to give round an emetic?"

"Yes, except of course to those who are already sick. That's all I can do." Lifting the telephone, Baird paused. "As soon as you can," he told her, "I suggest you organize some help to clean up a bit. Squirt disinfectant around if you've any. Oh, and as you speak to the sick passengers you'd better tell them not to lock the door of the toilet—we don't want any passing out in there." He pressed the button of the microphone. "Ladies and gentlemen, may I have your attention, please?" He heard the murmur of voices die away, leaving only the steady drone of the engines. "First of all," he went on, "my name is Baird and I'm a doctor. You are wondering what this malady is that has stricken our fellow passengers and I think it's time everyone knew what is happening and what I'm doing.

"Well, as far as I can tell we have several cases of food poisoning on board and I believe the cause of it to be the fish some of us had for dinner." An excited hubbub broke out. "Now listen, please. There is no cause for alarm. The passengers who have suffered these

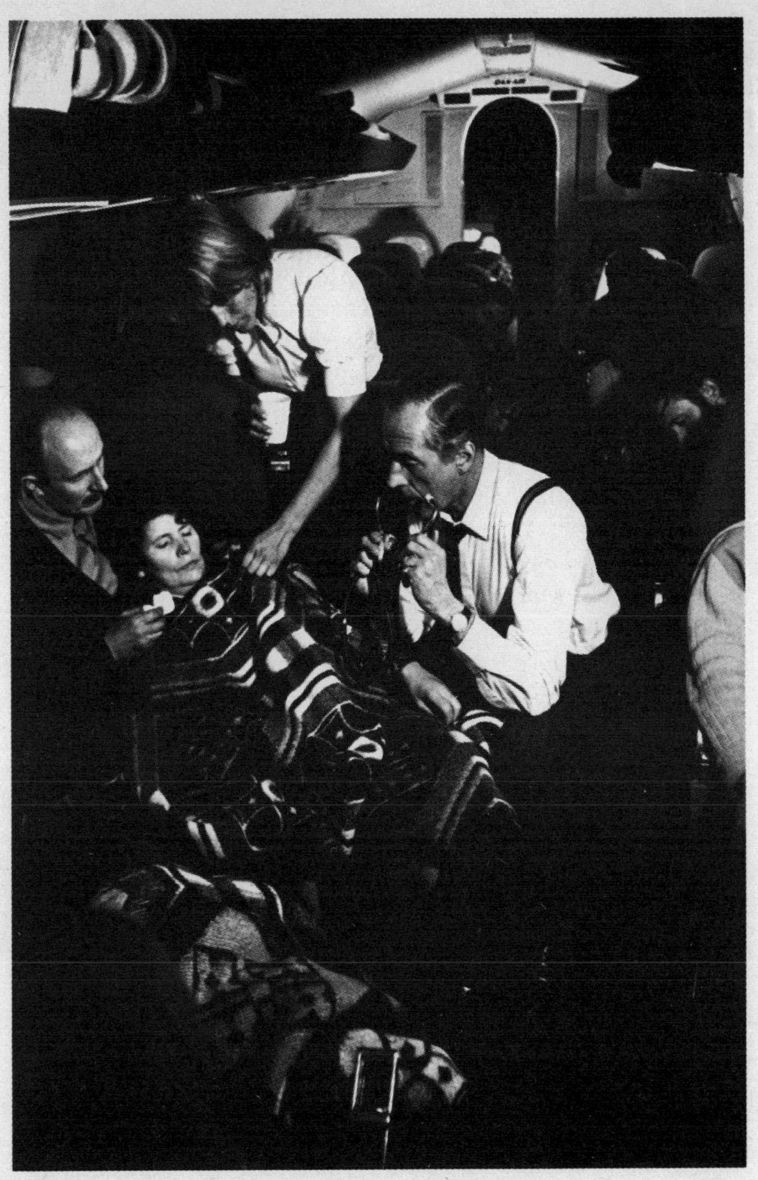

attacks are being cared for and the captain has radioed ahead for medical help to be standing by when we land. If you ate fish for dinner it doesn't necessarily follow that you are going to be affected too. However, we *are* going to take some precautions and the stewardess and I are coming round to you all. If you ate fish, we'll tell you how you can help yourselves." Baird took his finger off the button and turned to Janet. "All we can do now is to give immediate first aid," he said. "To begin with, everyone who had fish must drink several glasses of water—that will help to dilute the poison. After that we'll give an emetic. If there aren't enough pills in my bag we'll have to use salt. I'll start at the back here with the pills and you begin bringing drinking water to those people already affected, will you? Take some to the first officer too. You'll need help."

Stepping out of the galley, Baird practically cannoned into the lean, lugubrious 'Otpot. "Anything I can do, Doctor?" he said.

Baird allowed himself a smile. "Thanks. First, what did you have for dinner?"

"Meat, thank heaven," breathed 'Otpot fervently.

"Right. Then will you help the stewardess hand water round to the passengers who are sick? I want them to drink at least three glasses—more, if possible."

'Otpot entered the galley, returning Janet's rather tired little smile. In normal circumstances that smile of hers could be guaranteed to quicken the pulse of any man, but 'Otpot could see the hint of fear that lay behind it. He winked at her.

"Don't you worry, miss. Everything's going to be all right."

Janet looked at him gratefully. "I'm sure it is, thanks. Here's the water tap and there are the cups, Mr.—"

"The boys call me 'Otpot. For Lancashire 'otpot. You know."

"'Otpot?" Janet burst out laughing.

"There, that's better. Come on, lass, let's get started. A fine airline this is. Gives you your dinner, then asks for it back."

It takes a great deal to upset the equilibrium of a modern airport, but the control room at Vancouver, when Dun's emergency call came through, presented a scene of suppressed excitement. In front of the radio panel an operator transcribed Dun's incoming message straight onto a typewriter, pausing only to punch an alarm bell on his desk. He carried on imperturbably as a second man appeared behind him, craning over his shoulder to read the words. The newcomer, summoned by the bell, was the airport controller, Grimsell, a tall, lean man who had spent a lifetime in the air and knew travel over Canada as well as he knew his own back garden. He got halfway through the message, then stepped sharply back, cracking an order over his shoulder to the telephone operator.

"Get me Air Traffic Control quickly. Then clear the teletype circuit to Winnipeg. Priority message." Grimsell picked up a phone, waited a few seconds, then said, "Vancouver controller here." His voice was deceptively unhurried. "Maple Leaf Charter Flight 714 from Winnipeg to Vancouver reports emergency. Serious food poisoning among the passengers. The first officer is down with it too. Better clear all levels below them for priority approach and landing. Can do? Good. ETA is 0505." The controller glanced at the wall clock; it read 0215. He put down the phone and barked at the teletype operator, "Got Winnipeg yet? Good. Send this message. Starts: 'Controller Winnipeg. Urgent. Maple Leaf Charter Flight 714 reports serious food poisoning among passengers and crew believed due to fish served dinner on flight. Imperative check source and suspend all other food service originating same place. Understand source was not, repeat not, regular airline caterer.'" He swung round to the switchboard. "Get me the local manager of Maple Leaf Charter, Harry Burdick. After that I want the city police—senior officer on duty." He leaned over the radio operator's shoulder again and finished reading the now completed message. "Acknowledge that, Greg. Tell them that all altitudes below them are being cleared and that they'll be advised of landing instructions later."

On the floor below, an operator of the Government of Canada Western Air Traffic Control swivelled in his chair to call across the room, "What's flying in Green One between here and Calgary?"

"Westbound, there's an Air Force North Star at 18,000. Just reported over Penticton. Maple Leaf 714—"

"Maple Leaf 714's in trouble. They want all altitudes below them cleared."

"The North Star's well ahead and there's nothing close behind. There's an eastbound Constellation ready for take-off."

"Clear it, but hold any other eastbound traffic for the time being. Bring the North Star straight in when it arrives."

Upstairs, Grimsell had scooped up the telephone again. "Hello, Burdick? Grimsell here. Look, we've got an emergency on 714 ex-Toronto and Winnipeg. The first officer and several passengers are down with food poisoning. I called Winnipeg and told them to trace the source of the food. You'd better come over as soon as you can." He jabbed down the telephone cradle with his thumb and nodded to the switchboard operator. "The police—got them yet? Good, put them on. Hello, this is the controller, Vancouver Airport. . . . Look, Inspector, we have an emergency on an incoming flight. Several passengers and one of the crew have been taken seriously ill with food poisoning. We need ambulances and doctors out here at the airport. The flight is due in about five o'clock local time. Will you alert the hospitals, get the ambulances, set up a traffic control? Right. We'll be on again as soon as we've got more information."

Within five minutes portly little Harry Burdick had puffed into the room. He stood with his jacket over his arm, gasping for breath after his hurry and swabbing the moonscape of his face with a blue-spotted handkerchief.

"Where's the message?" he grunted. He ran his eye quickly over the sheet of paper the radio operator handed him. "It would be quicker to go into Calgary."

"No good, I'm afraid. There's fog right down to the grass everywhere east of the Rockies as far as Manitoba. They'll have to come through."

A clerk called across from his phone, "Passenger agent wants to know when we'll be resuming eastbound traffic. Should he keep the passengers downtown?"

The controller called back, "Tell him yes. We don't want a mob out here."

"Have you got medical and hospital help lined up?" asked Burdick.

"The city police are working on it."

Burdick shook a worried head. "Say, suppose the captain takes sick, Controller? Who's going to . . ." He left the sentence unfinished as the level gaze of the man opposite met his.

"I'm praying, that's all," said Grimsell.

FOUR

NEARLY FOUR MILES above the earth, the aircraft held her course. In every direction, as far as the eye could see, stretched the undulating carpet of cloud.

Inside the aircraft fear was taking root, like a monstrous weed, in the minds of most of the passengers. The hubbub of dismay and conjecture following the doctor's words had soon died away, to be replaced by whispers and uneasy snatches of conversation.

Baird had given Janet two pills. "Take them to the captain," he told her in a low voice. "Tell him to drink as much water as he can to dilute the poison. Then he's to take the pills. They'll make him sick—that's what they're for."

When Janet entered the flight deck Dun was completing a radio transmission. He signed off and gave her a strained grin. "Hello, Jan," he said. His hand was shaking slightly. "How are things back there?"

"So far, so good," said Janet. She held out the pills. "Doctor says you're to drink as much water as you can, then take these. They'll make you feel a bit green."

"What a prospect." He reached down into the pocket at his side and took out a water bottle. "Well, down the hatch." After a long draught, he swallowed the pills, pulling a wry face. "They taste awful."

Janet looked anxiously down at him as he sat before the panel of flickering gauges and dials. She touched his shoulder.

"How do you feel?" She was watching his pallor, the beads of perspiration on his forehead. She prayed to herself that it was just the strain he was undergoing.

"Me?" His tone was unnaturally hearty. "I'm fine." He looked over at the first officer, now prone on the floor, his head on a pillow.

"Poor old Pete," he murmured. "I sure hope he's going to be all right."

"That's up to you, isn't it, Captain?" said Janet urgently. "The faster you can push this thing into Vancouver, the quicker we'll get him and the others into a hospital." She stepped over to Pete and bent down to adjust a blanket round him, hiding a sudden tremble of tears.

Dun was troubled as he regarded her. "You think a lot of him, Jan, don't you?" he said.

"I—I suppose so," she replied. "I've got to like him during the past few months since he joined the crew and this . . . this horrible business has made me. . . ." She checked herself and jumped up. "I've got a lot to do. Have to hold a few noses . . . while the doctor pours water down their gullets."

She smiled at him and opened the door to the passenger deck. Baird was halfway along the starboard side, talking to a middle-aged couple who stared at him nervously.

"Did you have fish or meat?" Baird asked.

The man's bulbous eyes seemed about to depart from their sockets. "Fish," he exclaimed. "We both ate fish." Indignation welled up in him. "I think it's disgraceful that such a thing can happen. There ought to be an inquiry."

"I can assure you there will be." Baird handed them each a pill, which they accepted as gingerly as if it were high explosive. "Now, you'll be brought a jug of water. Drink three glasses each —four, if you can manage them. Then take the pill. It'll make you sick, but that's what it's for. There are paper bags in the seat pockets."

He left the couple staring hypnotically at their pills and in a few minutes, after progressing along the rows, had reached his own empty seat with Spencer sitting alongside it.

"Meat," said Spencer promptly, before Baird could put the question.

"Good for you," said the doctor. "That's one less to worry about."

"You're having a heavy time of it, Doc, aren't you?" Spencer commented. "Can you do with any help?"

"I can do with all the help in the world," growled Baird. "But there's not much you can do, unless you'd like to give Miss Benson and 'Otpot a hand with the water."

"Sure I will." Spencer lowered his voice. "Some of them back there sound in a bad way."

"They *are* in a bad way. The devil of it is I've got nothing I can give them that's of any real use. You make a trip to a football game—you don't think to pack your bag in case people get taken sick with food poisoning on the way. God knows why I threw in a bottle of emetic pills, but it's a good thing I did. In these cases, the serious thing is dehydration, the loss of body fluids. And I have nothing with me to help to preserve them."

Spencer rubbed his chin. "Well," he said, "thank God for lamb chops. I just don't feel ready for dehydration yet."

Baird frowned. "Perhaps you see some humour in this situation," he said sourly. "I don't. All I can see is my complete helplessness while people steadily get worse."

"Don't ride me, Doc," Spencer protested. "I'm only glad we didn't get sick like the other poor devils."

Baird passed a hand over his eyes. "I'm getting too old for this sort of thing," he muttered.

Spencer got to his feet. "Now, hold on there, Doc," he said. "You're doing a fine job. The luckiest thing that ever happened to these people is having you on board."

"All right, Junior," Baird retorted sarcastically, "you can spare me the salesman's pep talk."

The younger man flushed slightly. "Well, tell me what I can do. I've been warming my seat while you've been hard at it. You're tired."

"Tired nothing." Baird put his hand on the other man's arm. "Take no notice of me. I worked off a bit of steam on you. Feel better for it."

Spencer grinned. "Glad to be of *some* use, anyway."

"Until Miss Benson needs you, you'd better stay in your seat. There's enough traffic in the aisle already."

"I'm here if you want me." Spencer resumed his seat. "Just how serious is all this?"

"As serious as you are ever likely to want it," Baird said curtly and moved along to the group of football fans who had earlier imbibed whisky with such liberality. The quartet was now reduced to three, and one of these sat shivering, a blanket drawn across his chest. His colour was grey.

"Keep this man warm," said Baird. "Has he had anything to drink?"

"That's a laugh," replied a man behind him, shuffling a pack of cards. "He must have downed a couple of pints of rye."

"That's right," agreed another in the group. "And I thought Andy could hold his liquor."

"It has helped to dilute the poison," Baird said. "Has one of you men got some brandy?"

One of the men leaned forward to get at his hip pocket. "I might have some left in the flask."

"Give him a few sips," instructed Baird. "Do it gently. Your friend is very ill."

"Poor old Andy." The man with the flask unscrewed the cap. A thought struck him, "He'll be all right, won't he?"

"I hope so. Make sure he doesn't throw off those blankets."

As Baird stepped away the man with the cards flicked them irritably in his hand and demanded of his companion, "How d'you like this for a two-day vacation?"

Farther along the aisle, Baird found Janet anxiously bending over Mrs. Childer. He raised one of the woman's eyelids. She was unconscious.

Her husband seized frantically on the doctor's presence. "How is she?" he implored.

"She's better off now than when she was conscious and in pain." Baird hoped he sounded convincing. "When the body can't take any more, nature pulls down the shutter."

"She will be O.K., won't she? I mean. . . ."

"Of course she will," said Baird gently. "There'll be an ambulance waiting when we land. Then it's only a question of treatment and time before she's well again."

Childer heaved a deep breath. "It certainly is good to hear you say that."

Yes, thought Baird, but supposing I'd had the guts to tell the truth?

"You still think it was the fish, do you, Doctor?"

"I think so. Food poisoning can be caused either by the food just spoiling—the medical name is staphylococcal poisoning—or it's possible that some toxic substance has accidentally got into it during its preparation. I can't be sure which this is, but from its effects I'd suspect a toxic substance. We won't know until we're able to make proper tests in a laboratory. With the careful way in which airlines prepare food—the chances against this happening are a million to one. But our dinner tonight didn't come from the usual caterers."

Childer nodded. Funny how people seem to find comfort in a medical man's words, Baird reflected. Maybe we haven't come so far from witchcraft, there's always the doctor with his box of magic, to pull something out of the hat. Most of his life had been spent in coaxing, cajoling, bullying—reassuring frightened people that he knew best, and hoping each time that his skill had not deserted him. Well, this could be the inescapable challenge which he had always known would face him one day.

He felt Janet standing beside him. He questioned her with his eyes, sensing her to be on the edge of hysteria.

"Two more passengers have been taken ill, Doctor. At the back there."

"Right. I'll get to them straight away. Will you have another look at the first officer? He might like a little water."

He had barely reached the new cases and begun his examination before Janet was back again.

"Doctor, I'm terribly worried. I think you ought to—"

The buzz of the galley intercom cut across her words like a knife. Baird was the first to move.

"Quick!" he rapped out.

Moving with an agility quite foreign to him, he raced along the aisle and burst into the flight deck. There he paused momentarily, and in that instant something inside him, mocking in its tone but menacing too, said: *You were right—this is it.*

The captain was rigid in his seat, sweat masking his face and streaking the collar of his uniform. One hand clutched at his stomach. The other was pressed on the intercom button on the wall beside him. In two bounds the doctor reached him and leaned over the back of the seat, supporting him under the armpits. Dun was swearing between his clenched teeth, quietly and viciously.

"Take it easy," said Baird. "We'd better get you away from there."

"I did . . . what you said . . ." Dun gasped, squeezing the words out in painful jerks. "It was too late. . . . Give me something, Doc. . . . Got to hold out . . . get us down . . . she's on autopilot but . . . got to get down. . . . Must tell Control . . . must tell. . . ." With a desperate effort he tried to speak. Then his eyes rolled up and he collapsed.

"Quick, Miss Benson," called Baird. "Help me get him out."

Panting and struggling, they pulled Dun's heavy body out of the pilot's seat and eased him onto the floor alongside the first officer. Baird took out his stethoscope and made an examination. In a matter of seconds Janet had produced coats and a blanket; as soon as the doctor had finished she made a pillow for the captain and wrapped him round. She was trembling as she stood up.

"Can you do what he asked, Doctor? Can you bring him round long enough to land the plane?"

Baird thrust his stethoscope back in his pocket. In the dim light from the battery of dials his features seemed suddenly much older, and unbearably weary.

"You are part of this crew, Miss Benson, so I'll be blunt." His voice was so hard that she flinched. "Unless I can get all these people to a hospital quickly—very quickly—I can't even be sure of saving their lives. They need stimulants, intravenous injections for shock. The captain too. He's held out too long."

Barely audible, Janet whispered, "Doctor—what are we going to do?"

"Let me ask you a question. How many fish dinners did you serve?"

"About fifteen, I think. Most of the fifty-six passengers had meat."

"I see." Baird regarded her steadily. When he spoke again his voice was almost belligerent. "Miss Benson, did you ever hear of long odds?"

Janet tried to understand what he was saying.

"Yes, I suppose so. I don't know what it means."

"It means this," said Baird. "Our one chance of survival depends on there being a passenger aboard this airplane who is not only qualified to land it but who also didn't have fish for dinner."

FIVE

AS THE DOCTOR'S words penetrated her mind, Janet met his eyes steadily, well aware of his unspoken injunction to prepare herself for death. Until now a part of her had refused to accept what was happening. While she had busied herself tending the passengers, something had insisted that this was a nightmare: at any moment she would wake up to find the bedclothes on the floor and the clock on her locker buzzing to herald another morning. But now that sense of unreality was swept away. She knew this was really happening, to her, Janet Benson.

"I understand, Doctor," she said levelly.

"Do you know of anyone on board with any experience of flying?"

Janet cast her mind over the passenger list. "There's no one from the airline," she said. "I don't know . . . about anyone else. I suppose I'd better start asking."

"Yes, you'd better," said Baird slowly. "But try not to alarm them, or we may start a panic. Some of them already know the first officer is sick. Just say the captain wondered if there's someone with flying experience who could help with the radio."

"Very well, Doctor," said Janet quietly.

"Miss Benson—what's your first name?" he asked.

"Janet."

"Janet—I think I made some remark earlier on about your training. It was unjustified and unforgivable—the comment of a stupid old man who could have done with more training himself."

Some of the colour returned to her cheeks as she smiled. "I'd forgotten it." She moved towards the door, anxious to begin her questioning.

"Wait," Baird said. His face was puckered in an effort of

concentration, as if something at the back of his mind was eluding him. "I *knew* someone had spoken to me about airplanes. That young fellow in the seat next to mine. George Spencer. I forget exactly but he seemed to know something about flying. And he had the meat. Get him up here, will you? Then carry on asking the others too, in case there's someone else."

When she was gone, he knelt to feel the pulse of the captain. At the first sound of the door behind him, he jumped to his feet. Spencer stood there, looking at him in bewilderment.

"Hello, Doc," the young man greeted him. "What's this about the radio?"

"Are you a pilot?" Baird shot out, not moving.

"A long time ago. In the war. I wouldn't know about radio procedures now, but if the captain thinks I can—"

"Come in," said Baird.

He stepped aside, closing the door quickly behind the young man. Spencer's head snapped up at the sight of the pilots' empty seats and the controls moving by themselves. Then he wheeled round to the two men stretched on the floor under their blankets.

"No!" he gasped. "Not both of them?"

"Yes, both of them. Listen, can you fly this aircraft—and land it?"

"No!" Spencer put out a hand to steady himself. "Not a chance!"

"But you just said you flew in the war," Baird insisted.

"That was thirteen years ago. I haven't touched a plane since. And I was on fighters—tiny Spitfires about an eighth of the size of this ship and with only one engine. This has four. The flying characteristics are completely different."

Spencer's fingers, shaking slightly, probed his jacket for cigarettes. He shook one out. Baird watched him as he lit up.

"You could have a go at it," he pressed.

Spencer shook his head angrily. "I tell you, the idea's crazy," he snapped. "I wouldn't be able to take on a Spitfire now, let alone all this." He jabbed his cigarette towards the banks of instruments.

Baird shrugged. "Well," he said, "let's hope there's someone else who can fly this thing—neither of these men can." He looked down at the pilots.

The door opened and Janet came into the flight deck.

"There's no one else," she said. Her voice was flat.

"That's it, then," said the doctor. He waited for Spencer to speak, but the younger man was staring forward at the row upon row of dials and switches. "Mr. Spencer," said Baird, measuring his words, "I know nothing of flying. All I know is this. There are several people on this plane who will die within a few hours if they don't get to hospital. Among those left who are physically able to fly the plane, you are the only one with any kind of qualification to do so." He paused. "What do you suggest?"

Spencer looked from the girl to the doctor. He asked tensely, "You're quite sure there's no chance of either of the pilots recovering in time?"

"None at all, I'm afraid."

The young salesman ground the rest of his cigarette under his heel. "It looks as if I don't have much choice, doesn't it?" he said.

"That's right. Unless you'd rather we carried on until we were out of gas—probably halfway across the Pacific."

"Don't kid yourself this is a better way." Spencer stepped forward to the controls and looked ahead at the white sea of cloud below them. "Well," he said, "I guess I'm drafted." He slipped into the lefthand pilot's seat and glanced over his shoulder at the two behind him. "If you know any good prayers, start brushing up on them."

Baird moved up to him and slapped his arm lightly. "Good man," he said with feeling.

"What are you going to tell the people back there?" asked Spencer, running his eye over the gauges in front of him and racking his memory to recall some of the lessons he had learned in a past that now seemed very far away.

"For the moment—nothing," answered the doctor.

"Very wise," said Spencer dryly. He studied the bewildering array of instrument dials. "Let's have a look at this mess. The flying instruments must be in front of each pilot. That means the centre panel will probably be engines only. Ah—here we are: altitude 20,000. Level flight. Course 290. We're on automatic pilot —we can be thankful for that. Air speed 210 knots. Throttles, pitch, trim, mixture, landing-gear controls. Flaps? There should be an indicator somewhere. Yes, here it is. Well, they're the essentials anyway—I hope. We'll need a check list for landing, but we can get that on the radio. Where are we now, and where are we going?"

"From what the captain said, we're over the Rockies," replied Baird. "He couldn't turn off course earlier because of fog, so we're going through to Vancouver."

"We'll have to find out more." Spencer looked about him in the soft glow. "Where *is* the radio control anyway?"

Janet pointed to a switchbox above his head. "I know they use that to talk to the ground," she told him, "but I don't know which switches you have to set."

"Ah yes, let's see." He peered at the box. "Those are the frequency selectors—we'd better leave them where they are. What's this? Transmit." He clicked over a switch, lighting up a small red bulb. "That's it. First blood to George. Now we're ready for business."

Janet handed him a headset with the boom microphone attached. "I know you press the button on the mike when you speak," she said.

Adjusting the earphones, Spencer spoke to the doctor. "You know, whatever happens I'm going to need a second pair of hands up here. You've got your patients to look after, so I think the best choice is Miss Canada here. What do you say?"

Baird nodded. "I agree. Is that all right, Janet?"

"I suppose so—but I know nothing of all this." Janet waved helplessly at the control panels.

"Good," said Spencer breezily, "that makes two of us. Sit down and make yourself comfortable—better strap yourself in."

Janet struggled into the first officer's seat, taking care not to touch the control column as it swayed back and forth. There was an anxious knocking on the communication door.

"That's for me," said Baird. "I must get back. Good luck."

He left quickly. Alone with the stewardess, Spencer summoned up a grin. "O.K.?" he asked.

She nodded dumbly, preparing to put on a headset.

"The name's Janet, isn't it? Mine's George." Spencer's tone became serious. "Janet, this will be tough."

"I know it."

"Well, let's see if I can send out a distress call. What's our flight number?"

"714."

"Right. Here goes, then." He pressed the button on his microphone. "Mayday, mayday, mayday," he began in an even voice. It was one signal he could never forget. He had called it one murky October afternoon above the French coast, with the tail of his Spitfire all but shot off, and two Hurricanes had mercifully appeared to usher him across the channel like a pair of solicitous old aunts.

"Mayday, mayday, mayday," he continued. "This is Flight 714, Maple Leaf Air Charter, in distress. Come in, anyone. Over."

He caught his breath as a voice responded immediately over the air.

"Hello, 714. This is Vancouver. We have been waiting to hear from you. Vancouver to all aircraft: this frequency now closed to all other traffic. Go ahead, 714."

"Thank you, Vancouver. 714. We are in distress. Both pilots and several passengers . . . how many passengers, Janet?"

"It was five a few minutes ago. May be more now, though."

"Correction. At least five passengers are suffering from food poisoning. Both pilots are unconscious and in serious condition. The doctor with us says that neither of them can be revived to fly the aircraft. If they and the passengers don't get to hospital quickly it may be fatal for them. Did you get that, Vancouver?"

The voice crackled back instantly, "Go ahead, 714. I'm reading you."

Spencer took a deep breath. "Now we come to the interesting bit. My name is Spencer, George Spencer. I am a passenger on this airplane. Correction: I *was* a passenger. I am now the pilot. For your information I have about a thousand hours total flying time, all of it on single-engined fighters. Also I haven't flown an airplane for nearly thirteen years. So you'd better get someone on this radio who can give me some instructions about flying this thing. Our altitude is 20,000, course 290 magnetic, air speed 210 knots. Your move, Vancouver. Over."

"Vancouver to 714. Stand by."

Spencer wiped the gathering sweat from his forehead and grinned across to Janet. "Want to bet that's caused a bit of a stir in the dovecotes down there?" She shook her head, listening intently to her earphones. In a few seconds the air was alive again, the voice as measured and impersonal as before.

"Vancouver to Flight 714. Please check with doctor on board for any possibility of either pilot recovering. Ask him to do everything possible to revive one of them even if he has to leave the sick passengers. Over."

Spencer pressed his transmit button. "Vancouver, this is Flight 714. Your message understood, but doctor says there is no possibility whatever of pilots recovering to make landing. Over."

There was a slight pause. Then: "Vancouver Control to 714. Your message understood. Will you stand by, please."

"Roger, Vancouver," acknowledged Spencer and switched off again.

His hands played nervously with the control column in front of him, following its movements, trying to gauge its responsiveness as he attempted to call up the flying skill that had once earned for him quite a reputation in the squadron: three times home on a wing and a prayer. He smiled to himself as he recalled the wartime phrase. But in the next moment, as he looked blankly at the monstrous assembly of wavering needles and the unfamiliar banks of levers and switches, he felt himself in the grip of an icy despair. One wrong move might shatter in a second the even tenor of their flight; if it did, who was to say that he could bring the aircraft under control again? He began to curse the head office which had whipped him away from Winnipeg to go trouble-shooting across to Vancouver at a moment's notice. The prospect of a sales manager's appointment and a house on Parkway Heights now seemed absurdly unimportant. It would be damnable to end like this, not to see Mary again, not to say to her all the things that were still unspoken. As for Bobsie and Kit, he should have done more for those poor kids, the world's best.

He put a cigarette in his mouth and lit a match. "I don't suppose this is allowed," he said to Janet, "but maybe the airline can stretch a point."

SIX

WITH AN ACCELERATING thunder of engines the last eastbound aircraft to take off from Vancouver that night had gathered speed along the wetly gleaming runway and climbed into the darkness. Its navigation lights, as it made the required circuit of the airport, had been shrouded in mist. Other aircraft, in process of being towed back from their dispersal points to bays alongside the departure buildings were beaded with moisture. It was a cold night. Ground staff, moving about their tasks, slapped their gloved hands around themselves to keep warm. None of them spoke more than was necessary. One last slowly taxiing aircraft came to a stop and cut its engines at a wave from the indicator torches of a ground man. In the sudden silence the swish of its propellers seemed an intrusion. Normally busy Vancouver airport prepared itself with quiet competence for emergency.

Within the brightly lit control room the atmosphere was tense. Replacing his telephone, Grimsell, the controller, turned to Burdick. Perched on the edge of a table, the plump manager of Maple Leaf Airline had just finished consulting again the clipboard of information he held in his hand.

"Right, Harry," said the controller. "As of now, I'm holding all departures for the east. We've got nearly an hour in which to clear the present outgoing traffic in other directions, leaving plenty of time in hand. After that everything scheduled outwards must wait until . . . until afterwards, anyway." He addressed an assistant who sat holding a telephone. "Have you raised the fire chief yet?"

"Ringing his home now."

"Tell him he'd better get here—it looks like a big show. And ask the duty fire officer to notify the city fire department. They may want to move equipment into the area."

"I've done that. Vancouver Control here," said the assistant into his telephone. "Hold the line, please." He cupped his hand over the mouthpiece. "Shall I alert the Air Force?"

"Yes. Have them keep the zone clear of their aircraft." He turned to Burdick. "Have you any pilots here at the airport?"

Burdick shook his head. "We'll have to get help."

The controller thought rapidly. "Try Cross-Canada. They have most of their men based here. Explain the position. We'll need a man fully experienced with this type of aircraft and capable of giving instructions over the air."

"Do you think there's a chance?"

"I don't know, but we've got to try. Can you suggest anything else?"

"No," said Burdick, "I can't. But I sure don't envy him that job."

The switchboard operator called, "The city police again."

"Put them on," said the controller.

"I'll see the Cross-Canada people," said Burdick.

The controller lifted the telephone as Burdick hurried out of the room. "Controller speaking. Ah, Inspector, I'm glad it's you. That's fine. Now listen, Inspector. We're in bad trouble, much worse than we thought. First, we may have to ask one of your cars to collect a pilot in town and bring him here just as fast as possible. No, I'll let you know the address later. Second, in addition to the urgency of getting the passengers to hospital, there's now a very serious possibility that the plane will crash-land. I can't explain now but when the ship comes in she won't be under proper control." He listened for a moment to the man at the other end. "Yes, we've issued a general alarm. The fire department will have everything they've got standing by. The point is, I think the houses near the airport may be in some danger." He listened again. "Well, I'm glad you've suggested it. I know it's a hell of a thing to wake people in the middle of the night, but we're taking enough chances as it is. I can't guarantee at all that this plane will get down on the field. We're lucky that there are only those houses out towards Sea Island Bridge to worry about. We'll route her well clear of the city. . . . No, can't say yet. We'll probably try to bring her in from the east end of the main runway." Another pause, longer this time. "Thank you, Inspector. I'll keep in touch." The controller clicked the telephone back, his face etched with worry.

"The fire chief is on his way," reported his assistant. "I'm on to the Air Force now. They ask if they can give any assistance."

"We'll let them know, but I don't think so. Thank them." He returned to his study of the wall map as Burdick came into the room, breathing noisily.

"Jim Bryant at Cross-Canada says their best man is Captain Paul Treleaven. He's ringing him now. He's at home and in bed, I suppose. They'll get a police escort; I've told them we need him in the worst way. Do you know Treleaven?"

"I've met him," said the controller. "He's a good type. We're lucky he's available."

The switchboard operator broke in. "I've got Seattle and Calgary waiting, sir. They want to know if we got the message from 714 clearly."

"Tell them yes," answered the controller. "We'll work the aircraft direct but we'd appreciate them keeping a listening watch in case we meet with reception trouble."

"Right, sir."

The controller crossed to the radio panel and picked up the stand microphone. He nodded to the dispatcher who threw a switch to transmit.

"Vancouver Control to Flight 714," he called.

Spencer's voice, when he replied, spluttered from an amplifier high in a corner of the room. Since his mayday call all his conversation had been channelled through the loudspeaker. "This is 714. Go ahead, Vancouver. I thought you were lost."

"Vancouver to 714. This is the controller speaking. We are organizing help. We shall call you again very soon. Meanwhile do nothing to interfere with the present set of the controls. Do you understand? Over."

Despite the distortion, the asperity in Spencer's voice came through like a knife. "714 to Vancouver. I told you I've never touched a job like this before. I certainly don't aim to start playing fool tricks with the automatic pilot. Over."

The controller opened his mouth as if to say something, then changed his mind. He signed off and said to his assistant, "Tell reception to get Treleaven up here fast when he arrives."

"Right, sir. The duty fire officer is clearing all runway vehicles and gas wagons well under cover and the city fire department is bringing all the equipment they've got into the precincts."

Burdick said suddenly, "Hey, with the city departments onto this, we'll have the press at any time. Front page everywhere. I can just imagine it. Plane-load of people, many of them sick. No pilot. Maybe evacuation of those houses towards the bridge. And—"

The controller cut in, "Let Public Relations handle it. Get Cliff Howard here, at the double." Burdick nodded to the switchboard operator, who ran his finger down an emergency list and then began to dial. "Cliff will know how to play it. Tell him to keep the papers off our backs. We've got work to do."

Burdick picked up a telephone impatiently. "What happened to Dr. Davidson?" he demanded of the operator.

"Out on a night call. I've left a message."

"If he doesn't check in in ten minutes, get the hospital. That doctor on 714 is maybe in need of advice."

On the outskirts of the town a telephone was ringing incessantly. A smooth white arm emerged from bedclothes and groped slowly in the darkness for the switch of a bedside lamp. The lamp clicked on. With her eyes screwed up against the brightness of the light, Dulcie Treleaven, an attractive redhead, reached painfully for the telephone. She mumbled, "Yes?"

"Mrs. Treleaven?" demanded a crisp voice.

"Yes," she said. "Who is it?"

"Mrs. Treleaven, may I speak to your husband?"

"He's not here."

"Where can I find him, please? It's imperative that we contact him without delay. This is Cross-Canada."

"He's at his mother's place. His father is ill." She gave the telephone number.

"Thank you. We'll ring him there."

She replaced the receiver and swung her legs out of bed. As the wife of a senior pilot she was accustomed to unexpected calls for her husband, but part of her still resented them. Was Paul the only pilot they ever thought of when they were in a fix? Well, if he was having to take over a plane in a hurry, he would call home first for his uniform and gear. There would be time to make up a flask of coffee and some sandwiches. She drew on a robe and stumbled down the stairs towards the kitchen.

Two miles away, Paul Treleaven slept deeply on the chesterfield in his mother's parlour. That determined and vigorous old lady had insisted on taking a spell by the side of her sick husband, ordering her son to rest. The news from the doctor the previous evening had been encouraging: the old man had passed the dangerous corner of his pneumonia and now it was a matter of careful nursing. Treleaven had been thankful for a chance to sleep. Only thirty-six hours previously he had completed a flight from Tokyo, bringing back a parliamentary mission, and since then, with the crisis of his father's illness, there had been scant opportunity for more than an uneasy doze.

He was aroused by his arm being shaken and looked up to find his mother bending over him. "The airport is on the telephone," she said. "I told them you were trying to snatch some rest, but they insisted."

"O.K. I'll come."

Pulling himself off the chesterfield, he padded in stockinged feet to the telephone in the hall.

"Treleaven," he said.

"Paul, this is Jim Bryant." The words were clipped, urgent. "We're in real trouble here. There's a Maple Leaf Charter—an Empress C6, one of the refitted jobs—on its way from Winnipeg, with a number of passengers and both pilots seriously ill with food poisoning."

"What! *Both* pilots?"

"That's right. Some fellow is at the controls who hasn't flown for years. Fortunately the ship is on autopilot. Maple Leaf hasn't got a man here and we want you to come in and talk her down."

"It's a tall order." Treleaven looked at his wrist watch. "What's the ETA?"

"0505." Bryant said.

"But that's under two hours. We've got to move! Look, I'm on the south side of town. . . ."

"What's your address?" Treleaven gave it. "We'll have a police car pick you up in a few minutes."

"Right. I'm on my way."

"And good luck, Paul."

"You're not kidding."

He strode back to the parlour and pulled on his shoes without stopping to tie the laces. His mother held out his jacket for him.

"What is it, Paul?" she asked apprehensively.

"Bad trouble at the airport, Mother. There's a police car coming to take me there."

"Police!"

"Now, now." He put an arm around her for a second. "It's nothing to worry about. But they need my help." He looked round for his pipe and tobacco and put them in his pocket. He stopped in his tracks. "How did they know I was here?"

"Perhaps they rang Dulcie first."

"Yes, that must be it. Would you give her a ring, Mother, and let her know everything is all right?"

"I will. But what is the trouble about, Paul?"

"A pilot is sick on an aircraft due here soon. They want me to talk it down, if I can."

His mother looked puzzled. "If the pilot's sick, who's going to fly it?"

"I am, Mother—from the ground."

"I don't understand."

Maybe I don't either, Treleaven thought to himself five minutes later, seated in the back of a police car as the driver pulled away from the sidewalk and slammed into top gear. The speedometer crept steadily to seventy-five as the siren sliced into the night.

"Looks like a big night over at the field," remarked the police sergeant beside the driver, talking over his shoulder. "Every available car has been sent over to the airport in case the bridge estate has to be cleared. I'd say they're expecting a hell of a bang."

"You know what?" interjected the young driver. "I bet there's a busted-up Stratojet coming in with a nuclear bomb-load."

"Do me a favour," said the sergeant with heavy scorn. "Your trouble is you read too many comics."

They crossed the estuary to Sea Island, where police crews were already talking to bewildered homeowners in doorways, and sped along the last stretch of Airport Road.

At the reception building, Treleaven was out of the car, through the doors and had crossed the concourse before the wail of the siren had died behind him. He could move remarkably fast for a man of his size. His loose-limbed agility, combined with a solid physique and fair hair, had long made him an object of interest to women. His hard, lean features, angular and crooked, looked as if they had been inexpertly carved from a chunk of wood. He had a reputation as a disciplinarian and more than one crew member had had cause to fear the cold light in those pale blue eyes.

As he entered the control room, Grimsell stepped quickly over to greet him. "I'm certainly glad to see you, Captain," he said, and he gave him the story quickly. "Burdick has just got his president out of bed in Montreal. The old man sounds far from happy."

"What else can we do?" Burdick was pleading anxiously and deferentially on the phone. "Captain Treleaven, Cross-Canada's chief pilot, just walked in the door. We'll get on the radio with a check list and try to talk him down. . . . Of course it's a terrible risk, sir, but can you think of something better?"

Treleaven took from the dispatcher the clipboard of messages from 714, read them carefully, and consulted the latest weather reports. Then he laid the papers down, raised his eyebrows sombrely at the controller, and produced his pipe which he proceeded to fill.

Burdick was still speaking. ". . . I've thought of that, sir. Howard will handle the press at this end—they aren't on to it yet."

"What do you think?" Grimsell asked Treleaven.

The pilot shrugged without answering and picked up the clipboard again, drawing steadily on his pipe.

". . . ETA is 0505 Pacific Time," Burdick was saying with increasing exasperation. "I've a lot to do, sir . . . I'll call you as soon as I know anything more . . . yes, yes. . . . G'bye." Putting down the telephone, he blew out his cheeks with relief, then turned to Treleaven. "Thank you very much for coming, Captain."

Treleaven held up the clipboard. "This is the whole story?"

"That's everything we know. You'll have to talk this guy right down onto the ground. Can you do it?"

"I can't perform a miracle," said Treleaven evenly. "The chances of a man who has only flown fighter airplanes landing a four-engine passenger ship are slim, to say the least!"

"I know that!" Burdick exploded. "But do you have any other ideas?"

"No," Treleaven said slowly. "I guess not. I just wanted to be sure you knew what we were getting into."

"The biggest air disaster in years, that's what we're getting into!" shouted Burdick angrily.

"Keep your temper," said Treleaven coldly. "We'll get nowhere fast by shouting." He glanced at the wall map. "This is going to be very tough and a very long shot," he said. "I want that fully understood."

"You are right to emphasize the risk, Captain. We fully accept that," said the controller.

"Very well, then, let's get started." Treleaven walked over to the radio operator. "Can you work 714 direct?"

"Yes, Captain. Reception's good."

"Call them."

The operator switched to transmit. "Flight 714. This is Vancouver. Do you read? Over."

"Yes, Vancouver," came Spencer's voice through the amplifier. "We hear you clearly. Go ahead, please."

The operator handed the stand microphone to Treleaven. "O.K., Captain. It's all yours."

Holding the stand microphone in his hand, its cable trailing to the floor, Treleaven turned his back on the other men in the room, legs braced apart, staring unseeingly at a point on the wall map. His cold eyes were distant in concentration. His voice, when he spoke, was steady and unhurried, easy with a confidence he did not feel. As he began, the other men visibly relaxed, his acceptance of authority having relieved them of a crushing responsibility.

"Hello, Flight 714," he said. "This is Vancouver. My name is Paul Treleaven and I'm a Cross-Canada Airlines captain. My job is to help you fly this airplane in. We shouldn't have too much trouble. I see that I'm talking to George Spencer. I'd like to hear a little more about your flying experience, George."

Behind him, the flabby folds of Burdick's honest face had begun to shake in an uncontrollable spasm of nervous reaction.

SEVEN

SPENCER TENSED, shooting an involuntary glance at the girl in the seat beside him. Her eyes were fixed on his face. He looked away again, listening carefully. Treleaven was saying, "How many flying hours have you had? The message here says you've flown single-engine fighters. Have you had any experience at all of multi-engine planes, George?"

Spencer's mouth was so dry that he could hardly speak. He cleared his throat. "Hello, Vancouver. 714 here. Glad to have you along, Captain. But let's not kid each other. I think we both know the situation. My flying up to now has been entirely on single-engine aircraft, Spitfires and Mustangs—I'd say about a thousand hours in all. But that was thirteen years ago. I've touched nothing since. Over."

"Don't worry about that, George. It's like riding a bicycle—you never forget it. Stand by, will you?"

In the Vancouver control room, Treleaven pressed the cut-out button on the arm of the microphone in his hand and looked at a slip of paper Grimsell held out for him to read.

"Try to get him on this course," said the controller. "The Air Force have just sent in a radar check." He paused. "Sounds pretty tense, doesn't he?"

"Yes—who wouldn't be, in his shoes?" Treleaven grimaced reflectively. "We've got to give him confidence. Whatever happens, he mustn't lose his nerve." He released the cutout. "O.K., 714. This is Treleaven, George. In a minute you can disengage the autopilot and get the feel of the controls. When you've had a bit of practice with them you are going to change your course a little. When you start handling the airplane the controls will seem very heavy and sluggish compared with a fighter. Don't let that worry you. It's quite normal. Watch your air speed all the time you are flying and don't let it fall below 120 knots while your wheels and flaps are up or you'll stall. Now, one other thing. Do you have someone up there who can work the radio and leave you free for flying?"

"Yes, Vancouver. I have the stewardess here with me and she'll take over the radio now. It's all yours, Janet."

"Hello, Vancouver. This is the stewardess, Janet Benson. Over."

"Why, it's you, Janet," said Treleaven. "I'd know that voice anywhere. You're going to talk to me for George. Now Janet, I want you to keep your eyes on that air speed indicator. Remember that an airplane stays in the air because of its forward speed. If you let the speed drop too low, it stalls—and falls out of the air. Any time the ASI shows a reading near 120, you tell George instantly. Is that clear, Janet?"

"Yes, Captain. I understand."

"Back to you, George. Take this slowly and smoothly. I want you to unlock the autopilot—it's clearly marked on the control column—and take the airplane yourself, holding her straight and level. George, you watch the artificial horizon and keep the air speed steady. Climb and descent indicator should stay at zero. All right. Start now."

Spencer put his right forefinger over the autopilot release button on the control column. His face was rigid. Feet on the rudder bar and both arms ready, braced, he steeled himself.

"Tell him I'm switching over now," he told Janet. She repeated the message. His hand wavered for a moment on the button. Then, decisively, he pressed it hard. The aircraft swung a little to port but he corrected the tendency gently and she responded well enough to his feet on the rudder bar.

"Tell him O.K.," he gasped, his nerves taut as cables.

"Hello, Vancouver. We're flying straight and level." Janet's voice sounded miraculously calm.

"Well done, George. As soon as you've got the feel of her, try some very gentle turns, not more than two or three degrees. Can you see the turn indicator? It's almost directly in front of your eyes and slightly to the right. Over." Treleaven's eyes were closed with

the effort of visualizing the cockpit layout. He opened them and spoke to the dispatch messenger. "Listen. We ought to start planning the approach and landing while there's plenty of time. Get the chief radar operator up here, will you?"

Very gingerly Spencer extended his left leg and eased the control column over. This time it seemed an age before the aircraft responded to his touch and he saw the horizon indicator tilt. Gratified, he tried the other way; but now the movement was alarming. He looked down at the ASI and was shocked to see that it had dropped to 180 knots. Quickly he eased the control column forward. Then he breathed again as the speed rose slowly to 210. He would have to treat the controls with the utmost respect until he really understood the time lag, that was evident. Again he tried a shallow turn and pushed at the resisting weight of the rudder to hold it steady. Gradually he felt the ship answer. Then he straightened up, so as to keep approximately on the course they had been steering before.

Janet had lifted her eyes momentarily from the instrument panel to ask in a small voice, "How is it?"

Spencer tried to grin, without much success. "Tell him I'm on manual and doing gentle turns, coming back on course each time," he said.

Janet gave the message.

"I should have asked you this before," came Treleaven's voice. "What kind of weather are you in up there?"

"It's clear where we are right now," answered Janet. "Except below us, of course."

"Better keep me informed. Now, George, we have to press on. You may hit cloud layer at any time, with a little turbulence. If you do, I want you to be ready for it. How does she handle?"

Spencer, teeth clenched, looked across to Janet. "Tell him—sluggish as a wet sponge."

"Hello, Vancouver. As sluggish as a wet sponge," repeated Janet.

For brief seconds the group at Vancouver Control exchanged smiles.

"That's a natural feeling, George," said Treleaven, serious again, "because you were used to smaller airplanes."

The dispatch messenger cut in. "I've the radar chief here."

"I'll talk to him as soon as I get a break," said Treleaven.

"Right."

"Now, George," called Treleaven. "You must avoid any violent movements of the controls, such as you used to make in your fighter airplanes. If you *do* move the controls violently, you will over-correct and be in trouble. Is that understood? Over."

"Yes, Vancouver, we understand. Over."

"Now, George, I want you to try the effect of fore-and-aft control on your air speed. To start with, adjust your throttle setting so as to reduce speed to 160 and cruise straight and level. But keep the air speed over 120. The elevator trim is just to your right on the control pedestal and the aileron trim is below the throttles, down near the floor. Got it? Over."

Spencer checked with his hand, holding the plane steady with the other and with braced legs. "O.K., Vancouver, we're doing as you say."

Time ticked away as the speed slowly dropped. At 160 George adjusted the trim tabs and held up his thumb to Janet.

"O.K., Vancouver. We've got 160 knots on the indicator."

Treleaven waited until he had struggled out of his jacket before speaking. "Right, George. Try a little up and down movement. Use the control column as carefully as if it were full of eggs and watch your speed. Keep it at 160. Get the feel of the thing. Over." He put the microphone down. "Where's the radar chief?"

"Here."

"At what range will this aircraft show on your 'scope?" queried Treleaven.

"Sixty miles, thereabouts, Captain."

"That's no good for a while, then. Well," said Treleaven, partly to himself, partly to Burdick, "you can't have everything at once. Next call, we'll check his heading."

"Yeah," said Burdick.

"If he's stayed on the same heading," continued Treleaven, looking at the wall map, "he can't be that much off course, and we can straighten him up when he gets in our radar range. That Air Force radar check is a help."

"Can't he come in on the beam?" asked Burdick.

"Right now he's got enough to worry about. If I try to get him on the beam, he'll have to mess around with the radio, changing frequencies and a lot of other stuff. I'd sooner take a chance, Harry, and let him go a few miles off course."

"That makes sense," Burdick conceded.

The pilot turned to the radar chief. "I'll do the talking. He's getting used to me now. As soon as he shows up on your 'scope, feed me the information and I'll relay it. Can you fix up a closed circuit between me and the radar room?"

"We can take care of that," said the dispatcher.

"How about the final approach?" asked the radar chief.

"We'll handle that the same way," said Treleaven. "Directly we've got him on the 'scope and he's steady on course, we'll move to the tower. You report up there and we'll decide on the runway and plan the approach."

"Yes, sir."

"Dr. Davidson is downstairs," the controller told Treleaven. "From the information we've got he agrees with the diagnosis of the doctor in the plane. Wonders if it could be an outbreak of botulism. Shall we get the doctor up here and put him on the air?"

"No, Mr. Grimsell. It's more important right now to fly this airplane. We'll let them call for medical advice if they want it. I don't want Spencer's mind distracted from the job. But have Davidson stand by." Treleaven spoke into the microphone. "Hello, George Spencer. Don't forget that lag in the controls. Just take it steadily. Do you understand that?"

There was a pause. Then, "He understands, Vancouver. Over."

To Spencer it seemed as if Treleaven had read his thoughts. He had moved the column slowly forward, and then back again, but there had been no response from the aircraft. Now he tried again, easing the stick away from him. Imperceptibly at first, the nose of the aircraft began to dip. Then, so suddenly that he was momentarily paralyzed with shock, it plunged downwards. Janet bit hard on her lip to avoid screaming. The ASI needle began to swing round . . . 180 . . . 190 . . . 200 . . . 220. Putting all his weight on the column, Spencer fought to bring the aircraft back. In front of him the instruments on the panel seemed alive. The climb and descent indicator quivered against the bottom of the glass. On the altimeter the 100-foot hand whirred backward; the 1,000-foot hand less quickly but still terrifyingly fast; while the 10,000-foot needle had already stopped, jammed at its nadir.

"Come on, you slug, come on!" he shouted as the nose at last responded. He watched the altimeter needles begin with agonizing slowness to wind up again, registering gradually increasing height. "Made it!" he said in relief to Janet, forgetting that he was over-correcting.

"Watch it—watch the speed!" she exclaimed.

His eyes flicked back to the dial, now rapidly falling again. 160 . . . 150 . . . 140. Then he had it. With a sigh the aircraft settled down on an even keel once more and he brought it into straight and level flight.

The door to the flight deck opened behind them and Dr. Baird's voice called, "What's wrong?"

Spencer did not remove his eyes from the panel, "Sorry. I'm trying to get the feel of her."

"How are you doing?"

"Fine, just fine, Doc," said Spencer, licking his lips. The door closed again and Treleaven's voice came on the air. "Hello, George. Everything O.K.? Over."

"All under control, Vancouver," replied Janet.

"Good. What's your present heading, George?"

Spencer peered down. "Tell him the magnetic compass is still showing about 290." Janet did so.

"Very well, George. Try to stay on that heading. You may be a little out, but I'll tell you when to correct. Right now I want you to feel how the ship handles at lower speeds when the flaps and wheels are down. But don't do anything until I give you the instructions. Is that clear? Over."

Janet got Spencer's nod and asked Treleaven to proceed.

"Hello, 714. First of all, throttle back slightly and get your air speed steady at 160 knots. Adjust your trim to maintain level flight. Then tell me when you're ready. Over."

Spencer straightened himself and called over, "Watch that air speed, Janet. You'll have to call it off to me when we land, so you may as well start practising now."

He eased the throttles back. "What's the speed, Janet?"

"190, 180, 175, 170, 165, 155, 150 . . . That's too low!"

"I know. Watch it!"

His hand nursed the throttle levers, almost caressing them into the exact positioning to achieve the speed he wanted.

"150, 150, 155, 160 . . . it's steady on 160," Janet said.

Spencer puffed out his cheeks. "Phew! That's got it. Tell him, Jan."

"Hello, Vancouver. Our speed is steady on 160. Over."

Treleaven sounded impatient, as if he had expected them to be ready before this. "O.K., 714. Now, George. I want you to put on just 15 degrees of flap. The flap lever is at the base of the control pedestal and marked plainly: 15 degrees will mean moving the lever down to the second notch. The flap indicator dial is in the centre of the main panel. Have you got both of those? Can you see them? Over."

Spencer located the lever. "Confirm that," he told Janet, "but *you'd* better do it. Right?"

She acknowledged to Vancouver and sat waiting, her hand on the lever.

"Hello, 714. When I tell you, push it all the way down and watch that dial. When the needle reaches 15 degrees, pull the lever up and leave it at the second notch. All clear?"

"We're ready, Vancouver," said Janet.

"Right. Go ahead, then."

She prepared to depress the lever, then jerked her head up in alarm. "The air speed! It's down to 125."

Spencer's eyes flicked over to the air-speed indicator. Then desperately he pushed the control column forward. The lurch of the aircraft brought their stomachs to their mouths. Janet almost crouched in front of the panel, intoning the figures.

"135, 140, 150, 160, 170, 175. . . . Can't you get it back to 160?"

"I'm trying, I'm trying." Again he levelled off and jockeyed the controls until the ASI had been coaxed back to the required reading. He passed his sleeve over his forehead. "It is 160, isn't it?"

"Yes, that's better."

"That was close." He sat back in his seat. "Look, let's relax for a minute, after that." He managed to muster up a smile. "You can see the kind of pilot that I am. I should have known that would happen."

"No, it was my job to watch the air speed." She took a deep breath to steady her pounding heart. "I think you're doing wonderfully," she said. Her voice shook slightly.

It was not lost on Spencer. He said quickly and with exaggerated heartiness, "You can't say I didn't warn you. Come on, let's get going."

"Hello, George," Treleaven's voice crackled in the earphones. "Are your flaps down yet?"

"We're just about to put them down, Captain," said Janet.

"Hold it. I omitted to tell you that when the flaps are down you will lose speed. Bring it back to 140. Over."

"Well, I'll be—!" Spencer ejaculated. "That's mighty nice of him. He cut it pretty fine."

"It's probably hectic down there," said Janet, who had a very good idea of the scene taking place at the airport. "Thank you, Captain," she said, transmitting. "We're starting now. Over." At a nod from Spencer she pushed the lever down as far as it would go, while Spencer watched the indicator carefully.

"Right. Now back to second notch."

With infinite caution he cajoled the ASI needle until it rested steadily at 140.

"Tell him, Janet."

"Hello, Vancouver. Our flaps are down 15 degrees and the air speed is 140."

"Right 714. Are you still maintaining level flight?"

Spencer nodded to her. "Tell him, yes—well, more or less, anyway."

"Hello, Vancouver. More or less."

"O.K., 714. Now the next thing is to put the wheels down. Then you'll get the feel of the airplane as it will be when you're landing. When you are ready—and make sure you *are* ready—put down the landing gear and let the speed come back to 120. You will probably have to advance your throttle setting to maintain that air speed, and also adjust the trim. Is that understood? Over."

"Ask him," said Spencer, "what about propeller controls and mixture?"

At Janet's question, Treleaven said in an aside to Burdick, "Well, this guy's thinking, anyway. For the time being," he said into the microphone, "leave them alone. Later on I'll give you a full cockpit check for landing. Over."

"Tell him, understood," said Spencer. "We're putting down the wheels now." He looked apprehensively at the selector lever by his leg. It seemed a much better idea to keep both his hands on the column. "Look, Janet, I think you'd better work the undercart lever and call off the air speed as the wheels come down."

Janet complied. The arrest in their forward flight was so pronounced that it was like applying a brake, jerking them in their seats.

"130, 125, 120, 115 . . . it's too low."

"Keep calling!"

"115, 120, 120 . . . steady on 120."

"I'll get this thing yet," Spencer panted.

Treleaven's voice came up, with a hint of anxiety. "All O.K., George? Your wheels should be down by now."

"Wheels down, Vancouver," Janet reported.

"Look for three green lights to show you that they're locked. Also there's a pressure gauge on the extreme left of the centre panel, and the needle should be in the green range. Check."

"Yes, Vancouver. All correct."

"And say she still handles like a wet sponge," Spencer murmured, "only more so."

"Hello, Vancouver. The pilot says she still handles like a sponge, only more so."

"Don't worry about that. Now, put on full flaps for the proper feel of the aircraft on landing. Now follow me closely. Put full flap on, bring your air speed back to 110 knots and trim to hold you steady. Adjust the throttle to maintain the altitude. Over."

"Did you say 110, Captain?" Janet queried nervously.

"Yes, 110 is correct, Janet. Are you quite clear, George?"

"Tell him, yes. We are putting on full flap now."

Once more her hand pushed hard on the flap lever and the air speed started to fall.

"120, 115, 115, 110, 110. . . ."

Spencer's voice was tight with the effort of will he was making. "All right, Janet. Let him know. By God, she's a ton weight."

"Hello, Vancouver. Flaps are full on and the air speed is 110."

"Nice going, George. We'll make an airline pilot of you yet. Now we'll get you back to where you were and then run through the procedure again, with certain variations regarding props, mixture, boosters, and so on. O.K.? Over."

"Again!" Spencer groaned. "All right, Janet."

"O.K., Vancouver. We're ready."

"Right, 714. Using the reverse procedure, adjust your flaps to read 15 degrees and speed 120 knots. You will have to throttle back slightly to keep that speed. Go ahead."

Reaching down, Janet grasped the flap lever and gave it a tug. It failed to move. She bent closer and tried again.

"What is it?" asked Spencer.

"Sort of stiff. I can't seem to move it this time."

"Shouldn't be. Give it a good steady pull."

"It must be me. I just can't make it budge."

"Here. Let me." He took his hand off the column and pulled the lever back effortlessly. "There, you see. You've got to have the touch."

"Look out!" she screamed. "The air speed!"

It was 90, moving down to 85.

Bracing himself against the sudden acute angle of the flight deck, Spencer knew they were in a bad stall, an incipient spin. Keep your head, he ordered himself savagely—*think*. If she spins, we're finished. Which way is the stall? It's to the left. Try to remember what they taught you at flying school. Stick forward and hard opposite rudder. *Stick forward*. We're gaining speed. Opposite rudder. Now! Watch the instruments. They can't be right—I can feel us turning! No—trust them. Be ready to straighten. That's it. Come on. Come on, lady, *come on*.

"The mountains!" exclaimed Janet. "I can see the ground!"

Ease back. Not too fast. Hold the air speed steady. We're coming out . . . we're coming out! It worked! We're coming out!

"105, 110, 115 . . ." Janet read off in a strangled tone.

"Get the wheels up!"

"The mountains! We must—"

"Get the wheels up, I said!"

The door to the flight deck crashed open. There were sounds of crying and an angry voice.

"There's something wrong! I'm going to find out what it is!"

"Get back to your seat." This was Baird's voice.

"Let me through!"

The silhouette of a man filled the doorway, peering into the darkness of the flight deck. He lurched forward and stared in petrified disbelief at the back of Spencer's head and then at the prostrate figures of the two men on the floor. His mouth worked soundlessly. Then he impelled himself back to the open doorway and his voice was a shriek. "He's not the pilot! We shall all be killed! We're going to crash!"

EIGHT

WREATHED IN woolly haloes, the neon lights at the entrance to the reception building at Vancouver Airport glistened back from the wet driveway. At the turn-off from the main highway into the airport approach a police car stood angled partly across the road, its roof light blinking a constant warning. Those cars which had been allowed through along Airport Road were promptly waved by a patrolman to parking spaces well clear of the entrance to reception. Fire rigs and ambulances halted there for a few seconds to receive directions to their assembly points. A gleaming red salvage truck engaged gear and roared away, and in a small pool of silence the sound of a car radio carried clearly. "Here is a late bulletin from Vancouver Airport. The authorities here stress that although the Maple Leaf Airline flight is being brought in by an inexperienced pilot, there is no cause for alarm in the city. Residents in the airport area are being warned and at this moment emergency help is streaming out to Sea Island. Stay with this station for further announcements."

A mud-streaked Chevrolet swung into the parking lot and stopped abruptly. On its windscreen was a sticker: PRESS. A big thickset man, with greying hair, wearing an open trench coat, got out, walked rapidly over to reception and hurried inside. Dodging two interns in white coats, he made his way to the Maple Leaf Airline desk. Two men stood there in discussion with a passenger agent, and at the touch of the big man one of them turned, smiling in greeting.

"What's the score, Terry?" asked the big man.

"I've given the office what I've got, Mr. Jessup," said the other man, who was much younger. "This is Ralph Jessup—Canadian International News," he added to the passenger agent.

"I think Mr. Howard is about to make a statement in the press room," said the agent.

"Let's go," said Jessup. He took the younger man by the arm. "Is the office sending up a camera team?" he asked.

"Yes, but there'll be pretty full coverage by everyone."

"H'm. Remind the office to cover the possible evacuation of houses near the bridge. The same man can stay on the boundary of the field. If he climbs the fence he may get one or two shots of the crash—and get away quicker than the others. Who is this guy who is flying the plane?"

"A George Spencer of Toronto. That's all we know."

"Well, the office will get our Toronto people onto that end. Now grab a pay booth in reception here and don't budge out of it. Keep the line open to the office."

"Yes, Mr. Jessup, but—"

"I know, I know," said Jessup sadly, "but that's the way it is. If there's a foul-up on the phones in the press room, we'll need that extra line."

His coat flapping behind him, he strode across to the press room. Newsmen were already gathered, three talking together, another rattling at one of the typewriters on the large centre table, and others using two of the telephone booths that lined both sides of the room. On the floor were leather cases of camera equipment.

"Hi, Jess," greeted one of the men. "Where's Howard? Have you seen him?"

"On his way, I'm told. It's easy to see who's doing the work here." He indicated the two agency men in the telephone cubicles.

Abrahams of the Post-Telegram cut in, "We'd better start shouting for some action."

They turned as a youngish man entered, holding some slips of paper. This was Cliff Howard, high-spirited and energetic, and his crew-cut hair, rimless spectacles and quiet English ties were a familiar and popular sight at the airport.

"Thanks for staying put," he told them, and the two agency men hurriedly terminated their calls and joined the others.

"Let's have it, Cliff," said one of them.

Howard glanced down at the papers in his hand. There was a film of perspiration on his forehead as he said that one of the fifty-six passengers was at the controls of the plane because the pilot and co-pilot were ill. "Captain Paul Treleaven, Cross-Canada's chief pilot, is talking him down—but the authorities thought it advisable to take precautionary measures in clearing the area and bringing in extra help in case of accident."

"Come on, Cliff, what are you giving us?" protested Abrahams. "How does it happen *both* the pilots are ill?"

Howard shrugged uncomfortably. "We don't yet know for sure. It may be some kind of stomach attack."

Jessup interrupted, "Everything you've just said, our offices knew before we got here. What's the truth about the rumour of food poisoning? And who is the guy who's piloting the ship?"

Howard made a dramatic gesture of flipping notes to the floor. "Look, boys," he said expansively, "I'll lay it on the line for you. But if I stick my neck out I know you'll play along with me. We don't want to get the thing out of perspective. What's happening tonight is a big emergency—I won't pretend it isn't—but everything that's humanly possible is being done to minimize the risk. So far as my information goes, there has been an outbreak of sickness on the plane which may very possibly be food poisoning. The plane was late on arrival at Winnipeg and the normal caterers were not available. Food obtained from another firm included fish, and some of that fish, gentlemen, may, and I repeat *may*, have been contaminated."

"What about the guy who's taken over?" said a reporter.

"Luckily there was a passenger on board who had piloted before, and he took over the controls with the most remarkable smoothness. Name of George Spencer. He flew extensively in the war in smaller aircraft—"

"What kind of smaller aircraft?" Jessup demanded.

"Spitfires, Mustangs, quite a wide range of—"

"Hold it. This man was a fighter pilot during the war? And you mean that an ex-wartime pilot who was used to single-engine fighters has now, after all these years, to handle a multi-engine airliner?" Jessup said almost disbelievingly. There was a scramble as two or three of the newsmen broke away to the telephone booths.

"How long have we got before the crash?" Abrahams pressed.

Howard jerked round to him. "Don't assume that," he retorted. "She's due in round about an hour, maybe less."

"Suppose she overshoots into the water?" someone asked.

"That's not likely, but the police have alerted every available launch to stand by."

"Cliff," said Jessup, "how long will the gas last in this plane?"

"I can't say, but there's bound to be a safety margin," answered Howard, loosening his tie. He sounded far from convinced.

Jessup looked at him for a second or two with narrowed eyes. Then it struck him. "Wait a minute," he shot out. "If there's food poisoning on board, it can't be only the pilots who've gone down with it?"

"A number of passengers are ill, but there's a doctor on board who is giving what treatment he can. We have further medical advice available on the radio if required."

Jessup pursued relentlessly. "The time factor in food poisoning is everything. If those people don't get down pretty damn soon, they could die?"

"That's about it," Howard agreed, tight-lipped.

"But—but this is a world story! What's the position up there now?"

"Well, about ten, fifteen minutes ago—"

"That's no good!" Jessup roared. "Get the position *now*, Cliff. Who's duty controller tonight? Ring him—or I will, if you like."

"No, not for a while, Jess, please. I tell you they're—"

Jessup gripped the public relations man by the shoulder.

"This will be the biggest air story for years, and you know it. In an hour's time this place will be stiff with reporters, TV, the lot. You've got to help us now, unless you want us busting out all over the airport. Get us the exact present position and you can take a breather while we get our stories through."

"O.K., O.K. Ease off, will you?" Howard picked up an internal telephone from the table. "This is Howard. Control room, please? Hello, is Burdick there? Put me on, it's urgent. Hello, Harry? Cliff. The press are crowding up, Harry. They want the full situation as of now. They've got deadlines to meet."

"Of course!" snorted Burdick sarcastically in the control room. "Certainly! We'll arrange for the flight to crash before their deadlines. Anything for the newspapers!"

"Take it easy, Harry," urged Howard. "These guys are doing their job."

Burdick lowered the telephone and said to the controller, "Mr. Grimsell. Things are boiling up a bit for Cliff Howard. Do you think your Number Two could take a few minutes out to talk to the press?"

"I think so," answered the controller. He looked over to his assistant. "We'd better keep those boys under control."

"And no point in holding back," Burdick advised. "Tell 'em the whole thing—up to and excluding this," and he nodded to the silent radio panel.

"I get it. Leave it to me." The assistant left the room.

"The assistant controller is coming down, Cliff," said Burdick and rang off. He heaved his bulk over to the radio panel, mopping his face with a crumpled handkerchief. "Are you getting anything?" he asked in a flat voice.

Treleaven shook his head. His face was grey with fatigue. "No," he said dully. "They've gone."

The controller rapped to the switchboard operator, "Teletype Calgary and Seattle, priority. See if they're still receiving 714."

"Come in, 714, Vancouver Control to 714. Come in, 714," called the radio operator steadily into the microphone.

Treleaven leaned against the radio desk. "Well," he said wearily, "this could be the end of the line."

"Calling 714, 714. Do you hear me? Come in, please."

"I can't take much more," said Burdick.

"Hold it!" exclaimed the radio operator.

"Did you get something?" asked the controller eagerly.

"I don't know . . . I thought for a minute . . ." Bending close to the panel, the operator made adjustments to his fine tuning controls. "Hello, 714, 714, this is Vancouver." He called over his shoulder, "I can hear *something* . . . it may be them. If it is, they're off frequency."

"Tell them to change frequency," said Treleaven.

"Flight 714," called the operator. "This is Vancouver. This is Vancouver. Change your frequency to 128.3. Do you hear that? Frequency 128.3."

Burdick plumped back onto a corner of the centre table. "This can't happen—it can't," he protested in a gravel voice, staring at the radio panel. "If we've lost them now, they'll fry—every last one of them."

NINE

LIKE A MAN in a nightmare, his teeth clenched and face streaked with sweat, Spencer fought to regain control of the aircraft, one hand on the throttle lever and the other gripped tightly on the wheel. Within him, oddly at variance with the strong sense of unreality, he felt scorching self-disgust. Somewhere along the line, and quickly, he had not only lost altitude but practically all his air speed too. His brain refused to go back over the events of the last two minutes. Something had happened to distract him, that was all he could remember.

He felt an almost uncontrollable desire to scream. To scramble out and away from the controls and abandon everything. Run back into the warm, friendly-lit body of the aircraft crying out, *I couldn't do it. I told you I couldn't do it and you wouldn't listen to me. No man should be asked to do it. . . .*

"We're gaining height," came Janet's voice, incredibly level now. He remembered her with a shock and in that moment the screaming inside his head became the wild shrieks of a woman in the passenger compartment.

He heard a man shouting. "He's not the pilot, I tell you! We're done for!"

"Shut up and sit down!" rapped Baird clearly.

"You can't order me about—"

"All right, Doctor," came the adenoidal tones of 'Otpot, "just leave him to me. Now, you. . . ."

Spencer shut his eyes for an instant in an effort to clear the dancing of the illuminated dials. Behind him he could hear the woman passenger, sobbing loudly now. He shot a glance at Janet. In the greenish light from the instrument panel, her pale face looked almost translucent. He felt very ashamed.

"Trying to get the bus up as fast as I can," he said. "Daren't do more than a gentle climb or we'll lose way again."

Baird's voice called from the doorway, above the rising thunder of the engines, "What *is* going on in here?"

Spencer answered, "Sorry, Doc. I just couldn't hold her."

"It was my fault," said Janet.

"No, no," protested Spencer. "If it hadn't been for her we'd have crashed. I just can't handle this thing."

"Rubbish," said Baird curtly. Then his voice was raised loudly to address the passengers, "Now listen to me, all of you. Panic is the most infectious disease of the lot, and the most lethal, too." The door slammed shut, cutting him off.

Janet said calmly, "I ought to be reporting to Captain Treleaven."

"Yes," agreed Spencer. "Tell him what's happened and that I'm regaining height."

Janet pressed her microphone button to transmit and called Vancouver. For the first time there was no immediate acknowledgment in reply. She called again. There was nothing.

Spencer felt the familiar stab of fear. He forced himself to control it. "What's wrong?" he asked. "Are you sure you're on the air?"

"Yes—I think so."

"Blow into your mike. If it's alive you'll hear yourself."

She did so. "Yes, I heard all right. Hello, Vancouver. This is 714. Can you hear me? Over."

Silence.

"Let me," said Spencer. He took his right hand from the throttle and depressed his microphone button. "Hello, Vancouver. Hello, Vancouver. This is Spencer, 714. Emergency, emergency. Come in, please."

The silence seemed as solid and as tangible as a wall.

"I'm getting a reading on the transmitting dial," said Spencer. "I'm sure we're sending O.K." He tried again, with no result. "Calling all stations. Mayday, mayday, mayday. This is Flight 714, in serious trouble. Come in anybody. Over." The ether seemed completely dead. "That settles it. We must be off frequency."

"How could that have happened?"

"*Anything* could have happened, the way we were just now. You'll have to go round the dial, Janet."

"Isn't that risky—to change our frequency?"

"It's my guess it's already changed. All I know is that without the radio I might as well put her nose down right now and get it over."

Janet slid out of her seat and reached up to the radio panel. She clicked the channel selector round slowly. There was a succession of crackles and splutters.

"I've been right the way round," she said.

"Keep at it," Spencer told her. "You've got to get something. If we have to, we'll call on each channel in turn." There was a sudden, faraway voice. "Wait, what's that!" Janet clicked back hurriedly. "Give it more volume!"

". . . to 128.3," said the voice with startling nearness. "Vancouver Control to Flight 714. Change to frequency 128.3. Reply please. Over."

"Keep it there," said Spencer to the girl. "Is that the setting? Thank our lucky stars for that. Better acknowledge it, quick."

Janet climbed back into her seat and called rapidly, "Hello, Vancouver, 714 answering. Receiving you loud and clear. Over."

A relieved voice came back. "This is Vancouver, 714. We lost you! What happened? Over."

"Vancouver, are we glad to hear you!" said Janet. "We had some trouble. The airplane stalled and the radio went off. But it's all right now—except for the passengers, they're not taking it too well. We're climbing again. Over."

"Hello, Janet." This time it was Treleaven speaking, in the same measured manner as before but clearly with immense thankfulness. "I'm glad you had the good sense to realize you were off frequency. George, you *must* watch your air speed all the time. But there's one thing: if you've stalled and recovered, you obviously haven't lost your touch as a pilot."

"Did you get that?" Spencer asked Janet incredulously. They exchanged nervous smiles.

Treleaven was continuing: "You've probably had a bit of a scare, so we'll take it easy for a minute or two. While you're getting some height under you I want you to give me readings from the instrument panel. We'll start with the fuel-tank gauges."

While the captain was reciting the information he wanted, the door to the passenger deck opened and Baird looked in again, about to call to the two figures forward. He took in their concentration on the instrument panel and checked himself. Instead he entered quietly, closed the door behind him, and dropped on one knee beside the forms of the pilot and first officer, using his ophthalmoscope as a flashlight to examine their faces. Dun had rolled partly out of his blankets and was lying with his knees drawn up, moaning softly. Pete appeared to be unconscious.

The doctor readjusted the covers, wrapping them in tightly. He remained crouched in thought for a few seconds. Then he rose, bracing himself against the tilt of the steadily climbing aeroplane. Janet was relaying figures into her microphone. Without a word the doctor let himself out, carefully sliding the door closed.

The passenger deck resembled a vast casualty ambulance. At intervals along the crowded cabin sick passengers lay swaddled in rugs. One or two were quite motionless, scarcely breathing. Others were twisting in pain while friends or relatives watched them fearfully or replaced damp cloths on their foreheads.

Bending over the man he had recently thrust back into his seat, 'Otpot was saying, "I don't blame you, see? 'Appen it's better sometimes to let off steam. But it don't do to go shouting off in front of the others what's poorly, especially the ladies."

Temporarily subdued, the passenger, who was twice the size of 'Otpot, stared stonily at his own reflection in the cabin window by his seat. 'Otpot came along to the doctor, who patted his arm in thanks.

"You're quite a wizard," said Baird.

"I'm more scared than he is," 'Otpot assured him fervently, "and that's a fact. Doctor . . . what d'you make of things now?"

"I don't know," Baird replied. His face was gaunt. "They had a little trouble up front. It's hardly surprising. Spencer is under a terrible strain."

'Otpot put to him as quietly as he could, "What d'you really think, Doc? 'Ave we got a chance?"

Baird shook the question off in tired irritation. "There's always a *chance*, I suppose. But keeping an airplane in the air and getting it down without smashing it to a million pieces are mighty different propositions. Either way, it isn't going to make much odds to some of the folk here before long."

He squatted down to look at Mrs. Childer, feeling inside her blanket for her wrist and noting her pinched face, dry skin, and quick, shallow breathing.

Her husband demanded hoarsely, "Doctor, is there *nothing* we can do for her?"

Baird looked at the closed, sunken eyes of the woman. He said slowly, "Mr. Childer, you've a right to know the truth. We're making all the speed we possibly can, but at best it will be touch and go for your wife." Childer's mouth moved wordlessly, and Baird went on, "I've done what I could for her and I'll continue to do it, but it's pathetically little."

Childer found his voice. "I won't have you say that. Whatever happens, I'm grateful to you, Doctor."

"Of course he is," interposed 'Otpot heartily. "No one could've done more nor you, Doc. An absolute marvel, that's what."

Baird smiled faintly, his hand on the woman's forehead. "Kind words don't alter the case," he said. "You're a man of courage, Mr. Childer, and you have my respect."

The moment of truth, he thought bitterly: inside another hour we shall all very probably be dead. No romantic heroics—just the plain truth.

"I'm telling you," Childer was saying with emotion, "if we get out of this, I'll have everyone know what we owe to you."

Baird collected his thoughts. "What's that?" he grunted. "I'd give plenty to have two or three saline drips aboard." He rose. "Mr. Childer, if you can get her to take a little water now and then, so much the better. Your wife has lost a very critical amount of body fluids."

In the control room at Vancouver, Harry Burdick was replacing some of his own body fluid with a carton of coffee. In addition to the microphone held in his hand, Treleaven now had on a headset. He was asking, "Radar. Are you getting anything at all?"

From another part of the building, the chief radar operator answered in a conversational tone, "Not a thing yet."

"I can't understand it. They ought to be in range now."

Burdick volunteered, "Don't forget he lost speed in that last practice."

"Yes, that's so," Treleaven agreed. Into his headset, he said, "Radar, let me know the instant that you get something." To the controller, "I daren't bring him down through cloud without knowing where he is. Ask the Air Force for another check, will you, Mr. Grimsell?" He nodded to the radio operator. "Put me on the air. Hello, 714. Now, listen carefully, George. We are going to go through that drill again but before we start I want to explain a few things you may have forgotten or that only apply to big airplanes. Are you with me? Over."

Janet replied, "Go ahead, Vancouver. We are listening carefully. Over."

"Right, 714. Now before you can land certain checks and adjustments must be carried out in addition to the landing drill you just practised. I'll tell you when and how to do them later. Now I want to run over them to prepare you. First, the hydraulic booster pump must be switched on. Then the brake pressure must be showing about 900 to 1,000 pounds a square inch. Next, after the wheels are down, you'll turn on the fuel booster pumps and check that the gas feed is sufficient. Lastly, the mixture has to be made good and rich and the propellers set. Got all that? We'll take it step by step as you come in so that Janet can set the switches. Now I'm going to tell you where each of them are. Here we go. . . ."

Janet and Spencer identified each control as they were directed.

"Hello, Vancouver. We're O.K. on that."

"Right, 714. Check again that you are in level flight. Over."

"Hello, Vancouver. Yes, flying level now and above cloud."

"Right, 714. George, let's have 15 degrees of flap again, speed 140, and we'll go through the wheel-lowering routine. Watch that air speed like a hawk. If you're ready, let's go. . . ."

Already the first streaks of dawn were glimmering to eastward. Grimly Spencer began the procedure, following Treleaven's instruction with complete concentration while Janet anxiously counted off the air speed and operated the flap and undercarriage levers. Once again they felt the sharp jolt as their speed was arrested.

In the control room, Treleaven gulped some cold coffee. He looked haggard, with a blue stubble around his chin.

"How do you read the situation now?" Burdick said.

"As well as can be expected," said the captain, "but time's running short. He should have at least a dozen runs through this flap and wheels drill alone. With luck we'll get about three in before he's overhead—that is, if he's on course."

"You're going to give him practice approaches?" put in the controller.

"I must. Without them I wouldn't give a red cent for his chances. I'll see how he shapes up. Otherwise . . ." Treleaven hesitated.

"Otherwise what?" Burdick prompted.

Treleaven rounded on them. "We'd better face facts," he said. "That man up there is frightened out of his wits, and with good reason. If his nerve doesn't hold, they may stand more chance by ditching offshore in the ocean."

"But—the impact!" Burdick exclaimed. "And the sick people—and the aircraft. It'd be a total loss."

"It would be a calculated risk," said Treleaven icily. "If our friend looks like piling up all over the field, your airplane will be a write-off anyway."

"Hell, yes, I guess so," said Burdick uncomfortably.

"And with the added danger," continued Treleaven, "that if he crashes here, fire is almost certain and we'll be lucky to save anyone. Whereas if he puts down on the ocean he'll break up the airplane, sure, but we stand a chance of saving *some* of the passengers. With practically no wind the water is pretty calm. We'd belly-land him by radar as near as we could to rescue craft."

"Get the Navy," the controller ordered his assistant. "Air Force too. Air-sea rescue are already standing by. Have them put out offshore and await radio instructions."

"I don't want to do it," said Treleaven, turning back to the wall map. "It would amount to abandoning the very sick passengers. But it may be necessary." He spoke into his headset. "Radar, are you getting anything?"

"Still nothing," came the even reply. "Hold it, though. This may be something coming up. . . . Yes, Captain. I have him now. He's ten miles south of track. Have him turn right to a heading of 265."

"Nice work," said Treleaven. He nodded to be put on the air as the switchboard operator called across, "Air Force report visual contact, sir. ETA 38 minutes."

"Right." He raised the microphone in front of him. "Hello, 714. Have you carried out the reverse procedure for flaps and undercart? Over."

"Yes, Vancouver. Over," came the girl's voice.

"Any trouble this time? Flying straight and level?"

"Everything's all right, Vancouver. The pilot says—so far." They heard her give a nervous little laugh.

"That's fine, 714. We have you on radar now. You're off course ten miles to the south. I want you to bank carefully to the right and place the aircraft on a heading of 265. Repeat. 265. Is that clear? Over."

"Understood, Vancouver."

Treleaven glanced out of the window. The darkness outside had lightened very slightly. "At least they'll be able to see a little," he said, "though not until the last minutes."

"I'll put everybody on stand-by," said the controller. He called to his assistant, "Warn the tower, Stan. Tell them to alert the fire people." Then, to the switchboard operator, "Give me the city police."

Treleaven had slumped into a chair, his head bowed with a hand over his eyes, not hearing the confused murmur of voices about him. But at the first splutter as the amplifier came alive he was on his feet, reaching for the microphone.

"Hello, Vancouver," called Janet. "We are now on a heading of 265 as instructed. Over."

"Right, 714. You're doing splendidly," said Treleaven with an assumed cheerfulness. "Let's have it all again, shall we? This will be the last time before you reach the airport, George, so make it good."

Beside him the controller was speaking with quiet urgency into his telephone. "Yes, they'll be with us in about half an hour. Let's get the show on the road."

TEN

SPENCER tried to ease his aching legs. His whole body felt pummelled and bruised. In the effort of concentration he had expended enormous quantities of nervous energy: the moment he relaxed, he was left utterly drained of strength. He was conscious of his hands trembling and made no attempt to check them. All the time an interior voice, now every bit as real to him and as independent as the one in his earphones, kept telling him: *Whatever you do, don't let go. Remember, it was like this in the war. You thought you'd reached the end, with not another ounce left in you. But every time there was something left in the bag—one last reserve you never knew you had.*

He looked across to Janet, willing himself to speak. "How did we make out that time?" he asked her.

"We did pretty well," she said brightly. "I thought Captain Treleaven sounded pleased, didn't you?"

"Hardly heard him," he said, turning his head from side to side to relieve the muscles in his neck. "How many times have we done the flap and wheel routine now—three? If he asks us to do it once more, I'll. . . ." *Steady on*, his inner voice admonished him. *Don't let her see what a state you're in.* She had leaned over to him and wiped his face and forehead with a handkerchief. *Come on now, get a grip. Think of Treleaven: what a spot he's in.*

"Have you noticed, the sun's coming up behind us," said Janet.

"Why sure," he lied, lifting his eyes. Even ahead to the west the carpet of cloud was tinged with pink and gold, and the vast canopy of sky had perceptibly lightened. To the south, on the port beam, he could see two mountain tops, isolated like islands in a tumbling ocean of cotton wool. "We won't be long now." He paused. "Janet."

"Yes?"

"Before we go down, have a last—I mean, another look at the pilot and co-pilot. We'll probably bump a bit, we don't want them thrown about."

Janet slipped off her headset. As she rose from her seat, the door to the flight deck opened and Baird looked in. "I was just going to have a look at the captain and co-pilot, to make sure they're secure," she said.

"No need to," he told her. "I did it a few minutes ago, when you were busy."

"Doctor," called Spencer, "how are things with you back there?"

"That's why I looked in," said Baird tersely. "We're running out of time—but fast. I'd like to have had a diagnostic check with a doctor down there, but I guess it's more important to hold the air open for flying the machine. How long is it likely to be now?"

"Well under the half-hour, I'd say. How does that sound?"

"I don't know," Baird said doubtfully. "There are two patients in a state of complete prostration, and there are several others who'll soon be just as bad, unless I'm very wrong."

The earphones came to life. "Hello, 714. This is Vancouver. Over."

Spencer waved Janet back into her seat and she hurriedly donned her headset.

"Well, I'll get back," said Baird. "Good luck, anyway."

"Wait a minute," Spencer told him.

"This is 714," Janet was acknowledging into her microphone. "We'll be with you in a moment. Hold, please."

"Doctor," said Spencer quickly. "I don't have to fool you. This may be rough. Just about anything is liable to happen." The doctor said nothing. "They may get a bit jumpy back there. See that they're kept in their seats, huh?"

Baird replied in a gruff tone, "Do the best you can and leave me to take care of the rest." He thumped the younger man lightly on the shoulder and made his way aft.

"O.K.," said Spencer to the girl.

"Go ahead, Vancouver," she called.

"Hello, 714," responded the clear, confident voice of Treleaven. "Now that you've had a breather since that last run-through, George, we'd better press on again. You should be receiving me well now. Will you check, please? Over."

"Tell him I've been having a few minutes with my feet up," said Spencer. "And tell him he's coming in about strength niner." *Strength niner*, he thought. *You really dug that one up out of your past.*

". . . a short rest," Janet was saying, "and we hear you strength niner."

"That's the way, George. Our flying practice has slowed you down a bit, though that's all to the good as it will be getting light when you come in. You are now in the holding position and ready to start losing height. First I want to speak to Janet. Janet, when we make this landing we want you to follow the emergency crash procedures for protection of passengers. Over."

"I understand, Captain. Over."

"One more thing, Janet. Just before the landing we will ask the pilot to sound the emergency bell. And George—the switch for that bell is right over the co-pilot's seat and it's painted red."

"Can you see it?" asked Spencer without looking up.

"Yes," said Janet, "it's here."

"All right. Remember it."

"Janet," continued Treleaven, "that bell will be your warning for final precautions, because I want you to be back then with the passengers."

"Tell him no," Spencer cut in. "I must have you up front."

"Hello, Vancouver," said Janet. "I understand your instructions, but the pilot needs me to help him. Over."

There was a long pause. Then, "All right, 714," Treleaven answered. "I appreciate the position. But it's your duty, Janet, to see that all emergency crash precautions are taken before we can think about landing. Is there anyone you can explain and delegate this to?"

"What about the doctor?" suggested Spencer.

She hesitated, then pressed the button to transmit. "Hello, Vancouver. Dr. Baird will have to keep a watch on the sick passengers as we land. I think he's the best person to carry out the emergency drill. There's another man who can help him. Over."

"Hello, Janet. Very well. Leave the radio now, go aft and explain the procedure very carefully to the doctor. There must be no possibility of error." Janet laid aside her headset and climbed out of her seat. "Now George," Treleaven went on, "watch that you keep to your present course: I'll give you any corrections as necessary. In a minute, I'll give you a cockpit check of the really essential things. Some of them you'll remember from your old flying days. Be certain you know where they are. We'll have as many dummy runs as you like, but when you do finally come in the procedure must be carried out properly and completely. We'll start on the first check directly Janet gets back on the air."

In the control room at Vancouver, Treleaven looked up at the electric wall clock and back at the controller. "How much gas have they got?" he demanded.

Grimsell picked up the clipboard from the table. "In flying time, enough for about ninety minutes," he said.

"You figure there's plenty of time for circuits and approaches, don't you?" Burdick asked.

"There's got to be," said Treleaven. "This is a first-flight solo. But keep a strict check on it, will you, Mr. Grimsell? We must have plenty in hand for a long run-in over the ocean if I decide as a last measure to ditch."

"Mr. Burdick," hailed the switchboard operator, "your president is on the line."

Burdick swore. "Tell him I can't speak to him now. Tell him 714 is in holding position and his prayers are as good as ours."

The assistant to the controller, his hand cupped over an internal telephone, called to his chief, "It's Howard. He says the press are—"

"I'll take it." The controller seized the telephone. "Listen, Cliff. We're accepting no more non-operational calls. Things are far too critical now." He replaced the receiver with a bang.

Paul Treleaven stood by the radio panel, his fingers drumming absently, his eyes fixed on the clock.

Outside the airport, in the first light of dawn, the emergency measures were in full swing. At a local hospital a nurse hung up the telephone and spoke to a doctor working at an adjacent table. They hurried out and a few minutes later the overhead door to the vehicle bay of the hospital slid up, letting out two ambulances.

At the sound of a bell in a city fire hall, one of the few crews to be held on reserve slapped down their cards, snatched up their equipment, and raced for the door.

Near Sea Island Bridge, police were shepherding families from the group of houses into two buses. Most of the people had thrown street clothes hastily over their night attire. A small girl, staring intently at the sky, tripped over her pyjamas. She was picked up by a policeman and deposited in a bus. He waved to the driver to get started. . . .

"Hello, Vancouver," called Janet, a little breathlessly. "I've given the passengers the necessary instructions. Over."

"Good girl," said Treleaven with relief. "Now, George," he went on quickly, "the clock is running a little against us. First, reset your altimeter to 30.1. Then throttle back slightly, but hold your air speed steady until you're losing height at 500 feet per minute. You'll have a long descent through cloud."

Spencer spread his fingers round the throttles and gently moved them back. The climb and descent indicator fell slowly and a little unevenly to 600, then rose again to remain fairly steady at 500.

"Here comes the cloud," he said, as the gleams of daylight were abruptly blotted out. "Ask him how high the cloud base is below."

Janet repeated the question.

"Ceiling is around 2,000 feet," said Treleaven, "and you should break out of cloud about fifteen miles from the airport. Now, George, this is a little tricky. Keep a constant check on that descent indicator, but at the same time, if you can, I want you to pinpoint the controls in a first run-through of landing procedure. Think you can manage that?"

Spencer did not trouble to answer. His eyes fixed on the instrument panel, he just set his lips and nodded.

"Yes, Vancouver," said Janet. "We'll try."

"O.K., then. If anything gets out of hand, tell me immediately." Treleaven frowned in concentration as he looked at the blank spot on the wall, visualizing the cockpit of the aircraft. "George, this is what you will do as you come in. First, switch the hydraulic booster pump *on*. Remember, just fix these things in your mind—don't do anything now. The gauge is on the extreme left of the panel, under and to the left of the gyro control. Got it? Over."

He heard Janet's voice reply, "The pilot knows that one, Vancouver, and has located the switch."

"Right, 714. Surprising how it comes back, isn't it, George?" Treleaven pulled out a handkerchief and wiped the back of his neck. "Next you'll have to turn off the de-icer control. That's bound to be on and will show on the gauge on the right of the panel, just in front of Janet. The flow control is next to it. That one's easy, but the control must be off before you land. Watching the descent indicator, George? Next item is brake pressure. There are two gauges, one for the inboard brake and the other for the outboard. They're immediately to the right of the hydraulic boost which you've just found. Over."

After a pause, Janet confirmed. "Found them, Vancouver. They're showing 950 and—er—1,010 pounds—is it per square inch?—each."

"Then they're O.K., but they must be checked again before landing. Now, the gills. They must be one-third closed. The switch is right by Janet's left knee and you'll see it's marked in thirds. Are you with me? Over."

"Yes, I see it, Vancouver. Over."

"You can work that one, Janet. Next to it, on the same bank of switches, are the port and starboard intercooler switches. They're clearly marked. They will have to be opened fully. Make sure of that, Janet, won't you? The next and most important thing is the landing gear. You've been all through the drill, but go over it thoroughly in your mind first, starting with the flap movement and ending with the wheels fully down and locked. Full flap should be put on when the plane is very near touch-down and you're sure you're going to come in. I shall direct you on that. Is this understood by both of you? Over."

"Tell him yes, thanks," said Spencer, his eyes not leaving the panel.

"O.K., 714. When you're on the approach, and after the wheels are down, the fuel booster pumps must be turned on. Otherwise your supply of gas might be cut off at the worst moment. The switch for these is at five o'clock from the autopilot, just behind the mixture controls."

Janet was scanning the panel in a daze. "*Where?*" she almost whispered to Spencer. He peered at the board and located the little switch.

"There." His finger pointed at it.

"All right, Vancouver," she said weakly.

"Now the mixture is to be changed to auto rich. I know George has been itching for that, so I won't say any more—he'll handle that all right. Then you have to set the propellers until the green lights under the switches come on. They're just about touching George's right knee, I should think. Got them?"

"Pilot says yes, Vancouver."

"Lastly, the superchargers. After the wheels are down, these must be set in the take-off position—that is, up, on your aircraft. They are, of course, the four levers to the left of the throttles. Well, now. Any questions about all that? Over."

Spencer looked at Janet despairingly. "We'll never remember it all."

"Hello, Vancouver," said Janet. "We don't think we'll be able to remember it."

"You don't have to, 714. I'll remember it for you. There are some other points, too, which we'll deal with when we come to them. I want to go over these operations with you thoroughly, George, so that when I give the word you'll carry out the action without too much loss of concentration."

"Ask him about time," said Spencer. "How much have we got?"

Janet put the question to Vancouver.

"As I said, George, you've got all the time in the world—but we just don't want to waste any. You'll be over the airport in about twelve minutes. Don't let that bother you. There'll be as much time as you like for further practice." A pause. "Radar reports a course adjustment necessary, George. Change your heading five degrees to 260, please. Over."

Treleaven switched off his microphone and spoke to the controller. "They're well on the glide path now," he said. "As soon as we've got visual contact, I'll level them off and take them around for circuits and drills. We'll see how they shape up after that."

"Everything's set here," said the controller. He called to his assistant, "Put the entire field on alert."

"Hello, Vancouver," came Janet's voice over the amplifier. "We have now changed course to 260. Over."

"O.K., 714." Treleaven hitched up his trousers with one hand. "Let's have a check on your height, please. Over."

"Vancouver," answered Janet after a few seconds, "our height is 2,500 feet."

On his headset, Treleaven heard the radar operator report, "Fifteen miles from the field."

"That's fine, George," he said. "You'll be coming out of cloud any minute. As soon as you do, look for the airport beacon. Over."

"Bad news," Burdick told him. "The weather's thickening. It's starting to rain again."

"Get the tower," Treleaven told Grimsell. "Tell them to light up—put on everything they've got. We'll be going up there in a minute. I'll want their radio on the same frequency as this."

"Right!" said the controller, lifting a telephone.

"Hello, 714," Treleaven called. "You are now fifteen miles from the airport. Are you still in cloud, George? Over."

A long pause followed. Suddenly the radio crackled into life, catching Janet in mid-sentence. She was saying excitedly, " . . . it's lifting very slightly. I thought I saw something . . . yes, there it is! Do you see it, Mr. Spencer? It's right ahead. We can see the beacon, Vancouver!"

"They've broken through!" Treleaven shouted it. "All right, George," he called into the microphone, "level off now at 2,000 feet and wait for instructions. I'm moving to the control tower now, so you won't hear from me for a few minutes. We'll decide on the runway to use at the last minute, so you can land into wind. Before that you'll need to make some dummy runs, to practise your landing approaches. Over."

They heard Spencer's voice say, "I'll take this, Janet." There was a broken snatch of conversation in the plane, then Spencer came on the air again, biting off his words.

"No dice, Vancouver. The situation up here doesn't allow. We're coming straight in."

"He can't!" Burdick shouted.

"Don't be a fool, George," said Treleaven urgently. "You've *got* to have some practice runs."

"I'm holding my line of descent," Spencer intoned deliberately, his voice shaking slightly. "There are people up here dying. Dying! Can you get that into your heads? I'll stand as much chance on the first run-in as I will on the tenth."

"Let me talk to him," appealed the controller.

"No," said Treleaven, "there's no time for argument." His face was white. A vein in his temple pulsed. "We've got to act fast. By all the rules he's in command of that airplane. I'm going to accept his decision."

"You can't do that," Burdick protested.

"All right, George," Treleaven called, "if that's the way you want it. Stand by and level off. We're going to the tower now. Good luck to us all. Listening out." He ripped off his headset, flinging it down, and shouted to the others, "Let's go." The three men leaped out of the room and raced along the corridor, Burdick bringing up the rear. Ignoring the elevator, they bounded up the stairs and burst into the tower control room. An operator stood at the shining sweep of window, studying the lightening sky through night binoculars. "There he is!" he announced. Treleaven snatched up a second pair of glasses, took a quick look, then put them down.

"All right," he said, panting. "Let's make our decision on the runway."

"Zero-eight," said the operator. "It's the longest and it's pretty well into the wind."

"Radar," called the captain.

"Here, sir."

Treleaven crossed to a side table on which appeared a plan of the airport under glass. He used a thick chinagraph pencil to mark the proposed course of the aircraft.

"Here's what we do. We'll turn him so he begins to make a wide left-hand circuit, and at the same time bring him down to 1,000 feet. I'll start the pre-landing check here, then we'll take him over the sea and make a slow turn around onto final. That clear?"

"Yes, Captain," said the operator.

Treleaven took a headset that was handed to him and put it on. "Is this hooked up to the radar room?" he asked.

"Yes, sir. Right here."

The controller was reciting into a telephone-type microphone: "Tower to all emergency vehicles. Your runway is two-four. Two-four. Airport tenders take positions numbers one and two. Civilian equipment number three. All ambulances to positions numbers four and five. I repeat that no vehicle will leave its position until the aircraft has passed it. Start now."

Leaning down on the top of a control console, the captain flicked the switch of a desk microphone. At his elbow the spools of a tape recorder began to revolve.

"Hello, George Spencer," he called in a steady, even tone. "This is Paul Treleaven in Vancouver tower. Do you read me? Over."

Janet's voice filled the control room. "Yes, Captain. You are loud and clear. Over."

Over the headset, the calm voice of the radar operator reported, "Ten miles. Turn to a heading of 253."

"All right, George. You are now ten miles from the airport. Turn to a heading of 253. Throttle back and begin to lose height to 1,000 feet. Janet, put the preliminary landing procedure in hand for the passengers. Neither of you acknowledge any further transmissions unless you wish to ask a question."

Removing his hands one at a time from the control column, Spencer flexed his fingers. He managed a grin at the girl beside him. "O.K., Janet, do your stuff," he told her.

She unhooked a microphone from the cabin wall and pressed the switch, speaking into it. "Attention please, everyone. Attention please." Her voice cracked. She gripped the microphone hard and cleared her throat. "Will you please resume your seats and fasten your safety belts. No smoking, please. We shall be landing in a few minutes. Thank you."

"Well done," Spencer complimented her. "Just like any old landing, eh?"

She tried to smile back, biting her lower lip. "Well; not quite."

"You've got plenty of what it takes," said Spencer soberly. "Janet," he went on, his eyes on the instruments, "we haven't much more time. But I want to make sure you understand why I must try to get her down—somehow—on the first shot."

"Yes," she said quietly, "I understand." She had clipped her safety belt around her waist and her hands were clenched together tightly in her lap.

"Well, I want to say thanks," he went on, stumblingly. "You know, if anyone does, just how lousy I am at this. But taking turns around the field won't help. And some of the folks in the back are getting worse every minute. Better for them to . . . to take their chance quickly."

"I told you," she said. "You don't have to explain."

He shot her a look of alarm, feeling somehow exposed to her. She was watching the air-speed indicator; he could not see her face. He glanced away, back along the broad stretch of wing behind them. It was describing with infinite slowness the tiny segment of an arc, balancing on its tip the misty blue-grey outline of a hillside twinkling with road lamps. Sliding under the body of the aircraft, on the other quarter, were the distantly blazing lights of the airport. They seemed pathetically small and far away.

He could feel his heart thumping as his body made its own emergency preparations, as if aware that what remained of its life might now be measured in minutes, even seconds.

He heard himself say, "Here we go, then. This is it, Janet. I'm starting to lose height—*now.*"

ELEVEN

HARRY BURDICK lowered his binoculars and handed them back to the tower controller.

From the observation balcony which girdled the tower, the two men took a last look over the field at the gasoline tankers pulled well back from the apron and, clearly visible in the half-light, the groups of figures watching from the boarding bays. The throb of truck engines from the far end of the field seemed to add to the oppressive, almost unbearable air of expectancy which enveloped the whole airport.

Searching his mind for any possible fault, Burdick reviewed Treleaven's plan. The aircraft would arrive overhead at something just below 2,000 feet and then carry on out over the Strait of Georgia, descending gradually on this long, down-wind leg while the last cockpit check was executed. Then one wide about-turn onto the final approach would give Spencer maximum time to regulate his descent and settle down carefully for the run-in.

A good plan, one which would take advantage of the slowly increasing light of dawn. What would it mean to those of the passengers who were well enough to care? They would watch Sea Island and the airport pass beneath them, followed by the wide sweep of the bay, then the island getting shakily nearer again as their emergency pilot made his last adjustments to the controls. Burdick sensed, as if he were up there, the suffocating tension, the dreadful choking knowledge that they might well be staring death in the face. He shivered. In his sweat-soaked shirt, without a jacket, he felt the chill of the early-morning air like a knife.

"We are on a heading of 253." The girl's voice carried to them from the radio amplifier. "We are now losing height rapidly."

His eyes shadowed with anxiety, Burdick glanced meaningly into the face of the young man at his side. Without a word they turned and re-entered the great glass surround of the control tower. Treleaven and Grimsell were crouched before the desk microphone, their features bathed in the glow from the runway light indicators set into the control console in front of them.

"Wind still O.K.?" asked the captain.

Grimsell nodded. "Slightly across runway zero-eight, but that's still our best bet."

"Radar," said Treleaven into his headset, "keep me fed the whole time, whether or not you can hear that I'm on the air. Scrap procedure the instant 714 runs into trouble. Cut in and yell."

Burdick tapped him on the shoulder. "Captain," he urged, "what about one more shot at getting him to hold until the light's better and he's had—"

"The decision's been made," said Treleaven curtly. "The guy's nervy enough. If we argue with him now, he's finished." He continued in a quieter tone, "I understand your feelings, Harry. But understand his too, surrounded by a mass of hardware he's never seen before."

"What if he comes in badly?" put in Grimsell. "What's your plan?"

"He probably will; let's face it," Treleaven retorted grimly. "If it's hopeless, I'll try to bring him round again, unless it's obvious he doesn't stand a chance. Then I'll try to insist he puts down in the ocean." He listened for a moment to the calm recital of radar readings in his earphones, then pressed the switch of the microphone. "George. Let your air speed come back to 160 knots and hold it steady there."

The amplifier came alive as 714 took the air. There was an agonizing pause before Janet's voice intoned, "We are still losing height. Over."

Like a huge and ponderous bird, the Empress moved slowly over the Fraser River. To the right the bridge from the mainland to Sea Island was just discernible.

"Good," said Treleaven. "Now set your mixture controls to take-off—that is, up to the top position." He fixed his eyes on his wrist watch, counting the sweep of the second hand. "Take your time, George. When you're ready, turn your carburettor or heat controls to cold. They're just forward of the throttles."

"How about the gas tanks?" Burdick demanded.

"We checked earlier," replied Grimsell. "He's on main wing tanks now."

In the aircraft Spencer peered apprehensively from one control to the next, his face a rigid mask. He heard Treleaven's voice resume its inexorable monologue. "The next thing, George, is to set the air filter to ram and the superchargers to low. Take your time, now." Spencer looked about him wildly. "The air filter control is the single lever below the mixture controls. Move it into the up position."

"Can you see it, Janet?" asked Spencer anxiously.

"Yes. Yes. I have it." She added quickly, "Look—you can see the long main runway!"

"*Plenty* long, I hope," Spencer gritted, not lifting his head.

"The supercharger controls," continued Treleaven, "are four levers to the right of the mixture controls. Move them to the up position also."

"Got them?" said Spencer.

"Yes."

"Good girl." He was conscious of the horizon line dipping and rising in front of him, but dared not release his eyes from the panel.

"Now let's have that 15 degrees of flap," Treleaven instructed. "Down to the second notch. The indicator dial is in the centre of the main panel. When you have 15 degrees on, bring your air speed back slowly to 140 knots and adjust your trim for level flight. As soon as you've done that, switch the hydraulic booster pump on—extreme left, by the gyro control."

Through Treleaven's headset, the radar operator interposed, "Turn on to 225. I'm getting a height reading, Captain. He's all over the place. 900, up to 1,300."

"Change course to 225," said Treleaven. "And watch your height—it's too irregular. Try to keep steady at 1,000 feet."

"He's dropping off fast," said the operator. "1,100 . . . 1,000 . . . 900 . . . 800 . . . 700. . . ."

"Watch your height!" Treleaven warned. "Use more throttle! Keep the nose up!"

"650 . . . 600 . . . 550. . . ."

"Get back that height!" barked Treleaven. "Get it back! You need 1,000 feet."

"550 . . . 450 . . ." called off the operator, calm but sweating. "This isn't good, Captain. 400 . . . 400 . . . 450. . . . He's going up. 500. . . ."

For a moment, Treleaven cracked. He swung round to Burdick. "He can't fly it!" he shouted. "He can't fly it!"

"Keep talking to him!" Burdick spat out, seizing Treleaven's arm. "Keep talking! Tell him what to do."

Treleaven grabbed the microphone. "Spencer," he said urgently, "you can't come straight in! Listen to me. You've *got* to do some circuits and practise that approach. You've enough fuel for two hours' flying. Stay up, man! Stay up!"

But Spencer's voice came through. "I'm coming in. Do you hear me *I'm coming in*. There are people up here who'll die in less than an hour, never mind two. I may bend the airplane a bit—that's a chance we have to take. Now get on with the landing check. Wheels down, Janet."

"All right, George, all right," said Treleaven heavily. He had recovered his composure, but a muscle in his jaw twitched convulsively. He spoke with his former crispness. "If your undercarriage is down, check for the three green lights, remember? Keep your heading steady on 225. Increase your throttle setting slightly to hold your air speed now the wheels are down. Adjust your trim and keep all the height you can. Right. Check that the brake pressure is showing around 1,000 pounds. Then open the gills to one third. D'you remember, Janet? The switch is by your left knee and it's marked in thirds. Answer me only if I'm going too fast. Next, the intercoolers. . . ."

As Treleaven went on, his voice filling the hushed control tower, Burdick moved to the plate glass window, searching the sky low on the horizon. The dawn light was murky, retarded by the thick cloud banks. He heard Treleaven instruct a gentle 180-degree turn to the left, to bring the aircraft back for its approach, impressing on

Spencer to take it slowly while the last checks were carried out. The captain's precise monotone formed a sombre background to Burdick's frantically worried thoughts.

". . . Now advance your propeller settings," Treleaven was saying, "so that the tachometers give a reading of 2,250 r.p.m. on each engine. Don't acknowledge."

Spencer repeated the r.p.m. figure to himself, as he made the adjustment. "Janet," he said, "let me hear the air speed."

"It's 130 . . ." she began tonelessly, "125 . . . 120 . . . 125. . . ."

In the control tower Treleaven listened to the steady voice from the radar room. "Height is still uneven. 900 feet."

"George," said Treleaven, "let your air speed come back to 120 knots and adjust your trim. Repeat, air speed 120." He looked down at his watch. "Take it nice and easy, now."

"Still losing height," reported the radar operator. "800 feet . . . 750 . . . 700. . . ."

"You're losing height!" rapped out Treleaven. "Open up—open up! You must keep at around 1,000 feet."

Janet continued her reading of the air speed: "110 . . . 110 . . . 105 . . . 110 . . . 110 . . . 120 . . . 120 . . . steady at 120. . . ."

"Come up . . . come up!" Spencer growled between his teeth, hauling on the control column. "It doesn't respond! It doesn't respond at all."

"125 . . . 130 . . . 130 . . . steady on 130. . . ."

"Height coming up to 900 feet," intoned the radar operator. "950 . . . on 1,000 now. Maintain 1,000."

Treleaven called to the tower controller, "He's turning onto final. Put out your runway lights, except zero-eight." He spoke into the microphone. "Straighten out on a heading between 074 and 080. Watch your air speed and your height. Keep at 1,000 feet until I tell you."

In one series after another, the strings of lights half-sunken into the grass beside the runways flicked off, leaving just one line on either side of the main landing strip.

"Come out of your turn, George, when you're ready," said Treleaven, "and line up with the runway you'll see directly ahead of you. It's raining, so you'll want your windscreen wipers. The switch is down at the right on the co-pilot's side and is clearly marked."

"Find it, Janet," said Spencer.

"Hold your height at 1,000 feet, George. We've taken you a long way out, so you have lots of time. Have Janet look for the landing light switch. It's in the panel overhead, a little left of centre."

"Can you find the switch?" asked Spencer.

"Just a minute . . . yes, I've got it."

Spencer stole a quick look ahead. "My God," he breathed. The lights of the runway, brilliant pin-points in the blue-grey overcast of dawn, seemed at this distance to be incredibly narrow, like a short section of railway track.

"Correct your course," said Treleaven. "Line yourself up straight and true. Hold that height, George. Now listen carefully. Aim to touch down about a third of the way along the runway. There's a slight cross wind from the left, so be ready with gentle right-rudder." Spencer brought the nose slowly round. "If you land too fast, use the emergency brakes. You can work them by pulling the red handle immediately in front of you. And if that doesn't stop you, cut the four ignition switches which are over your head."

"Janet, if I want those switches off it'll be in a hurry," said Spencer. "So if I shout, don't lose any time about it." His throat was parched.

"All right," Janet replied. She clasped her hands together to stop them shaking.

"It won't be long now. What about the emergency bell?"

"I hadn't forgotten. I'll ring it just before touchdown."

"Watch that air speed. Call it off."

"120 . . . 115 . . . 120. . . ."

"Begin descent, 400 feet a minute," said the radar operator. "Check landing gear and flaps. Hold present heading."

"All right, George," said Treleaven, "put down full flap. Bring your air speed back to 115, adjust your trim, and start losing height at 400 feet a minute. I'll repeat that. Full flap, air speed 115, let down at 400 feet a minute. Hold your present heading." He turned to Grimsell. "This is it. In sixty seconds we'll know."

They listened to the approaching whine of engines. Treleaven reached out and took a pair of binoculars the controller handed him.

"Janet, give me full flap!" said Spencer. She thrust the lever down all the way. "Height and air speed—call them off!"

"1,000 feet . . . speed 130 . . . 800 feet, speed 120 . . . 700 feet, speed 105. We're going down too quickly!"

"Get back that height!" Treleaven shouted. "Get back! You're losing height too fast."

"I know, I know!" Spencer shouted back. He pushed the throttles forward. "Keep watching, Janet."

"650 feet, speed 100 . . . 400 feet, speed 100. . . ."

Eyes smarting with sweat in his almost feverish concentration, Spencer juggled to correlate speed with an even path of descent, conscious with a deep, sickening terror of the relentless approach of the runway, nearer with every second. The aircraft swayed from side to side, engines alternately revving and falling.

Burdick yelled, "Look at him! He's got no control!"

Keeping his glasses levelled at the oncoming aircraft, Treleaven snapped into the microphone, "Open up! Open up! You're losing height too fast! Watch the air speed, for God's sake. Your nose is too high—open up quickly or she'll stall! Open up! *Open up!*"

"He's heard you," said Grimsell. "He's recovering."

"Me too, I hope," said Burdick.

The radar operator announced, "Still 100 feet below glide path. Fifty feet below glide path."

"Get up—up," urged Treleaven. "If you haven't rung the alarm bell yet, do it now. Seats upright, passengers' heads down."

As the shrill warning rang out in the aircraft, Baird roared at the top of his voice, "Everybody down! Hold as tight as you can!"

Moving clumsily in his haste, Childer tried to gather his motionless wife to him, then leaned across her as far as he could. From somewhere mid-ship came the sob-racked sound of a prayer and, farther back, an exclamation from one of the rye-drinking quartet, "God help us—this is it!"

"Shut up!" rapped 'Otpot. "Save your breath!"

In the tower, Grimsell spoke into a microphone. "All fire-fighting and salvage equipment stand fast until the aircraft has passed them. She may swing." His voice echoed back from the buildings.

"He's at 200 feet," reported radar. "Still below glide path. 150 feet. Still below glide path. He's too low, Captain. 100 feet."

Treleaven jumped to his feet, holding the microphone in one hand and the binoculars in the other. "Maintain that height until you get closer in to the runway. Be ready to ease off gently. . . . Let down again. . . . That looks about right."

"Damn the rain," said Spencer. "I can hardly see." Ahead he had only a blurred impression of the beginning of the runway.

"Watch the air speed," cautioned Treleaven. "Your nose is creeping up. Straighten up just before you touch down and be ready to meet the drift with right rudder. . . . All right. Get ready to round out. . . ."

The end of the runway, two hundred feet across, slid under them.

"Now!" Treleaven exclaimed. "You're coming in too fast. Lift the nose up! Throttles right back! Hold her off. Not too much! Be ready for that cross wind. Ease her down, now. Ease her down!"

Undercarriage within a few feet of the runway surface, Spencer moved the control column gently back and forth, trying to feel his way down onto the ground, his throat constricted with panic because he now realized how much higher was this cockpit than that of any other plane he had flown, making judgment almost impossible. For what seemed an age, the wheels skimmed the runway, making no contact. Then with a jolt they touched down. There was a shriek of rubber and a puff of smoke. The shock bounced the aircraft right into the air again. Then the big tyres were once more fighting to find a purchase on the concrete.

A third bump followed, then another and yet another. Cursing, Spencer hauled the control column back, all the nightmare fears of the past few hours now a paralyzing reality. The grey stream below him jumped up, receded; jumped up again. Then, miraculously, it remained still. They were down. He eased on the toe brakes, then held them hard, using all his strength in his legs. There was a high-pitched squeal but no drop in speed. From the corner of his eye he could see that they were already more than two-thirds down the length of the runway. He could never hold the aircraft in time.

"You're landing too fast," roared Treleaven. "Use the emergency brakes! Pull the red handle!"

Spencer tugged desperately on the handle. He hauled the control column back into his stomach, jammed his feet on the brakes. He felt the tearing strain in his arms as the aircraft tried to slew. The wheels locked, skidded, then ran free again.

"Cut the switches!" he shouted. With a sweep of her hand Janet snapped them off. The din of the engines died away, leaving in the cabin the hum of gyros and radio equipment, and outside the screaming of tyres. Spencer stared ahead in fascinated horror. With no sound of engines, the aircraft was still travelling fast, the ground leaping past them in a blur. He could see now a big checkerboard marking the turn at the far end of the runway. In the fraction of a second his eyes registered the picture of a fire truck, its driver falling to the ground in his scramble to get away.

Treleaven's voice burst into his ears with the force of a blow. "Ground-loop it to the left! Hard left rudder!"

Spencer put his left foot on the rudder pedal and threw all his weight behind it, pressing it forward savagely. Veering suddenly from the runway, the aircraft began to swing in an arc. Flung over to the right side of his seat, Spencer struggled to keep the wings clear of the ground. There was a rending volume of noise, a flash, as the undercarriage ripped away and the aircraft smashed to the ground on its belly. The impact lifted Spencer clean from his seat. He felt a sharp pain as his safety belt bit deeply into his flesh.

"Get your head down!" he yelled. "We're piling up!"

Gripping their seats against the maniacal violence of the bouncing and rocking, they tried to curl themselves up. The aircraft continued to slither crabwise, ploughing grass in vicious furrows. With a screech of metal it crossed another runway, uprooting the runway lights, showering fountains of earth into the air.

Blood appeared in the corner of Spencer's mouth from a blow as yet unfelt. He waited for the inevitable tip-over, the splintering crash that would disintegrate into a thousand fiery pin-points of light before they were swallowed into darkness.

Then, quite suddenly, they were moving no longer. For the space of seconds there was no sound at all. He braced himself against the awkward sideways tilt of the deck and looked over at Janet. Her head was buried in her hands. She was crying silently.

In the passenger compartment there were the murmurs and rustlings of people incredulously finding themselves still alive. Someone laughed hysterically, and this seemed to let loose half a dozen voices speaking at once.

He heard Baird call out, "Is anyone hurt?"

The noises melted into confusion. Spencer closed his eyes. "Better open up the emergency doors," came the adenoidal tones of 'Otpot, "and then everyone stay where he is."

From the door to the flight deck, jammed open in the crash, he heard the doctor exclaim, "Wonderful job, Spencer! Are you both all right?"

"I ground-looped!" he muttered to himself in disgust. "We turned right around the way we came. What a performance—to ground-loop."

"Rubbish—you did magnificently," Baird retorted. "As far as I can tell, there are only bruises and a bit of shock back here. Let's have a look at the captain and first officer—they must have been thrown about some."

Spencer turned painfully to him. "Doctor, are we in time?"

"Yes; just about. It's up to the hospital now."

Spencer tried to raise himself in his seat, but at that moment he became aware of the sound of crackling. He felt an upsurge of alarm. Then he realized that the noise was issuing from his headset which had slipped to the deck. He reached down and picked it up, holding one phone to his ear.

"George Spencer!" Treleaven was calling. "Are you there?"

Outside there was a rising crescendo of sirens from crash tenders and fire trucks and ambulances. "Yes," he said, "I'm here."

Treleaven was jubilant, behind him were sounds of excited conversation and laughter. "George. That was probably the lousiest landing in the history of this airport. So don't ever ask us for a job as a pilot. But there are some of us here who'd like to shake your hand, and buy you a drink. We're coming over, George."

Janet had raised her head and was smiling tremulously.

He couldn't think of a thing to say to her. There was no adequate word of thanks. He knew only that he was intolerably tired and sick to the stomach. He reached over for her hand and grinned back.

Arthur Hailey

When Arthur Hailey's first television play was screened by the BBC it caused a remarkable sensation. Telephone calls jammed the BBC switchboard, to be followed by a deluge of enthusiastic mail. At this time Arthur Hailey considered himself to be primarily a playwright, so that when the idea occurred to him that his play might be turned into a book, he looked round for an experienced novelist with whom he might collaborate.

As luck would have it, he turned for advice to two authors who, under the pseudonym of John Castle, had written a brilliantly successful World War II novel, *The Password is Courage*. Hailey's project caught their fancy, and they got down enthusiastically to work. The resulting novel, *Flight into Danger*, captured all the tension and authenticity of Hailey's original play and has been equally successful.

Since then, of course, Arthur Hailey has gone on to become in his own right what the *Sunday Times* magazine has described as ". . . one of the most successful novelists of all time". One by one his books climb quickly to the top of both British and American best-seller lists, and many of them have proved major attractions to the film companies. The enormous authenticity of his work is the result of meticulous preparation: Hailey will devote as much as a full year to preliminary research before planning the outline of his book or starting to write.

His expertise in *Flight into Danger* comes from his years as an RAF pilot during the war. He was born and educated in England, then emigrated to Canada in 1947, where he worked at first in sales and advertising before turning to scriptwriting. He and his wife and three children now live—as befits the family of a phenomenally successful writer—overlooking a lagoon in the Bahamas.

HALIC: THE STORY OF A GREY SEAL
Ewan Clarkson

HALIC

The story of a grey seal

A CONDENSATION OF THE BOOK BY

Ewan Clarkson

ILLUSTRATED BY DENVER GILLEN

PUBLISHED BY HUTCHINSON, LONDON

Grey seals are enchanting animals, full of high spirits and innocent curiosity. Holiday-makers round Britain's rocky coasts will often have found themselves watched by secret, whiskered faces, bobbing gently or playing in the wake of each in-coming wave.

Yet few of us know where the grey seal comes from, or where he goes. His world is mysterious, his cry a haunting, almost-human sound: small wonder then that sailors once pictured mermaids singing piteously on the distant rocks.

The truth behind the grey seal's myth and mystery is no less fascinating. In this book the wild beauty of his life is vividly recreated, his dangers, his delights, his restless voyaging. Nature lovers and all who enjoy a well-told story will relish Halic's unusual, enthralling adventures.

THE BEGINNING

HE WAS born on the running tide. The sea and the rain cleaned him, the wind dried him, and the sun-hot stones warmed his body. He was an Atlantic grey seal, and his name was Halic.

It was October, and the dying breath of summer hung warm and fragrant over land and sea. To the east lay the mainland of Wales, and westward the island of Ramsey. All around were small islands and outcrops of eroded rock, mere skeletons of stone.

Earlier in the afternoon, as the tide ran north through Ramsey Sound, boiling and foaming over the ragged knives of Half Tide Rock, something had roused his mother from slumber. Perhaps it was the urgent quickening of life that caused her to hang upright in the clear water, head and shoulders exposed to the air.

Then the cow seal half-rolled on the surface, dived, and swam purposefully, her fore flippers pressed to her sides, towards a small stony beach on the landward side of Ramsey Island. As she surfaced twenty yards from shore, her arrival was marked by the beachmaster, a bull seal ten summers old, whose massive head and strong muscular neck were scarred by many fights.

The bull had won and claimed this beach, along with the two cows that now lay sunning themselves near their calves. Ceaselessly he patrolled offshore, lest some other male usurp his beach and his cows. In the following weeks he would court the nursing cows relentlessly, until they succumbed to his wooing. Now, roaring his anger, he arrowed through the water towards the newcomer.

As the bull drew close the cow struck at him, but he recognized her sex and swerved away. Her white teeth snapped on empty air as he sheered off, leaving her to make her way to the beach between the large boulders. Taking advantage of the Atlantic swell, she hauled out and slowly dragged her body a few feet from the surge of the tide, levering herself forward on her fore flippers. Then she rested, dozing in the hot sun.

She was quite young, this being her fifth summer, and this was to be her first calf. She was in perfect condition, a land mammal who had adopted the sea as her home, returning to land only to give birth to her young. In the water her coat of short fine hair had appeared to be silvery, mottled with dark grey. Now, as the sun dried her, it became a drab brown. Her head, smaller and rounder than the bull's, widened gracefully to the curve of her shoulders, which tapered away to her tail and the broad, leathery blades of her hind flippers. Her eyes were large, round, and dark below stiff curving whiskers; her ears were almost invisible.

It was very quiet. The other seals slept too, stretched out on the stones. Only a mewing gull broke the silence. To the southwest lay the Atlantic; it seemed to breathe with a steady rise and fall. To the south and east lay the Sound, a narrow gut of turbulent water caught between the island and the mainland. Across it giant slabs of purple slate rose vertically from the sea, buttressed by wind-carved sandstone and weathered granite. On the cliff tops lay heather and golden splashes of gorse. Beyond, fading into the hills, glowed the mellow hues of the land. From time to time, as the tide rose, the cow seal heaved herself farther up the beach. The sun moved on, and as the light faded and the tide had yet an hour to run Halic was born.

He arrived quite suddenly. One moment his mother was lying quietly on her side. Then she gave a low moan, made a convulsive heave, and it was all over. The calf's sudden appearance seemed to startle her, for she spun around, breaking the short umbilical cord. Halic lay at the edge of the tide, and while his mother gazed at his small white form a wavelet broke over him.

He moaned and shifted, and his mother, sniffing him nervously, shied away in alarm. He moaned again, louder, and began twitching convulsively away from the cold stinging spray. His mother made no effort to help, but watched continuously until at last he lay above the high-water mark. Here he fell asleep, exhausted, and his mother left him, to clean herself and swim in the cool sea.

When he woke it was night and the moon was full. His mother lay beside him, offering him comfort and shelter. He crawled towards her, nuzzling her flanks. After some inexpert fumbling he found her teats and drank the rich yellow milk on which he was to grow so fast. He slept again, and with the dawn came a gentle rain, cleansing his soft white fur of birth stains. The sun shone, the wind blew kindly, and Halic took his first look at his world.

THE BEACH, small and steeply shelving, was composed of tightly packed pebbles. Towering cliffs isolated it from approach except by sea. This environment was kinder than it seemed. The stones dried quickly, were smooth to Halic's body, and there was no sand to irritate his eyes or skin.

He was aware of the smell of seaweed and salt water, of the strong, musky scent of his own kind. He was aware too of the less pleasant odour of crude oil. The beach was contaminated with dark sticky clots of the substance, and the pelts of the other calves were stained with it.

He heard the rattle of stones as a seal moved over the beach, the bellowing roar of an outraged parent when one of the other seals approached too near its calf, the plaintive mewing of gulls, but above all the rhythmic sound of the sea.

The surge and hiss of the Atlantic swell, the slap and gurgle of wavelets trickling through rocks, the deep double boom as a wave thudded into a crevice, compressing the air until it exploded, throwing tons of water against the rock—these sounds, and the song of the wind, were his heritage. They were to be with him all his life.

Halic's dark eyes watered a little as he raised his muzzle and stared about him. Like all seals, he was born with his eyes open and could see well from birth. He had no internal tear ducts, which explains why, out of water, a seal's cheeks are always wet with tears. And when he was restless or disturbed tears would roll down his cheeks even more copiously. Near him he saw the sleek and dappled flank of his sleeping mother. High up the beach, its rotund little body pressed tight against the cliff, lay the elder of the other two calves on the beach, also sleeping. At the far end of the beach the second calf lay unattended. It was a few days older than Halic, weak and sickly, and it wailed miserably, moving its head slowly from side to side as it waited for its mother to return.

Clumsily Halic shuffled across the stones to his mother's side. She roused and leaned forward. Their muzzles touched briefly and then she lay back. In response to his caress her two breasts, normally flat and hidden, rose up through her fur, and Halic began to feed. As he sucked she caressed him lightly with her flipper. This rapid "flippering" was the only gesture of affection she showed for her calf.

A young cormorant was fishing nearby unworried by the seal—for grey seals never touch seabirds. Halic finished feeding and lay still, watching the sea. He looked very wise. Seals are, in fact, most precocious infants. At birth Halic had already grown and shed some of his milk teeth and had started to molt his white baby coat.

At birth he weighed twenty-nine pounds; he would gain more than three pounds each day. His mother's milk was over ten times richer than cow's milk. During the nursing period his mother would not feed herself but would draw on her reserves of fat built up during months of rich summer feeding. Sleek and plump now, by the time Halic was weaned she would lose nearly two hundred pounds, almost a third of her body weight.

For the first few weeks of his life Halic was more vulnerable than he would be ever again. It was vital for the success of his species that this nursery period should be as short as possible. Meanwhile, he slept and ate.

All the seals had a seemingly limitless capacity for sleep. Indeed, it seemed their natural mode of existence. They awoke only when stimulated by danger, hunger, or other driving need. As soon as those needs were satisfied, back they went to sleep. Now, with little fear of danger and no desire to feed or hunt, the cow seals had only to feed their calves, drowse on the stones, and conserve their energy. Sometimes a seal might yawn and stretch, idly scratching her hide with a fore flipper. Then she would smack her lips contentedly, her heavy eyelids would droop, and her head would sink gently onto the stones. What seemed to the human observer an interminably long confinement was perhaps to the seals quite a short interlude, unnoticed except during brief periods of consciousness.

During this time the master bull did not feed either. He too slept for long periods, in the water or on the beach, and during his waking hours patrolled just offshore, ever ready to intercept a trespasser. Each time a cow seal entered the water to play and relax, the bull would approach; but she would warn him off with slashing white teeth and bristling whiskers. He would remain in attendance, but at a respectful distance.

A challenge came at dusk on the first day of Halic's life. The tide was almost full, and the cows lay high on the beach, sheltering the calves with their bodies from the impact of the small waves. An uproar broke out and they gazed with mild interest in the direction of the noise. The challenger bull, a lusty unscarred youngster, had come quietly into the Sound along the edge of the rocks. By the time the beachmaster noted his arrival the challenger was between him and the beach.

The beachmaster was still in full vigour, for the strain of fasting had not yet begun to tell. Berserk with anger, the older bull reared up from the water and the sea boiled as he struck at the imprudent stranger whose teeth were chopping at his throat. In the nick of time the younger bull turned his head away from the terrible jaws that could crush his skull like an egg. Instead, the beachmaster took him by the neck and shook him as a terrier shakes a rat.

Wrenching free, the young bull fled. A black mist of blood hung in the water for a moment. Then the sea cleared, the master bull returned to his station, and the cow seals slept. Later the young bull lay sleeping on a flat rock south of the island. His wound had stopped bleeding and shone white in the moonlight.

THE WEATHER remained fine and calm. There were now five cows and four calves on the beach, joined occasionally by the bull. At high tide the herd was a little cramped for space. As the tide rose, mother and baby would stay in position until the calf was awash in the swell. Then came a general reshuffle as the herd moved up the beach, each seal endeavouring to secure a place for herself and her calf by aggressive posturing and a savage display of teeth. At last the herd would settle down for a time, only to repeat the performance as the tide rose higher.

When Halic was a week old he began to explore the sea. Anxiously guarded by his mother, he wriggled, like a fat grub, into the water and let the waves wash his body back to the beach. As he gained strength and confidence he began to investigate narrow channels and pools among the rocks. He rode out to sea on a receding wave and then flippered frantically shoreward, only to find the next advancing wave carried him there. His mother hovered nearby, ready to slip beneath him and support his weight if he found himself in difficulty. If the master bull came too near she would knock him sideways with the fury of her attack. Meantime Halic would bumble about, practising little dives, which invariably failed because he had not yet learned to empty his lungs of air before submerging. He would stand on his head, his hind flippers working furiously in the air, only to bob up again like a cork. But his fore flippers were stronger now, and soon he would master the art of diving by pulling himself under with one sidewise stroke.

Exploring the crannies of the rocks, nosing through the fringe of weed that hung there, he played with pebbles and chased, but never caught, small crabs and butterfish. He found snails and crunched them up, savouring the strange taste and letting the water wash the shell fragments from his tongue and jaws. When he was tired he would haul out onto the stones, bawling until his mother came and fed him. Then, lulled by the security of her side and bloated with rich creamy milk, he would drift into slumber, to wake only when the rising tide nudged him up the beach.

Of the five calves born on the beach that autumn, only three remained. One had been stillborn and the weakling calf had died. The bodies had lain among the stones until the tide took them away. The eldest calf was now three weeks old and its mother had ceased to feed it. Too fat to care, it dozed in the sun while its mother played in the sea with the master bull.

Small incidents marked the passing of the days. A young raven flew in from the sea and hurtled straight for the cliff face. At the last moment he catapulted high into the air, soaring over the island before he turned back out to sea and repeated the performance. His arrival disturbed a pair of rock doves, perched on a ledge below the cliff top, and they sped away towards the mainland.

A thousand feet above, a large hawk hung stiff-winged in the sky. He was one of the few surviving peregrines. Now he marked the doves as they climbed towards him, and he dropped from his position, speeding his plummeting dive with swift incisive wing-beats. He hit one of the doves and it spiralled downward towards the waves. The hawk caught it a foot above the sea and flew off with his burden.

But for long periods the Sound looked empty of life. Most of the birds had gone, heading far out to sea to winter in the Atlantic. They had come to land only to mate and raise their young, and now the nesting sites were empty.

The weather was deteriorating. The wind had suddenly backed south and on the third day, after a very high tide, was gusting strongly. Sudden squalls hit the beach as the tide rose and darkness fell. The seals were restless, and their sobbing wails rose above the clamour of waves and wind.

The youngest calf was safe, wedged in a niche of rock on the lee side of the beach. The eldest swam out, away from the danger of the breaking waves. But Halic, now fourteen days old and seventy-nine pounds in weight, lingered, reluctant to forsake the land. His mother called anxiously and returned to his side again and again, trying to lead him into deeper water. Several times he followed for a few yards but then returned and lay wailing and moaning, as the waves broke and crushed him against the stones.

At last the whole beach was awash. Halic, in danger of being smashed against the foot of the cliff, suddenly found himself riding a wave higher than the rest. The next moment he was in the open sea. For a while his mother managed to keep by his side. Ahead of them lay The Bitches, a chain of jagged rocks that stretched out into the Sound. Here the sea boiled and thundered in a maelstrom of foam. Halic went spinning and sliding forward on the tide. When he reached calmer water he was a hundred yards from his mother. He never saw her again.

THE WANDERER

Dawn broke grim and grey. The wind had abated somewhat and a steady rain seemed to flatten the waves. North of the island and miles from land, Halic floated on the sea. He had survived the ordeal of the storm and the danger of being cast up on a mainland beach where he would have been at the mercy of farm dogs and men. He had lost his mother, but he would not have fed from her much longer.

A thick layer of blubber insulated him from the cold. It would nourish him in the weeks to come, as, slowly, he learned the art of catching his prey. This blubber was so densely interlaced with blood vessels that he had fifty percent more blood than other mammals of comparable size.

His rich blood supply meant that he could go for long periods without breathing. He was further aided by a sphincter muscle close to his heart that could slow down his heartbeat from a hundred and twenty beats a minute to less than ten. Now, as he slept on the surface of the sea, a sensation of coldness in his flippers roused him every five minutes or so, and he raised his head, eyes still shut, to take a dozen breaths before sinking back into slumber. Waking on the ebbing tide, he turned and began to swim with the flow south and west of the island on which he had been born.

He soon discovered it was easier to swim underwater. From time to time he was joined by great shoals of fish, swimming all around him. Below him their jade-green and blue-black markings merged with the shadows of the sea; above, their silver bellies and flanks matched the broken light that filtered down from the surface; from the sides, their shimmering flanks betrayed their presence. Halic chased them as he had chased the crabs and butterfish in the rock pools. The fish easily evaded him and sped on, but their numbers were so vast that they continued to pass him for a long time.

The rain had stopped and the clouds were breaking as he came at last to the small islands west of Ramsey. Here he hauled out to doze on a small flat rock which was exposed at low tide. He woke to darkness and the rising tide. Now the islands were shadows in a black and silver sea. From time to time the scene was lit by a spear of light from the South Bishop Lighthouse.

Halic could hear other seals nearby, sobbing and moaning above the hiss of wind and waves. He swam to a sloping rock slab where some yearlings lay. He hauled out beside them and slept fitfully. At dawn when the others tumbled off the rock into the waves, Halic followed. But he soon lost them and found himself heading south again, across the wide mouth of the bay towards distant islands.

As the sun rose the sea ahead seemed to boil. Mackerel had found a shoal of tiny immature cod and were scything into their ranks. A small school of bass, lean grey wolves of the sea, joined them, taking mackerel and cod impartially. Then seven dolphins arrived; their triangular black fins cut through the water at terrible speed. They encircled the shoal, then attacked, killing and feeding while the rest of the fish fled. Halic watched from a respectful distance. The dolphins were bigger than he was.

When they moved away he swam into the area, moving cautiously about six feet below the surface. Thousands of silver scales dislodged in the melee shimmered in the waves. Halic saw a mackerel, still alive but swimming slowly, its spine broken by a dolphin. He killed it, then bore it in triumph to the surface, shaking it, throwing it from him, and retrieving it. For some time he made no attempt to eat it. Suddenly his instinct told him what to do. He bit into the fish near the neck, raised both fore flippers, and, still holding firmly with his teeth, pushed the mackerel violently away from him. In this manner he tore a strip of flesh from the fish, then swam after it for repeated bites. When he was finished he looked for more easy prey, but found none.

Halic's swimming was improving rapidly. He learned to journey over the seabed with his hind flippers waving from side to side and his fore flippers hanging down to act as stabilizers and keep him on an even keel. When he had to move fast these fore flippers pressed close to his sides to cut down water resistance. His judgment of distance was improving too and he found he was able to swim for longer periods of time without feeling exhausted.

He was losing the white coat of his babyhood, and the mottled grey of his new pelt was beginning to show around his head and flippers.

The islands to the south were nearer now, their russet walls rising sheer from the white foam that surged around their base. Once these islands had been prized for their produce. Crops were grown and sheep reared. Seals were butchered for their hides and oil. Seabirds were harvested and their eggs collected at nesting time. Now the islands were nature reserves for the seabirds and seals to breed and live in peace.

The wind blew cold from the north and whipped up a stinging spray. Halic took shelter in the lee of an island and slept for the first time on the seabed, undisturbed by wind or waves. When his body needed oxygen he would rise to the surface and, still sleeping, recharge his bloodstream. Then, with a lazy wave of his flipper, he would turn and sink headfirst to the clean sand bottom. Flatfish, plaice, and sole lay there in dense packs, burrowing into the sand so that they were hidden from view or moving slowly over the seabed in search of marine worms. A dogfish hovered nearby ready to pounce on any flatfish that ventured too close.

Halic broke surface as the sun was setting. Other seals played in the water around him, and on a small beach two cows rested with their calves. When Halic approached, however, the master bull warned him away. He swam off into the darkening waves, still heading south.

His horizons were limited, physically as well as metaphorically. He could only raise his head a foot or so above the water, and often his view was obscured by waves. His vision underwater was good, but objects at a distance seemed dim and blurred.

Had he not been swept from his island birthplace by the sea he might have been content to spend his life there, for only a few grey seals ever venture far. Yet he was not alone in his wandering; other seals had travelled farther than he. It was through the migrations of these wanderers that new colonies were formed.

The grey seals' habitat ranges from the eastern seaboard of North America to the coast of Norway, but Great Britain is their last stronghold.

For centuries man has persecuted the seal, shooting the adults for their flesh and oil and clubbing the calves for their skins. Where there are many calves, the hunters grow tired, their aim less sure. So from time to time a calf is skinned before it is dead.

Only on remote islands, where the breeding beaches are inaccessible, can seals survive extermination. Their numbers are dwindling, except in Great Britain, where they are given protection of the law.

On his journey southward, Halic followed a course along a current which was part of a great slow eddy swirling back to the southwest from the Bristol Channel. Whole days would pass when he seemed alone in a world of tumbling grey water. At other times the sea would be alive with great shoals of mackerel. Sometimes he met squid. They often changed colour as they swam, now blushing dark red, then paling to pink or yellow. The colour cells in their skin were elastic, and by extending and contracting them they could instantly change their hue.

Once Halic dived at a squid, which paled to a dead white and released a thick black cloud of ink. The ink hung in the sea, retaining the shape of the squid, and Halic snapped at it while the squid itself disappeared.

From time to time Halic saw ships: small rusty coasters with cargoes of timber, oil tankers, and trawlers returning to port with their harvest of fish, followed by gulls that wheeled and screamed over the stern. For thousands of years man had fished in the sea. When the railways came and fresh fish could be transported inland and sold before it went bad, the fishing fleets grew to meet the new demand. As fish grew scarcer, the boats sailed into the icy wastes of the North Atlantic, harvesting the sea, not only for fresh fish for human consumption but for fish to turn into fertilizer and cattle food.

The oceans became dumping grounds for all sorts of waste, and Halic often investigated floating debris—wood, bottles, plastic containers of all kinds. The plastic, unaffected by sea or weather, might float for weeks or lie on a beach for years.

The sea held many surprises. One evening a shoal of basking sharks broke surface close to Halic, who, after one glimpse, crash-dived and sped away. Although later he was to grow familiar with these harmless giants, his first sight of them filled him with terror. The smallest was more than twelve feet in length, the largest nearly thirty. Swimming at full speed from the seabed, these normally lethargic creatures rocketed into the sky to a height of twenty feet, then fell back with a resounding splash. This was to rid themselves of sea lice, which clung to their gill arches and fins.

They had spent the summer cruising over the sea at a snail's pace, their backs showing above the water and their great fins and tails waving in the air. Their food consisted of shrimps and mollusks, and larvae of crabs and fish, which they obtained by swimming with their great shovel mouths open. The food was sieved by their gill plates, collected on their tongues, and swallowed. Their gill plates were frayed from continual use; eventually the sharks would come to rest on the seabed and grow a new set.

One by one the sharks ceased their acrobatics, and Halic was alone once more in a twilit sea. He passed by the two lighthouses on the Isle of Lundy and in the days that followed, as winter bit into the sea, he romped in the waves, riding the white crests before plummeting down to the troughs thirty feet below, or dived through a wave a split second before its crest engulfed him. He travelled south and west, butting into the wind, passing great rafts of seabirds riding out the storms.

Halic was now a very different seal from the one washed off the beach three weeks ago. He was the mottled grey of a young adult and slimmer, for he had not fed since he caught the crippled mackerel. But little by little he grew more expert in hunting. He learned to prowl over the seabed, watching for the faint flutter of sand that betrayed a buried plaice. He caught small turbot and brill, often when they were feeding and unaware of his presence. He used the twin pads of gristle below his nostrils to locate other prey when it was dark or the water was deep. These pads kept him aware of every small movement, probably by picking up vibrations; it was as if he owned his own echo sounder. And all the while, he drifted slowly down the coast.

In turbulent weather he swam well out to sea and dived down into the twilight of the ocean. When the sun shone, and the sea was calm, he came inshore, nosing into the rocky coves and inlets, swimming along underwater canyons by the side of weed-bearded cliffs, or cruising through tessellated grottoes where fish played like birds and red anemones clung like rubies to the stone. He came upon caves which no man knew existed. These caves might be halls lit with dim green light, with lofty roofs supported by giant pillars of stone, or they might be little more than dark hollows in the rock. Sometimes they were filled with strange music as the sea surged in.

Halic liked to listen to the music as he lay on the cold weed-covered slabs of rock. Sometimes he answered with moaning wails that to human ears sounded mournful but to Halic were comforting and entertaining. Sometimes he sang at sea, especially when the moon shone full. Then superstitious fishermen would tell each other it was the ghost of a drowned seaman.

In the caves Halic often met other seals. He joined them in hunting parties. Together they robbed the fishermen's lines, which had been set with baited hooks where the sea floor was too rough to trawl. The seals would eat the small fish hanging on the hooks, and those too big to tear away they mutilated, biting great chunks from the living flesh. Whenever the men found the damaged fish, they vowed to shoot every seal they saw.

On a bright morning in early December, Halic discovered a strange object bobbing in the waves. It was a mine, set more than a quarter of a century ago when Great Britain was at war with Germany. It had been overlooked when the minefields had been cleared after the war. Now gales had torn it loose from its mooring on the seabed. As Halic played with enough high explosive to sink a ship, other seals joined him, levering the deadly brittle horns with their flippers and spinning the mine around. As it drifted towards the cliffs, Halic succeeded in riding it for a few minutes before it tipped him back into the waves.

At last the seals left the mine and headed back out to sea. A herring gull perched on it as it neared the cliffs but flew away screaming as the mine lurched in the foam. For a few moments it bobbed, dark and gleaming in the white water, and then the cliff face was torn asunder as it exploded.

Far out to sea the seals panicked, crash-diving under the waves. When Halic surfaced he was again alone, and he swam on. In a day or two he drifted back to the coastline where the flatfish were easier to catch than the swift strong codling that were arriving offshore from the north. In January the sea temperature dropped and snow squalls blew in. Life was at its lowest ebb as the fish, conger eels, crabs, and lobsters moved away into deeper water to spawn or to shelter from the cold. Halic was so well insulated that he could have withstood far lower temperatures.

HALIC HAD not yet come into contact with mankind. But one evening, as the tide flowed and the lights of a nearby town began to glow faintly in the dusk, he swam into the mouth of a broad estuary, questing for the food which swarmed there—rag worms, colonies of mussels, tiny shrimps, prawns, sand eels, water snails, and shore crabs. He came upon flatfish feeding on the crabs. His teeth clamped down across the largest, and he bore the fish flapping to the surface. Far away in the dusk a dark shadow stirred, but in his preoccupation with the flounder Halic paid no heed.

After he had finished eating, he swam off in search of fresh victims.

The fisherman, watching Halic from the shadows at the water's edge, reeled in his line, removed the bait, and moved quietly up the hill to his cottage. Putting away his fishing tackle, he picked up a small-calibre rifle and left the house once more. The moon was rising now and the tide beginning to ebb. Halic remained in the estuary, listening. Above the faint noises from the town, the soft wind in the trees, and the plop of a rising fish came other sounds, a metallic clatter, the creak and splash of oars.

Halic hesitated. He was aware of impending danger but uncertain of what form it would take, so he hung in the water, his head a round black silhouette in the moonlight. Very faintly he could make out the dark shadow of a boat. The rowing ceased but Halic still waited, puzzled and curious. Slowly the boat swung around, and all at once the bowed back of the oarsman became a menacing shape as the moonlight shone on his white face and two white hands gripping a glittering rifle.

Halic dived with the report. In his mind the sound, the flash of the gun, and the image of the man were welded together by the searing pain of the bullet that ripped across his neck. He passed under the boat and away out to sea. Behind him his blood trailed like black smoke in the tide.

Never again would he trust mankind, or boats. Henceforth he would keep to the open sea or the sanctuary of the high cliffs. Now he swam far away from the land and its dangers. Dawn was silvering the sky before he slept.

Though his wound bled profusely, it was little more than a graze across the back of his neck which quickly healed in the clean salt water and eventually left a white scar. Halic forgot it as he journeyed on down the coast, drifting silently over mud, rock, and sand.

The sea held many secrets. Wherever boats were numerous the seabed bore unmistakable evidence of mankind. Rubbish littered the floor. Commonest and most indestructible were bottles, many of which had been adopted as homes by sea creatures. A jar which had once contained face cream moved slowly and jerkily over the

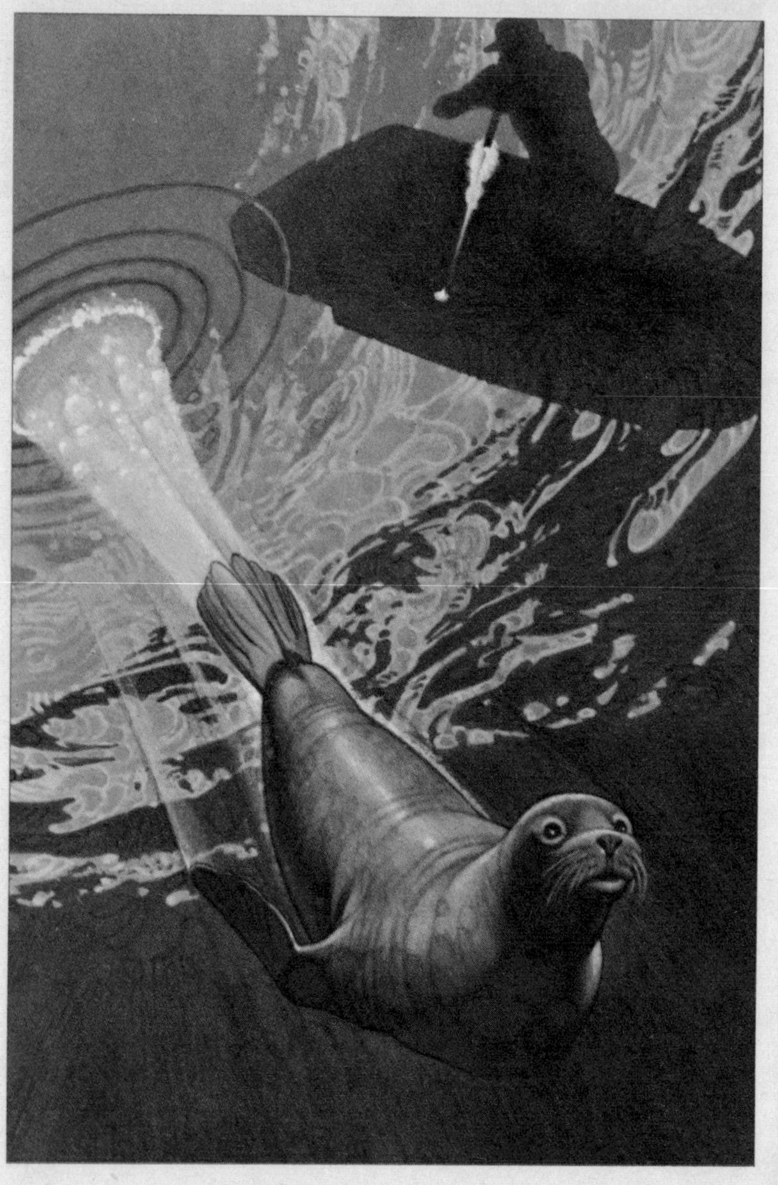

stones, sprouting antennae and claws. It had been appropriated, instead of the more customary whelk shell, by a hermit crab. Blennies, small fish, had also discovered that wide-necked bottles were superior to shells for laying their eggs. So the manufacturers of pickles and coffee contributed to the spread of wildlife.

Where rivers flowed into the sea, they carried other, grimmer burdens. Insecticides, sprayed over the land, were washed into the sea by heavy rains. Shellfish absorbed these as they sieved the seawater, and the deadly chemicals lodged in their tissues. The fish ate the shellfish and accumulated even more poison, storing it away in their fat. By the time Halic ate the fish the original trace of chemical had increased a hundredfold, to be stored in his fat.

Seabirds were being poisoned in the same way, though as yet the doses were too small to be fatal. Many land birds and animals, however, along with freshwater fish, had succumbed to the poison. For the sea creatures it was perhaps only a question of time.

Now the days were lengthening, although the nights were still cold. Halic came to a tiny remote bay, cut off from the land by high cliffs, where a narrow fissure opened up into a cave with a floor of smooth stones and flat rocks. Offshore the stones gave way to smooth sand, rich shoaling grounds of plaice and other flatfish. Here Halic lingered. He was now almost six months old.

THE BLACK SPRING

SPRING CAME. In the sea the tiny jewellike plankton grew and multiplied in the warmth and light of the sun. Whole areas of the sea were stained amber and emerald by them. To feed on the plankton came hordes of tiny animals, and these in turn were cropped by shoals of small fish. Larger fish harried these shoals, and Halic joined in the feast. Forsaking the shelter of his cave, he drifted south and west, keeping to the open sea, but never far from land.

The day had been warm, and a dense white mist rolled in from the sea as dusk fell. Ahead of Halic stretched a chain of rocks. The needle-sharp peaks just visible above the water were the remains of what, centuries before, had been a pattern of islands. When the tide turned, he hauled out onto a ledge and slept.

Dawn came, but still the cotton-wool blanket of fog blotted out all detail. As Halic roused, he was aware of a muffled sound, a regular beat. A ship was approaching cautiously through the fog. As the throb of its engines grew steadily louder, Halic plunged into the sea and swam, conscious of a great black wall looming up, of a screaming bow wave, and the deafening beat of the ship's propellers as they cut by him through the sea. The tanker sailed straight onto the reef and its knifelike granite cut her steel hull as though it were paper. The ship came to a shuddering halt, then, like a stricken whale, lurched over. Her cargo of thick black oil began to flow from the ragged gash in her flank.

From her stern came a tiny flame that grew until it towered higher than the ship. For a brief moment it lit the whole scene, reddening the sea and staining the mist; then it was extinguished by a giant explosion that sent a shower of debris flying into the air. As Halic looked, the crew leaped overboard and boats were lowered. One, laden with men, headed straight for Halic, who swam away through a sea littered with flotsam. Once he tried to dive but found himself entangled in a massive coil of rope. He surfaced and swam strongly towards the distant shore. Still the boat followed him, and only when he reached the cliffs did it turn aside and head for a tiny cove. Later that day a group of excited men tried to explain how they were led to safety by a grey seal.

As the tide ebbed, the stricken tanker settled more firmly onto the reef, and all that day her oil spilled down the rocks and drifted slowly away. Within the next two days over a hundred miles of coastline were polluted.

So came the Black Spring. Where oil pitched on the shore, life went out. The air reeked with coal-tar fumes. At first with stunned disbelief, then with near panic, men tried to fight the oil, spraying it with strong detergent in an attempt to emulsify and sink it.

For Halic it was the beginning of a long nightmare. The sea was crowded with boats, as the Royal Navy and fishermen joined forces. On land, giant vehicles crawled down the steep hills, bringing soldiers and drums of detergent. On the beaches men struggled, in high winds and bitter stinging rain, to manhandle the heavy drums into position. At times the quantity of oil was so great that sprays had no effect, and the men desperately poured the undissolved detergent into the running tide.

For several days Halic skulked just offshore. So far he had avoided the oil, but everywhere he saw puffins, shearwaters, and guillemots, their feathers clogged with it, dead or dying in the swell. The birds had been gathering in thousands offshore before moving to their nesting sites on the coast.

Halic came at last to a tiny cove, its shingle beach still clean. Here he found a cave with ledges of rock stretching far back into darkness. He swam in on the rising tide and slept peacefully for the first time since the morning of the wreck.

The cove held its quota of casualties from the oil. In crevices and among the boulders above high-tide mark, seabirds crouched, unable to feed or fly, awaiting death. From time to time, as the tide rose, the waves brought another victim to join their ranks. A pitiable black object would pitch, struggling, on the sand, try to stand, and finally crawl away from the sea that had betrayed it. All along the coast men, women, and children were working to save the oiled seabirds by taking them to centres where they were bathed, fed, and warmed. The work was arduous and unrewarding, since most of the victims were too near death to save.

On the second day after Halic's arrival, a boat came edging around the base of the cliffs and landed on the beach. Two men and a woman began to gather up those seabirds still alive among the stones, wrapping each in a strip of rag and laying it in a basket. Alone in his cave, Halic listened as their footsteps drew steadily nearer. He heard their nailed boots crunching the gravel. Then there was silence as they stopped outside the entrance.

The older man spoke. "It's strange we haven't come across any seals yet. There must be a few along this coast. We'd better check the cave."

The second man went back to the boat for nets, rope, clean sacks, and a flashlight. Dumping his gear at the mouth of the cave, he led the others in through the narrow gap. Halic lay motionless, his dark eyes watching the thin pencil of light play around the cave. It swept over him, blinding him, and the woman let out a gasp. "What a beauty, and still quite young too! What is it, a cow or a bull?"

The older man shook his head. "Difficult to be sure, but judging by the markings, a bull. He's quite clean. No trace of oil."

The younger man grunted. "He won't stay clean for long, with those oil slicks just outside the bay. Besides, if any of the locals find him, they'll knock him on the head. They've no great love for seals around here."

"You think we ought to take him?" queried the woman.

"Just as well," agreed the older man. "We can drive him across country and release him off the north coast. There's no oil up there. We can keep him in the shed overnight."

They unpacked the nets and as the woman held the flashlight the two men advanced slowly towards Halic, the net spread between them. Halic moved with surprising speed towards the entrance. But he was too late. Next moment he was entangled in the net and the weight of the two men pinned him to the floor. Still bundled in the net, he was thrust into a sack and borne slowly away.

Halic was unhurt but both men were bleeding; one had a gash in his leg from a razor-edged rock and the other a badly bitten thumb. They grumbled good-naturedly as they stumbled down the beach with their captive. The woman followed with the remainder of the gear, and after they had settled Halic in the boat she dressed her husband's leg and her son's thumb.

Halic lay in the dusty dark shed, conscious of a misery such as he had never known. The wooden floor was hot to his skin and the atmosphere stifling to lungs accustomed to the purest of air. Beside him were two tin tubs, one holding fresh water and the other a little seawater in which floated several dead mackerel. The fish were stale, the water tepid. Halic ignored both.

Relief, of a sort, came when one of the men entered the shed and threw a bucket of water over him, and again when both men entered with a large wooden crate, which they laid on its side. Crawling over to it, Halic found it lined with fresh weed. Grateful, he crawled inside and slept.

When he woke the moon was high in the sky and its beams through the dusty window flooded the shed with soft light. Halic's bed was warm and the weed was beginning to decompose. Desperately he moved around his prison, seeking the sea, tearing at the boards until his flippers were red with blood. He came at last to the door, where a cooling breeze blew through a crack, and here he rested, his muzzle pressed to the gap. When his captors opened the door, Halic almost fell out.

The shed stood at the top of a sloping vegetable garden and Halic took off across the plot with remarkable speed. He gained the hedge and was struggling to force his way through when his captors came up and bore him back to the shed. As the door closed behind him he realized he was no longer alone.

The newcomer was an old bull. His life had been rich and sensual—until the clinging oil sickened and half suffocated him. Now he lay on the floor of the shed, breathing harshly. From time to time he moaned. Towards dawn he vomited oil and blood. His moaning ceased and, as day broke, his great head dropped forward.

They came and took Halic away, leaving the corpse of the old seal. Once more, despite his struggles, he was netted, bundled into a sack, and laid in the back of a truck. For a long time he swayed and bounced in the sack, nauseated by the movement and deafened by the engine's roar. At last the truck stopped and he felt himself lifted up. He began to struggle as he heard the muffled boom of the surf. They laid him down on the beach, and light blinded him as they ripped away the sack. The air was deliciously cool and laden with the smell of salt, and the sun was warm and golden. Ahead the green wall of the sea rushed towards him, and a cold spray spattered down over his face and back. Next moment he was gone.

He had no clear objective in mind except a desire to rid himself of those tainted shores. He swam fast and far, and whether led by instinct, memory, or an inherited navigational system, he set course for the island of his birth. Three days after being freed he was playing in the rippling waters of Ramsey Sound.

THE SPRING GATHERINGS

SINCE FEBRUARY the grey seals had been arriving at the storm beaches and outlying rocks of Ramsey Island, as they had done each spring since the dawn of history. It was a time for sociability, for meeting and playing together in the shallow waters, or for sleeping and sunbathing on the beaches and rocks.

Apart from small frictions, life was amiable. The big bulls, who would be at each other's throats during September and October, now lay side by side or passed in the sea without more than a halfhearted yawn of warning. The cow seals, in a coquettish mood, sought to arouse the indolent bulls, who responded without fire or vigour. Not all the play was sexual, yet the allure of love was always hovering near, a strange sweetness in the air that heightened the joy of living. A pair of voluptuous virgins came up on either side of a lordly bull as he swam, nibbling his neck and caressing him with their bodies. He was at last roused enough to join in the dance, and the foam flashed as he seized one of the pair and their grey curving bodies met and entwined in the act of love.

The adult cows, with their neat rounded heads, gentle curves, and dark eyes, were as a rule easily recognizable from the battle-scarred roman-nosed bulls, with their powerful wrinkled necks and massive doglike jaws. Important physical changes were taking place in the bodies of the cows. They had mated in the autumn, two or three weeks after the births of their calves, with the master bull who was guardian of their beach, but the fertilized egg had lain dormant throughout the winter. Perhaps the stimulus of the spring dances evoked the glandular reactions necessary for the egg's development, or perhaps the glandular activity prompted the behaviour. Certainly the social life of the seals was geared to the survival of the species. The autumn matings ensured that the strong master bulls sired calves. The spring dances might ensure the fertility of these sowings, or they might serve to impregnate those females who by chance had missed the autumn rites.

Stimulated by the excitement and activity, the adolescent seals chased each other through the surf, wrestled and fought, or carried on endless games of tag around the outcrops of rock. Shyly, Halic joined a small group of calves of his own age at one end of the beach, where they basked in the sunlight. The calves were distinguishable from the rest of the herd by their small size and slenderness and by the colour of their pelts. During the winter Halic's mottled grey had faded, and his coat when dry was now pale beige. As the summer wore on, he would shed this coat and by winter would once more be sleekly grey.

In May the mackerel returned to the Sound, their summer feeding ground, and here the seals found them and tore into the densely packed shoals, gorging until they were replete. Halic gained weight rapidly as he fed on the rich, oily flesh.

With the coming of the mackerel, the spring gathering gradually broke up and the seals grew less social and more preoccupied with feeding. From now until the autumn the adult seals would build up the reserves of blubber which would support and nourish them through the long fast of the breeding season. For the younger seals life in the summer was not quite so earnest. Groups of young adolescents still played around the rocks.

Halic remained detached, like other seals his age. Often he could be seen alone in the water by the rocks, playing with a strip of weed or a piece of cork, apparently content. For days at a time he deserted his beach and went exploring far out to sea, to the rich hunting ground of a chain of rocks which rose thirty feet from the seabed. He soon discovered where he easily could find a meal. In a narrow submarine ravine hung a virtually indestructible fishing net, stretched by the tide between two sheer walls of rock. It might have broken away from a fishing boat or been swept away from some beach on a high tide. Now it was set permanently, for marine organisms had cemented it firmly to the rock.

Halic visited the spot regularly, once unwittingly driving

a panic-stricken flock of mackerel into the waiting meshes. Although this was the only such net he ever found, their number was increasing all around the coast as fishermen forsook the old nets of twine, which rotted quickly, in favour of the newer, lighter nylon nets. Each drift net or trawl that was lost went on fishing, year in and year out.

Conger eels lived in cracks and crevices among the rocks. Occasionally one would emerge, its long grey body undulating as it searched for food. One of the eels was a giant, more than three times as long as Halic and as thick around. The first time Halic saw him was when he went to investigate a violent struggle taking place near the rocks. An octopus was fighting to overpower a lobster. Barely had it succeeded when Halic saw the great eel glide towards the octopus. The octopus saw the eel and, paling, released a cloud of ink and shot off towards the rocks. The eel surged forward and grabbed the octopus, which promptly wrapped its arms about the eel's head, to no avail. The conger simply threaded its tail through a coil of its body, thus tying a half hitch in itself, and slipped through the knot, brushing the octopus off. Next moment it had seized its prey by the head, and the arms of the octopus hung limp. Halic kept a respectful distance. He was too small to attempt to deal with the conger; he might well have come off second best in the tussle.

Halic was able to stay out on the reef for long periods because, like all his kind, he drank little. In the main, he got all the moisture he needed from the fish he ate. He would hang about the reef for several days and then quite suddenly go back to the island, hauling out and falling asleep as though he had never been away. Each time he returned he was a little sleeker, a little heavier, and his coat shone paler as the sun dried it. Life at sea was richer and far more rewarding than it was close inshore.

AT DAWN one day Halic found the headless corpse of a half-grown seal in the shallow water of a rock pool. He approached it warily and sniffed, shying away in alarm. Other seals examined it, then turned away, vaguely disturbed.

The next tide took the corpse away, and the seals forgot. They slept, played, and departed for prolonged fishing expeditions. But something was wrong. Some did not return and others would swim in from the sea, exhausted and blowing, their eyes filled with terror. They would leave the beach reluctantly and swim warily, hugging the high cliffs. The entire colony grew nervous.

Then, one day, an old bull swam slowly and wearily in and lay in the water at the tide's edge, trying to haul out. When at last he succeeded, it was seen that his left fore flipper was missing, and a great wound ran from his jaw to his flank. The wound festered. For a few days he lived on, but he had lost too much blood and finally died. He lay with his eyes wide open, staring out over the sea as though waiting for it to come and claim him. Next morning his corpse was gone.

Halic swam far out in the bay. There was ninety feet of water between him and the sand, and a fresh wind whipped the wave caps. He had fed well and was drowsy. Suddenly he was jolted awake by the hiss of an indrawn breath, louder and more terrifying than anything he had ever heard.

For a brief moment he gazed at the tossing green wilderness surrounding him. Then, at the sight of three tall black fins slicing through the water towards him, he crash-dived. As he turned seaward he caught a glimpse of a gigantic black shape, with dirty white markings, great jaws armed with vicious teeth, and small glittering eyes.

A bloodthirsty trio of killer whales had moved down to the islands from the Arctic. They were the most accomplished assassins of the sea, combining great strength and speed with a voracious appetite and a grim intelligence. The big male was almost thirty feet in length, and his dorsal fin towered seven feet above the waves. The females were half his size but still formidable in speed and strength. They roamed the seas of the world, from Greenland to the Antarctic, killing whether they were hungry or not, harrying porpoise and seal. They banded together in packs of up to sixty to attack other whales.

Within moments the killers were gaining on Halic, but a split second before the male struck, Halic turned and shot towards the shore, skimming close to the seabed and raising flurries of sand.

He had won some distance, for the killer whales lacked his ability to turn swiftly. But they gained on him once more, and he darted away at a tangent as the male struck again, gouging into the seabed and plowing a great furrow in the sand. Then Halic doubled back, passing so close to one of the females that her teeth grazed his flipper, drawing blood. He longed to surface, to draw breath. His heart was hammering, his head was pounding, and his body felt stiff and heavy. Yet he knew instinctively that once he left the seabed he was doomed, for the killers could encircle him. So he fled on, twisting and turning, desperately seeking shelter, a rock, a cliff face, even a dense jungle of weed. Once he was actually buffeted by a great tail as, aching with fatigue, almost beaten, he twisted away.

Then quite suddenly he was alone. Dimly he was aware that the sea had grown lighter, that the sandy bed was shelving steeply upward, and that he was being rocked by the motion of the waves. As he surfaced, gasping and blowing, he looked frantically around for his pursuers.

He saw them a hundred yards away, patrolling just beyond the shallow waters of the bay which had proved his salvation. The killers knew that if they followed him they could find themselves stranded on the beach. Now they waited, ready to attack again the moment Halic left his sanctuary.

Satisfied that he was no longer in danger, Halic drifted off to sleep, rocked by the waves and carried shoreward by the surf. Every so often he would awake and start out to sea, but always the menacing fins hung offshore. Rain clouds were gathering, and the wind was freshening from the north, breaking the steady rhythm of the surf and imparting an uncomfortable lop to the water. Halic began to feel seasick. He was unable to dive into deep water and reluctant to haul out onto the beach, for it was not protected by cliffs or isolated in any way. Nearby lay a road, and its noisy traffic unnerved him. He was almost tempted to make a run for safety out in the ocean.

The porpoises saved him. They came swooping into the bay after a shoal of mackerel and were within range of the killers before they suspected anything. At the last moment, as they realized their danger and turned to flee, the killers surged among them, their great bodies rising above the waves, and within moments the bay was boiling with the struggles of the doomed porpoises. Soon, deep in the sea, the killers wolfed the remains of their victims. The other porpoises fled and then the killers departed too, leaving behind no trace of their work save streaks of red on the foam-capped waves.

Halic swam cautiously down the coastline away from the island. Darkness came early as the wind increased in force, driving black clouds low over the surface of the water. Stinging rain fell in fierce squalls. Halic turned and swam out to sea. Overhead seabirds wailed as they were storm-tossed through the sky like scraps of white paper. At last Halic slept, and throughout that wild night and all through the following day, as the gale blew itself out, he lay as if dead, not once opening his eyes or caring where he was. When he woke, fresh and ravenously hungry, the sun sparkled on a heaving, tumultuous sea. He went hunting for food.

SEASCAPE

FAR OUT AT SEA a dumpy black and white bird floated on the oily swell. It was a little auk, or dovekie, and the gale had blown it from its northern feeding grounds. Now, slowly but steadily, it was making its way back.

The dovekie was one of the many birds which had forsaken the land for the sea, returning to remote and inaccessible shores only to breed and raise their young. Such a way of life had once proved so successful that, at breeding times, they thronged cliffs and rocks from the Faroes to Brittany, and although they were slow to breed and produced but one youngster at a time, rafts of feeding birds darkened the surface of the sea.

For centuries their chief enemy had been man. To the tough, self-sufficient islanders of the past the seabirds were an annual crop, important to survival in a harsh life. At first they took adult birds and eggs from the most accessible breeding stations. Those in remoter places were spared, and the predations of man made little difference to their numbers. Indeed, the bird population perhaps benefited by being relieved of overcrowding.

But as world trade grew the number of sailing vessels multiplied. These ships carried large crews and were often ill-provisioned, so that it became the custom to call at the breeding places of seabirds to supplement the ship's rations with fresh eggs and meat. One bird in particular, the great auk, was the chief victim of these raids. They stood almost three feet high, and one carcass provided more than enough food for a hungry man; the eggs were correspondingly large and were collected by the bucketful. Because the great auk was flightless, it was powerless to escape marauders. By 1850 there were no great auks left in the world.

The other seabirds, the guillemots and razorbills, the puffins, shearwaters, petrels, kittiwakes, and terns, managed to survive, although frequently in reduced numbers. But a new and more insidious menace threatened them. With the coming of the internal-combustion engine, mankind began to need vast quantities of oil. It was the habit of a tanker's master, after discharging his oil, to wash the residue from the holds into the sea. Beaches all over the world became fouled by tar. Legislation made it an offense for a tanker to clean its bilges at sea, but it was impossible to enforce. The law and the punishment acted as no deterrent. Meanwhile seabirds died by the thousands, their feathers matted with oil.

Many of the cliffs and islands where the birds bred had been declared sanctuaries by law. The birds, however, spent most of their lives at sea, and even when they were nesting they returned to the ocean to catch fish for their young. So for much of the time they were totally unprotected.

The majority of the oil slicks were comparatively small and in time broke up. But the guillemots, razorbills, and puffins swam underwater to catch fish and often surfaced under an oil slick. Indeed, sometimes it seemed that the oil actually attracted them, perhaps creating an illusion of calm water. Slowly but surely these birds were going the way of the great auk.

The dovekie was soon out of sight among the waves, and Halic was once again alone in the silent, peaceful wilderness of the sea. He had now journeyed farther south than ever before, passing far to the west of Land's End and the Scilly Isles, then through warmer waters and under sunny skies into the Bay of Biscay. Ahead of him stretched a rocky coastline very similar to that of Cornwall, with high cliffs, sandy bays, and small wooded estuaries.

In the months that followed he drifted slowly eastward along the north coast of Spain, from Corunna to Santander. Here the light was stronger than on his native coasts, and the sea illuminated to far greater depths, and here for the first time Halic found shoals of tuna, the rovers of the Atlantic.

Tuna live long and some grow to weigh over a thousand pounds. They can swim at speeds up to nine miles an hour, and they never stop swimming. By the time they are fifteen years old some have travelled over a million miles, inscribing great arcs in the ocean from America to Britain and back.

Most of the tuna Halic saw were small, approximating three pounds. They made excellent eating, and he gained weight fast on the rich fare. The tuna had fed on sardines, the small silvery fish that glittered by the millions in the warm sunlit sea. Thousands of tons of sardines were harvested by Spanish and Portuguese fishermen each year.

Many times, as Halic explored the seabed that lay off this wild and rocky coast, he passed over ancient wrecks which had sunk centuries before and now lay rotting in the ooze. The surface of the sea was littered by more recent wreckage. On an afternoon in late summer, under a clear sky, Halic spotted a dark shape that wallowed on the surface of the sea and moved from time to time in a curious, jerky fashion. Puzzled, Halic swam closer.

It was a dead pony. It had died of seasickness and had been thrown overboard from a ship transporting animals from England to the Continent. Now the corpse bobbed in the sea as a pack of sharks tore at it.

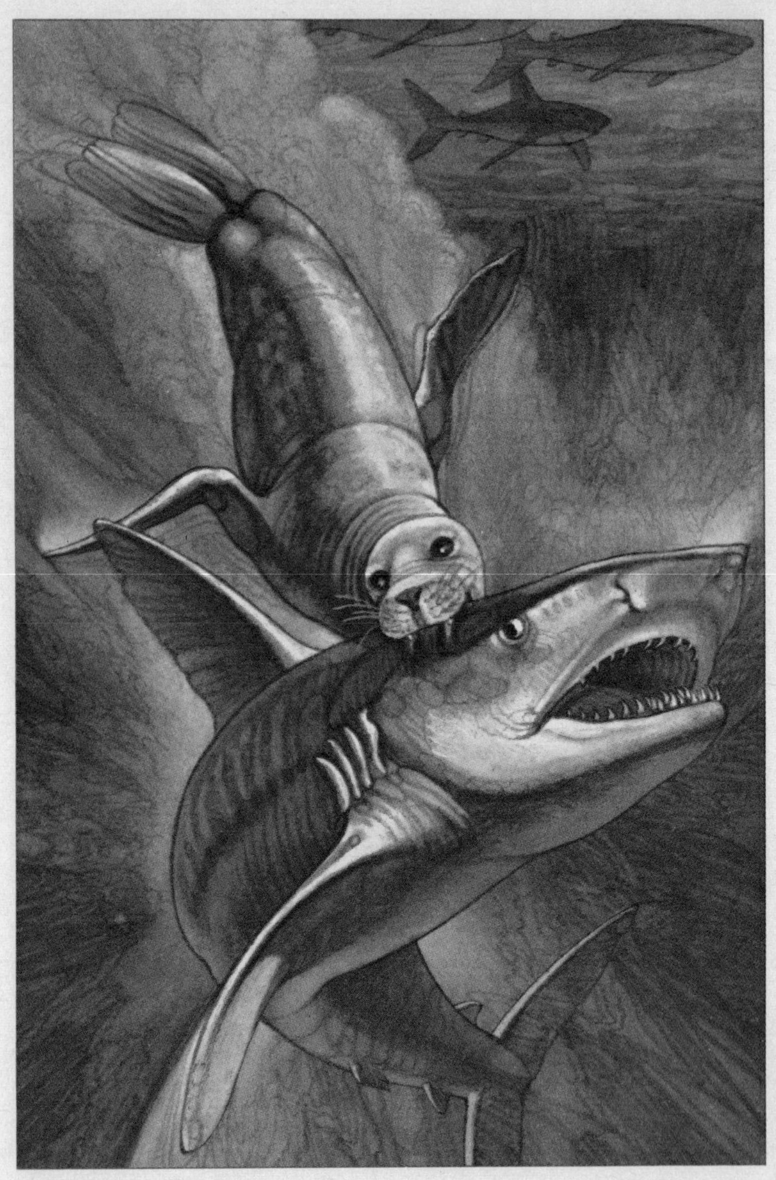

Halic realized the danger too late. The sharks were all around him, silent and menacing, as he swam warily away. He was almost clear when a small blue shark swam towards him. Halic increased speed slightly, but his enemy gained on him until he could see the irregular sharp white teeth in the wide gash of its mouth. He slowed down, waiting until the shark was underneath, cutting up to attack with lightning speed. Then he dived, caught it at the back of the neck, and bit deep into its backbone.

The shark pulled free and flapped wildly in the water as Halic fled. Its tail swung in widening arcs until, incongruously, the shark caught it in its jaws and held on tight, spinning like a wheel through the sea. Blood drifted down towards the other sharks, and within seconds the cripple had been torn to pieces by the rest of the pack.

Halic sped on over the seabed until the water grew shallow and sunlit and he could see his own shadow, black against the sand. He surfaced to find himself off a small gravelly cove surrounded by towering cliffs thickly clad with heather and juniper. Here he hauled out and fell asleep on the stones.

When he woke it was dark, and a hot gusty wind was rustling through the heather, sending small twigs rattling down onto the beach. He lay listening, his head raised and his muzzle sniffing the air. Above the slap and crash of the waves he heard again the sound that had waked him, the call of his own kind, faint and pitifully weak. He moaned in answer, and when the call came again he dragged himself over the stony beach towards the sound. In a crevice in the rocks he found a cow seal lying quite still. She made a feeble effort to raise a flipper in greeting.

Halic soon fell asleep again. He woke at dawn, better able to see her. She was extremely emaciated, and her lower jaw hung loose. It had been shattered by a rifle shot many weeks before. The wound had healed, but the jaw was so deformed that she was unable to eat. Halic did not understand, but he stayed by her side, not out of pity but because he gained comfort from her presence.

A pair of eyes watched the seals as they lay in the thin light of dawn. The man was old and gaunt, but the eyes, under bushy white eyebrows, were keen, and the hands that held the telescope were steady. All his life he had been a hunter, climbing far into the mountains in search of deer, bear, and lynx. His joy had been in the long stalk and the quick clean kill. For days now, ever since he had heard from fishermen of the plight of this seal, he had sought her, tramping miles along the cliffs and scanning the sea for hours under the hot sun. Now, with a quick indrawn breath that told of his disgust and pity, he laid down the telescope and reached for the rifle at his side.

It was a long difficult shot. The faint click as he eased the cartridge into the breech caused Halic to raise his head, effectively blocking the man's aim. The man lowered the rifle and waited, as the dawn light drew stronger. Slowly Halic sank back, and now the hunter had the cow seal in his sights. He drew in a slow breath, cuddled the stock to his cheek, and squeezed the trigger.

With the report, Halic exploded into action. He caught one glimpse of the cow seal as her eyes closed and a fountain of red blood spurted on the rocks. Then he was gone, the green water closing over his head as he made out to sea.

The hunter watched through his sights as the seal died. Then he rose and made his way back along the cliff.

THE THREAT OF THE SPEAR

WINTER CAME, and Halic rode the gales far out in the tempestuous waters of the Bay of Biscay. The fish had gone to their winter quarters to the west in readiness for spawning. With them had gone the whales, dolphins, porpoises, and sharks; all denizens of the upper sunlit waters dependent, directly or indirectly, on the plankton bloom. Now the sea lay fallow, waiting for spring.

Yet there was still plenty of food for Halic—skate, dogfish, pollack, wrasse, and whiting. He put on weight and was now heavier and stronger than a man, with powerful muscles and jaws like a leopard. He had molted again and wore the grey livery of an adult seal. He drifted north and by late spring reached Brittany and the island called Belle-Île. Here the surf leaped in white fury at the weatherworn rock, and its music roused in Halic nostalgia and unrest. The shallow waters and high-ramparted cliffs evoked half-forgotten memories of Ramsey Island.

Throughout the long hot summer he slowly journeyed north, following the cliffbound coastline with its multitude of tiny green islands. The seas were crowded with vacationers and red-sailed fishing boats. Halic managed to avoid attention, hugging the cliffs or swimming deep down among forests of weed and sponge. One day he swept into a clear inlet protected by a cliff. He swam on his back, for in this way he was better able to locate his prey. He took three small bass, then continued to quest around, for three small fish were less than a snack to him.

In a small hollow at the base of the cliff an octopus lay guarding her eggs, fifty five-inch clusters of about a thousand each, which hung from the roof of the miniature cave. When the octopus saw Halic she paled, fluttered with fear, and pressed close into the sheltering cavity in the rock. Halic seized one of her arms and pulled. The octopus held on to the rock, and the arm came away. Halic swallowed it and swam back. This time he grasped her by the mantle, bit into her brain, and killed her. Then he surfaced and tore her to pieces, bolting the remnants without attempting to chew them. The eggs in the cave he ignored.

Halic's dealings with the octopus had been watched by a young man who lay on the cliff. Pale and dark, with the smooth soft muscles of a townsman, he came to the coast each year and roamed the shallow seas, seeking fish to kill with his spear gun. Now, as he gazed down at Halic asleep in the limpid waters of the inlet, he thought that the seal's pelt would make a handsome rug or, perhaps, a jacket.

He made his way down the cliff and out onto the long arm of rock. Carefully he donned his rubber suit and flippers, adjusted his mask and cylinders of compressed air, checked his spear gun and his long knife. He then entered the water on the seaward side of the rock and swam quietly around into the inlet. He peered ahead, his finger curled over the trigger of his gun, and breathed slowly, struggling to remain calm. A thin stream of bubbles trailed behind him, rising wavering to the surface.

At last he could make out a grey form rippling in the waves. Halic was much bigger than he had seemed from the cliff top, bigger than the man himself. For a second the diver wondered whether he would not be wiser to depart quietly, but the instincts of the hunter urged him on.

At that moment Halic stirred and, as the man watched, sailed languidly to the surface to breathe. Foolishly the man followed and the disturbance of the water woke Halic, who instantly crash-dived, sprinting towards the head of the inlet. He turned and saw the man swimming slowly towards him, the white hands gripping the gun. Halic swerved as the man's spear inscribed a gleaming arc and passed to one side.

Halic swam to bypass the man in order to gain the open sea, but the diver turned to intercept him. Halic now saw one white hand, armed with the knife. His jaws closed around the wrist, feeling the wrench as the diver, in agony, struggled to free himself, and the knife sank flickering to the seabed. Almost fainting with pain, the man was pulled to the sea floor.

But Halic had no desire to prolong the fight. He released his hold, chopped once, with terrible force, deep into the muscles of the man's shoulder and neck, and then swam with all speed out to sea. Somehow the man regained the rocks and painfully divested himself of his gear before losing consciousness. Hours later he was found by some vacationers and taken to a hospital. By the time he had convinced the authorities of the truth of his strange adventure, Halic was fifty miles away from land.

Halic swam northwest and at dawn of the third day came to the Scilly Isles. Here, amid savage riptides and overfalls, he fed for the first time since his encounter with the man and hauled out on a sheltered pebble beach to sleep in the morning sun.

The sound of seals, sobbing and wailing above the crash of the waves, roused him as night was falling. In the darkening water two seals played, their heads visible in the foam. Halic called and they turned, staring, hanging upright and motionless in the sea. They were yearling cows from the rocky fastnesses of North Cornwall who had strayed south during the summer, meeting by chance in the maze of channels and tide races that swirled and eddied between the islands.

They welcomed Halic, and the trio stayed together in the weeks that followed, using the same beach and playing in the shallow surrounding seas. The cows were much smaller than Halic and a little in awe of him. They would wrestle and fight, teasing him, but never allowed him more than the smallest intimacy.

All the while, Halic played at being a beachmaster, guarding his chaste harem against a challenger who never appeared. During the day, when the cows lay hauled out on the stony beach, he patrolled in the sea, and if a seagull or cormorant landed near he surged towards it with snapping jaws and angry bark.

Each lump of floating driftwood, each cluster of weed or flotsam was carefully investigated. Every unusual sound caused him to hang upright in the water, listening intently until he was sure all was well. Even when he lay dozing beside the cows on the warm pebbles he never quite relaxed, and when either of the cows left the beach for the water, Halic followed and drove her shoreward if she strayed. The two cows seemed to enjoy this attention and grew anxious when he was not close at hand.

The weather remained fine well into the winter. Fishing was good and the seals fed well. Halic's desire to reproduce his own kind was not strong enough yet to affect his appetite.

By December the three were beginning to drift apart, going off on long, lone fishing trips around the islands. On one of Halic's trips, ten miles to the west, a sudden gale ended the three seals' association. The wind drove mountainous seas before it, carrying Halic north and east, past Land's End and Cape Cornwall. When at last the gale abated he lay in a fishless twilit sea six miles northwest of St. Ives.

Here, during World War I, an admiralty transport vessel had struck a mine. The crew took to the boats and the ship sank quickly, to lie on the stones a hundred feet below. The sea gradually claimed her for its own and cemented her firmly into place. She began to rust, her woodwork rotted, her furnishings decayed, and her metallic frame became carpeted with a dense growth of corals and ascidians, sponges and sea fans. The effect was that of some exotic rock garden planted with ferns and cacti, muting the stark outlines of the wreck.

She became a shelter for shoals of small fish and crustaceans—shellfish, crabs, and lobsters. Then the predators also took up residence. Starfish carpeted the bridge. Small fish darted in and out of the portholes and hovered on stairway and companionway. An octopus lived in an empty cupboard. Conger eels, some of immense size, prowled the caves of the holds. The wreck grew less and less like a ship and more like a submarine castle, surrounded by shimmering shoals of silver and gold fish.

Hungry after his enforced fast in the gale, Halic dived to scour the seabed in search of prey, gliding over the ship's rime-encrusted deck. Fat pouting hung in streamers by the rigging, and Halic took them as they scattered, crushing each one before swallowing it whole. He caught ten before he surfaced, leaving behind him a trail of glittering silver scales. He dived again, now in a spirit of exploration. He swam to the gaping hole where the mine had struck. Beyond the opening all was darkness and silence. The jagged entrance was like the jaws of a killer whale, and Halic hesitated, feeling instinctively that somewhere within danger threatened. At that moment a large, eel-like ling drifted around the stern. Halic struck at it as it came within range, his jaws closing around its flank and tail. Crippled, the ling struggled away towards the hole in the wreck.

Halic followed into the darkness of the hold, his nervousness forgotten in the excitement of the chase. Next moment he turned a complete somersault in the water and shot out of the wreck as though fired from a gun, not stopping until he reached the surface. In his brief moment in the hold he had caught a glimpse of eight powerful arms and two tentacles, surmounted by an enormous eye. Two of the arms had clasped the ling and bore it towards a giant body which lay shrouded in shadow. Halic had chanced upon the lair of a giant squid, a species rarely seen near the continental shelf. Usually they stay far out in the deep Atlantic. They may grow to more than fifty feet in length and their only enemies are the whales, especially sperm whales, which dive to a thousand fathoms or more in pursuit of them.

Halic now swam out from the coastline, away from the wreck. As hail and cold rain lashed the sea, he slid deep under the waves and slept, to dream of the call of his kind beckoning him back to the waters of his birth.

RETURN TO THE ISLANDS

SPRING CAME early to the Pembroke coast and warm rain plumped the dry soil of the cliff tops. A flush of pale green lit the carpets of heather and blueberries, and wild daffodils nodded beneath the bare branches of trees where thrushes sang in the soft evening light. The night skies were alive with the flutter of bird wings, as swallows, martins, wagtails, and warblers, travellers from the far south, mingled with the winter visitors, fieldfares, starlings, bramblings, and redwings, who were departing for the north and east.

Some birds, blown offcourse by high winds, flew on over open seas until, exhausted, they dropped to their death in the waves. Others crashed into the rigging of ships, and hundreds more flew straight into the glare of lighthouses, dashed themselves against the glass, and fell broken onto the rocks below. Still the survivors pressed on, driven by the instinct to migrate.

Halic heard the travellers pass overhead as he journeyed through the darkness, heading north to the island of his birth. He could smell land now and quickened his speed, swimming without apparent effort, hour after hour, as day and night passed.

As the morning sun sent shafts of light onto the beach, Lugo, a young cow seal, idled on the edge of the tide. She had been born in a cave of the mainland cliffs across the Sound from the beach where Halic had spent his first weeks. She was a year younger than he and very palely marked, the silver of her back lightly speckled with grey. A yellow plastic ball, broken from a fishing net, came drifting by on the ebb. Lugo followed it, diving under to balance the ball on her head and then trying to grasp it in her jaws. She pursued it to the mouth of the Sound.

Far out in the bay a small black dot appeared. It drew nearer and nearer until the two seals met. The newcomer was larger and darker than Lugo, but she at once allowed him to join in her game. As he rolled in the sea a white scar showed on his neck. Halic, the wanderer, had come home.

For a while they played together, but Halic was weary. He swam away, and Lugo abandoned her toy to follow him up the Sound. Together they hauled out on the beach where he had been born, and Halic fell into deep slumber. Lugo lay beside him.

It was again the time of the spring gatherings and the courtship dances. An immense bull lay on a rock, the outline of his head silhouetted against the sky. A group of cows sprawled on the stones, repulsing the halfhearted overtures of a young bull who retired, waving a placatory fore flipper each time he was rebuffed. At last he meandered down to fall asleep in shallow water.

Lugo and Halic were the only adolescent seals on the beach. During the weeks that followed they fished and played together, and slept and sunbathed as the days grew longer and the sea warmer.

The power of spring exuded from the pale light of the sun and the warm breath of the salty wind. It shone from the bright eye of the adder coiled among the heather roots and glistened on the watery backs of the spawning frogs. It echoed from the hum of busy insects and the laughing cry of the gulls. It penetrated the dark earth and lit the dark waters, so that they burgeoned with life. It had an intoxicating force that no creature could deny.

The wine of spring flowed in the blood of the seals and sent Halic and Lugo racing through the sea, calling to each other and chasing each other through the waving forests of kelp. Their games reflected their exuberance and their high intelligence. Halic would find a piece of driftwood and dive, clutching it in his jaws. Lugo would follow and when deep in the water Halic would release his prize. Then the two seals would race after it as it rocketed upward, striving to catch it before it broke the surface.

Sometimes Halic would loll in the waves holding a stick in his jaws, enticing Lugo to come and take it. As she drew near he would fling it away with a shake of his head. Then both would launch themselves after it. If Halic reached the stick first he would seize it and race off, with Lugo in hot pursuit. At other times both would arrive at the goal, and then the stick would be forgotten as they locked in mock combat, wrestling and rolling in the waves. At such times Halic would try to grasp Lugo by the nape of her neck, embracing her with his flippers, while Lugo, half excited and half fearful, would face him and nibble at his face and neck until he was forced to release her. Soon they would race away through the waves, their desires forgotten.

Their parting, when it came, was sudden. Halic had found a lumpsucker stranded by the tide. These obese, ungainly fish laid vast numbers of pink eggs in shallow water at the low-tide mark. The males guarded the eggs, anchoring themselves to stones by a powerful sucker on their undersides, and remained at their posts even when half exposed to the air.

Halic was hungry, and when Lugo came to join him he growled a warning to keep away as he bit at the fish, still clinging grimly to its stone. Innocently, Lugo ignored the warning and came closer. Halic snapped at her. Taken by surprise, she bit back. Unluckily, she caught Halic on the nose, drawing blood. Berserk with pain and rage, Halic flung himself at her and rolled her over and over into the waves. Terrified, Lugo fled, and as Halic returned, grumbling, to the lumpsucker, she swam away down the Sound. South of the island she fell in with a band of adolescent seals and drifted away with them to the rocks that lay to the west. Soon she had forgotten Halic.

On a gusty morning in May, Halic spotted a stranger in the Sound. She was a female tope, a kind of shark, and her long grey form cut the water with a speed and grace surpassing Halic's.

In the weeks that followed, the ravens and the seabirds saw her from the cliff tops, cruising along below the surface of the water, and from time to time the seals saw her crescent fin cutting like a knife through the waves. Most of the time she kept deep down, for her prey was fish, particularly the flatfish that abounded in this part of the bay. She established a regular patrol, from Porth Clais Rock to Sylvia Rock, circling out to sea and then back again. She soon discovered a wide depression in the seabed already known to the seals. Into this hollow the tide brought rotting debris which the marine life converted into a rich supply of fish food. Here the bottom-living fish browsed in dense packs. Halic visited the spot throughout the year and seldom went away hungry.

Then one day he found the depression deserted, save for a huge skate and a pair of dogfish which fled in panic. For the past few days the tope had swept into the crater every few hours, chopping into the ranks of helpless flatfish. Now the survivors were scattered over the bay. Mystified, Halic swam away.

A small white cruiser, sturdy and well equipped, now came purring across the bay. In the cabin two deep-sea anglers, father and son, studied the flickering red line on the echo sounder. When they found the hollow they lowered a yellow marker overboard and sailed the boat a few yards uptide, dropping anchor.

Earlier they had caught a supply of fresh mackerel to use as bait. Now the man and his son each chose a fish, cut a fillet from one side, threaded it onto his steel hook, and lowered it. The tide carried the baits down to the hollow, but the big skate had gone in search of plaice which hid in the sand beneath the shallow waters. The two baits lay ignored.

The older man in the boat was impatient. Hunched over his rod, he grumbled, "Two hours without a bite!"

The son made no answer. Long and lean, he was content to dream, to admire the translucent white of a gull's wing against the sun. He watched the black oval of a seal's head as it hung in the surge of a breaking wave. He hoped his father wouldn't spot it, but he did. "Look at that villain! That's why we aren't catching any fish. Look what he's got! Wish I had a rifle with me."

Halic lay close to the rocks, tearing up a pollack and keeping a wary eye on the boat. But the son still made no comment. Something about the seal, the burning stare of the large dark eyes, the gesture of pushing the fish away with its flippers, prompted an odd train of thought. Did man descend from the trees or did he come out of the sea? The young man half smiled at the thought. In his mind's eye he saw tropical shores washed by warm seas, and a breed of animals, monkeylike, their bodies immersed up to their waists, foraging among the weed-covered rocks.

It all fits, the young man thought, dreaming on as he watched Halic. Even to our liking for shellfish. It might account for the shape of our teeth, so unlike those of other mammals.

"WAKE UP! YOU'RE ON!"

His reverie shattered by the old man's shout, the son came to with a jolt. The tip of the rod was jerking as though alive, and the reel drum was revolving as the line paid out. Carefully he inserted the butt of the rod in the harness around his waist and let the fish run. The reel picked up speed. Deep down the tope ran like a grey ghost over the sunlit amber sand. She was crushing the bait slowly with her teeth. With a last savage bite she gulped it.

When she felt the first wrench of the hook her panic sent her scorching far out to sea. As she slowed, she felt a heavy pull which brought her veering back towards the boat. The fisherman cranked wildly at his reel to keep the line from going slack, but he was only half prepared for the jolt as the tope turned again. His rod bent until the tip touched the sea, and the knuckles of his right hand came down on the gunwale with a sickening crunch. He let the fish run until she came rocketing to the surface. The two men gasped as for a moment they saw her silhouette against the sky, her wildly thrashing tail threatening to sever the line. Next moment she was down again, zigzagging through the waves, shaking her head in an effort to throw the hook. Then she settled to runs of short duration. But she still had such savage power that, pump as he might, the fisherman could gain no more line.

Slowly, as the minutes stretched into an hour, the fish weakened. Finally she could only roll feebly as she was drawn through the water to the boat. At last she lay dead on deck, and the young man, nursing his injured hand, stared at her as his father set the boat leaping at full throttle across the bay. In time he would relive the excitement of the battle and enjoy the rewards of his success, the trophy and the prize. But now he felt only depression and remorse at being the killer of such a magnificent fish.

It was September, and Halic swam through the Sound heading for the stony beach where two cows already lay with their calves. He was now in his sixth year, lean, muscular, and powerful, and although he had not yet attained full growth, he weighed well over five hundred pounds. During the last spring's gathering he had been prone to sudden outbursts of aggression or fits of jealousy. The other seals had begun to avoid him.

Now, as he thrust towards the breeding beach, the sight of the master bull patrolling offshore sent him surging forward in angry defiance. The two bulls met in a welter of foam, rearing half out of the water as they feinted and sparred with bared teeth. Halic struck first, but the older bull twisted sideways, and Halic's teeth sank into the back of his neck. Then they rolled over and over in the shallow water until the heavier bull tore free and returned with surprising speed to the attack, rearing out of the water, angry eyes staring and white teeth menacing, his mane fringed with red. Halic felt a violent blow over his heart and the beachmaster's teeth in his neck. A ponderous weight forced him down until his back scraped the rocks; then he was shaken and pummelled as he twisted frantically. Fear replaced anger. With a last desperate effort he broke free and fled, blood streaming behind him.

He did not stop until he reached the southern tip of the island. Then he hauled out and slept. When he woke his wound had stopped bleeding, and although his neck was stiff and his chest still hurt, he felt hungry and alive. He slid into the sea and went fishing, his wound stinging from the salt water.

Later, at night, across the bay in the moon's pathway of milky light, Halic first saw her.

She waited, her neat round head silver in the moonlight, as he swam towards her. Their muzzles touched briefly as they met, in

a seal's greeting. Then she turned and swam slowly away, while Halic followed and drew alongside her. Together they roamed through the sea, and from time to time her flank would touch his. Filled with a fierce desire for possession, he would swim over her, trying to grasp the nape of her neck with his strong white teeth. Each time she evaded his embrace, but turned towards him with playful love bites. Neither Halic nor Lugo remembered that once before, long ago, they had played together.

Day followed night, and Halic grew more demanding, but Lugo was not ready to consummate their love. Everywhere she went Halic went, in a fever to possess her, and several times she let him grip her gently with his jaws as his flippers enfolded her. But each time, as he curved his body for the final act of love, she broke away.

Once, as they hung languidly in the waves, a strange seal swam up to Lugo, and Halic came awake with a roar of rage that sent the seabirds whirling like snowflakes. Leaping clear out of the water, he hit the stranger so hard on the flank that he sank in a silver cloud of bubbles and spray. As he surfaced again Halic lunged, sinking his teeth deep and spinning around in a savage attempt to tear out the other's throat.

His grip broke and the stranger was gone, diving below the waves and swimming fast from Halic's terrible wrath. Satisfied that he had conquered, Halic turned back to Lugo. She was swimming away, with many a backward glance and swerve of her flanks, into the green shadow of a tall underwater cave. There she waited for him, and, still filled with the pride of battle, he took her first roughly and savagely, then more gently. In the cave, still united by the act of love, they slept.

That night, as the moon rose with the tide, the sea was lit with blue-green phosphorescence and rocks shone green in the dark. As Halic and Lugo swam out of the cave their bodies glowed with the fire caused by tiny animals called noctilucas—night shiners. Every tiny movement of the water caused them to glow, and there were millions of them in the sea around the island.

In the days that followed, Halic and Lugo repeatedly enacted their rites of love, at times briefly and spontaneously, at others, especially after a prolonged flirtation, slowly, so that they often lay united for an hour or more. Each night, so long as the invasion of noctilucas persisted, they danced like green ghosts; but slowly, as the fire of the noctilucas died, so the fires of passion in Lugo and Halic began to fade.

Winter was coming—announced by the whistle of the curlews as they flew inland to the waterlogged meadows, echoed by the wild geese as they flew in from the snowy Northlands. The bracken on the cliff tops turned yellow, then russet. Gradually, Halic and Lugo drifted apart. Seals do not share the raising of their offspring. Halic would in all probability never see or recognize his calf. In another year he would win his own breeding beach, with several females. This was the way of the seals.

THE BROTHERS

AT THE entrance a line of corks marked the site of a drift net, laid to trap the larger fish swimming into the cove. In the darkest hour of the night the corks twitched violently; a very young seal had found the net and was stuffing himself with trapped fish. Then he fell asleep on the rocky bed of the cove. At dawn the throb of diesel engines woke him and he surfaced to breathe, only to find his exit to the sea blocked by a boat. He panicked and swam straight into the net.

To the two brothers in the boat, now hauling in the net, the sudden jerking told them they had caught a seal. The men were farmers and part-time fishermen. Toil and poverty had hardened and embittered them; the younger of the two had an artificial leg, the result of a tractor accident some years before. Now instead of a good catch of fish they were going to land a worthless seal. One of them nodded grimly to the other, who picked up a heavy wrench and laid it on the thwart. They wanted revenge.

The net was almost all in the boat, and the seal was thrashing to free itself when the younger brother picked up the wrench and struck. The seal's shout of defiance died in a gurgling scream as it plummeted into the water. Without a second glance the two men hauled in the rest of the net, still with quite a number of fish in it, and headed back to harbour.

The killing of the seal was an unlawful act, as grey seals were protected from September to the end of December each year. The men knew this, but it added a certain relish to their defiance of hated authority. They knew nothing about conservation; in their view seals were vermin. In the local inn that night they were voluble in their complaints against them.

For centuries mankind had hunted seals, at first for their oil and hides, then because of their habit of robbing nets and long lines. Though there was an abundance of fish, man begrudged the seals their share.

By 1900 the grey seal population had dwindled alarmingly. Since the period of greatest mortality was when the seals were calving, government regulations were enacted to forbid the killing of seals during this time. This law had the desired effect and over the years the grey seal grew in numbers until once again the complaints of fishermen began to make themselves heard.

A fresh problem also arose which gave the authorities cause for alarm. Grey seals, like all animals, acted as hosts to parasites. One of these was the codworm, which in its reproductive stage lived in the seal's stomach. The seal droppings contained the eggs of the worm, and when the eggs hatched, the larvae swam among the plankton and established themselves in the small crustacea. These in turn were devoured by fish, the worms to be embedded in their muscle walls. In due course the fish would be eaten by the seals and the worms would become adult, to repeat the cycle. They caused little harm to their hosts, but housewives complained when infected fish were sold. It was useless to tell them that the worms were harmless when cooked.

As a result, culls were arranged in those areas where seals were most numerous. Cows and calves were slaughtered by government officials or individuals working under license. No cull was planned for the seals of Ramsey Sound, but at the inn that night, as beer flowed and discussion centered around seals, the two brothers were egged on by the sympathy of the others in the bar.

Later, back in their farmhouse, they decided on a secret plan. The older man grinned. "The way I see it, it's better that one of us stays in the boat. We leave at dawn, sail quietly up to that beach where the calves lie, and shoot as many of the big ones as we can before they take off. You hold the boat just offshore, and I'll knock the youngsters on the head. Then there'll be a few less of the blasted things to rob our nets."

The younger man stood up, stretching. "Well," he yawned, "we'll see what the weather's like in the morning. I have an idea it's going to blow the slates off."

He was correct in his forecast. During the night the wind increased in force, and by morning low scudding clouds sent cascades of rain sweeping over the land, while out in the Sound white storm caps showed above the gray sea as the waves pounded the rocks at the base of the cliffs.

Lugo lay on the beach where years ago Halic himself had been born. For two days now she had felt listless and heavy. As evening wore on the storm abated. Lugo grew restless, rolling from side to side and moaning softly. Then in the dark hour before dawn her calf arrived, a bull calf, small but well formed, the son of Halic.

Dawn broke too bright and clear. Out in the Sound the seas still ran high. Already dark clouds were massing ominously on the horizon. In their open boat the brothers were tense and uneasy. Even with the engine at full throttle they seemed to make little headway against the tide and rising wind which drenched them with spray. But at long last the beach was in sight. Seven cows, five of them with calves, crowded onto the narrow strip. The seals watched curiously as the men swung the boat broadside to the shore.

The beachmaster died first, his face blown away by a charge of shot. Three of the cows were hit as they stampeded clumsily into the sea. Two died instantly, the third swam feebly away, until at last she drowned. Before the men could reload their rifles the other cows had gained the sea, but one more died as her head showed briefly above the water. Lugo escaped, leaving her calf bleating helplessly below the cliff.

The boat wallowed in the storm waves crashing on the beach, and above the whistling of the wind the younger man shouted to his brother: "Don't try to land. It's too dangerous, and the calves will die anyway."

In answer the brother picked up an axe handle, jumped over the gunwale, and waded ashore. As the first calf lay staring up at him, he killed it with two blows of the axe. Another calf was struggling through the boulders down the steeply shelving beach towards the sea. As the man leaped across the weed-covered rock towards it the calf spun around to face him, snarling and snapping at his foot. For a brief moment the man swayed, struggling to keep his balance. Then he fell heavily, screaming as his thigh splintered beneath his weight. Dimly he heard his brother shouting above the roar of the sea. "Going for help. . . . Can't land. . . . Tide ebbing. You'll be O.K."

He was aware only of an intense rage at his own helplessness, at his brother for abandoning him, and, most of all, at the seals, who were the cause of his predicament. His last thought, as he drifted into unconsciousness, was regret that he had not got the calf.

Waves were breaking over the stern of the little boat as the younger man, with engine at full throttle, fought to keep up enough speed to prevent the boat from being swamped. He was coming to the chain of rocks known as The Bitches, and now, crouching low in the stern, he cursed the sea and his useless limb as the engine coughed, then died.

The fuel! The reserve tank! He dropped the tiller and scrambled forward. The reserve-tank tap was corroded from lack of use. It snapped off as he forced it over. The tide took the boat and spun it around, lifting it high before it sank stern first into the sea.

The man's hollow artificial leg buoyed him up but forced him to float upside down. For a long time he struggled with the harness that kept the leg attached. At last he struggled no more. The sole of his boot, upturned to the sky, marked his slow journey as the tide carried him south, out of the Sound.

With the force of the wind against the tide, water began to creep stealthily back over the stones. Pain roused the man on the beach as the sea lifted and dropped his injured leg. Feverishly, he struggled higher. Twice he passed out again, recovering as the tide plucked at his heels. At last, delirious with pain, he reached the base of the cliff, where the calves lay wide-eyed among tangled driftwood, watching him. With one last desperate effort he stood up, bracing himself, as the tide sucked at the stones around his one good foot. Then, wearily, he slithered down, and the waves broke over him, battering him to death against the rocks until at last his body was pulled away by the undertow.

Out in the darkening sea Lugo waited for her calf to join her. The surviving calves were struggling among the grinding driftwood, flung back each time they tried to gain the safety of the open sea. Now a wave higher than the rest swept diagonally along the cliff face. It carried two of the calves out to sea. But Lugo's son and another died, thrown twenty feet into the air by the breaking wave, and crushed as they fell back on the rocks below.

DAWN CAME. Halic ranged to the north, his mood as grim and relentless as the sea around him. On a small beach at the tip of the island two cows lay with their calves. Purposefully, Halic swam towards them.

A warning bellow from the master bull told him he had been spotted, but he merely quickened his speed. The beachmaster waited offshore, his doglike head drawn back into the folds of skin that wrinkled his massive neck. He was a very dark bull, and his bared fangs were yellow and curved. Now he surged forward to meet Halic, rearing out of the water to strike.

Quickly, Halic slipped aside and struck the master bull hard just under his heart, driving him below the waves. Next moment the bull surfaced. The two seals reared and clashed together, their teeth rattling like sabers. Halic fell back. The beachmaster had him by the neck and was thrusting him down. Halic rolled, tearing himself free, to turn and catch the beachmaster at the side of the throat. They rolled over and over before sinking out of sight. Long minutes later the waters erupted in a fountain of spray as the seals exploded into the air, each still roaring defiance.

Slowly the beachmaster was weakening. He was bleeding from a score of bites and his injured flipper was swollen. They were now in shallow water close to the beach, and Halic's blows sent the beachmaster crashing against the stones. Halic struck downward and his teeth laid his adversary's head open.

It was the end. The beachmaster tore free, and Halic, too weary to follow, watched him make off through the waves; then he hauled out onto the beach and collapsed in sleep.

When he awoke the sun was setting. He lay at rest, his muscular body scarred from battle, looking out over the Sound towards the brooding hills of Wales. A little distance away the two cows lay on the stones, accepting the presence of their new master with wary calm. The younger of the two fed her calf; the older watched her youngster sleeping at the foot of the cliff.

Halic had reached maturity, and here on this island sanctuary he would spend the rest of his life.

Between Halic and the mainland lay the turbulent Sound, where the tide raced to and fro, and the wind, cold and clean, ripped the whitecaps from the waves to hurl them against the jagged rocks. Beyond the Sound the cliffs rose sheer from the sea, forming a formidable barrier to what was, for man, a wild and inhospitable place. This was the Sound of the seals.

Ewan Clarkson

The story of Halic evolved from a visit Ewan Clarkson made some years ago to the rugged coast of Pembrokeshire, where he first saw the grey seal in its natural habitat. He was struck then by the purity and beauty of the environment. And when he learned later of a grey seal calf that had been tagged in that area and subsequently identified off the coast of Northern Spain, the book was under way.

His interest in animals dates from his childhood in Cumberland. As the result of a paper on the balance of nature which he wrote as a schoolboy, he developed what was to become a lifelong concern with man's place in nature. His interest in zoology led him to a Bachelor of Science degree, after which he worked for seven years as a veterinary officer with the People's Dispensary for Sick Animals.

With his marriage and the births of his two children, Bruce and Sheila, he moved to Devon and became a writer, feeling that an urban environment was no place in which to raise a family. He is passionately interested in conservation and hopes in his writing to preserve a record of fleeting natural beauties and to communicate to others the serious dangers threatening their very existence.

In 1967 he was an eyewitness to the tragedy of the *Torrey Canyon*, when she spilled her massive cargo of oil into the sea off the Cornish coast. He believes that the survival of such rare species as the grey seal, though protected by law, cannot be assured as long as the possibility of such appalling pollution hazards exists.

His first book, *Break for Freedom*, published in America as *Syla the Mink*, was acclaimed as a "classic" and his second, *Halic*, has been a still greater success, even being translated into Japanese. In addition to his books, Ewan Clarkson has written many articles and short stories and has worked at most aspects of animal husbandry, including dog-breeding, mink-farming and zoo-keeping. He is a keen fisherman and believes that "in the main the *modern* sportsman has done more to help conservation than a great many preservationist societies".

GREEN DARKNESS
Anya Seton

GREEN DARKNESS

a condensation of the book by

ANYA SETON

ILLUSTRATED BY TERRY GILBERT

PUBLISHED BY HODDER & STOUGHTON, LONDON

As a poor relation in the Tudor household of Sir Anthony Marsdon at Medfield Place, beautiful young Celia Bohun's life was protected but perilous. Many things were expected of her: above all, that she should make an advantageous marriage. To think instead of following the passionate longings of her heart was folly. She would be destroyed, and the conscience-tortured object of her love also. For Stephen was a priest, and married already to Mother Church.

The tragedy of these two young people left echoes in the places where they had lived and loved, intimations of it lingering down the years to intrude finally on the private unhappiness of another Celia, wife to another Marsdon, Sir Richard, the twentieth-century owner of Medfield Place. Were her ghostly experiences there attributable to no more than the grief of these long-dead souls? Or was there not in their past distress some clue to the outcome of her present pain?

Anya Seton believes that human life has many levels, and as many states of consciousness. In this richly-textured tale she resolves vividly and movingly the mistakes of yesterday in the greater wisdom of today. It is a story of love, and anguish, and a strange spiritual journey, and final joy.

Prologue

In the ancient manor of Medfield Place in Sussex there is a huge vellum-bound book containing entries made by the Marsdon family from A.D. 1430 until September 15, 1967, when the death of Sir Charles Marsdon is noted. All but one of the entries are terse dates of births, marriages and deaths.

The exception is as follows:

All Hallowes Eve. Ye 31. yeare of hir Majesties reine, & a tyme of rejoicingye since our fleete has sunk ye wickede Spaniarde. England may now with God His Will live in peace under oure most vertuous Queene.

My selfe Thos. Marsdon Esq. beinge yet quite younge but mortal sicke desire to writ of a bye-gone tragick matter my Father tolde me of on his dethbedde. I have tryed to discover the bodye of the wretched girle which is for certaine welle hid atte Ightham Mote but Sir Chris: Allen & his vexatious ladye heatedlye denye all knowledge, his aged wittes are addled, but she hath a mad wolfishe eye. I wisht to give the girle a Christian berial since it was bye my unckle Stephen she was brote incontinent to her doome. He too suffered grievous paine and dyed in violence I knowe not how. Which unshriven deeds bringe sorrowe to our house.

Stephen was monke of Benedict Order in the troubled reines of King Edward & Queene Marye (God rest their soules) he was house priest first at Cowdraye Castle in West Sussex, after at Ightham in Kent.

A terrible lust was sente him bye the Devil, and he broke his sacred vowes. God punished him & the partner of his downfalle. Yet myselfe havinge known deepe tragickal love, can find in me naught but pitye for those tormented soules. I did question an olde sheepherd he said that the spectre of a black-habited monke was seen both at Cowdraye & Ightham Mote & that he hadde yt from his granddam the poore girle was put away alive, & quick with childe.

I am feable and can no more. I command my heires God his wille permiting to take measures of layinge the ghoste and to finde the murdered girle for Xtian berial.

Medfielde-Ann: Dom. 1588

PART ONE: 1968

Chapter 1

Celia Marsdon, young, rich and unhappy, sat huddled in a lounge chair at the far end of the new swimming pool, vaguely listening to the chatter of the weekend guests. Across the pool, above the privet hedge and the rose-laden pergola, sprawled the cluttered roof line of the Sussex manor house, Medfield Place. Richard's home. Her home, now. "Lady of the manor".

Every brick and beam of Medfield Place—the Tudor half-timbering of blackened oak, the Georgian bay window, the Victorian library wing, the glass garden room—was dear to Richard. The young architect who was supervising repairs wanted to remove the additions made during Queen Victoria's reign by the only Marsdon baronet who could be called wealthy; but Richard was adamant; and, indeed, the manor house triumphed over any architectural incongruity. It nestled placidly, as it always had, between two spurs of the South Downs—those quiet, awesome hills looming purplish-green against the East Sussex skies.

Celia took off her dark glasses, shut her eyes and tried to relax. Why should she be frightened? Why this lump in her throat which could not be swallowed, this sense of suffocation? You have everything a woman could ask for, Celia said to herself.

She had been told this a hundred times, especially by her mother, Lily. Celia glanced along the poolside to where Lily was rapt in conversation with one of those exotic characters she was always finding.

This one Celia rather admired, to her own surprise. True, he was a Hindu and practised Yoga, but he had firmly refused to let Lily introduce him as a guru; he was, he said with his pleasant manner, a doctor of medicine. He had studied at Oxford and at Guy's Hospital so long ago that he must be sixty. Yet his brown face was ageless, and his body, as now revealed by swimming trunks, was young and lean and supple. His name was Jiddu Akananda. Celia had had little chance to talk to him, but she had noted wise, kindly eyes and a sense of humour.

Lily Taylor was past fifty and managed not to look it. Celia smiled indulgently as she heard her mother's enthusiastic Midwestern voice rise in response to something the Hindu said. "But, of course! Every intelligent person believes in reincarnation!"

"Well, *I don't*," remarked the elegant Duchess of Drewton with her usual smiling assurance. "Lot of nonsense."

Celia examined the Duchess. Dowager Duchess, actually, though Myra was barely thirty; her old duke had recently died and the title had passed to a nephew. Combating someone's statement, as she had Lily's, was one of Myra's ways of being provocative. And she *was* provocative, that long gleaming auburn hair, the wide sensual mouth. Celia noted that Myra glanced often towards Richard.

Celia, too, looked at her husband. He had just executed a perfect swan dive and was blandly ignoring the applause. Yet did he, with a sidelong glance, respond to Myra? One never knew with Richard any more. The world, and Lily, who had come over on an extended visit, thought him a model of charming courtesy. He had a beautiful smile. It seemed to occur to nobody but Celia that the smile never reached his long-lashed hazel eyes.

I love him so desperately. Her hands clenched. I *think* he still loves me, though something has gone wrong, very wrong.

It seemed to begin with a visit to Cowdray Castle and Midhurst last autumn. Hallowe'en it was; the woodlands were yellow and russet, and there was a tang in the air. She and Richard had made love the night before, with ecstatic fulfilment even more joyous than during their honeymoon. The glow still enclosed them as they left Medfield Place in the Jaguar for Midhurst. Richard drove slowly, for him, along the hedge-lined byways. "I'll be glad to see old Holloway again—friend of my father's—and your romantic little American heart will be charmed by the Spread Eagle Inn. It's frightfully ancient."

"My romantic heart is charmed by Sussex, by England, and especially by my husband," Celia said, cuddling against him.

He rested his cheek against her curly brown hair. "Foolish poppet," he said. "It's not quite the thing to be in love with a husband."

"Look, darling, the bonfire on that hill—is it for Hallowe'en?"

"I suppose so, though we usually reserve those for Guy Fawkes Day," he said. "Remember the Gunpowder Plot, when the wicked papists tried to blow up Parliament? The Marsdons were Catholics in those days. We didn't become meekly Protestant until the eighteenth century."

"And you regret the conversion?"

"Lord no! Though sometimes I've had strange—well, dreams."

She pounced on this, for he rarely made a personal admission. "Dreams? What kind of dreams?"

He withdrew a trifle. "Lunatic fancies, not worth recalling."

She sighed. Always the door slammed shut.

"You make rather a fuss over Hallowe'en in the States," he continued conversationally.

"Just fun," Celia said. "Dress up and carve jack-o'-lanterns."

"You new and careless race." Richard sighed. "Almost untouched by the ancient evil, which yet casts its shadow on us all."

She was silent, never knowing quite what he meant when he talked this way. It was dusk, and they were driving through Easebourne, only a few miles from Midhurst, when Richard said, "That building to your left was a nunnery before Henry the Eighth dissolved it, along with the monasteries. The church has some rather good effigies of Cowdray Castle's former owners."

"Who were they?" she asked. English history had always interested her, but now that passionate love had made her part of England and its past, she had begun a fascinated study of it.

"The old family of de Bohun, until the fifteenth century. Then the Brownes. There is an elegant marble effigy of Anthony Browne, the first Lord Montagu, kneeling above his two wives; one wife was a Lady Magdalen Dacre, who must have been remarkably tall, to judge by her statue. Shall we take a quick look at the ruins of Cowdray Castle?"

Celia felt a quiver of delight. After a rootless girlhood, what joy to belong to an ancient established family, though she was not yet accustomed to being a baronet's lady—an elevation brought about some weeks ago when old Sir Charles died in a nursing home.

They turned through a gate and down an avenue of horse chestnuts, past a fourteenth-century granary and a row of cottages where yellow light shone through small windows, to the fire-gutted shell of a Tudor castle.

Richard stopped the car and led Celia by the hand into shadowy roofless rooms. "The chapel was there to the right, as I remember," he said. "And here, the remnants of the Great Hall."

She looked up at a huge stone window from which the glass had long ago vanished, her hand clutching Richard's. "I feel queer," she said, "as if I'd been here before. Is that the minstrels' gallery up there? See those wooden stags high on the walls?"

Richard did not answer. There were no figures now on the ruined walls; but the caretaker had once told him that this was called Great Buck Hall, from eleven statues of stags—or bucks—representing Sir Anthony Browne's crest which had been there. "One gets queer feelings from old places," Richard said reprovingly. "Strong vibrations of the past, or I suppose your mother would say you *had* been here in another life. Actually, the psychologists call it *déjà vu*, the *illusion* of having already experienced something."

Celia was not listening. "The Hall is crowded with people dressed in silks and velvets," she murmured. "There's music from viols and lutes. The smell of flowers and new green rushes on the floor. We are waiting for the young king."

"You devour too many historical romances." He shook her arm. "Come along, the Holloways will be wondering."

"I'm very unhappy because *you* aren't here," said Celia, unhearing. "You're somewhere nearby, in hiding. I'm afraid for you."

"Come *along*!" Richard cried. "What's the matter with you?" He dragged her back to the car. At once the impression of a dream which was not a dream evaporated. Celia fished out a cigarette. She felt dazed and a little foolish.

"That was funny." She laughed shakily. "For a moment, I—"

"Never mind," he snapped. "Forget it!" His vehemence was almost like fear. She was puzzled, a trifle hurt by it.

They entered Midhurst through winding shop-lined streets, crossed the market square and parked in the courtyard of the Spread Eagle Inn. As she stepped into the low-beamed bar, she was again conscious of some twitch of awareness. Nothing as marked as in the ruins. Yet she had to give it momentary attention before shaking hands with John and Bertha Holloway.

John Holloway was a prosperous antique dealer who had, over the years, acquired a number of the Marsdon treasures. Now that Sir Richard had a rich American wife, he was gradually buying back the heirlooms his father had been forced to sell. John had written to Richard that a splendid sixteenth-century court cupboard from Medfield Place was being angled for by an American museum, and Richard was interested.

Holloway glanced at Celia, who was gulping her Martini very fast. Somehow *not* the type one would expect Sir Richard to settle for. Small and dark, nice eyes, good ankles, yet nothing striking. Of course there was the money. But Richard was no fortune hunter. Marriages were ever inexplicable.

"Another round before we feed?" he asked Richard, who shook his head, smiling.

Celia started. "I'd like one," she said. "After all, it's Hallowe'en, we ought to celebrate."

Richard's heavy black eyebrows rose a trifle as he laughed. "I'm not really wedded to a tosspot. This round's mine, please."

"I've taken the liberty of ordering dinner," remarked John. "Dover sole and Aylesbury duckling. They do them rather well here. I hope that's all right, Lady Marsdon?"

Celia jumped. "Oh, of course. I adore . . . sole and duck."

What's the girl so nervous about? John thought. Have those two had a row? If so, it was not an auspicious time for bargaining.

But once in the dining room, Celia's unease began to fade. She listened politely to Bertha's breathless account of a committee on which she had served with Lady Cowdray; she listened to a general discussion of antiques. Finally, during a lull, she remarked that Midhurst seemed to have great historical interest.

"Oh, yes," said Bertha. "John knows all about the old days here. There's a funny hill the locals think is haunted."

"A haunted hill?" Celia asked. "Tell me about it, Mr. Holloway." Did she feel or imagine a sudden strangeness in Richard? He was skilfully dismembering his duck, but she thought that the long sensitive hands she so loved grew tense.

Holloway smiled. "St. Ann's Hill has, it's true, a peculiar atmosphere. The footpath's a shortcut from here down to the River Rother, and thus to Cowdray Castle."

"Was there once a castle on St. Ann's Hill, too?" Celia asked involuntarily, ignoring a faint interior warning.

"Oh, yes," answered Holloway. "For centuries the de Bohun family had a stronghold on 'Tan's Hill'. You can still see bits of wall. And they say there was once a Druid temple."

"Fascinating," said Celia. "And what about the ghosts?"

John Holloway laughed. "There are several. The most popular one is the 'black monk'. My great-aunt claimed she saw him."

"Why *black* monk?" asked Celia, smiling.

"The Benedictine habit, I suppose. The theory is that one of Cowdray's chaplains got tangled up with a village wench."

Richard said sharply. "Ghosts come sixpence the dozen. Holloway, if I'm to examine the court cupboard, I think we should go along."

CELIA, lying by the swimming pool at Medfield Place, forced herself to remember what had happened next. I don't know what came over me. I insisted on exploring St. Ann's Hill then and there. I escaped from the showroom and went up alone. Mist swirled around me, yet I knew my way. At the top of the footpath I turned right and clambered up a sharp rise. I reached some moss-grown stones and knew they had been part of a wall. Then inside the wall I saw a wavering light and a tall shape. I cried out to it with wild longing. But it disappeared. I must have run back to the Spread Eagle, for I was sitting by the great fireplace crying when Richard and the Holloways rushed in. They had been looking everywhere for me. Richard's eyes blazed with anger I had never guessed possible. He bundled me into the car, called me drunk and hysterical, said I'd seen nothing on the hill. And that night he did not sleep with me.

Dear God, it's now been seven months. He moved to the dressing room, and we've never mentioned Midhurst. Yet the night before we had known such bliss in each other.

She opened her eyes at a stirring by the poolside and saw that Dodge was approaching with a tray of drinks. Dodge was the kind of butler they kept saying one couldn't find any more. But one *could*—with American dollars—along with Mrs. Dodge for cook, plus a housemaid and daily help from the village. If necessary, and it was not yet, there was Richard's old nanny, who helped the household in many little ways while she waited for the empty nurseries to be inhabited again. I *should* have got pregnant when Richard wanted me to, Celia thought, and felt a clutch of confused panic. She had been afraid of pregnancy.

She bent and strapped on her sandals. She felt beaten, helpless. What would her father, whose millions were paying for all this, have said about her marital dilemma? The scarcely known father who had died of cancer seven years ago, when she was sixteen. Probably he'd have said, "Oh, talk to your mother, baby. I don't know what to tell a girl. Now if Lily and me'd had a *son* . . . ." He never realized how often he said that, nor how much it hurt her.

Dodge came back to announce that luncheon was served. Walking along the poolside, Celia marshalled her guests.

"As you are," she said. "In the garden room. Dodge simply won't serve out here, it upsets his dignity.

Myra laughed. "You're learning fast, my sweet. I live in positive terror of *my* butler." Her laugh displayed flashing white teeth and Celia saw the long green eyes turn again towards Richard. You'll get no place in that quarter, Myra dear, Celia thought. She swallowed hard against the lump in her throat. Crazy, she said angrily to herself, and led the way to the garden room.

She paused at the foot of the long glass table as she gestured her guests to their seats. There were places laid for eight. Five guests plus Lily and themselves. To balance Lily, there was the Hindu doctor; to balance Myra, the divorced knight, Sir Harry Jones, a former member of Parliament who was handsome in a ruddy, jovial way and had a bold, admiring stare. That he and Myra were lovers, as commonly reported, Celia felt to be unlikely. Then there was George Simpson, Richard's London solicitor, a small man with a squeaky voice who, though his firm had served the Marsdons for three generations, had never before been invited as a guest to Medfield Place. Celia was starting to sit down when she saw Richard's slight inquiring frown and realized that the seat on his left was vacant.

"Oh, dear," she said to George Simpson. "I'm so sorry. I didn't realize Mrs. Simpson wasn't here. Is she still sick?"

George's mouth twitched. "She said she'd be down to lunch."

Celia turned to Dodge. "Will you inquire after Mrs. Simpson?"

Dodge said, "Certainly, my lady," and Celia was amused at the distaste he managed to convey. Mrs. Simpson had taken to her bed, pleading a headache, immediately upon arrival last night, but Celia had been made aware that with the butler the Simpsons had failed, on sight, to pass muster.

There was a pause around the table in the garden room until Dodge reopened the door from the main house. Edna Simpson "made an entrance". There was no other phrase for it. With slow and measured steps the stout, big-jawed woman preceded the butler, bowed towards Richard, and Myra on his right, then more casually towards Celia.

"Pardon me, I'm sure I had no notion of the taime."

The men rose, and Richard murmured inquiries about Edna's health while he held her chair. "Quaite, quaite recovered, thank you, Sir Richard. This luvely country air after smoggy London."

Heavens! Celia thought. Where does she come from? Celia did not recognize, as the English did, the North Country accent, curbed by a genteel effort at disguise.

The woman was staring in disdain at the rest of the company, half-naked in swimsuits, beach robes and sandals. Drinking, too—precisely what she had expected from the Americanized aristocracy. Lady Marsdon's mother, a woman of her own age, sat there tarted-up like the rest of them. And that *black* man next to her. Edna did not, however, look at Celia or examine the dislike she felt for young Lady Marsdon. Nor had she noticed that the sick headache had come on last night at the moment she met Celia and Sir Richard. She had a tonic for all discomforts that might plague her. It was contained in a plain quart bottle labelled BELL'S ANODYNE TINCTURE. That this green fluid, smelling of peppermint, consisted of thirty per cent alcohol was known only to her chemist and would have horrified Edna, who had joined a temperance league at fourteen. The tincture had done its usual soothing work last night, and a few swigs had proved restorative this morning. She addressed herself to Myra and Richard.

The salmon mousse was delicious, but Celia could not eat. Richard was watching her. The dark brooding look which she could not interpret. Had it always been there?

Her mind slithered back to those shimmering days on the ship. Love at first sight, yes. And yet what actually happened had been more like recognition. It was a year ago last May on the *Queen Mary*. After her father died, it had been travel, travel. And Lily had decided to visit England again. "After all," she said, "it was our ancestors' homeland."

Lily, who knew how to manage these things, had been seated at the captain's table. Celia was at a nearby table with a dull couple from London and an Englishman called Richard Marsdon.

And it happened, just like that, Celia thought. We fell in love between the vichyssoise and the guinea hen.

That evening they watched the dancing, listened to the orchestra, talked little. Richard made one personal remark. "Your Christian name is Celia," he said. "It's always attracted me. I once bought a rather—well, bawdy recording of a sixteenth-century song about a Celia."

She gave an excited laugh. "I'm glad you like the name."

"Would you like to dance, Celia?" he said.

The rest of the voyage was a delicious haze. Richard, she learned, had been born in a very old house in East Sussex, his family was poor, he had won a scholarship to Balliol at Oxford and graduated, "I assure you, with no particular aptitude for anything but reading and undue introspection."

Puzzled, she asked why "*undue* introspection", and he shrugged. "I'd a tendency to brood, which I later offset by travel—I hope."

He had accepted a job doing legwork for a famous journalist. Just now, working in New York, Richard had received a telephone call from the family solicitor, George Simpson, who had told him of his father's massive stroke, "and I'm needed at Medfield Place at last." Since his father's condition had stabilized, he'd decided to return by sea instead of air. "On such apparently chance decisions one's future seems to hang." This was the only acknowledgment he made of the attraction between them until the last night out.

They had climbed to the boat deck after dinner and sat down on a locker under one of the lifeboats. "Land," said Richard quietly. "I can smell England."

She shivered, but not from the damp wind. Richard put his arm around her. She relaxed against him, wanting nothing more, held fast in a timeless moment. With faint astonishment she felt Richard begin to tremble. She did not move as he drew away. But he spoke suddenly in a harsh voice. "I want you, Celia. You know I want you. As you want me. But I'm *afraid*. At least, there's a barrier."

She tried to speak lightly. "A barrier? What barrier?"

His long flexible hand clenched on his knee. "It goes far into the past, something I read, partly. I want you," he repeated very low, "yet I want to be *alone* . . . to serve God."

Celia drew back, incredulous. "Serve God," she repeated.

"Of course you don't understand. I don't myself."

She had no time to puzzle over this thing, for he grabbed her against him in a kind of frenzy. He kissed her hair, her neck, and then with violence her mouth, which opened to his in total response. She felt a savage joy in the closeness of their bodies.

"Naow, naow—ye two!" said a stolid voice from the deck beside them. "Captain 'e don't like fun and games up 'ere!"

Celia was confused, but Richard got up and gave the night watchman a slight nod. "Quite right. Though this lady is my fiancée, and we were not exactly indulging in fun and games."

Richard and Celia walked silently down to the main deck. At her cabin door her mouth trembled as she looked at him. "Did you really mean that I was your fiancée? What about the—barrier?"

He took her hand and kissed the palm. "Our marriage is predestined," he said. "On the outcome we must take our chances."

They landed next day at Southampton, and after that life bustled on like a speeded-up film. Celia and her mother stayed a week at Claridge's, making financial arrangements and buying a trousseau. Celia saw Richard only once, when he came up from Sussex to give her a beautiful engagement ring. It was made of heavy gold—two hands clasping an amethyst heart. "And all the Marsdon wives have worn it, back to, oh, Tudor times, at least."

"I'm somewhat daunted at the prospect of running Medfield Place," she said, wishing he would hold her close, not show such haste and urgency. "Do you think I can?"

"No fear," he said gently. "You can, and your money will help."

She had grown used to his frankness about material things, but she frowned. "Are you sure that isn't all you want me for?"

Richard laughed. "You know bloody well it's not. I've met plenty of willing heiresses. But never wished to fall in love."

The marriage took place in a registry office. "It's practical, I suppose," Lily said, "with Sir Charles so sick. My dear child, do you realize how lucky you are! You're madly in love, and it's the sort of marriage I've always prayed you'd find."

Yet, thought Celia a year later at lunch in the manor's garden room, she doesn't guess how wrong it is going now. "Yes, *indeed*," she said brightly to Sir Harry. She was searching for a clue to what his question had been when Richard's voice saved her.

"What are your plans for this afternoon, Celia?"

It was Lily who answered. "How about an expedition?"

Myra spoke up languidly. "What expedition, Mrs. Taylor?"

"To a place in Kent, about an hour from here, where nobody lives but *ghosts*. The owner's an American who's not there now, but one can get in by appointment. I've got the phone number."

"Do you by any chance mean Ightham Mote?" Richard's tone was so cold that Lily gaped at him while she nodded.

Celia managed to laugh. "*What* kind of a moat?"

Dr. Akananda looked at her. "No," he said involuntarily. "Please do not pursue this." But nobody heard him.

"Your mother," Richard said frigidly, "is speaking of an old manor house which I visited when I was twelve and found exceptionally oppressive."

"But Richard, darling," Myra protested, glad to annoy her host, whom she was finding tiresomely unresponsive, "it sounds divine. Absolutely creepy."

"Dodge," Richard said, standing up, "no doubt her ladyship would like coffee served by the pool."

Richard glanced at his watch and said he had suddenly remembered an appointment with his tenant farmer. He excused himself with impersonal courtesy.

"Quite the most mysterious man I know," remarked Myra. "Very polite lord of the manor, but one feels there's a positively smouldering Heathcliffe somewhere."

"Richard simply forgot he had to see Hawkins," Celia retorted. "They're building a new pigsty."

Myra yawned. "How dreary. Mrs. Taylor, what time would you like to start? I'll drive my car and take Harry." Harry's prominent eyes glistened expectantly. "And will *you* come with us, Mrs. Taylor?" Myra added, giving a little purring laugh at Harry's change of expression. Though for eight years Myra had been a faithful wife to her old arthritic duke, she had no more scruples than her wild border forebears. She enjoyed playing amorous games. But her mischief-making was tempered by good nature and an inborn sense of responsibility. Many a tenant near her father's Cumberland castle spoke of her with warm gratitude.

Lily forgot Richard's odd behaviour and enthusiastically outlined her plans. "If you don't mind, my dear?" she asked Celia belatedly.

Celia smiled acquiescence. What *was* the matter with Richard?

Edna Simpson lumbered up from her chair, her bulldog face red. Nobody had consulted *her* preferences. Rude, brazen American women! Her glare turned towards Celia. He'll soon tire of that stupid little thing, if he hasn't already. "My headache's returning," she announced. "I'll rest this afternoon, if it is quaite convenient to have tea sent up?"

"Of course," Celia said, startled by the malevolent stare.

They all drifted into the house, and Celia went to find Richard. Nanny was in his dressing room laying out his dinner clothes. "There," she said lovingly, and saw Celia standing in the door. "He'll not be here, m'lady." Her quick voice could be cutting, but for Celia there had been from the first only gentleness.

"Has he gone down to the farm already?" Celia asked.

"I doot it, m'lady. Ye might try the library. 'Tis in this mood he at times consults that great ponderous book o' the Marsdons."

"What book?" said Celia, sighing. "Oh, Nanny. . . ."

"Aye, puir lady, there's a deal he keeps to himself, always has. 'Twas the week after the first Lady Marsdon died that I came here to tend him. I never nursed so solemn and quiet a weanling."

"Did he mind when his father married again?" Celia knew only that Richard was twelve when Sir Charles had remarried, and still at Eton when his stepmother had been killed in a car crash.

"To be sure he minded. Times I heard him weeping i' the night. Starved for love he was, and not a body tó gi'e it to him but me. That minx his father wed had nae more heart than a weasel."

"I must find Richard," Celia said, and hurried downstairs. The library was very large and panelled in fumed oak. It smelled musty, unaired. Celia found Richard standing in an alcove, frowning over a large open book on the lectern.

"What *are* you reading, darling?" Celia asked softly.

Her husband jumped. "I thought you'd gone to Ightham Mote." The murky light that shone through the Victorian stained-glass windows gave Richard's face a strange defencelessness.

"I won't go if you don't want me to. Oh, my dearest, why—"

"Why *what*? Do as you like. I'm off to the farm."

She stiffened, her heart began its erratic thumps. "Could I see the book?" she asked. "See what interests you so?"

He laughed curtly. "By all means. It's the Marsdon Chronicle, covers over five hundred years of family history."

It was huge, bound in thick yellowed vellum, open at a page of crabbed writing in faded ink. She squinted. "I can't read this."

"I didn't think you could." He shut the book.

She put her hand on his. "Richard, is there something in it which you feel gives the past a bearing on the future?"

"Isn't the past finished for ever?" He glanced down at her hand, at the heavy Marsdon ring, and she felt a chill.

"Richard, for God's sake, what *is* wrong? We were so happy. I don't think it's another woman, but wives are often fooled."

Richard's eyes softened and he spoke with the teasing tenderness she had not heard in all these months. "No, poppet, no other woman. One's quite enough. You've married a bloody-tempered bloke is all. Nor does he understand himself." He kissed her hard and quickly, in the old way, his hand gently cupping her left breast. "Go put some clothes on, you're scandalising this library."

She looked down and realized that her robe was open, exposing her bikini and a good deal of slim, tanned nakedness. "Sorry," she said, laughing with wild relief. She snatched the robe together.

"I'm off," he said. "Is it the Bent-Warners for dinner tonight?"

"Yes, you suggested them. Will they fit?"

"Nobody," said Richard, smiling, "would fit this extraordinary house party. The Simpson woman is a disaster. A secret toper as well, according to Dodge, who had it from the new housemaid."

"Heavens," said Celia, "I suppose that explains her baleful glares. Poor woman."

"You're a nice child. But *I* feel that the female is sinister."

Chapter 2

Celia and all the guests except the Simpsons set out for Kent at half-past three. George Simpson had wanted to go, but he knew better than to oppose Edna when she smelled of peppermint. "You don't have to toady to vulgar Yanks to keep Sir Richard's business,

George. He's not going to that Ightham Mote. Mind you don't go either. I don't laike the sound of it."

As George went out, shutting the door softly behind him, Edna's annoyance shifted to puzzled questioning. There was no reason to dislike the very name of a place she had never heard of before; or the name Celia, let alone the young woman herself. Well, I've a right to my fancies. She reached for more tincture and drifted rapidly into snorting sleep.

Myra led the way to Ightham in her Bentley, Lily sat beside her with a map; Harry sat in back smoking his pipe. In the Jaguar were Celia, with Dr. Akananda beside her. He was very quiet, an inward listening expression on his bronze face.

"England must be a very old story to you, Doctor," Celia said, and was startled by the gaze he turned on her—it looked like pity.

"Why do you look at me like that?" she cried involuntarily.

Akananda smiled apology. "I'm sorry, Lady Marsdon, it's that I'd like to offer my help during the trials that may await you. I tried to stop your coming here today, but you didn't hear me."

"Do you predict futures?" asked Celia, alarmed. Light seemed to radiate from him. *That's* idiotic, she thought.

"I'm not a fortune-teller, no." Akananda smiled. "But through long discipline I receive more impressions than most people can. I was trying to prepare you for a grave ordeal. I am permitted, even commanded, to help you as best I can. Though we must all pay our Karmic debts, the divinity which is above Karma is ever merciful; through God's help and your own actions you *may* be able to reduce a sword-thrust to a pin-prick."

Celia stared ahead. "I used to believe in God when I was little, but my father laughed at religion and said common horse sense was enough for him."

"And you agree?"

"I think so," Celia said. "I got cynical. Mother took up Theosophy. I've seen her involved with astrologists who charge five hundred dollars for a 'reading' that could mean anything. And faith healers. And a Yogi in California who preached purity, and tried to seduce me. It was awful."

"And now you fear she's entangled you with another?"

Celia coloured. "Oh, I don't mean *that.* I trust Mother. I—"

"Your mother," he said, "is a fine woman. She seeks the truth and often glimpses it. The bond between you is very strong."

She nodded, uncomfortable. "Oh, Mother's all right. My whole *life* should be all right now. It will be, I'm sure."

Akananda sighed. "There's something you desperately want—to understand your husband. And you are *not* sure. There are from the past appalling obstacles, I'm afraid, between you and your desire." It was an authoritative statement.

Celia's jaw tightened. "I don't know what you're getting at."

"Child, your deep self knows. Why are your hands trembling?"

"Nerves," she said angrily. "Everyone gets nervous symptoms sometimes. Stop probing. You've no right to, and I don't like it."

"That's reasonable." He spoke with patient dignity. "However, I *am* a physician and a psychiatrist. I am also a disciple of a great world teacher, Nanak."

"Is he *dead*?" she asked.

"He no longer inhabits a body," said Akananda. "He's passed beyond the disciplinary Karmic need to reincarnate."

"Oh," she said, "I know half the world believes in rebirth, even the Bible suggests it. But why can't we remember past lives?"

"Remembrance would usually be an intolerable burden, which all-merciful God spares us. For that matter, Lady Marsdon, do you consciously remember the first year or two of *this* life?"

"No, but what difference does it make?" Celia was tired. She resented his having disrupted her hopeful mood. "You don't seem to be the sort of man who would bother to come to a silly weekend house party," she said crossly. "Especially as you hardly know us."

He hesitated before he spoke. "I don't want to annoy you, child, but I believe I've known you and your mother before this lifetime, though I don't know where. There's a reason for my presence. Also, you have known some of your house party before. The great Karmic law has now brought you to the brink of a precipice where a battle will take place."

"Indeed," said Celia, shrugging. "I hope the good guys win." She suddenly felt tired. "Oh, look down there! That house must be the one we're going to. Why, it really *does* have a moat!"

Myra turned her Bentley through the gates and Celia followed. The five got out of the cars and were quiet for a while as they gazed at the manor house gilded by the afternoon sun. Secluded, solitary, enchanted, Ightham lay dreamlike within its encircling moat.

"Marvellous, Mrs. Taylor," Sir Harry said.

A middle-aged woman came briskly over the stone bridge towards them. "Mrs. Taylor's party?" she inquired, smiling.

Lily smiled back. "May I introduce the Duchess of Drewton, Sir Harry Jones and Dr. Akananda. Then my daughter, Lady Marsdon."

The guide glanced at Lady Marsdon, who had drawn away from the others and was staring at the stone tower with extraordinary intensity.

"Now," she said, "we'll start our tour here on the bridge. The original fortified manor house was built about 1370. You will find a list of most of the early owners on the back of the leaflet." She handed out pamphlets. "That'll be sixpence each if you wish to keep them."

Myra declined hers graciously. "I'm afraid I'm not all that keen on crawling over old houses," she said. "Are you, Harry?" He shook his head. "Then we'll wait for you in the gardens."

"Well," said Lily, "*we* want to see everything." She looked at Dr. Akananda, then at Celia. "What's the matter with *you*, dear?" she said. "You act moonstruck."

Celia jumped. She looked hastily down at the moat. "I was watching the swans." Two of them were gliding under the bridge among the green weeds.

The guide led her party on into a cobbled courtyard, where she unlocked a massive oak door. "This leads to the vestibule, then into the Great Hall."

They filed into the Hall, which was suddenly flooded with sunshine through the tall mullioned windows. The guide pointed out the original oak roof timbers, the grotesque fourteenth-century corbels, the Flemish tapestries, and Lily exclaimed with delight. The doctor watched Celia. Her face was flushed, her uneven breathing audible. He took her arm and led her to a bench below one of the windows, noting her pounding pulse.

"Now we'll proceed to the old crypt, then upstairs," said the guide. "Is there something wrong, Lady Marsdon?"

Celia heard the question from a vast distance. She licked her lips. "I'm all right. I guess it's the heat."

Lily made a move towards her daughter, but was stopped by a shake of Akananda's head. "I'll take care of her, Mrs. Taylor."

She was reassured and turned back to the guide. "I can't wait to see the rest of this fascinating place. What's that little door next to the big door on the wall? It doesn't go anywhere."

The guide smiled. "That's a niche where they found the skeleton of a girl when they rebuilt this wall in 1872. I'm afraid she'd been walled up alive."

Lily gaped. "Where's the skeleton now?"

"No doubt," said the guide, "the bones were dispersed—"

"Who was she?" Lily asked. "Doesn't her ghost do some haunting?"

"I've never heard mention of the ghost of the walled-up girl, but there are other legends—ghostly hoofbeats, a black monk with a rope around his neck, that sort of thing." Then the guide determinedly shooed Lily back into the vestibule.

Celia remained on the window seat with Akananda. Her face was now pale, and glistening with sweat. She slumped against the doctor. "Deathly sick," she whispered. "Can't breathe."

Akananda put a firm hand on her forehead. She felt the sustaining pressure and straightened slowly. "Where are Mother and the guide?" she asked in a little-girl voice. He saw that her pupils were widely dilated.

"They have gone to see the rest of this place."

"This place," she repeated. Then she spoke in a startlingly unfamiliar cadence. "This is a place abhorrent. Yet I cannot flee. For I must see him. My love awaits me in secret. Jesu, forgive us!" She crossed herself with a wavering, uncertain motion.

Akananda understood what she, enmeshed in the results of a bygone tragedy, could not. His thought sped to the exalted ashram in the Himalayas where he had passed some of his boyhood, under the guidance of Guru Nanak. With the yearning memory went a humble prayer for wisdom.

"Come out into the garden, my child," he said, putting a hand on Celia's arm. "You've had enough. Already the protective veil is torn."

"Let me be!" she cried angrily. "I must tell him." She stroked her belly. "It hath quickened. I felt it move this morn."

Akananda, watching her, saw a subtle change, as though a different face were shedding a reflection on that of Celia Marsdon.

"Lady Marsdon," he said in a cold tone designed to reach through to her, "do you mean you are pregnant by Sir Richard?"

"Will you mock me?" she cried. "Stephen is my dear love. . . ."

She whirled around and ran through the door. With Akananda after her, she flew up the heavily carved stairs. On the landing she put her hand to her lips. "I hear voices. None must know. *She* found us once." Celia flattened herself into a corner.

The voices were those of the guide and Lily, who were in the room called the solar, examining the window through which ladies of bygone days watched male revelry in the Great Hall below. "And now," said the guide, "we go through towards the Priest's Room and the Tudor chapel. The chapel was built about 1521, during the reign of Henry the Eighth . . ." Her voice died away.

"They are gone," Celia murmured to herself as she walked slowly through the solar. "Might he be at the altar? Not so late at night, though he *does* pray overmuch."

She entered a bare cubicle which contained a fireplace and led into the chapel. "Stephen," she whispered urgently. "What's that . . . black, hanging there . . . ?" She moved to the fireplace, raising her arms high. Then she fell to her knees with a scream so piercing that it shrilled right through the manor.

From deep in the house the guide and Lily came running. They stood for an appalled moment staring at Celia crumpled on the floor, with Akananda bending over her. "Dear Lord!" cried Lily distractedly. "Surely that terrible noise wasn't *Celia*!"

Akananda did not hesitate. There would certainly now be no escape from suffering, but he would spare the poor mother what he could. "Was there some special noise?" he asked. "I was preoccupied with Lady Marsdon. She fainted."

The guide at once showed exasperated relief. "You can depend

on it, 'twas the plumbing." She helped Akananda lift Celia. "We'll take her to a bed in the owner's wing, poor thing."

"She's never fainted before," said Lily, much alarmed.

But within twenty minutes Celia seemed completely recovered. She told no one that she couldn't remember a thing since she'd set foot on the moat bridge. The guide showed them out, accepted the fees and her tip, then vanished.

Myra and Harry greeted them amiably. But even Myra's gaiety was penetrated by something odd about Mrs. Taylor and her daughter—their silence, and on Celia's face a haunted look. Myra disliked uncomfortable situations and dealt with this one briskly. "The pubs must be open," she said. "Let's get fortified."

IT WAS SEVEN O'CLOCK when they arrived at Medfield Place. Richard, in evening dress, asked cordially, "Enjoy yourselves?"

Myra gave Richard her lazy smile. "We missed you, darling. I hope you built a *divine* pigsty!"

"Quite. A sanctuary for supersows. Celia, you seem a bit fagged, but I'm afraid the Bent-Warners'll be here shortly."

"Oh, yes," she answered after a minute. "I'll go and change."

The Bent-Warners? Who were the Bent-Warners? She mounted the steps very carefully, as though uncertain of her balance.

Richard watched her, frowning. He drew Lily into his study. "Anything wrong with Celia?" he asked. "She seems strange."

Lily hesitated. "She had a kind of fainting spell at Ightham Mote . . . but Dr. Akananda says she's all right. I thought maybe she was—" She stopped, a flush sprang up on her cheeks.

Richard's gaze hardened. "Pregnant? I assure you she's not. Nor do I consider that Hindu an adequate physician. If she's not better when I go up, I'll call Dr. Foster."

"That's a good idea," Lily murmured, dismayed by his abrupt tone. Lily shut her eyes and strove to clear her confusion with one of her favourite aphorisms: "We live by an invisible sun within us." She tried to *feel* the interior glow, which had never before failed her—but it did now. And being a woman of action, she left the study and went and knocked on Akananda's door.

He greeted her without surprise. "I just wanted to . . . to ask you . . . well, about Celia," she said. "And Richard's so rude, which he's never been until today, and what *really* made Celia faint? Everything is suddenly queer." Her eyes filled with tears.

Akananda looked at her sadly. But it was not the time for explanations. "We'll both pray," he said.

"I guess I'll go to church tomorrow," Lily said. "It always makes me feel better. But you don't believe in Christianity, do you?"

"Of course I do," Akananda said, laughing. "The Lord Christ was sent from God to show the way, the truth and the life to the western world. The Lord Krishna, the Lord Buddha—their teachings come from the same source. I'll gladly go with you to that charming village church. One can more easily touch God in appointed places."

Lily agreed with him. "I really do know that prayers are answered. I don't know why I got so upset."

"Prayers," he said gravely, "are always *heard*. They are *answered* according to divine law. Prayers are really desires. And desires, good *or* bad, are fulfilled according to their strength. Violent desires inevitably set the machinery in motion. As long as there's violence there will be retribution in this life or succeeding ones. I believe you understand this intuitively."

"Well, yes," said Lily, "in a way." Though she wondered what a speech about violence had to do with a fainting spell or the unexpected sharpness of a son-in-law.

CELIA was sitting at her dressing table, applying eye shadow, when Richard came into her room. "I hear you fainted at Ightham Mote. What happened?"

"Nothing special," she said coolly. Deep inside her something stirred. Hostility to Richard. She had no memory of Ightham Mote, little of the ride home; but she was aware of this shift in feeling.

Richard stared. That chill remoteness instead of her usual eager warmth. "Well, I'm glad you're all right again," he said uncertainly. "You didn't look it when you got back. I was worried."

Her grey eyes examined him quietly. "*Were* you, Richard?" She rouged her lips a cherry red, which further astonished him. She had always worn pale lipsticks. She stood up in her brief lacy slip and dropped a simple tangerine chiffon sheath over her head. "Zip me up, please!" He obeyed clumsily, and when his fingers touched her back, she shuddered and drew away.

She brushed her dark hair into a high pile on her head and clipped on crystal earrings as big as golf balls. They gave her a strange, exotic look.

He frowned. "I thought you didn't like stuff like that."

"Not my image?" asked Celia sweetly. "Harry brought them as a guest gift." She opened a sealed bottle of Shalimar, a long untouched Christmas present. "I think," she added, "that I'll seduce Harry, be fun to take him from Myra."

If she had suddenly hit him in the face he could not have been more shocked. Teasing—but nothing like this—had once been part of their love-making when they were close, *had* been close. His look darkened. Mrs. Taylor had thought Celia pregnant. But he hadn't touched her in—well, a long time. Why not? Because sex had suddenly grown repugnant. *You should not have married!* He heard the words in his head.

"The seating arrangements tonight," said Celia, pulling a stack of gold-rimmed cards towards her. "I'll write them fast. I shall put Harry beside me," she added.

Richard swallowed. "If you're being so childish as to try and make me jealous, the effort's wasted."

"Don't flatter yourself," she said. Their eyes met in anger. That behind the anger was fear neither of them perceived.

THEY ALL SAT DOWN to dinner at nine in Medfield's gloomy great dining room. The Victorian baronet had decorated it with purple brocade and painted the original woodwork in a muddy brown. Purple plush curtains shut out the evening sunlight. The light of thirty candles on the mahogany table and in sconces wavered over ten ancestral portraits, proof of the long-established lineage which so thrilled Celia.

The Bent-Warners, who had expanded the house party, were an ebullient young couple. Pamela was a pretty, chattering blonde, and Robin sat on Celia's right and made her laugh with his amusing talk. The laugh was high-pitched and shrill.

Lily inspected her daughter anxiously. What had come over the girl? Her cheeks were flushed, her eyes glittered like those extraordinary crystal hunks she wore. While she laughed, her bare shoulder was pressing against Harry's, and he looked startled and pleased. Lily put down a forkful of crab *ravigote* and pushed her plate back. Celia could not be tight, she had taken no cocktails or wine. Then she was coming down with something. That would explain the fainting, too. Right after dinner we'll see if she has a temperature.

Richard was also watching Celia. He made no pretence of listening to either Pam's chatter or Myra's husky blandishments. Myra flicked his cheek with her finger. "*Must* you glower so tiresomely, my lad? I've seen a side of you this weekend I never suspected."

"Men are perhaps more complicated than you quite realize, dear Myra." He raised his glass in a mocking toast.

She laughed. "Well, Harry isn't complicated. He's just plain susceptible. I might be glowering a bit myself, seeing that heavy-lidded bedroom look he's giving your Celia, but actually I think it's funny." And she did. Imagine that little mouse of a Celia suddenly acting sexy, and looking it, too. As though somebody had switched a light bulb on. That this phenomenon was designed to pique the mysterious Richard, Myra had no doubt, and that the ploy seemed to be succeeding, she thought admirable.

Another close watcher of Celia was Edna Simpson. During her tincture-induced afternoon nap Edna had suffered a recurrent nightmare. Her host and hostess were in it, though they did not look like themselves. Sir Richard had no face, and he had a long black snake around his waist. She wanted to grab the snake and make it bite Celia Marsdon, who stood spread-eagled against the wall of a high-vaulted room. The dream-Celia had long fair hair, which she would not keep decently bound in a kerchief. Another of her crimes was the depth of her laced bodice. So vile a creature should be destroyed. God said so. God was perched on top of a silver crucifix, shouting "Kill!" as the sound of the cars returning from Ightham Mote had roused her. She was pouring out more tincture when George walked in.

"Ye dumb bustard," she snarled. "Ye made me slosh me tonic."

In twenty-six years, for all her tempers, George had not seen her like this.

"You shouldn't go down for dinner," he cried anxiously.

Edna hiccupped and slumped on the bed. "Must keep an eye on that mealy-mouthed minx."

But her brain had cleared, and resplendent in her new evening frock of navy blue satin with white polka dots, she sat now, like a massive monolith, beside Sir Harry, whose entire attention was devoted to his hostess. Celia's altered appearance and actions gave Edna a venomous satisfaction. Little slut, she thought.

After the chocolate *soufflé* the men remained in the dining room and Celia led the ladies to the drawing room for coffee. She poured, she chatted, and she brightly refused Lily's whispered request that she take her temperature. But below these actions she was empty. Celia had gone off somewhere, far away, into a cramped cold space. Someone else was using Celia's body.

As soon as the men joined them, she jumped up crying. "It's Saturday night, let's dance! We'll go to Richard's music room."

Harry laughed, while eyeing Celia with new admiration. Looks like a gypsy suddenly. Astonishing little beasts—women.

Myra cried, "I didn't know you had a music room, Richard!"

Everyone looked at Richard, who removed his unfathomable gaze from his wife. "'Music room' is a bit grand for the old schoolroom. I have records which appeal to *me*. Nothing modern."

His tone piqued Myra. "Let's see what he *has* got! He obviously doesn't want us to. Are his records naughty, Celia?"

"I don't know," answered Celia, in a voice as brittle as Myra's. "I've never been in there. Richard keeps it locked."

Myra's mocking eyes turned from Richard's stormy face to Celia's flushed one, and she perceived that the girl was under great tension. She felt a sudden flicker of feminine alliance. "Bluebeard's closet, is it, Richard? Unlock the ancient schoolroom door or we'll suspect the worst!"

Richard reddened, but he controlled himself. "By all means, Myra, but your lurid hopes will be disappointed. I lock the place simply to keep out housemaids who disturb everything."

This was not quite true. Richard had locked that door since he was twelve because it represented the only privacy he had had from his stepmother. He resented Celia's idiotic wish to expose it to these people as he resented her extraordinary behaviour tonight. Yet he was aware of her as he had not been in months, aware that she was alluring, arousing a crude lust deep within him.

Silently he led them upstairs—all but Edna, who sat in glassy silence. "The Chamber of Horrors," he announced, unlocking the door and switching on the single electric light. The room was quite large because the Victorian baronet had produced nine children. Battered desks and stools were piled against a wall. On a plain deal table stood the stereo, above a rack of records. The speakers had been placed at either end of a long bookshelf.

There were other objects in the room which only Akananda saw. At the far end a cupboard door had been removed, thus forming a shallow alcove. Within its shadows he could see a *prie-dieu*, or kneeling chair, in front of a makeshift wooden altar that held two candlesticks and a silver and ebony crucifix. Akananda knew at once that the crucifix was very old, and knew with equal certainty that Richard did not wish it to be noticed.

"You win, Richard," cried Myra after a rapid survey. "I have never seen a duller place." She swooped down on the record rack. "'Gregorian Chants—*Kyrie Altissime*'. Heavens!"

"Would you care to hear it?" Richard asked with elaborate courtesy. "It is a plain chant as sung by monks for centuries."

"I suppose I brought this on myself, didn't I!" Myra said ruefully. She glanced at the others and was aware of that tension which had seemed to arise so often during this interminable day. "Well, put the thing on—do, Richard," she said impatiently.

The schoolroom was suddenly filled with male voices, chanting, beseeching. "Kyrie eleison, Christe eleison". Akananda saw Celia's back go rigid. Then in Richard's eyes he caught a look of anguish and what seemed to be tears. "Lord have mercy . . . Christ have mercy." Poor fellow, Akananda thought. I believe he's chanted this himself in the past. He does not quite *know* it, but he feels it, as I do.

When the record ended, Myra lit a cigarette. "Definitely damping to the spirits. You *are* rather peculiar, darling."

"No doubt," said Richard. He was replacing the record in the rack when Harry, who had been squinting at the titles, gave a pleased cry.

"You're human after all Richard! 'A Lusty Young Smith', 'A Maiden Did a-Bathing Go'. Here's one about *you*, Celia! 'Celia, the Wanton and Fair'. Didn't Richard ever play that for you?"

"No," Celia whispered. "No, I've never heard it."

"Those songs are not for mixed company," Lily said. "We'll go back downstairs and play bridge."

In the drawing room Edna still sat in glassy silence. Since Celia at once regained her feverish glow and began to flirt with Harry, and Richard uncharacteristically ignored his guests and poured himself a stiff brandy, Lily tried to retrieve the evening. An impossible feat.

Suddenly Celia put her hand on Harry's arm and suggested quite audibly that he might like to see the garden by moonlight.

"*Well*—of all the brazen . . ." began Edna loudly, watching Richard, who was pouring more brandy. Myra joined him.

"Are you the jealous type, my sweet?" she asked. "Because if Celia returns the same chaste wife she left, I don't know Harry."

Richard's look stopped her. It was murderous; his body trembled. "Good Lord, Richard," she said apologetically, "I was only joking. No need to go all primitive."

He smiled then, a smile more frightening than the anger. "All women are whores," he said blandly.

Myra started. "Well, thanks, dear—that's one viewpoint," she said as he walked away. He sat down on the sofa beside Edna Simpson, who bridled with gratification. The look she gave Richard was positively doting.

Good God, Myra thought. This whole party's too damn uncomfortable. I'll remember an important date tomorrow. Give Gilbert a ring and we'll go out somewhere. Fed up with Harry anyway.

Just as the party broke up, Celia and Harry came back from the garden. Celia made polite farewells to the Bent-Warners, and as her guests all seemed ready for bed, she said her good nights with the same high-pitched brightness she'd had all evening. Lily saw no perceptible difference in her good night to Harry, though Edna was sure she saw a signal. So *that's* it! There wasn't time in the garden, but they'll get together later when it's safe. Poor Sir Richard. Funny thing, she thought, I took a fancy to him straight off. As if I'd seen him somewhere. That wench! Cuckolding him in his own house. Ye'll not get away with that, my girl!

Edna lumbered upstairs ahead of the others and, leaving her bedroom door ajar, took two long pulls from the tincture bottle. As the party came up she watched everyone through the crack in the door. The Duchess went to her room, Sir Harry to his, which was next to the Marsdons'. The doctor murmured to Mrs. Taylor, then they both disappeared into their own rooms. George came in and gaped at her. "Aren't you going to undress, my dear?"

"In my own good taime," she said. "Go to bed, George. In the dressing room. You snore, and I need my sleep."

He obeyed without comment. Edna was shockingly altered. He didn't know what to do. It was a long time before he slept.

Edna lurked behind the door in the dark, and presently saw her host and hostess enter their suite in utter silence. Now to wait until two doors opened stealthily, Celia Marsdon's and Sir Harry's. She settled her bulk on a chair and watched.

IN THE MARSDONS' bedroom Richard stood staring at Celia with a black intensity. "You aren't," he said without expression, "the woman I thought I'd married. I never should have."

Her spasm of sick fear Celia noted objectively. She took off the earrings. "No doubt you are quite right, Richard. Divorce may be a trifle difficult in England, but certainly can be managed."

"The Marsdons don't get divorces. . . . I didn't mean that. I . . ." He heard the wavering in his own voice and was angered afresh. "Did you enjoy yourself with Harry Jones? Did you enjoy forcing me to open the schoolroom to show your power?"

She did not answer, and he watched her slide out of her flame-coloured dress, then her slip and panties. Naked, she began brushing her hair with slow voluptuous strokes, arching her slender back. Richard watched the insolent, taunting woman until the throbbing of his head descended to his loins. "By God," he cried hoarsely, "*that's* what you want! But you'll not get it here!"

He grabbed her wrist and jerked her across the room. "Richard, you hurt me!" she cried in terror. "Let me go!" She slapped his face, then let out a strangled scream as he cut his hand across her windpipe with a quick karate chop. She went limp, and he picked her up, threw open their door, carried her down the passage to the old schoolroom and flung her on the floor, where she lay gasping, naked, half-stunned.

Richard went into the alcove and lit the two candles. He then removed his clothes and hung them carefully on the *prie-dieu*. He went to the gramophone, put on a record, and turned up the volume.

Celia moaned and put a groping finger on her larynx, where he had hit her. "Hurts," she whispered. "You hate me, Richard!" She stared up at him in the candlelight. "What are we *doing* . . . ?"

He clapped his hand roughly over her mouth. "Listen!"

Above the ancient instruments a tenor voice was singing:

"Celia the wanton and fair
Hath now no need to despair
She hath used shameless art
To inveigle lust's dart
And she shall suffer it now
And she shall suffer it now. . . ."

"No!" she cried against his hand. "Not like this, not in hate."

But he pinned her down and raped her savagely.

Neither of them heard the door open, nor knew that a polka-dotted bulk stood over them. Until the song ended, and Edna's voice rose shrill. "I've caught you, you filthy whore. Hanging's too good . . . God Almighty, *you*, Sir Richard!" Gasping, Edna stumbled backward out of the door and shut it with a resounding thud.

Celia heard the thud. She lay tight and still, waiting for the next thud—the slap of a trowel against mortar. And beyond the thuds, in the shadowy Hall, that gloating woman's face was watching.

Richard turned off the gramophone, put on his trousers, and looked down at Celia. "I'm sorry, my dear," he whispered, "terribly sorry. It was disgusting, all of it. My behaviour and that unspeakable woman's. . . ."

Celia's eyes strained towards the wall, unblinking. "How long, Stephen?" she said faintly. "How long must it take to die?"

"You won't die," he said sharply. "I'm sorry I behaved like such a bastard. Here—" He bundled her inert body into his shirt.

"You are going to let me die," she said. She did not speak again.

Beneath Richard's guilt there was horror. Why did she call me *Stephen*? He carried her back through the passages to their room. She was hardly breathing as he laid her on the bed. Suddenly she reached her arms straight up above her head, her fingers curled as though grasping at a ledge. Her face flushed purple, she began to gasp.

"It's all right now," he whispered, trying to take her hand. "I was beastly, you must forget—Celia, put your arms down!"

But her only response was a bubbling sound from her throat.

"Oh, my God!" he cried, and rushed out of the room.

Chapter 3

Mellow sunlight illumined the garden room as the guests straggled in for Sunday breakfast. Harry came first, then George Simpson, and finally Myra. They helped themselves from the hot table, and the impassive Dodge poured coffee.

After breakfast they drifted towards the pool, where they riffled the Sunday papers and were silent.

"No host or hostess—or Mrs. Taylor?" Myra asked finally. "I mean, it's past eleven, and one might reasonably expect—" She broke off; they all stared at each other as they heard an ambulance siren in the drive.

Lily Taylor rushed from the house in her dressing gown. "It's Celia," she cried. "Dreadfully sick, going to the hospital."

There was a startled pause. Then Myra clasped the older woman's arm. "I'm so *sorry*, Mrs. Taylor. How dreadful for you."

"Poor woman," said Myra, as Lily sped back into the house. "And poor Celia. Obviously we must clear out. I'll give you a lift back to town, Harry. I do wonder where Richard is. Not one to go to pieces in an emergency, I'd think, but he's been acting very strangely. Oh well. . . ." She went off to summon a maid.

Upstairs in the Marsdon bedroom the elderly Dr. Foster, who had been summoned by Richard, spoke to Akananda with impatient condescension. "Hysterical seizure," he barked. "But bound to admit I've never seen the like of those arms! And the *eyes*!"

The eyes showed white as a terrified mare's, and the arms were still rigid above the head, the fingers clutching. Both doctors had tried to lower the arms and found them unyielding as iron.

"Not quite dead," went on Foster. "Pulse of around thirty."

"I believe she may live," Akananda said, "though the adrenalin seems to have had no effect."

Foster shot an annoyed glance at Akananda. There was something fishy. Girl looked as though she was dying of fright. "Where is Sir Richard?" he asked. "He ought to be here."

"He is absent. Nor is he needed. Shall we take her now?"

Foster called the ambulance attendants. The men lifted Celia onto the stretcher, and Akananda went to get Lily from her room, where he had asked her to stay. "Come along now," he said gently. "We're off to the hospital."

"But where's Richard? Where did he go after he roused you?"

"I don't know," said Akananda. "We'll look for him later. *Pray*, Mrs. Taylor—for your daughter and for Sir Richard."

"Not for *him*," she said. "He's run away. It's inhuman."

All *too* human, Akananda thought. That glimpse he had had of Richard as he cried hoarsely, "Celia—go to Celia. I'm frightened." If he'd ever seen guilt and horror on a face . . . What could possibly have happened to bring on these disasters? In all his medical career he had never felt as helpless as he did now.

Dodge had kept the servants in their quarters. But there was one member of the household he could not control, and when Lily set foot on the ambulance step, Nanny flew out of the manor. "Wha' ails her ladyship?" she cried shrilly, blinking down at the inert body on the stretcher. "The lass isna *dead*—"

"No, no," said Dr. Foster. "See if you can find Sir Richard."

"The young master—what's he done?" Her voice trembled.

"He hasn't done anything that I know of," said Foster

impatiently. "He simply isn't here. Carry on," he said to the driver.

Nanny watched the ambulance career down the drive. As she re-entered the house, the Duchess was descending the stairs, all dressed for town. Myra said kindly, "Is there anyone to bring my car around? I'm so sorry her ladyship is ill. We'll all leave at once. But would you know where Sir Richard is?"

"I wouldna, Your Grace. But he'd tak' shame if ye left wi'out a fareweel. The gardener's lad'll get the car—but will ye no bide?"

Myra hesitated. She longed to be out of this subtly menacing atmosphere, but it seemed necessary for someone to take over, at least temporarily. "I'll wait here," she said, indicating the drawing room, where Harry soon joined her.

"Extraordinary," Harry kept saying. Dammit, he thought. I wish I'd never come down this weekend.

George Simpson, struggling to rouse his wife in their bedroom, shared Harry's view in this most fervently. "Get up, Edna. We have to leave. Lady Marsdon's very ill, been taken to the hospital."

Her eyes focused slowly. "Lady Marsdon . . . ? Very ill?" She smiled with malicious triumph. "Hope she dies."

George grabbed her thick shoulders and yanked her upright. "Before God, I don't know *how*, but I think you're drunk!"

She sagged back onto the pillow, her mouth open.

George gazed down at her. What'll I do? Can't let anyone see her like this. I *can't* have seen that gloating look on her face.

NANNY, searching for her young master, went first to the library, where the Marsdon Chronicle was kept. The room was empty, but the great vellum book rested in its accustomed place. Nanny opened it at random. Beside an entry made in 1588 there was a faint pencil line. She could decipher but a few words of the strange script. "All Hallowes Eve . . . unshriven deeds bringe sorrowe to our house . . . terrible lust . . . murdered girle . . . at Ightham Mote . . ."

"'Tis this he moithers over," she murmured. "Evil fra' lang ago, yet here again amangst us. The Lord ha' mercy." And so where would he be? Aye, to be *sure*. She trudged to the old schoolroom.

"Master Richard," she called softly. There was no sound inside.

The door was locked. "'Tis only Nanny. Open up!" Her ears caught a faint rustling noise. Her heart thumped heavily. Twenty years ago she had stood rapping at this very door when the lad was twelve. "Open up! Sir Richard!" she cried in the nursery tone of command. "I'll get them to break the door in!"

After a moment she heard a hoarse response. "Leave me alone!"

She steadied herself against the door. "Master, her ladyship is gone to hospital. Come down to your guests."

Silence. Then a shout. "For God's sake, let me *be*!"

No pleading or exhorting elicited a further sound. Nanny at last plodded back to the drawing room. "Your Grace," she said to Myra, "may I speak private wi' ye?"

Myra rose and followed her into Richard's study. "He's locked himsel' i' the old schoolroom," Nanny said. "He willna come oot. Doom ha' laid its dreadful hand on the Marsdons."

Myra smiled. Her own nanny had been much like this. "I'm sure there's no need to fear doom just because Lady Marsdon is ill and Sir Richard wishes solitude. We'll leave for London, and you must give him our sympathy and farewells when he appears."

Nanny's black eyes looked sadly up at the beautiful, impatient face. "He will *not* appear, Your Grace." It was a flat statement and unpleasantly convincing.

Myra exhaled and sat down. "I don't understand."

"No," said Nanny. "Ye dinna understand. I'm sore afeard, Your Grace, and there's nobody else here I weesh to tell why to."

Myra sighed. "Sit down then, and tell me."

It began with the death of Richard's mother when he was two and Nanny had come to take care of him. The servants told her the baby had used many words, but he didn't talk for months afterwards. He didn't cry either, nor smile. Sir Charles—"verra grim, he was"—said the boy ought to be taken to a London doctor, which Nanny fiercely resisted. She loved her charge and never doubted he'd come right. "An' he did, Your Grace. The whilst he was three ye never saw a brighter bairn."

Half-listening, Myra received the impression of a lonely little boy, who talked and walked in his sleep, who insisted that his name was Stephen and that Stephen had been very wicked in another life.

Only Nanny knew about this phase. Anyway, it all stopped when she got him a collie pup. "'Twas the making o' Master Dick. When the dog was shot, he could never bear another near him. He loved that dog wi' all his heart, an' he felt that whatever he loved came to a bad end."

"The dog was shot?" said Myra with some sorrow. "What for?"

"Sir Charles thought it had rabies. He didna wait to mak' sure, nor told the lad why. It was the year everything happened to the puir lad. Sir Charles had no been a tender faither before he wed that woman, but after *she* got hold o' him, he'd do naught but sneer at Master Dick an' call him crazy. He didna even bother wi' schooling him. Until afterwards . . . The vicar tutored the lad."

Myra frowned. She saw the pattern, saw even how Celia's sudden illness could present a threat so great that Richard might be driven to escape. But then he must be really unbalanced. She found that hard to believe. "After all," she said aloud, "he's not to blame—"

"He thinks he *is*, Your Grace. And so do I. Fra' the past. When he was Stephen. 'Tis i' the Marsdon Chronicle."

"*Really*, Nanny," said Myra, so astounded that she laughed.

"I've spoke to nobody o' this, nor would now, save that Sir Richard is behaving as he did near twenty years agone." Her voice dropped. "I fear for him so, come nightfall, that's when it happened afore."

"What did?" Myra forced herself to ask.

"We broke in. . . . He was hanging fra' the auld gas fixture."

Myra's green eyes widened. "How frightful! But he isn't that miserable child any more, Nanny, you really mustn't imagine—"

"The curtain cords be still there, Your Grace."

Myra shivered. She also had the inborn British distaste for emotionalism and for interference in anyone's private life. Nevertheless. . . . "You want me to speak to Sir Richard?"

The old Scot surprised her. "No, Your Grace. I want ye to telephone the hospital and summon the Heendu gentleman, he's the pairson to help us. They'd no listen to me."

Myra saw the truth of this. But the urgency, the explanations—how embarrassing if Nanny's fears were all imaginary. Yet the steady piteous gaze touched her. "Very well," she said.

A HUSHED and anxious group stood around the flat white bed where the unconscious girl lay motionless. Glucose dripped into one arm, a blood-pressure gauge was attached to the other. The mercury showed only a feeble flicker. Foster pressed his stethoscope harder against the ribs. "I fear she's going. . . ."

Lily gave a sobbing gasp. There had been hope a few minutes earlier. Celia had responded to oxygen and to Akananda's slow, monotonous commands. "Relax, Celia. Let your arms go. Shut your eyes. Relax. Go limp." After five minutes she had shivered once, then the rigid hands had come forward, the eyelids shut. Both nurses had been greatly relieved at the disappearance of that ghastly stare. But they shared Dr. Foster's conviction that the patient was dying.

"Get the mother out of here," Dr. Foster barked, and to Akananda, as the nurses gently shoved Lily through the door, he added, "Cardiac arrest—we might massage."

"That may mean breaking ribs," Akananda said. "Danger of puncture and it won't help. She'll *not* die now. I've seen several cases of suspended animation in India. In Western terms, this is a form of catalepsy."

"I've never seen anything like it," said Foster. "If she does recover, what about brain damage? And what the devil do we do with her now?"

"Get a psycho-neurologist. I recommend Sir Arthur Moore."

"Yes." Foster was relieved. Arthur Moore was the best.

When Foster had left, Akananda put his hand gently on Celia's forehead and concentrated on receiving some impression from her brain. At first he felt nothing but a dense blackness. Celia Marsdon, he said silently, where are you now?

He enfolded himself with her in the blackness. Suddenly a tingle ran up his arm and a scene slid into his mind: a hilltop crowned by greenery; a grey, mossy stone wall, and the ruins of a chapel with a thatched hut attached to it. Outside the hut stood a black-robed monk, his arms around a girl in a blue skirt and laced bodice, a girl with long tumbling yellow hair. The little scene vibrated with emotion—a frenzied longing and desperation. Then the vision disappeared.

"Doctor!" a young nurse was saying insistently. "A phone call from Medfield. It's the Duchess of Drewton."

"Very well. Don't touch or disturb the patient, will you?"

After Akananda spoke to Myra, he found Lily Taylor waiting miserably in the hall. "I'm going back to Medfield for a bit," he said. "Come and take some rest. There's nothing to do here at present." He hesitated. "I think that Lady Marsdon, due to some great shock, has been jerked back into the past, her past life and Sir Richard's, and for that matter, yours and mine. It was then that the violent emotions and actions were initiated, those which are inexorably showing their results today."

"But Celia's dying. How can we stop it? Oh, God, I don't understand. . . ." Lily covered her face with her hands.

"With divine mercy we may stop it." He spoke with more assurance than he felt. He hurried Lily to the car.

Myra awaited them on Medfield's doorstep, with Nanny just behind her. "Do hurry, Doctor!" Myra said.

Akananda inclined his head. "But I must be alone. Will you please wait with the others in the drawing room." He mounted the great staircase, Nanny stubbornly following. She waited outside his door while the Hindu, inside, purified his mind for the struggle. He knelt and chanted, very low, words from the Atharva-veda. Then he waited . . . until the quiet English bedroom dissolved around him into golden-white light—the illumination of compassionate wisdom—as he raised his arms with touching palms in the universal gesture of prayer. He arose, left the room and nodded to Nanny. "We will go to the schoolroom now."

The door was wide open when they arrived. Richard sat writing at a desk. "Oh, thank God," Nanny gasped. "Ye frightened me so."

"I'm not twelve years old *now*, Nanny," he said coldly, and turned to Akananda. "How is Celia? I presume she is in hospital."

"She is very ill, Sir Richard. You must go to her."

"Has she asked for me, or indeed, perhaps *Harry Jones*?"

Even Akananda was shocked by the tone and implication.

"She's near *dead*, lad," Nanny cried. "Ye *mun* see her."

Richard stood up. "I've done Celia quite enough harm. It's better that we never meet again. Her mother will look after her."

Akananda sought for the wisdom he had felt a few minutes earlier—wisdom to combat the inflexibilities, distortions and cruelties of the human will. "What do you propose to do, Sir Richard?"

"Rid my house of everyone connected with my disastrous marriage. Live henceforth quite alone, as long as I *choose* to live."

"'Tis the curse fra' the Chronicle," Nanny sobbed.

"Bah! Morbid clap-trap! The book is closed."

"That," said Akananda sternly, "in your case is impossible. Circumstances have reproduced themselves in this life so that you may have a chance to redeem your past mistakes. You and Lady Marsdon both. Now you are compounding the evil."

"I neither understand nor wish to listen to you, sir. Nanny, I'll move to the red bedroom. See that Lady Marsdon's effects are cleared out of Medfield Place." And Richard stalked out.

"He's no *truly* heartless," Nanny said. "Oh, Doctor, ye heard him, '*as lang as I choose to live*'."

"I know. Will you show me the Chronicle you spoke of?"

They made their way to the library and Akananda studied the entry Nanny pointed out to him. As he traced the Elizabethan writing, certainty grew. Here was the key to Celia's past.

"Ightham Mote." He looked again at the reference to its Tudor owners. "'Sir Christopher Allen & his vexatious ladye . . . she hath a mad wolfish eye.'" There came to him the image of Edna Simpson, glaring at Celia and doting on Sir Richard. Had the woman last night somehow echoed an old crime?

He turned to Nanny. "We're dealing here with great mysteries, you know," he said.

"Aye," said Nanny, "and great confusion. I'm sore afeard."

"Try not to worry," Akananda said. "You had better follow Sir Richard's orders, since there is no reaching through to him now."

They left the library and Akananda went to the drawing room. His assurance that Richard was quite all right but wished to be alone was taken by Myra and Harry as dismissal. Myra jumped up. "Well, let's get going. Good-bye, Mrs. Taylor, I do hope Celia recovers soon."

In the drawing room Lily and Dr. Akananda heard the departing purr of the Bentley, the diminishing crunch of gravel on the drive.

"I must hurry back to Celia," Lily murmured. "Richard will come with me, of course."

Akananda said, "Mrs. Taylor, I must talk to you."

The weight in Lily's chest grew heavier, but she understood him. "What is it with Richard?" she asked. "He's not *really* all right, is he?"

"No," said Akananda. "He wants to repudiate his marriage, wants every evidence of it removed from Medfield."

She gasped. "Has he gone crazy? He *loved* Celia!"

"He's not medically insane. Violent emotions are blind forces, often strong enough to carry beyond one lifetime."

Lily fished out a handkerchief. "If I could only understand . . . ."

Akananda touched her shoulder. "I'm nearly as much in the dark as you are." He paused. "By the way, I think the Simpsons are still here." His sensitive perceptions were aware of a black focus inside the house. "Wait for me. I'll deal with them." He went up to the Simpsons' door and knocked.

"Coom in, then," said a woman's voice. Akananda obeyed and paused on the threshold. "Lumme! I called the maid!" Edna clutched a kimono around her billowing flesh.

"Mrs. Simpson." Akananda bowed slightly. "Mrs. Taylor asked me to see how you were. There've been grave troubles at Medfield today. The other guests have left."

Except for a dull headache, Edna had recovered from the effects of the tincture and had decided that the dimly remembered events of last night were one of her bad dreams. "Lady Marsdon is ill?" she said genteelly. "Yes, Mr. Simpson told me." She indicated George, who was gazing at his wife with bewilderment. "I've been quaite ill m'self. But if Sir Richard and Mrs. Taylor are downhearted, we'll stay on and cheer them up."

Akananda could see around the woman a muddy dark aura with zigzag flashes of crimson. And he knew she was as unconscious of the evil emanating from her as was her husband. "Mrs. Taylor is off to the hospital, and Sir Richard is unwell. Someone will drive you to a train."

"We'll be packed in a jiffy," said George, "won't we, m'dear?"

And Akananda, watching with the clairvoyance he could sometimes command, saw a change in Simpson's aura, which had been faint and grey, as he talked to his wife. And more amazing, there was a change in Edna's. There's actually some love between these two. Then with a shock of precognition he saw flames leaping around a bloated screaming face. He shuddered and spoke his polite farewells in a kinder tone.

THERE WAS no change in Celia. The nurse watched Akananda in silent contempt as he examined the patient. "We need that bed," she told him. "Hospital's here to care for the *living*, and this woman isn't."

Akananda nearly agreed. He could find no vital signs of life.

"Do you think Richard would let us take her home?" whispered Lily desperately, stroking her daughter's limp hand.

Only if she were really dead, Akananda thought. If then. Nanny had told him in a horrified whisper that Sir Richard had cut into ribbons the new oil painting of Celia which hung in the stairwell.

The hours dragged by as Lily and Akananda waited. It was nearly midnight when Sir Arthur Moore arrived, exuding confidence and amiability. He went straight to the bed, clicked on the top light himself and took Celia's wrist while he peered intently at her face. "Ring up Dr. Foster," he said to the hovering nurse. As she vanished he muttered, "The girl's certainly dead, but. . . ."

He was suddenly aware of a man and woman across the bed. "Sorry," he said to the anguished, pretty, middle-aged woman. "You the mother?" As Lily nodded mutely, Sir Arthur turned to the man. "Jiddu!" he cried. "Is it Jiddu Akananda?" He stared at the chiselled brown face, the slender body in well-cut tweeds. One of the most brilliant students at Guy's and later at The Maudsley. "What in blazes are *you* doing here?"

"Trying to prevent this young woman from totally relinquishing her present body, and to prevent others from forcing her to."

"Indeed," said Sir Arthur, shaking his hand. "Same old visionary! You haven't altered a bit. Must be thirty-five years. What've you been doing with yourself?"

"Calcutta, London, research—very quiet compared to *your* career, Arthur, and I need your help now."

"Yes, tell me *all* about this case," said Sir Arthur.

Lily, overlooked by both men, wandered out to the waiting room.

Akananda talked for ten minutes while his colleague listened carefully.

"Clinical death is no longer so simple to establish," Moore remarked as Akananda paused. "The transplant chaps are finding that out. Until true *rigor* sets in, I'll hold off the ghouls for you."

"Thank you," said Akananda. "I prayed you would."

"The husband," said Sir Arthur, "sounds a proper stinker."

"He is behaving like one," agreed Akananda. "But he's acting out evil compulsions from the past, and suffering greatly. Sir Richard is in a dangerous state of fugue, repudiation of present reality. This poor girl, as you see, is in even greater danger. Also from the past."

Sir Arthur nodded dubiously. "That was a curious remark, Jiddu, that you were trying to prevent others from forcing her to relinquish her body. Sounds like murder. You can't mean *that*?"

"Murder is exactly what I mean." Akananda gazed at his colleague. "It was murder before, and will be again unless . . ."

"You mean the girl's *poisoned*?" Sir Arthur jumped up.

"No, no. This isn't that sort of poison. What I was about to say was that we need abreactive therapy." Akananda was choosing his words carefully, hoping to satisfy his friend. "Reconstruction of the original traumata in order to cause a curative catharsis."

Sir Arthur grunted. "Gobbledygook, old boy. In plain English, you hope to bring the girl out of this cataleptic trance, or whatever it is, by making her unconscious live through and accept the disasters she's trying to escape from?"

"Something like that," Akananda answered. He hesitated, longing to win his friend's entire cooperation for a venture into the past. But he knew that frankness might provoke doubt, even hostility. Arthur was an excellent psycho-neurologist. He would accept possible regression into any past—even foetal—of the palpable body of a patient. But of any life existence before the womb or beyond the grave he had always been scornfully contemptuous.

"Unconscionable time that G.P.'s taking," Sir Arthur said, then jumped. "Good God, what was that?" He whirled around and stared at the bed. "I thought I heard her speak." He pulled out his handkerchief and wiped his forehead. "Did you hear anything?"

The Hindu had not. "What did you hear her say?"

"It sounded like 'Stephen'."

"Ah-h," said Akananda on a long drawn breath. "You heard what she was thinking, Arthur, a cry from her soul."

"My dear chap!" Sir Arthur exploded. "This case is peculiar enough without muddling it. I had a simple hallucination."

Akananda, seeing his friend shaken, said mildly, "If you can believe in television, Arthur, vibrations continually surrounding us and only made pictures or words by a properly tuned receiver—"

"Rubbish, no parallel at all. I'm not a bloody wireless!" Moore heard footsteps outside and cried, "Thank God, this must be Foster. Now we can get cracking!"

Dr. Foster appeared and Sir Arthur plunged into the directives and practical arrangements at which he was adept.

BY THE next morning Celia was installed in a luxurious room at the London Clinic. The electroencephalogram showed minimal brain-wave function. The prognosis was black. Akananda stood by while Sir Arthur himself cautiously administered shock therapy. Celia's brain waves were unaffected.

"I've never seen anything like this," he finally confessed. "Ten years ago she'd have been embalmed by now. Jiddu, you have a free hand. What do you want to do?"

"Be entirely alone with her, uninterrupted."

Sir Arthur sighed. "Very well. Some damn-fool Indian trick?"

"Perhaps." Akananda smiled. "I'm going home first to rest."

"Well, good luck," said Sir Arthur. "Give me a ring if there's any change. I'll check in tomorrow." He moved majestically down the corridor ignoring the flutter of nurses.

Akananda went to Lily Taylor in the waiting room.

"Any news?" she asked hopelessly. Her anxious face, without make-up, looked young and defenceless, he thought.

"Nothing new," Akananda said gently. "I'm going to try an experiment later—one I must be alone to do."

"Can't I do *anything*?" she cried. "It's awful just to wait."

He nodded. "I suggest that you take a taxi to some spiritual place where you will sit quietly for at least one hour. Where do you wish to go? St. Paul's? Or one of the smaller churches?"

She was tearing little scraps off the magazine cover she had in her hand.

"Lily Taylor, look at me!"

She raised her head slowly and met his stern, concentrated eyes. "There *is* a church I might pray in. I was there once years ago. It's across the river, Southwark—a cathedral. I liked it. They call it St. Saviour's, I think, but that isn't its real name." She stopped, startled by a shiver down her back. She tried to look away from Akananda, but she could not.

"What used to be its name?" he asked. "Quickly! Don't think!"

"St. Mary Overie. The priory was given to the Montagus."

"Ah-h," murmured Akananda, "Montagu." She had given him a clue he needed. During his internship at Guy's he had lived in Southwark and had himself been drawn to St. Saviour's. He had been uncertain how to guide Celia in his attempt to penetrate her past life. That she had been a part of some Tudor period seemed likely in view of the Marsdon Chronicle and the recurrence of the name Stephen, but there was no other lead, aside from her behaviour at Ightham Mote. He knew that Montagu, from the mother's own buried memory, now provided one.

"Take this, my dear," he said, giving Lily a capsule. "It'll calm you. Then go to St. Saviour's which was indeed once called St. Mary Overie. You should be able to pray there."

Akananda saw Lily into a taxi, then took himself to the British Museum. There he spent two hours consulting *Burke's Peerage* and the *Dictionary of National Biography*. Enlightened, he walked to his flat and immersed himself in meditation.

The night staff had come on when Akananda returned to the Clinic. "Lady Marsdon's condition seems quite unchanged, Doctor," said the capable young Irish nurse. "Will you be wanting glucose?"

"Nothing," he answered smiling. "And no interruptions for *any* reason. I shall lock the door and take all responsibility."

"'Tis like her spirit's stifled. I pray you can save her, Doctor."

Akananda locked the door after the nurse, then sat by Celia. She was an alabaster effigy, chill and remote as a medieval tomb. Her chest did not move. Had the tiny flicker of life really been snuffed out? He clasped her hand tightly, trying to propel vital force into her body. His firm grasp encountered cold metal, and he saw that she was wearing a heavy amethyst heart-shaped ring over the plain gold wedding band. The Marsdon ring. He had casually admired it on the night of his arrival at Medfield, and Sir Richard had said, smiling, "The lady of the manor's badge of servitude." Akananda slipped it off and laid it on the night table. He thought he saw a tremor flit across the ashen face. Tentatively he moved the wedding ring. There was no doubt this time. He felt the hand quiver.

Greatly relieved, he spoke. "The Marsdon 'badge of servitude' is gone from you, Celia. You wish to keep the wedding band?"

But she had gone back into her faraway void. He put his hand on her forehead. "Take me back to where you are, Celia. Trust me." He thought of one of his master's teachings: There was no such thing as circumscribed time. All time existed *now*. Sweat gathered on his forehead as he tried to block out the sound of London traffic. "Is *Stephen* with you?" No response. "Montagu . . . Cowdray . . . Ightham Mote. . . . Are you afraid, Celia?"

The skin under his hand grew colder, and he knew an overwhelming sense of defeat. The years of his Western training jeered at him. What a fool Arthur Moore would think him!

Akananda saw a luminous white figure on the hospital wall. From it flowed pity and authority. Akananda prostrated himself on the floor. When St. Marylebone's bells rang ten o'clock, Akananda rose, his face wet with tears, and he knew with certainty what he must do to redress the wrongs he had inflicted and to help those now again in danger. He must relive with them the past.

With assurance now, he pressed his bunched fingers between Celia's eyebrows. "Where are you, Celia? *Answer me!*"

Her bluish lips moved and he heard a faint whisper. "In Great Buck Hall, waiting for the young King. The family is in sorrow, but we must hide this. There's gay music from the minstrels' gallery. I smell thyme and lavender amongst the new rushes on the floor. I'm afraid for Stephen . . . they've locked him up."

"Yes . . ." said Akananda. But there was one more link necessary. "Who am I, Celia?" he said quietly. He felt the faint motion under his hand. "Who *am* I?"

She spoke. "You are Julian, Master Julian."

The gap was bridged. He leaned his head against the wall.

PART TWO: 1552–1559

Chapter 1

At Cowdray Castle, Monday, July 25 of the Year of our Lord 1552, Great Buck Hall was decorated as it had never been in the five years since old Sir Anthony Browne had completed alterations. On high brackets around the walls he had vaingloriously placed life-size wooden statues of eleven bucks as reminders of the Browne crest. From their antlers now dripped flowery garlands. On the oaken floor there was new carpeting of sun-dried rushes from the River Rother, strewn with lavender and thyme. In the minstrels' gallery the musicians practised a madrigal. For young Sir Anthony Browne was welcoming the boy-King, Edward, to Cowdray.

Celia Bohun gloried in a new gown, lovingly made for her by her aunt, Lady Ursula Southwell, out of peacock brocade. There was a demure cap, which framed the soft shining ripples of Celia's corn-coloured hair. The new finery was one of Ursula's many kindnesses to the orphan girl who shared her blood and also shared her anomalous position at the castle. Ursula and Celia were de Bohuns. Their family had lived here at Cowdray for nearly four centuries. When the impoverished Bohuns had been forced to sell all their property to the Browne family, Ursula, nearing sixty and long since widowed, had gratefully accepted from Sir Anthony Browne's father a small upper chamber in the castle and a seat just above the salt at the long, trestled dining table. Celia stood with her aunt in Buck Hall, eagerly savouring her first glimpse of assembled nobility. Her cheeks glowed, her long bluish-green eyes sparkled.

Sir Anthony and his wife, Lady Jane Radcliffe, daughter of the Earl of Sussex, were circling the Hall to greet important guests and to make a last tour of inspection. They were both dressed in crimson velvet embroidered with gold and pearls. The splendour suited Anthony, who was tall, and stoutly built for a man of twenty-five. Beside him Lady Jane was puny and shrinking, her eyes red from weeping. Three days ago their infant son had died of a convulsion. The little coffin stood not in the chapel as it should have, but in an alcove off their bedchamber. No Masses were to be said for the tiny soul until after the Protestant king had left, and there must be no mention of the tragedy to cloud the royal visit.

Sir Anthony gave Lady Ursula a quick nod, then caught sight of Celia. "Hallo-o!" he exclaimed. "Who may *this* be?"

"Celia Bohun, Sir Anthony," said Ursula, flushing a little. "My niece. I trust I've not offended in letting her come today."

Anthony shook his head amiably, uninterested in the connection or in Ursula, a charge he had inherited from his father and seldom saw. The girl's from that bastard branch of the Bohuns, he thought, staring at Celia. "So fair a maid is ever welcome," he said. "How old are you, poppet?"

"Fourteen, sir. Last month, on St. Anthony's Day, your own name day, an't please your lordship." She curtsied.

Anthony chuckled at Celia's pert reply. He noted the innocent provocativeness of the full breasts, the slight protrusion of her red underlip, and the square uptilted chin. "This luscious fruit is ripening fast, eh, lady?" he said to Ursula. "We must find her a husband. Perhaps even a squire if I can spare a dowry."

Ursula spoke up quickly. "The girl is as apt to learn as she is comely, sir. I'm teaching her to read, and Brother Stephen gives her religious instruction."

Anthony's eyes flashed. "We do not mention the priest, madam! Nor see him while the King is here. You have been warned!"

Ursula reddened. "Aye, sir, pardon. It was a slip."

"There must be no slips." Sir Anthony's father had succeeded in keeping the precarious favour of King Henry VIII, and Anthony was equally formidable in his effort to keep the favour of Henry's bigoted young son. A harder task, Anthony thought, for young Edward was swayed daily by the real enemy, the real danger: the Duke of Northumberland—a man mad for power and now virtual King of England. Praised be God, Northumberland was occupied on the Scottish border at this moment, but he had his spies everywhere near Edward. "There must *be* no slips," Anthony repeated.

As the couple moved on, Ursula whispered to Celia, "I'm shaken. Let's mount to my chamber to watch for the approaching heralds."

Celia obediently followed her aunt up circular stone stairs to the small comfortable room near the servants' attic on the third storey. The room contained Ursula's few treasures—her four-posted marriage bed, her carved dower chest, her Italian X-shaped chair; and hanging on the wall, her husband Sir Robert Southwell's sword in its gilt-encrusted sheath. Near the bed hung her ebony crucifix. There were, besides, two unexpected objects on a shelf: a small ephemeris for computing the daily positions of the stars, and a neat roll of horoscopes tied with a golden cord. Ursula practised astrology; she had received instruction twenty years ago from the Duke of Norfolk's Italian astrologer while she and Sir Robert were visiting the Norfolks at Kenninghall.

Celia rushed to the window seat and peered through the diamond panes to catch a first glimpse of the King's procession. There was nothing yet to be seen and she turned into the room frowning. "My lady aunt, *why* must Brother Stephen be hid?"

The girl's voice lingered over the young priest's name, and Ursula felt a twinge of foreboding. "I've been wrong not to tell you, Celia. Three days agone, when we knew that the King would come here, Sir Anthony gathered us all in the Hall and gave his commands. He said that, though we were Catholic, and as devout a family of the True Faith as could be found, we owed yet temporal allegiance to our King and must respect his heretic views. That during the royal visit there would be no Masses; nobody was to cross himself or mention saints. That our chapel would be stripped of its holy statues, even the crucifix!"

"Surely a great lord like Sir Anthony may do as he pleases."

"Obviously not," answered Ursula tartly. "Don't you know that a year ago Sir Anthony was thrown in the Fleet like a common criminal for hearing Mass at his mansion in Southwark? True, he stayed in prison only six weeks for he has powerful friends."

"But he had Masses *here*, until just now," protested Celia.

"Aye," said Ursula, "and, Cowdray being far from London, he will resume them. But no need for the King's men to know this."

"How very odd." And Celia thought with increased fear about Brother Stephen.

HER FATHER, the bastard Bohun, Celia could scarcely remember. When she was three he had been stabbed to death in a tavern brawl, defending the family name. Celia and her mother, Alice, had lived thereafter in a garret at the Spread Eagle Inn in Midhurst. The little girl ran errands and her gentle pretty mother served as barmaid. Then this last September Alice suddenly took sick and died. Master and Mistress Potts, the innkeepers, had Celia serve ale in her mother's place, but she was dazed and lost, and she wept much in the night. She had nobody to turn to. That her father had been raised at nearby Cowdray Castle with his two half-sisters, the child had no idea.

Jack Bohun had been a man of fierce family loyalty, perhaps all the stronger because he was not legitimate. He had deeply resented the sale of Easebourne, Cowdray and large pieces of Midhurst to the Earl of Southampton. Later, when old Sir Anthony inherited the properties, Jack had quarrelled with his half-sister Ursula for becoming a dependant of the Brownes. Ursula had accepted the break with Jack realistically. But she inquired from time to time about the welfare of her brother's widow. Through Cowdray's servants she heard of Alice's death and the plight of little Celia, her niece. One day she rode into town to the Spread Eagle Inn and asked after the Bohun girl. She was shown to a small black-beamed chamber off the pot room, and looked up with no more than charitable curiosity when a slender frightened girl came through the door.

"Pray sit down, sweeting." Ursula's voice quavered. She felt as though this child were hers. The little face had a nascent beauty;

the abundant hair, properly cleansed, would be a rich buttercup yellow. There was a promise of vibrancy and allure which Ursula had never had.

"Celia," she said gently, "you are my niece. And since you have none who belongs to you now, and nor do I, 'tis time we knew one another."

Celia stared, suspecting one more of the cruel jests—in which the world abounded.

"Your father was my half-brother," said Ursula tenderly.

Ursula had no means of her own. She could not ask Sir Anthony to take in another dependant, nor did she wish to introduce Celia as a servant at Cowdray. Celia therefore went on living and working at the Spread Eagle, but visiting Ursula often.

Ursula's ambition for the girl grew as her love did; she began to feel that her rough-cut jewel was capable of great brilliance and set about remedying her lack of education. The absence of any religious training must also be rectified. Accordingly, she waited outside the Cowdray chapel after Mass one day and explained her wishes to the Brownes' house priest, Brother Stephen.

Stephen was a tall young man, made taller by the black Benedictine robes. His care for the household of two hundred souls was diligent. Otherwise, he kept to himself, choosing to live in a stark cabin attached to the wall of the ruined chapel on top of St. Ann's Hill.

Courteous as always, he smiled at Ursula's request. "It's true, Lady Southwell, that your niece should have religious instruction; but what woman in her station has use for Latin and arithmetic?"

"I do not, good Brother, expect Celia to remain in her present station," said Ursula. "I've cast her horoscope; she has Jupiter and Venus in benign aspects and most auspicious stars, too."

Stephen laughed. "Nonetheless, God's will *alone* determines us."

"To be sure. God's will rules the heavenly bodies, too." It occurred to Ursula that the monk had a dignity and aloofness which made him seem older than his twenty-seven years. "At least *see* the child," she added softly. "She's virtually a pagan."

"That's dreadful!" cried Stephen. "Tell her to come to me on St. Ann's Hill at noon tomorrow." He said, "*Benedicite*," and strode out of the castle. He crossed the River Rother and clambered up the hill. Entering his hut, he blew the smouldering embers and swung the crane holding the pot of stew over the fire to heat.

STEPHEN MARSDON had been born at Medfield Place in East Sussex. Since the days of the Conqueror a Marsdon younger son had been given to the Church. When Stephen was nine, his father had taken him the day's journey to Battle Abbey and entered him as a sub-novice. The boy was happy, excelled at sports and studies, and was popular with the other boys. He knew also that the teaching monks favoured him. He had overheard the Abbot saying, "Stephen Marsdon will be an abbot himself one day, mark my words!"—a prediction which delighted him.

On May 27, 1538, when Stephen was thirteen, Abbot Hammond assembled his community after vespers and made a speech, during which his voice trembled with helpless rage. His Gracious Majesty King Henry VIII had decreed that monasteries were to be dissolved. It now seemed that this most monstrous decree was to affect Battle Abbey, too. Unthinkable! Battle Abbey, founded in holy thanksgiving by William the Conqueror on this exact miraculous site, to be dissolved like lesser foundations!

The boys discussed the extraordinary announcement later in nervous whispers. Only one of them professed admiration for the King. "Now *there's* a man who will get what he wants!"

"What's that?" asked Stephen, still dazed by the Abbot's news.

"Gold, property. He'll get 'em from the monasteries."

"But he *can't* just grab for himself what belongs to God," faltered Stephen.

"Oh, can't he just!" The boy guffawed. "You'll soon see."

And Stephen did. The boys were sent home and magnificent Battle Abbey was methodically stripped. Gold and silver, furniture, even the marble from the high altar, were carted away. Then King Henry bestowed the Abbey itself upon Sir Anthony Browne—a grant made doubly infamous by the fact that Sir Anthony was supposed to be a good Catholic.

Stephen's father shared his stunned indignation. The only course now open to a youth with a true vocation was to go to France. He chose for Stephen the Benedictine Abbey of St. Martin at Marmoutier, near Tours.

It happened that Stephen rode back to Battle Abbey to say farewell to the old Abbot on the very day that Sir Anthony was celebrating his new ownership. Stephen reined in his horse at the Abbey gates, astonished to see the courtyard crammed with horses and lackeys. As he watched, one of the lackeys threw a giggling kitchen wench down on a pile of hay and pulled up her skirts while the other servants cheered.

In a few minutes the man got up, and another took his place on top of the woman, whose lewd excited laughter Stephen plainly heard. He jerked his bridle and fled down the road, retching, his heart pounding, sweat trickling down his neck. He flung himself off the horse and doused his head in the wayside brook, then rode soberly back—avoiding the Abbey—to find Abbot Hammond.

At a tavern Stephen was told that the old man's lodging was in the next street. The Abbot opened the door to Stephen's knock.

"Ah, my son," the old man cried, embracing Stephen.

"Oh, Reverend Father," Stephen said, "I've come for your blessing, since I go next week to France. Holy Mother of God," he added, "our Abbey . . . they were fornicating in the cloister!"

"Ah," said the Abbot with a heavy sigh. His wise eyes examined the boy. "I understand you still wish to take the vows?"

"I was born to be a monk," said Stephen. "I wish no other life."

The old eyes misted at the boy's sincerity; but John Hammond knew human nature.

"You will have many a battle to wage with the Tempter, my son. These battles may not be against chastity; I think you have not a lascivious nature. Certainly not poverty; you have no undue attachment to personal possessions. But—"

"Not obedience to my superiors; I'll never fail in that."

"The test may come in a form hardest for you to endure." He paused. "You hate old Sir Anthony Browne, don't you?"

"Why, to be sure, Father. I detest him and all his line. He's a traitor to God. He should give back the Abbey."

"That is not so simple, my child. The King gave it to him. And

Sir Anthony is servant to the King. Also, I believe he has found a way to ease his conscience."

"There can *be* none!" Stephen cried. "There is no way."

"You may have to change this opinion someday," said the Abbot with a faint smile, "when your vow of obedience is tested."

STEPHEN, eating his mutton stew fourteen years later in the little hut on St. Ann's Hill, knew at last what the Abbot had meant. Old Sir Anthony had, "to ease his conscience", tried to find positions for all of Battle Abbey's evicted monks. And he had even then determined to have Stephen Marsdon at Cowdray, once he had taken his vows. He favoured Sussex men, and knew of the Marsdons, who came from long-established Saxon blood as the Brownes did *not*.

In 1548 Sir Anthony had died. The younger Anthony tried in all respects to carry on his father's policies. It was thus that the horrified Stephen was sent by his order from France to Cowdray—and found himself fully as rebellious as Abbot Hammond had foreseen. He had loved the cloisters and the companionship of his fellows, and in his heart had always expected to progress up the Church scale to an abbacy. Instead, there was Cowdray, and ministry to a household who lived on money which belonged rightly to God. And his brother, Tom, had warned him when he'd stopped for a visit at Medfield on the way; he had come home to a "mighty unsettled country, where the cat jumps to the right today and the left tomorrow".

Stephen prayed duly for release if it were God's will. He thought back with longing to the warm glow of that week in Medfield. He had been startled to find how dearly he loved his childhood home, more startled to find himself envying Tom, master of Medfield's abundance, the contented husband of pretty Nan suckling their infant son. He had done penance for those moments of envy.

Stephen finished his mutton, and then, because it was February 2, Candlemas Day, he went to the crumbling chapel. He took with him his cherished painting of the Virgin, which he had carried back with him from France, along with a black and silver crucifix. There, alone, he performed the forbidden ritual of the Purification of the Blessed Virgin. As he reverently lit three candles and knelt before the Virgin, her mysterious smile seemed to widen. He felt a bursting love in his chest, and his loneliness dissolved in a flood of healing and joyous submission.

He was still joyful next morning at Cowdray chapel. Six o'clock Mass was attended by all the servants, and today by the four ladies of the house. There was Sir Anthony's girl-wife, the frail-looking little Lady Jane. Beside her was the haughty young dowager, the late Sir Anthony's widow, Lady Geraldine, of the rambunctious clan of Fitzgerald, who had been dispossessed of their Irish estates by King Henry VIII. Her father, the Earl of Kildare, had died in the Tower, accused of treason, and her brother, Lord Gerald Fitzgerald, rightful Earl, was supposed to be lurking on his Irish estates, wondering what King Edward's attitude would be under the new power of the Duke of Northumberland. Then there was Mabel, Sir Anthony's sixteen-year-old sister, a fat discontented girl. There was also Ursula, Lady Southwell, whose greeting Stephen returned as he left the chapel.

He was back in his hut, cutting himself a slab of bread and cheese, when, as the castle bell clanged noon, he heard a timid knock on his door. He opened it and stared at a girl in russet wool whose yellow hair tumbled out from under her kerchief down to her waist. He felt a shock of puzzled recognition, he knew, not the face, not the shimmering sea-blue eyes, but the person behind them.

"Lady Southwell, my aunt, said I might come," she said nervously, as he did not speak. "I'm Celia Bohun."

"Aye," murmured Stephen, who had forgotten. As he stood there collecting himself, he looked very black and forbidding.

"I don't want to pester ye, Brother," she faltered, blushing.

"No, no," Stephen said briskly. "Come in, child. Sit down. Can you say the Creed?"

Celia was dismayed by his peremptory tone. "Not—not well." She began hesitantly. "I believe in one God . . ."

"In *English*?" Stephen said sharply. "I know 'tis the law at present, but it's wrong, Celia. You must learn the Latin."

He clasped his hands and began reverently. "*Credo in unum Deum. . . .*" The sonorous words meant nothing to her, but she listened with startled pleasure to his beautiful voice and joined his "Amen" in a whisper. He looked at her and suddenly smiled. The smile transformed his sombre face, and she smiled back.

"I could *never* learn that, Brother Stephen."

"You *can*, Celia. The true Credo, the Paternoster and the Ave Maria; and the catechism. For today, recite the alphabet." He soon put her at ease. She answered readily and the hour went fast. Finally Stephen rose, smiling approval. It was agreeable, he thought, to be moulding a mind while leading the spirit towards a state of grace.

As Celia turned to go she glimpsed the small painting of the Virgin. "Oh-h," she cried. "So beauteous. I ne'er saw a woman so comely. Is't a picture of your mistress, sir? Do ye love her?"

Stephen frowned at the blasphemous implication until he suddenly realized the extent of her innocence and smiled instead.

"I adore her," he said quietly. "My poor child, that is the Blessed Virgin Mary. God's Holy Mother."

Celia blushed, thinking that the long eyes and fair hair in the portrait resembled her own. "I'll come on the morrow?"

For an instant he wished never to see her again, but he had never in his life broken his word.

"At noon," he said.

SO HAD BEGUN, nearly six months ago, Celia's noontime visits. Stephen never admitted to himself how he looked forward to them. Nor did Celia know why she worked so very hard to win his rare warm smile. And now, sitting in the window seat on July 25, watching for the King to come, she was acutely aware of Stephen's present danger. She understood why Sir Anthony dared take no risks that Northumberland's spies might smell the presence at Cowdray of a Benedictine monk. But she could think only of Stephen's suffering. He'd been hidden in a stinking secret room off the cellars near the latrine pit.

Suddenly there was a blare of trumpets, and the Cowdray cannons began to boom.

"They're here, Aunt!" Celia cried. "That must be the King, riding alone. He's but a meagre lad!"

"To be sure, child, he's not full grown, and near died of the pox last spring, God preserve him. We'll go down now, Celia. Hold yourself proud. Bohuns have as much right as any in the land to meet the King."

Chapter 2

The royal banquet proffered by Sir Anthony Browne—who kept a master cook trained in France at the court of King Henry II—was sumptuous. It consisted of exotic dishes the young King Edward had never tasted, for he had been kept to simple fare by order of his careful tutor, Sir John Cheke. Cheke, however, was recovering from desperate illness, and not with his charge in the Great Buck Hall. So Edward gorged himself with beef spiced with cinnamon, a rabbit pasty and a fat capon leg. Though accustomed only to ale, he drank a large goblet of wine from Sir Anthony's well-stocked cellar. And he could not refuse to taste the cook's masterpiece, a marchpane confection six feet high representing the royal arms in full colour.

"In truth, Sir Anthony," Edward said to his host with a boyish chuckle, "you have marvellously banqueted me. I shall so write to Barnaby in France. I wish he were here. I miss him."

"I grieve, Your Grace," answered Anthony, smiling, "that you should lack for anything. Would I could conjure Master Fitzpatrick to Cowdray this moment!" As he spoke he considered the King's affection for the Irish lad, Barnaby Fitzpatrick, who had been raised with him. The connection might be useful. Barnaby was related to Anthony's stepmother, Geraldine. He glanced down the table to where that lady was murmuring intimacies to Edward Fiennes, Lord Clinton. Clinton, a widower of forty, had managed to sustain his career at court after King Henry's death by allying himself matrimonially with the all-powerful Duke of Northumberland. Clinton was now Lord High Admiral of England. If the Lady Geraldine could entice him, it would be a helpful alliance, Anthony thought, and a relief to have that vixen out of Cowdray.

Anthony now forced his errant mind to consider the young King himself. Edward had turned to Sir Henry Sidney, his boon companion. "Harry" was clever, amiable, and married to Northumberland's daughter, Mary Dudley.

Suddenly Edward addressed Anthony. "We're weary of sitting at table, Sir Anthony. I've not yet spoken to all your guests. I hear there are several so-called papist nobles amongst them."

"Aye," said Anthony. "*Erstwhile* Catholics who have seen their errors. They are utterly loyal, Sire."

"My father loved your father, Sir Anthony, and the sons shall be friends. I'll now mingle with your company. There are other rooms where we can be more at ease?"

Anthony bowed and motioned to the massive, richly carved new staircase which led up to the long gallery. The King ascended alone, Harry Sidney following close. Anthony gave his arm to Jane and was perturbed at her dragging footsteps.

"Brace yourself, my lady," he whispered, "you must make the presentations!" As an earl's daughter she outranked her husband.

The King affably admired a new Flemish tapestry of unicorns and virgins wandering through a misty forest, and stationed himself in front of it on a velvet-covered court chair. There was an uncomfortable pause while Sir Henry murmured something in his ear. The boy sighed acquiescence.

"My lady," he said to Jane, "Harry tells me that yonder near the door there are a clutch of Dacres." He smiled faintly. "I know *of* them, to be sure, but have never met any."

The listening Anthony went to round up the Dacres. They had travelled down from Cumberland to summer with some cousins. In presenting them Jane and Anthony were hesitant on the matter of precedence.

Geraldine Browne had been watching from beside Lord Clinton, and she now glided up. "Your Majesty—" she threw a little, contemptuous glance towards her stepson and his sickly wife—"may I present to you Lady Dacre of Gilsland and Greystoke, who lives at Naworth Castle in Cumberland. Her lord, Warden of the West Marches, is at present engaged in the Scottish border disputes. Lady Dacre has here three of her children."

"Ah . . . so?" said the King, grateful for this concise, clear introduction. He extended his hand to Lady Dacre.

She gave the thin young fingers a hearty kiss. "Much honoured, Your Grace—God gi'e ye health! These're ma youngsters." Lady Dacre thrust forward Sir Thomas, a huge youth with bristly red hair, and Leonard, an even taller young man, who held one shoulder higher than the other by reason of a broken, badly twisted collarbone. "An' here's ma braw lass, Maggie." Though only fourteen, Magdalen, also amazingly tall, was neither gawky nor self-conscious. She, too, kissed the King's hand heartily.

Anthony was relieved to see that the King was amused. The Dacres' clothes, like their manners, appeared homespun among the jewelled velvets and lace ruffs. Uncouth border lords, Anthony thought, rough and independent as the wild Scots whom they constantly fought. Yet there was about them an imposing dignity.

The King was already tired. "We will proceed to the chapel for evening prayers," Edward said, taking Sir Henry's arm as he swayed in an attack of the transient weakness he had felt since his sickness in the spring. He straightened. "Your chaplain is waiting, I presume?" he said to Anthony.

"My own chaplain is ill, Sire. The Midhurst vicar is here to conduct prayers."

The company jammed themselves into the denuded chapel. Edward, after one satisfied glance around, was fortunately too tired to heed the mumbling rendition of the English prayers he himself had helped to write. But the evening was not yet over.

URSULA AND CELIA had remained in the Hall with the lesser folk while the privileged ones went upstairs. Ursula felt hurt and disappointed. She had expected, foolishly, that in some way her darling would be noticed. When the steward announced portentously that they must assemble in the chapel for "evensong", Ursula said sharply to Celia, "Whatever these heretic prayers are, *you* say a Paternoster and an Ave to yourself."

But in the chapel Celia forgot. She was too interested in the girl who stood beside her. They *all* stood in this strange ceremony which apparently permitted no kneeling. The girl's head was a span higher than her own. A bush of red hair curled loose on the broad shoulders. She smiled at Celia, showing broad, even white teeth. "I canna hear a word o' this gobbing," she whispered, "an' 'tis hot as hell's pit in here."

"*Sh-h*," whispered Celia, giggling.

"I'm Magdalen Dacre," said the girl. "Who are *you*?" Her clear brown eyes examined Celia with friendly admiration.

Sir Thomas Dacre whispered to his brother, Leonard, "Yon's a tasty dish next to Maggie." Leonard examined Celia, who reddened under their stares.

Magdalen chuckled. "The Dacres admire ye, lass, have a care, there's na woman born safe fra' those two cock-a-hoop gallants."

Celia understood the tenor of Magdalen's remarks and was pleased. She felt the first delicious stirrings of feminine power which lasted through the vicar's Amen.

The Dacres knew nobody among the crowd, so they drifted out with Celia to the courtyard and chatted. Lady Ursula, meanwhile, made inquiries of the steward about the trio. The answers pleased her. For all their rustic ways, the Dacres of the North were powerful Border Barons. The elder son, Thomas, was married to Lady Elizabeth Neville, daughter of the Earl of Westmorland. She examined the second son. A pity his shoulder was awry. Groping in the hitherto unknown maze of maternal ambition, Ursula walked benevolently out to join the young people in the courtyard. Thus they all heard the herald's trumpet.

Edward was on his way to bed. He recognized the special flourish reserved only for the arrival of a king's messenger. "Could it be a letter from Barnaby?" he said to Harry Sidney, and forgetting his weariness, he ran down to the courtyard.

The messenger fell to one knee and smiled up at the eager-faced boy. "Letters from France, Sire." Edward nodded happily. "Also, Sire," said the messenger, "I have conveyed a gentleman hither, from London." He indicated a man who stood waiting by the entrance.

The man, in a scholastic gown with fur collar, and a square-cornered black hat, was unmistakably a physician. His ebony staff was engraved with the Aesculapian symbol, and an orange-red jacinth stone—sovereign preventive of plague—which dangled from his copper neck chain, confirmed his profession.

"You there!" called Edward. "Come and state your business!"

The man bowed and said in a deep voice, slightly accented, "I have been sent to you, Your Majesty, by Master John Cheke. My name is Julian Ridolfi, once of Florence. I took my doctorate of medicine at Padua, though I have been long in this country."

"*Cheke!*" cried Edward. "I don't believe he sent you. There are royal physicians if I wanted one. My health is excellent. I don't need a *foreigner*. I believe you are a Spanish spy!"

Silently Julian tendered a letter, but the angry boy knocked it from his hand. "A forgery," he shouted. "We bid you leave at once!" He stamped back into the castle, the onlookers with him.

Julian Ridolfi stood stiffly alone. Ursula put her hand on her niece's arm. "Stay—wait a bit!" she said. "I think the doctor may be the astrologer who instructed me at the Duke of Norfolk's."

Julian showed none of the effort he was making to master his humiliation. Since the princely Norfolk family, who had employed him, had plunged into disgrace—the old Duke imprisoned and his son beheaded—Julian had eked out a living by collaborating with a surgeon-barber in Cheapside, and by casting horoscopes. By great good fortune John Cheke's manservant had come to be cut for a stone in his bladder. Julian had treated him with a concoction for disintegrating the stone. The servant, delirious with gratitude, had mentioned this to his master. And one day Cheke summoned Julian to his home.

The two men liked each other, and they shared a deep interest in astrology and alchemy. Julian was only nominally a Catholic and amiably agreed to Cheke's Protestant tenets.

Julian's great chance had come when John Cheke was smitten with plague. Under Julian's treatment Cheke was recovering well. So when he began to fret about the strenuousness of the royal progress, he dispatched Julian to Cowdray. From this mission Julian, knowing himself to be far abler than the English doctors, expected an appointment as court physician. The King's hysterical outburst he knew to be a symptom of the very overtaxing which Cheke dreaded. And he was disturbed; the royal lad had about him a death look. And strong in Julian, amidst many less altruistic traits, was the desire to heal.

As Julian stood in Cowdray's courtyard, the lights were gradually extinguished in the castle. Ursula walked up to the discredited doctor. "Are you not the Italian astrologer whom I met with the Norfolks at Kenninghall?"

"I do not understand you, madam," Julian said warily. Reference to that attainted family was dangerous.

"I'm *sure* when I hear you speak! You taught me some astrology, you physicked my husband, Robert Southwell," cried Ursula.

Julian vaguely remembered, but he did not welcome the lady's indiscreet speech. "I believe you are mistaken," he began, but Ursula shook her head, glancing at the hovering gatekeeper.

"You've no place to go, have you?" She put her hand under his elbow and hustled him out the gate. It was then that Julian noticed Celia, who seemed as startled as he. "We saw it all. There'll not be a bed in Midhurst tonight—at any price," Ursula said. "And you cannot trudge back to London."

Julian sighed. She spoke the simple truth.

"Besides, the King may change his mind," she went on.

"You can have my garret at the Spread Eagle," said the girl suddenly. "I may sleep in your room, my lady aunt, mayn't I?"

Celia's offer was precisely what Ursula had in mind and she loved her niece all the better for it.

As for Julian, experience instilled renewed suspicion. What had these two to gain by this? "You are most courteous," he said. "But, madam, will you forbear to speak of the Norfolks? You must see that such an association is perilous in these times—for both of us."

"Aye, I will respect your wishes," said Ursula. "But, sir, I pray you to cast Celia's horoscope. I feel that I've made errors."

Julian looked at the girl's lovely face and bowed.

"We must hasten, sir," Ursula breathed. "It grows dark."

They took the shortcut to town, across the footbridge over the River Rother and up St. Ann's Hill. At the top Celia stumbled and made a queer sound, half-gasp, half-moan.

"Are you hurt?" asked Julian. "Did you twist your ankle?"

"No," whispered Celia, choking. The emptiness of Stephen's hut pierced her chest. While she had been laughing with the Dacres and absorbed in Master Julian, Stephen was shut up like a foul beast. Suddenly she was sick at the danger she now knew him to be in. Her heart was thumping when they all arrived at the inn.

The place was jammed with roisterers. It sounded like Bedlam, Julian thought grimly—London's new hospital for lunatics.

Celia and Ursula were guiding him to the outside stairs when a harassed little man dashed out the door and caught sight of Julian's robes. "Pray, sir, come, my wife is taken bad."

In the parlour a stout woman lay twitching on the rushes, her face purple as a plum. Julian felt her pounding pulse and smelled her breath. The woman was drunk. "Get her to bed," he said to the husband. "No need for concern."

"'Tis not the plague, sir? God and His Holy Mother save us!"

"It is not," answered Julian, who had seen all forms of plague.

The man held out a gold coin. "Christopher Allen, Esquire, of Ightham Mote in Kent, will ever be friend to ye, sir."

Julian accepted the coin. "I give you good-night, squire." Ursula and Celia were waiting patiently to show him to his garret. Why, he wondered, should he feel such a glow of warmth towards two kindly women he had never seen before? It was like opening a shuttered window onto a sunlit garden.

Celia, next to her aunt in the great tester bed at Cowdray, did not sleep that night. Thinking of Stephen, she felt his suffering in her own body. Yet what her mind returned to, again and again, was the sight of that fat, empurpled woman on the floor of the Spread Eagle parlour. At that time she had felt only shocked curiosity. In recurrent memory there was a growing fear which reason would not allay.

So fearful did she become that she finally slipped from bed and, kneeling below Ursula's crucifix, said an imploring Paternoster. As dawn brightened the sky she opened the casement window and sniffed at the new day's air. It smelled of damask roses and gilly-flowers, of dewy grasses and sheep dung. Quickly she dressed and ran into the garden, intent only upon freedom.

THE REMAINDER of the King's visit to Cowdray held nothing discomfortable. Edward was in high spirits, and Sir Anthony provided the amusements which Edward enjoyed. Geraldine had so succeeded in the enslavement of Lord Clinton that he proposed marriage. At dinner they asked the King's blessing.

Edward knew the importance of proper marriage among his nobility. And surely Northumberland approved of Clinton. Edward wished the Duke were here to advise, for he was afraid of him. But he said grandly, "You have our royal consent."

Lord Clinton hastily drew a ruby signet ring from his thumb and put it on Geraldine's finger. The betrothal was accomplished.

Celia watched the pantomime from the other end of the hall. Leonard Dacre had found means to sit next to her, and she had been listening absently to his North Country wooing, most of which she did not understand. Finally the young man, increasingly fired by both her beauty and her indifference, cried, "By God, lass—will ye no *look* at me? Am I so ill-favoured?"

She gave him a small puzzled smile. "I'm bemused," she said.

The smile further undid him. Its charm, its dimple, its mysterious unawareness. He had never had a rebuff. The Dacres took women, high or low, when they wanted them. He and Tom kept tallies, and Leonard knew his prowess. "Where do ye lodge, lass? Wi' yonder lady aunt? Or at the tavern?"

"At times the one, at times the other," answered Celia.

"By the Virgin, will ye play cat and mouse wi' a *Dacre*!"

"'Tis dangerous to swear by *her*," Celia cried. "Dangerous especial for—" She stopped, her eyes wet with tears.

"Ye love a lad who is in danger?" Leonard asked sharply.

"It is so," said Celia, bowing her head.

Jealousy released the instinct to lay hands on a desired possession. Leonard grabbed her by the neck, upturned her face, bit her lips and forced his hand into her bodice. Celia's response was instant. She clouted his ear with a resounding slap.

The pages guffawed. The great redheaded lout had no business sitting here, anyway. Leonard darted a furious glance at them and stalked up the Hall, where he squeezed in beside Magdalen and received his sister's spirited teasing in silence.

Sir Anthony saw the bit of byplay even while he parried an embarrassing question from the King: Were his tenants properly convinced of the diabolical errors in the old religion?

"Oh, entirely so, Your Grace," said Anthony quietly.

The King went on to discuss with enthusiasm the new royal chaplain, John Knox. "He and Archbishop Cranmer often do not agree on points in my beloved new Prayer Book."

Anthony suppressed a smile. He was touched by the boy's pride in the Prayer Book and delighted to hear that the fanatical Knox was subjected to any criticism whatever.

"The Duke will soon join me on the progress," Edward went on, half to himself. "At Salisbury, I believe. He draws me a plan of new fortifications on the borders. My lord Dudley's ideas are of surpassing cleverness. He hath even suggested a new devise for the succession."

Anthony was startled into an impolite "*What*?"

Edward stiffened, he raised his chin in that gesture so like his father's.

"You will forget my allusion, Sir Anthony."

Anthony smiled gravely and babbled on about the border troubles until Edward was not sure that he had spoken of the succession at all.

But on Anthony a sinister light had burst. He guessed, for the first time, what Clinton and Geraldine had been aware of much sooner: Somehow, the sequence of the succession decreed by Henry VIII himself—the Princess Mary, to be followed by the Princess Elizabeth—was to be altered. Somehow, those Dudleys were going to seize the throne. Both Princesses were as royal as Edward—Mary more so, since her unhappy mother, Catherine of Aragon, had also been Spanish royalty. He had always felt great pity for the unfortunate Princess Mary, whose religion was his own. He had less sympathy for the Protestant Elizabeth, who was currently living in neglect at Hatfield House.

Anthony's speculations were checked by the need to provide the next entertainment for the King. He had sent for a troupe of mountebanks, who tumbled and juggled and came in with a clever little dog dressed in a monk's habit. The King shrieked with laughter at their tricks, and so did all the company who crowded in the courtyard. Celia had begun by laughing, too. Then the dog's trailing black robes, the sham tonsure, suddenly appalled her.

Somewhere below must be Stephen. He could perhaps hear the raucous merriment.

She could not bear it. She slipped away and crept up the old stone staircase to Ursula's room.

AT THE SPREAD EAGLE that evening Julian was enduring the company of the Allens from Ightham Mote. Emma Allen had recovered from her drunken fit, of which she remembered nothing. She was full-bodied and quite comely, with glossy black hair, and eyes of remarkable brilliance—reptilian, Julian thought, a lizard's eyes. She talked all through supper, recounting her life history and the reason for the Allens' presence in Midhurst. Emma Saxby was born of prosperous yeoman stock, and had a younger sister, Nan, who had married one Thomas Marsdon of Medfield Place. Recently a matter of inheritance had arisen between her and Nan. Their father had made what Emma considered an unfair will, leaving certain holdings away from herself. The Allens were vexed also by another financial uncertainty. Emma had been a novice at Easebourne Priory—which now belonged to Cowdray Castle—at the time of the Dissolution. The dowries which had been sent to the Priory with the novices had disappeared. Nobody knew where.

So the Allens had decided to brave Sir Anthony Browne himself, and on the way they had stopped at Medfield to see which way the wind blew on the inheritance. The wind blew stormy. Tom Marsdon had stated flatly that wills were wills. But the Allens had learned something that might help at Cowdray.

"Tom Marsdon's younger brother, Stephen, is *house priest* at Cowdray! Fancy the luck. Now we can get Sir Anthony's ear!"

Julian's attention was at last riveted. "But, my dear madam, the Brownes, indeed all of Cowdray, are Protestants!" He knew this from Cheke. "They'd have no Benedictine monk as chaplain."

"I'm no fool," Emma said contemptuously. "I've been speaking wi' the landlord here. He wouldna say this nor that, but *I* trapped him. They've a priest, all right, but he's hid. We must wait till the King's gone. It's simple." She squared her jaw. "When *I* intend a thing, 'tis good as done. And when *I* want a thing, I'll get it, God heeds me when I speak."

Julian looked at her sharply. His perceptions quivered. The sudden ruthless note in her flat voice and the way those strange eyes narrowed, he was reminded of a lunatic he had once seen in Bedlam.

The impression passed at once. Emma got up, smoothing her skirts. "Now that we happen here, whilst the King is, we must try to get a glimpse of him," she said, chuckling. "That'll be something to tell our little Charles, won't it, Kit? Our son," she explained to Julian, "six years old, come Christmastide, and the apple of our eyes, since he looks to be the only one!"

So natural and maternal a remark convinced Julian that his own predicament was inspiring him to overwrought fancies. He bade the Allens good-bye and went out to the stables to confer with the ostler, who asserted that there was not a horse nor an oxcart for hire today in the whole of Sussex. Julian went up to Celia's hot attic room sunk in despondency.

THE NEXT MORNING Anthony and Lady Jane waited by the gatehouse until the last flourish of trumpets faded at the end of the long royal procession. Then he put his arm around her and crossed himself. "Blessed Saint Mary, my dear, it is over."

She gave a sob, leaning her face on his shoulder. "Now our babe . . . he can be brought down to the chapel. . . ."

Anthony nodded. "And that wretched monk released. God forgive me, I've scarce thought of him. But we've still got the Dacres. And Clinton. I daren't release the priest until Clinton leaves."

"Anthony," said Jane, "I can bear no more. . . ." And she fainted.

Lord Clinton left the next day for Greenwich, where he had urgent business. Geraldine was so content with her prospects that she became kinder to everyone and took charge of Cowdray. With Jane so ailing, Anthony was grateful.

After Clinton's departure Geraldine directed Anthony to release the house priest. "Let him bury the babe, then get rid of him. I do not wish him in a house I am associated with."

"My lady," Anthony said coldly, "I wish you well, but I will not discharge my chaplain. And whatever your secrets may be with my Lord Clinton, I wish no part of them."

"Are you *certain*, Anthony? I know you well. You would like to be called 'my lord'. You have toadied the King these last days!"

"I have simply respected the King's known views and wishes," Anthony cried, furious at the partial truth. Damn the bitch, he thought. He had started towards the south wing, bent on releasing the priest at once, when he was distracted by the sound of laughter coming from Lady Ursula's room. He found the door ajar and looked in. Leonard and Thomas Dacre were playing cards, throwing half-crowns on the table while Magdalen Dacre egged them on. Handsome wench, Anthony thought. Healthy and wholesome as an oak. What an armful in bed. Then he caught sight of Celia, looking out the window. But there was *beauty*!

It was Magdalen who felt the watcher at the door and looked around. "Ho! Sir Anthony!" she cried, laughing. "Will you chide the gamesters? I vow they cheat!"

Leonard and Thomas sprang to their feet. Anthony felt constraint. They were his own age, but they made him feel old, the powerful host, the intruder. "Nay," he said, smiling, and waved them to sit down. "'Tis snug here," he said pleasantly to Ursula. He looked up at her crucifix and crossed himself. He was tired of dissembling. "All those who are *in* and *of* my house will go to Mass tomorrow morn at six," he said harshly.

Celia's heart was beating fast. She had been imagining all sorts of disasters. She said to Anthony in a low firm voice, "For the Mass, sir, will you not need your priest—Brother Stephen?"

There was accusation in the clear gaze. "You are right, child. Would you like to come with me now to release him?"

"Aye," Celia said. Ursula's indrawn breath did not touch her.

"Well, then—" said Anthony, and motioned her out the door.

They circled down the old stone staircase to the dank, dimly lit cellars. The stench of the latrine pit was sickening.

Anthony swung open a tiny door. They peered in and could see nobody. "Brother Stephen!"

"No food, only water," muttered a voice, and a dark shape stirred on a pile of straw.

Celia squeezed through the door and ran to kneel by him. "'Tis *me*, Celia," she cried. "And Sir Anthony himself. You're free!"

Through fevered mists Stephen heard the girl's beseeching frightened voice. "Begone . . . Celia . . . in your hair are golden snakes. . . ." His hand raised to cross himself, then fell limp.

"Delirium," said Anthony grimly. "Wait here."

She obeyed, crouching beside Stephen, wetting his hot hand with her tears until Anthony returned with two stout varlets.

They found a rat bite on Stephen's thigh when they laid him on a counter in the scullery. They forgot Celia as they stripped him. She shrank back, shocked, troubled, fascinated. She had not imagined how well made Stephen's body was, with broad shoulders and narrow hips, the muscles rounded, the flushed skin as smooth as her own. As she looked further, her cheeks grew hot; she felt the heat in her scalp, and she turned away.

"God's nails—look at that!" Anthony poked a finger around a puffy mass of proud flesh from which yellow-green pus trickled. Red streaks ran down Stephen's swollen leg; he winced when Anthony touched it, and shivered with a violent chill. "I doubt he'll live," Anthony said sadly. "We should send for the barber."

"Sir Anthony!" Celia's voice was hoarse as a raven's. "There's a physician at the inn. The one Master Cheke sent to the King. I'll fetch him!" She darted out.

Thus it was that Julian was installed at Cowdray, though not in the manner he had hoped and expected.

DURING THE WEEK of his struggle for life, Stephen lay in a small chamber near Ursula's. That lady did most of the nursing, while Celia wandered about Cowdray in anxiety.

Julian used all his skill to save the patient. Nevertheless, the fever mounted for three days. Then on the fourth morning Julian entered the sickroom and saw great improvement. "*Benissimo*. . . ."

Stephen opened his eyes. "Who are *you*?" he whispered.

"A physician, and you'll recover. There *was* grave doubt."

"Our Lord hath shown infinite mercy," said Stephen after a moment of wonder. "The Blessed Virgin be praised."

"Praise her by all means, but a bit of earthly gratitude is also fitting," Julian said dryly, "to little Celia Bohun, who summoned *me*—and to my own ministrations. And to the Lady Ursula. . . ."

By the middle of August, before the Feast of the Assumption of the Virgin Mary, Stephen had begun to chafe at his confinement. He was able to walk around his room, and this day he greeted Julian's morning visit with a determined smile. "Good day, Doctor, you see I'm nearly well. I intend to celebrate our Blessed Lady's Mass for my Cowdray flock."

"They'll be glad to have you back. Lady Jane still weeps because her poor babe had to be buried by the Midhurst vicar."

Stephen nodded sadly. "I have prayed for its soul."

Julian smiled. He had grown fond of Stephen, in whom he recognized a lonely spirit not unlike his own. "You enjoy thinking you save souls, don't you, my friend? As I do saving bodies. Have you read your Plato, Ovid, Virgil on the subject of souls?"

"Of *souls* . . . ?" asked Stephen. "What do you mean?"

"Of their belief that our souls return over and over to earth in new bodies, that the choices for good or evil made in one life may determine the next incarnation."

"There is but one incarnation," Stephen said gravely. "That of our Blessed Lord. You blaspheme, Master Julian."

"I simply point out what many better minds than yours or mine have believed. Followers of Jesus apparently did. *The resurrection of the dead*—does that mean the soul must descend again into the decayed corpse it has just gladly left behind?"

"The bodies will be made new—the *same* bodies."

Julian suddenly laughed. "We won't quarrel about it, Stephen. I wasn't born for strife." He poured a glass of wine. "Here, drink this! I've tired you. Lie down for a bit!"

Stephen obeyed, ashamed of the sudden weakness in his body.

"One would never suspect your priesthood to look at you," Julian observed with dry amusement, inspecting his patient.

Since he had been able to get out of bed, Stephen had worn a maroon velvet dressing gown lent by Sir Anthony. It was an elegant garment, faced with yellow satin and furred with squirrel. He looked as darkly virile and fashionable as any young courtier.

"They've taken my habit to wash," said Stephen. "It'll be back tonight. I've no mind to be decked in this thing."

"Ah," said Julian. "You do enjoy renouncing the sensual." But, he added to himself, I think you have not met temptation. "I should tell you," he went on, "that you have kinfolk below in the courtyard, champing around for a sight of you."

"Kinfolk?" Stephen frowned. "I have none now but Tom."

"Their name is Allen. Mistress Allen is sister to your brother's wife. I've had trouble keeping her at bay. Something about a lost dowry at Easebourne Priory sixteen years ago."

"What can I do about that?" said Stephen.

"Promise *anything*," Julian chuckled, "that'll get her out of the Spread Eagle. She's driving the landlord mad, and me, too."

The doctor ushered the Allens into the sickroom. Emma Allen exuded obduracy and will. "Brother!" she cried loudly. "I thought ye'd never mend!" She plopped on her knees to receive his blessing, looking up at him with a provocative stare.

"I don't see how you think I can help you, Mistress Allen."

Her husband said nervously, "Emma was diddled out o' a hundred sovereigns. Sir Anthony'll know what happened to 'em."

"Why have you waited so long, and why can't *you* ask him?"

Their lengthy answers made Stephen's head spin. But he knew it was his duty to help a Catholic who had been hurt by the Dissolution, so he promised to get them an audience with Sir Anthony and hastily signed the cross in the air for dismissal.

"That woman!" said Julian, as the door swung to. "Thunderous effluvia surround her. She stinks like sulphur. And the lewd desirous looks she gave you!" Julian poured a ruby liquid into a noggin. "Remember to take this after I've gone. I'll teach you to make it. 'Tis most strengthening."

Stephen looked at the man who by saving his life must have been an instrument of God's will. He would miss Master Julian. Impulsively he put his hand on Julian's arm. "I thank you, my friend, and shall pray daily for the welfare of your soul."

Julian smiled. "By all means. That odd invisible vapour is *your* concern, as the body is mine. Hark, there's a knock!"

It was Lady Ursula with the monk's cleansed habit. "Welladay, good Brother! Here's a marvel of recovery." She thought how handsome he looked in the velvet gown and was glad Celia could not see him. "Your habit. You'll wish to don it at once."

"Aye, Lady Ursula. You *are* good to me. I'll hear confessions tomorrow night. Will you tell the others? I must go now and speak to Sir Anthony about a matter."

"In that case," said Julian, "I'll take this time to cast Celia Bohun's nativity for you."

Ursula flushed with pleasure. "In my chamber, Doctor," she cried eagerly. "I've all that's needed."

They found Celia in her aunt's room doggedly stitching on a strip of tapestry. She rose and curtsied, her sea-green eyes anxious. "How does *he* do?" she asked fervently of Julian.

"Very well indeed—cured, in fact," he answered, observing her sudden radiance. So . . . what's this? In love with the priest? Poor child.

"How old are you, *carina*?" he asked.

"She's scarce fourteen," put in Ursula. "'Tis all down on this parchment. I've had to guess at the hour of her birth."

"Ye'll tell me a good fortune, sir, won't you?" asked Celia.

Julian glanced at the gillyflowers she had stuck in her bodice, at the dimpling mouth, at the rich golden hair, and had to restrain a desire to touch her. "I tell only what the stars foretold at your birth. Naught but good, I'm sure." Yet he had a foreboding. "She should leave," he said to Ursula. "I need solitude."

"Oh, to be sure," said Ursula, considering how to prevent the girl from seeing Stephen, who was now at large. "Run down to Midhurst for me, dear, buy me a skein of crimson silk, I've none left." She handed her a sixpence.

There was a rebellious glint in the girl's eyes, but she curtsied and left. The two older people looked at each other as she closed the door. "I have guessed what perturbs you," Julian said. "You should not fret. But it *would* be better if there were distance between them. The little one is beautiful."

"Aye. Magdalen Dacre asked us north to visit at Naworth in Cumberland and I think we'll go. Leonard Dacre is enamoured of Celia and would suit, though I hope for a better match."

"Possibly," said Julian. "Now let's get to work."

With Ursula's astrolabe, and an ephemeris he always carried in his bag, Julian worked fast, making occasional comments, but as he studied the position of Celia's planets Ursula saw his eyebrows draw together.

"There are afflictions . . . self-undoing." Violent early death, he would have decided, but his sympathy for these two women was strong, and predictions were not infallible. "Afflictions to be surmounted," he said lightly, smiling at Ursula. "Come, lady, look not so doleful. There is *hope* of a brilliant marriage."

Ursula jumped at reassurance. "Oh, Master Julian, I love Celia. Perhaps God *will* safeguard her if I have faith enough."

She moved to the open window. "Here she comes now." Then she saw Stephen enter the courtyard, saw their pleasure as they greeted each other.

She called out, "Celia! Come! I'm waiting!"

"It is unwise, my lady," said Julian, "to show your fears or to press her unduly. They are both completely innocent as yet."

"Aye. But we'll go to Cumberland as soon as—" She broke off as Celia rushed in.

"Here's your silk, Aunt!" She waved a crimson skein. "I met Brother Stephen below! I vow he seems better than before his illness. He says he'll start my lessons next week again!"

Ursula gave her thanks and a fleeting smile, and said, "Master Julian, pray will you look at Celia's palm?"

He was immensely reluctant to do so, but Celia danced up to him, holding out both hands. He took them in his, gazed at them briefly and dropped them, shrugging. "I see little to interpret." He bowed and said, "I bid you good day."

Julian went down the passage to his room, poured himself a glass of wine and tried to deny what he had seen. Very short life lines on both palms stopped with an "island" on the Mount of Venus; and the malignant cross on Saturn on the right hand at the base of the ring finger—well, she did have a star on Jupiter, which was good. Prognostications do go awry. In any case, I am a physician, not a soothsayer.

He combed his hair and went off to find Sir Anthony to take his leave. With his patient cured he would be off now to London, to St. Thomas's Hospital, where he would be near the court and his patron, John Cheke.

By nine o'clock that evening Anthony, having spent a long day disposing of tenants' problems, gave a great yawn and pushed back from the supper table. The day had ended with unexpected requests from members of his own household. The first—Stephen's—had resulted in an interview with an importunate matron named Emma Allen, about an Easebourne dowry. When he told her he had no idea where it was, she collapsed in sobs. Anthony, generous by instinct and aware of the immense benefits the Brownes had derived from the dissolution of the monasteries, had given her some gold and a slightly flawed diamond ring. Clearly relieved to get anything, she had accepted them avidly and hurried away.

Anthony had also been generous with Julian, giving him a purseful of coins, with thanks for his successful doctoring.

The interview with Lady Ursula had been the most disquieting. Anthony was startled that she should ask to take a journey that seemed to him dangerous, and at the same time strangely hurt that any of his household might desire a protracted absence from Cowdray.

"At your *age*, lady," he'd said sharply, "and with that—that fair young maid? Impossible. I thought Celia happy at Cowdray."

"She does not know of this plan," said Ursula. "There are reasons"—she took a long breath—"reasons why she must go. Sir Anthony, I humble myself to ask this of you."

"*What* reasons?" asked Anthony. "Explain yourself."

He saw her face fall, but the eyes met his proudly, until he saw this pensioner he had long taken for granted as formidable, and was reminded of the five hundred years of de Bohun pedigree. "I can't give you reasons," she said with dignity, "except that they have to do with the avoidance of a grave threat to Celia's soul."

Shaken, he had granted permission and wished her Godspeed.

Chapter 3

The hazy red August sun had scarcely risen when the Cumberland-bound party set out from Cowdray. Anthony had made handsome provision for them. Ursula and Celia were mounted on quiet, sturdy geldings. There was a stout mule to carry the coffers and bedding, and for escort, Wat Farrier. Wat was Cowdray's keeper of the horse and supervisor of gamekeepers.

As a boy he had shown such quickness of wit that old Sir Anthony had sent him to school. Wat had later seen much of the world, accompanying the old man on military and diplomatic missions.

During the last five years Wat had chafed at the restricted life of Cowdray, fond as he was of young Anthony. He was, therefore, delighted with this expedition, for it also involved a secret errand which might liven the trip.

He glanced at his charges. The Lady Ursula, for all her years, rode easily. The girl was another matter. She gripped the pommel, her left foot was turned wrong in the stirrup. Pretty lass, though, or would be if she didn't look so stiff, solemn and ill-tempered.

As they plodded through Easebourne, Ursula studied the silent Celia. Blessed Saint Mary, the child looks blasted! But I've got her away. New sights, new people, will soon dispel the gloom. "Only think, sweeting!" she cried. "*London* tomorrow night, or next. You'll see the Bridge, the Tower, all the palaces!"

Celia, her strained eyes staring, answered nothing, and except for the *clop-clop* of hoofs and the barking of farmhouse dogs, there was no sound for some miles. She had scant awareness of anything but the black hollowness in her chest. Desolation. I hate him, I hate him.

Celia had gone to Stephen on Tan's Hill last evening. She had laid careful plans for escape. For three days she had been secreting bread, cheese, salted fish in a cache under a yew tree, and she had arranged to hide in the garret of old Molly O'Whipple, who, though esteemed for her herbal remedies, was held to be a witch. No one would have looked for her there. Thus had been Celia's plan, formed by the frantic desire to remain near Stephen and the certainty that he wished her to. For when yestermorn in chapel she had knelt for his blessing, he had touched her hair, her neck, and she thought she had heard him murmur, "Don't leave me, beloved." The shock of secret bliss had sustained her through supper last night, when she had been laughing, airy, as Sir Anthony kindly toasted the voyagers. Then she had excused herself, saying she wished to bid farewell to some newborn puppies in the stable.

Once outside, she had sped down to the footbridge and up the rough hill path. She had expected him to be waiting for her.

He had been digging a garden plot. His habit was kirtled high, and he looked younger, less monklike than she had ever seen him. Celia called out a joyous, "Stephen! I'm here, at last!"

Stephen dropped the spade, turning on her a startled face.

"Ye stare so, love." She laughed. "Ye knew I'd come."

Stephen's intake of breath was clear. "No," he said. He pulled down his habit and became the tall, black forbidding figure she knew too well. "Celia, why are you here?"

"D'ye think I'd go off a thousand miles from thee? I saw your eyes. You touched my neck, you *asked* me to bide."

"I said *naught* but the *Benedicite*." Nor had he, yet all that day he had been appalled that his hand, of its own will, had caressed her hair, stroked the petal-smooth neck as she knelt before him. "To be sure you're going."

She heard a hesitation in his voice. "I've saved food. I'll hide awhile at Molly O'Whipple's and come to you nights up here."

"Celia . . ." Stephen found the needed coldness to say, "this is disobedient, ungrateful folly. You've no more wits than a titmouse. How long do you think to hide? What would you do after?"

"Why—" she said, faltering, "you'd win them over and I'd go back to Cowdray. We'd be nigh each other."

"What for?" said Stephen. "I don't want you near."

She gasped. "Stephen, you *do* want me nigh!" And she threw her arms around his neck. He felt the soft pressure of her body and his own body's shameful response as she kissed him. Her lips lit a dizzy flame he had felt before only in wicked dreams. He jerked back.

"Slut!" he cried, and pushed her so hard that she fell to the turf. "You're a little fool, Celia Bohun." And he stared down with savage joy at her abasement. "These are Satan's tricks."

Celia leaped to her feet. Chin high, she confronted him. "Aye—meaching house priest! Ye're right. I'm a fool. I've been a love-sick mooncalf. Never fear, I'm off to Cumberland. There'll be men there joyed to see me. I bid ye farewell, Brother Stephen!"

She tossed back her hair and melted into the forest dusk.

"Blessed Jesu—" Stephen's eyes stung and watered. He walked

slowly into the little chapel and knelt. *"Ave Maria gratia plena . . ."* The words were dry as the rustling leaves.

He went into his hut, and the beautiful face of the Virgin seemed to smirk with leering reproof. He covered the picture with the purple linen pall which shrouded her in Lent. All that night he walked on Midhurst Common.

WAT FARRIER two days later guided his charges into Southwark, while church bells rang out noon. "Blessed Mary, what a din!" remarked Ursula. "I'd forgot the town was so noisy." Below the church bells from both sides of the Thames there was a constant rumbling of carts, horses' whinnies, barking dogs and street cries. "Who'll buy? Who'll buy?" "Scissors and knives, to grind—to grind!"

"Used to be vastly *more* noise," remarked Wat, indicating Sir Anthony's town house, "when the priory bells rang, too."

Along with Battle Abbey, King Henry had presented the priory of St. Mary Overie to the elder Browne. Ursula had, so far, no particular scruples about sacred places turned secular, yet as she looked at the great priory's church next door, now rechristened St. Saviour's and used by the parish, she was dismayed. The chapels adjoining the church had both been boarded up, the fair Gothic stonework daubed with plaster. One had become a bakehouse, the other housed a drove of squealing pigs.

It occurred to Ursula that it was from here that Anthony had been hauled off to jail for hearing Mass. It was truly a dangerous time for Catholics. At Cowdray she had scarcely realized this.

Wat showed his party into the erstwhile cloisters, planted now with turnips and greens. Four of the priory rooms had been sparsely furnished, and in one of them the caretaker, a doddering monk kept on by old Sir Anthony, was discovered snoring on a straw pallet.

"Wake up, Brother!" cried Wat. "We've come from the master!"

The old man jumped. "There's been no Masses, ye can look . . ."

"Nay, nay," said Wat. "We come from Sir Anthony."

Celia kept her eyes away from the monk and whisked into practical matters—laying their bedding, kindling a fire to cook dinner. Action keeps miseries at bay—this she had learned in childhood. During the days of travelling her gnawing black hurt had receded. Now she walled it off in a secret cell.

The next two days they spent seeing London. Ursula was as excited as Celia as they rode from the Tower to Westminster, gaping at the palaces along the Thames. But they constantly encountered ruins—priories, convents, hospitals, churches.

And the streets were full of starving beggars. "'Tis horrible," said Ursula as a scabrous woman suddenly screamed and died before their eyes. "Nobody cares for them now. Nobody cares for the old, the sick, the poor." She herself had doled out all she dared from the purse Anthony had given her for expenses.

"Yet, dear Aunt," Celia ventured, "Wat says King Edward is founding a new hospital; that he's not unmindful of the suffering."

Ursula shook her head. "I doubt that pale, spineless lad can help his people, nor will live to do so," she said indignantly.

They were approaching London Bridge, bound home to the south bank of the river, when this exchange took place. Its immediate result was like a thunderbolt. A rough hand clamped down on Ursula's shoulder, a sardonic bearded face was thrust close to hers. "I heard ye plain, mistress, and ye'll answer fur it. Thou, too, maiden," he said to Celia. He was dressed in helmet and padded doublet, and carried a pikestaff with which he prodded Ursula.

"Answer for what?" cried Ursula. "Don't you *dare* touch me!"

"Treason, that's wot. Ye'll answer to the Duke." He seized the bridles of both geldings and turned them round as the bridge traffic paused to watch. Ursula heard fearful murmurs. "Duke's man . . . Northumberland."

"Holy Saint Mary," cried Ursula, "I'm Lady Southwell, this is my niece, we are but passing through on our way to the north."

"An' calling on the saints, too! I smell a papist. Come along!"

Ursula met Celia's uncomprehending gaze. "It seems we must go with this knave, my dear. 'Tis some foolish blunder he's made."

The girl nodded. She had never heard the word "treason" and was more exhilarated than frightened as the Duke's henchman herded them to Durham House where the courtyard was thronged with petitioners and miscreants under guard. The Duke's steward walked pompously to Ursula's guard. "His Grace'll want a look at these." Few of the throng looked around as the women were hustled into the palace.

In the presence chamber John Dudley, Duke of Northumberland, sat on a canopied throne. He was an ugly man of fifty, soberly dressed as became a Calvinist. His eyes, like smoky glass, were ruthlessly appraising. "Good day, lady," he said to Ursula; he waited until she had curtsied. "My guard reports wicked—nay, treasonable—speech from you."

Ursula stood tall and quiet. "I remember no such thing, Your Grace. Eavesdroppers and spies oft hear wrong."

The Duke knew this to be true, and an elderly provincial widow seemed hardly worth his time. "You made derogations anent the King's Grace and his health. And you swore by a saint."

Ursula hurried to answer the second accusation. "I was so startled at disrespectful treatment to one of my rank, Your Grace, that I may have forgot and used words from the old religion."

Northumberland stiffened, aware that she had evaded him. "What's that chain around your neck?" he shouted.

Ursula flushed. Several of the courtiers in the chamber turned to watch. Celia, for the first time, felt danger.

The Duke made a gesture to his guard, who tore off Ursula's neck chain, revealing the small ivory crucifix attached to it. "Ah," said the Duke, smiling. With precise deliberation he twisted the crucifix off the chain and broke it in two.

"You are *indeed* forgetful, lady, of English law. And you, maiden, have you hid on you these prohibited, idolatrous trinkets?"

Celia shook her head, her luminous eyes staring. "No, sir."

"And where do you live, maiden?"

"We stop in Southwark, my lord, at Sir Anthony Browne's, on our way to Cumberland. But we come from Cowdray."

Cowdray! That undoubted nest of papacy. He had permitted Edward to visit there only because Anthony Browne's support might be extraordinarily helpful. "Lord Clinton!" He suddenly bawled to a nobleman who had just entered the chamber.

Clinton made his way through the crowd. He stopped, astonished, when he saw the two women.

"Ye know them?" said the Duke.

"I've seen them at Cowdray," said Clinton. "What's amiss?"

"The old lady's a papist and was heard speaking very indiscreetly of the King. I'll let her off if you vouch for her."

The Duke was treading warily. He had but recently gained Lord Clinton to his cause. Clinton was about to marry Anthony Browne's stepmother. The Lord High Admiral was not a man to offend.

"To whom do you go in Cumberland?" the Duke asked Celia.

"To the—the Dacres, at Naworth."

Here was a surprise! The Duke had just returned from conferences with Lord Dacre, who was so vital to the defence of the Scottish border that a blind eye must be turned to his Catholicism.

"Some Dacres were at Cowdray when the King was," Clinton snapped. "The King's Grace liked them. A pox on it."

But Northumberland had one more question to put. "Do you call, perchance, at Hunsdon on your way north, maiden?" In the young face, as in the old, he saw genuine bewilderment.

He turned to Ursula. "You know who resides at Hunsdon?"

"No, Your Grace," said Ursula with complete truth, "I do not."

"You may go, lady." The Duke tossed her the chain. "But guard your tongue and mind the trinkets you wear, or ye'll end behind bars, as you almost did today."

Celia gasped, and clutched at Ursula's hand. They did not speak until they were back in the priory, telling Wat their story. He knew much of which they had no inkling and was far more dismayed than they were.

"Wat . . . where's Hunsdon?" Celia asked thoughtfully.

"*Hunsdon?* Was there mention o' Hunsdon?"

"Aye," said Ursula. "His Grace asked if we were to stop there on the way north. I've never heard of the place."

Wat sighed. Those two lived at Cowdray as sequestered as in a nunnery. Their ignorance was becoming dangerous. He spoke firmly. "The Lady Mary's at Hunsdon. In Hertfordshire. And we *are* stopping there."

Ursula swallowed. "The *Princess* Mary?" she said incredulously.

"Not so called now, another thing ye'd better remember or ye'll get the lot of us hanged yet, m'lady."

"What have we to do with the Lady Mary?"

"Message from Sir Anthony," he said briefly. "Natural to pay our respects. She's still heir to the throne."

"*Still?*" cried Ursula, pouncing. "There's no question about it. 'Twas in the late king's will. Everyone knows that!"

"Knowledge's one thing," he said, "wot happens is another. The Lady Mary's a stubborn Catholic, the saints preserve her!"

"And Princess Elizabeth is *not*," said Ursula, frowning.

"The *Lady* Elizabeth is not. The King's Grace now dislikes both his sisters. Won't see either of 'em."

"Nonetheless, he *can't* alter his father's will."

"A king may do as 'e pleases." Wat was no surer of the vague conspiracy to disinherit the Princesses than was Sir Anthony. But rumours ran fast underground, and Wat had enjoyed a drinking bout with Lord Clinton's valet. The fellow had hinted at the Duke of Northumberland's ambitions.

"You may take Mistress Celia to the bear-baiting," said Ursula to Wat. "I wish to be quiet. Guard her well."

"Ye'll bide here?" asked Wat. "Aye, rest, lady."

Ursula wanted to be alone. She pulled the broken gold chain from her waist pouch and stared at the twisted link which had held the crucifix. A longing for guidance seized her—she knew not where to find a priest—for sanctuary then, some hallowed place where she might see the dear familiar symbols which had ever been channels towards prayer and inspiration. She looked out the window at St. Saviour's four little spires, put on her mantle, went downstairs into the old cloister park and so entered the church.

Its bleakness confounded her. The painted windows had been smashed. A bare oak communion table on the altar steps was all there was in the chancel. Her slow footsteps echoed through the empty nave.

There was no place to sit, but she knelt on the bare medieval tiles in the chancel and began to tell her beads on the rosary her mother had given her fifty years before.

The world has gone mad, she thought. I'm an old woman, and I don't know what to do. They could have put us in prison. They're strong—strong and evil. Our Dear Lord and His Blessed Mother have fled this land. Yet, if Celia can be safe. . . . Her love for the girl was warm and real.

Uncomforted, Ursula went back to her priory room to wait for Celia's return.

WHEN URSULA'S party reached Hunsdon on the following afternoon, they were soaked from a steady downpour and very hungry. But unknown visitors were rare and viewed with suspicion, so it was a long time before Princess Mary's steward, Sir Thomas Wharton, appeared.

He listened with a frown as Wat explained. "We come, sir, from Cowdray. I've a message from Sir Anthony Browne he wants delivered to Her Grace *in person*."

Wharton noted Wat's badge with the Browne buck-head crest on it. But he knew the King had recently visited Cowdray. Moreover, there was the alliance between Browne's stepmother and Lord Clinton, a known Dudley-ite.

"Give *me* the message, fellow," he said. "I'll relay it."

Wat's eyes hardened. "Master wants it delivered in person."

"Her Grace is unwell. Be off with ye!" cried Sir Thomas, angered by Wat's tone. Then he started, as they all did, at a deep voice.

"What's ado, Sir Thomas? Who is it?"

They looked up and saw a woman's head in a jewelled coif leaning out of the window. "Bring them in!"

When they entered the Hall, Princess Mary was standing by a great snapping fire awaiting them. How small the royal lady was, Ursula thought, as she and Celia curtsied. The Princess's hair, once the true Castilian gold, had faded to drab. Her thin mouth was stubborn, her eyes set in a frown of pain. Though Mary was but thirty-five, she looked old. Ursula watched as Wharton spelled out his suspicions of Sir Anthony's intent. She saw that his attitude would prevail and they would all be packed off into the cold drizzle again. Noticing a gold crucifix among the other jewels on Mary's chest, she reached in her pouch and drew out her shabby rosary, waited until the gesture caught Mary's eye, then slowly kissed the silver cross.

The Princess started, her face was transfigured. Her thin lips relaxed into a singularly sweet smile. "Ah-h," she said. "You are welcome to Hunsdon in the name of our Blessed Lord."

They were invited to spend the night. Mary had for weeks been both anxious and bored. The memory of her miserable girlhood with her adored, repudiated Spanish mother—the fears, the dangers—never left her. She prayed for forgiveness when hatreds overpowered her, hatred of the magnificent father, who had replaced her royal mother, Catherine, with Anne Boleyn, the whore. And hatred of Elizabeth, the innocent result of that sham marriage.

Mary, who was well trained to recognize the scent of danger, smelled whiffs of it around her now. She was forced to celebrate Mass in secret; her sisterly letters to Edward remained unanswered. But she had never doubted her position as present heir to the throne. This was her father's decree, it was also divine decree. She loved her brother and, in hopeful moments, felt sure she would somehow regain his affection and her position at court. Ursula's account at supper of the King's visit to Cowdray did not shake her in this.

After supper Mary retired to her privy chamber and summoned Wat Farrier. "What is the message you so press on me?" she asked.

Wat had been startled at first sight by the Princess's meagreness in contrast to her deep voice. Now, in her smile, in the set of her head, he saw a likeness to her father. An aura of royalty. She was not the poor little wisp he had thought.

From inside his jacket he drew out a small gold signet ring.

"'Tis this, Your Grace—pray will ye examine it close?"

Mary took the ring, observed the carved buck's head.

"If it comes to Your Grace again by *any* hand, Your Grace must beware of aught else ye've heard. Of *any* summons."

"You speak in riddles, my good fellow. *What* summons?"

But Wat knew only what Sir Anthony had made him memorize.

"May I go now, Your Grace? I've a hard ride tonight to London. I'll come back for my ladies tomorrow."

He reached his hand out respectfully for the ring. Mary gave it to him, impressed as she had always been by male strength. Her head ached. She could think only of the soothing potion Lady

Wharton would give her—and oblivion for part of the restless night.

In the morning Wat returned from London, where he had deposited the signet ring with a certain goldsmith in Lombard Street according to Sir Anthony's command. By noon the Cowdray party was able to set forth again for the north.

Chapter 4

By the time they reached Cumberland ten days later, Ursula was as sated by travel as Celia was enlivened. For both, the crimson-heathered moors, the flaming orange bracken, and now the mountains—rocky, misty-topped—were astounding. They plodded miles without seeing even a shepherd's stone cot. The language became incomprehensible. Instead of bread, they were given dry oatcakes, and messes of entrails for meat; instead of good ale, there was water or a white liquid so fiery it burned their throats.

Ursula's spirits flagged. Few south-countrymen had a liking for scenery so startling, so primitive. They were not aware of any romantic beauty in wilderness. "I doubt we should have come."

"Oh, but yes, Aunt!" cried Celia. "I never guessed any place could look like this! Mysterious, grand—one can breathe deep. . . ." She did so, her cheeks glowing, though she could not explain the glad yet awed response in her heart to the blackish mountains, the grey implacable crags, and the nut-brown lake of Ullswater.

Ursula sighed. I'm a foolish woman, she thought, looking at black storm clouds which had massed in the northern sky. Her plan of escape now seemed as stupid as its reasons. The Dacres' invitation had been so casual, her later decision to accept it so impulsive, the Benedictine monk seemed so remote.

When at last they came in sight of Naworth Castle, Ursula was burning with fever, and Wat beside himself with anxiety for his party's safety. He had twice been misdirected. They had been caught in sleet and driving rain and bitter wind. Only Celia was still exhilarated. But Naworth, however welcome a sight, looked forbidding indeed. Ursula thought of the luxurious elegance of Cowdray. She sat her horse dejectedly while Wat went off to beg admission at the bolted portal.

Celia glanced anxiously at her aunt, whose teeth were chattering. She, too, thought of Cowdray and the secret wish in her heart welled up and exploded into one word—Stephen. No. She would not let herself think of Tan's Hill and its inhabitant.

Wat came striding back with a tall girl in russet cloth who waved her arms. "Welcoom, welcoom—ye puir things. Sech a journey!"

Magdalen bestowed a kiss on Celia and helped Ursula down from the saddle as Lady Dacre herself came out to greet them.

During the next hour the forceful Dacre women took charge. Ursula was put to bed, and Celia was given a stool near the fire. Wat disappeared to the servants' wing.

Magdalen explained to Celia that all her brothers had gone on a Border raid and only the old baron, Lord William Dacre, remained at home.

"Leonard'll be glad to see ye, hinny," said Magdalen, laughing. "We all are, dinna doot it."

Celia blushed with delight, prepared to enjoy herself at Naworth. That night in Magdalen's bed, curled close and warm, she savoured the scent of peat smoke and heather, listening to the lowing of distant cattle.

A FORTNIGHT later Celia longed to leave Naworth and had no means of doing so. The Dacre men had come back from harrying the Scots. They had burned many farmsteads and had taken some fine Scottish cattle. Young Sir Thomas gave his father a vociferous account of it in the Hall, while the men roared out their war cry.

Celia shrank as Magdalen, sitting next to her, bellowed, too. The Dacres were so large, so noisy and so numerous. Besides Tom and Leonard, there were four younger boys, all with wiry red hair, all stinking of sweat, horse dung and drink. The hounds, yelping and scrabbling for bones tossed to them, increased the confusion.

Celia glanced at Leonard and tried to imagine him as a husband. Magdalen had made it obvious that she had this in mind, as Ursula did. The second son of the powerful Dacres would be a wonderful match for a penniless orphan. Leonard was big, rough, crude, but there's nobody else for me, Celia thought. An eon of spinsterhood stretched ahead of her, and the deep walled-off hurt quivered.

Yet when Leonard's attentions began on the morrow, they made Celia shrink. He pawed her, pinched her buttocks, called her his bonny, but there was never a word of love. She felt besieged.

The early days of October shattered any lingering romantic notions she might have had about him. Even Ursula was warning her never to be alone with Leonard, to guard her maidenhead.

One night he sought out Celia and grabbed her around the waist. "Coom outside, hinny," he cried, "we'll walk a bit i' the gloaming."

"I don't want to," she said. "I'll stay here."

The young man flushed. "God's bones!" he shouted, lifting her from where she sat. As she struggled he grabbed her wrists in one hand and plunged the other down her bodice, wrenching her right breast with such violence that she screamed, whereupon he covered her mouth with a savage bite.

"*Have done*, Len!" He reeled at a resounding blow on his cheek and turned to see Magdalen, her amber eyes sparking with fury. "Let her be, ye randy tup! Ye shame us all!"

Celia's knees gave way as Leonard released her and confronted his sister, who was nearly as tall as he—and twice as brave.

"Go on away, Len." Magdalen had always daunted him. He slunk away. His sister now turned to the sobbing Celia. "Aye, he's torn your bodice, the scurvy wencher. He'll maybe askin' your aunt fur ye arfter this. He's a dolt to think he'd get ye otherwise, but the Dacre men're dimwitted."

"I'll not *have* him, Maggie. I can't abide him."

Magdalen did not answer, but she thought to herself that poor Celia had no choice, if Leonard *did* proffer honourable wedlock. But Len would be no worse than most. And anyway, when did a girl's wishes have any bearing on marriage?

ON ALL HALLOWS EVE, the last day of October, Leonard's thwarted passion for Celia finally overcame him. This happened in the Hall while the sky outside was lurid with bonfires lit to ward off bogles, witches and other evils which roamed that night. At one end of the Hall the young folk threw nuts on the fire, having named each one secretly for a possible sweetheart.

Celia did not notice that Leonard rose and joined his parents at the far end of the Hall until Magdalen touched her on the shoulder. "M'lord an' lady want ye, hinny."

Lord and Lady Dacre sat frowning slightly in their carved oak armchairs. Leonard stood behind them, staring at the floor. Ursula, seated in a lesser armchair, gave Celia a quick excited smile. "We've—we've something to tell you, sweeting."

The old Baron nodded solemnly. "Aye, lass, Leonard wants ta wed ye. Sence he wants ye so bad, we'll no deny him."

Lady Dacre's large kind face broke into an encouraging smile. "Coom, dear," she said. "We'll treat ye like a dotter. Have no fear."

"I don't want to," said Celia on a long gasp.

Magdalen squeezed her hand. "Hush, luv," she whispered. "'Tis best." She turned to her parents. "Leonard's been too rough. Celia's a delicate lass. Ye great booby!" she cried to her brother. "Tak' her hand, kiss her pure, ye clod."

Leonard, trembling slightly, slowly obeyed. The girl shrank in every fibre. "I'd rather not wed at all," she cried.

"Tush," said Lord Dacre, who had no patience with girlish whims. He had settled the matter. Lady Dacre saw Celia's reluctance as shyness, to be resolved in time. Ursula quelled misgivings by telling herself that if the girl's disinclination had to do with that monk at Cowdray, indeed this was no time for softness.

"'Tis settled, Celia," she said briskly. "My lord and lady have proposed the marriage take place December twenty-ninth."

"Aye," said Lady Dacre, smiling, "we'll wed ye proper i' church, then mak' a gladsome revel o' it."

Leonard suddenly guffawed, and gave Celia a crudely lustful look. "A merry, merry night, we'll have, eh, lass!"

Nobody heeded Celia's whisper. "I won't. I'd die first."

THE DAYS sped on inexorably. Celia's misery settled to apathy. When she could not avoid Leonard, she answered him dully, grateful that he now felt a respect for her and did not touch her.

Christmas Day came and its burst of feasting and music. The piper skirled; there was a fiddler and a flutist; there were carols and North Country ballads. They ate wild boar. As master of the revels for the twelve days of Christmas they selected a Lord of Misrule. This year it was the third Dacre son, George.

"Yule! Yule! saith the Lord o' Misrule," George boomed. "Every man to make merry and each play the fool! Fetch all the servants into the Hall!"

Cooks and scullions, stableboys, dairymaids, shepherds, swineherds, hunters, archers crowded in. They drank and jigged and shouted and stamped while the piper led them in reels. Celia found herself grabbed by a new partner almost before she had finished greeting the last. Everyone danced, even Lady Dacre and Ursula, and the wassail bowl was often replenished.

At dawn they fell into bed exhausted. Celia had managed to forget the approaching marriage, and just at cockcrow she dreamed of Stephen, the Stephen she'd hoped for at their farewell on Tan's Hill, clutching her in his arms, saying, "Never leave me, my love," and when he kissed her they became one being. Shining contentment lasted until Celia was awakened by Magdalen shaking her shoulder.

"Och, there, slugabed, 'tis late. Were ye dreaming o' your bridegroom wi' that daft wee smile on your face?"

"Of Stephen," whispered Celia, sick with loss.

Magdalen nodded. "That's apt," she said, "sence 'tis his day."

This was St. Stephen's feast day—so also *her* Stephen's name day. . . .

"Hasten," cried Magdalen. "We'll be late, an' ye knaw that annoys Faither, and there's much ta do fur your weddin'."

"I can't wed Leonard," said Celia flatly, her eyes like ice.

"Whish, hinny!" Magdalen pulled Celia off the bed. "Wake oop!" Celia allowed herself to be propelled down to the chapel, but her long apathy had vanished. She would not marry Leonard. As fire burned and snow was cold, she *could* not wed him.

She glanced at the Baron as he and his lady followed the Mass with brisk devotion. Flat refusal, she knew, would do no good. The Dacres were kindly, but the Baron never altered his decisions. Magdalen had laughed about one Dacre marriage, where the bride had been trussed up, then carried screaming to the altar and jabbed with a dirk until she panted out the vows.

So what to do? Feign illness? Deception clever enough to fool Magdalen or Ursula was beyond her. If she told them she was with child? No, they wouldn't believe that either. Blessed Mother, what *can* I do? The chapel walls closed around her like a tomb.

"Coom, lass," said Magdalen, nudging her. "Jesu!" she added sharply. "Ye're white an' wambly as a lamb newborn! Coom, ye need to break your fast," and she conveyed Celia into the Hall.

Ursula was already there with Lady Dacre, sorting out favours to be bestowed on the wedding guests. "Celia's wedding'll be like a dotter's," Lady Dacre had said, and had raided her coffers of bows and trinkets she'd been storing against Maggie's marriage. "We'll send to London fur more when your time cooms," she said, smiling at Magdalen as the girls joined them.

"I suppose none of the Nevilles'll come," Ursula said. Certain that the Dacre generosity must overwhelm Celia with the grateful rejoicing she herself felt, she did not see the look on Celia's face.

"Only Tom's puir wife, Bess," Lady Dacre said, sighing. "He's gan ta fetch her fra' Dacre Castle. I hope there'll be na trooble."

The Lady Elizabeth Dacre—"Bluidy Bess" as they called her from her habit of sucking blood and marking her breast with a bloody cross—was a Neville, and as mad as her brother, the Earl of Westmorland, imprisoned for trying to murder his father and wife. When Lady Bess's bad fits came upon her, she was sent, with her devoted old nurse, blind Janet, attending her, the thirty miles from Naworth to Dacre Castle. That she should now be brought to Naworth to honour Celia's wedding added to Ursula's happiness. Celia, however, saw the news as yet another nail in her coffin lid.

By twilight of that day Celia's desperation was very great. She slipped out to the courtyard and, hopeless, crouched against the wall. A fine powdery snow began to fall, but she paid no attention. There was bustle in the kitchens, she heard snatches of laughter and the squeals of the bagpipes. Jock the piper was practising for her wedding. Blessed Virgin help me. She prayed with all the force of her despair. Time passed and still she did not move, and her golden hair whitened with snow. She did not raise her head when the gates swung in and a party of horsemen came through. She only dimly heard voices. "What's that?" "Why 'tis a lass!"

Looking up then, Celia thought there had been a miracle. That an angel had come down from heaven to comfort her. A tall whitish figure stood beside her and spoke in a low sweet voice. "What troubles you, puir maiden?"

Celia gave a shaking sigh and reached out her hands towards the figure. "Help me," she whispered. A hand took hers, but its touch startled her—so clammy cold. She saw then that the hand was encased in a drenched velvet glove.

Sir Thomas, having also dismounted, came peering. "Why, 'tis little Celia Bohun!" he cried. "Bess, 'tis Leonard's bride!"

"Ah," said Lady Bess, "sma' wonder she shivers an' hides."

"Coom inside, Bess, lass, all o' ye!" Thomas waved his arm to the servants who had accompanied him from Dacre.

Pine logs crackled in the Hall, and the Baron and his wife gave Thomas and Bess a hearty welcome, smacking kisses on their daughter-in-law's cold cheeks, determined to think her better, relieved that there was no strange look in her large dark eyes.

"Eh, there, Tom," grunted the Baron, "I vow Lady Bess'll gi'e ye a son yet; ye'll tak' a go at it this night, won't ye, lad?"

"Aye," answered Tom. Not for worlds would he have admitted that the thought of bedding his wife gave him gooseflesh. "She's a'reet. Janet says she's drunk no bluid the past month." And indeed, despite the coarse white robe she insisted on wearing, Bess looked again like the lovely Neville bride he had been so glad to win. "A wedding," he said to his father, "will gladden the lot o' us. Where's Leonard?"

"Handlin' some complaint o' my crofters. He'll be coomin' in."

"We found his lass huddled i' the courtyard. Na doot they've had a lover's tiff." Both men looked at Celia, now sitting quietly by Magdalen. "A bonny beauty," said Tom appreciatively.

Celia went to bed that night hopeless, and again she dreamed, this time of Master Julian. It *was* the Italian doctor, but changed. His face had become clean-shaven and lean, and his brown eyes, intense and pleading, were sending a beam of light into her brain. "Celia!" Something he urgently wanted her to do, something she could not do. She shut her eyes tighter against the command. Another voice said, "I think there was a quiver . . ." and she heard a strange roar of honking, hooting—noises she did not recognize. She sat up in bed, trembling, waking Magdalen.

"Maggie, I'd a dream, it was so real. Master Julian, the doctor who tried to see King Edward. . . . He was trying to help me. . . ."

"Havers!" Magdalen pulled up the blankets. "Mun ye waken me fur sech bletherin'?" She turned over and slept.

As Celia lay staring up at the blackened beams, the dream's reality faded. But when day dawned she felt strangely purged from desperation. She knew that the wedding would not take place.

ON THE MORNING of December 28 this certainty was confirmed. It had been a boisterous night of whistling wind and driving hail. Nobody but blind Janet heard the commotion in the bedchamber where Thomas slept with Lady Bess. When Janet managed to arouse the Dacres, it was almost too late to save Thomas. And Bess was dead in a pool of her own blood. She had fumbled her attack on her husband, but the knife which she had plunged into her own breast had pierced straight to her heart.

Celia and Magdalen learned of the tragedy when, in the Hall, they met young George Dacre. He was blanched; there was sweat on his forehead. "It's Bess," he said. "She's dead. Tom near so, but our mother says he'll do. Bess turned Tom's dirk on 'em both. 'Tis sick'ning." He glanced at Celia. "There'll be na wedding the morrow, m'lass! Funeral instead."

"Yes," said Celia. "Oh, poor, poor thing."

Magdalen gave a sob and threw her arms around Celia. Celia wept with her, but her truly pitying sorrow was tinged by gratitude. Awful as the tragedy was, it had been her release. And Bess, so gently asking in the courtyard—"What troubles you, puir maiden?" —was, after all, the helping angel Celia had mistaken her for.

Chapter 5

At the beginning of June, 1553, Celia and Ursula, with a yeoman sent by Lord Dacre to accompany them, set out for Cowdray, unsure of their welcome. Ursula had written twice to Sir Anthony, but no answer came. There was such fearful unrest on the border that spring that the old baron sent his household to the greater safety of Dacre Castle. Provisions grew short, and so did tempers. Though the Dacres were too kind to say so, it was obvious that the southerners were a nuisance. Ursula made up her mind to leave.

Magdalen and Celia kissed good-bye outside the great postern. "Matters didna turn oot as we hoped, hinny," said Magdalen. "Na doot God's will—I'll send ye a prayer noo an' agen."

"Farewell, Maggie dear," whispered Celia, sighing, yet glad that the past months of sorrow and strain were over.

By the time the travellers reached London, the hedgerows were dappled with wild roses, and Celia had begun to laugh again. They went straight to the priory of St. Mary Overie, where they expected to lodge. But the town house was shuttered and barred, the cloister filled with rubbish.

Ursula had no money left. She had been sure of finding the caretaker-monk, at least.

She sent the Dacre yeoman out in search of a neighbour.

"I found one scared old woman," he reported. "Says the old monk's dead—and Sir Anthony's not been here at all."

Ursula frowned, then her face cleared. "Master Julian! He'll help us! They'll know at St. Thomas's Hospital where he lives."

As the weary horses plodded towards the hospital's dingy pile, Celia suddenly gave a happy cry; there was Julian, just going in the door. He gave a grunt of astonishment as he recognized the women.

"*Mirabile!* Where did *you* drop from?" He frowned.

Ursula and Celia explained their plight.

"Then you know nothing of the news." He glanced over his shoulder nervously. "Can't talk here—you've no money at *all*?"

Ursula shook her head, humiliated by Julian's gruffness.

"I can lend you a few pence to get you to Cowdray," he said coldly. "You don't know of the marriage? The King's condition?"

They shook their heads, staring at him.

Julian examined the Cumberland yeoman. "You can water the horses yonder," he said, and shoved the two women into the hospital hall. "Now listen. A fortnight ago, on May twenty-first, the Duke of Northumberland married off his fourth son, Guilford

Dudley, to Lady Jane Grey, Edward's half-cousin. The King has altered his will, declaring Lady Jane his successor. Most have signed the devise for the succession. Northumberland commanded Anthony Browne to sign, but Sir Anthony sent word that he could not leave Cowdray. King Edward is said to be furious. He has been ill, and *I've* at last been summoned." Julian's eyes shone with a sudden gleam of trimph. "John Cheke—Sir John now—has prevailed on His Majesty to see me. I go to Greenwich tomorrow. I'll cure him yet!"

"I'm sure you will," said Ursula slowly. "But if Edward *should* die, the crown now goes to Lady Jane Grey . . . and thus, in effect, to her father-in-law? What of the Princesses?"

"The Lady Mary is a Catholic, the Lady Elizabeth's true religion is uncertain, and either one might marry a foreign prince."

"You approve this monstrous plan!" Ursula rounded on him.

Julian stiffened. "I am a physician, Lady Southwell, I've nothing to do with moral judgments. I shall cure the King and these complications will not arise."

Ursula understood too clearly why he did not want to be seen with those connected to Sir Anthony. "I'm sorry we bothered you," she said. "I can see that you mustn't offend the Duke or the King."

Julian gave her a faintly apologetic smile. "Hasten to Cowdray and, as you wish Sir Anthony well, talk *submission* to him, for he has lost the King's favour." He turned and hurried down the hall.

Celia and Ursula, hurt by Julian's coldness, proceeded to Sussex.

THE PRESENCE chamber at Greenwich was filled with solemn-faced courtiers when Julian was ushered in. John Cheke led him to the sickroom.

"His Grace is worse," he said. "There *was* improvement last month when the Duke brought in a midwife who gave him secret potions, but now he vomits incessantly."

Julian had faith in himself and felt a great surge of hope, seeing himself triumphant and secure at last. He nodded, and followed Cheke into the King's room. Edward lay flaccid, his face on the hand of his friend, Sir Henry Sidney, his harsh breathing filling the room. His eyes were glazed, the lids lashless, the chicken-claw hands had lost their nails. The boy's belly was greatly swollen and his bloated face was a patchy bronze. The stench was so unpleasant that even Julian faltered.

"He's been poisoned," Julian cried furiously.

"*Poisoned!*" Cheke gasped. "You're mad. Wickedly mad."

But Sidney's eyes filled with tears. He had suspected this for some days.

"What kind is it?" He formed the question soundlessly.

"Arsenicum," Julian answered curtly. He had seen arsenic poisoning under the Medicis. Edward's condition was unmistakable. That midwife's magic potions had given the lad new vigour for a month—just long enough for him to disinherit his sisters.

"What you said"—Cheke jerked at Julian's sleeve—"must *never* be mentioned—'tis too monstrous."

"I can make him more comfortable," said Julian tonelessly. "Fetch hot bricks, well padded." He held a vial to the boy's blue lips.

Suddenly Edward raised on his elbow and his eyes lit on Julian. "That spy!" he cried, jumping half out of bed. "He's a foreigner—a papist! What does he *here*! Guard!" A convulsion seized him.

Julian withdrew in haste, nor looked behind him as he left. He rode slowly back to town along the riverbank.

His situation was far worse than it had ever been. Cheke would never forget the King's shocked cry. Nor would Northumberland, who would certainly hear of it. When Edward dies, Julian thought, I'll be in grave danger. I am so now. I must escape. To Italy. But how? There was no money to bribe a passage to France. All the ports were guarded; everyone knew Northumberland was preparing for a crisis. Yet, perhaps, some fishing smack out of Norfolk? Among the Duke's own fishermen there'd been a boy whose arm he'd saved from amputation. The boy had come from Yarmouth. If I can find him. . . .

Julian acted rapidly. He went to his lodgings and changed to an old jersey doublet, leather breeches and felt hat. He cut his robes off at the knee, to serve as a cloak. And he shaved his beard. Even his own eyes could see how much younger he looked. He rather liked the transformation. He let himself out at the back door just

as men in the Duke's livery knocked at the front. In a quarter of an hour he had quitted London and was on his way to find the fisher-boy of Yarmouth.

URSULA AND CELIA arrived in Cowdray on the day after Julian started his flight. As they passed through Easebourne, they saw that Cowdray's meadow was dotted with booths and coloured pavilions.

"'Tis festival time!" Ursula cried gladly. Every June the lord of Cowdray had held a midsummer fair for Midhurst. The gay scene at once raised the spirits of the voyagers from Cumberland.

"Why, here comes Mabel," said Celia, as they turned up the avenue of great oaks towards the castle.

Anthony's young sister was very elegant in her mauve satin riding suit, but her round face looked gloomy. She reined in her palfrey. "God's greeting," she cried. "Here's a wonder! We thought you settled forever in the north!"

"I—I hope we're welcome," said Ursula hesitantly.

"Oh, to be sure, but Cowdray's doleful nowadays. Anthony'll hardly speak, and Jane's ill—she's with *child* again."

"Brother Stephen is well?" Celia asked in a casual tone.

"Aye," Mabel shrugged. "His penances are overstrict. I wish we had a merry house priest like the Arundels'." She sighed. "Anthony *promised* we'd go to London once Jane's delivered, but lately he won't talk about it."

They entered the courtyard, and the steward came hurrying out. Sir Anthony, he said, might be found in his study. He did not bother to show them upstairs, so Ursula led the way.

She knocked on Anthony's door more loudly than she meant to because her heart was sinking. They could hear an exclamation and the scraping of a chair. The cabinet door was flung open by Stephen. They saw him flush. "*B-Benedicite*—" he stammered, looking at Celia with a startled expression.

The girl, suddenly calm, sketched a small mocking curtsy and raised her chin.

"Welladay!" cried Anthony, peering around his chaplain. "'Tis my Lady Ursula, *and* the fair little niece. A very paragon of beauty, with northern roses in the cheeks. Come in, come in!"

Anthony was cloaking displeasure at the interruption, as well as the fact that he had forgotten the girl's name. "We thought we'd lost you to the Dacres."

Ursula shook her head. "I wrote to you twice, explaining." She smiled anxiously. "We won't be a trouble to you."

Anthony was touched. Impulsively he kissed Ursula on the cheek. "My dear lady, this was your home before it was mine. I only fear you'd be safer in the north. From day to day I expect to be hauled off to the Tower. And have Cowdray confiscated."

Ursula gasped. "They couldn't do *that*!" she cried.

Anthony pointed to an open letter from which two red seals depended. "That is the tenor of this missive. The King has come to hate me since I would not sign for the new succession."

Ursula stared appalled at Anthony. "They don't accuse you of *treason*!"

"Not quite—not yet." A muscle twitched beside Anthony's eye.

"Courage, my friend," Stephen said, resting his hand on his patron's crimson velvet shoulder. "Our Blessed Lady will protect you, you've stood up for both divine and earthly justice!"

"Ah, Stephen," said Anthony warmly, "*your* faith is a comfort!"

The two men exchanged affectionate looks, and Ursula thought how wrong she had been about Stephen. I need never have insisted on that Cumberland trip. "May I come to confession tonight, Brother?" she asked. "I'm in sore need."

Anthony wondered what Lady Ursula could possibly have on her conscience. But the girl—*Celia*, that was her name—tempting as a peach, *she* might have a thing or two!

"How old are you now, Celia?" he asked.

"I was fifteen, sir, on St. Anthony's Day. We were nigh Oxford then. There was a great thunderstorm, my gelding cast a shoe, and a spider ran across my arm. It seemed ill-omened, alack!"

Anthony laughed, now remembering her amusing pertness. He turned to Ursula. "I'm glad you're come, for my Lady Jane's with child and most unwell. She weeps incessantly."

"To be sure I'll help!" cried Ursula, immensely relieved to be needed. "And Celia—I'll find ways to make her useful."

Anthony turned back to the threatening letter on his writing table. It must be answered—the royal messenger was waiting. "We'll send a copy to that Cranmer," he said to Stephen. His lip curled. "My Lord Archbishop Cranmer—a good Catholic once. He signed the old king's will, which fixed the succession, and now signs Edward's which changes it." Anthony banged his fist on the table. "What's to be expected from a *married* priest!"

"Very little, sir," said Stephen calmly. "He is, to be sure, *not* married in God's eyes, and thus a fornicator."

Fornicator, Celia thought, what an ugly word. And with what contempt Brother Stephen speaks it. She looked at the young man's mouth—full, red, flexible—impossible to believe she had kissed it—or that for a second he had certainly responded.

"Shall I go to Lady Jane?" asked Ursula tentatively.

"Aye, pray do." Anthony gave her his warm smile. "And Celia'll companion Mabel, who wanders about like a lost pup."

Stephen now stared at Celia like a reproving elder. "Celia may also repair the altar cloths and the chasubles."

"Excellent!" cried Anthony, though startled by the young monk's tone. And the look in the girl's beautiful eyes—was it resentment? At this moment, when Ursula totally relinquished the notion that there had ever been anything between Stephen and Celia, the idea first occurred to Anthony.

"I'm not very skilled wi' the needle," Celia said slowly.

Stephen had not finished. "Also," he went on, "I think it expedient for Celia to return daily to the Spread Eagle."

"Holy Saint Mary," Celia cried with a tremble of anger. "Have *you* perchance been appointed to direct my future?"

Anthony chuckled, for the girl looked rather like an outraged golden kitten, but he was puzzled. "Come now, Brother Stephen—"

"Celia," said Stephen, speaking as though she weren't there, "has intelligence. She can keep her ears open—"

"Oh-h," cried the girl, "you mean a kind of spy?"

Stephen smiled. "London carters, sheep traders, sailors going to their ships—they all blab of much *we* never hear."

Anthony nodded as he saw the monk's idea. He was under what amounted to house arrest. He had no access to news. His trusted servant, Wat Farrier, was lodged near the palace in Greenwich with instructions for the moment he heard that the King had died.

"Will you try Brother Stephen's plan, Celia?" Anthony said.

"Need ye ask," cried the girl, her eyes sparkling. "I'd do anything for you and Cowdray, and 'tis like a game!"

"I wish it were," said Anthony.

THE NEXT THREE WEEKS at Cowdray passed in mounting tension. Celia walked daily into Midhurst. Each dusk she reported privately to Sir Anthony, sorry that there was so little to tell.

On St. John's Eve the fair closed with the traditional bonfire. Anthony, Ursula, Celia and Mabel stood a little apart. "'Tis the finest we've ever had," said Anthony. And no doubt the last, he thought. He drew himself up as two horsemen came trotting across the meadow. One, the meagre little squire of nearby Stedham, and the other, John Hoby, the King's steward at Petworth, both vociferous Protestants, and both, he knew, enemies.

"Good evening," said Anthony. "You've come to our bonfire?"

"I see ye celebrate the vigil of St. John," said Hoby, dismounting, and doffing his hat.

Anthony answered with sarcastic caution. "How can you think so, Master Hoby, since saints are forbidden in England. The bonfire is for Midsummer Eve. That's not prohibited yet, I believe?"

Hoby grunted. "Ye jest, Sir Anthony?" He stared around. All these yokels enjoying Sir Anthony's bounty were attached to Cowdray and would—most of them—be loyal; but there weren't over a hundred fighting men in the lot. Hoby's instructions were to watch and wait until word came to strike. His was to be the honour of arresting Sir Anthony for treason, but clear evidence of papistry might hurry the matter and greatly add to his acclaim.

"I regret, sir," he boomed above the roaring of the fire and the drunken shouts of the merrymakers, "that ye have shown so little meekness of spirit to the request of the King's Grace."

Anthony bowed, wondering if the men at Petworth had broken the seal of the letter he had sent by the King's messenger. "My wife's condition prevents me from leaving Cowdray."

Hoby found something attractive about this stubborn man. His plight was hopeless. You couldn't help feel a pang of sympathy.

The Browne men were none of your mealymouthed nobles—their stock three generations ago had been as plebeian as his own.

Hoby put his hand on Anthony's arm. "Ye know there's trouble brewing, sir, ye might go to Cornwall, but don't make a try for the Continent. Not the meanest fishing tub'll get by unsearched."

"My dear Master Hoby, are you suggesting that I bolt? I know all the approaches to Cowdray are guarded."

Hoby spoke softly. "If ye went Stedham-way tomorrow night mayhap you'd not be noticed."

"Planning an ambush? Or are you really prepared to wink at my escape?"

"I'm giving ye the chance," Hoby muttered.

"*Why?* You loathe the Faith, you're the Duke's man."

"I mislike needless bloodshed, sir, or frightening women."

"By the Mass," Anthony breathed. He saw that Hoby was sincere, and thereby how great must be his own danger if such a man were moved to pity. "I thank you, Master Hoby," he said quietly. "But I'll bide in my own home and take what God sends me. Will you join me in a flagon?"

"Nay." Hoby regretted his impulse the instant he heard "by the Mass", that sickening papist oath. "We'll not meet again in amity, sir." He mounted his horse and called to the squire.

As they rode off, Anthony scowled towards the fair, where the last kegs of ale and savoury pies were being consumed. He turned suddenly to Ursula. "Is this as it was in your father's time, lady? Does it remind you of your girlhood?"

She heard the appeal and smiled at the boy that lived still in this big handsome man. "'Tis much more lavish, sir."

He sighed. "Ah, those were simpler, happier days. . . ."

"The Lady Jane seems better, sir," Ursula said. "D'ye know, I believe there're two babes i' her womb!"

Anthony jumped. "Holy Saint Mary! *Twins?* How wondrous! Ah, lady, I thank you!" He bent quickly and kissed her.

Ursula pressed his hand. "I wish Master Julian were here. . . ."

"Surely he wouldn't concern himself with midwifery?"

"He knows many potions to relieve pain, and has a tender heart. I wonder if he *has* cured His Majesty."

"We must pray so," said Anthony. But whether or not the King recovered, with the new succession Anthony's personal plight would continue. May God blast Northumberland, he thought.

Chapter 6

On Thursday, July 6, 1553, at dusk, King Edward died in Henry Sidney's arms. He died after saying quite clearly, "Lord have mercy upon me—take my spirit." The royal physician, Dr. Owen, bent over the hideously decayed body. "At last, poor royal youth."

"Stay with him," said Henry, tears running down his cheeks. "I must tell the Duke, who wants the utmost *secrecy* at present."

"I'd forgot you were the Duke's son-in-law. I mislike this hole-and-corner death. No last rites, nor even prayers."

Henry flushed. He started to reply when, with a tremendous thunderclap, lightning flared into the death chamber.

"'Tis a warning, Henry Sidney!" cried the doctor. "Tell His Grace to heed it!"

"'Tis an ordinary storm." But Henry's voice was trembling.

Wat Farrier knew of the King's death only ten minutes after the Duke heard of it. Wat was outside the palace's back kitchen when Betsy, a laundrymaid whose favour he had been cultivating, came scurrying down from the royal apartments with a hamper of filthy bed linen. "He's gone," she whispered as she dumped the linen into a vat. "I heard 'em say so."

"Ah-h," Wat breathed. "Ye certain, m'dear?" She nodded, and Wat gave her a warm kiss. "Thankee, lass."

Within the hour Wat was banging on the goldsmith's door in Lombard Street. "'Tis time!" he shouted through the crack which finally opened enough to admit him. "Tom must make haste! They sent her a summons yesterday laying a subtle trap. She's probably left Hunsdon, he may meet her on the London road. He must put it in her *own* hand. Has 'e the nerve?"

"He's my grandson," snapped the goldsmith, opening a small ebony box to show Wat the buck-crest ring still safely in it, before he hobbled out of the room. Within minutes hoofbeats were pounding on the cobblestones. The old man returned. "I'll thank ye to leave now," he said. "If aught goes wrong, I've ne'er set eye on ye."

"Ye'll be glad enow fur the reward if all goes well," Wat snorted. But he quitted the shop and went back to a wharfside inn in Greenwich to await developments.

He had three days to wait before the news rocked London. King Edward was dead. Jane Grey Dudley was proclaimed Queen of England. Cries of "Long live Queen Jane!" burst from Northumberland's archers, carefully planted among the crowds. Shocked protests were suppressed by force. The Londoners were dazed. Even Protestants were appalled. Why had Jane, a chit of sixteen, descended from the daughter of Henry VII, been given precedence over Edward's *sisters*, the Lady Mary, even the Lady Elizabeth, both of King Harry's own get? Placards all over London announced that because Mary was a papist and half-Spanish, King Edward had set aside her claim by will.

For four more days Wat waited around in Greenwich, loosening tongues with ale, until at last he was rewarded with some real news. A fishing smack from Yarmouth arrived with a load of herring for the palace. Her master could not, after a pint or two, contain his excitement. The Princess Mary was at Framlingham Castle! East Anglians of all degree were rallying round her. The fisherman grinned. "They say she was warned of a trap. Northumberland's men were arter her. But she got clear an' hightailed it north—brave as a lion, like her dad. They're solid for her up Yarmouth way."

"God bless her," said Wat. "I'm off to join her." He looked around defiantly, aware that as matters stood his assertion was treason.

But he was cheered. "We'll join ye!" The master nodded. "If we must be ruled by a queen, better the roightful one!"

Wat had a fleeting thought for Sir Anthony at Cowdray, but there was nothing yet for him to do. So with eleven companions, Wat headed north instead of south. All along the way they found ferment. Church bells pealed for Queen Jane one hour and Queen Mary the next. They heard that the Duke was marching to "fetch in Lady Mary, captive or dead", burning and pillaging and rousing angry opposition as he went. And only an hour after Wat's party joined the hordes outside Framlingham Castle, a royal herald galloped among them.

"*London's* proclaimed Queen Mary! Long may she reign!" he yelled, then blew a great blast on his trumpet.

The crowd gave a collective gasp.

A rich squire, one of Mary's staunch supporters, came running from inside the fortress. "Did I hear aright? Has the *council* proclaimed Queen Mary in London?"

"Aye, sir. An' the order's out for Northumberland's arrest."

"Jesu!" And then the crowd fell suddenly silent, riveted by the appearance on the drawbridge of a small pale woman in violet velvet, riding a white palfrey.

"Long live our good Queen Mary!" the herald shouted as all the men uncovered. "Defender of the Faith!"

Her pinched face brightened. She pulled up her jewelled crucifix and kissed it. "A miracle!" she cried in her deep voice. "By our Blessed Lord and His saints. And I thank you, too, all my loyal followers."

There was riotous rejoicing that night outside the castle. Wat, ever attracted by the sea, joined a group of sailors. One of the most fascinating tellers of tales was a bosun called Jack Tate, who had set forth on a search for a northeast passage to India. But he only got as far as Amsterdam when he took sick, and the crew, fearing it was plague, dumped him. His eyes were still blood-red, he had purple patches on his face and an ugly running sore by his mouth.

"I don't know why I don't 'eal," Tate said ruefully. "I wonder would our new Queen touch it fur me?"

"N'doubt," said Wat, noticing, as he spoke, a shabbily dressed man staring at Jack Tate. "Sit down," said Wat, "don't loom o'er us like that. Ye want to hear about Jack's venture?"

"*Da vero*," the man said. "I was thinking I could cure him. I am a physician—Julian Ridolfi—and aren't you, my good man, master of the horse for Sir Anthony Browne at Cowdray?"

"Aye," Wat admitted after the moment it took him to realize that there was no more need for secrecy. "By God, and are *ye* the foreign longbeard wot healed our Brother Stephen o' rat bite? Ye've come down i' the world, old cock!"

"Certain changes became imperative if I were to be a stowaway to the Continent—now not necessary." He smiled suddenly.

"How would ye heal me?" Jack asked curiously.

"Your disease is called scurvy," said Julian. "I'd have you drink milk and new-pressed cider, eat raw, chopped greens—"

"Faugh!" cried Jack. "Me belly heaves at the thought."

"Then you will die before your time," said Julian. He saw how unlikely the sailor was to follow his advice, and he turned back to Wat. "You'll be off to Cowdray now?"

Wat sighed. "Aye, sir—and wot'll *you* do, Doctor?"

"Hitch my wagon to the new star," answered Julian. He jerked his head towards the castle. "I hear they've no physician."

"They'll never believe *ye're* one, lookin' like that. Wait though, can ye weasel your way in to Sir Thomas Wharton? He's the Queen's steward and would know about Sir Anthony's buck-crest ring that was sent to warn 'er. Tell 'em ye was Sir Anthony's leech. Here's me own buck emblem to prove it."

"*Santa Maria!*" Julian cried gratefully. He pressed Wat's hand and strode off towards the drawbridge.

Wat, filled with the glow of one good deed, wrapped his cloak around him and went to sleep.

ON JULY 20 Cowdray and its inhabitants reached the depths of despair. Jane Grey Dudley was Queen of England. It was done; the incredible infamy which would certainly ruin Anthony.

"At least the suspense is over," said Anthony. "Hoby's men will come for me any time now, and I'll not resist." Even Celia saw how useless resistance would be. Cowdray was a lovely glass-traceried manor house, not a fortress. And though Anthony was generally liked, Midhurst could not be counted on to help its feudal lord as it would have in the old days.

At nine o'clock of that morning Celia hurried miserably to Midhurst. Since breakfast the Lady Jane had been screaming. Screams that terrified Celia, as did Ursula's anxious face.

"Go for Goody Pearson, child. She delivered the Mayor's lady.

She can help the Lady Jane. And hasten!" cried Ursula. "I've sent for Brother Stephen. Cut o'er Tan's Hill, and if ye meet him, tell him *hurry*!"

Celia sped off. She had been avoiding St. Ann's Hill, but today that was unimportant. She met Stephen at the footbridge over the Rother. "Is't bad?" he asked.

"Aye," she said with a half-sob, "frightful, horrible screams." She noted that he held the box containing materials for the last rites. She crossed herself, while her face crumpled.

Like an arrow shafted to his heart, Stephen suddenly knew what the girl was feeling. He raised her chin and kissed her on the forehead. "Have faith, my child!" he whispered in a voice so tender that she stood gulping as he ran towards Cowdray. Then she streaked on into Midhurst.

She was stopped by a throng in the marketplace. She was too dazed to grasp what was happening.

"What's this!" she said aloud. "'Tis not market day," and she tried to shove between two stocky leathern shoulders.

The man on the right looked down at her. "Hold still, pretty one, or ye'll be crushed."

Then she saw what they were all staring at. "*Another* proclamation!" she cried angrily. "A pox on Queen Jane! *Lady* Jane is dying at Cowdray."

"Listen!" hissed the man, and shook her.

The herald put the trumpet to his lips and blew a stave, then his voice boomed, "The Lady Mary Tudor is hereby and henceforth proclaimed Queen of England, Ireland and France." He crossed himself. "*In nomine Patris, et Filii, et Spiritus Sancti.*"

For an instant the crowd was so startled by this public exhibition of the forbidden words and gesture that they scarcely took in the reason for them. The mayor raised the first voice. "Long live Queen Mary!" The crowd roared, "Long may she reign!"

What'll this mean to *us*? Celia thought, and then in sudden panic broke loose from the crowd.

The midwife's cottage was bolted and empty. Disconsolate, Celia trudged back to Cowdray. By the porter's lodge she met Sir Anthony, his fists clenched, his ruff torn off, his white lawn shirt open across his hairy chest like any ploughman. "Where have you been, you little jade?" he shouted.

"I went to Midhurst for the midwife. I couldn't find her."

"Nor'll need to." He drew a ragged breath. "My wife is dead."

Celia's arms raised instinctively to comfort him, but he was as forbidding as stone. "The babe . . . ?" she whispered.

Anthony made an angry sound. "They'll never live. Two o' them, shapeless as misbegotten rats—Why are the bells pealing like that in Midhurst?" he cried. "They should be tolling for my lady's passing. She was only twenty."

"The bells, sir," Celia said gently, "are being rung for the Lady Mary's Grace. She is now Queen of England!"

Anthony started. "Mary is Queen . . . ? *Mary?*"

"Yes, sir. I heard the proclamation."

"Holy Blessed Virgin!" Anthony quivered, then burst into wild hysterical laughter. Celia put her hand on his arm. He stopped laughing and allowed her to lead him into the Hall, where his retainers were silently gathered.

THREE DAYS later it seemed that the twins would live. Stephen had christened them Anthony and Mary just before he administered the last rites to Lady Jane. Ursula had found a wet nurse, and after Anthony's heirs finally accepted her breasts, they began to look more like babies. Anthony, by then, had little time for wonder that his heirs lived, nor even to grieve for Jane, so immediate was the change in his fortunes.

While Lady Jane still lay in state in the family chapel, Wat came galloping home. His dismay upon seeing that the Browne standard flew at half-staff was soon mitigated.

"God rest her," Wat said, when the porter explained. He ran on into the great house and encountered Stephen emerging from the chapel. "Greetings, Brother! Oh, 'tis sad indeed, but ye must be gladsome ye can gi'e her a true showy funeral right i' our Midhurst Church."

Stephen looked startled. He had lived all his days in a climate of persecution and secrecy. "Are you *sure*, Wat, that the Princess Mary will bring back the true religion? And she's not crowned yet."

"Rest easy," said Wat. "Country's behind 'er. Ye should see—crucifixes back on the altars, vestments out. And Northumberland fast in the Tower."

Wat hurried on, while Stephen made his way to St. Ann's Hill.

During the months of furtive anxiety he had hidden his candlesticks, altar cloth and silver-gilt crucifix in a locked coffer. He had also hidden his painting of the Virgin and the purple veil he had covered her with on the evening of Celia's visit. All that seemed a century ago. The tumult, the shameful longings were past.

Joyfully, he replaced the altar furnishings and the precious painting, and kneeling on the chapel's leafy ground, addressed her with abounding love. It was there he still was when he heard the angelus ring out from the village church. *The angelus!* He sprang up from his knees. I can go to the church for vespers! I'm free to go into town! He pulled up his cowl and leaped over the ruined wall.

As Stephen walked into the church, the congregation turned and the vicar stammered in mid-prayer. The Black Monk's appearance confirmed the changes that were being rumoured.

Most of the town of Midhurst, and all of Cowdray, eagerly returned to the comfort of the old religion. Traffic between castle and town grew as free as it had once been, and everyone basked in Sir Anthony's summons to join the Queen's triumphal entrance to London. Sir Anthony deserved special favour from Her Majesty, that was clear. Wat thrilled the Spread Eagle pot room nightly with the story of how the buck-crest ring had saved the Queen's life.

In the castle Mabel had ceased pouting now that she was to have her visit to London, enhanced by the delicious prospect of the coronation. Celia, too, was to go. And Brother Stephen would accompany the Cowdray party as chaplain. Blessed Mary, but life is good, Celia thought. One has only to wait.

Chapter 7

Sir Anthony Browne arrived at Southwark with his family and some thirty retainers on September 28, the day on which Mary moved from Whitehall Palace to the Tower, from whence English monarchs proceeded to Westminster Abbey for coronation.

Anthony's house, the old priory of St. Mary Overie, had been transformed. A small army of plasterers and labourers had refurbished all the rooms, and new, elaborately carved furniture had been made by a master craftsman.

Anthony was pleased by his womenfolk's delighted cries, but he had been summoned to Whitehall and dared not tarry.

"Come wi' me, Stephen," said Anthony. "I need your brains—there's a skein of plots to be unravelled."

Celia heard this request. Stephen, *don't* go! she thought. She knew the feeling of fear was unreasonable.

"Anthony," Mabel cried, "won't you be seeing Lord Gerald Fitzgerald? Tell him I've made a purse for him." Her stepmother's brother was the only man who had ever kissed her.

"Oh-h?" said Anthony. He had barely noted some flirtation between Mabel and the Irish youth. "I'll certainly *not* see Fitzgerald. He's cooked his goose along wi' Clinton and my precious stepmother. He signed for Lady Jane Grey, y'know. I'll find you a *worthy* husband," he added impatiently, "but it can't be tomorrow. Come along, Stephen!"

Stephen went. Celia leaned out the window to watch. His cowl slipped back and the sun brought auburn lights to his thick dark hair, the tilt of his head almost hiding the tonsure. He looked as handsome and arrogant as his master, and she heard his rare laugh ring out. She stared down with longing. Stephen did not look up.

TWO DAYS LATER Wat Farrier guided Ursula with Celia and Mabel to places reserved for them on one of the wooden stages erected along Mary's route from the Tower. Anthony had picked an excellent site for his womenfolk, just below a triumphal arch constructed from thousands of massed lilies, roses and heliotrope topped by a fifteen-foot figure of an angel with a trumpet. The flowers' perfume was enchanting and did much to offset the smells of massed humanity. Though they had long to wait, Celia was so bedazzled that time did not drag for her, but the others were not so happy. The hard bench hurt Ursula's skinny rump, and Mabel's fashionable steel corset was uncomfortably tight. And then a wind sprang up, swirling dust, and Ursula began to cough.

"You look overgrim, lady, for such a glad occasion," said a voice behind her. Startled, she turned and saw Master Julian.

"Blessed Jesu!" She forgot her discomfort. "What do you *here*?"

He wore new doctoral robes; his foursquare cap was pulled down at a rakish angle to prevent it from blowing off; his grey eyes twinkled; and she thought how well he looked.

"I am here, Lady Southwell," he said, smiling, "because I helped make the mechanism for yonder arch, erected by my fellow Florentines. The angel performs according to plans made by Master Leonardo da Vinci for a Medici pageant. Good day, Celia, and Mistress Mabel," he added as the two girls turned.

Celia's face lit up. Despite the coldness of their last meeting, she admired the doctor. "Oh, sir," she cried, "you joined the Queen's Grace at Framlingham, didn't you? Wat was full of the story."

"At least I no longer am fleeing for my life," Julian said with his sardonic smile, fingering a new gold chain from which hung his jacinth stone. The night Mary left Framlingham for London, she had suffered one of her blinding migraines. Julian, having no remedies with him, had picked some cowslips and mashed them with cow urine. "This will help, Your Grace," he said in his deep, commanding voice. "You will feel well."

Mary's headache indeed vanished, and she gave Julian a gold sovereign, with which he had bought these new robes. Then Mary had forgotten him; but Julian, certain that the future was brightening, had knocked on the door of a Florentine merchant in Lombard Street and asked for lodging until after the coronation. He had repaid his host by helping design the mechanical angel.

Another half hour passed before the vanguard cleared the street, strewing it with fragrant herbs before the mounted esquires came riding up, followed by the exalted clerks of the chancery, the signet, the privy seal and the council, and then the lesser knights—banner and banneret. Celia was the first to pick out Sir Anthony, who turned and waved to them. The judges and justices, the Knights of the Garter, the Queen's household—all filed by. And then, between trumpet flourishes, the peers, two by two. And the lord mayor.

The crowd hushed as Mary's splendid chariot approached, drawn by six white palfreys. Mary was effulgent in blue velvet and silver cloth, furred with ermine. Her head was covered by a gold cap, diamond-and-pearl studded, and so heavy that she constantly had to stiffen her neck. Her small pale face was strained. She seemed older than her thirty-seven years. She has no stamina, Julian thought gloomily. She'll not last long—and then what?

As if in answer to his unphrased question, a crimson velvet chariot followed the Queen's, carrying a girl of twenty, chastely dressed in silver-white, an expression of gentle demureness on her face, her Tudor hair uncovered and blazing. The populace, suddenly magnetized, burst from its awed hush and roared out blessings on the Princess Elizabeth. "Harry's true daughter!" "Look at 'er 'air!" "And English, through and through."

"So the moon pales when the sun comes out," Julian observed.

A hundred paces from the flowery arch, Julian's Florentine host darted out to the Queen's chariot. The Queen looked puzzled, as they could all hear the buzzings of clockwork and the creak of bellows inside the angel. Julian held his breath. The great arms quivered and raised the trumpet. Six deafening blasts of compressed air shrilled through the figure's lips, shouting what might be interpreted as "Ma-ri-a Re-gi-na".

The horses reared and stamped. Mary laughed delightedly—like all the Tudors, she adored boisterous novelties—and from every window the applause thundered.

As Julian helped Ursula and the girls down to the street, a middle-aged couple came up to him. "Ah," said Julian, "these, Lady Southwell, are Squire and Mistress Allen from Kent, and their son, Charles."

"Oh, we met at Cowdray last summer," said Emma Allen in her loud Kentish twang, "when we were there to see my relation, Brother Stephen. Will ye all sup wi' us at the King's Head? We must drink to the Queen's Grace."

What's she after *now*, Julian thought, remembering her assertion at the Spread Eagle: "When I intend a thing, 'tis good as done."

Ursula had started to accept the invitation when Celia interrupted. "My head aches, Aunt. You go. Wat will take me home."

"Oh, sweeting," cried Ursula, "we'll all go back."

"*No*," protested Mabel, angry tears brimming over.

"If you will permit it, Lady Southwell," said Julian, "I'll escort Mistress Mabel and return her at a proper hour."

Ursula sent Julian a warm look of gratitude. He marvelled again at the feeling of protection both Ursula and Celia aroused in him. He again received the impression that he had somehow before met the baleful force of an Emma Allen and had savoured the appeal of the aunt and niece.

BACK AT THE PRIORY in Southwark, Ursula put Celia to bed and made her swallow a mug of heather mead, which brought back a little colour.

"I don't think I'm ill, dear Aunt—I was affrighted by that woman."

Ursula frowned. This sounded feverish. "Mistress *Allen?*"

Celia shuddered. "I saw an adder last year. It had those eyes. There's danger," Celia said flatly, her hand to her throat. "Stifling . . . Master Julian speaks . . . says, 'Celia, come back!'"

A chill ran up Ursula's spine. "I've given you too much mead," she said. "Master Julian is supping at the King's Head."

The girl sighed. She stared imploringly at Ursula. "Must it happen, Mother? Can't we stop it? Don't you see, I *love* Stephen! But I'm so afraid. Make the doctor . . ."

"Holy Blessed Mary." Ursula reached for her rosary. Holding the crucifix, she went to the door. "Wat!" she called. "Wat! Mistress Celia's ill. Get Master Julian."

Wat glanced at the now sleeping girl and thought she looked entirely healthy, but he obeyed. He found Julian at the King's Head, in earnest conversation with a younger man in doctoral robes, and Mabel sitting disconsolately alone. The Allens had joined a more convivial group.

Julian listened to Wat's message. "Bah!" he said. "'Twas a green girl's attack of megrims. Lady Ursula frets overmuch. Now you're here, Wat, take Mistress Mabel home. I've important matters to discuss." His companion was Dr. John Dee, alchemist and astrologer, whom he had met at John Cheke's and who was now propounding some very shrewd ideas on personal advancement.

Wat nodded. "Come along, mistress," he said to Mabel.

On their return to the priory, Lady Ursula turned on Wat. "How *dared* you come back without him? You didn't tell him how ill Celia is. May the Saints punish you!"

Wat lifted one eyebrow and escaped rapidly.

Ursula found herself trembling: How to explain why Master Julian's refusal to come had frightened her into fury? Or the terror Celia's incomprehensible ramblings had provoked, with that reference to Stephen? She called me Mother, Ursula thought, while love gathered itself into a wave. She sat down by the sleeping girl and gently touched her arm. *"Can't we stop it?"* she had said. "Stop *what?*" Ursula whispered. She shook herself, went to her *prie-dieu* and knelt. But no words came. I'm going mad, she thought. Stephen is no threat. It was blasphemous to think so.

MARY was crowned next day, on October 1, by Stephen Gardiner, Bishop of Winchester, since no other loyal Catholic prelate could be found. Cranmer, the Archbishop of Canterbury, had been imprisoned for heresy. Northumberland had been executed.

During this autumn the priory household enjoyed itself. Anthony brought company home nightly from court. Ursula and the two girls savoured a gaiety they had never known. Celia did not remember her strange attack. She bloomed, while discovering the delights of airy dalliance.

Mabel might well have been jealous, except that her stars also turned favourable. On the feast of All Saints, Anthony brought new guests home, among them Gerald Fitzgerald. He had had the brotherly kindness to warn Ursula. "Tell Mabel to wear her best gown and speak softly. Though I doubt Fitzgerald will rise to the lure. If it could be Celia—a thousand pities she's not nobly born."

They both looked at the girl, who was laughing as the Kentish knight, Sir Thomas Wyatt, tried to teach her to play the lute. Then Ursula glanced at Anthony. He was not a nobleman himself.

Perhaps catching Ursula's thought mirrored on her face, Anthony said gravely, "The Queen has promised me a peerage upon the occasion of her marriage. A viscountcy, for which I will select the title of Montagu, in deference to my paternal grandmother. I shall ponder well before I choose the Viscountess Montagu."

The priory's small Hall was jammed that evening for what was ostensibly a revel in honour of the feast day. Anthony had commissioned John Heywood to be master of the revel. A robust man in his fifties, a zealous Catholic and a wit, he had been something of a court jester to the Queen's father, and Anthony had selected him for an experiment this night. They together had most carefully determined on a way to test the wind of opinion as it might be expected to blow on a momentous matter.

Sir Thomas Wyatt remained near Celia as the guests drifted in. He had drunk a great deal of Anthony's best wine, and as he took the lute and began to sing, he tried to squeeze her waist. She merely laughed at him. He was in his thirties and seemed old to her, and she knew he had a wife in Kent. She listened to his compliments happily with one ear and kept one eye on her aunt for the signal which meant "Important guests—get up and curtsy!"

"I know a song for you, cruel maiden," said Wyatt. He began in a loud tenor: "*O Celia, the wanton and fair, hath ne'er the need to despair, she hath used shameless art—*" He broke off with annoyance as Celia moved away.

She was staring at Anthony's chaplain, who had suddenly appeared and pinned on the girl so dark and piercing a gaze it was as though he had never seen her before.

She gave a nervous laugh as Stephen walked up to her. "Celia—the wanton and fair?" he said angrily. "Willing target for Wyatt's adulterous darts? You learn London ways apace."

"You, too, have altered among the great folk, Brother Stephen," cried Celia angrily. "I note your new gold crucifix."

Stephen itched to shake her. He said stiffly, "The Bishop of Winchester gave me this. And has shown me how to present the True Faith in the world."

"No doubt," said Celia. She went over and joined Ursula, who was greeting Gerald Fitzgerald. Mabel, in her rapture at Gerald's presence, looked almost pretty; and Gerald, with his impish grin, seemed glad to see her. "The Fitzgeralds are no longer disgraced, thanks to our gracious Queen," Anthony had told Ursula.

During the elaborate supper Celia was seated next to a stout elderly knight, Sir John Hutchinson from Lincolnshire, who ate greedily. Sir John had discovered the girl on his left. Fresh and innocent as a primrose. He was startled by a flicker of romantic interest such as he had not felt in years.

John Hutchinson, long a widower, had been married to a scraggy little cousin of Lord Clinton's. The connection had abetted his own rugged abilities in building his career as wool merchant, ship owner, and finally Member of Parliament. Protestant convictions like his would be unpopular under the new régime, but it was not in Sir John's nature to disguise them. Nor to consider them very important. The export of Lincolnshire cloth—that was important, and no whims of a meagre middle-aged woman, queen or not, could sway him.

He put down a forkful of roast quail and addressed Celia. "You are related to Sir Anthony?" he asked.

"Nay," she said, taking her eyes away from Stephen, down the table. "I am a Bohun. Cowdray land once belonged to my father's folk, and Sir Anthony gives shelter to my lady aunt and me."

"Aye . . . indeed . . ." Sir John nodded. Pensioners, he thought. Poor child. "Your mother?" he asked softly.

Celia looked up, startled. Nobody ever mentioned her mother. "She was a Londoner," said Celia. "She never told me much." Her brows drew together in dismay. There was so little to remember.

John Hutchinson watched the changing expression on Celia's beautiful face and fell in love, totally, irrevocably. "Your name, darling?" he whispered. "Your Christian name?"

"Celia, sir," she answered with a touch of her natural pertness.

He smiled tenderly and said, "A beautiful name, 'Celia'—and one already dear to me."

She looked at him more attentively. He was clean-shaven, his silvered hair still thick and dark at his forehead. His mouth was broad and well shaped, since he had lost no front teeth. He was dressed in a maroon velvet gown; the ruffles around his thick neck were spotless. His nails were trimmed, and he had a great ruby ring on his thumb. A heavy gold chain ended in a golden sheep—the emblem of his guild—and rested on his substantial paunch. Did my father look like that? Celia wondered. She guessed he could never have exuded this air of assured worth.

As the minstrels finished a madrigal, John Heywood disappeared behind a curtained box, and Anthony looked for a moment at Stephen. Stephen touched his crucifix as invocation, and Anthony nodded slightly, thinking how fortunate he was in his house priest. Vastly useful Stephen had become.

Three loud knocks behind the box silenced the company, and little red velvet draperies drew back to disclose twin golden thrones on a dais. The audience laughed as a small wooden figure moved jerkily across the stage. None of the English had ever seen a puppet show, and it took them several minutes to recognize the marionette as their Queen. The little figure beat its breast at every third step, then clasped its hands in supplication towards the cross painted above the thrones. Suddenly the puppet stiffened and flopped into the right-hand throne.

The curtains fell together and then parted to disclose a canvas sea. On it glided a carved wooden galleon, its square sails each painted with an over-size Spanish coat of arms. The galleon glided back and forth carrying a male figure on the bow, his black sugar-loaf hat decorated with a golden lion. The curtains fell to an uneasy silence.

The curtains parted again, to show the Queen sitting on one of the twin thrones. The galleon moved into view, and the black-hatted figure jumped off and advanced towards the Queen, who flew off the dais and held out her arms. The two figures intertwined, and, touching hands, mounted to the thrones. A large placard then popped up behind them: England's royal arms under a gold *M*, and a *P* over the Spanish crest; the two linked by ribbons and cupids.

Sir Thomas Wyatt jumped to his feet, his sword half-drawn. "Browne, you must be mad!" he cried shrilly.

"Soft, *mon chevalier*," said the French Ambassador, de Noailles.

Henry Sidney was staring grimly up at the rafters. Renard, the ambassador from Spain, was smiling a little. Others were blankly puzzled. A few were looking at Wyatt. Reputedly a superb soldier, he had been threatened by the Inquisition on a sojourn in Spain. He was trembling so hard that his sword rattled in its scabbard.

"The man is Prince Philip o' Spain," he cried. "That Browne

would *dare*—every trueborn Englishman'll fight against becoming Spain's vassal!"

At this moment Sir John, who was wondering how soon he could decently leave, spoke up. "Let one Spaniard knock at my gates an' I'd set the hounds on him. Too many foreigners in England already, takin' bread from the mouths o' honest Englishmen."

The other knights all murmured, "Aye, aye, well said."

"Now that we've seen Master Heywood's little novelty," Anthony announced smoothly, "shall we have a caper?"

Chapter 8

On January 6, 1554, Celia, shivering and coughing, awoke to the sound of sleeting rain and seven bongs from St. Saviour's. Ursula had already risen for early Mass. 'Tis the feast of the Three Kings, Celia thought. Epiphany. Twelfth Night—the end of Christmas—and the beginning of what? Ever since All Saints' Day the weather had been bad, Anthony and Stephen were rarely at home, and one of Mabel's frequent colds had seized both Celia and Ursula in a violent form. Celia lifted her head and found that it still throbbed. She flopped back and shut her eyes. She opened them again as the bed curtains were parted and a chambermaid tendered her a mug of steaming ale.

"Good morrow, miss. Lady Suthell sent me up ter rouse ye."

Celia sighed. "Good morrow. Aye, I must drag myself to Mass."

"Ye needn't, then," said the woman. "God don't *want* ye to!"

It took a moment for Celia to understand this extraordinary statement. Then she looked up. This must be the new chambermaid, a freckle-faced woman with a sweet, rather stern smile.

"You're called Agnes, aren't you?" Celia said.

"Agnes Snoth, widow. I've come from Kent and am now spreading the Gospel according to his Holy Word, an' accordin' ter m'station in life, which be lowly." Her smile deepened.

"You mustn't say such things," said Celia. "That's *heresy!* How did you *get* here, anyway?"

"Oh, I went to Lady Suthell wi' some writin' from Mistress Allen o' Ightham Mote. I was nurse ter Master Charles."

"Mistress *Allen?* But the Allens're true Catholics!"

"I hadn't seen the light m'self then. Master Rogers at Paul's Cross converted me. An' I thank God fur it. I wants ter save *thee*, poppet."

The woman spoke with calm certainty, and Celia did not know what to say. She looked at the mug of hot ale; it smelled deliciously of nutmeg and apple.

"I can't drink this before Communion," she said.

"'Twas why I brung it. There's naught in the Bible about feast days, holy water, or praying to idols made by human hands."

"There isn't?" said Celia, startled. She had never read the Bible. "How would *you* know, Agnes?"

"Because I read the Scriptures fur m'self, Englished by Master Rogers. Sir John Cheke had me taught. Took me a year."

Celia frowned. Cheke. Tutor to the deluded King Edward. "He's in the Tower for *treason*, Agnes. I'll have to ask Brother Stephen to set you right, or we can never keep you here!"

"Oh, poor sweeting. D'ye think any scoldin from some man i' a long frock'd sway me from God's true word. Ye've but ter *read* it—I've got the Book m'self, an' ye won't need those wicked mummeries. Our Blessed Lord saith that when two or three're gathered together in His name, that's church enough."

The shining in Agnes's face, the wholeheartedness of her, perturbed Celia. Of course, the woman was wrong. She noted the poor thing had a twisted limp. Maybe she was simpleminded, too.

"Clubfoot," said Agnes cheerfully, seeing Celia's glance. "I can work as well as any wench, but lots don't want ter hire me. The Chekes had to turn me out when he was put in prison, and I couldn't find work, more than a crust or two. Our Father ne'er promised we'd have *no* trials, but He knows what we have need of. He told me i' a dream to use the writin' Mistress Allen give me."

Celia couldn't imagine Mistress Allen employing this woman. And she said so.

"Oh," said Agnes, "she hated the sight o' me."

"She couldn't've if she wrote you a character."

Agnes was silent while she stirred up last night's embers in the fireplace. Mistress Allen's reference had been a bribe. Agnes had gone to the kitchen one night and surprised her, drunk and half-naked, in the arms of a lusty young scullion. "Well, no matter why," said Agnes. "She gi'e it me."

Celia drew breath and began to cough. As the spasms lessened she drank the ale and banished all thoughts of Mass.

Agnes watched the pretty, downcast face. "The Blessed Lord'll find ye a good husband, miss—if ye talk to him straight."

"Agnes, stop talking like that or I'll have to tell my aunt."

"I'll do wot God tells me ter do," said Agnes gently. "An' he's allus wi' me—in me heart."

I wish there were *something* in *my* heart, Celia thought, as she got up and dressed. But how could she be envious of a clubfooted serving maid? Precisely at the moment that she finished adjusting her everyday kerchief and peered absently into her mirror, she became aware of what it was that really made these days so drear. It was the recurrent sight of Mabel's dithering delight in Gerald's attentions—and the fact that Stephen had totally avoided her since his wrathful speech at the All Saints' Day revel.

Celia walked slowly down to the Hall. She heard her aunt's voice and wondered, without much interest, who was there. Then in an instant she was smothered in a hearty embrace. "God's greeting, hinny. By the Mass, it's been a lang while!"

"Maggie!" exclaimed Celia, drawing back to stare. This was a new Magdalen. Dressed in green velvet and a cloak furred with the finest miniver, this young woman was every inch the daughter of an ancient noble line. For the first time Celia was struck by the difference in their stations.

"A bit o' surprise, eh, lass?" asked Magdalen, her leaf-brown eyes twinkling. "Ye'll niver guess what I'm doing i' London. The Queen's Grace—God bless her—has appointed me a maid o'honour."

She accepted their enthusiastic congratulations in her downright way, then examined Celia. "Ye luik a wee bit peaky, lass."

"We've both been ill," Ursula interjected. "'Twas good of you to visit us, Maggie. We've been dull and housebound."

But Magdalen, still fond of Celia and shocked by her obvious despondency, was struck by a sudden idea.

"Do ye go tonight, you an' Lady Southwell, to the Queen's Twelfth Night revels?"

"Celia and I? To court—to Whitehall?" asked Ursula, astounded.

"Sir Anthony's mebbe heedless, bein' so caught up wi' great matters, but did he think on it, he'd na want ye droopin' lak this. The palace's open wide this night. I'll send a groom fur ye at three."

She bestowed another hug on Celia, and hurried off.

QUEEN MARY was happier on that Twelfth Night than she had ever been in her life. She sat graciously on her throne, her pinched little face transfigured into comeliness. For the Spanish emissary had just brought confirmation from Prince Philip of her heart's desire—the marriage contracts. Soon, after years of neglect and frustrated virginity, she would have someone worthy to love. She loved him already. Her rapture infected her guests. They milled through the state chambers, enjoying a courtly freedom reminiscent of King Henry's best years.

Anthony was standing near the throne conversing warily with the Earl of Pembroke, whose views on the Spanish marriage were known to be adverse, when he was astonished to see Magdalen Dacre come in shepherding Ursula and Celia. He excused himself from the Earl and went to meet them, beaming and contrite.

"Aye, sir," said Magdalen. "You neglect your womenfolk!"

Anthony laughed and thumped his breast. "My ladies, I'm glad to see you," and he was, though he did not know what to do with them. By no stretch of propriety might they, as "commoners", be permitted to sup in the banqueting hall.

Understanding his embarrassment, Ursula quietly pulled Celia away. "You were good to bring us, Magdalen. Celia and I can fend for ourselves now."

Across the room she saw Julian Ridolfi; he was somebody to talk to. And they threaded their way through the horde to where he stood with a lean young man in a black skullcap.

"We meet always by chance," cried Julian.

"Evidently," said Ursula, "since you do not choose to visit us, even after an urgent summons."

Julian laughed. "Dear Lady Southwell, Wat said there was no need, and I see Celia well. Thin, perhaps. . . ." And he introduced them to his friend, John Dee, the Queen's astrologer.

"We might give the young mistress a sample of our *elixir vitae*," said John Dee, bowing sedately towards Celia.

"*What* do you want to try on me, sir? It sounds fearsome."

Julian laughed. "'Water of life', little one. We've been concocting it in our laboratory on Paternoster Row."

Celia's head throbbed as her aunt talked eagerly to the two doctors about the arts of alchemy. She wished she were at home. But I'm at *court*. I should be happy, she said to herself.

A man touched her arm, saying, "Mistress de Bohun?"

She looked up at Sir John Hutchinson. "You startled me, sir," she said. Her smile was radiant at the sight of an admiring face.

"I've thought o' ye so much since I met ye, Mistress Celia," Hutchinson stammered. "Did ye think at all o' me?"

"Once and again," she said, lying kindly. "I've been ill." The reminder brought on a brief spasm of coughing.

"Ye shouldn't be abroad in this weather," cried the knight. "Ye should be cared for, cosseted . . . your lady aunt's neglectful."

"What's all this?" Ursula turned, hearing his raised voice. "Sir, I know we've met, but confess I've not your name."

"John Hutchinson, knight, from Boston, Lincolnshire, widower, member o' the Merchant Adventurers' Company, worth about ten thousand pounds, even at the present sorry rate." His shrewd blue eyes looked directly into Ursula's. "I never beat round the bush," he said. "Waste o' time." She caught his meaning, of which she saw that Celia was unaware. "I'll stop by the priory tomorrow morn," he added. "Take her home, my lady, and mind she keeps out o' draughts." He bowed and swung away.

Ursula bit her lip. How dared a fat old cloth merchent tell her how to treat Celia! How dared he covet her treasure!

"Ah, you are perturbed," said Julian softly. As had sometimes happened to him in regard to Ursula and Celia, the present slipped out of focus. It seemed that he stood alone with them in a place of shadows, tied to them by poignant threads of sympathy—or that they were all three entangled in a cobweb from which he might free them—if he truly wanted to. As he looked now at Ursula, another face shimmered behind the rawboned Anglo-Saxon features, a young face, with olive skin and wistful eyes. One he had loved and grievously hurt—some time before memory began.

"Leave London," he whispered. "Take Celia to Cowdray!"

"*Cowdray!*" Ursula recoiled. "But Sir Anthony needs me here."

"Go tomorrow," Julian breathed. "There is safety there."

"And since when are you so concerned for our safety?"

Julian sighed. His foreboding vanished. "My apologies, lady—I see that the Queen has left for the banqueting hall. Shall we seek supper, too?"

Sir John Hutchinson did not come to the priory the next morning because the infatuated knight had waylaid Sir Anthony after supper in Whitehall. "The old merchant is besotted over your Celia," a laughing Anthony told Ursula two days later. "He wishes to wed her at once and cares naught for dowry. He seems to think she loves him. To be sure, he's old, but Celia widowed would be rich—"

Ursula caught her breath. "Why then did you send him off?"

Anthony was astonished. "The man's a canting *Protestant*! She'd be undermined—a wife obeys her husband."

"Blessed Jesu," Ursula breathed again. "Sir Anthony, we're not too much burden? I try . . . We both try to be of use. . . ."

Anthony picked up a letter from his desk. "You are . . . you're most useful," he said absently, frowning at the missive.

He made an exasperated noise, but his face cleared as Stephen walked in. "Where have you been? What's this Latin drivel mean?"

It was a letter from Renard, and Stephen scanned it rapidly. "The Ambassador's spies report that rebels may try to attack London from here. He asks you to rally and arm all your men."

"I don't believe it. Things've died down since All Saints' Day. That hothead Wyatt has gone home like a lamb to Kent."

"The lamb is mustering an army in Kent," said Stephen dryly. "We too have our spies reporting at the Bishop's Palace. And 'tis not only Wyatt."

"*What* army? cried Ursula.

Anthony had forgotten her. "It'll all blow over, Lady Ursula."

"*What* will?" asked Ursula, drawing herself up, her eyes stern.

"If we are to be endangered, I *demand* to know precisely why."

"And you should, lady," said Stephen suddenly. "You remember our puppet show? Many Englishmen fear that the Queen's marriage would make us vassals of Spain and of His Holiness the Pope. To prevent this, some Protestant factions are about to revolt. And their darling is the Princess Elizabeth."

"I see," said Ursula, thoughtfully. "Thank you, Brother Stephen. And thank you, Sir Anthony, for your handling of Celia's matter."

Stephen jerked his head up and frowned. "What of Celia?"

"Oh," said Anthony, "she's enchanted that old John Hutchinson from Boston. I suppose he wants to beget a son while he can."

"It's indecent," said Stephen in a curiously muffled voice.

"Nay. It will be hard to find her as good a match."

"Wi' her tricks, she'll find *someone*," said Stephen.

"I mislike that," Ursula snapped. "You've grown hard, Brother Stephen." And she swept out of the room.

Anthony chuckled. "Cease glowering, Stephen, and help me with the list o' my retainers. 'Twill take time to get 'em here in this bloody weather."

"So you believe *now* there'll be a revolt?" said Stephen.

"Aye. Renard's no fool. I see the danger." Anthony buried his head in the inventory of his armories. "There's a falconet on the turret of this house. We'll need it to defend the bridge. I suppose Hobson'd know enough to prime and fire it." He entered zestfully into preparatory measures.

ON JANUARY 31 the rebel army was seventeen miles from Southwark, and there was no longer any doubt as to a national crisis. Sir Thomas Wyatt had conquered Rochester and sent a defiant message that he meant to imprison the Queen. Panic flared over London. Many of the citizens were sympathetic to the rebels; the monstrous spectre of Spanish rule outweighed loyalty to the throne.

On February 1 Anthony galloped home and raced up the priory stairs, followed by Wat. "London's arming for the Queen at last!" he cried. Ursula, Celia and Mabel stared at him with alarm. During the last days the women had grown accustomed to guards in mail and a small encampment of men in the cloister.

"Round up our men, Wat, and quick!" said Anthony, wolfing down a meat pasty. "We've got to march 'em over London Bridge before it's blown up, which has been ordered to keep Wyatt on this side of the river."

Celia listened with a feeling of unreality. It all sounded like some frightening play. I wish I were far away, she thought, with someone I love to hold my hand. Her reverie was broken by the appearance of Stephen. He, too, was intense. She heard Anthony order him to put on a linked-mail shirt, saying, "Those heretics'll not respect the cloth. I want you here to guard the women. I'll leave ye four men. You don't have to bear arms, but you can give orders."

Stephen refused the mail shirt offered him. Instead, he inspected his charges. Ursula looked tight-lipped and composed; Mabel doleful because she had not seen Gerald since the crisis started. He looked then at Celia and encountered her brooding gaze full on. It gave him a shock. Since he had so angrily admonished her on All Saints' Day, he had felt he rather disliked her—a foolish child, best ignored. But the look from those unwavering eyes was not childish, nor was there any trace of coquetry. There was both intimacy and something withheld—an ancient wisdom—and he could not look away; heat seared his veins. He grabbed his crucifix and jerked around to the others.

"Kneel!" he commanded. "We will pray for divine help."

Astonished by the harshness in his voice, they obeyed, echoing prayers which seemed rather battle commands than invocations.

SIR THOMAS WYATT'S troops marched into Southwark two days later. He had received along the way one bit of catastrophic news after the other. He was now bereft of all support save his Kentishmen and a few Londoners who had joined him at Rochester. Nevertheless, he held his head high; he rode his horse proudly; and to frightened faces peering through shutter cracks, he called, "We'll not harm *you*. Come out, true Englishmen, 'less ye wish to be ground 'neath the iron heel o' Spain!" But the citizens remained quaking behind their barred doors.

Wyatt marched straight for London Bridge and found the centre drawbridge lying in pieces in the Thames. On the other bank he saw that a battery of guns was mounted. He decided to repair the bridge despite the danger of bombardment, for no boats were left on the south bank of the Thames. Anthony, stuck on the London side and seeing a thousand moving lights in Southwark, cursed his decision to leave the priory so ill-guarded.

Wyatt did his best to rally his army. He told them that they would be delayed for a day or so in Southwark, that they must pay for their food and drink, and commit no vandalism, that victory was at hand. His men cheered, and a work force shovelled and banged at the frozen earth to make a trench against the possible bombardment.

At eleven in the bitter chill night there came the disturbance at the priory's portal which Stephen had been expecting. He gathered the women in the Hall, nine of them. They heard the gun butts thud on the huge oaken door, the crash of a shot through glass. "Stay here, everyone, don't budge," Stephen said.

He barred the Hall door behind him and walked down the stairs. He saw Anthony's guards securely bound, the entrance filled with armed men. Wyatt himself, sword drawn, met him at the stair's foot. "*Benedicite*," he said ironically. "Methought Sir Anthony's mansion admirable for my headquarters."

"You promised no violence," said Stephen, instinctively stretching his arms to guard the staircase. "Yet look at my guards."

"Sir Anthony might've left you a braver lot. I see you've a falconet on the north turret. I've a mind to send up a few gunners to keep the cannon aimed in the proper direction."

Stephen's voice rang strident and clear. "I forbid you in the name of God to mount these stairs."

Wyatt stared at the tall black figure with its outstretched arms, and the beliefs of his childhood made him wince—but only for a moment.

"Out of my way, Brother."

He struck Stephen a fierce blow on the shoulder with the flat of his sword, knocking him to his knees, and gestured to his men. "Tie him up. The rest come with *me*."

He leaped up the staircase ahead of some thirty men and unbarred the doors to the Hall. One woman shrieked. Ursula spoke with freezing dignity. "Your entrance lacks ceremony, Sir Thomas. What have you done with Brother Stephen and our guards?"

Wyatt bowed. "You've naught to fear, lady. Only I need a guide through this warren o' passages. *You*, my poppet"—he touched Celia on the arm—"I sang you love songs, you may repay them now."

"And if I will not go?" said Celia. The other women gasped.

"Go with him, Celia," cried Mabel, "or we'll all be killed!"

"I doubt that," said Celia. "Sir Thomas is a courteous knight, for all his views are misguided. I'll go, no need to make a pother." And she smiled in her most enchanting manner.

Wyatt was taken aback, and then delighted. He swept Celia out of the Hall and rebarred the great door. The girl laughed, all her miseries eclipsed by giddy excitement. She liked the rough grasp around her waist, the cold hardness of his mailed shirt against her arm. "*Celia the wanton and fair*" he had sung. She felt in these wild thoughtless moments only the joy of being wanted—and of escape.

She led Wyatt and his men to the door leading up to the turret, where old Hobson guarded the falconet, then drew back, waiting among the rafters. She was aware of a scuffle above her, then Wyatt's triumphant shout, and the men climbed back down the ladder carrying something. "'E's still alive. Tough old bastard," said a voice.

The bundle was old Hobson, and a blackish trickle ran from his lips. "Blood . . . ? You've killed him?" Celia recoiled, staring at Wyatt.

"Nay, nay, sweetheart," said the knight impatiently. "He'll recover. Now, Celia, I want a chamber that o'erlooks the river."

"There's only my room," she said in a thin whisper. Hobson had been a merry old man. And now he was grotesque, tongue lolling, throat rattling.

Wyatt whirled the girl around so she could not see Hobson. "To your chamber, my dear," he said softly. The girl would need forcing now. "'Tis *only* that I may have a view of the bridge." He lifted a strand of her hair and kissed it. "Here's the shining net which has caught me in its meshes, snared fast, in thrall to love."

She quivered and took him mutely to the room she shared with Ursula. It was warmer there, embers glowed ruddy in the grate. "Yonder is the riverside window," she said.

Wyatt laughed. "A pox on the window! I see only the bed, sweetheart, and a goodly one, too." Struggling and cursing beneath his breath, he began unhooking his chain-mail shirt.

"What are you doing?" whispered Celia.

"Don't act the innocent," said Wyatt, savagely breaking one of the tangled tapes of his hose. "We've not much time."

"Time. . . ." Celia shrank against the cupboard, her arms across her breasts in the immemorial gesture of threatened virginity.

He looked at her with swift lust. "You were warm enough i' the Hall. I'm not going to play the gallant now. I've not had a woman in weeks—an' ye *brought* me here!" He strode across the room and ripped open her bodice with one violent tear. Celia screamed and scratched his face.

"Scream away, you little bitch," he panted, pinioning her arms. He was dragging her to the bed when the door opened and Stephen stood there, appalled. He had been untied by the guards to give old Hobson the last rites, and then had gone searching for Celia.

Wyatt dropped the girl and shouted, "Get out, you eunuch!"

Stephen went white. In one lithe motion he hit Wyatt full on his bearded jaw. The knight grunted and collapsed on the rushes. Stephen and Celia stood frozen, side by side.

Wyatt sat up slowly. As his vision cleared he gaped up at the two who stood over him. "'Odsbody—the monk an' the maiden. Ye bestow your charms in odd quarters, my dear." He got up carefully, pulled on his hose and armour and went to peer out the window. "By God!" he cried. "There's a boat—"

There was a rumble and white flash. The priory's old stones vibrated. "Sir Anthony's falconet!" Wyatt cried in triumph. "Thank ye, my dear." He made Celia a mocking bow and ran out.

Stephen and the girl turned with one accord and looked at each other. Celia saw his face, naked, young, defenceless, as she had never seen it. She drew a sobbing breath. "Oh, my dear, dear love." He held her close, yet as though she were sacred—trembling, feeling her naked breasts against his chest.

"Holy Virgin, forgive me," he whispered, and kissed her soft open lips. She staggered and clung. He lifted her onto the bed.

"Dear love, dear heart—" She moaned, pressing against him.

He spoke in a groan so violent it sounded like anger. "I love thee, Celia, my God—forgive me."

"Nay, nay" she whispered. "What more can God give?"

It was a whispered "Jesu!" and a stifled sob which at last they heard. Stephen turned slowly onto his back, then rose. Celia looked up into her aunt's contorted face. "Cover your paps!" Ursula cried, and threw her head-veil over the girl. "Oh, monstrous—"

"Aye, monstrous," Stephen said in a voice of great sadness. "But she is *not* harmed, Lady Ursula. I love the girl more than myself, almost more than my vows. I did not know it till now."

"You base priest," Ursula groaned. "How should I believe you?"

Stephen held his crucifix in his hand. "I swear by this."

"Ah," breathed Ursula, "so much for *this* time, Stephen Marsdon, and I'll not call you 'Brother'. Yet when your lusts return—and hers—nay, don't answer! I know a remedy!"

Stephen bowed his head. "So do I, lady."

Chapter 9

Defeat gathered around Wyatt like the rain clouds. The rebellion was finished three days later when Wyatt surrendered at Ludgate outside the city walls. He was taken to the Tower, and hysteria died down.

Anthony, in high spirits, came home to the priory. "Not much disturbance, was there?" he asked jovially.

"Enough," said Ursula sombrely.

Anthony was at once sympathetic. "Wyatt's breaking in must have frightened you. And poor old Hobson. Still, it only lasted a few hours, I hear. Haven't seen Brother Stephen."

Ursula tightened her lips. She was dreading this moment. "Sir," she said, "Celia must wed Sir John Hutchinson."

"*What?*" Anthony's mind was full of the Queen's problems. But Ursula was still speaking.

"Pray, will you summon Sir John at once?"

Anthony gave her his full, startled attention. "But my dear Lady Southwell, what sea change is this? And what does Celia say?"

Ursula flushed. "Celia will obey. We can avoid . . . more ghastly sin." She clenched her hands. "I don't know how to tell you."

Anthony wondered that this composed lady should show so much distress, and he questioned her gently. But as he understood, anger and shock churned his stomach. That Wyatt had tried to rape Celia was bad enough. But that shameless girl and *Stephen*—his brazen avowal of love. "Jesu!" he cried. "She may be wi' child."

"He swore not. Yet it seems he holds his vows lightly. Celia stares at me—with eyes of hate." Ursula's voice broke.

CELIA was married to John Hutchinson on February 22, in the church porch of St. Saviour's. Her only attendants were Ursula and a rather contemptuous Mabel. Anthony, stiff-lipped, gave her away. Since Sir John had flatly refused to attend a nuptial Mass, there was none. The little party trailed back into the priory, where Anthony had ordered a wedding feast. His anger had waned after he talked to Stephen, and his natural generosity prompted him to some of the observances due any maiden married from his house.

Sir John had accepted Celia's hand with a trembling joy embarrassing to see. Nor had Celia needed forcing into marriage, as Anthony had feared. "Sir John seems kind," was all she had said, "and I shall be glad enough to live in Lincolnshire."

Anthony suspected, and Ursula knew, that Celia's behaviour resulted from a note Stephen had sent her. In Anthony's final interview with Stephen, the young monk's face had been a granite wall. "I am sailing, sir," he said, "for Marmoutier with letters from Bishop Gardiner. I shall retire to the cloister."

"But I *need* you, Stephen." Anthony quite forgot his wrath. "You're more than chaplain, you're my friend—"

"Whether I ever return will be my superior's decision," said Stephen. "May our Blessed Lord and his Holy Mother hold you in their keeping, sir."

Now Anthony glanced at the silent bride beside him, then looked down his table at the few guests—Sir John's groomsman, Master Babcock; Master Julian, whom Ursula had suddenly asked;

and Mabel, fidgeting. 'What a celebration!' Anthony shouted to his minstrels, and raised his goblet. "Wassail to the bride, wassail to the groom!" He turned to Celia, bowing. "Come, my lady, we'll begin the dance."

Celia started and looked behind her.

Anthony laughed. "'Tis *you* are 'my lady'. You've wed a goodly knight. Sir John, *you* dance wi' your bride!"

Sir John rose majestically and took Celia's hand. Her fourth finger now wore a heavy golden ring made of two hands clasping a large amethyst heart. She clutched his arm. "There, there, poppet. We'll drink the loving cup together instead, shall we?" And he hefted the great silver punch bowl filled with mulled claret.

"Long life!" cried Anthony.

"We thankee, Sir Anthony, for this splendid wedding feast," Sir John said, bowing. "My little bride seems a-weary, we'd best be leaving now."

"The lacerated heart repairs itself, my poor lady," said Julian to Ursula as they watched the Hutchinson chariot lumber off. "It's not the marriage you hoped for, yet no tragedy either."

"She hates me. Had I been her mother I'd've had more wisdom."

"This happens to blood mothers, too," said Julian.

IN SIR JOHN HUTCHINSON'S lodgings in London, his servants had prepared a festive little supper, but Celia refused the food John awkwardly pressed on her and poured herself noggins of mead.

"God blast it, Celia, ye've drunk enough for a barrowman!"

"I wish to be sotted," she said. "Better so."

"Look, my dear. Ye needn't be bedded tonight. I wish for a son, and I want thee, but by God, ye frighten me."

"I'm sorry," Celia said. "You're a good man, Sir John."

"*Not* Sir John. I'm thy husband! What are ye *doing*, Celia?"

She had suddenly risen and picked from a vase two Christmas roses, tucking one behind each ear. They gave her an exotic fairy look. She moved near him, raising her white arms in a gesture of supplication, and suddenly his fear left him. Beneath the mummery he saw the despairing child. He lifted her in his arms and carried her to the bed. Gently he undressed her and drew her head against his shoulder, where she nestled and went to sleep at once. The bells rang out for midnight. "Stephen," Celia whispered.

John held himself very still. Stephen? How little he knew of this girl. But presently he slept, too.

FOUR DAYS later the Hutchinsons arrived at Sir John's manor, Skirby Hall, a mile outside of Boston. Celia's misery had lessened with each mile away from London, as their party rode single file along the dykes, through the marshlands, though she found none of the exhilaration she had felt in Cumberland. Her only positive pleasure was Juno, the mare Sir Anthony had given her in happier days at Cowdray.

From time to time she looked down at the pouch which hung from her girdle and which held Stephen's note. Why keep it? She knew it by heart: "After you make your confession, as *I* shall—we will pray God to forget what happened, nor think on it ever again ourselves."

"I shall think as I please," said Celia to Juno. She had not gone to confession since Wyatt invaded the priory. Her entire interest in religion had sprung from Stephen. She thought of his cherished portrait of the Virgin, her rival—I hate her. She suddenly fished in her pouch for the note and flung it into a muddy drain.

"Ah, sweet, there's Skirby Hall," John was saying with a quiet triumph. "They've the banner flying. Ye'll find a goodly welcome."

Indeed it was overwhelming. The road was lined with people shouting greetings. "Sa young, sa fair, lucky master." She heard it whispered all around her.

John laughed, swept Celia up in his arms and carried her over the threshold. "We'll make a son yet, darling," he whispered. She smiled a little and kissed his cheek.

Yet, much later in John's great bed, that which he so desired became impossible. She nestled against him. "Ah, this is sweet . . . to be held close like a father. Would that you *were* my father, sir."

His arms stiffened, then fell away. He sighed heavily.

"Have I said wrong?" she asked. "I didn't mean to."

"Hush," he said. "Sleep now, I've much to do on the morrow."

After that night he did not touch her again. Celia, though aware that she had somehow failed him, was deeply relieved. Capably she learned her duties as lady of the manor, and learned, too, to feel the still and hazy beauty of the fenlands. She scarcely noticed John's joviality vanish as a brooding peevishness grew. Juno's sprained fetlock, or the ailments of a mongrel puppy she called Taggle, caused her far more concern.

John, for his part, observed that with her skin grown rosy and golden from her summer rambles, Celia was becoming a woman of great beauty. But as he remembered the wild allure she had shown him on the night of the wedding, his gouty toe gave a throb and he said one day in sudden anger, "Ye'll bide home more now as the days be drawing in." Then noting her stricken face, he added, "I'll teach ye draughts an' read ye the Bible."

"The Protestant Bible?" she said faintly. "'Tis forbidden me . . . Stephen said—" She stopped. "If you wish it, sir."

"Who the devil is Stephen? Ye mentioned him once before!"

"He was house priest at Cowdray."

"Oh, indeed. I warrant ye've forgot a' that nonsense."

"Aye," said Celia after a moment. "I've forgot it."

ONE MISTY AFTERNOON in October Celia wandered out to a grassy knoll near the fen, Taggle flopping at her heels. She sat on an old willow stump. John had gone to town that day, worried about an overdue cargo ship, and they would not sup until he returned. She felt, as so often at gloaming time, an infinite hush, as though something were going to happen, and yet it never did. Then she saw a horseman.

Good, she thought, now we'll sup. But it was not Sir John. She watched him turn up towards the Hall. Then she ran to the gatehouse. "*Wat!*" she cried. "Wat! Come in! I'm *glad* to see you!"

Wat grunted. "God's greetin', miss—m'lady. 'Tis worse gettin' to this bloody back o' beyond than Cumberland. Have ye anyone'll gi'e me a drink?"

"To be sure, come to the Hall. Oh, Wat, how is my aunt?"

"Ye've not heard from her . . . nor written neither?"

"I can't write well," she said, flushing. "I thought she might—Wat, will *you* carry a message to my aunt?"

"Aye, Lady Suthell's not forgot ye." He looked at her curiously. "D'ye get any news at all midst these Godforsook bogs?"

"I know that the Queen was wed to Philip of Spain. But they detest the marriage round these parts, and don't speak of it."

"Ah-r-r," said Wat, lifting the flagon of ale she'd poured. "Lot o' England feels that way. As ye should know from Wyatt's Rebellion. The poor toad." Wat crossed himself. "All spring the bleedin' heads was a-rollin'."

Sick pangs darted through Celia. The debonair Wyatt had sung to her, desired her. "Has there been danger for Sir Anthony?" she asked in sudden fear.

Wat laughed. "*Sir* Anthony's the Viscount Montagu, and apple o' the royal eyes."

"Wedded?" she asked in a low voice, after a moment.

"No, though I'll wager he'll pick Lady Maggie. But Mistress Mabel's the Countess of Kildare, Lord Fitzgerald having got hisself turned back into earl. Ye ne'er saw such doins at Cowdray."

Celia was swamped by the sense of exile; and Wat, experienced in human faces, had no trouble reading hers.

"Lookee, Mistress Celia, yer aunt loves ye, but ye parted cool, an' she's too proud to push in. She asked me to tell ye that." Wat looked around the Hall. "Ye've a nice manor here, an' a title, an' the babes'll keep ye content."

"There'll be no babes," said Celia, hugging Taggle.

"Ah-r-r, indeed," said Wat, startled, then comprehending. "Ye must get ye a charm. Must be some wise-woman nearby."

Celia flushed. "There's the water witch," she said very low. "I've heard the servants. They're terrified of her."

"Taradiddle," said Wat. "Ye've got courage. Try 'er. 'Tis yer wifely duty. Ye can allus be shriven later, the priest'll understand."

Celia looked away. The thought of the water witch was repugnant, and yet subtly fascinating. She was reputed to have green seaweed hair and tremendous magical powers.

"I see no priests. This is a Protestant household."

"By God, I'd forgot! Sir John better change his tune. England's papist—and Spanish—all the way." Wat made a wry face. "Brother Stephen'd have a fit at ye turnin' heretic."

Celia tensed. "Did he officiate at Mabel's wedding?"

"Ye must know he left fur France," said Wat. "To some place called Marmateer, his old abbey."

Celia's heart bumped against her ribs. Amid the pain so long suppressed there was bitter relief. He was far away. She'd not have to think of him again, as he had commanded.

WAT'S suggestion of the water witch took root in Celia's mind. It would be an adventure—and if it *should* bring Sir John the son he so wanted—aye, it was worth a try. The wrecking of one of his ships on the Yorkshire coast gave her the opportunity she wanted. John would be gone a week.

As soon as he'd left, she summoned the maid who had mentioned the water witch, and questioned her further. Did she know of a guide who would take her to the witch's habitat? The woman's stolid face showed fear. "Nabody goes nigh there."

"But," said Celia, "you say somebody takes her food on Fridays."

"'Tis Daft Dickon from Frampton parish does that."

"Aye, so. Thank you," said Celia with her charming smile.

Celia curled up on her window seat and began excitedly to make her plans. And then an odd thing happened.

She heard voices. A woman, speaking English with an unfamiliar accent, said, "I doubt Lady Marsdon'll last much longer, Doctor. *I* think we *must* call Sir Arthur back. Excuse me speaking plain, sir, but what *she* needs is proper medical procedure."

A male voice answered. "She has reached a crossroads; the outcome is in the hands of God." She could not quite hear it all. Some of his words were gibberish. "Electroencephalogram?" He sounded vaguely like Master Julian. Then it all slid away as Taggle gave a sharp yelp and shivered, while his neck fur rose.

"What ails *thee*, sweet?" said Celia, laughing. She stooped to pat him, but he cringed and snapped.

Celia rode Juno into Frampton next day and found Daft Dickon. He lived with a grandmother, who snatched at Celia's shilling, then shrugged her shoulders. "Thou canst goo the morrow, being Friday. Effen thee looks on *her*, thou'rt lost." Dickon, she explained, was safe, since God protected the dim-witted from witchcraft.

The next day Daft Dickon was waiting for her, a great woven hamper at his feet. There was no road, but Dickon led the way with certainty until she could hear the lapping of seawater on the shingle.

"Yon's witch hut," he said. "Dickon goos no furder." He dumped the hamper down, turned, and began to walk away.

Seized by panic, she ran after him. "Dickon—I'll be lost in those fens." This did not reach him. She pulled his head down, uncaring by what method she could force him to stay, and kissed him. "*Wait* for me!"

He gave a strangled gasp, and she knew she had won. As she stumbled towards the hut, carrying the hamper, she heard him crooning, "Dickon bides . . . Dickon bides . . ."

The hut was set back, safe from the tides, in a crevice of brown rock. Celia walked resolutely up to the door and knocked.

"Good day, mistress," she called. "I've come to see you, brought your provisions."

The door opened a crack. "You are brave," said a voice. "Enter, then!" The door was flung wide, and Celia shrank back.

The water witch was naked, covered only by her thick, wavy white hair, which fell to her thighs. The woman advanced a step into the sunlight. And then Celia saw the scars on her face and legs, the distorted feet.

"Holy Jesu," Celia whispered. "What happened to you?"

"I was burned for being witch in France. My lover save me."

"Horrible," Celia whispered. "The cruelty . . ."

"*Justice*. I *am* a witch!"

Celia wanted to flee, yet could not. She was terrified, fascinated. "I—I brought your hamper," she said feebly.

"You came not for *zat* reason." The eyes were amused. "You need not fear me if your heart is pure." Her beautiful tapering hands were unmarred, for they had been tied behind the stake as her burning began. She put one on Celia's arm. "Enter," she said softly. "It is good to talk . . . so many years I have not."

The hut smelled of the sea and was very clean. There was a wide couch in the corner made of sacking stuffed with dry kelp. The fire was burning driftwood, flickering blue and green. But Celia's eye was held by a round table and an X-shaped armchair more exquisite than anything at Cowdray.

The woman nodded. "Milor', from love, then pity, tried to give me some comforts. He was *noyé* . . . drowned, sailing back."

"How could you know he was drowned?" Celia asked.

"I know much others cannot. I am Melusine," said the woman.

Celia saw now that the long eyes fixed on her—mockingly, tenderly—were the yellowish green of a cat's, and the pupils long instead of round. Again fear touched her.

Melusine went to a huge oaken coffer and took out a filmy gown, grey, and decorated around the neck with pearls, in a fashion long forgotten.

"This is how I *was*," she said, slipping into it. "Many men loved me. *Alone*, I feel better to be naked." She gestured towards the kelp mattress. "Lie down." She handed Celia some dry flowerets. "And put these in your mouth!"

As Melusine began to talk, her voice was like distant music. Melusine de Lusignan. There had always been a Melusine, back beyond the reaches of time, born of a fountain, yet possessed of a mortal soul. One day there was an English duke who wished to be king. If Melusine used her great powers to insure the king's death, the duke would raise her to be even, perhaps, his queen.

Celia stirred. It was like the romances of kings and fairy spells that Ursula used to read her. And was there not even a water sprite called Melusine?

Melusine's voice was gathering urgency. The king would have died. But that Medici woman caught her with the wax image. She, too, was versed in the black arts.

"The Medici woman?" said Celia.

"Catherine de Medici, yes . . . she had me burned."

Celia's head suddenly cleared. Catherine de Medici was *real*, the king was real—King Henry, who lived on the other side of the water which washed these shores. And this strange woman, half-crazed by what she had undergone, whether witch or not—Celia jumped up. "Dickon's waiting, I didn't mean to stay so long."

Melusine's eyes widened to their sad, mocking look. "First . . . the love philter you came for! Some gallant who spurns you?"

"No, no," cried Celia. "My husband—he can't—"

"Ah-h, you came to *help* him? Then do this!" With a faggot she drew a pentacle on the sandy floor. "Five points like this. Then put this powder in the centre." She drew a tiny vial from a sack. "Then say 'Ishtareth' three times and place the powder in his drink. He will make a son in you, for this powder is from the mandrake root."

Celia frowned. "It might harm him."

"If you wish only good to your husband, there'll be no harm. Now repeat 'Ishtareth'. Ishtar was goddess of love." She put the vial in Celia's hand. "*Adieu*, we shall not meet again. The great tide on All Hallows' Eve—I go with it."

"Melusine!" cried Celia with a yearning which was almost love.

But the woman pushed her out. "*Adieu*," she said inexorably.

By the time Celia reached Skirby Hall she was ashamed of the whole episode. When John came home she welcomed him warmly. But she never gave him the water witch's powder.

Chapter 10

In the summer of 1558 John Hutchinson died. Then days later a letter summoned Celia back to Cowdray. It was delivered by an elegant young gentleman-usher named Edwin Ratcliffe, now attached to Lord Montagu's enormous household, who had several other commissions in Lincolnshire.

"Blessed Jesu!" he breathed when the widow rose gravely to meet him. Celia, in her mourning robes, reminded him of a nun, but never was a nun so beautiful.

Edwin dropped to his knee and extended the parchment with its buck-head seal. "From Lord Montagu," he said.

"I wonder that he heard of my loss so soon," Celia said.

"I b-believe"—Edwin blushed—"that it is another matter."

She looked at him and became aware that this was a comely young man and that there was a kindling in his round blue eyes—an expression she had not seen for so long.

"But I've made you no welcome," she cried. "Forgive me." She moved to the bell rope. "There are only two servants now. You see, there was naught left but debts. Sir John's heir leaves me here on sufferance awhile, but he is angry."

Edwin was shaken by a surge of feeling so unaccustomed that he did not recognize it. He was betrothed to the daughter of a neighbouring squire at Petworth and would marry, joining the two manors, when he reached his majority in November. She was pleasing enough, but she inspired none of the odd sensations evoked by the lovely widow. As the old maidservant shuffled in with a flagon of ale, he gazed at Celia, moonstruck.

"Wassail," she said. "I know not your name, sir."

"Edwin Ratcliffe, my lady," he said quickly. Her skin was luminous, like a golden pearl. He did not touch his drink.

She slowly broke the seal on Lord Montagu's letter. Addressed to Sir John Hutchinson, it announced the marriage of the Viscount Montagu and Lady Magdalen Dacre at the chapel royal on the fifteenth of July. The Queen's Grace was present, and her health being poor, the wedding was exceeding small.

"Ah-h, I'm pleased that I—that *we* were remembered," Celia said. Then she saw that there was an enclosure. It was signed "Ursula Southwell". Bittersweet pain, resentment, even anger shook Celia. The handwriting was extremely shaky. She couldn't make it out.

"Can you read this, sir?" she asked. "I cannot."

"I believe it says, 'Celia, I implore you, come to me. I pray Sir John will permit. So I may die in peace.'"

"She is dying?" Celia whispered.

"I know not, lady. She keeps to her chamber at Cowdray. . . . Lady?" he said timidly after a silence. "'Tis a piteous plea. I—I can escort you. In truth"—Edwin was fundamentally sensible—"wi' matters here as they are, what else can you do but go?"

CELIA left Skirby Hall forever five days later. She rode Juno and carried Taggle in a little basket behind the saddle. All her other possessions made a very small bundle. Sir John had not meant to leave her so. Celia had shed tears for him, but as they rode, she at last let joy come through. She was going home to Midhurst. She was only twenty, and Edwin's every glance told her that she was desirable.

By the time they came in sight of Cowdray's crenellated roof, the young man was in fact thoroughly besotted. He had begun to make feverish plans for breaking his betrothal. Once his parents met Celia they would agree—who could resist her? With so recent a bereavement, perhaps he should wait a little. But Edwin did not like to wait. As they turned into Cowdray's avenue he burst out, "Lady! I love thee—I must have thee!"

Celia reined in Juno. "What's this, sir?" she said smiling. "You ask me to be your leman? I find you forward."

"Nay, nay, lady," cried Edwin. "I wish thee for my wife!"

Celia fingered Juno's mane. "You are kind, sir," she said.

"I did not mean to speak so soon—but Celia . . ."

"I cannot answer yea or nay," she said gently. She knew him to be years younger than she in feeling and experience. Yet was not *any* love better than none? And then her heart began to quake as they drew up to the porter's lodge.

The porter—a new one—spoke respectfully to "widowed Lady Hutchinson". "M'lord an' lady'll not be back from Arundel till supper, lady. Master Ratcliffe'll show you where to wait."

"'Tis Lady Ursula Southwell I came to see," said Celia evenly, "and I can find my way. Nay, sir," she said to Edwin, who was clearly unwilling to leave her, "I must go alone."

Ursula was so altered that Celia stopped dead, clenching her hands. The rugged face had shrunk to a pale wedge from which sad hollow eyes stared at Celia. "My darling child." Ursula held out a fleshless hand.

Celia knelt and put her forehead on the hand which moved to caress her face.

"In black?" Ursula queried. "Not Sir John?"

Celia nodded. "Oh, *why* did you send me away?" she sobbed. "Why did you never come? I thought I hated you."

"I know," Ursula whispered. Through her rapture of relief a grey mist swirled. "The drops, sweetheart—the cordial!"

Celia reached for the vial, poured a few drops and held the cup to Ursula's mouth. She waited, tears brimming, until the gasping breaths grew softer. There was an aura of neglect in Ursula's room that smote her.

"Who cares for you, aunt?"

"Why, they come . . . now and again . . . the servants. There used to be Agnes Snoth, d'you remember her, dear? At the priory? She was good to me."

"Aye. The Protestant with the clubfoot. What happened to her?"

"She was burned for heresy. So many burnings, they sickened me, but Sir Anthony—his lordship—always agrees with the Queen's Grace. Heretics must burn." Ursula had begun to shiver. "I could hear their screams when I ventured across the river."

"Don't," Celia said, appalled. "My lady aunt, forget!"

"I can't forget. . . ." In a few minutes Ursula was quiet enough to tell the story.

The Queen had thought herself with child, but when no babe came forth, only a bladderful of wind and putrid matter, King Philip had contemptuously gone off to Spain. The Queen saw this as evidence of divine wrath, that she had been too lax with heretics. So the burnings began. Not only were the great folk burned—the bishops, the Archbishop Cranmer—but anyone so misguided as to doubt any tenet of the Holy Catholic Faith. At Cowdray, Agnes Snoth had been caught reading her Protestant Bible and had gushed forth a stream of heresy. Lord Montagu sent her home to Kent, where she was burned with others at Canterbury.

"After that," said Ursula, "*I* was shunned. Agnes had been dear to me. . . ." Her head went limp against the pillow.

Celia's mouth tightened as she wiped Ursula's damp forehead. So Anthony had virtually sent a crippled servant to the stake. "How Lord Montagu must have altered since he wed *me* to a Protestant."

"Aye." Ursula found breath again. "But that was before the *Queen* grew fanatic. Celia, I had not written because I felt you didn't wish it. When Wat brought me your message, Montagu forbade me to communicate with you. Since the discovery of Agnes's heresy, I've been almost a prisoner—until they saw I wouldn't last the summer out. *Now* do you forgive me?"

"With all my heart," Celia said soothingly. But death shadowed the chamber.

"I've a stain on my soul," said Ursula suddenly. "May the Blessed Virgin forgive me. I've got Agnes's Bible and have *read* in it—it's under that floorboard near the window."

Celia stared at the bolted door, then lifted the loose piece of planking and picked up the book slowly. "'Tis like the one Sir John would read to me from. I know the pictures."

"Aye!" Ursula's voice shook with fear. "Hide it quick!"

Celia hesitated. "Can it be so great a sin to read this?" she mused. "In here is the story of our Lord Jesus."

Ursula started up in the bed. "*Celia.* It's forbidden by our faith. Throw the book into the Rother. Blessed Mary, if they knew *you* had read it—"

"Hush, dear aunt. I'll rid you of the book when I can." Gently Celia took Ursula's trembling body in her arms. She now had serious doubts as to her own reception here. When she heard the familiar hoofbeats on the Easebourne road, she looked out to see flashing plumes and galloping horses. The two figures riding ahead must be Anthony and Magdalen.

Hounds bounding along beside them reminded Celia that Taggle was still in the basket, along with her bundle, at the porter's lodge. She left the now dozing Ursula and ran down to release Taggle. As the Montagus came up the avenue, she stood clutching her squirming dog, with her chin high, just within the courtyard.

Magdalen saw the shadowed figure first. "Begock! 'Tis Celia Bohun! In widow's weeds? That man is dead? He didn't infect ye wi' his wickedness, lass?"

Celia gazed up into brown eyes which were no longer loving. "Lady Magdalen, you know my poor aunt sent for me. I'll not be a nuisance."

"Nay, nay." A touch of the old warmth softened Magdalen's voice. "Ye're welcome back ta Cowdray for the nonce, is she not, my lord?"

Anthony looked blank. He had just heard at Arundel that the Queen's condition after another false pregnancy was serious and that she had definitely named the Protestant Elizabeth as her heir. His heart was heavy with fears for the future. He roused himself and stared at the widow. She had caused Stephen's departure, wed a Protestant. Still, no call upon his hospitality had ever been refused. "Aye, my Lady Hutchinson," he said, unsmiling, "of course. What have you with you? Children, no doubt?"

"No babes, my lord," said Celia. "I've only my dog and Juno, the mare you gave me. Sir John died a ruined man."

"I'm sorry for your sake to hear so," said Anthony coldly. "My lady, you will attend to this? I want a bath and drink."

Magdalen turned majestically to Celia. "We will gan in, my dear, and tak' some wine. Ha' ye seen Lady Ursula?"

Celia nodded, her control wavering. The Viscountess Montagu appeared formidable. The impression faded only slightly when they were installed in Magdalen's parlour, a charming apartment with much of the Dacre in it. A servingman hurried in with a tray bearing a flask of claret and two goblets.

"We'll chat a bit," Magdalen said. "But I do not weesh to hear of your time wi' that heretic. Where's your beads?" She looked sharply at Celia's girdle.

"In my bundle." Celia felt herself flush. She had not told her beads in years.

Magdalen seemed satisfied. "What're your plans, Celia? After your puir aunt goes to God." She crossed herself.

Celia flushed deeper. "I—I've not had time to think, lady."

"Ye've no money at all? Syon. Yes, we'll get ye into Syon!"

"Syon?" repeated Celia faintly. A nunnery! Surely they had not the power to shut her away against her will. Yet, the alternative? A life like Ursula's? Eternal dependence on patronage? To die neglected and forgotten? She thought of Edwin Ratcliffe. Aye, that would be better. At least I'd not die a virgin.

"I'm glad for sweet pity's sake, your aunt's got ye here. Ye may order what ye like to mak' her passing easier."

This sounded more like the old Maggie. Celia, slightly relieved, curtsied and returned to Ursula. She was now stuck in a pattern of waiting for a future she could not guess. She dined in the Hall each noontime, though the Montagus no longer did. Nor did Edwin, though he found means to waylay her, and she knew his passion grew.

One night when Ursula slept—as she almost constantly did—

Celia looked towards Ursula's crucifix and remembered how passionately she had prayed to it the time when Stephen was imprisoned in the cellar. Suddenly that far-off pain invaded her again. How strange it should still be there. She wrenched her eyes away from the crucifix to where the Bible lay hidden. What had all those burned Protestants found there to give them courage to endure the most terrible of deaths?

Celia pushed up the concealing plank, took the dank tome on her lap and opened it at random. Slowly she spelled out the seventh chapter of First Corinthians. It left her dismayed. There was no doubt that Saint Paul considered virgins and widows who did not remarry far more blessed than other women. Celia was both and did not feel blessed at all. She read with growing vexation and puzzlement. Nowhere did she find the suffering gentle Jesus, the Redeemer of her Latin prayers. There was no guidance, no comfort here for her. The Catholics were right. In guilty contrition she went to Ursula's *prie-dieu* and gabbled off a Paternoster. But at the last clause she paused. *Why* should an all-loving Father *lead* His child into temptation? Why must He be implored not to?

At that moment in Ursula's draughty chamber, Celia renounced God. She would cease to worry about religion. She would guide her life by her own will. All else was lies.

ON NOVEMBER 17 Queen Mary died at St. James's Palace, and the whole of England shifted balance. Anthony and Magdalen were roused at midnight by Wat, who leaped off his lathered horse and plunged upstairs into the Montagu bedchamber without ceremony. "It's happened, my lord," he panted.

Anthony sat up. "God give her peace, she had little here."

"Ye best get ye quick to Hatfield, my lord—swear allegiance to the new one. They've all been runnin' there the last week."

Magdalen's eyes watered. "Did she die peaceful, Wat?"

"She did. Heard Mass at five, expired at six."

"Ye mun get ready," said Magdalen.

"For what?" said Anthony dully. He felt empty, lost.

"To go to *Hatfield*, my lord, like the rest!" cried Magdalen. She got out of bed, regardless of Wat. "Elizabeth is now your queen,

Anthony Browne, and if you prize being Viscount Montagu—if you value your head—you had better swear allegiance."

"Her ladyship's right, my lord," said Wat. "The Commons is wild wi' joy. They've got a true Englishwoman."

"Bring mead to his lordship, Wat, to hearten him. My lord, I niver thought ta see *you* wambly when your duty's clear. I'd ride wi' ye, except I'm three months gone—a perilous time, they say."

Anthony rose, a handsome man of thirty, and reached for his day linen. "But I'll not compromise my faith to satisfy the—"

"She'd *niver* ask it!" cried Magdalen with assurance. "She's a canny lass, and ye've the knack to please her, Anthony."

AT HATFIELD Anthony found his new sovereign suitably dressed in filmy black, and deep in converse with Sir William Cecil, whom she had immediately appointed her Secretary of State. As Anthony, kneeling, swore his allegiance, her tawny eyes inspected him contemplatively.

"We know how well you served our late sister," she murmured. "And have no doubts of your fealty, my Lord Montagu." She spoke with the faintest tinge of question.

"In all *temporal* matters, Your Grace, I will serve *you* with all my heart," answered Anthony, looking her straight in the eye. He added softly, "What man could resist so fair a mistress?"

Much as she loved flattery, Elizabeth had long ago learned to listen for the underlying ring of truth. She appreciated Lord Montagu's courage. The religious convictions of most courtiers yielded fast to expediency. Also, his bold glance told her that he did indeed think her fair, that he recognized both her charms and her regal dignity. There was, he saw at once, the strength and flexibility of Damascene steel in this young woman. She had indeed been sired by King Henry. During the evening the Queen gave him occasional friendly smiles—but he was removed from the Privy Council. Men long in eclipse had reappeared. Anthony would hold no official position in the new reign.

Anthony returned to Cowdray, in melancholy mood, for the Yuletide. Magdalen forbore vexatious topics until her lord had rested for the night. The next day was Christmas Eve, and after breakfast she told him, "The Lady Ursula is dead. I've had her laid out in the chapel, since she was born at Cowdray."

Anthony crossed himself. "She had the last rites?"

Magdalen shook her head, frowning. "Celia did not summon the priest till next day. The lass has not even prayed beside the bier."

"For sure the poor lady died in a state o' grace," said Anthony. "We'll have Masses said. 'Odsbody, enough of funerals! Tomorrow we'll rejoice. Christmas games!" Anthony's eyes sparkled. "Edwin is Lord o' Misrule. Must see him at once, help me cast off dull care!"

"My lord," said Magdalen reluctantly, "Edwin is gone."

"Gone?" Anthony stared at her.

"Home. Battling wi' his faither. Edwin's gone daft. He vows he'll wed Celia. He broke his betrothal the day he coom of age."

Anthony snorted. "That Celia! I'll deal wi' her."

"It's na so easy. She's in her room, grieving. And we can't send her to Syon. With the Protestants, it'll be suppressed again."

"Aye," said Anthony, frowning heavily. "It is already."

The Christmas festivities proceeded without either Celia or Edwin. Edwin was being ostentatiously treated as the victim of an attack of madness. Celia stayed in Ursula's chamber, having no heart for merriment. Ursula had died in her sleep, her head resting on Celia's shoulder. Celia had loved Ursula. Now new fires must be lit, new plans laid.

Ursula's will left Celia all she possessed. For Celia the meagreness of the inheritance was transfigured by the delight of ownership. She rearranged the chamber. She explored the great court cupboard, found many items to enhance her beauty and rejoiced that they were hers. In the chest she found Ursula's wedding gown, a satin overdress sprigged with tiny embroidered flowerets, faded to a rich cream, with silver bands and silver belt now tarnished black.

Celia tried it on. The bodice could be tightened, the silver polished. I shall wear this at *my* wedding, she thought. She determined to marry Edwin. The two prime obstacles, Squire Ratcliffe and Anthony, she was sure she could manage. After her aunt's funeral she would choose her time. Meanwhile, she discarded her cheap widow's garb and altered Ursula's best black velvet weeds, knowing that the velvet enhanced the beauty of her skin.

The funeral was held on December 27. Anthony and Magdalen attended the Mass at Cowdray Chapel, but they did not go to Easebourne Church for the burial service. Celia walked alone, followed by a handful of retainers who had known Ursula.

Once back at Cowdray she made her plans. The time to approach Anthony, she decided, was when he was mellowed by the Twelfth Night festival. She had already exchanged messages with Edwin through Robin, the page who had waited on Ursula. He was so dazzled by Celia that he gladly loped the seven miles to the Ratcliffes for the sake of her thanks.

The twelfth and last day of Christmas came in a crisped sparkle of icy trees. Cowdray was lavishly decorated with holly and spruce. The fine weather was a happy omen, and Celia felt exhilarated.

On Twelfth Night the Christmas revels climaxed with the traditional "dance of fools". Celia trusted that amid the carousing the presence of an extra "fool" would not be noticed. There were always twelve fools—for the months of the year, for the days of Christmas—dressed as court jesters. Their identities were secret. There were stacks of old costumes in Cowdray's attics, so Robin had had no trouble smuggling one to Celia.

By dusk she was ready. The long parti-coloured hood came to her waist and covered her bosom. The baggy trunks hid her hips. She had made a sad clown mask out of parchment, on her hands she wore gloves to hide the amethyst wedding ring.

She stole downstairs when she saw the commotion in the courtyard. They were lighting the bonfire near the fountain. The twelve fools were milling around by the gatehouse, along with three hobbyhorse clowns, amid much laughter. Celia joined the group without anyone noticing.

As was the age-old custom, Anthony himself soon appeared and cried, "Welcome, sir fools! Will ye dance Christmas out for the lords of Cowdray?"

"Aye, if ye do *our* bidding tonight!"

Anthony made a sweeping bow. "Ye shall be masters here."

The fools, jingling their bells, leaped in the air, then jogtrotted into the Great Buck Hall. Magdalen, splendid in gold and green brocade, came down from the dais to greet them. The ticklish moment for Celia was the first step of the dance, when the fools formed six couples and bowed to each other. An odd man would be noticed at once. She managed to hide behind one of the hobby-horses in a patch of shadow. But the next measure was an intricate leaping, darting mêlée, and she moved in with the fools, copying their every leap.

Then came the part of the dance she counted on. The group dissolved, and each fool ran around the audience, tapping now one, now another, and crying—muffled through their masks—"Come hither, wretched wight, we'll purge—we'll purge!" Soon all who had been tapped followed the cavorting fools from the Hall to the chapel. Here they all began to riot, thumbing noses at the crucifix and performing all manner of obscenities, while the company roared with mirth and the music became wilder and wilder.

The house priests and Anthony looked on tolerantly. Anthony had drunk far more than usual; he, too, enjoyed this one night of debasement when he was *not* Lord Montagu, and irreverence towards him, as to the chapel, satisfied a need for masquerade, for momentary freedom from restraints. When one of the smallest fools capered up and thumped him on the shoulder, hissing "Come," he was delighted. "Surely, good fool, where shall we go?"

Highly amused, Anthony allowed himself to be tugged up the grand staircase and into his small wainscoted study. The fool pushed him into a chair, then turned the great key in the lock.

"What d'ye want of me?" said Anthony, suddenly wary.

"Obedience, as you have sworn," cried the fool, ripping off the hood and mask. The girl's golden hair tumbled to her waist. Her face was of startling beauty.

Anthony gasped. "'Odsbody," he whispered. "'Tis Celia!"

"Aye, 'tis Celia," she said with a peal of laughter. "And you've vowed to do my bidding." She moved nearer and he saw the upturned breasts through her shift. He lunged and grabbed her.

"Is't *this*, my little demon? Aye, 'tis a night for lust."

"Nay," she said, slithering from his hold. "Not that you displease me, sweet, but surely you're not the man to rape a virgin!"

"*Virgin!* Madam, you mock me! *Who* is virgin?"

"I am a virgin," she repeated quietly. "Sir John was unable."

Anthony drew back, staring, was slowly convinced, then stricken by remorse. "Poor little lass. What would you have me do, Celia?"

"Arrange my marriage to Edwin Ratcliffe. *You* can do it."

Anthony looked at her beseeching face. Aye, he had this power, and he had helped sentence her to those sterile years. Celia was a de Bohun, and beautiful, and the lad adored her. He could spare some farmland for a dowry. Why not?

"When you were a capering fool, my pretty," he said, smiling, "I swore to obey you. I can do no less for a fair woman."

Celia knelt and kissed his hand. "You're not angered with me?"

Anthony stroked the soft shining hair. "'Twas a merry jest and proves your wit. Edwin is lucky!"

Chapter 11

Queen Elizabeth was crowned on January 15, 1559, a date picked by Dr. John Dee from meticulous calculations in Elizabeth's horoscope. Julian and Dee had drifted apart, and Julian now found himself as subtly but firmly ousted from the new court as Anthony was. Elizabeth, who knew that her popularity was based on her fully English blood, evinced distaste for all foreigners.

Occasionally Julian wondered what had happened to Ursula or Celia. When Anthony, at Queen Mary's funeral, had invited him to Cowdray for Yuletide, he had been gratified. Though saddened to find that Ursula was dead, he was pleased when Magdalen invited him to stay on for her confinement. He was also pleased to be near Celia, to see her so radiant and assured. For Anthony kept his Twelfth Night promise, and Celia's marriage to Edwin was set for Sunday, April 9, safely ahead of Magdalen's term.

On the Thursday afternoon before the wedding, it rained. Celia sat with Magdalen and her ladies in the private parlour. All of the old friendship had returned. Celia, sewing on Ursula's wedding dress, thought: all is well.

She was, therefore, dismayed when, as once in Lincolnshire long ago, she heard voices. There was a woman's, choking with grief. "Sir Arthur, I can't stand this! She's losing ground. I don't care *what* Akananda says. As for Richard, he's shut up in that room, and Nanny's so frightened. She says he raves about those stupid Simpsons, and mortal sin. What's *happened* to those two?" There was some masculine murmuring in response, then silence.

Celia gazed vaguely around Magdalen's parlour, puzzled. The eerie voice had not sounded like Ursula, yet she thought of Ursula. But the names were meaningless.

Magdalen looked at her and laughed. "What ails ye, hinny?"

Celia shook herself. "I heard a woman's voice, most doleful."

"Och," said Magdalen, "it'll be a cow down i' the byre." She yawned. "I'd lay doon a wee bit, but that my lord'll be back any moment fra Lunnon. Sech a broil with all the daft changes the Queen's Grace wants. She would put us back to Englished Mass an' Prayer Book, and to be supreme head o' the Church. *Daft!*"

Celia was not much interested. The Ratcliffes were Catholic, but they would doubtless conform, as Anthony had when Edward was king, denuding the chapel, hiding the priest.

Brother Stephen. She could think of him calmly now, as one long dead. The feelings she had suffered, even those moments of forbidden love at Southwark, had happened to a foolish child. She was about to be Edwin's bride. A dear lad, courteous and accomplished. There would be comfortable years, babies, residence in a charming manor. She would be near Magdalen and Anthony, received at Cowdray as an equal. Her happiness rushed back.

It was Celia's last placid day.

ANTHONY came home late. They sat down to supper in the privy dining room to which both Celia and Julian were invited. Anthony, scowling, ate his roast lamb and drank his sack in silence.

"The Queen is now head of the Church, my lord?" Julian finally ventured.

Anthony gave a sudden bitter laugh. "So it be. Queen Elizabeth has transformed herself into His Holiness the Pope. I, Viscount Montagu, alone gainsaid this monstrous shift."

"But the bishops?" interjected Julian.

"Voted nay, much good it'll do 'em in the Tower!"

"The *Tower* . . . Oh, Anthony, could ye na ha' kept *mum?*"

"I meant to, Maggie. 'Twas that stiff-necked monk Brother Stephen. He's returned from France and has been serving in Westminster as junior to Abbot Feckenham. He prayed at me all one night. Told me the curse o' Cowdray would strike us all. Said 'twas the only way to avert punishment for my father's sin in taking Easebourne, the priory, and Battle Abbey."

There was a stunned silence, broken at last by Julian. "I congratulate your courage, my lord. Is the Queen very wroth?"

"She was much displeased, Cecil said. Yet for the love her father, King Harry, bore mine, and the esteem in which she held *me*, she would take no harsh measures at present. However." Anthony went on, "she's sending me out o' the country. On a trumped-up mission to Spain and King Philip."

Magdalen paled again. "When—when mun ye go, my lord? Blessed Jesu, not afore this wee one's born!"

"Cecil gave me a month to prepare. Poor wife, don't look so doleful. This is better than the Tower, whence so few return."

To Magdalen the long sea voyage seemed as dangerous. Her fears broke out in anger. "God blast that meddlesome monk! I wish I'd him here—I'd show him what I feel!"

Anthony said something to the yeoman behind his chair. "*That* is a wish I can grant, lady. Would others were so easy."

Celia suddenly took Anthony's meaning and her heart lurched.

"*Benedicite*," Stephen said quietly. Magdalen was too startled to speak for a moment.

Celia could not look up. His deep voice seemed to race into her breast, where it churned up such turmoil that she shuddered. Julian saw her head down, saw her whitened knuckles as she gripped the table. *Dio*, can it still be thus? He examined Stephen. Tall, broad-shouldered; the same dark, lean face; a mouth that would be sensual on another man. Julian felt masculine strength, hardness of stone, heat of fires well banked. This man should never be a monk. . . . Julian paused and chided himself. Yet he had dedication—a rare and wondrous quality, one he himself had lost.

"Ye know Doctor Julian, don't ye, Brother?" said Magdalen.

"Aye," said Stephen, smiling. "He cured me once of a rat bite."

"And perchance ye know M'lady Hutchinson?"

Stephen started to make a courteous disclaimer. Then Celia raised her face. Their eyes met in a long fulminating gaze.

Stephen's intake of breath struck Julian like a thunderclap. He saw the tremors which seized Celia. *Dio mio!* They are drowning in each other's eyes. Quickly he upset his wine.

The mopping up gave Stephen time for control. "Ah, yes, Mistress Celia and I met in my Cowdray days." But Celia was still incapable of saying anything. Bitter fluid rose in her throat.

"Stephen," Anthony said, "you'll come with me to Spain, as my confessor? After all, ye got me into it. If I acquit myself well, the Queen's Grace may be mollified."

The young monk shook his head. "'Twould be agreeable, but Abbot Feckenham has plans for me to go to Ightham Mote in Kent as chaplain to Sir Christopher Allen."

Celia shivered. She could not stop herself from shivering.

"Allen?" cried Anthony. "Not that odious woman! Sorry, Stephen, she's some kin o' your brother, Tom's, isn't she, but that's no reason to bury yourself. What's Abbot Feckenham up to?"

"He sends me to a house where there is no trace of compromise or heresy. Such few homes left in England must be supported."

"Bosh!" said Anthony. "How long can ye stay wi' us?"

"I've a fortnight, but I wish to see Tom at Medfield."

"Och, then," Magdalen cried, "ye'll assist at Celia's wedding Sunday! That'll please ye, eh, hinny?"

Stephen spoke before Celia need respond. "I must leave here *Saturday*, but I wish Lady Hutchinson the greatest happiness."

Celia slumped, and would have fallen, but Julian caught her. "I'm all right." Celia sat up straight and looked at Stephen. "I believe brides are given to vapours. Aren't they, Brother Stephen?"

He could not answer her. Magdalen said, "Brother Stephen, ye may tak' the blue chamber whilst ye're wi' us."

"I've a fancy, if you permit, to go back to St. Ann's Hill."

"It's no guid shelter," protested Magdalen, but Stephen was determined. He bowed his thanks and asked to be excused.

"Yon's a guid priest," said Magdalen, "fur all he looks like a fighter."

"My lady," Celia said, "I'm queasy, may I go to my chamber?"

No! thought Julian. He half-rose from the table. I could stop her, whatever her plan. But his thickly cushioned chair was comfortable, and he had not finished his delicious marchpane tart.

Celia intercepted Stephen in the courtyard. "Stephen, I *must* speak with you—God, I never knew 'twould be like this again."

He raised his chin. "We've naught to say to each other."

"We *have*. I saw it in your eyes! I must talk to you. *Only talk*—" she stammered. "I need your counsel. I'll come later up Tan's Hill."

"*Nay!*" he cried. "I forbid it. Leave be, Celia!" He pushed her aside and almost ran through the gatehouse.

"Blessed Jesu help me!" Celia whispered. Then she clamped her lips at the instinctive supplication.

She found Robin in the scullery. "Which page is to carry the requirements to the stranger monk on Tan's Hill tonight?"

The order had just come. Robin would go himself. She smiled. "Good. Be sure the holy brother's ale is not sour. Bring it to me to taste before you take it."

Robin did not dream of questioning. He took up the tankard of foaming ale and waited like a good dog outside her door, while she ransacked the coffer for the vial the water witch had given her. Breathing hard, she took a brand of dead charcoal from the brazier, pushed aside the rushes on the floor and drew the five-pointed star. She put the vial in the centre. "Ishtareth," she said three times, then poured the powder into the tankard.

"Dear Robin," she said, as she opened her door, "you're a great comfort to me." He bobbed his head and took the tankard.

While she waited for the castle to quiet down, Celia arrayed herself in the bridal dress and combed her hair into a cascade of gold. Then she opened a silver bottle—essence of gillyflower—that Edwin had given her to use on her bridal day. "Ishtareth," she said, and laughed as she rubbed the spicy carnation scent on her neck and arms. And the laugh sounded strange, as though it came from someone else.

She put on her black cloak, pulled the hood close around her face and ran down the stairs. When she scrambled across the rubble of the old Bohun stronghold, she saw light in the hut. The door was on the latch, but she went in, letting her cloak slip off as she advanced towards Stephen, holding out her arms.

"Celia . . . I forbade this . . . don't look at me like that!" He covered his eyes. "*Maria Beata—Miserere mei.*"

"Ah," Celia said sweetly. "*She's* not here now. *I* am, Stephen. And I wear my bridal gown for you. None but you."

"Christ!" he cried. "Why did I come back to Cowdray!"

"You've drunk but little of your ale," she said, looking into the tankard. "We'll drink together, a loving cup, my dearest."

"I don't love thee, Celia, I don't want thee. I wore the hair shirt, I scourged myself. I've made my vows. There can be nothing but hell if we should commit so—so horrible a sin."

"But you'll not refuse to drink to my bridal, Brother Stephen?"

"I'd not be churlish to you," he said. He took the tankard and quaffed of the ale. "To your health, and to your bridegroom's."

"I thank you," said Celia. "How good it smells in here. The pallet is new-stuffed with meadow grass and thyme, and do you smell the fragrance I am wearing? 'Tis gillyflower and woos the heart to languorous ease. . . . Stephen, look at me!"

He turned slowly, against his will. Crystal teardrops glistened on her cheeks. Her lips quivered like a child's. "Nay, darling," he whispered, "don't weep." His arms raised of themselves, he pulled her close, and gently kissed her mouth. It opened to his.

She spoke but once more. "Love so wondrous sweet can*not* be wrong." And the honeyed fire consumed them, until they lay quiet, her head buried on his shoulder.

When the Midhurst Church bell rang out for six o'clock Mass, Stephen groaned and turned away.

"Nay, love—we are one. It was always meant to be."

He sprang up from the pallet, yanking his habit around his nakedness, and ran out into the grove of oaks. There he stood, a figure as stiff as the tree trunks. A thrush began to trill its song, which the country people heard as "Did he do it? For sure he did."

Stephen looked up at the bird. "You may well mock me." And

so the devil jeers at me, he thought. He went to the well and sluiced his head and neck. He was encased by a sense of doom.

Finally Stephen returned to the hut. "You must go, dear," he said gently. "Make some excuse if they've missed you. I'll leave today."

"You *can't*! You can't leave me again! Not *now!*"

"What else is there? You'll be happy with Edwin Ratcliffe."

"And *you?* You'll be happy? You can forget this night?"

He shook his head. "But I don't expect happiness. When I dare pray again, 'twill be for mercy. Our carnal love—"

"Carnal love!" she said fiercely. "Is that all *I* mean to you?"

He touched a gleaming tendril of hair which partly covered her breast, then snatched his hand away. "Go, Celia!"

"If I didn't love thee, I could hate thee, Stephen Marsdon!"

As she dressed he sat on the pallet, his face in his hands.

JULIAN AWAKENED that Friday morning in a very bad mood. There was a darting pain behind his eyes. A chill wind whistled around the window. *Santa Maria!* He pulled the blankets close around his shoulders, craving Italian sunlight with a passion. Once Lady Montagu was delivered, he'd go home.

A knock on his door cheered him. The servant would make a fire. "Enter!" he cried, and was disappointed to see Celia.

"F-forgive me, Master Julian," she said, taken aback by his angry face. "I—I thought you might—that you would help me."

Julian crouched in his blankets and looked at her. The egotistical arrogance of the young! And of beauty. Some subtle change in that beauty; the sea-blue eyes were dark-circled; there was a red mark on her neck. "The monk, no doubt," he said. "I'm not interested in your lechery."

She flushed scarlet. "It's *not* lechery! It's love, Master Julian, *love!* Can you not understand that?"

"Ah, yes, extremely pleasurable." A buried string reverberated . . . guilty discomfort under olive trees . . . Greek columns . . . supplication and denial.

"It's *torment*—he's leaving! Yet he loves me, he must." She crumpled onto a stool. "I gave him the water witch's powder."

"You *what*?" said Julian. "You did what?"

It all came out in muffled broken sentences. Melusine. The mandrake root. Mandragora, Julian thought, the most powerful of herbs. Yet, given the look he had seen exchanged between Celia and Stephen, what herb was needed? Human passions could generate enough magic without potions. He felt unaccustomed fear. "What did she say, this witch, when she gave you the powder?"

"That if my heart was pure, that if I used it only to—to help my husband—there was no danger."

"And did you?" he asked.

She shook her head slowly. He saw her widened eyes go blank. "I love him. Naught else matters."

Julian sighed. "If naught else matters, why disturb me?"

She clasped her hands. "Tell Stephen we can flee to the Continent. We could be wed. He can remain a priest. He need only give up his unnatural Benedictine vows."

"You ask too much, Celia. And you do not understand the man you say you love. You think only of yourself. You'll get over this madness, and marry as you should. Go now—and on the way back to your chamber, find somebody to bring up wood."

Her great eyes fixed on him strangely. "You don't care what happens to me or Stephen—yet, I felt . . . I fancied you were trying to help me—a kind of dream, I was dying. . . ."

"My dear girl, you're overwrought. You'll soon forget."

"*Will I?* I'll give order for the wood," she said, and left.

Julian felt dismay, tinged with anger. The effrontery of trying to embroil him in this sordid affair! It could ruin him with the Montagus. I hope Lady Montagu delivers soon, he thought. I need the gold. I'll hasten the birth, rupture the membrane.

England—what had possessed him to waste all these years in a place so alien? Sayings of Plato darted through his bafflement. He had once amused himself with Plato's certainty of transmigration, how each soul selected its life, how the experience of the former life generally guided the choice of the later one. *Was* that the answer? Julian went to his coffer and pulled out an old notebook in which he had written down precepts which had struck his fancy.

One by a Florentine historian in the court of Alessandro de Medici: "Whatsoever has been in the past or is now, will repeat itself in the future, but with the names and surfaces of things so altered that he who has not a quick eye will not recognize them."

Possible, thought Julian uncomfortably. Here was a fourth-century saint, Gregory of Nyssa: "It is absolutely necessary that the soul be healed and purified. If this does not take place during its life on earth, it must be accomplished in future lives."

Future lives, Julian thought. What a wearisome prospect.

"So that finally purged of self-will, purged of desires, the soul becomes one with God." Who said that to him forty years ago at Padua? Black eyes like ripe olives. The visitor from Mecca . . . but he wasn't a Moslem, or was he? What was . . . *Nanak!* That was his name!

Julian no longer wanted to remember Nanak, yet for a moment he forced himself. Something to do with a succession of rebirths in which one experienced the result of every act, thought, especially strong desire. "Be careful what you crave for," Nanak had said, "since you will eventually get it."

Why, the young Julian had persisted, could he not remember past lives, if such he had had. "Sometimes," Nanak finally said, "*if* it's for the soul's good, one remembers. Maybe to redress old wrongs. Remember this, that sins of omission will be punished by the law as certainly as acts of violence."

Suddenly vexed with himself and the whole memory, Julian got up. I desire warmth, sunlight—and I do not intend to wait for some possible future life to attain them!

CELIA did not appear for dinner, but nobody missed her. Her absence at supper would not have been noted either, except that Edwin Ratcliffe had ridden over to see his betrothed.

The Montagus received him cordially, if somewhat absent-mindedly, and sent the nearest page to fetch Celia. The page happened to be Robin, and when he came back after a long time, his young brows were furrowed. "I can't find her, my lord—Juno's gone, but she left her little dog." Robin swallowed a sob. "There's a note writ to you."

"Her *mare* is gone?" said Anthony, refocusing his mind. Anthony read the note twice, then passed it to his wife.

Milord—I can not wed Edwin Ratclif. Pardon forgette me—Celia. Robbin muste care for Tagle.

"'Tis some coy trick," Magdalen said. "She wants ye to find her, Master Ratcliffe."

Anthony chuckled. The thought of the fool's dance on Twelfth Night sent heat to his loins even now. "Yes, Edwin, go find the naughty lass."

Edwin flushed. "She seemed to love me, though I was never sure." He bowed and went off. Beneath his humiliation was certainty: Celia was gone from his life as suddenly as she had entered it. His infatuation extinguished itself almost as completely. He mounted his horse. He debated for just a moment—then pricked the animal towards the Petworth Road and home.

In Cowdray's privy chamber the Montagus looked at each other, "Why has Celia fled?" asked Magdalen.

Remembering suddenly the occasion for the girl's first marriage, Anthony started. Stephen had left this morning. Nay, there could be no connection between Stephen and Celia now. A pox on Celia!

Chapter 12

On August 1 Celia trudged into the village of Ightham in Kent. She had spent nearly four months in flight, first heading instinctively towards London, and then, when her shillings were gone, sleeping in a field with Juno. Arrested for trespassing, she was threatened with the pillory, but released in return for Juno. She kissed the mare farewell and walked through Southwark without a glance towards the priory. She applied for work in a tavern and returned to her girlhood duties, working without hope or plan.

Celia was often awakened now in the morning by a clutch of panic and a bout of nausea. Three days ago she had incurred first the lust, and then the fury, of one of the tavern's best customers, who grabbed her as she came up from the cellars with a flask of Malmsey. Aroused with disgust she swung the flask upward and felled him. The landlord dismissed her, and Celia set out for Kent.

The village of Ightham swarmed with visitors. It was Lammas quarter day, the day when loaves made of the first ripe grain were consecrated. Farmers, cottagers and shepherds were clustered before the George and Dragon. Nobody noticed Celia, who wore a laced bodice, cut-off skirts and a kerchief on her head. Her wedding ring she kept in a pouch she wore around her neck. She went into the George and asked for ale and a bit of bread. The barmaid said, "A ha'penny fur the ale, chuck, but the Lammas bread's free. They allus send loaves from the Mote."

"Ah-h," said Celia. "You mean the Allens at Ightham Mote?"

The barmaid nodded. "Sir Christopher keeps up the old ways. Wot be ye doin' here? Come for the hop pickin'?"

Celia was grateful for the simple friendliness. She smiled and her dimple appeared. The barmaid stared. "Why, chuck, ye'd be fair as a blossom was ye not so thin. Ye don't look a worker."

"I'm a worker. Any posts you know of?"

"I'll think on't," said the barmaid. "Me name's Nancy. Wait i' the kitchen whilst I carry the trays outdoors."

The ale and the fine white Lammas bread had relieved Celia's fatigue by the time Nancy came back bearing news. "M'lady Allen 'as just thrown out her scullery maid. Found she'd a big belly and couldn't name the father. Give her a beating. Very harsh is m'lady when she's in her cups. But the steward, Will Larkin, he'd no be hard on ye. He's in the pot room and ye can arsk him now."

"I've no references," said Celia, and she told Nancy why she'd been dismissed from the tavern. The girl exploded into laughter. "I've wanted to do that m'self. What's your name, chuck?"

"Cissy," said Celia after a moment. "Cissy Boone."

"Well, Cissy, ye speak ladylike. Write yer own reference. Pen and ink i' the parlour."

Cissy Boone is a trusty servente [Celia finally achieved], *Lyved fore year with me in Lincs. I commende hir. Ladye Hutchinson.*

The rest was simple. Steward Larkin was impressed by the note. He helped her into the oxcart and headed for the Mote.

To Celia, Ightham Mote seemed a typical old manor house, with a moat from an earlier age that looked somehow sinister.

"Lot o' ghosts at Ightham," the steward told her cheerfully.

"These old places've seen a lot o' murder. Don't do to dwell on it."

Celia's heart beat fast as she accompanied the steward across the bridge into the cobbled courtyard. "If they're i' the Hall," Larkin said, "ye'll have to wait. My lady don't like disturbings at her food. An' don't 'ee dare set foot outside servants' quarters *ever*."

"Aye, sir." Celia tingled with the sense of Stephen's nearness.

It happened that my lady was in good humour. They had broached the March beer and found it excellent. Her son, Charles, was blossoming under the new chaplain's instructions. So was Emma. She accepted the steward's report affably. "Good, Larkin. I'll see the wench in the buttery."

Celia was as silent as she dared be during the interview. Emma approvingly noted that the reference was signed by a "ladyship". She saw nothing in the thin, downcast face to remind her of a beautiful girl she'd taken a dislike to at Queen Mary's procession.

"All found and a shilling every quarter day," Emma said. "Mass each morning. You *said* you were raised a Catholic?"

"Aye, m'lady."

"No fooling about wi' the men!" added Emma, though she was satisfied that this scrawny bit of woman was not likely to be tempting. "Ye can bed i' the far attic wi' the other maids, an' I don't expect to see you again until my birthday."

"Aye, m'lady," said Celia, and raised her eyes once. Lady Allen at forty-three was still handsome in a full-blown way.

During the next two days she obeyed orders exactly. There was a great deal to do. The indoor staff was small because Emma was a penny-pincher. Apart from the cook, there were three maids and one servitor, Dickon Coxe, to wait on table. Emma Allan took little interest in housekeeping, yet fiercely criticized anything which discommoded her. She arose in the morning bleary-eyed for the ten-thirty Mass. The staff's Mass was at six.

The chapel glowed with rich panelling. Tying her kerchief so as to hide her face, Celia sidled into the back pew. The sight of Stephen, magnificent in a green and gold chasuble, cut her breath. She felt her love was so tangible that he *must* notice her, though he never looked her way. At the end of Mass she returned to the great jumble of pots and skillets to be cleaned.

"'Tis man's work, that," said Dickon, passing through the scullery. "Had I time, Cissy, I'd gi'e ye a hand. Ye seem delicate."

"I'll make do," said Celia, though her back was aching.

"There be ways to get on in this house," said Dickon slyly.

"Aye?" said Celia, reaching for another pewter dish.

"When ye're sent to pantry, slip a pouch o' sugar loaf or nutmeg under yer skirts. I sell 'em in Ightham, we split profit. Ye won't get catched, either, my lady's so fuddled wi' drink. Only mind her temper if ye cross her. She near broke the back o' that last scullery maid. And she killed one o' the hound's pups. Stumbled over it on her way to bed. She wrung its neck."

"Killed a puppy!" Celia shivered. But nothing could sway her, now. "How does the new chaplain?"

"*She* dotes on him. Touches his arm whilst they talk. 'Tis 'Oh, Brother Stephen . . .'" said Dickon in falsetto. "I ne'er met a monk before—this 'un wears a hair shirt under his habit."

The hair-shirt penance made Celia angry. Why must he punish himself, and her, for the happiest moment of their lives? She vowed to fight for the new life inside her as she hadn't for her own.

That evening Celia broke the rules. First she went out to the garden to find a clump of gillyflowers, and picked two of the fragrant pinks. Then she crept up the back stairs and began exploring the house. She found a room called the "solar", which had one small interior window into the chapel so that invalids might see the altar, and another which looked down into the Hall. Celia pressed close to the grille and stared.

Emma and Christopher Allen sat side by side at the head of the table, Charles next to his father, Stephen by Emma, while Larkin ate in isolation below the saltcellar.

Though Stephen had not felt her presence in chapel, this time he was disquieted. She heard him say to Emma, "I've the odd feeling someone's watching us."

"I'd never think *you* one for fancies, Brother Stephen." She prodded him in the ribs and bestowed on him a languishing look.

Stephen drew away, revolted by the woman's infatuation. "I see the mason's made progress with the niche for your new safe." He pointed to a spot below where Celia stood.

"Aye," said Emma, "but the wall's three foot thick, and he's mortal slow."

Celia left the grille and wandered on, and at last the survey of the Mote's topography was rewarded. She found what was certainly Stephen's room—a wooden cot made up with unbleached linen; a chest with his missal lying on it; his picture of the Virgin.

Celia paused beside the image. "I'll win him yet and be damned to you!" But she heard her blasphemy with a prick of fear.

She plucked a dozen hairs from her head and tied them around two gillyflowers into a bowknot. She put the offering on Stephen's pillow. Their clovelike scent pervaded the room. Would he guess? She felt a great lifting of the spirits.

STEPHEN found the gillyflowers and was perturbed. There was no one with such hair at Ightham Mote. At least it couldn't be Emma Allen who put them there. Burnished gold. No, he thought. She's married to Edwin Ratcliffe. But his hand trembled as it held the gillyflowers. The scent troubled him. He put them inside his coffer, and felt himself rushing towards a precipice.

He sat down on his cot and thought determinedly of pleasant things. His brother, Tom, and his family had made him very welcome at Medfield. Tom was virtually the local squire, and Nan kept pace with him. Nan happily resembled her sister Emma in colouring only. She had given Tom two more babies after little Tom, now a bright, sensitive five-year-old. One evening Tom had shown Stephen a large vellum-bound book in which he wanted his brother to write down all the Marsdon names, births and deaths that the two of them could remember. "Ye know, Stephen," said Tom, "we've got a *crest*, us Marsdons. It's on great-grandfather's old silver goblet."

"Sure enough, Tom. A cockatrice, and the French for 'Beware'. Beware of temptation—and *pride*." He smiled.

"Well, I *be* proud," said Tom, "proud o' the Marsdon stock."

But between them they could go no further back than their great-grandfather, born in 1430. Nan blushed with pleasure when she saw her own name written: "Thomas Marsdon married Anne Saxby, Martinmas A.D. 1550." But she looked at Stephen with troubled eyes. "Oh, I wish ye weren't a monk, Brother. Ye'd be such a fine husband and father. And I wish ye weren't going to Emma."

"Why so?" asked Stephen.

Nan frowned. "Emma's m'own sister. But I was allus afraid of her. She used to snare birds, then twist their necks and keep the corpses. Still, she's well married to old Kit, and I know she cleaves to the true Faith."

Stephen, since his arrival at the Mote, had been aware of the cruel beating of the scullery maid, the killing of the puppy. He had expected some remorse during confession. There was none, and questions drew only puzzled blankness. He had concluded that Emma Allen remembered nothing of her drunken lapses. He must, he resolved, increase his efforts to regulate the spiritual behaviour of the household.

He stood up and took off his robe, then removed the hair shirt. His skin was angry red. The abbot had only commanded the penance for three months, but Stephen had worn the hair shirt for four. He decided the penance was completed and that he might hope now for divine forgiveness. His disciplined mind forbade wonder about those gillyflowers.

CELIA awoke anxiously on the next morning and jumped out of bed. "Wot's ado?" asked Alice, the nursemaid, yawning.

"There's a fine golden sunrise," said Celia, "and I'm going a-walk after Mass." She had lugged a tub of rainwater up to the attic, and Alice watched with interest as Celia washed her hair.

"It do come pretty. I didn't guess—allus a kerchief hiding it," Alice said.

Celia rubbed gillyflower essence on her skin, then put on a clean shift and her other skirt, a fine green wool, made from one of the Lincolnshire gowns. She turned away as she laced her bodice.

Alice suddenly giggled. "Who is he, Cissy, m'dear?"

Celia laughed gaily. "A ploughboy in Ivy Hatch. We're to wed."

"Fancy that, ye sly puss. When'd ye meet him? Must've been some months back, since I believe ye're breedin'!"

"*Nay!*" Celia cried. "My belly's ever been plump."

"Have a care, Cissy, ye know what *she* did to th' last 'un."

"I know. Tell cook I'll be down i' time for breakfast dishes."

Celia had observed that after early Mass, Stephen always walked up to a copse of beeches. Today she skipped Mass and hurried there to wait for him. When she saw the tall figure come up the grassy slope, her palms began to sweat. She hid behind a tree. Suddenly he leaned down and picked a purple mallow.

Celia took a deep breath and came around the tree. "May I have the mallow, Stephen," she asked, "in return for gillyflowers?"

His head jerked up. He stood as though turned to marble, staring at Celia, at her face framed by curtains of golden hair.

"May I have the mallow flower, my dearest?" she said, and took it from his hand. "Now we've exchanged love tokens—" He grabbed her to him with an inarticulate cry. He had no defence. He melted in the fire she kindled. On the moss beneath the beeches, they lay in mindless joy—until a shepherd's horn blew from down the hill.

Stephen stirred. "How can this be? You wed Edwin Ratcliffe."

"Could you *think* so? I never loved any man but thee, Stephen."

"Nor I any woman." And in the saying came the first realization. "You left *all*—you left Cowdray, your marriage—for *me*?"

"Aye, Stephen. And for your babe—here, in my belly."

"God forgive us! Holy Blessed Virgin, what can we do?"

She said quietly, "You can take me, and the babe, to Germany mayhap? We could—" she faltered, afraid of his expression—"marry there? Priests can be married in Germany—Martin Luther was once a monk."

"Marry? Would you damn me to heresy like that!"

"I don't ask it," she said, "but if you love me . . ."

"I love thee above all human beings, but that matters not. I must pray. God will grant us an answer."

"Will he?" said Celia. "Or your Blessed Virgin? I doubt it—if they even exist. You and I must decide this."

Stephen looked horrified. "So to my conscience I must add your loss of faith. Oh, my poor child, pray to Our Lady, as I will."

Suddenly she looked up at him. "I'm afeared—something terrible is going to happen. Can't we leave here together *now*?"

"We must wait for guidance. And surely there is *no* babe. I cannot believe it—unless 'tis punishment for our odious love."

"*Odious* love—poor Stephen, and is it so hateful to you?"

She reached up and put her arms around his neck and pressed her mouth on his. Again passion overwhelmed him like a fiery cloud. The world narrowed to one ecstatic moment.

Again they lay quiet on the moss. "My love," he whispered.

"Aye. And is *this* love not nearer to thee than the other—*her*, in your picture?"

He recoiled. How dared she question? Why must she speak?

"Leave be, Celia—I—there's the next Mass—though I'm no longer worthy to celebrate it, God forgive me."

Celia watched angrily as he smoothed his robes and tied the knotted scourge around his waist. "Jesu," he said, "why did you come? I thought you happily wed." And he ran down the hill.

A great sob rose in Celia's throat. For the first time she began to comprehend her lover's terrible dilemma. With searing insight she saw it: If I make him go to Germany, break his vows to marry me, he'll truly hate me. Master Julian said I did not understand him. I'll run away . . . a few more days . . . then I'll go. When? A voice cut through her chaos. "August eighth," it said. She looked around in fear. But no one was there.

When she crossed the moat into the servants' door, she found Dickon Coxe outside the scullery. "Ye look forespent. Yer boy'll be a lusty one, eh?" So Alice had been talking! "Ye needn't go so far afield." He grabbed her, fumbling her breasts.

She spoke through her teeth with venom. "Don't you dare touch me, you scurvy thieving little runt, you make me puke."

Dickon's eyes narrowed. "Thanks. I'll no forget that."

Celia knew abstractedly that she had made an enemy. While she scoured and rinsed, her mind plodded in dreary little circles. Leave now, I can't leave, I *must* see him. Pray, I can't pray. Until finally she could not think at all.

The next day, Sunday, August 6, was to be the Transfiguration of our Lord on Mount Tabor. It was also Emma Allen's forty-fourth birthday. It became clear to Stephen that she regarded this coincidence as a special mark of divine favour. After her confession on

Saturday evening she rose from her knees and sat on the other stool. "We must chat a bit, Brother." Her smile jarred him. She was so close that her ample knees pressed against his. She smelled of spirits.

"Lady Allen," he said quietly, "is it possible that—well, that you imbibe certain strong drink which may injure your health?"

"Oh, nay, indeed not—though 'tis kind in you to consider my health. Ye know, I believe you're like *Him*."

Stephen reacted violently. "I am in no way like *Him*, Lady Allen." This was too much. "I must leave Ightham Mote. I'll ask the abbot to send you another chaplain."

"Nay, dear. The Queen ousted Feckenham last month. Ye've no master but *me*. And here ye'll bide."

Stephen rose abruptly. "There's many of your household waiting to make confession, Lady Allen. *Benedicite!*" And he spoke with such authority that she went.

Drunk, Stephen thought, merely that. Yet for a moment he had felt the presence of something "other" and most evil. Until midnight he gave penances and granted absolutions. All the time, in a shut-off part, he felt his own great sin, his sickly longing for Celia.

Emma begrudged money spent, but on this feast day she gave free rein to her husband's generosity. In a new crimson gown she presided at the long table set up in the courtyard, responding to toasts with little beaming nods. But her darting eyes missed nothing, and she beckoned to Larkin. "Where's the new scullery wench—Cissy? I don't see her wi' the other maids."

"I'll go see, m'lady." The steward bowed and scurried off.

He finally found Celia in the buttery examining her wedding ring. "Cissy?" he quavered. "My lady wants ye i' the court."

"I don't feel merry," she said.

"Come on, do," said Larkin. "Just make yer bob an' say, 'I wish ye good health, long life'. Why today 'tis the Mote's great Gaudy Day!"

Celia burst into a peal of laughter. "So be it," she said. She gave her head a toss, then smoothed the golden hair she had not that morning troubled to bind.

With a flourish that was nearly insolent, she curtsied to Sir Christopher, to Stephen, to Emma Allen. "I would've come sooner, my lady, but I thought me forbidden outside servant quarters. May you enjoy many another Gaudy Day!"

Emma stared. This indecent wealth of golden hair, the wide turquoise eyes, was there something familiar? Emma's black brows drew together. "Thankee, my gel, ye may go get some food." As Celia went off swinging her hips, Emma turned to Stephen. "I believe she's lewd. What's your thought, Brother Stephen?"

He could not answer, his throat was too choked with longing and apprehension.

Celia danced, and she ate and drank greedily. She was hungry as she had not been for days. When the Mote clock struck eight, she slipped away, making occasion to pass near Stephen. "My love," she whispered, "I'll come to thee tonight. Leave the door open."

He flushed, started to speak, to say he knew not what, but she was gone, flitting across the courtyard.

Celia was apparently sound asleep when Alice and the chambermaid staggered up from the festivities, talking loudly.

Celia judged it wise to stir. "Be quiet, do, I'm a-weary."

Alice giggled. "Ye didn't seem weary when ye was dancing—all the lads was eyein' ye, but then yer own body wan't there."

"Aye, that's right," said Celia. She lay very still until the other two were snoring, then slid carefully out. She glided down the wooden steps, testing each one for creaks. At the second storey she listened carefully. There was only the distant barking of a dog.

And then, for a moment, she heard a woman's voice, bright and brisk. "And now," it said, "we go through towards the priest's room and the Tudor chapel. The chapel was built about 1521, during the reign of Henry the Eighth . . ."

Celia leaned for support against the panelling. She was breathing fast, but there was no more sound. Mice, to be sure, or maybe ghosts. Her love and purpose repossessed her and she moved surely to Stephen's door. It was ajar, as she had known it would be. Stephen stood next to his cot. Neither of them spoke. He opened his arms and she went into them.

Chapter 13

Emma Allen had ceased to enjoy her festival after Celia appeared with her insolent beauty. She had been watching the girl when she paused by Brother Stephen, and had not missed his expression, like none *she* had ever seen. And the way he bent tenderly down—suspicion was too monstrous. Yet Emma's unease grew. At nine o'clock she stopped the Gaudy Day, ignoring Sir Christopher's protests. "But, my dear, they look forward to this day all year."

"I've had enough. And I'll thank ye to let me be."

"Ye don't feel poorly, my dear?" He spoke anxiously. He never understood his wife's moods, nor quite realized that they had been growing stranger. He was fond of her, proud of the son she had given him and proud of Ightham Mote. And he wished to keep up the traditions of manor lord. But he rarely gainsaid his wife. When the musicians left on this night, he went placidly to bed.

Emma did not. She walked around the courtyard for a while, then went up to the chapel and knelt, her ears alert. Soon she heard footsteps not twelve feet away. She waited a few minutes, then rose stealthily and crept to Stephen's door. She heard his voice. "My dear love, we *will* fly to France."

Opening the door a crack, Emma could see gleaming tresses falling off the bed to the floor. She backed away silently.

"The door's open," Celia whispered. "I saw a face."

"Nay, darling. There's nobody there."

"I'm affrighted," she whispered, shrinking against him.

"No reason. Everyone's asleep. We'll be gone tomorrow."

"There's my ring," she said. "Poor Sir John's ring. Stephen, put it on! It'll make a—a kind of marriage between us . . . before we have to sell it." With difficulty she forced it onto his little finger.

"And what can I give to *you*, my love?"

"Ye've given the babe inside me. Do you believe it now?"

"Aye. My child. Almighty God, I wish I were Tom—squire of Medfield. But I thought I had a vocation. . . . I *did* have . . ."

Celia sat up straight. "There'll always be that between us, Stephen? Can you change your whole nature—for me?"

"Hush," he said. He kissed her, and she drew away.

"Something will punish us," she said in a small dead voice.

"Rubbish, it is I should be talking thus. My foolish one, hush. We'll soon be in London, and they'll never find us there."

She leaned over and kissed him softly on the mouth. Then she gave an agonized sigh. "Farewell," she whispered, but he did not stir as she left. No longer furtive, she walked back and observed without surprise that there was a light in the solar. She paused, holding her mantle tight around her. Emma Allen stood there, flanked by Larkin and Dickon.

"Here's the priest's whore," said Emma triumphantly. "Ye know what must be done!"

The two men stood gaping. Dickon said, "Ah-h," and licked his lips. Both stared at Celia. Neither moved.

"Very well, ye cowards." Emma made a low animal sound and lunged. Her hands closed around Celia's neck and twisted.

THE NEXT DAY Stephen, after Mass, went to the beech wood and waited until time for family Mass. He was partly relieved that Celia did not come. By the grey light of morning his plan seemed impractical. He looked at the amethyst heart ring Celia had put on his finger and was worldly enough to be able to assess its probable value—not sufficient to pay their passages to France and support them for long. Other means must be found.

He performed his priestly duties that morning with calm and precision. He was not astonished that Lady Allen did not come to Mass. Sir Christopher murmured that his lady was ailing. Therefore, she did not grace either the dinner or supper table. Nor did the steward. By evening Stephen ceased to think that Celia was showing common sense and began to hunger for sight of her. He went to the scullery and found Alice angrily banging dishes.

"Aye, Father?" she said bobbing.

"I was—well, wondering where—where the new scullery maid was? Didn't see her at Mass this morning."

"Oh, *her*," said Alice. "I suppose she's took off. Has a lover in Ivy Hatch she's hot for. Has left us shorthanded."

Stephen wandered up to the beeches. Tomorrow she'll be here.

There *is* no man at Ivy Hatch, she had said that to quiet the other maids. Then, of a sudden, doubt clashed in him like cymbals—her allurement as she'd listened to Thomas Wyatt's singing; even last night—provocative, dancing, laughing with those yokels. Was one of *them* from Ivy Hatch? It *is* my child, unless. . . . She has told other lies. Mad with a jealousy he never knew existed, he paced back and forth among the tranquil beeches.

It was past midnight of that August 8 when Stephen walked back to the manor determined to see if Celia were in the attic. Stephen groped his way through the unlit passages. At the foot of the backstairs he paused. There was a strange noise in the Hall, a gritty, rhythmic, slapping sound, and a crack of light beneath the door. Stephen held his breath. He opened the door and saw Emma Allen sitting at the end of the table. She seemed to be chuckling—a low bubbling sound. Larkin cowered by the fireplace. It was Dickon who made the slapping noise with a mason's trowel as he fitted a brick into the niche, then dipped into a bucket of mortar and plaster.

"What's this?" said Stephen, his voice unsteady. "Lady Allen, 'tis an odd hour to be sealing up your strongbox!"

"And an odd hour for *you* to be abroad. Ye seek your leman?" Her eyes focussed slowly on Stephen. "Near finished, Dickon. Only two, three more bricks."

Dickon looked at Stephen in terror and dropped his trowel.

The steward whimpered, "I'd naught to do wi' it, sir—she was near dead anyways—poor maidy. I didn't know . . . what the bundle was we carried up from the dungeon. I swear I didn't."

Emma smiled. "O' course ye knew, Larkin. So did Dickon. Ye knew that Christ in his shining robes'd want ye to wall up the priest's whore. 'Twas always done so. . . . An' now ye'll not be tempted, dear," she said to Stephen. "We'll be easy together here at the Mote."

Stephen stared at them for one more second, then he flung himself at the bricks and wet plaster, pulling them down until he saw what was crouched inside, shrouded in brown sacking.

"He mustn't touch her!" Emma screamed. "She's near dead!" She seized the trowel and hit Stephen on the head, stunning him.

"Drag him away," Emma said. "Bind him down in his bed wi' sheets—then, Dickon, come back and finish the job." She rattled a purseful of gold coins. "Ye can live like a lord."

"As ye like, lady. Come on, Larkin, gi'e me a hand wi' *him*."

Emma gaped at the hole in the wall. "That must be filled. . . . Naught there but a lustful scullery maid. . . ." She picked up the trowel and began slapping on the mortar herself.

The next morning Stephen did not appear for the servants' Mass. It was Alice who found him hanging from the beam near the confessional, his knotted scourge around his neck.

ON MICHAELMAS DAY, September 29, Cowdray Castle celebrated with glorious profusion, for Anthony had returned from Spain and his new son, Philip, was to be christened that day. Geese were roasting and apples baking, and Easebourne and Midhurst were decked as never before. There was music at the Spread Eagle, and morris dances in the streets. The bell ringers added to the joyous din. Queen Elizabeth had sent a tiny gilt cup to the infant Philip. The Bishop arrived from Chichester to perform the christening.

Julian alone did not share in the rejoicing. Each day since the baby's birth he had started to plan his return to Italy. He dreaded the English winter, yet lacked the energy to leave.

On August 7, Julian had had a dream, a stifling nightmare in which he thought himself bound in a dark hole with Celia, struggling to escape, and heard her muffled voice moaning his name. He had not thought of Celia since she had run away. Why should he dream of her with suffocating remorse, as though he had wronged her? Celia—a headstrong girl who had thrown away a good marriage and loving friends, and admitted to witchcraft.

Julian grew increasingly morose and viewed the Michaelmas festivities with a sour eye. The instant the christening ended he left to find a quiet sunlit bench, and was irritated when one of a party of galloping horsemen drew rein and hailed him. "Master Julian, by God!" It was Wat Farrier, a trifle drunk. "Ye're the very man. I wouldn't want to plague m'lord on sech a day. Ye can pick the right time. 'Tis the monk."

"Monk? What monk?" Julian was exasperated.

"Stephen, o' course. He's dead, God rest him. His brother, Squire Marsdon, he's at the Spread Eagle, an' wants m'lord's advice."

Julian's knees weakened. Why should the news of Stephen's death bring with it the stifling miasma he had felt in the nightmare of Celia? "When did he die?"

"Last month, I think. I got the feel there's summat fishy."

"I'd better see Marsdon," he said. "May I have your horse?"

"Sure," said Wat. "I'll give ye a hoist. . . . There ye be!"

Julian found Tom Marsdon in the pot room, grim-faced, and explained his presence.

Tom said, "Aye—my poor brother mentioned ye. When d'ye think it'll be seemly to see my Lord Montagu?"

"What for? Brother Stephen must be buried long since."

"That's just it," said Tom. "He should be buried at Medfield wi' the Marsdons, but my sister-in-law, Emma Allen, won't give up the coffin. Keeps it i' the chapel. I rode to the Mote, but I got no satisfaction. I thought my Lord Montagu might write a word to Lord Cobham, who is Lord Lieutenant o' Kent."

"I see," said Julian slowly. "What did your brother die of?"

Tom's face, so like Stephen's, grew more sombre. "I don't think Christopher knows. But I asked the nurserymaid, she turned grey an' had hysterics. Somethin' ain't right."

Julian's intuition seeped through his wall of inertia. "Was there any mention of a girl called Celia?"

Tom frowned. "Never heard of such. Stephen was a godly monk. There'd *be* no girl in his life—I'd kill anybody who said so!"

Julian inclined his head. "I understand, Master Marsdon. I will approach Lord Montagu for you tomorrow."

The next morning Julian caught Anthony just before he set out stag hunting. "Brother Stephen, my lord . . . he's dead."

Anthony crossed himself. "How—how can that be?"

Julian told him briefly of his talk with Tom Marsdon.

"Shocking," said Anthony. "Truly regrettable. He would've been useful to me i' Spain. Tell the secretary to write to Cobham. You'll know what to say, give it to the Marsdon brother. And tell him there'll be a Requiem Mass here after the guests've left."

A WEEK later Julian and Tom Marsdon descended the hill to Ightham Mote. Tom was armed with an order from Lord Cobham. A hearse hired in Ightham rattled behind them. Tom had expected another hostile reception, but what with Emma's sullen refusal to leave her bed or speak for days, Christopher had been forced into command. He was pleased to receive the visitors. "Hearty welcome, brother Tom," he said to Marsdon. "And Doctor. I remember ye kindly from Midhurst—time o' Queen Mary's procession, too. Emma, my dear, ye remember Master Julian, the physician?"

Emma, greatly improved, sat at the table cracking hazelnuts. "Aye," she said. "Pray sit down." She turned to the servitor. "Bring sack."

"Glad to see ye better, sister Emma," said Tom uncertainly. "I fear I've returned on no pleasant errand. There's a hearse a-waitin' for Stephen's coffin. I've an order from Lord Cobham."

Christopher looked anxiously at his wife, but she smiled blandly. "'Tis natural ye'd want him buried at Medfield."

So reasonable a speech at once reassured Tom, but Julian, seeing the dilation of pupil in the strange eyes, felt an emanation of ancient evil—not entirely from her, though she was its focus.

What then was wrong? He looked around the Hall. His glance was drawn towards a large rectangle of darker plaster in the wall near the entrance. Sir Christopher noticed his stare.

"That's where my lady's strongbox is. Newly bricked in and mars the Hall. I've ordered a Flemish tapestry to cover it."

"I want it uncovered," said Emma, "to keep an eye on it."

Julian, baffled and uneasy, could find no reason for the formless suspicions he had arrived with. They were invited to spend the night, and Tom, who was naturally convivial, had begun to think he had made too much ado in running to Lord Montagu and then Lord Cobham. He was delighted when his brother-in-law suggested they sing a round. "Though not too merry," Emma said, "wi' our brother lying dead i' the chapel. Are the Marsdons given to fits, Tom? It was like a fit struck him."

Julian was inclined to agree with Tom that they had been over-imaginative, when he felt a sudden clap of certainty. There was death in the Hall, murder had been done. The woman was evil and would go unpunished. His gaze passed again to the rectangle of new plaster, and even as he looked, the centre glowed with a soft light. In the midst appeared Nanak's face. The heavy-lidded eyes that Julian had seen so many years ago in Padua held both compassion and rebuke.

Leave me alone! Julian said to it in his head. What would you have me do?

Early next morning the Medfield company left for Sussex. Emma did not come down, but as the men were sliding the coffin into the hearse, Christopher said to Tom, "Emma, she wants ye to take this ring. Seems 'twas found on Stephen's little finger."

It was a heart-shaped amethyst ring held by two golden hands.

Julian stared down at the ring in Tom's horny palm. He knew what it was—Celia's wedding ring, the one put on her hand by Sir John Hutchinson at the priory in Southwark five years ago, the one she had worn at Cowdray six months ago.

As the cortège plodded up the lane, Tom was halted by an old man.

"Ye got her in there?" he stabbed a bony finger towards the hearse. "The poor fair maidy—so ye got her outa the wall?"

"Nay, nay, gaffer," Tom was kindly but brisk. "'Tis my brother Stephen Marsdon's body I'm taking home."

"I didn't do it, ye know," said the old man earnestly. "My lady did, I swore I wouldn't speak of it, an' I haven't. I didn't know what we brought up from the old dungeon, 'twasn't hardly breathin' anyways, m'lady'd wrenched her sa good."

Julian clutched his pommel. Tom made an exasperated sound as the old man held onto his horse's rein. "I'm Steward Larkin," he said. "I simply want ye to know *I* didn't do it. I never would, e'en if she *was* the monk's whore."

Julian saw scarlet flame up on Tom's neck. "Ye're daft," Tom growled. "Whoever tends ye should *be* here. *Loose my rein.*"

"She were wi' child, too," said Larkin, dropping his hand. "I'm glad she's gettin' Christian burial so her soul can rest."

"Your brains're addled, ye old turdygut!" Tom spurred his horse and galloped ahead. Julian caught up with him on the brow of the hill. The two men looked in each other's eyes. "Did ye hear that madman?" cried Tom. "The terrible things he said!"

"You must make what you like of it, Master Marsdon." Julian paused a moment. "The man's maundering."

Tom gazed hard for a moment at the doctor, whom he had come to respect. "Aye, to be sure," he said.

"All the same," Julian added softly, "I believe there was truth in what the steward said."

Tom heard him and clamped shut his mind, as shutters are slammed against windows to keep out the cold and fearsome dark. "Hops," he said, pointing to a field of vines already stripped by the pickers. "They do well here. I've a mind to plant 'em at Medfield. I vow they might make me a mint—"

"*Da vero*," said Julian, "we should all plan for our future comforts, and not permit disquiet to enter our lives."

PART THREE: 1968

Chapter 1

Sir Arthur Moore swept into the London Clinic and banged on Celia Marsdon's door. "Open up, Dr. Akananda! This has gone on long enough!" He was relieved to have the door unlocked at once, then startled at the Hindu's face; the man had aged ten years. "God, you look terrible! How's the patient? The hospital thinks I've gone mad to permit these shenanigans."

Akananda drew aside and pointed to the bed, Sir Arthur gaped. "I'll be damned! Brought her round, have you?" He bent over Celia, fingers on pulse, pinched her cheek and watched the blood flow back. "What's the *brain* doing? You never know with cataleptics."

"Her mind . . . will gradually clear." Akananda collapsed into the armchair. "It's been a struggle," he said faintly.

Sir Arthur looked at his colleague with sudden sympathy. "Don't know what you did, Jiddu, but the woman's come out of the grave. Was it hypnotism? You need a bracer, my boy."

"A cup of tea would do it, Arthur." Akananda smiled wearily. "As for this one"—he indicated Celia—"there's more to be done—but not just now. Later we might do the HCG test."

"*What?*" said Sir Arthur. "You think the girl's pregnant?"

"Yes," said Akananda.

"But the mother *said* . . ." Sir Arthur shrugged. "Mrs. Taylor's waiting outside now, by the way, along with the Duchess of Drewton and Sir Harry something."

"So . . . they were, then, also close to her before."

"Look here, old boy. You've *had* it. Want a tranquilizer?"

"I shall be tranquilized," said Akananda, "when I've finished achieving a balance for those to whom I owe it."

Sir Arthur gave him a startled glance. The man made no sense—but look at the patient, sleeping like a healthy baby. "Dammit all, Jiddu, you ought to write this up."

Akananda smiled. "You can hardly write that Celia Marsdon has just lived through a former life in Tudor times, and I with her, guided by my master who was once named Nanak."

Sir Arthur tried to laugh, but there was something about Akananda—a sureness, an impressive quiet. "You were raised to all that stuff, of course. But no, I don't see it at all."

"She will recover, freed from the past; but the end is not yet for the others—for redress, for redemption."

"Very pious sentiments." Sir Arthur grunted. "There was a preacher—I've tried to forget it—*he* talked that way . . . redemption and the lot."

"Truth is naturally universal," said Akananda. "Arthur, we should summon Mrs. Taylor, poor lady."

When Lily Taylor saw Celia sleeping as she had in childhood, she could not restrain a sobbing choke. She kissed her on the cheek, then smoothed the matted curls.

Celia opened her eyes. "Aunt Ursula? Have I been ill?"

"No, no, darling," Lily cried. "I'm your *mother*."

Celia considered this, and nodded. "Aye, to be sure—you almost were—you wanted to be, at Cowdray. And Sir John, he *was* my father this time. He got the riches he wanted, but he didn't get the son. Only me."

Lily looked anxiously at Akananda. "She *looks* normal, but she's delirious. Oh, Doctor, will her mind be all right?"

He nodded. "She has almost made the transition."

"From what?" Lily asked sharply.

"From the far past and its evils."

"The evil's *now*!" Lily cried. "I mean, I guess my baby's come through, I pray you're right. But Richard. . . ."

"Yes. Sir Richard has a worse Karma to understand and expiate. I'll go to him tomorrow, when I've rested."

"I don't understand what makes you help us," Lily said.

"Doctors usually try to help," said Akananda. "Yet *that* time in Tudor England was not the first in which I failed you two." Lily did not hear him. She had seen a movement on the bed, a groping hand. She took it in hers, the fingers clung, and she began to cry softly. He looked tenderly down on them both. "You may stay with Celia, but please don't talk. Let her rest."

Lily nodded mutely.

AKANANDA'S visit to Medfield next day was considerably delayed. He stopped at the Clinic to see his patient and found her sitting up, in a pink bed jacket. "I had such strange dreams. You were in them, Doctor, only you had a beard." Her face puckered. "Something terrible had happened. . . ."

The colour was good, Akananda observed, but there were still signs of strain around the eyes. A pleasant little face; but it held none of the beauty of Celia de Bohun. *This* face would not lead its owner towards wantonness and destruction.

He thought of the moment at Medfield—*Lord, only four days ago*—when this Celia had suddenly merged with the other one—the wild sparkle, her reckless disappearance into the garden with Harry—her defiance. Harry Jones. It was hard to believe that he had once been Anthony Browne, Lord Montagu—and yet Akananda thought so. If the law of Karma *could* be neatly explained, he wondered what had happened during the rest of Lord Montagu's life to make the soul this time inhabit such a common-place man. As for the Duchess—perhaps she had not altered much from Magdalen Dacre. She had been a great lady then, she was so still. Born in a Cumberland castle, she had again moved south with marriage.

Akananda briefly considered the painful experience he had lived through during the last few days, and the purpose behind it. All these people had undoubtedly been brought together at the Marsdons' house party last week so that there might be a chance of resolving an ancient tragedy which was still producing tragedy.

Suddenly Celia said, "Where's Richard? I want him."

Akananda started. The fascinating puzzles of the past were not paramount. The central dilemma remained. "Why, Sir Richard, too, has been ill," he said.

"Oh, poor darling," said Celia. "He was acting rather feverish before the house party. I'm longing to see him." She looked at her left hand. "Where's my ring—the Marsdon ring? I had it. . . ."

Akananda opened the bed-table drawer. "Is this it?"

Celia took the ring and smiled. "Of course. I seem to have forgotten a whole lot. Did I have an accident . . . ? Richard hasn't been *hurt*, has he?"

"*No*," said Akananda with such conviction that Celia relaxed. "Sir Richard has *not* been hurt. I want you to stop talking now and to sleep dreamlessly for three hours." He moved his hand slowly in circles, then smoothed her forehead. "Sleep, Celia. You will awaken refreshed. Sleep. Awake refreshed." He had hypnotized many patients, but never had he had so receptive a subject. He saw her eyelids droop, and left the room. He found the nurse in the hall. "Don't disturb her today—no getting up."

As he passed the waiting room, a man darted out and clutched his arm. "Doctor . . . *please* . . . I've been here an hour, they won't tell me anything!"

Akananda couldn't quite place the contorted face.

"You know me, Doctor. George Simpson. We met at Medfield. I want to know how Lady Marsdon is."

"She's doing well. No need to be so excited about her."

"'Tis Edna, Doctor. She's in hospital—very bad. But the only thing she said before the pain got so bad was 'Celia'—and knowing that was Lady Marsdon's name, and that *she* was so ill, I came to inquire."

He had Akananda's full attention now. "Sit down. Tell me."

"It was last night. She was burned," the little man said with a gulp. "People in the next flat heard her screams—her kimono had caught, she was all in flames—they rolled her in the carpet." George put his hands over his eyes. "They doubt she'll live."

Akananda put his hand on the man's shoulder. "I'm deeply sorry. Can you tell me how it happened? It's better if you talk."

"Must've been the spirit lamp," answered George dully. "Lit it to make a cup of tea . . . she wasn't quite herself maybe. Had a—a tincture the chemist gave her. When she'd taken a lot. . . ."

Akananda spoke soothing words to Simpson, but he felt immense relief. The law of Karma had worked in the great agony and purging of seemingly accidental fire. There was a link which only he could discern. Edna Simpson's accident had happened at the moment Celia had been reliving *her* death at Emma Allen's hands.

"Shall I ring the hospital for you?" he asked. "They're more likely to give me the information than you."

George nodded. The doctor reached for the phone and spoke for some minutes. As he put the receiver down softly, George said, "She's gone . . . ?" Akananda slowly bent his head.

JIDDU AKANANDA and Lily Taylor arrived at Medfield Place that evening in the chauffeur-driven car she had rented in London. Lily felt strength flowing from the Hindu's quiet presence.

A last-minute check on Celia had confirmed steady improvement. She had asked for a Bible, and was quietly leafing through it.

"You don't think that a sign of abnormality?" Lily asked. "She's always been something of an agnostic."

"I think you'll find her changed in many ways," he replied.

They were well into Sussex when she roused herself. "If Richard won't let us in, I suppose we can go to the Star."

The Hindu chuckled. "I thought of that. I've already made reservations. I trust I'm improving in care for your comfort."

"You've been wonderful through all this—" Lily paused.

He put his hand suddenly over hers. She jumped with startled pleasure, then let her hand go limp under the tingling warmth.

"What do you see?" he asked very low. "What do you feel?"

"Why," said Lily, "it's foolish, but I had a flash—white columns, like a Greek temple, against a blue, blue sky. I felt love, grieving . . . a man who deserted me and—our little girl."

"Yes, just so." Akananda spoke tenderly. "My love for you is still there—but in a higher form. You may trust it, now."

Lily caught her breath. From any other man this would have been an overture; from him it couldn't be. The melting and release she felt were not physical.

"While Celia was in great danger, you prayed in Southwark Cathedral. Do you know why you were drawn to that place?"

"No . . . and it didn't help. I kept having a feeling there was something behind the church, buildings, unhappy buildings. I went to look. There were only warehouses."

"There *was* unhappiness for you once where those buildings stand. It was Lord Montagu's priory four hundred years ago."

"Did *I* live there?" asked Lily in a whisper.

"Yes. But there's no need for you to puzzle over it. Here we are."

The car drew up at the entrance to Medfield Place, and the chauffeur opened the rear door. "Seems to be nobody about, madam."

He pushed the bell. Nothing happened. "Is there some staff, madam? I could go round to the back entrance."

"There *was* staff," said Lily unhappily. "Oh, Doctor . . ."

"You may have a wait, my dear," Akananda said. He got out of the car and walked around to the garden, fragrant with roses, stocks and carnations. At the swimming pool he was seized by a frightening question. But he was at once reassured. He knew Richard was alive and in that house. He tried, as he had been taught, to gather together the golden forces into his body, into his brain—fighting an immense desire to be free from turmoil, misery, effort. Let them all help themselves now, he thought. *Celia* is saved. His own expiation would continue. He had felt, since the ordeal in the London Clinic, a stricture in his chest, darting pains in his left arm. He knew he had sacrificed his splendid bodily health.

Akananda turned sharply away from the pool; he was aware of music coming from the house. Gregorian chant—adoration, to the Virgin, to God . . . as he had heard it in this house last week.

The door of the garden room was open. He followed the sound. The door of the old schoolroom was open, too, and Richard was kneeling in the tiny makeshift chapel. He jumped up when Akananda stood beside him.

"Get out of here!" he shouted. "How dare you spy on me! How the devil did you get in?" The eyes were savage, dangerous.

"It's very beautiful—this old church music," Akananda said mildly. "I'd like to listen with you."

"You were here when Celia died," Richard cried. "Get out, you spy! I sacked the servants and locked the doors."

"Well, yes," said Akananda, smiling, "I suppose you did, except the garden door. My Latin is rusty. What are they singing?"

"A *Salve Regina.*" Richard's eyes were wary, perplexed.

"Let's sit down," said Akananda. "It's hard to listen to music standing, don't you think? By the way, your wife is *not* dead—I came to tell you she's at the London Clinic, and doing very well."

"You're wrong. I killed her, I and that Simpson woman. And by God, Celia deserved it. 'Celia the wanton and fair'."

"Edna Simpson *is* dead," said Akananda with trepidation. How far and how fast dared he go? "Fatally burned in a fire. *She* is dead. Celia is not. Now, Sir Richard," he said in a measured voice, "I'd like you to go to bed. We can listen to the music in the morning." He saw renewed tension in his eyes. "Did you sack Nanny, too?" he asked pleasantly. "Or is she still here? Shall we go see if she's around? She's devoted to you."

"Devoted . . ." Richard repeated. He shuddered. "There *is* no devotion. Only betrayal. You, *too*!" He rounded on Akananda, his upper lip curled in a snarl that gave the doctor, for all his experience, a thrill of primitive fear.

He *must* overpower the man, and do it with his will alone. "Touch your crucifix, Stephen Marsdon!" he cried in a voice so penetrating that Richard started. He shook his head like a goaded bull.

"Do as I command you, Brother Stephen," said Akananda. "You vowed obedience to your superior. *I* am your superior!"

Richard wilted slowly under the force behind the doctor's eyes. He dragged himself to the altar and put his hand on the wooden

shaft, below the nailed silver feet. "*Domine non sum dignus . . .*" he said in a muffled voice, and began to tremble.

Akananda took Richard's hand. "Come. We'll find Nanny."

LILY was admitted to Medfield Place by Akananda, through the front door, over an hour later. She saw at once how tired he was.

"You *found* him, didn't you?" she whispered.

He nodded. "I gave him a sedative. He's sleeping."

The tranquilizer had begun to take effect before Richard saw the slashed portrait of Celia in the stairwell. "See! I told you I killed her," he shouted furiously. "She betrayed me!"

Akananda kept his charge on the move, his anxiety mounting. He was sure the little Scottish nurse must be nearby, but he dared not leave Richard alone. They had wandered through most of the great house, before it came to him. Of course—with all his knowledge of the past, which in Richard's disordered brain was so gruesomely intermingled with the present, he should have guessed.

"Did you put Nanny in the cellar?" he asked casually. Richard looked at him through drooping eyelids and yawned. Akananda pushed him into a chair. "Sit there! Don't move," he commanded.

He turned on the cellar lights and called, as he had all through the house. This time he heard a faint reply. At the far end of the cellar he saw a little wooden door, bolted by an iron bar. He found Nanny sitting on a pile of cast-off household implements. The tiny resolute figure greeted Akananda with one sobbing cry. "God be thankit, Doctor. Oh, but he frighted me. He's gan daft, ye ken."

Akananda wasted no words. "How long have you been here?"

"Yester nicht. I'm a wee bit thirsty, but how's *him*?"

"In the kitchen. Hurry!"

The little woman pelted up the stairs ahead of him. She saw Richard, hunched in a chair, and threw her arms around him. "A naughty lad, ye are, playing tricks wi' yer auld Nanny."

Richard looked at her in a dazed way, then his head fell on her poplin-covered bosom. "I'm sleepy."

The next morning Richard slept on heavily as Medfield Place, in Lily's competent hands, rapidly returned to its normal appearance. She and Akananda threw away Celia's slashed portrait. A call to the London Clinic brought reassurance about Celia. And a temporary housekeeper was hired from the village.

"Should we do anything to the schoolroom?" asked Lily.

Akananda frowned thoughtfully. "Let's go and look."

The bright morning light exposed nothing sinister in the shabby room with its coal grate, its battered desks and benches, the ink-stained drugget on the floor.

"The place certainly needs a cleaning," said Lily. "What's in that closet—an *altar?*" She stared at the candles and crucifix.

"Yes," said Akananda. "Sir Richard's chapel."

"But he isn't Catholic, he sneers at religion. Any kind."

"Nonetheless, he *was* devoutly religious once—and the contents of that rather pathetic little cupboard saved him last night."

"Prayer," she said softly, "the redeeming light. . . ."

He smiled. "You understand, my dear. I think we mustn't touch this room now. Let Sir Richard decide when he's able to."

She nodded. "You know, I remember hearing somebody say that the Marsdons' old chapel, their first one, was built in this wing. Do you think it was here?"

"Very probably. The Marsdons retain stronger links with the past than most—especially Sir Richard, though his haven't been quite conscious."

"Yours *are*," she said. "Oh, I wish I could remember."

"Remembrance can cause great suffering. Imperfect, uncomprehending remembrance nearly killed Celia and Sir Richard."

"I learned a poem once, I forgot who wrote it," Lily sighed.

> "'*Twas the moment deep*
> *When we are conscious of the secret dawn*
> *Amid the darkness that we feel is green . . .*
> *Thy face remembered is from other worlds,*
> *It has been died for, though I know not when,*
> *It has been sung of, though I know not where.*'"

She broke off, blushing. "I feel there's something *true* in it."

Akananda put his arm around her shoulders and kissed her cheek. "There *is* something true about it, my dear, and *you*, at least, will always feel the hope of secret dawn."

Chapter 2

On the fourth of July, Celia came home to Medfield Place. The Marsdons' car twisted deftly through London traffic. Akananda sat in front with the chauffeur Lily had hired.

"Why didn't Richard come for me?" Celia asked her mother.

"He's been sick, too, you know," said Lily. "He still isn't very strong."

When Lily had told Richard they were fetching Celia, he'd said only, "I suppose she should come, if she's well enough. I married her."

"He's much better, he knows who she is," Akananda had said. "But much is still unresolved."

Celia was dressed in a violet linen frock which became her clear, tawny skin, and the soft dark hair was rumpled and a little boyish. Yet Lily noted a new maturity. Celia looked older now than her twenty-three years, perhaps it was the hint of sadness, perhaps pregnancy. The test result was positive.

As they crossed southward on London Bridge, Lily glanced at Southwark Cathedral. "Does this church bring back any—anything to you?"

"Why, no," said Celia. "Should I feel something about it?"

"I guess not, it's just that Dr. Akananda said . . ."

Celia interrupted, frowning. "I don't think I like that man."

"He saved your life, Celia," said Lily sternly. "And we need his exceptional skills for Richard. No matter what anybody says, your life, and your baby's, depended on Jiddu Akananda."

Conflict was so rare between this mother and daughter that it disturbed them both. Lily at once changed the subject. "Did you find what you wanted in the Bible?" she asked smiling.

"I found," said Celia, accepting the olive branch, "many verses that had meaning and comfort I'd never seen in them."

The meeting between Richard and Celia was like that of polite strangers. Richard came out on the steps as the car drew up. "It's a pleasure to welcome you back to Medfield Place. Sorry you were ill. I believe tea's laid in the drawing room. We've a whole new staff. Your mother's been most efficient." He nodded to Lily. "And Dr. Akananda? So you've come down for a breather? Splendid."

Akananda bowed gravely, but he was watching Celia. He had seen her eyes widen. She had held her face up to be kissed, but deftly hid the motion by shifting her handbag to the other arm.

"Some tea would be great," she said. "How are *you* feeling, Richard? Funny we should both get sick at the same time."

She'll do, Akananda thought. She's handling this right. It would be better if he and Lily cleared out, but he did not dare. As they sat at tea, he concentrated until he saw the emanations around Richard. There was still danger in them. And the girl—my Celia—his chest twinged. He had felt her hostility at once. Justified in view of the past lives, but saddening.

They dined at eight, and watched television until Lily suggested that a girl just out of the hospital must get her rest. Richard nodded and said he believed that the master bedroom was in order.

"Where are *you* sleeping, Richard?" Celia asked him evenly.

"In the red room. There's a maid to look after you."

"Where is Nanny? I should've thought she'd greet me."

"Oh, no," said Richard. "She never greets guests. Have a nightcap?" he added politely to Akananda, who shook his head. "Then off to bed with you all!"

"Are *you* going to bed, Richard?" said Celia quietly.

He blinked. Her voice penetrated his private world, and he looked at her more closely. Pleasant voice, but not English. A small, chic, brown-haired foreigner—yet one who had some right to question.

"Might spend a while in the library," he said reluctantly. "Fascinating lot of books my ancestors have gathered."

"And the most fascinating of all is the Marsdon Chronicle?" Celia spoke in the same neutral tone, but she flushed, remembering the last time she had been in the library, in her bikini, the last time he had shown her any real love. And after that—the visit to Ightham Mote—fear, and a long void. A black tunnel.

"I don't expect the family archives to interest you," Richard said. "You had no part in them."

"But she *did*!" said Akananda from the foot of the stairs.

Richard stared at the Hindu in perplexity. "Well, I suppose I did enter our marriage in the Chronicle—or intended to—"

Celia made a small choking sound. She knew that Richard had not recorded their marriage, and a sea of desolation washed through her.

Akananda looked at Celia's hand clutching the banister and said, "Sir Richard, your wife bears the Marsdon bridal ring; you gave it to her. But she also gave it to *you* on a certain occasion."

"Nonsense," said Richard, though he stared at the amethyst heart. "You make me uncomfortable, Doctor. You're a psychiatrist, aren't you? I suppose dealing with crackpots makes you—"

"A bit of a crackpot, too?" Akananda took it up. This is coming faster than I expected, he thought, and deep in his mind, he asked for guidance. "Lady Marsdon," he said, "as physician delegated by Sir Arthur for your care, I wish you to go to bed."

Celia clutched the banister harder, her eyes flashed. "I'm not a child, Doctor, I don't need you to tell me what to do. Leave me alone with my husband!" But on the last word her voice wavered.

"Courage, my child," said Akananda, so low that Celia did not hear, though she glanced at him and felt a far-off comfort.

"I guess I *am* a bit wobbly. See you tomorrow, Richard." Slowly she went up the stairs, accompanied by Lily.

"Carnations." Akananda plucked one from the vase on the hall table. "Delicious fragrance. The gillyflower of centuries past."

"I hate the smell," said Richard. "Are you going to turn in?"

"I wonder if you'd be so good as to show me the library? I'm one of those who likes a book to go to bed with. Even a whodunit."

Richard smiled. "Lord, yes, my father had a lot of them."

Richard walked to the library and switched on the lights. The pseudo-Gothic room contained thousands of books. The windows were open to the sultry July air. Akananda hoped there would be a storm, any outside aid to explode the tension.

"Here are the detective stories," said Richard.

"Actual mysteries are perhaps more exciting, don't you think?" Akananda said, moving into an alcove which held the older books. "I've heard so much about your Chronicle. I mean," he said carefully, "I got some idea, possibly quite wrong, that there was a mystery in your own archives, some past puzzle not yet solved."

Richard stiffened and his face grew black. "Who said so?"

"Your unconscious mind remembers. I wish it to become conscious. *Sir Richard, sit down!*" said Akananda, indicating an armchair. "You obeyed me in the schoolroom, though you've forgotten. You will obey me now, for my purpose is to help you."

"Leave me alone! You can't! I don't want help!"

"Oh, yes, you do, Sir Richard. You will surrender to your hidden self. I'll get the Chronicle. I know where it is."

He reached up for the great vellum-bound book and thrust it in Richard's hands. "Find the passage which has so long disturbed you. Read it to me. Quick!"

Though Richard looked at the page, he spoke from memory: "All Hallows Eve, the thirty-first year of Her Majesty's reign . . ." He jerked back his head. "This is just a lot of stuff about some monk who seems to have got a girl pregnant."

"What happened to the girl, Richard?"

Both men jumped, and gaped at Celia. She stood at the corner of the alcove, very still, wearing a shimmering yellow silk robe.

"There's going to be a thunderstorm," said Celia. "You know they scare me." She smiled up into her husband's face with tenderness and pleading. "What did happen to the pregnant girl?"

Richard passed his hand over his forehead as if to brush away cobwebs. Akananda moved quickly out of the alcove and back to the mystery stories. He heard with relief a rumble of thunder.

"Let's read it," he heard Celia say. "Let me read it, too—if you'll help me, all those squiggles and the funny spelling."

He listened to the duet of voices, Richard's angrily reluctant, prompting Celia when she hesitated. Celia's voice alone finished the excerpt. "Find the murdered girl for Christian burial."

There was a long silence, broken only by thunder.

"Do you think you were once Stephen, and I that walled-up girl?" Celia's question was clear, gentle, assertive—yet tinged with sadness. The Hindu held himself tense, his body quivered.

"*Yes, by God, I do!*" It was a strangled cry, which shocked Akananda into immediate awareness as a physician. He touched the syringe in his pocket. With a man like Richard one never knew.

A sudden breakthrough into realization—alone with the woman he had loved, hated, betrayed his vows for, and then ended his life, believing *she* might have betrayed *him*.

"But then," said Celia, in the same calm tones, "you could hardly give those old bones a Christian burial *now*. The guide at Ightham Mote said they'd been 'dispersed'—I'd rather not try to find them, and what would they mean, anyway?"

Rain began to spatter heavily on the tiles, but Akananda could still hear Celia. "Richard, my dear love—or Stephen, if you wish—that's all finished. *I* am carrying your child *now*, in the present—shall it not have welcome, and a father, as the other one did not?"

For a long time there was no answer. There was thunder again, then a lull, during which Akananda heard a different sound—that of a man's broken, barely audible sobbing.

ON AUGUST 8, at four o'clock, the village of Medfield and certain guests from London gathered in the church. Sir Richard and Lady Marsdon had decided on a religious ceremony to supplement the registry marriage in London. The church, not normally High Church, reeked of incense, many candles were lit on the altar, and the choir quavered raggedly through old Latin chants. Just before the final blessing there was a slight divergence, which startled a few. It consisted of prayers for the repose of the souls of Stephen Marsdon and Celia de Bohun.

"That's creepy," whispered Myra to Harry Jones, who was sitting next to her in a side pew. "And look at this." She pointed to a shiny new brass inscription above the old marble tomb in the niche beside her. STEPHEN MARSDON OSB. 1525–1559. REQUIESCAT IN PACE.

"Got a 'Celia' in the obit, too," Harry whispered back. "Whole thing's peculiar. A couple of R.I.P.'s tacked onto a *wedding*! But then, Richard always was an odd duck."

"It's touching, somehow," Myra murmured, kneeling and bowing her auburn head as the rector began the prayer.

"Let us pray—for the souls of Thy departed servants, Stephen and Celia. Unto God's gracious mercy and protection we commit them. The Lord bless them, and keep them. The Lord make His face to shine upon them, and be gracious unto them. The Lord lift up His countenance upon them, and give them peace, both now and for ever more. . . ." He lowered his hands majestically and put them on the shoulders of the couple, who were kneeling at the altar rail. He went on smoothly to finish the marriage service as Sir Richard had asked. "God the Father, God the Son, God the Holy Ghost, bless, preserve, and keep you . . . that ye may so live together in this life, that in the world to come ye may have life everlasting. Amen."

Richard and Celia Marsdon rose. They looked long into each other's eyes, while the organ wheezed, blatted, then burst into Mendelssohn's triumphal march. They proceeded down the aisle, Celia in a long chiffon gown of a subtle cream colour which made her look taller, and Richard imposing in the conventional cutaway with a small white carnation.

Lily and Akananda followed the bridal couple out. On the faces of the American mother and the Hindu doctor were expressions of quiet joy. The peals of the church bell shook the little belfry while the Marsdons paused beside the lych-gate to greet their guests.

Myra rushed up and kissed Celia. "Oh, my dear," she said, "*thank you* for asking us!" She glanced at Harry, who stood beaming beside her. "May God bless you both," she added. "You've had a rough time." Myra had inquired every day at the Clinic, and she had had two unhappy dreams about Celia. "I'm very fond of you, hinny—as we say in the north."

"Do we now have dancing on the green?" Harry asked. "Touch of Merrie England as it was? Actually, I'm glad I don't live back in those days. I'm satisfied with the present."

"So am I," said Richard. He put his arm around Celia and smiled down at her. She leaned against him, radiant.

Akananda supported himself against a buttress and watched. Though his soul was full of gratitude, he was staving off exhaustion. He saw George Simpson, with his puckered anxious face, coming over to him, and smiled a greeting.

"Nice wedding," George said. "Edna'd have liked it. She was so partial to Sir Richard."

"Ah, yes," said Akananda. He was almost drained of emotion, yet still capable of feeling pity for the good man's grief.

"Are you ill, Doctor?" cried George suddenly. "Come and sit down." He propelled Akananda to the bench in the lych-gate.

"Thanks," whispered Akananda. "I do have these—these spells, lately. It'll pass." He reached in his pocket for a capsule.

The wedding guests were leaving the churchyard, many on foot, since it was less than a mile to Medfield Place. The Marsdons had gone ahead. The church bells pealed on.

Akananda sat huddled on the stone bench, which had been built six hundred years ago for the resting of coffins before they were carried into church for burial rites.

He raised his head at a touch on his shoulder. Lily Taylor stood beside him. "You don't feel well?" she said anxiously. "I came back for you. Celia's going to cut the bridecake—all the old customs Richard wouldn't have in London—and she won't start until you come. Richard wants you there, too. I'm sure you can manage," she said gently.

Akananda rose from the lych-gate bench, he took Lily's arm. "They and you *shall* be happy today," he said, "I, too. Whatever errors may occur in the future, several tragic wrongs *have* been redressed by love, by knowledge and by the Grace of God."

He paused and smiled at her. "These particular lingering debts from the past are finally paid."

Anya Seton

"Reincarnation," says Anya Seton, "still seems to me the only logical explanation for life's inequities, and half the world believes in some form of it today." Miss Seton came by her interest in the subject naturally: her father, the famed naturalist Ernest Thompson Seton, considered he was the reincarnation of an American Indian; her mother felt that at one time she had been an Egyptian priestess.

Miss Seton believes that she too lived before—in fourteenth-century England. In fact, when doing research for a novel set in that period, she often had Celia Marsdon's experience—knowing well a house or a castle she'd never been in before.

Miss Seton's first "quiver of interest" in the *Green Darkness* story came in 1968 on a visit to Ightham Mote, the medieval manor house which is a key setting in the book. There she heard about the "walled-up girl", and viewed the niche in which she had been discovered in the 1870s. The present American owner of the lovely and mysterious Mote in Kent welcomed Miss Seton there many times, and permitted her use of private notes and his excellent library. The Cowdray sections of her novel resulted from Miss Seton's long stays at the Spread Eagle in Midhurst, frequent examination of the Cowdray ruins, and study of local literature. Characters in the Tudor section of *Green Darkness* were assembled with historical accuracy: the lord of Cowdray, Anthony Browne, Viscount Montagu, and his lusty wife, Magdalen Dacre, were well-documented, as was Julian, the Italian physician-astrologer. Celia and Brother Stephen were more shadowy characters, but they too really existed.

Daughter of a respected writer, Miss Seton has written some of the great best-sellers of our time, three of which—*The Winthrop Woman*, *Devil Water*, and *Avalon*—have appeared in previous volumes of Condensed Books.

THE STRANGE FATE OF THE MORRO CASTLE

Gordon Thomas and Max Morgan-Witts

The Strange Fate of the Morro Castle

A CONDENSATION OF THE BOOK BY

Gordon Thomas & Max Morgan-Witts

PUBLISHED BY COLLINS, LONDON

On Wednesday, September 5, 1934, the luxury liner *Morro Castle*, carrying 336 passengers, set sail from Havana, bound for New York. Her captain, Robert Wilmott, was a frightened man, convinced that attempts had already been made both on himself and on the safety of his ship. Within two days Captain Wilmott was dead, apparently of a heart attack. Seven hours later the *Morro Castle* caught fire.

Fanned by gale force winds, the flames spread with terrifying swiftness. Fire-fighting equipment was faulty, the liner's lifeboats were inadequate. Although several other ships came swiftly to the rescue, 134 passengers and crew lost their lives. Conspicuous for his bravery during the fire itself was George Rogers, the *Morro Castle*'s radio officer, a man whose criminal background curiously enough included heavy police suspicion for at least one case of arson . . . .

Gordon Thomas and Max Morgan-Witts have written a spell-binding account of the disaster. Interviews with eye-witnesses—survivors, rescuers, investigators—have helped to emphasize the human drama in the *Morro Castle* story, a tale of incompetence, tragedy, heroism, and quite possibly murder.

Prologue

In 1884 an editorial in the *Daily Spray*, a journal circulating in the Asbury Park area of New Jersey, U.S.A., suggested one way for Asbury Park to improve its resort status.

> We want a first-class shipwreck. Why? To make Asbury Park a famous winter resort. There is a very comfortable berth for a big ship between the fishing pier and the Asbury Avenue Pavilion.
>
> She should strike head-on, so that her nose would ram the Baby Parade grandstand, and her tail might hop around even with the end of the pier.
>
> We could accommodate her all winter.
>
> Pontoon or suspension bridges could be built from the pier and the pavilion, so that the ship could be used as a casino.
>
> We need a spectacular ship.

Fifty years later, almost to the day, the newspaper's demands were fulfilled.

This is the story not only of how it happened, but of why.

A Likely Suspect

Somebody on board wanted to kill him.

No record exists of the exact moment Robert Wilmott, captain of the *Morro Castle*, a cruise liner shuttling between New York and Havana, Cuba, finally came to this conclusion. But it was certainly before his ship docked in Havana on September 4, 1934.

To the passengers aboard the *Morro Castle*, Wilmott was a public-relations press release come true. He epitomized the advertised enchanted world of a sea cruise, in which there is no death or danger. A liner captain was expected to be either a Valentino or an old sea dog, and Robert Wilmott had chosen the latter role. He was big-boned, with a face crimped by the weather, deep-set eyes and a head of greying, close-cropped hair. He liked his pipe. He regaled passengers with tales of rounding the Horn and roaring through the China Sea. It was not all myth either: in September 1933, he had spent seventy-five continuous hours on the bridge steering the *Morro Castle* through a hurricane.

For four years now his ship had been the pride of the American Merchant Marine, the flagship of the eastern seaboard smart set, a haven for those eager to forget about the Depression and Prohibition. On this, the 174th voyage, her reputation as a floating gin-mill remained intact. As usual, nearly every stateroom was filled.

But during the summer of 1934, a series of events had occurred which endangered both the *Morro Castle* and her master. On July 29, a meal had been served that made Wilmott ill enough to suspect poisoning; on August 4, an attempted strike had threatened to wreck the liner's tight schedule; on August 27 a fire had started in No. 5 hold, which contained high explosives.

At first Robert Wilmott tried to isolate each of the incidents, but on the present run from New York to Havana, they had gradually become linked together in his mind. As a result, since the ship's departure from New York on September 1, he had shunned virtually all social obligations on board. He now confined himself to his cabin, not eating, drinking only bottled water. Apart from the first officer, who reported at regular intervals, his only caller was the chief radio officer bringing messages from the radio shack.

Captain Wilmott's absence aroused immediate speculation on board; by the time the *Morro Castle* berthed at the Ward Line pier in Havana that Tuesday, even the tourist passengers were wondering why their captain had relinquished the helm. The ship's officers' bland reassurance that there was nothing to worry about pacified only the least sceptical. Meanwhile, in assessing responsibility for the attempted arson, murder, and strike action, Robert Wilmott had made one grave mistake.

He suspected the wrong person.

STOREKEEPER WILLIAM O'SULLIVAN and Seaman John Gross shared the captain's belief that the fire had been started deliberately. On Wednesday 5 September, deep in number five hold, they sat on a pile of sacking and watched Cuban stevedores stack a cargo of bananas, eggplants, and peppers. From where they sat the two men could clearly see the scorch marks on the bulkhead near where the fire had started. The *Morro Castle*'s smoke-detecting system had on that occasion alerted the bridge; the flames were extinguished by a firefighting mechanism which pumped pressurized carbon dioxide gas into the hold. The incident had been over in moments, but ever since O'Sullivan and Gross had been detailed to guard the huge steel-lined hold whenever it was open.

The theory of incendiarism was supported by several clues; a small train of charred pieces of cardboard led away from the initial fire point; the heat generated was unusually intense, suggesting a chemical agent had been used. The fire had been extinguished only a few feet from crates marked "sporting goods", a regular consignment in the *Morro Castle*'s Havana-bound cargo. "And those crates," said O'Sullivan, "contained enough guns and ammunition to blow the ship all over the Atlantic!"

The storekeeper understated the situation. For a whole year the *Morro Castle* had been a floating arsenal. Certainly none of her passengers had any inkling of this; neither had the American Bureau of Shipping. Built with a low-interest government loan of $3,422,181, the liner had been designed for conversion into a troop carrier in the event of war. But at no time had the Ward Line or its parent company, Atlantic, Gulf and West Indies, informed the government that a vessel "certified for ocean passenger service" was going to be involved in gun-running to the Cuban dictatorship.

In one month, August 1934, the *Morro Castle* transported over one hundred crates of assorted weapons to Havana—kegs of high explosives, drums of gunpowder, cannon powder, smokeless powder, cartridges, bullets, and shells. This arsenal was always unloaded at night by soldiers of the Cuban Army. Storekeeper O'Sullivan had stumbled on this traffic in July 1934, when a longshoreman revealed to him the true contents of the crates. Since then O'Sullivan had kept a careful tally of weaponry going to Cuba.

To him the motive for starting a fire near the "sporting goods" was clear. To prevent these explosives from reaching Cuba, somebody was desperate enough to risk sacrificing a whole ship's crew and passengers; to murder, if necessary, up to 750 people.

Exactly who would take such chances, O'Sullivan could not say with certainty. But he hazarded a guess.

"Communists," he told Gross. "They're the ones behind it!"

Certainly Communism had had a toehold in Cuba for some years before the *Morro Castle* was launched. In May 1919, a handful of professional revolutionaries slipped ashore at Guantánamo Bay, to spread a "workers' revolution" against U.S. domination on the island.

Since 1903 U.S. interests had exercised virtually complete control over Cuba's political and economic affairs. Seventy-five per cent of Cuba's arable land was controlled by U.S. companies; while control in the telephone and electric services exceeded ninety per cent; and for $2,000 a year the U.S. rented military bases at Guantánamo Bay.

During this time, the Americans did little to improve conditions for the local population. Statistics showed that in 1920 there was only one doctor for every 3,000 people; a third of the population had intestinal parasites; the average per capita income was two dollars a month; six out of every ten rural children never went to school.

Dedicated to the abolition of colonialism, the revolutionaries rapidly gained ground in the 1920s. Their immediate goal was to overthrow the corrupt and repressive ruling junta; their ultimate hope was the removal of U.S. influence from the island.

In the interests of stability, successive U.S. administrations openly supported the dictatorship. In 1933 the U.S. Ambassador to Cuba, Sumner Welles, said that the prime qualification for any Cuban president must be "his thorough acquaintance with the desires of the U.S. Government [and] his amenability to suggestion or advice which might be made to him by the American legation". At the same time powerful business interests organized shipments such as those in the *Morro Castle*.

FOR THOSE ON the watch for evidence—real or imagined—of Communist agitation, the *Morro Castle* had been a special focus of attention since her first voyage. The flamboyant Havana police chief, Captain Oscar Hernandez, was one who expressed particular concern. The more conservative Harold Brust, a one-time detective-inspector with Scotland Yard's Special Branch, was another.

Brust's responsibility at the Yard had been political agitators. In 1929, he retired from police work to join the Cuban National Syndicate, which looked after the interests of the island's tourist trade. Early in 1931 Brust provided the Havana police with information which led to the arrest of six Spaniards who had booked passages on the *Morro Castle*. Their luggage contained explosives. They admitted to being Communists. Then, in March 1934, he again uncovered evidence pointing to a Communist plot to sabotage the ship, and there was a spate of arrests.

Now, in September, Brust had warned Captain Hernandez of yet another potential threat to the ship by Cuban Communists.

There may well have been a new plot against the ship. Brust's previous warnings had been timely and correct. And in fact, the Cuban Communists were anxious to make headlines; destroying an American ship that was secretly transporting arms to Cuba would ensure that. But in his most recent warning to the Havana police, Brust had been adamant on one point: it would be "at least a full month before they will make a move". Unfortunately, on a visit to the ship's captain that Wednesday morning, Hernandez omitted to mention this last detail.

Hernandez—in his white suit and floppy hat, cheroot clamped in his mouth, looking a little like Groucho Marx—simply warned the captain to be on the watch for a Communist agent. The mysterious fire, the poisoning attempt, and the strike threat, said Oscar Hernandez, were all "classic symptoms of the presence of Reds". With his worst fears thus confirmed, Captain Wilmott accepted the police officer's diagnosis. In all his thirty-one years with the Ward Line, Robert Wilmott had accepted the obvious. He was the archetypal company man, not given to questioning.

Since childhood he had had only one ambition: to command a passenger ship. Born in London, he left England in 1902 as a deck boy on a freighter to New York. Ten years later he was third officer on a Ward Line cargo boat. He climbed the promotional rungs of the Ward Line with dedication. The reward came in November 1930, when he was fifty-two, command of the company's flagship, the *Morro Castle*.

On his first day aboard, he committed to memory the ship's vital statistics: gross tonnage, 11,520; net tonnage, 6,449; displacement, 15,870; length overall, 508 feet; length between perpendiculars, 482 feet; beam moulded, 70 feet 9 inches; depth moulded to shelter deck, 39 feet; total cargo space, 335,000 cubic feet; type of machinery, twin-screw turbine-electric drive; shaft horsepower, 16,000; boilers, 6 watertube. Though few passengers understood these specifications, he regularly recited them in his speech of welcome after dinner on the first night at sea.

Ponderously firm and earnest, Robert Wilmott had enjoyed a largely trouble-free life. Now that he had been given a label that he could instantly apply to the events of the past few months, he wasted no time. As soon as his visitor left, he locked his cabin, picked up the telephone and called Chief Officer William Warms. "Bill," he said, "There's a Red in the radio shack. Get some irons."

IN FACT, that Wednesday morning, George Ignatius Alagna, the captain's "Red in the radio shack", had already learned that his promising career appeared to be in jeopardy. At 11.30 a.m. he received a message from the Radiomarine Corporation of America, his employers, that he was to be relieved of his post as first assistant radio officer when the voyage ended. There was no mention of a new assignment. At the age of twenty-two, the slim, dark, handsome Alagna faced a bitter lesson: his concern for the welfare of others had probably cost him his future.

George Alagna had joined the *Morro Castle* in June. Like all radio operators, he was leased to the ship by the Radiomarine Corporation, which had a virtual monopoly on radio men within the American Merchant Marine. The pay was good—eighty dollars a month—and Alagna was one of the three operators on the *Morro Castle*.

The junior member of the communications team was a nineteen-year-old, heavily muscled, blond Finn named Charles Maki. Off duty, one of Maki's favourite pastimes was to lie on his bunk contemplating the bulkhead overhead, which he had covered with pictures of muscle-men clipped from body-building magazines. Maki would lie there and flex his biceps, giving an excellent imitation of his heroes.

Stanley Ferson, chief radio officer when Alagna first joined the *Morro Castle*, was an altogether different personality. A lifetime of crouching over a transmitter seemed to have permanently isolated him from ordinary human contact. Alagna exchanged no more than a handful of words with him.

On one trip, Maki was taken ill and a newcomer was drafted into the radio room. To his fury, Alagna was reduced to the most junior post. Only one thing stopped him from making a heated protest—the sympathetic attitude of the newcomer, George White Rogers.

Physically, Rogers was an extraordinary sight. He had curly grey hair, and blue eyes buried in a flabby face. His neck was a fold of flesh connecting a massive head to shoulders that sloped sharply. His hips were many inches larger than his chest. He had a quiet, cooing voice and a smile which seemed to have been permanently set years before.

On his first night aboard Rogers had taken Alagna aside. He said he was specially assigned by the Radiomarine Corporation to get information allowing them to sack both Ferson and Alagna. Apparently somebody on board had stuck a knife into them, but before acting, the Radiomarine wanted positive proof that they were no good. Rogers said too that he had already formed a favourable opinion of Alagna, but still reserved judgment on Ferson.

It was an extraordinary tale, but to Alagna, inexperienced and not a little gullible, it was believable.

Rogers had tapped a well of resentment in Alagna, who angrily spat forth a catalogue of complaints: the food was little better than pig swill; working conditions were appalling; the officers seemed to have stepped out of the nineteenth century.

Rogers suggested a solution: "Organize a strike just before the ship sails on the next trip from New York. You will get all the backing you want." Rogers said he would be unable to participate. His involvement might compromise his "undercover work". That, too, seemed reasonable to Alagna.

Exactly a year before, militant action by seamen had shattered the complacency of American shipowners. In August 1933, the crew of the *Diamond Cement* had staged the first sit-down strike in America, demanding higher wages and improved working conditions. Waterfront workers along the entire East Coast had backed them. The shipping line finally capitulated to the crew's demands. It was a great victory for the seamen.

The foundations for that strike had been carefully laid; the reinforcements to sustain it had been readily available. George Alagna had neither of these prerequisites. All he had was his enthusiasm.

On Saturday, August 4, 1934, Alagna, clutching a copy of the *Marine Workers' Voice*, the official organ of the Marine Workers International Union, approached a number of the crew and junior officers an hour before sailing time. He urged them to walk off. The call to strike was a total failure. The officers looked on Alagna as a dangerous radical willing to risk their livelihoods in an era when ships' officers would sign on as watchmen to make a living. The deck crew was not much more sympathetic. Most of them had nothing in common with the well-spoken college graduate, whose conditions on board were undoubtedly better than theirs.

Captain Wilmott wanted to fire Alagna at once, but the Radiomarine Corporation said it was impossible to find a replacement at such short notice. So Alagna was temporarily reprieved. But he was shunned by virtually all the officers and crew. The only exception was Rogers.

On August 11, Stanley Ferson walked off the *Morro Castle* when she docked in New York. With his departure, Rogers became chief radio officer, Alagna regained his old position as first assistant radioman, and Maki returned to complete the team.

Alagna now found it difficult to relax. He had started to get "the creeps". He believed somebody was trying to waylay him, for the trouble he had caused. "I thought several times that I heard footsteps hurrying along behind me in the shadows of the deck. But each time, when I swung round to investigate, the deck would be vacant."

It may have been this stress which finally sealed Alagna's fate. On this trip, one day out of New York, as the *Morro Castle* steamed through the Florida Strait on her way to Havana, Alagna had been on radio duty. Suddenly he raced to the bridge and accused the watch officer, Second Officer Ivan Freeman, of jamming the main radio transmitter.

It was a ridiculous and improper allegation, and Captain Wilmott sent off a signal to the Radiomarine Corporation demanding the immediate removal of Alagna on their return to New York. The Corporation agreed. They knew that if they had sided against Alagna over the strike, it could have been construed by other militant radiomen as an attack on their rights. But Captain Wilmott's charge of personal misbehaviour was a different matter.

When Alagna received the message that his service on the *Morro Castle* was to be terminated, he sat alone for a while in the silent radio room contemplating the events that had brought such a sudden shift of fortune. Then he crumpled the message and walked into the cramped living quarters he shared with the two other men.

Rogers lay stretched out on his bunk, asleep. Though the wall thermometer read 100°F., the radio chief was fully dressed.

Alagna was struck by the fact that he had never seen Rogers undressed. Whenever the chief radio officer changed from one faded uniform to another, he retired to the privacy of the toilet. Into that tiny cubicle he invariably took a small bag. It was Maki who had discovered it contained puffs, powders, and lotions.

"You want something, George?"

With a shock Alagna realized that Rogers had been watching him for some moments without giving any signs of doing so.

HAD ALAGNA known that he was now suspected of arson, he would have laughed incredulously, but as far as Captain Wilmott could see it was only a small step from trying to stage a strike on his ship to actually trying to destroy it. After the warning from Hernandez, he now regarded Alagna as a committed Communist who would use arson and poison to get his own way, although he had no evidence linking him with either.

He explained to his chief officer, William Warms, that he wanted George Alagna clapped in irons for the return voyage and handed over to the FBI in New York. Warms, however, although he agreed that Alagna was a dangerous *agent provocateur*, argued against this plan because of the difficulties it posed: bad publicity for the Line; the possibility of the Radiomarine Corporation's demand for an independent inquiry; undue concern among the passengers; the refusal of the other two radiomen to work with a depleted staff; and, most importantly, the ship's lack of adequate irons.

As an alternative, Warms suggested keeping a "close watch" on Alagna until the ship reached New York, at which point the radioman would become somebody else's problem.

Captain Wilmott finally agreed.

WILLIAM WARMS, the tall, raw-boned chief officer, had had a chequered career. He had first gone to sea at the age of twelve, his wages two meals a day and a dollar a month. He had immersed himself in sea lore to cushion some of the hard knocks that a turn-of-the-century sailor had to take. By the time he was sixteen he had buffeted around all the oceans of the world. He had sailed with captains who carried Bibles under their arms and with some who forbade drinking, gambling, or "going with dirty women".

Those wrathful skippers had moulded Warms into a God-fearing man who had little enthusiasm for fancy living and was intensely proud of his own climb up the promotion ladder. In 1918, after nine years of service, the Ward Line made him captain of a fruit boat. He did well, and other commands followed: his enthusiasm for his work overcame the discomforts of shunting around the world picking up anything from copra to lemons.

In 1926, Warms became master of a small passenger liner named the *Yumuri*. He worked the crew as hard as he drove himself. Yet, unaccountably, he ignored the cardinal rule of sea captaincy: take every precaution to ensure the safety of passengers and crew. He never held any lifeboat or fire drills on the *Yumuri*.

Three members of the engine-room staff filed a complaint. Warms lost his licence for ten days, and the Ward Line "beached" him. After an agonizing year ashore he was given command of the Ward cruise liner *Agwistar*. In 1928 two fires mysteriously broke out on board. Once more the issue of proper fire precautions came under scrutiny: again Captain Warms lost his command.

To his dying day Warms would maintain he had been a scapegoat. His dourness became more marked. For a year he went about his business, a mere name on the list of employees to those in the Line's head office. But with seamen, Warms had established a reputation as probably the best cargo officer in the American Merchant Marine, and it was this reputation that influenced Captain Wilmott. He needed a first officer who knew the fastest way to load a hold—and how to keep his mouth shut. For the cargoes the *Morro Castle* carried, Warms had proved ideal.

Now, in the privacy of his own cabin, Warms was considering a new idea: if Captain Wilmott continued his strange behaviour the company was bound to make him take a rest. If this happened, would the Ward Line give First Officer Warms a third chance?

Charade

To the passengers, the ship's cruise director—on the *Morro Castle*, his name was Robert Smith—was the front-desk manager, the man in the blue blazer and raffish cap who was always on hand with some new amusement.

The Ward Line's brochures were confident that the passengers' expectations would be met: "The Cruise Director is a genial chap

Getting

...with the Ship

You will find your stateroom comfortable and the room service excellent no matter what the location.

You'll want to give consideration to the position of your deck chair — it's important for those morning and afternoon naps.

The Lounge is a fine and handsome clubroom.

For those with "kiddies" there is the ideal children's Playroom, with its ever careful attendants.

The Smoking Room has everything that appeals to the masculine liking for informality and solid comfort.

The pastry chefs on the "Morro Castle" have the subtle touch that makes them artists.

WHETHER it be in the homelike seclusion and privacy of your own stateroom, or in the public places of the "Morro Castle," you will find an unusual degree of genuine luxury that contributes not only to your comfort, but that appeals as well to your appreciation of the really fine things of life. Every detail of this superb pleasure craft has been designed with the utmost skill to combine all the elements of true beauty and ultimate utility. Abundance of ligh both natural and electrical floods all the public places, while th wholesome daylight streams through the windows of the stateroom making them cheerful indeed. For your hours of idleness in th pleasant sea air, comfortable deck chairs in desirable locations leav nothing to be wished for.

Acquainted
..with your Cruisemates

Every afternoon the ponies gallop over a measured course with all the thrill and suspense of a horse race on the turf.

Mask parties will be another gay feature. Here you may show your genius in costume designing.

Who doesn't like to dance? The Dancing Deck is ideal, and in the moonlight it's simply gorgeous!

The attractive Tea Room is the ideal place to entertain your friends

Many pleasant minutes will be spent watching for porpoises, sailfish and other denizens of the deep.

THERE is such a big variety of amusement and wholesome recreation aboard the "Morro Castle" on your Havana Easter Cruise that you will not find a moment of idleness for the lack of something pleasant to do. The Cruise Director is a wizard with more diverting tricks up his sleeve than Merlin the Magician. It will be something new, something different, when it is least expected. He's a versatile young man, and knows how to keep the ball a-rolling. If you tire of one game there will be others to choose from. Dancing, of course, the universal pleasure, on the moonlit deck under the bright stars of the Tropics, or on the waxed floor of a ballroom fit for a palace. Social chit-chat over a cheering cup in the Tea Room; the carnivalesque merriment of the Mask Parties; the excitement of the horse races—whatever suits you best, whatever fits into your mood will be yours—for a good time.

with an abundance of new and smart ideas that will keep you interested all the time."

On this particular Wednesday noon, Robert Smith was in the process of staging one of those "new and smart ideas"—what the ship's itinerary called "a get-together".

On the trip from New York there were 318 passengers. Thirty-two of them, mostly Cuban, had been using the ship simply as a means of transport to Havana. They travelled tourist in the stern of the ship. Another, larger group on board consisted of the 102 members of the Concordia Singing Society of East New York. Occupying almost the whole of C deck, they were a self-contained group, dining, playing, and dancing as a block. Smith had left both these groups to their own devices. That left him with just under two hundred people to amuse for six days—and a series of get-togethers was a safe, guaranteed way of doing so.

With a glad-eye smile for the ladies, Smith watched the group assemble on the pier at Havana. Representatives of the American urban middle class, most of them were from the cities of the East Coast, and were on the cruise just for "a hell of a big time", but many of the unattached women were searching—in earnest—for husbands. Robert Smith calculated that the single women outnumbered the bachelors by about two to one.

Once the *Morro Castle* docked in Havana, the majority of passengers spent their time ashore on conducted tours, and Cruise Director Smith was now about to bundle them into a flotilla of open cars. "Now listen to this!" he announced, and with the air of a man who had paid for it all out of his own pocket, he outlined the festivities ahead. "First, a visit to a typical Cuban farm. An amazing revelation, folks, of tropical luxuriance. Sugar cane, pineapples, coconuts, tobacco, and, for the ladies, a world of flowers. On the way back you will visit the world-famous Tropical Gardens, drive down the Avenue of Bamboo Trees and the Royal Palm Drive to the Country Club Park, La Playa, the Yacht Club. On to Old Havana, with its winding streets and balconied houses. Then, back on board ready for sailing time—and new games!"

They shouted approval, climbed into the cars and thundered away from the pier. Smith watched them go, beaming happily.

FOR DR. JOSEPH BREGSTEIN, however, the 1168-mile run to Havana had been exactly fifty-eight hours and forty minutes of bitter disappointment.

The thirty-four-year-old widower dentist had paid out over two hundred dollars for a first-class twin-bedded stateroom on a trip he hoped would be an "exciting time" for himself and his nine-year-old son, Mervin. A promise from one of his patients, a high official of the Ward Line, to introduce them to the captain of the *Morro Castle*, seemed to assure the success of the adventure.

Two years had passed since the death of Joe Bregstein's wife. The scars were still there, but in recent months Joe had fallen in love again. It had been a gentle courtship. Both Joe and his fiancée wondered how Mervin would react. In New York there had not been a real opportunity to find out. Joe intended to raise the subject on the voyage.

Unfortunately, as the *Morro Castle* headed towards Havana, nobody seemed to remember the promises of special treatment. No one, in fact, seemed to be the least bit concerned about the Bregsteins' comfort.

Joe Bregstein, never a pushing man, decided to let matters take their course. After briefly exploring the ship, father and son had gone for an early dinner. Assigned to a corner table, they sat virtually alone in the dining room full of white tables, glittering with institutional silverware. The white-coated stewards seemed distantly polite.

The food, when it came, was hardly first-class fare: "the sort of stuff you would get in a summer hotel," Bregstein recalled later. "There was turkey and duck, both with the kind of stuffing which tastes like kitchen soap. The salad dressings seemed to have been bottled years before. Mervin couldn't eat the stuff they offered on the menu. I asked for a couple of lamb chops. The waiter said they weren't on the menu so they couldn't be served. I reminded him this was first class. He shrugged as if he couldn't have cared less. I insisted, so he went away and eventually returned with the chops.

"In one of them was a nail which had obviously been slipped in after the meat was cooked. I called the headwaiter, and he apologized as if he had been doing so all his life on the ship."

Other things disturbed the dentist. There were no life jackets in his cabin; there had been no lifeboat or fire drills. He also noticed that some crew members doubled up on jobs; deckhands would don stewards' jackets to help out during the cocktail hour.

Disturbed by all he saw, Joe Bregstein had not yet found an opportunity to bring up with Mervin the subject of his forthcoming marriage. Nor had the sojourn in Havana offered an appropriate moment. As soon as father and son stepped ashore, they were surrounded by a bevy of guides eager for their business. At the Cathedral they ran the gauntlet of priests with collection plates, and the beggars gave them no rest. Bregstein decided to wait for the heart-to-heart talk until they were on their way back to New York.

JOE BREGSTEIN'S discoveries were evidence of a crack in the *Morro Castle*'s façade. The carefully-nurtured story that she was manned by "the cream of American seamen" was apparently just a fable. Crew troubles had plagued the ship since her second voyage. Her schedule allowed only seven hours in New York every Saturday. In that time the crew had to refuel and load cargo and a fresh group of passengers. Only officers were allowed ashore. Crew members wishing to leave the ship had to sign off, thereby giving up their jobs in an era of unemployment.

This led to acrimony and dissension, which, over the years, degenerated to the point where the *Morro Castle* increasingly drew only seamen of poor quality, many of whom could hardly speak English. Four days previously, while the ship was in New York, forty of the deck crew and a dozen stewards had been sacked for a variety of offences including drunkenness, theft, and assault. Already scheduled for dismissal after this trip were eight stewards, an electrician, five deckhands, and radioman George Alagna.

PASSENGER WILLIAM PRICE was a thirty-eight-year-old New York police patrolman on vacation with his wife Mary. On the morning of September 5, they had spent several exhausting hours ashore buying cigars, perfumes, and souvenirs. Now they leaned over the ship's rail, watching boys diving for coins in the foul water.

Bored with throwing dimes into the sewage the Prices were about to go to their stateroom on D deck when a shrill whistle sounded on the port side. There was a pounding of feet, and somebody shouted, "Break out da hose, for Chrissake, break out da hose!"

Warning his wife, who was crippled, not to try to move from where she was, Price raced across the promenade deck to discover the most unusual scene: the *Morro Castle* was having its first fire drill in three months.

First Officer Warms had given the order. It is almost certain there would have been no fire drill if Captain Wilmott had been in full command. Three months earlier, on June 16, 1934, in violation of the regulations of the Bureau of Navigation and Steamboat Inspection, and at the risk of endangering the lives of everybody on board, Wilmott had banned all further fire drills.

His order could lay him open to prosecution, imprisonment, and the certain loss of his master's licence, but the basis for his decision was simple. In May, during a fire drill, a woman passenger had fallen on a deck made wet by a leaking joint connection between a fire hose and its hydrant. She fractured an ankle and hired a good lawyer, and the Ward Line settled out of court for $25,000.

Captain Wilmott, after a visit to the shipping line office, ordered the *Morro Castle* deck fire hydrants capped and sealed; 2,100 feet of fire hose was locked away, along with nozzles, outlets, and wrenches for each length of hose. As a result, one of the fastest and most luxurious liners became from that moment on a floating fire hazard in all but its cargo holds. If a fire started in any of the passenger areas the only pieces of equipment readily available to fight it were ninety-four portable fire extinguishers.

How this extraordinary situation could have gone undectected can be explained in part by the fact that the annual government inspection of the ship had been carried out in May, 1934, a month *before* Captain Wilmott issued his order.

But other questions raised about a routine re-inspection by another team of government inspectors on August 4, 1934 remain largely unanswered. Crew members insisted later that the inspection was little more than "a walk around and then a drink with the captain". Officers maintained it was a "thorough going-over". If this was so, why were the secured fire hydrants not noticed? Why did the ship's officers and crew remain silent?

The reports filed on the August re-inspection no longer exist. Concerning the silence of officers and crew, remarks made years later by Third Officer Clarence Hackney and Seaman John Gross may provide a clue. "When making a living means not being difficult, then you are not difficult."

Certainly, the fire drill ordered by William Warms was a charade. He refused to allow any water to be used—in case another passenger should be injured—and without water, there was no way to test the single 42-foot length of hose he ordered removed from the ship's storeroom for the drill.

Taking their cue from such lax leadership, the handful of men on the hose treated the drill like carnival time. They lugged it up and down the deck, but they did not couple it to a hydrant. Ports, deadlights, convention valves, deck baffles, fireproof valves, and watertight doors—none were tested.

Seaman Gross regarded the whole affair as a "damn fool pantomime. There weren't enough men at the hose. We just rolled it out and played it around".

FOR DR. CHARLES COCHRANE this cruise was intended as his first complete vacation in three years. He was accompanied by his sister, Catherine, a woman of delicate health who, he believed, would benefit from the sea breezes.

Few on board knew he was one of New York's most distinguished physicians, chief of the urological staff at Kings County Hospital in Brooklyn. From previous experience Charles Cochrane knew the inevitable problems which would arise if it were generally known that he was a doctor. "A doctor is somebody to be consulted at the first rumble of pain. People do so without a second thought—though they would never dream of consulting a bank manager about financial problems if he was on vacation with them."

Tall, elegant, and naturally reserved, Dr. Cochrane had insured privacy for his sister and himself by booking the most expensive pair of suites on the *Morro Castle*, staterooms one and two on A deck. Each cost $160 for the seven days. Forward of all other passenger accommodation and immediately beneath the navigating bridge, their location provided a superb panoramic view of the ocean ahead.

Apart from the absence of the captain from their dinner table, the cruise so far had been what Dr. Cochrane expected. Catherine already looked better, and he had finally been able to relax.

The rumours about the captain did, however, concern him. He dismissed as preposterous the gossip that the captain wanted to be relieved of his command, or that the visit aboard of a senior police officer that morning had been linked with some incident in Robert Wilmott's past life. On the other hand, Dr. Cochrane was disturbed by the captain's almost complete seclusion in his cabin and his strained look during his few public appearances. Such obvious signs of distress in a man charged with the safety of all on board were not reassuring.

On September 5, at five o'clock—an hour before they were due to leave Havana—Dr. Cochrane and his sister were alone on the sun-deck watching the last hold being filled with a cargo of salted hides. The stench was awful. Catherine Cochrane wondered aloud whether the smell would spread to the rest of the ship. Her brother assured her that "the men on the bridge" knew how to control it.

Indeed, Third Officer Clarence Hackney had just received orders from Captain Wilmott on how to do so, but in twenty years at sea Hackney had never been given such a baffling command. He had been instructed that once the hold with the cargo of skins was sealed, the ship's smoke-detecting system was to be turned off and was to remain switched off until the last passenger had disembarked in New York.

The system was the most sophisticated early warning of a fire hazard then available. It was composed of twenty-seven lines of piping leading from various cargo spaces to a cabinet in the wheelhouse. An exhaust fan drew a continuous sample of air through each pipe to the cabinet: the system was so sensitive that, Hackney knew, "anybody having a smoke in the hold would have been spotted at once".

This system, in fact, had indicated the fire in No. 5 hold two

The turbo-electric liner Morro Castle. *Twelve lifeboats, six on either side, were suspended from A deck and hung directly over the promenade of B deck. On the diagram B deck is tinted grey.*

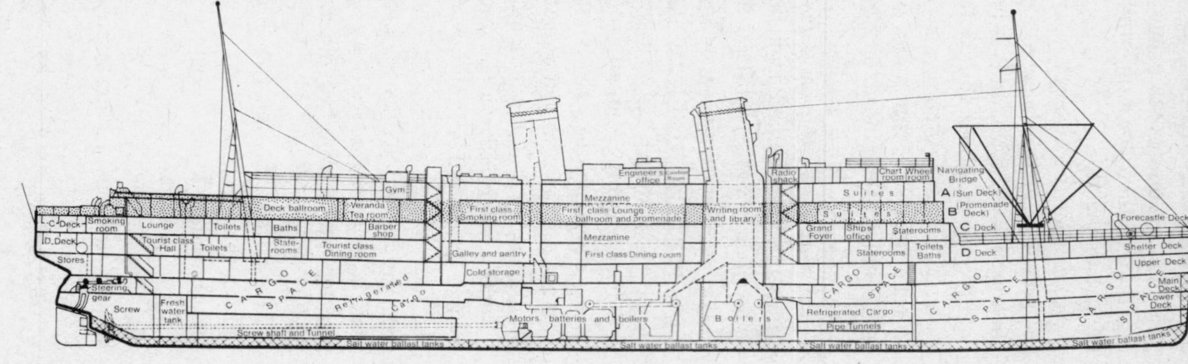

weeks previously. With this order from Captain Wilmott, the cruise liner was no longer afforded such protection. At the time, the only explanation Clarence Hackney could give for the change of procedure was that Wilmott was "putting the passengers in front of everything".

At 5.15 p.m. he shut the valves in the cabinet tubes.

DR. EMILIO GIRO and his brother-in-law, Rafael Mestre, had planned to travel to New York with another line, but were unable to get berths. At the last minute they had found a vacant double stateroom on the *Morro Castle.*

The tall, dark-eyed Mestre was twenty years old, rich, and single. His infectious laugh and his enthusiasm for life charmed everyone he came in contact with. As he bounded up the gangway, the first thing he checked was the number of pretty, unattached girls on board. Mestre was in luck: there were plenty to ensure him a good time all the way to New York.

Emilio Giro was thirty-four years old, well-off, married, with an infant daughter. An outstanding endocrinologist, Dr. Giro was going to America for two months of research.

A cautious man, he approached the *Morro Castle* as if she were a patient. First, he formed an overall impression of her shape, size and colouring: black-hulled, rising to a towering white superstructure, the ship was sleek and graceful and quite the largest he had ever travelled on. Next, he inspected the stateroom. It was compact and planned with care. On the back of the door Dr. Giro read a notice, framed in glass, in English and Spanish:

TO ALL PASSENGERS

The necessary number of life preservers for adults and children will be found in each stateroom.

Directions for Use:

Slip the arms through the shoulder straps and secure the belt across the body and under the arms.

Your lifeboat is: No. 10. Your lifeboat station is B deck.

Emilio Giro located a life jacket under each bed. Then he set off to find lifeboat No. 10.

ACCORDING TO her shipbuilder, the *Morro Castle* was a "three-deck, complete superstructure, with combined forecastle head and long bridge, forming a flush deck forward; double-bridged, with an overhanging promenade deck of steel, as are the companion hoods, enclosures, skylights, domes, and the like".

For their part, the interior designers had succeeded in eliminating any hint of the sea in the passenger compartments. False casement windows accented a décor which mixed something called "olde English" with the wilder moments of the Italian Renaissance. A shattering canvas of what looked like the Mad Hatter's tea party being held in the forecourt of Windsor Castle dominated the dining room. The first-class lounge resembled the drawing room at Versailles during the time of Louis XVI. Redwood, satinwood, ebony and rosewood combined to provide false walls, ceilings and doors. Travelling first class on the *Morro Castle* was like putting to sea in the Waldorf-Astoria.

Tourist-class accommodation for ninety-five passengers was located aft. Here, the rich panelling and carpeting gave way to paint and linoleum and the ventilation system, which pumped carefully measured sea air into the first-class areas, here carried the sniff of engine-room oil and cooking fat.

Dr. Giro located lifeboat No. 10 on the port side of A deck. The boat was made of steel, and would hold at least seventy people. At first he was puzzled that his embarkation station was below on B deck, the promenade deck. Then he realized that for easy access, seamen would lower the boats to the level of the deck below, where the passengers could "just step in".

Satisfied with his inspection, Dr. Giro went below to the promenade deck to watch the final preparations before departure. He was not in time to see the huge, waddling figure of Chief Radio Officer Rogers puffing his way to the wireless shack. Dr. Giro was probably the only man on board qualified to recognize Rogers for what he was—the victim of an unusual disease, adiposogenital dystrophy, also known as Fröhlich's syndrome, a pituitary disorder which frequently produces social maladjustment.

Rogers was carrying two small bottles. One contained sulphuric acid; the other nitric acid.

GEORGE WHITE ROGERS was born with the pituitary disorder on June 9, 1901, in New York City. His mother, Lulu, suffered from a similar glandular disturbance. It gave her a rotund figure—poor equipment for husband-catching. Yet in 1897 she had met and married George Rogers, Sr. He was a reticent man, with strong religious convictions. During the week he drove a dray cart; on Sunday he read aloud from the Bible. There was very little communication between the two, and the arrival of baby George four years after their marriage did nothing to awaken any true intimacy between them.

In August 1906, George Rogers, Sr., took his family west to San Francisco, attracted by newspaper reports that there was big money to be made by anyone willing to work hard to rebuild the city shattered by earthquake and fire. The reports proved to be untrue. There was work, plenty of it, but there was no fortune to be made hauling rubble with a horse and cart.

In the spring of 1907 George Rogers, Sr., died of a chest infection; a few weeks later Lulu Rogers joined him in the municipal cemetery in San Francisco. George was taken to live with his maternal grandmother in nearby Oakland.

At the age of seven George developed an alarming symptom. In a month he gained almost fifty pounds, most of it around his hips and thighs, the upper arms and the back of the neck. The disproportions were accentuated by the thinness of his lower arms and legs.

Taunted increasingly by the neighbourhood children, George Rogers must have been a pitiful sight—an enormous boy, wearing cut-downs of his grandfather's clothes. By the age of twelve he weighed 170 pounds. His knock-knees, soft facial features, and short, pudgy hands made him even more susceptible to ridicule.

He had also become painfully aware of the classic symptom of his illness: he was sexually underdeveloped. His genitals were minute. His hairless skin seemed inordinately feminine, and his voice never deepened into a manly register. The effect of all this on him was devastating: the fat child became a secretive and reclusive adolescent.

By the age of eighteen, the psychological harm was deep. In an attempt to stimulate sexual growth, George Rogers would rub his genitals with various quack lotions and ointments. In his mid-twenties, he added five years to his actual age, in the belief, he once confided, that he would be "more respected".

By the time he joined the *Morro Castle* he was literally obsessed with his sexual immaturity. Although he had married, the union had been a disaster. That failure had increased his hatred for his body, which now weighed 250 pounds; and the memories of cruel teasing by neighbourhood children became a painful carry-over to adulthood.

At numerous stages of his life, the craving for recognition went out of control. At the age of thirteen he claimed he was descended from one of the original Pilgrim families; at sixteen he went around San Francisco dressed as a ship's officer. Three years later, when he applied for a job as a shore telegraphist, he stated he had been a wireless operator since 1910, the year of his ninth birthday.

Rogers worked his way through that and other jobs. Invariably he was given his walking-papers. Now, after three months in the *Morro Castle*, it had happened again: the Radiomarine Corporation told him a few hours before the ship sailed from New York that this was to be his last trip. His dismissal followed a confidential investigation by the Corporation.

Rogers believed—mistakenly—that a number of people on the ship had been questioned during the inquiries. At some point during the voyage to Havana, nursing his hatred, believing himself once more the victim of unfounded injustice, he finally allowed his paranoiac fantasies a free rein. When, at exactly six o'clock Captain Wilmott took his ship out of Havana harbour past the rock fortress whose name she had taken, Rogers's fantasies were real enough for him to act.

Playing with Fire

By 6.30 p.m. life on board the *Morro Castle* had established its normal cruise pattern.

Aft, on B deck, the ship's orchestra was playing hits from the Twenties, and while the passengers danced to the "Tiger Rag" and

"Tea for Two", the ship's headwaiter, Carl Wright, moved graciously through the first-class dining room. A tall, fine-boned man, he had a European-hotel-trained reserve, which gave the dining room the class that the more snobbish passengers demanded. They relished his conversation, always liberally sprinkled with French words. One passenger remarked that he even had the ability to make a bottle of soda water taste like vintage sparkling wine.

Tonight, Wright was hard-pressed to maintain his image of polished sophistication. Five stewards had returned to the ship drunk that afternoon. All would be sacked when they reached New York. For the time being, they were confined to their bunks. This depletion in his staff did not augur well.

Wright's foreboding increased when he was informed that Captain Wilmott intended that night to keep his first dinner date with his passengers for many days. The captain had an unnerving habit of sweeping through the dining room, mentally noting a knife out of alignment, and making an issue of it afterwards.

Meanwhile, Eban Starr Abbott, chief engineer of the *Morro Castle*, was well into his normal evening routine. Satisfied that all was functioning smoothly in the engine room, he bathed and dressed carefully in an immaculate white uniform with gold braid at the cuffs and epaulettes.

For four years, the boxlike cabin between the ship's two smokestacks had been his home at sea. At the end of the last voyage, Eban Abbott had removed an item of property from his cabin: a photograph of his wife Ada. "There were goings-on in the ship that he didn't want me to be any part of," Mrs. Abbott later recalled. He cringed, he told her, at the gin-and-sinning at the nightly gala balls. Naturally, she took him at his word. Yet, Eban Abbott certainly played his part in entertaining the passengers, particularly the many women on board. He was a very passable sleight-of-hand artist with a handkerchief or coins, and even the Cubans admired his ability in executing a rumba.

He had joined the Ward Line in 1909. For twenty years he sweated through the tropics or buffeted across the Bay of Biscay on cargo boats. Then in 1929 he was promoted to one of the key posts in the American Merchant Marine: chief engineer of the

Morro Castle, the fastest turbo-electric vessel afloat. By her maiden voyage on August 23, 1930, Abbott knew the caprices of every generator and armature, the position of every switch and circuit-breaker. On her first trip to Havana, she clipped twelve hours off the record.

Only one thing had marred the situation for him: the first officer of the *Morro Castle* was William Warms. Abbott and Warms actively disliked each other. In the four years since the maiden voyage, the dislike had deepened to the point where Abbott openly referred to that "worm on the bridge", and Warms talked of that "stuffed tailor's dummy in the engine room". But this evening Captain Wilmott had at last settled the situation by politely suggesting that the chief engineer transfer to the Ward Line's other turbo-electric liner, the *Oriente*.

Eban felt strongly that Wilmott didn't want him to go, but that for unexplained reasons the captain had to please Warms.

AT ABOUT the same time, First Officer Warms decided to stroll past the radio shack to check on George Alagna. He had been reporting to the captain on his every move. As he passed by the door to the shack, he saw that Alagna was on duty.

Suddenly, the bulk of George White Rogers filled the doorway. Rogers called out softly. "Mr. Warms?"

The first officer turned, and Rogers walked towards him.

"Mr. Warms. I'd like to see the captain. I have some information for him."

"About what?"

"Best I tell the captain first."

During the conversation a bland, fixed smile remained on the chief radio officer's lips. It was that, more than anything Rogers said, that Warms found disturbing.

For some time, Warms had felt uneasy in the presence of the chief radio officer, and this brief encounter only exacerbated his feelings. "There was something about George that didn't make you anxious to tangle with him," he was to say later.

There were, in fact, good reasons for Warms to be suspicious. Unknown to the officers on the *Morro Castle*, Rogers was a recidivist of long standing. Crime gave some meaning to his life. Crime helped him forget the emptiness and devastating guilt he felt about his sexual underdevelopment. Crime boosted his ego and provided a substitute for personal involvement with other people.

The principal of the California school that Rogers attended had discovered his first known crime: stealing skates from other children. It was a pointless piece of thievery: thirteen-year-old George, weighing nearly two hundred pounds, was far too clumsy to balance on any skates. He had stolen to get even with those who tormented him about his size. George was let off with a warning.

Nine days later he broke into a house and stole a radio set. He confessed at once, but this time he was not so fortunate: he was committed to a reform school, the Good Templar's House in Vallejo.

During adolescence the psychotic tendencies he had already shown became more deeply rooted. He began a series of petty thefts from other inmates in the home. His language became vulgar and salacious. He would not work.

In March 1915, the Templar home asked that Rogers be moved elsewhere. He was committed to the Boys and Girls Aid Society in San Francisco, a place with a policy of firm discipline. But beating did not arrest the development of the boy's disturbed personality. Amazingly, not once was he seen by a doctor. Even a cursory medical examination would have indicated physical abnormality, and a psychiatrist would have recognized his psychotic characteristics. According to one psychiatrist who later examined Rogers's record, "there was clearly a basic disturbance of the feelings; this disturbance was periodic; in between there were periods of normality".

Extended silences now alternated with an intolerant, often domineering manner. The conflict between his inner world and the world around him grew. The Society's reports show that he had been involved in several acts of petty stealing, and had also committed sodomy on a younger boy in the home.

This last was the final straw for the Aid Society. Almost overnight they found him a job—as assistant wireless operator on a schooner sailing out of San Francisco. It was a job Rogers actually wanted. He was paroled, and on May 12, 1917, went to sea.

Rogers later said it was the glamour of the job that attracted him. It is doubtful whether he found much glamour on the schooner: he got ten dollars a month and his food. Even so, he acquired sound training in wireless telegraphy.

For more than two years there is a blank in the official records on George White Rogers. Later in life Rogers teased questioners about this period, hinting at wild and romantic voyages, that he had been shanghaied, married a girl in China, and fought in a South American revolution.

When he did reappear, he weighed more than 250 pounds and apparently had found religion. In September 1919, when he joined the U.S. Navy, he stated he was a Jehovah's Witness.

Rogers had one of the shortest naval careers on record. It lasted eighteen weeks. Poor eyesight was given as the official reason for his dismissal.

From 1920 to 1929, he drifted through the zany era of ragtime, Dixieland and the Charleston within the strange world of New Jersey's Hoboken. He felt at home among the shabby shops, the foreign sounds, the unkempt streets. Somewhere along the line he met and married Edith Dobson.

He held one job after another in quick succession. It was a period of drifting into near-poverty and social isolation, but if Edith Rogers was aware of what was happening to her husband, she said nothing. She had openly questioned his authority only once. She wanted to go to a relative's funeral. Her husband forbade her, threatening to kill her dog, to which she was inordinately devoted. She went. He poisoned the dog.

By 1929 Rogers had become fascinated with the possibility of murder in which the evidence is totally destroyed. Arson seemed to fall nicely into that category. Rogers maintained that his interest was no more than an intellectual exercise. But there is evidence that he went beyond that. He started a collection of scientific books and magazines on the subject and experimented with timing fuses and reactions between various acids. His experiments reached a climax when he believed he had reproduced the time bomb which caused the famous "Black Tom Explosion".

That explosion had occurred at a New Jersey factory during

World War I. Rogers believed the fire could "only have been caused by an incendiary fountain pen clipped to a workman's pocket when his working coat was hung up for the night in a closet". He advanced a plausible explanation of how it could have been done. "An incendiary fountain pen was filled with acid which ate down into a combustible powder through a thin membrane of copper." The thickness of the copper controlled the time it took to melt. The device was designed to produce a chemical reaction that generated intense heat, and simultaneously released oxygen to spread the fire.

Then, in March 1929, while he was employed by the Wireless Egert Company in New York, a mysterious fire broke out at the plant. Police files noted: "It was Rogers's custom to arrive for work at 8.30 a.m. The morning of the fire he was on the scene at 7.30 a.m. He unlocked the door and let the firemen in."

By then the blaze was burning fiercely. Salvage experts concluded it had been started by a chemical timing device. Rogers was questioned for days. The set smile never left his lips. In the end he was released. The police file stated that Rogers was "suspected of the arson".

Although he had got off scot-free, Rogers's first real encounter with the police had frightened him. The bullying, the crude jokes about his misshapen body, and the final admonition that next time "they'd throw the book" at him, were traumatic. After destroying his bombs, chemicals and the electronic equipment he kept in his back room, he took to his bed and remained there for weeks.

When he re-emerged, he returned to his old method of getting even: stealing. Each time he committed a theft, he was caught. He promptly returned the goods, and persuaded the owner not to press charges. The astonishing thing about every episode is that the owners went along with him. Rogers had found that if he presented the "problem" of his body in the right way, it elicited pity. The police role was itself a curious one: on at least two separate occasions he confessed and was never brought to court.

But somewhere down the line, George White Rogers may have sensed that his luck could not hold. In March 1934, he decided to return to sea. The officials at the Radiomarine Corporation had no inkling that Rogers had a long record of crime and mental disturbance when they renewed his licence. Nor did the Ward Line officials. Rogers, with his set smile and long silences, might have appeared to be an oddball, but there was no way a lay person could know he was genuinely disturbed.

Rogers joined the *Morro Castle* in June 1934. He liked it. It took him away from America, away from the police, away from their questions, and as chief radio officer his salary was $120 a month.

But this was not enough for Rogers. He started to pocket charges to passengers for radiograms. However, he overlooked the fact that at the end of each voyage, inspectors from the Radiomarine Corporation checked the books against the money a chief operator handed in. Rogers failed to doctor the books and was found out in a bit of thieving worth only a few dollars. He now knew that in less than three days his career at sea would be terminated, unless something dramatic occurred to change the course of events. Rogers already had a plan to ensure that change. He placed the bottles of sulphuric and nitric acid on the shelf above George Alagna's bunk.

Later that evening he casually strolled over to the shelf, removed the bottles, and turned to Alagna. "What are you going to do with these, George?" he asked.

AT PRECISELY 7.30 P.M., William Warms and Eban Abbott arrived in Captain Wilmott's cabin. The pre-dinner meeting was a ritual at sea, a chance for the ship's three senior officers to discuss informally the day's run.

The cabin was furnished with three sofas upholstered in blue, several easy-chairs and tables, lamps, a grandfather clock, and blue curtains on the scuttles. Along one bulkhead stood a cabinet which converted into a bar. A connecting door led to the captain's night cabin. It held a double bed, bath, and toilet. A speaking tube above the bed was connected to the bridge. A telephone stood on a side table.

The chief engineer's report was short: the engine room and his men were working normally.

The first officer reported the five stewards who had been logged for drunkenness. He made no reference to the "fire drill" he had authorized, and Captain Wilmott did not mention his order to seal off the smoke-detector system.

At 7.45 p.m. the three officers began their rounds—a brisk tour of the bridge, the promenade deck, and the first-class dining room—to show both passengers and crew that the ship was under benevolent, yet effective, command.

Their inspection of the bridge required only a few moments. The complex of equipment—master gyrocompass, course recorder, bearing repeater, steering repeater, and radio-direction-finder repeater—seemed to be in order. The azimuth, electric sounding machine, depth recorder, barometers, chronometers, and the fathometer all indicated that the ship was on course and on time.

The three men proceeded quickly to the promenade deck, which was enclosed at the forward end with storm windows. The glass sheeting swept back to midships, where it gave way to 125 feet of open rail, lined with deck chairs, empty at this hour. Beyond lay the deck ballroom, where the orchestra was playing Gershwin and Berlin tunes.

After a brief look into the veranda café—a jungle of potted plants and palm trees—the captain's party strode down to D deck. Captain Wilmott wanted to check the galley area. Neither of his fellow officers could recall such a digression from the normal evening rounds. To Abbott it seemed further proof of the captain's preoccupation with the apparent attempt to poison him on July 29.

On that day Captain Wilmott had ordered an afternoon snack of one of his favourite dishes, finnan haddie, brought to his cabin. He had only eaten a mouthful when he became aware of a peculiar taste. He inspected the haddock. It did not appear spoiled, yet afterwards he developed severe stomach cramps, diarrhoea, and a temporary disturbance of vision. By the time the ship's surgeon, Dr. de Witt Van Zile, diagnosed it as food poisoning and treated the captain accordingly, the suspect haddock had been dumped overboard with other garbage.

After recovering, Wilmott conducted his own investigation.

Finnan haddie had been on the first-class dinner menu the same day; yet none of the passengers who ate it complained of any side effects. The portion of fish for Wilmott had been selected from the cold store by a kitchen boy. It was then washed and prepared by another kitchen hand. An assistant chef poached it and placed it on a tray. A steward carried the tray to the captain's cabin. Had one of these four people doctored it? If so, why?

The captain had little direct effect on the lives of the galley staff. Had one of the kitchen hands been acting on behalf of another crew member? Certainly, there were a number of seamen who hated the captain as the nearest available symbol of the Line.

Dr. Van Zile took no steps to confirm, or even to report the captain's suspicions. The captain flatly stated that somebody had tried to kill him, yet the one man who could have been expected to pursue the matter further—the ship's doctor, with his knowledge of poisons—did nothing. Doctor Van Zile was, by all accounts, not a person of great initiative. Even so, he had a duty to report a statement as unusual as Captain Wilmott's to the Ward Line. He did not. Instead, he told the whole story to his close friend, Chief Engineer Abbott, who later discussed the matter with his wife, Ada. She advised him that if somebody was trying to get the captain, Abbott had best stay out of it.

That is precisely what Abbott did.

There is one final question. Why didn't Robert Wilmott report the matter himself? There is no ready answer to these questions. But the evidence suggests that even the master and officers of the *Morro Castle* were genuinely afraid that reporting anything untoward to the Line might lead to their dismissal.

"CAPTAIN, SIR, is everything in order?" Headwaiter Carl Wright had come into the kitchen the moment he was alerted of the captain's presence there.

The master of the *Morro Castle* nodded, and turned back to the rows of crab hors d'oeuvres. He picked a dish at random. "Serve me this one at dinner," he ordered Wright, and proceeded into the first-class dining room.

The dining room extended through two decks with a mezzanine

supported by tall pillars at the well opening. Above the well opening in the mezzanine ceiling was a mural depicting Perseus rescuing Andromeda. Wilmott's table was immediately beneath the painting; the tables of Warms, Abbott and Dr. Van Zile fanned out on either side.

SEVENTY FEET FORWARD of the first-class dining room, with its silver-and-gilt baskets of fruit, the deck crew used stale bread to sop up the last of the greasy stew.

The air in the crew's mess reeked of sweat, cigarette smoke, dirty clothes, and liquor. This jungle of bare rivets and steam-pipes was a world with its own laws and its own standards; few of the ship's officers ventured into it. Thieving was commonplace; so were drug-running, bootlegging, and fighting.

At sea the crew formed small groups and aired their complaints over their tin plates at mealtime. Storekeeper William O'Sullivan and Seaman John Gross discussed a recurring theme: the lack of proper safety precautions on the *Morro Castle*. Ship's Watchman Arthur Pender agreed that the situation was "catastrophic".

Pender, a licensed first mate for ocean-going liners, had been to sea for sixteen years. Four months prior to this voyage he had been hired by the Ward Line at fifty dollars a month to be partly responsible for the ship from midnight to 6.00 a.m. In his years at sea Pender's overwhelming concern about safety regulations had made him unpopular with more than one master. On the *Morro Castle* he had compiled a "potential disaster dossier".

He had discovered that the fire doors were not equipped with sirens or bells, standard on all first-class passenger vessels. Also, four of the ship's lifeboats were virtually useless; in an emergency-lowering, the first two forward boats on either side would come down outside the enclosed promenade decks and it might well be impossible to open the heavy glass windows in order to get into the boats. Pender noted, too, that during the rare fire drills the crew never handled more than two hoses, one forward and one aft. Most of the crew had no actual training with fire hoses. The fire-screen doors were never closed during fire drill. Almost every regulation had been broken.

Pender also discovered something that dismayed him even more. The ship's Lyle gun—a line-throwing apparatus—and the drum of powder used to fire it, had been moved from the bridge, on Captain Wilmott's orders, as "it might get some Cuban excited into thinking we were an armed ship". Third Officer Clarence Hackney had ordered the seamen to roll the Lyle gun and the drum of powder into the space between the ceiling of the first-class writing room and the deck above. The overriding consideration to Hackney was that it was easily accessible from the bridge in an emergency. He overlooked the fact that all there was between twenty-five pounds of dangerous explosive and the writing room below were thin sheets of board covered with plaster.

The seamen who stowed the gun and powder barrel had carried the apparatus past the wireless room. When Chief Radio Officer Rogers stopped them to ask what they were doing, they had told him the purpose of their mission. He said he never knew the compartment existed.

IN THE FIRST-CLASS dining room, Carl Wright had solved the problem of the shortage of stewards by drafting waiters from the tourist-class restaurant, among them Sydney Ryan. Ryan, who had never worked in first-class before, was astonished at the variety of food offered: the crabmeat hors d'oeuvres were followed by a choice of roast goose, baked ham, or steak; trays of vegetables accompanied each entrée. Ryan's job was to assist in replenishing wine and liquor glasses. By the time the ice cream and fresh fruit compôte were served, it became clear to him that many of the passengers were quite drunk.

In one corner, members of the Concordia Singing Society had linked arms and were singing the classic German drinking song, "Ein Prosit, ein Prosit, der Gemütlichkeit". Ryan marvelled at their boisterous freedom, at the casual way they ordered up rounds of drinks, or pushed aside plates still half-covered with the remains of dinner. He calculated that each singer had consumed in one meal's food and drink the equivalent of his own week's salary.

All evening, attention centred on Captain Wilmott's table. His presence after three days caused an understandable stir. Dr. Giro, who was seated two tables away, observed that Wilmott ate very little and sipped only iced water. There were also two doctors at the captain's table, Charles Cochrane and a Dr. Theodore Vosseler; both were aware of a seeming nervousness in Wilmott's conversation. He told his table guests that the "pressure of work" was responsible for his absence during the outward-bound voyage.

As soon as dinner was over, he excused himself and hurried to his cabin, anxious to keep his appointment with George Rogers, to find out "What other tricks that radical's up to . . . ."

The Storm Rises

At 8.45 p.m., George Alagna turned the radio receiver to the six-hundred-metre frequency, the distress waveband, for the mandatory three-minute "listening out" period observed by all ships at fifteen minutes before and fifteen minutes past each hour.

Charles Maki watched Alagna fine-tune the instruments. Maki himself sometimes found it difficult to locate the frequency, and on several occasions Rogers had given him a tongue-lashing on his failure to switch smoothly across the wave bands. Maki knew his career as a radioman would be terminated abruptly if Rogers made a report to the Radiomarine Corporation. Rogers, however, chose not to file any official complaint; instead, he kept Maki on as a personal whipping boy. Maki took it all quietly. If anybody had suggested to Maki that his perfectly proportioned body was a constant reminder to Rogers of his own physical failings, he would undoubtedly have shaken his head in bewilderment.

At 8.48 p.m., Alagna again adjusted the apparatus and turned it over to Maki to send a handful of passengers' messages. When Alagna was satisfied that the Finn was on the proper frequency, he went into the adjoining room where the operators slept.

Two things had bothered Alagna all evening. First, how had Rogers been able to tell him that the bottles on the shelf over his bunk contained acid? There were no labels on the bottles, and the contents were odourless. Then, how had they got on to the shelf? He was positive they had not been there until Rogers had returned from his trip ashore. For any stranger to reach the room he would have had to come through the radio shack, and there had been no callers that day. There seemed to be only one answer: either Maki or Rogers had placed the bottles there.

Now, alone in the room, Alagna was struck by something else. The two bottles were gone. And when he slipped out on deck again, so was George White Rogers.

ROGERS'S INTERVIEW with Captain Wilmott exceeded Rogers's wildest hopes.

He had planned his story with care. It was a simple one: for weeks, he told Wilmott, he had suspected that Alagna was capable of stirring up trouble. Now he even had proof: the discovery of the two bottles of dangerous acids.

The captain was so shaken that he accepted without question the chief radio officer's statement that he had thrown the bottles over the side immediately on discovering them. "I think the man is crazy!" Wilmott ranted. "In New York he started a riot because he wanted to get off the ship without having his crew pass stamped by the immigration authorities." The more Captain Wilmott talked about Alagna, the more irrational he became. The most trivial rumours were magnified, until Alagna suddenly became the epitome of every Communist agitator the captain had ever heard about.

The captain finished his tirade, "Mr. Rogers, I want you to take the key to the emergency room and I want you to put it in your pocket. I do not want the key anywhere that man can get it, because I do not trust him."

What precise damage George Alagna could do to the radio compass, which was the only item of importance kept in the emergency room, Captain Wilmott did not explain.

Rogers listened gravely. He had no need to do anything else; the captain's fears were now firmly established.

The captain already had Alagna under surveillance by Warms. Now the chief radio officer had established his own role as the captain's contact within the radio shack, reporting regularly on the operator's activities.

As Rogers left the cabin, Captain Wilmott thanked him again for disposing so promptly of the two bottles of acid. He had no reason to suspect that the chief radio officer had kept them.

AS MIDNIGHT approached, Raymond Aloysius Egan leaned over the port rail, peering into the night. Embarrassment, more than anything else, made Egan, a twenty-seven-year-old bachelor, reluctant to join in the evening's entertainment, and face another round of well-intentioned prodding for him to pick up one of the single girls on board and have a "good time". Egan was a Roman Catholic priest, but he did not choose to explain this. He felt that seamen and vacationers were ill at ease when a clergyman was aboard.

Far in the distance a light broke the darkness. Egan wondered what it was.

"Miami."

Father Egan turned around, startled. Standing behind him was George White Rogers. The chief radio officer explained that the light came from the city of Miami, ten miles away on the Florida coast. The next landfall to watch for was Port Everglades, he told the priest.

Nodding good night, Rogers proceeded down the deck. Father Egan marvelled that such a big man could move so quietly.

AT 9.00 A.M. next day, Thursday, September 6, Cruise Director Smith's voice came over the dining-room loudspeaker: "Good morning, everybody. This is your cruise director speaking. Are we happy? Everybody? Good, good, good! . . ."

First he gave them the weather forecast: it looked like a wet day. Never mind, there was plenty to do: miniature horse-racing, bingo, indoor quoits. For the ladies, the beauty parlour was open all day. And "don't forget, folks, tonight there's the grand elimination dance with lots and lots of prizes!"

THAT MORNING Captain Wilmott locked himself in his cabin. He opened it only to First Officer Warms, to whom he announced: "Acid—that's what they'll use. Acid to destroy me with!"

Warms beat a hasty retreat. If the captain continued to behave like this, the Ward Line was bound to retire him. For William Warms that could mean only one thing: a real chance of sewing an extra gold stripe around his cuff.

He was as excited as he had been that day, long ago, when he had first gone to sea.

TO JOE BREGSTEIN the voyage was becoming unbearable; his feelings about the food had long since been overridden by his worries about safety on board. When a number of seasoned passengers remarked that morning on the absence of boat drills, it heightened his apprehension.

Joe Bregstein felt worried enough to question the first ship's officer he came across on his way to lunch, Chief Engineer Abbott. The chief engineer smiled reassuringly. He asked Bregstein if this was his first trip, and when Bregstein told him it was, he nodded and said the dentist's fears were very natural among first-trippers. There was absolutely no need for any worry, Abbott told him: "The *Morro Castle* is the safest ship afloat." As a measure of good faith, he offered to give Bregstein a guided tour of the ship. Bregstein arranged to meet the chief engineer the following morning. The excursion would be a last-minute surprise for his son Mervin.

AT MANY OF THE TABLES lunchtime gossip focussed on Captain Wilmott's absence and on the weather.

When the radio room received warning of a gale, force seven, bearing down in a wide sweep from Newfoundland, the news was conveyed to passengers by Cruise Director Smith. "But," he assured them, "that won't spoil the fun. A tea dance, bingo, and indoor horse-racing in the veranda café are still scheduled."

Carl Wright placated guests at the captain's table: "The master is on the bridge making sure everything is shipshape if the storm becomes really bad." Wright had no way of knowing if this was true; he was just repeating what Warms told him to say.

Meanwhile, Chief Engineer Abbott insisted to his table guests that *his* engines could withstand any amount of pounding.

At the table hosted by Dr. Van Zile, news of approaching bad

Captain Robert Wilmott: "*Acid—that's what they'll use. Acid to destroy me with.*"

Chief Engineer Eban Abbott: "*A hundred hoses wouldn't make any difference now.*"

Chief Radio Officer George White Rogers: "*Guess I was too busy getting out the SOS to notice the colour of the flames.*"

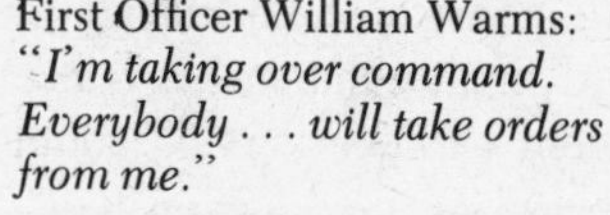

First Officer William Warms: "*I'm taking over command. Everybody . . . will take orders from me.*"

weather, the captain's absence, and extra bingo sessions made no impact, favourable or otherwise. By the end of lunch, his guests had worked their way through several pitchers of planter's punch and interminable toasts to a "wonderful time".

"I DID THE BEST THING possible by dumping them overboard, George, the best thing all round. You've got to believe that."

Alone, sitting on his bunk, George Alagna recalled the words of the chief radio officer. They did not make sense. Alagna had not brought the bottles aboard, nor had he known of their contents. There was only one way to interpret Rogers's statement: in dumping the mysterious bottles, the chief radio officer implied that he had helped Alagna—and at the same time implicitly accused him of intending to commit a crime. The longer Alagna thought about it, the more upset he became.

AT 4.15 P.M., George Rogers tuned into the six-hundred-metre distress waveband, ordered Charles Maki to "listen out", and left the radio shack. He walked the few feet to the chartroom, unlocked the door, entered and locked the door behind him. Precisely what he did in the chartroom is not known. There could be a perfectly innocent explanation: he could have been checking out the radio compass. He might even have been using it, as he had done previously, to pick up a shore music channel. Or George White Rogers might have escaped to the chartroom to brood—and plan. For he had just realized his role as the captain's informer was over.

Earlier he had gone to Captain Wilmott's cabin to make his first report of the day on Alagna's activities. He knocked and found the door locked. When he identified himself, Captain Wilmott ordered him to go away and stay away. Whatever his reason, Captain Wilmott had literally locked out the chief radio officer from further consultation.

Rogers found himself in an all too familiar situation. When he reached New York he would be out of a job and would again face police harassment. For a reasonably well-balanced man, facing unemployment in a jobless world would be difficult. For Rogers, physically and mentally disoriented, the prospect could well have been too much. If anything could turn his mind to thoughts of revenge, the moment when Captain Wilmott ordered him away was tailor-made.

ON THE BRIDGE the watch changed. Third Officer Clarence Hackney made up the log and handed it over to Second Officer Ivan Freeman. The rpm indicator on the control board showed 145, giving a speed of nearly 20 knots. With the weather closing in, it was too fast for passenger comfort. Freeman ordered a reduction to 17 knots.

The reduction in speed came too late for Catherine Cochrane. The plunging and pitching had finally made her sick. Her brother prescribed sips of iced water, salted, and rest in bed.

The gale was a relief to Headwaiter Carl Wright. It considerably reduced the number he could expect for dinner, and provided a cast-iron story, should the captain continue to be absent from meals.

The gale, in fact, brought Captain Wilmott out of his cabin. When he joined Warms on the bridge the first officer gave him the latest weather report, and Captain Wilmott authorized a further reduction in speed.

For a while the Captain stood staring ahead into the storm. Then he turned to Warms and said: "I don't feel good, I will take an enema and lie down." He walked back to his cabin and locked the door after him.

AT MIDNIGHT the watch changed. For the last 73.5 miles the run north had averaged a speed of 16.2 knots. Fourth Officer Howard Hansen ordered an increase to 18 knots: most of the passengers were probably in bed, anyway. From then on he ordered regular course corrections which took the ship past Frying-Pan Shoals, and Diamond Shoal. At 5.00 a.m. the most difficult part lay ahead—navigating past Cape Hatteras, the most treacherous stretch of coastline. The Cape Hatteras lighthouse had still not been sighted when Howard Hansen handed over the watch to Third Officer Clarence Hackney and went below for breakfast and a morning's sleep.

"IN THE EVENT OF COLLISION, five electrically operated watertight bulkheads seal off the ship. They just press a button on the bridge!"

For an hour Joe Bregstein and his son listened as Chief Engineer Abbott recounted an endless stream of "safety facts". He told them the decks were covered with a fireproof lightweight sheathing laid on the plates. An electric fire-detecting system was installed in all staterooms, and in officers' and crews' quarters thermostats provided early warning of any temperature increase. There was also the smoke-detecting system, and seventy-four steel cylinders of carbon dioxide gas, located at strategic points around the ship, fed a complementary smothering system through which the gas could be pumped under pressure.

Abbott did not tell the Bregsteins that this system had been rendered virtually useless from the moment Captain Wilmott had ordered the smoke-detecting system turned off. Nor did he say that the protection offered by the fire-detecting system did not extend to the public rooms.

All the same, Eban Abbott's list of life-saving gear was impressive: in addition to the lifeboats, with a total capacity of 816 passengers, there were a dozen box floats, each capable of carrying 17 people, 18 lifebuoys, each capable of supporting two people, and 851 life preservers, of which 78 were designed for children. In all, there was equipment to save nearly three times the ship's complement.

Like any good performer, the chief engineer reserved until last the tour's climax—the engine room.

There was something boyishly enthusiastic in the way Eban Abbott described *his* engines. He led the Bregstein's across catwalks and down clanking steel ladders, pausing briefly for a lecture on the generators that supplied electricity, air conditioning, and refrigeration.

To Joe Bregstein it seemed a different world from the one he saw topside. It was a hot and noisy place and "the men had that honest look about them which comes from a hard day's toil".

He would probably have retained that image of the engine-room crew, but for one incident: he noticed a Cuban, with an open paint pot, painting a pipe adjacent to an open furnace door. It was an obvious fire risk, he pointed out to Abbott. The officer looked unhappy and said he couldn't really say anything. "I just don't start up anything with these people," he told the dentist.

Bregstein wondered how the chief engineer would face a real crisis, if he found it so difficult to exert his authority in such a simple situation.

BY FRIDAY AFTERNOON the continuous rain, the grey sea, and the whistling wind had produced almost universal gloom among the passengers. Many had missed lunch, their appetites gone because of the pitching and tossing of the ship. The tea dance had been a gelid affair; the bingo and horse-racing were poorly patronized.

By five o'clock Cruise Director Smith was reduced to making regular announcements: "Remember, folks, this is Friday—the *last* day! There is still one last grand fling left—the captain's farewell dinner and gala ball. Come one, come all to the crowning event of your week—the end of an epoch in your life."

EARLIER IN THE DAY, Captain Wilmott had complained to Warms of a backache and general tiredness. The doctor had prescribed "some medicine". Nevertheless, at exactly 5.15 p.m. Wilmott undertook the one social obligation he could not avoid—the traditional farewell cocktail party for a favoured few of the first-class passengers. On this trip there were only four guests, all from the Captain's table: Dr. Cochrane, his sister, and Dr. and Mrs. Vosseler. It was a restrained affair. Catherine Cochrane was still recovering from seasickness. None of the guests were great social drinkers. Captain Wilmott apologized for his continued absence, but pleaded that weather conditions made it imperative for him to remain on the bridge. The party broke up around 6.00 p.m. He repeatedly assured his guests that any storm could not be as bad as the hurricane he had faced a year before, when the waves had been up to sixty-five feet high.

CHIEF ENGINEER ABBOTT was about to dress for dinner when the engine room called. Assistant Engineer Antonio Bujia reported that one of the fire boilers had a fuel blockage.

"Can you clean it?"

"Not without shutting down."

Abbott climbed into a boiler suit, and stepped out of his cabin and into the elevator specially installed to take him down to the engine room. When he stepped out of the elevator, he noticed that the buffeting from the sea sounded like not-so-distant artillery.

The blockage was in No. 3 boiler in the forward fire room. After thirty minutes the chief engineer knew the only way to clear the blockage was to strip down the feeder system, something which could be done only in port. He ordered the faulty boiler closed down. It would mean that the *Morro Castle* would not be able to reach 20 knots for the rest of the voyage. Nor would the engine room be able to meet any sudden call for maximum water pressure to the fire hydrants.

He picked up a telephone and dialled the captain's cabin. There was no reply. He called the bridge. Second Officer Ivan Freeman told him Captain Wilmott was not there. Again Abbott dialled the captain's cabin. He could hear the number ringing. After a few minutes he called the bridge and reported the loss of boiler pressure. He also said he had been unable to get a response from the captain's cabin.

Evan Abbott took the elevator back to his cabin, washed, and dressed. Then he set out to discover why Captain Wilmott had not replied.

Moments later First Officer William Warms stood in the captain's night cabin, shocked and horrified. Slumped over the side of the bath, half-dressed, lay the body of Robert Wilmott, his eyes open, but obviously dead.

Who Killed the Captain?

Warms closed the captain's eyes and hoisted up Wilmott's trousers. He wanted the body "to look decent", he explained later. He looked at his watch: it was 7.48 p.m. About three minutes had passed since he knocked on the door. Receiving no reply he had pushed it open, walked across the day cabin, and found the body.

On that basis Warms put the time of death at just before 7.45 p.m. This estimate was based on the fact that eighteen minutes earlier—at precisely 7.30 p.m.—Warms had seen Captain Wilmott alive.

Warms had gone to the captain's cabin with the latest weather report, and found Wilmott seated on the toilet in the night cabin. Nearby was a tray of food that Wilmott had picked over: a slice of melon, scrambled egg, toast, coffee, and a pitcher of iced water.

Warms delivered his weather report: "Captain, it is a little thick, but everything is all right." When he asked the captain how he felt, Wilmott assured him that he felt "all right".

Warms had then gone back to the bridge, where he discovered the weather had worsened. In addition to the heavy rain, there was fog. Second Officer Freeman suggested reducing speed. Warms agreed, and ordered Freeman to blow the fog horn as well. When Warms returned to the captain's cabin to report further on the ship's progress, he found Captain Wilmott dead.

Standing at the door of the night cabin now, it occurred to the first officer that it would have been virtually impossible for the captain to have toppled naturally off the lavatory seat and into the bath. Clearly something had forced him to move, trousers around his knees, towards the bath. Had he felt an urgent need for a drink, and tried to reach the bath's cold-water tap? It was possible—yet only a few feet away, on the tray of food, stood the pitcher of iced water. Had a sudden feeling of nausea driven the captain towards the bath? Warms did not pause to ponder further. He unstoppered the speaking tube linking the captain's cabin with the bridge. The speaking tube was answered by Fourth Officer Howard Hansen, who had reported early for his watch. Warms ordered him to locate Robert Tolman, the ship's purser, and to come with him to the captain's cabin immediately.

While Hansen sought the purser, Warms telephoned the ship's surgeon. He ordered him to the cabin, adding: "Bring your bag."

At that moment Chief Engineer Abbott walked in. In his search for the captain, the engineer had followed the usual route of Wilmott's evening rounds. In the dining room, Wright had reported no sign of the captain.

Abbott was surprised to find Warms in the day cabin, looking fearful. The chief engineer began to explain: "One of the boilers has gone. I'm looking for the old man—"

"He's dead. In there." The first officer motioned towards the night cabin.

Abbott walked across the day cabin. He stopped short when he saw Wilmott's body. "Maybe he's just fallen—"

"He's dead! I'm taking over command. Everybody, including *you*, will take orders from me."

In the circumstances Warms, as the senior deck officer, would assume command automatically, even though Abbott outranked him. But it seemed to Abbott that Warms was being a little insensitive, and that he saw the captain's death as his big chance to have another shot at being captain.

Abbott's feeling was reinforced by the arrival of Purser Robert Tolman, followed by Fourth Officer Hansen and Dr. Van Zile. Tolman, a dignified man with impeccable manners, was principally concerned with passenger welfare; his contact with the other deck officers was limited. The only reason Warms has the purser here, the chief engineer thought, is to swear him in.

In a group they moved into the night cabin.

Dr. Van Zile knelt beside the body and felt for a pulse. He ordered Captain Wilmott to be lifted onto the bed. The purser remarked on the body's colour. "It's quite blue," he said.

Dr. Van Zile ignored this—as he did Fourth Officer Hansen's attempt to resuscitate Captain Wilmott. He simply filled a hypodermic needle and injected a colourless liquid into a vein in Wilmott's arm.

What the injection was has never been ascertained; it may have been adrenalin. The doctor probably assumed there was still life in the body, and was attempting to revive the captain.

Hansen now ceased attempts at resuscitation. He too was puzzled by the blue colour, and also noted that there were no marks of violence.

Finally, Dr. Van Zile announced: "The captain is dead." It was 8.15 p.m.

"I will prepare the necessary papers," said Tolman.

Warms nodded, murmuring, "Very good." He stepped to the bedside and glanced at the body. "God bless his soul." Turning to Abbott and Hansen, he said, "Lay him out and dress him up. Then switch off the lights and turn the key over to me."

Without waiting for a reply, Warms walked from the cabin followed by Dr. Van Zile and the purser. In the corridor he turned and asked the doctor: "What was the cause of death?"

"He died of indigestion and heart failure," the doctor replied. Without an autopsy, it would have been difficult for Van Zile to have been more explicit, but his reply was misleadingly simple. It was only a statement of symptoms. Indigestion is a term so imprecise as to be almost valueless, and most people die of heart failure. It can happen quickly, or it can be the result of chronic heart disease causing a deterioration over years. Robert Wilmott had suffered from a "nervous stomach" and high blood pressure. But there was no history of chronic heart disease.

Warms, troubled by Dr. Van Zile's verdict, said to him: "I believe there are other doctors on board. Why not get them to confirm your findings?"

FOLLOWED BY the purser, Warms walked to the bridge, where Second Officer Freeman was standing watch. "Wilmott is dead," he said to Freeman. "I have assumed command. You are promoted to first, Clarence becomes second, and Howard, third. Go below and tell every member of the crew you see that I am now the master."

Next Warms ordered the purser to notify the Line.

The purser walked into the chartroom and wrote out two identical radiograms: one to Thomas Torresson, the Ward Line's marine superintendent, the other to Victor M. Seckendorf, the company's passenger traffic manager. The message read:

WILMOTT DECEASED 7.45 P.M. ACKNOWLEDGE WARMS

Warms initialled the radiograms and told the purser to take them to the radio room. Turning to the business of sailing the ship through appalling weather conditions, he told the men on the bridge, "I'm not leaving here, come what may."

IN THE NIGHT CABIN Eban Abbott and Howard Hansen completed the task of laying out Robert Wilmott's body. Resplendent in his uniform, his arms folded across his chest, he lay in the centre of the bed. A steward removed the captain's dinner tray, saying news of the captain's death had stunned the kitchen staff. Why Abbott allowed the steward to remove the tray—particularly in view of the suspected previous attempt on Wilmott's life—is not clear. Undoubtedly the chief engineer, like his colleagues, was under a great deal of emotional stress.

Howard Hansen wondered, as he noticed the captain's face turning black, whether the surgeon's diagnosis of the cause of death was satisfactory. He left Abbott in the captain's cabin and closed the door behind him.

GEORGE ALAGNA awoke with a start. Rogers was shaking him. "George, George," he said. "The old man's dead."

It took a few seconds for the words to penetrate. When they did, Alagna looked up and noticed that Rogers seemed to be smiling.

"Go back to sleep," Rogers said soothingly. "You can't do anything." But, as he left, the chief radio officer called over his shoulder, "Looks like a busy night for me."

Alagna noticed the excitement in Rogers's voice. Inexplicably he began to think that the captain might have been murdered.

WAS ROBERT WILMOTT MURDERED?

Since that Friday night, numerous investigations have led to one significant probable cause of death: poisoning. It must be added, however, that the question of whether Captain Wilmott was poisoned is impossible to prove. A more careful investigation by Dr. Van Zile might have provided a concrete basis for this hypothesis. But medical authorities today emphasize the virtual impossibility of determining the cause of sudden death without an autopsy.

In the months following his death, suspicion fell upon the Cuban Communists, who murdered Captain Wilmott, it was said, as a gesture against the Ward Line for shipping arms to the island's dictatorial regime. Yet he was probably not murdered for political purposes. It would have been pointless: the Ward Line would simply have replaced him with another captain and the arms traffic would have continued. Later speculation on who might have murdered Captain Wilmott centres around the figure of George White Rogers.

Three volumes on the case compiled by Police Captain Vincent Doyle of Bayonne, New Jersey, and exhaustive investigations by Wilmott's lifelong friend Captain George Seeth provide further evidence. As far as is known, Doyle and Seeth never met. Yet, somewhat astonishingly, both came to the same conclusion: that Rogers poisoned Wilmott as a deliberate act of retaliation.

The evidence presented by Doyle and Seeth differs in certain details. In Doyle's version, the radio officer sought revenge because he believed Captain Wilmott had discovered the evidence which would result in Rogers's dismissal for dishonesty. Seeth believes Wilmott had discovered Rogers's involvement "as a key member of a smuggling ring among the members of the crew".

This ring had operated from the first voyage, smuggling drugs and liquor into New York. From time to time New York customs officers arrested crew members caught moving contraband off the ship.

On at least two occasions, suspected informers in the crew had met with "accidents". One had disappeared overboard at sea; the other had been crushed under a load of cargo in No. 2 hold. Seeth believes that Rogers was responsible for transmitting and receiving details of contraband to an accomplice ashore.

According to Doyle, Rogers obtained the poison used against Wilmott during the ship's stopover in Cuba; he does not indicate what type it was. Seeth believes the poison was an irritant which in ordinary circumstances would not have been fatal; but Rogers knew it was powerful enough to kill the captain, who had a weak stomach.

He suggests that Rogers got to the captain's food tray during one of his visits to the galley for coffee. It is possible: the kitchen crews were in the middle of final preparations for dinner. The sight of the chief radio officer pouring himself another coffee would cause no comment.

FATHER EGAN sensed a growing tension among the diners around him. At first he put it down to the ship's motion. The priest himself was unaffected by the swell, but stewards performed ballets of equilibrium as they carried away trays of uneaten food.

Some of the guests wore costumes, but the majority of first-class passengers were in evening dress, a tradition for the captain's farewell dinner. Father Egan wore his clerical collar. He had carefully weighed the matter before deciding. There was the question of embarrassment to other passengers, for he still believed they would be uneasy in the presence of a cleric on a "fun cruise". On the other hand, he wanted to do what was "fitting" for such a special occasion. His appearance in clerical garb *had* caused a momentary flutter in the dining room which was quickly superseded by something more significant.

For some moments all had been aware that neither the captain nor any of his officers had yet appeared for dinner. Attempts to question the waiters about it proved fruitless: they expressed baffled surprise. The passengers were becoming disgruntled. It was, after all, the captain's farewell dinner.

Coffee was being served when Headwaiter Carl Wright appeared from the kitchen, white-faced and trembling. News of Captain Wilmott's death had reached the cooks. Shortly afterwards Dr. Van Zile appeared in the dining room. He whispered something to Dr. Cochrane and Dr. Vosseler. The two doctors rose with apologetic smiles and followed the ship's doctor out of the room.

It was a little after 8.30 p.m.

ON THE BRIDGE, William Warms glanced through the papers the purser had prepared to formalize his position as captain.

Warms paced the bridge steadily, issuing orders in a quiet voice. Tolman was reassured. It seemed that the crisis and the assumption of command had brought Warms a new knowledge and authority.

Warms handed back the papers. Needles of water hit the bridge windows. Far below the sea was a bubbling mass of white flecks over which the ship rose and fell.

"The passengers, sir . . ." Tolman paused. "Shouldn't they be told about Captain Wilmott?"

"Not yet." Warms was silent, thinking about something. "I'll get Mr. Freeman to make the announcement later."

Outside the wind whistled through the rigging.

"Can I get you something to eat, sir?" Tolman asked.

"Later," Warms replied.

With a final nod Tolman beat a dignified retreat.

BY NINE O'CLOCK Chief Engineer Eban Abbott was accustomed to the ritual: there would be a knock on Captain Wilmott's cabin door, and Dr. Van Zile would lead yet another distinguished-looking passenger into the night cabin where the body lay. Abbott, seated in a corner of the day cabin, had not stirred from there since he and Hansen had laid out the body. He had made no attempt to contact the engine room or the bridge. The death of Robert Wilmott seemed to have induced in him a severe and deep-rooted trauma. The tragedy for Eban Abbott, and everybody on board, was that it remained undetected or misinterpreted.

During the time he sat in the cabin, half a dozen doctors came and went. Each spent a few minutes in the next room, and then departed. Later, those who attached any significance to the discoloration of the body ascribed it to a condition sometimes found after a severe heart attack. Although it was an acceptable medical deduction, it was not necessarily the right one: poisoning could also produce discoloration.

If the doctors noticed the silent chief engineer, sunk in his chair in the corner, they made no comment.

When Abbott finally left Wilmott's cabin he went to his own. He undressed, then telephoned the engine room, and was told "All O.K. down here." Still confused by Wilmott's death, he fell asleep wondering why Warms had made no attempt to contact him.

ACTING CAPTAIN WARMS peered through the bridge windows into the night. There was nothing to be seen all around the ship except black sea streaked with white. He turned to his new senior officer, Ivan Freeman.

"All hatches battened down and secured?"

"Yes, sir."

"All watches at regular strength?"
"Yes, sir, plus a lookout forward."
Satisfied, Warms nodded.

THE CHANGE IN COMMAND had a profound effect on the seamen in the forecastle. Among the older hands the death was regarded as a bad omen. Several said they would sign off and try to get a berth on another ship for a trip or two until the danger had passed. No one doubted that Warms would be confirmed as captain, but there was a division of opinion as to his fitness for command. Some, like Storekeeper O'Sullivan, wondered whether he had that "magic thing with the passengers", while others, including John Gross, believed Warms would be a hard taskmaster, cracking down at the first sign of careless seamanship.

Joe Spilgins, a twenty-six-year-old deckhand in charge of six starboard lifeboats, hoped the new captain would reintroduce proper safety rules: "Half the guys on the ship never even raised or lowered a lifeboat. Most of them wouldn't know how." Spilgins drew a chorus of approval when he said that if it was a choice between a captain with personality and one who practised a stricter adherence to safety standards, he'd take the latter every time. "Hell," he grinned, "if they want a personality as a captain they should stick Smithy on the bridge!"

WHILE THE DISCUSSION between the seamen grew more intense, "Smithy"—Cruise Director Robert Smith—took it upon himself to stop all further speculation in the first-class dining room. On hearing the news of Wilmott's death, he marched briskly to the captain's table. The room was suddenly very still as the cruise director clinked a spoon against a glass. When he spoke his voice was flat, almost emotionless.

"Ladies and gentlemen. A great tragedy has befallen us. The captain is dead . . . ." He paused. "Captain Wilmott passed away earlier this evening. First Officer Warms has assumed command." Again he paused. "There is no cause for alarm—only sorrow. I request, out of respect for Captain Wilmott, that all the usual activities of tonight be cancelled."

Heads nodded in stunned agreement.

Before any questions could be asked, the cruise director left the dining room to repeat the news to the tourist class.

AT 10.28 P.M. the tension in the radio room was broken by an incoming radiogram, addressed to the ship's purser. It read:

PLEASE CONFIRM QUICKLY MESSAGE SENT BY WARMS TO SECKENDORF REGARDING WILMOTT GIVING DETAILS WARDLINE

Rogers looked at the message intently, then shook his head. "They don't trust him," he said. He handed the radiogram to Maki. "Take it to the purser."

Maki turned and walked out of the room.

"It's bad, George, bad for Warms," Rogers said. "When they cable the purser, it's going over the head of the man in command."

At 10.40 p.m. a priority radiogram was sent to the Ward Line:

CONFIRMING MESSAGE FROM WARMS STOP WILMOTT DECEASED ACUTE INDIGESTION AND HEART ATTACK SEVEN FORTY FIVE THIS EVENING STOP ALL PAPERS FOR ENTRY IN ORDER TOLMAN PURSER

IN THE VERANDA CAFÉ, Rafael Mestre was keeping time to a rumba record with a set of maracas, watched by an admiring group of girls. The session was brought to a sudden halt by Cruise Director Smith, who appeared to be hunting down any sign of frivolity. Mestre smiled, shrugged, and walked away with the girls.

On the promenade deck, members of the Concordia Singing Society were slopping beer and singing at the tops of their voices. The cruise director cut them short in mid-chorus.

By around eleven o'clock most people understood that wild parties were not thought appropriate. All the same, a number of passengers made an attempt to sustain a festive atmosphere. This was, after all, the last night of the voyage. Inhibitions began to dissolve as the drinking and singing continued.

Stewards Sydney Ryan and Daniel Campbell wanted the party to break up early. The public rooms had to be made ready for the new passengers who would board the *Morro Castle* the next day.

However, it was not until 2.45 a.m. that the party showed any signs of abating. By then, it had dwindled to two women in trailing evening gowns and their escorts in tuxedos. Campbell and Ryan were collecting empty glasses. Campbell looked sourly at the quartet. "If you're planning to get some sleep before we dock," he said, "you'd better get to bed."

One of the women giggled. "Who wants to go to bed? I'm not going to bother." Her companions agreed.

At exactly 2.50 a.m. Sydney Ryan paused in his glass-collecting and turned to Campbell. "Dan. You smell it?"

Campbell wrinkled his nose. "Come on," he said.

Both smelled smoke—coming from a long way forward.

Fire at Sea

At 2.51 a.m. the night watchman reported to the bridge that he had just seen and smelled smoke coming out of one of the small ventilators near No. 1 stack. The ventilator led from the first-class writing room on B deck.

Warms rushed to the ventilator. A trickle of smoke emerged from the opening. He ran to rouse his first officer, Ivan Freeman.

"Ivan! Get up! Fire!"

Back on the bridge, the acting captain ordered Hackney: "Go down below and find the source of the fire and let me know the situation *fast.*"

As he ran from the bridge Hackney grabbed a fire extinguisher.

By this time Campbell and Ryan had reached the door of the writing room. Smoke, like low-lying smog, carpeted the room.

"It's in that locker!" Campbell shouted.

The locker contained spare jackets for the stewards. It was situated immediately below the false ceiling on top of which lay the Lyle gun and the barrel of gunpowder.

Opening the locker, Campbell saw a mass of flames. Quickly, he slammed the door, blistering his hands in the process.

As both men ran from the room to raise the alarm, they passed a fire extinguisher on the wall near the writing-room door.

It was the first mistake by members of a crew poorly trained in fire drills. If Campbell and Ryan had turned that extinguisher on the fire *at once* it might have made a critical difference.

Three vital minutes passed before Clarence Hackney arrived. He yanked open the locker door and a wall of flame rushed out. Hackney backed off and emptied his fire extinguisher into it, but a dozen extinguishers could not have contained the inferno now raging around the lockers.

Choking from the smoke, he ran from the writing room.

He had made the second fatal mistake. Solid-steel fire doors had been built into entrances to the public rooms to deal with just such an emergency. It would have taken Hackney only a few moments to isolate the writing room from the rest of B deck by lowering its fire door. He did not take that preventive measure. Smoke billowed after him as he ran through the lounge towards the telephone near the smoking room entrance. He dialled the bridge.

"It's pretty bad," he told Warms. "We better get water on it."

"Break out the hose and I'll get you the men," Warms ordered. "Get all the fire hydrants uncapped—fast!"

The acting captain had reacted swiftly. He called down to the engine room: "I want all water pressure possible."

"We've got a boiler still out," a voice replied. "What do you want the pressure for?"

"Fire," retorted Warms. "Get all you can to the hydrants!"

On the bridge the sounds of the storm breaking against the ship drowned out conversation.

Warms ordered a textbook change of course, heading the ship into the wind to reduce the effect of the squall. He also ordered the bridge lookout to rouse the seamen in the forecastle.

It was 2.55 a.m.

Ivan Freeman had gone straight from his cabin to B deck—to be met by a wall of smoke billowing across the lounge. Behind it he could see flames.

When he reached the bridge, he told Warms: "It's bad. We should run for the beach in case we have to get the passengers off."

Warms calmly walked over to the fire-detecting system. Each light represented a thermostat in a stateroom or the quarters of officers and crew. The system did not cover the public rooms. Not a single light flashed red on the board. Reassured, Warms told Freeman: "We can hold her. Get down and take charge." He then telephoned the engine room and left word for Chief Engineer Abbott to call him the moment he got there.

Warms turned to the helmsman and checked the course: the *Morro Castle* was cutting through the Atlantic at the fullest speed possible, almost due north, into the storm.

At that moment Clarence Hackney rushed onto the bridge. "It's getting worse! We'll need every man on the hose!"

Warms did not hesitate. He set off the general alarm. "Get all the passengers out," he told Hackney. "Use tin pans! Anything you can get hold of to wake them!"

It was 3.00 a.m.

The quartet of drinkers at the bar moved towards the lounge doorway, sipping their highballs. Suddenly Stewards Campbell and Ryan and Watchman Arthur Pender rushed past them, clutching fire extinguishers.

The smog in the lounge had become so dense that it masked the fire beyond.

"Can't you stop all that smoke?" shouted one of the girl passengers. "It's going to ruin my dress."

"You best all report to your life stations," Campbell said.

"Why? It's raining outside. Anyway, I want another drink . . . ." The man's drunken demand faded as a fork of flame darted out from the smoke. "Run for it!" he shouted. "The ship's going to go down!"

Seamen and passengers fled.

Panic had arrived on the *Morro Castle*.

FATHER RAYMOND EGAN sensed the panic the moment he stepped out of his stateroom. The corridor was filling with half-dressed passengers awakened by stewards hammering on their doors.

Father Egan had put on his clerical garb, believing that in a crisis it would be useful for people to know his office. He was right. The moment he appeared, people turned to him. But before the priest could act, the corridor lights flickered out.

"She's sinking!" a voice screamed in the darkness.

"She's not!" Father Egan roared. "They're just switching the power supplies." The conviction in his voice stilled the panic immediately around him. From farther down the corridor came shouts, curses, and grunts, as passengers became bottlenecked at the foot of the staircase.

Father Egan forced his way along the corridor, deflecting groping hands and stumbling over feet. "Stay still! All of you! Wait until the lights come on!" he commanded.

The bedlam on the staircase slowly died away. At that moment the lights returned, revealing the bodies of men and women sprawled up the staircase. The scene was terrifying. Ordinary, thoughtful people had been turned into a fear-crazed rabble.

The priest took charge quickly. He told the passengers to return to their cabins, dress in outdoor clothes, put on their life jackets, and go to their boat stations immediately.

"And don't panic," he admonished.

EBAN ABBOTT, awakened by the alarm ringing above his head, walked naked from his cabin to the one next door, occupied by his first assistant, Antonio Bujia.

Bujia was struggling into a boiler suit. Abbott muttered dazedly: "When the bell rings there is a fire—?"

Bujia finished dressing and left without saying a word.

Abbott returned to his cabin, and carefully dressed in the formal mess kit he had worn the night before. Then he telephoned the engine room.

Bujia answered. Three pumps were working to supply water for the firefighting crews, but already the smoke was drifting down into the engine room, and "every minute seemed like an hour".

"Do the best you can and keep things going," Abbott said.

"All right."

Abbott put on his cap with its gold braid and straightened his jacket. Sartorially satisfied, he stepped out of his cabin.

Walking past the elevator that would have taken him directly to the engine room, he made his way to the promenade deck. There he watched a fire crew, supervised by O'Sullivan, struggling to couple a hose to one of the hydrants. The hose had had to be brought from the top deck; then the hydrant uncapped.

"Open the valve! Open the valve!" Abbott ordered.

"The valve *is* open!" shouted O'Sullivan.

The engine room was clearly unable to supply the necessary sustained pressure.

"Permission to throw deck chairs overboard?" asked Seaman John Gross. "Something to cling to if we have to jump."

The chief engineer nodded and the firefighters abandoned their hoses and started to hurl chairs over the side. Caught by the wind, the canvas furniture flapped clear of the boat, dropping into the sea well astern.

Abbott continued on his way, still shocked. He walked down a companionway to C Deck, where a group of girls from the Concordia Singing Society asked what they should do. Abbott told them to go up to the boat deck and wait there.

Coming up the stairway from D Deck was Bujia. Abbott peered at him. "What are you doing? Where are you going?"

"To the bridge. I called you through the telephone and speaking tube and got no answer. Everything is running good. But we cannot stay down there much longer."

The two men looked at each other. Wisps of smoke were drifting around the staircase.

"Go back and stand by. I'll go to the bridge," said Abbott. With those few words he changed his whole future; he would regret them all his life.

Shocked and disorientated though Abbott still was by Captain Wilmott's death, he had been moving, albeit in a roundabout way, down towards the engine room. But Bujia had brought Abbott head on with reality: the engine room, in his assistant's estimation, had shortly to be abandoned.

There was only one course of action open to Abbott. It was to go down to check the situation himself.

It was Abbott's responsibility to ensure that the men in the engine room performed their duties fully through the growing crisis. He abandoned this responsibility when he ordered Bujia back below and rapidly climbed to the safety of the open deck.

DR. EMILIO GIRO was making his way up to the boat deck. After the first sharp whiff of smoke, he knew there was trouble. He smiled encouragement to his brother-in-law, Rafael Mestre. Mestre grinned back, but Dr. Giro could see the fear in his face. As they climbed, they noticed a phenomenon others would also notice: the smoke was being driven down on them.

Near the first-class lounge, the two Cubans watched fascinated as the fire ran along the paint, wood, and chintz. There was no one there to stop it. "Remember, if we get separated, we are in lifeboat number ten," Dr. Giro repeated. Mestre nodded and crossed himself as they continued upward.

ON C DECK, Cruise Director Smith found near-panic among members of the Concordia Singing Society as smoke suddenly swirled overhead and down the corridor.

He moved quickly among them. "Down! All of you. On your knees! Hold on to the ankles of the person in front of you. And keep your heads down!" He took position at the head of the crocodile, leading it in a painful crawl along the corridor under the smoke and up a stairway to the ballroom on B deck. "Get to your lifeboat positions. They'll swing the boats down to you," he said. Then he ran back below to help other passengers.

BEYOND THE CURTAIN of smoke that swept across the deck, Storekeeper O'Sullivan hefted a fireman's axe, swung it in a wild arc, and smashed the corridor window of stateroom No. 2 on A deck. Behind him stood Dr. Cochrane and Dr. and Mrs. Vosseler.

Smoke poured out of the shattered window. At that moment the first officer, Freeman, appeared. "Up top. All of you!" he ordered.

"My sister is in there," said Dr. Cochrane.

"We can't get to her from this side, sir," O'Sullivan told Freeman. "I'll try from the other side!"

"Very well! But the rest of you up top!" repeated Freeman.

Dr. Cochrane started to protest. Freeman cut him short: "We'll get her, sir."

Without waiting for further discussion Freeman followed O'Sullivan around to the port side of the luxury-stateroom complex.

Dense smoke billowed everywhere. The two men felt their way down the deck, barely able to breathe. Finally they reached the cabin Catherine Cochrane was believed to be trapped in. Freeman lifted O'Sullivan through the window.

Inside, the seaman's flashlight was useless. He called out, but there was no answer. The bed was empty, but seemed to have been slept in. He searched the floor of the stateroom and, finding no one, assumed Dr. Cochrane's sister must have escaped. O'Sullivan was almost unconscious by the time he got back to the window, where Freeman waited to drag him out.

The brave rescue attempt had failed. Unable to see, O'Sullivan had entered the wrong cabin. Catherine Cochrane had been overcome by smoke as she slept two staterooms away. Soon others would die, with terrible speed and finality, as the fire roared down passageways and sealed them off.

ON THE BRIDGE, Warms looked on the smoke as an indication that the fire was being doused. As he turned to check the ship's course, a light on the fire-detecting system flashed red: a temperature of 160° F. was being reported from stateroom No. 5. Suddenly the whole system flashed on.

"My God! They're all going," Warms cried.

His first terrible miscalculation had come when he executed the textbook turn into the wind to meet the storm. Warms had overlooked the effect this would have on the fire. For over ten minutes, the *Morro Castle* had travelled head on into the squall, and the wind, gusting at over 20 knots, had acted as a giant bellows, fanning and speeding the flames the length of the ship.

FAR BELOW the bridge, Chief Stewardess Lena Schwartz finally identified the strange sound she had been hearing: the *Morro Castle* was moaning, like a whimpering child. Since the alarm had sounded, Mrs. Schwartz and the other stewardesses had run from stateroom to stateroom, waking the passengers. Mrs. Schwartz's calmness did much to reassure them as she offered a hand with life jackets, guided people to the quickest route topside, repeating over and over, "There's probably nothing to worry about." But that deep, sorrowful whine, coming from nowhere, yet everywhere, sent a sudden chill through her.

"Help me!" The voice came from an outer cabin near the stern. "Help! Please help me!"

Lena Schwartz ran towards the voice, plunging from one empty cabin to another. The cry was clearer, but as she got closer, it seemed to come from outside the hull. The stewardess rushed to a porthole, opened it, and peered outside. A few feet away, a woman was sitting on the rim of her cabin porthole, feet dangling over the sea, the wind tearing at her nightdress. She looked at Mrs. Schwartz, abject terror on her face.

"Don't move!" the stewardess shouted. "Just stay there and I'll come and get you."

At that moment the ship lurched, catapulting the woman into the sea. Mrs. Schwartz caught a brief glimpse of the body bobbing in the ship's wake. Then it was gone. She turned, tears of fear and anguish streaming down her face.

THE SHIP'S LURCH had been the result of another command Warms gave to the helmsman. "Hard to port!" The *Morro Castle* rose and fell as she turned in towards the New Jersey coast.

Warms hoped the manoeuvre would help contain the main fire. Although the lights were flashing on the fire-detecting system board, indicating intense heat as far down as C deck, he believed that he still had time to contain it.

The ship tossed and heaved around towards the distant coast. Spray blew across the forecastle. The liner wallowed, broadside to, and then came onto its new course.

Suddenly an explosion rocked the bridge. Warms rushed to a portside window. A flash burst across the promenade deck near the writing room. The powder keg for the Lyle gun, hidden in the false ceiling, had exploded.

THE EXPLOSION opened the door to full-scale panic. Dr. Joseph Bregstein and his son reached the promenade deck moments later to find passengers stumbling blindly, or walking around in circles, spellbound by terror. Women screamed and men swore like maniacs. The crew, panicking, pushed passengers aside—men, women, and children. For a moment the ship's whistle cried, helpless and despairing. The flames roared on hungrily.

Bregstein's eyes smarted from the smoke. Red flames blazed into the sky. The heat on the deck was searing. The dentist could smell wood burning. Safety glass in the deck doors was melting; the metal door frames began to buckle.

The wind appeared to be rising. Large waves, like hills, lifted the *Morro Castle* up, held her trembling for a moment, and then plunged her down again. Joe Bregstein, young Mervin clinging tightly to him, tried to hold on to his sanity. Everything around him assumed strange shapes by the light of the flames. As father and son huddled near the open rail of the promenade deck, a gang of sailors appeared carrying ropes. They fastened them to the rail, then uncoiled them over the sides. The ends of the ropes trailed in the water. A seaman shouted that when rescue came, passengers could scramble down the ropes to safety.

Joe Bregstein looked down at the water. It suddenly seemed much farther away than it had a few minutes before. He looked aft, his apprehension growing.

Down the deck another father and son had also been watching the sailors snake the ropes over the side. The man lifted his child onto his back, throwing one leg, and then the other, over the railing. For a moment he sat there, holding on with his hands, peering down at the sea. Then he let go of the rail.

Bregstein watched them hit the water. The sea closed over their heads. They seemed to go under forever. Then they shot to the surface. Somehow, the boy still clung around his father's neck. The man snatched at a rope and held on to it, screaming, "Help, help, help us." But there was nothing anybody could do. In the glare of the flames Bregstein could see that the sea was crashing the pair against the side of the ship. Then a wave swept completely over them and they were gone. The rope hung slack.

Sickened and terrified, Joe Bregstein clutched his own son close to him and wondered how long it would be before rescue ships arrived. He automatically assumed that the moment the fire had been discovered, an SOS had been sent.

GEORGE WHITE ROGERS had handed over his watch to Maki at midnight. He had then gone for a "breath of air". Twenty minutes later he had returned and gone to bed.

When the fire alarm sounded, George Alagna had had to shake him quite hard to wake him. The two men then dressed quickly and joined Maki in the radio room.

Evidence of fire was quite apparent from the radio shack. The room was filling with smoke, and when Rogers went to the door he could see the reflection of flames just below and forward on the port side. Rogers signed the radio-room log, saying that he was summoned to duty to take over what was apparently a distress watch. Turning to Alagna, he said, "Go up to the bridge and see what orders the mate has to give you."

It was just after 3.00 a.m.

Moments later, Alagna returned, ashen-faced. "The flames are taller than the radio room," he told Rogers. "I tried to get to the bridge, but I couldn't make it."

Rogers took the news calmly. He tried to call the bridge by telephone—without success. Apparently the electrical circuit had broken down. Picking up the speaking tube, he tried to call the bridge again. All he could hear was a loud roaring noise.

Once more Alagna was ordered to go to the bridge and "obtain whatever orders it was possible to obtain."

This time the smoke cleared momentarily, allowing him to reach the bridge. He arrived just in time to hear Warms give the course change for the New Jersey shore. He yelled to Warms that he had been sent up to the bridge by Rogers.

Warms paid little attention to him. When Alagna repeated what he had said, Warms finally answered "All right." He appeared to be obsessed by something of great importance. Alagna assumed it was the fire.

Alagna was wrong. The sight of the radio assistant had brought to mind all the suspicions Warms and Wilmott had nursed on the voyage—suspicions that Alagna was a "radical", capable of any act, possibly even arson.

Alagna returned to the radio room and reported what had happened on the bridge.

Rogers shook his head. "Go back to the bridge and ask again for orders when we are to send an SOS," he said.

Alagna made a third journey to the bridge.

In the radio room the smoke was thickening. Maki shifted uneasily. "Shouldn't we do something?"

"We wait for orders. That's what the regulations say."

Rogers settled back. Several minutes later he looked at his watch. Alagna had been gone for three minutes. He turned to Maki: "Go soak a towel in the washbasin so that I can breathe through it. Then go to the bridge and find Alagna."

Maki did as he was told, and then left. He would never return to the radio room. For a while he would wander aimlessly around the deck; finally he would jump from the ship.

Alone, Rogers went to the doorway. The fire was spreading. Black smoke was everywhere. When he resumed his position in front of the transmitter, he noted the time: 3.13 a.m.—thirteen minutes since the general alarm, and still no order to transmit an SOS.

Alagna reappeared. "The whole place is on fire," he shouted. "We'll be caught like rats in a trap."

"Are we to send the distress message?"

"I dunno. They're a bunch of madmen up there . . . ."

"Go back and ask the mate again," ordered Rogers.

Alagna began a fourth trip to the bridge. As he left the door, the transmitter crackled to life.

IT WAS THE FREIGHTER *Andrea S. Luckenbach*, steaming a parallel course ten miles seaward of the *Morro Castle*. At 3.14 a.m. her radioman contacted the U.S. Coast Guard station at Tuckerton, New Jersey. "Do you have any news of a ship burning off Sea Girt?" asked the operator.

"Haven't heard of any," came the reply.

The operator took the reply to the bridge where the ship's captain and first officer were peering west through binoculars.

"There's a glow over there," said the first officer.

The operator reported his conversation with Tuckerton. Both officers lowered their glasses, believing they had made a mistake.

ROGERS SAT, transfixed by the exchange between the cargo ship and the Coast Guard station. If the fire was now visible ten miles away, the situation was critical enough for the seriously disturbed mind of the chief radio officer to see there was the possibility of becoming a hero.

Regulations governing the sending of distress signals at sea are strict: no SOS can be sent without the express order of the captain. But it would have been proper for Rogers to have sent a message such as "Fire on *Morro Castle* off New Jersey. Awaiting orders from bridge."

The time to send such a message was now, yet instead of a distress signal, Rogers sent: "Standby. DE KGOV."

KGOV was the call sign of the *Morro Castle*.

"KGOV wait three minutes," ordered Tuckerton radio station.

Rogers immediately stopped sending.

ON THE BRIDGE, Alagna stood, almost mesmerized by the extraordinary scene. Warms had just discovered Eban Abbott lurking in a dark corner of the bridge. In his dress uniform, Abbott looked as if he were going to the captain's ball. He began to shriek, "What will we do? What will we do?"

"What are *you* doing *here*?" Warms screamed. "Why aren't you below to see to it that my orders are obeyed—"

"It's too late—"

"God damn it, get below and organize things. We need water!"

"A hundred hoses wouldn't make any difference now—"

"Captain, the water pressure's gone!" Second Officer Hackney brought the news to the bridge. "It's hopeless down there."

The lack of fire drills had produced its deadly effect. Seamen who abandoned their hoses in the face of the spreading flames had also failed to turn off the hydrants. The engine room's capacity to provide a thousand gallons of water a minute was quickly dwindling. In twenty minutes the pressure had been halved, then cut to a third. Now it was only a trickle.

Warms turned to his chief engineer. "What's happened to that pressure?" he screamed. "*Answer* me! D'you hear, *answer* me!"

But the chief engineer sat, crouched in the corner, repeating:

"It's too late. Too late . . . . A hundred hoses wouldn't help . . . ."

The radioman stepped towards Warms. "Mr. Warms. Do you have any orders for the radio room."

"Orders? Can you send an SOS?"

"Certainly! That's what I've been coming here for—"

Warms turned his back on the radioman, preoccupied.

Convinced that the bridge was being run by lunatics, Alagna turned desperately to Hackney.

"What's our position?" he asked.

"Sea Girt. And get it off fast," ordered Hackney.

Nightmare

FATHER EGAN estimated that the crowd of passengers huddled aft on C deck numbered nearly one hundred. Indifferent to the driving rain, their eyes were drawn to the raging fire.

The priest moved among them, calming them, urging those who wanted to pray to do so.

"Father." A woman touched his sleeve. "My husband. He's still down there on D deck. He went back to get a topcoat for me—"

"Stay here. I'll go and look for him."

"I'll come with you, Father." The voice belonged to Steward Sydney Ryan. Together, the two men left the stern. Ahead the fire crackled from port to starboard.

Near the barber shop a couple of stewards were kneeling beside a badly burned child, whom they had pulled clear of a burning cabin. In places the child's flesh had peeled back to the bone. He kept repeating, "*Mi madre*! *Mi madre*!" As Father Egan knelt to administer last rites, the child died.

EVEN IN HIS UNDERSHIRT and shorts Headwaiter Carl Wright still retained much of the dignity of his office. He had organized a party of waiters on C deck. In twenty minutes they had evacuated a dozen passengers from their cabins.

Some passengers were openly resentful. One man threatened to report the steward who awakened him. Some were drunk, one a young Cuban woman who had been having an affair with one of the men on board and was quite put out at being taken from her boy friend's bed.

But by 3.20 a.m., the mood on C deck changed. Flames flashed suddenly through the door of cabin 226, situated directly below the writing room. Passengers started to scream. The lights failed. Wright anticipated the panic a split second before it came. He had enough time to flatten himself in a cabin doorway. A tangle of bodies hurtled past him. People pushed and shoved like animals. Men hit women, women clawed back.

Wright watched the flames coming down the corridor, licking at the ceiling and shooting down the walls in a roaring red glow. He heard the piercing cry of a child. Bent double, he ran down the corridor. In cabin 234 he found a little girl cowering in a corner, too frightened to move. Wright picked her up and ran as the flames came roaring through the walls.

CHIEF STEWARDESS SCHWARTZ and Stewardess Ragne Zabola climbed up to D deck, the older woman turning to smile encouragement to her friend.

"I wonder where Sydney is?" Miss Zabola asked more than once. "I hope he's all right." She and Sydney Ryan had been good friends since joining the ship.

"He's probably up on deck waiting for you," said Mrs. Schwartz. "When we get there it probably won't be as bad as we think."

But when they reached D deck, her confidence began to evaporate. They found themselves ankle-deep in water that gushed from a couple of uncapped fire hydrants.

Both women squinted against the smoke rolling down on them. The smarting pungency came from the combination of heavy paint, laminated panelling in staterooms, and the highly inflammable varnish that had made the *Morro Castle* a thing of beauty, and that now helped turn her into a floating charnel house.

The women could hear the fire crackling overhead and were aware of the wind howling in through broken portholes—ready-made flues allowing oxygen to feed the inferno. Suddenly behind them they heard a dull roar. The fire had reached D deck.

"WHICH WAY to lifeboat number ten?" Up on B deck, Dr. Emilio Giro asked the question with polite diffidence.

A sailor shouted over his shoulder, "Forget the lifeboats! Jump"—then vanished into the smoke.

Giro turned to his brother-in-law. "Jump? But I can't swim."

"It's the only chance," Mestre answered.

Giro considered the words carefully, as he might consider the opinion of a trusted medical colleague. "Very well. I will jump," he said gravely.

The decision made, he took off his coat, folded it carefully, and placed it on the deck. Next he took off his shoes. He wondered whether he should also remove his shirt and trousers; he would find it easier to stay afloat without them, but there was also the matter of the cold—and the matter of propriety. A few feet away a group of men and women knelt in prayer. Turning his back on them, Dr. Giro walked across to the rail. The sea was covered with pieces of debris and bodies.

Dr. Giro started to weigh all the factors scientifically. He knew that his life jacket alone would probably not support him in the storm. A piece of wood, he thought, could become waterlogged. Then it occurred to him—he needed a body to hang on to.

He stared down again into the sea. Then he turned to his brother-in-law. "Take care of Sylvia and the baby for me . . . ."

"You'll make it," said Mestre, embracing the doctor.

The two men stepped apart. Giro noticed that Mestre wasn't wearing a life jacket.

"I'll jump from lower down," said Mestre. He turned and ran down the deck into the smoke. It was useless to go after him.

Dr. Giro walked to the rail and sat on it. He swallowed deeply, closed his eyes, and jumped.

The coldness of the water was followed by another sensation—a pounding against his ears, the feeling that his stomach was being forced up and up into his chest and then a terrible choking feeling, as if he were being strangled. Curiously, he had expected this. Something told him that, medically speaking, he was experiencing no unusual symptoms. As long as he didn't open his mouth he was still safe.

He shot to the surface, coughing and spitting, close to the ship. The black hull rose up like the side of a cliff. Coming down the cliff was the fire, showering the water with sparks. On the decks Giro could see people. They seemed to be dancing along the rail, little figures jumping up and down, waving their hands, like puppets in a carnival sideshow.

As the waves tossed him around, Dr. Giro felt as if he were being pulled down. He began to swallow sea water, then spat it out and closed his mouth. He kicked and flailed, repeating to himself, "You can't drown. There's Sylvia and baby Sylvia." Then he saw a corpse floating a few feet away, face down.

He reached out and got his arms around its neck. As the body turned over, Dr. Giro could see it was a man, about fifty, dressed in pyjamas. His face had been terribly burned. He placed both arms around the body's waist and started to kick out with his feet, slowly and steadily. It was a long way to shore.

FATHER EGAN and Sydney Ryan emerged from the furnace heat of C deck, unsuccessful in their search for the missing husband. Their eyes streamed from smoke.

The man's wife rushed towards them. She seemed on the verge of saying something when, with a scream of pain, she twisted forward. A great splinter of glass, shaped like a jagged triangle, had pierced her back. She was dead before they could move.

The heavy plate-glass windows of the ballroom had shattered in the heat. Showers of smoke-blackened, heavy glass flew through the air. Any one of the fragments was capable of killing.

"Duck under the thwarts!" shouted Seaman Gross.

His warning was too late for some: a man and two women were sliced down where they stood.

AMIDSHIPS ON THE STARBOARD side, Seaman Joseph Spilgins wondered where the officers were, where the lifeboat crews had gone, where the passengers had disappeared to. For twenty minutes, with flames scorching the air, he had waited to launch the first lifeboat. Through the smoke straggled a small group of people: three young women passengers, a few stewards, and a sailor. Spilgins helped the women into a boat. The others scrambled in after them.

Spilgins released the brake and dropped the lifeboat over the side. He knew that lifeboats are not lowered from a ship under way, but under the circumstances, it seemed essential to use any means of escape at hand. The wire falls whined in the sheaves as the boat shot down to the sea. He looked down. Something had gone wrong. The lifeboat was being towed alongside the ship by one of the falls. Its hysterical occupants clung like leeches to a plunging, terrified animal. A man fell over the side and was hauled back by the sailor as the lifeboat scraped against the *Morro Castle*.

The sailor grabbed a hatchet stowed in the stern and cut the wire. They were free. As they drifted clear of the liner, another lifeboat, red-hot and flaming, came loose from its fastenings, pitched out over the ship's side, and crashed into the sea a few yards away.

ACTING CAPTAIN WARMS was unaware that at least one lifeboat had been launched without his authority and that passengers were jumping into the sea. The calmness of a few hours before was gone. It was understandable: Warms had never imagined he would assume a command again under such circumstances, nor could he expect his chief engineer to fail him at a crucial moment.

The helmsman spun the magnetic compass wheel to bring the ship on to a new course. "No response, sir!"

"Now Goddammit! *Get* her around!"

"Sir—"

"Get her *around*!"

But the wheel spun slackly. The *Morro Castle*'s helmsman had lost control over her rudder.

Warms ran out to the wing of the bridge to check how fast the stern was swinging. A blast of heat scorched his face, singeing his eyebrows and hair. Tall columns of flame leaped as high as the mast amidships. Against this background Warms saw blackened figures run and plunge over the side.

For moments he peered aft, unwilling to believe his own eyes.

"Captain. Fire's totally out of control."

Warms turned at Ivan Freeman's words. "Ivan. They're jumping back there." Warms shook his head in wonderment. "Get forward and let go the anchor." The two men rushed back onto the bridge.

"They needn't have jumped," muttered Warms. "There's plenty of life gear for everybody." There was, but panic and inefficiency had rendered it useless.

AT EXACTLY 3.25 A.M. Alagna returned to the radio room shouting, "O.K., send it."

Rogers began to transmit. "*Morro Castle*. Twenty miles south of Scotland Lightship. Ship afire. Need immediate assistance."

Alagna's and Rogers's versions of the events that followed are similar, but Rogers's testimony puts him in a more heroic light—and heroic he was, even though his motives may be questioned.

Rogers suddenly became conscious that his feet were so hot he couldn't stand it. He felt the floor with his hand. He withdrew it quickly. "I had a white towel over my face. I could hardly breathe any longer. I had gotten about halfway through the distress message when the corner of the radio-room table that housed the receiver batteries exploded. The room became filled with a sulphuric gas, probably because the hot deck was boiling the acid pouring from the batteries.

"The receiver was completely out of commission. But I continued to send the SOS, realizing that the transmitter was still functioning. Then, the auxiliary generator suddenly stopped. I staggered to the wall and hung on for several seconds. Then I fixed up the connections and I heard the generator start again . . . . I was just staggering around . . . my feet were burning bad . . . the towel was already practically permeated with smoke. I could not hold out much longer. Then there was an explosion in the auxiliary room and the radio generator stopped completely."

Alagna was shaking Rogers. "Come on, Chief, get out of here."

Rogers pushed him away and said, "Go back to the bridge and see if there is anything else!"

Alagna returned once more to the bridge. Acting Captain Warms ordered the radio room evacuated; the ship was being abandoned.

Back in the radio room, Alagna found Rogers barely conscious. He pulled him towards the door. They managed to get onto the bridge. The ship was covered by the smoke and flames aft. They paused, wondering which way to turn next.

On the port side of the bridge, Warms was struggling with a screaming passenger whose girl friend was trapped in a cabin.

"Put him in a boat," Warms gasped.

A few feet from the bridge, a lifeboat had been prepared for lowering. The sailors bundled the man towards it.

Behind them came Chief Engineer Abbott, mumbling, "There's nothing more we can do in the engine room without choking to death . . . ." And as the sailors dumped the passenger in the lifeboat, Abbott stepped into its stern. "Lower away," he ordered.

The kindest interpretation of Abbott's action is that he was still deeply shocked. But the fact remains that this lifeboat, with a capacity of seventy, then held only eight people, six of whom were members of the crew. Indeed, of the first eighty people lowered away in lifeboats, seventy-three were crew members.

Acting Captain Warms shouted from the bridge, "Don't lower that boat! Keep it at the rail for passengers."

Eban Abbott continued to order the boat to be lowered.

As it slid down, Abbott tore off his bars and gold braid.

"IT WAS A MOMENT of shame for all who believe in the tradition of the sea," Warms recalled later. Yet Warms himself was not without fault. The nearly thirty minutes he let pass between the discovery of the fire and the sending of an SOS has never been explained adequately. His brief explanation—that he didn't want to alarm the passengers by triggering off an immediate full-scale rescue operation—was accepted.

Some knowledgeable seamen have said that sending out an SOS was the last thing a captain would do in those days. An SOS that was not strictly necessary could attract undesirable publicity, and would undoubtedly dim a captain's prospects of promotion.

Perhaps if somebody other than Alagna had visited the bridge to get permission to send an SOS, Warms might have paid more attention; and certainly the fire spread much faster than he had allowed for. Whatever the reasons, there is one inescapable fact; by the time the SOS *was* sent, the *Morro Castle* was beyond help.

ROGERS AND ALAGNA picked their way forward of the bridge. The chief radio operator recalled later that as he looked aft, he could hear portholes cracking from the heat inside.

They scrambled to the forepeak, joining a small group of people around Warms, who had a flashlight in his hand.

"Hackney," said Warms, "there is a ship out there. See if you can raise her."

Hackney started to wink out the call sign of the *Morro Castle* to the steaming *Andrea S. Luckenbach*.

The freighter's blinking system cut in: "Do you need assistance?"

Hackney flashed out: "Immediately. Five forty passengers."

"We will send a boat," came the reply. It seemed an inadequate response, but the *Luckenbach* carried only two boats.

Warms looked at the superstructure, flaming aft from the bridge, virtually dividing the ship in two. In the forepeak were Ivan Freeman and Clarence Hackney, as well as Rogers and Alagna, the watchman Pender, Storekeeper O'Sullivan, a handful of seamen, and Dr. and Mrs. Vosseler.

The wind which sent shivers through them also protected them from the blaze roaring through the rest of the ship.

"We'll all be safe soon. I got off the SOS," said Rogers.

C DECK, near the stern, was crowded with people. The cruise director was trying to calm them. Somebody had brought a bedspread on deck. Lena Schwartz tore it up into little pieces and wet it so that the people could have a piece to put to their noses to keep the smoke from choking them. Some of the men asked why she didn't jump. "I am *the* stewardess on the ship," Mrs. Schwartz said. "I must stay."

Steward Sydney Ryan and Stewardess Ragne Zabola had been holding hands by the rail. Mrs. Schwartz turned to give them strips of cloth, but they had jumped.

Horrified, Mrs. Schwartz rushed to the rail. Far below she watched the couple thrashing desperately to get clear of the stern. Then they were sucked under.

"The propellers must have cut them in two," Mrs. Schwartz recalled. "It was horrible, horrible."

HEADWAITER CARL WRIGHT sensed that if he didn't jump soon, he and the little girl he carried would die. But Wright knew the danger of jumping from the stern. He turned and inched his way towards midships. It was a nightmare journey. A sailor's hand had been sliced off and he was walking around, appealing for help, trying to use his other hand as a tourniquet. With a scream, the man jumped overboard. A woman passenger lay face down on the deck, either trampled to death or suffocated.

Clutching the child tightly to him, the headwaiter jumped overboard. Swimming steadily, he was carried away from the *Morro Castle*. Around him the sea was filled with corpses and people clinging to debris. He started to swim towards a lifeboat.

When the waves swept over the child's head, he lifted her and told her to spit out the water. Wright listened to her heart but could hear nothing. "I carried the poor little tot on towards the boat because I didn't want to abandon her."

The boat drifted off into the night before he could reach it. Wright clung to the child for two more hours. Other passengers swam up, begging him to release the body and help the living. "It broke my heart," he said, "when I had to set her body adrift."

PATROLMAN PRICE and his wife Mary stood on C deck. They had watched others go over the side and knew they must jump even though Mary Price was crippled. Finally, with the assistance of a passenger, Patrolman Price got his wife's legs over the side, tied a lifebelt around her waist, looped the rope and around a hawser, and lowered her down into the water near a lifeboat.

The survivors in the lifeboat ignored her. Price kept shouting, "Pick her up! Pick her up!" But instead they shouted for him to jump. They did not pick up Mrs. Price from the water until William Price slid down a rope. When the policeman got into the boat he found his wife dead.

ANOTHER PATROLMAN on board, Charles Menken, had helped his wife jump from C deck, then followed her into the water. He had been stunned by a falling body and nearly drowned.

"When I regained my bearings, my wife wasn't anywhere to be

seen. I spent an hour looking for her, swimming from one corpse to another. Then I found her, lying on her back, floating like she was in a pool. She just turned her head and looked at me, and said, 'Charley', and I said 'Annie'.

"Then we just held hands, floating, as the waves kept smashing at us."

"MY FRIEND is still in her cabin," cried a woman passenger.

Cruise Director Robert Smith nodded. In the past hour his heroism had cost him burns on his face, hands, and body. He edged towards the curtain of flame. "The heat was scorching the inside of my mouth, and I was scared," Smith recalled. Then through the fire he saw it—an isolated, moving ball of flame.

"It's my friend!" shrieked the woman behind him.

The fireball staggered down the corridor; the whole body seemed to be aflame. As the horrified Smith watched, the flames gushed up above the body, and it rolled back along the corridor into the inferno.

Smith grabbed the woman passenger and ran out to D deck. He scooped her into his arms and jumped overboard. He would support her for hours before both were rescued.

ON C DECK, half a dozen passengers were trapped by fire in a corridor. Rescue was impossible. Father Egan knelt at the edge of the fire. The heat burned the skin off his knees. Raising his hand, he spoke the words of absolution. Then he rose, clothes smouldering, and ran back on the deck, tears streaming down his face.

"Father! You've got to jump. Everybody's going!"

The priest nodded to the seaman. Crew and passengers were swarming over the side.

RAFAEL MESTRE had been trying to steel himself to jump overboard but his courage failed him. "Then I saw this woman," he recalled. "She was weeping because she had no preserver. I gave her one I found, strapped it on her, and threw her as far out as possible from the side of the ship."

Before he could reconsider, the young Cuban sprang over the

side. He swam steadily for an hour before a boat found him. In it was the body of the woman he had given the life jacket to. She had drowned.

SEAMAN LEROY KELSEY peered intently through the pouring rain over the prow of his lifeboat. "Sea Girt," he bellowed. "It's the light at Sea Girt! And look . . . !"

A red star shot up into the sky. Somebody on shore was firing a rocket to guide them.

"Come on," he said, "let's break out the sail, we don't want to be out here forever." They rigged it, and squared away towards the shore. Then Kelsey started to sing. A handful of people picked up his chant:

"Roll, Jordan, roll,
I wanna go to heaven, when I die,
To see ol' Jordan roll."

The *Morro Castle* was a faint glow far on the port side, and the light from Sea Girt blinked more clearly through the murk. Soon they were able to pick out individual lights on shore. Then they heard the dull roar of the surf. A dark mass of water piled up astern, the sea hissed and the boat pitched skyward and dropped sickeningly in a smother of foam.

Into the surf came a man with a line in his hands.

"Jump," he yelled. "But watch the surf and undertow."

The men tumbled waist-deep into the sea, and then helped the three girl passengers over the side. The lifeboat survivors were dragged ashore.

The man called out: "Who are you? Where are you from?" Kelsey replied, "Survivors—from hell."

The Rescue Armada

Between 3.00 a.m. and 3.25 a.m. fourteen separate Coast Guard stations received "positive calls" that a large ship was blazing a few miles out to sea. The Coast Guard lookouts saw nothing. They decided to wait. It was therefore not until the *Morro Castle*'s SOS was picked up by the Navy that a general alert went out along three hundred miles of coast.

On paper, the Coast Guard commanded a small armada of ships in the disaster area.

Twenty-five miles away from the burning *Morro Castle* cruised the large patrol boat *Cahoone*, but, with only two inexperienced operators on board, the *Cahoone* did not pick up the repeated order to speed to the rescue until 4.00 a.m.

The cutter *Tampa*, berthed in New York harbour, also missed the original order, and sailing was delayed until 5.39. Alongside her lay the *Sebago*, her boilers stripped for a routine overhaul, her radio shack deserted. She did not sail for fifteen hours. None of the dozen seventy-five-foot patrol boats within the area was equipped with radio to direct them.

Four fast Coast Guard patrol boats had been detached from their regular New Jersey coastal watch to trail a rum smuggler five hundred miles north of New York, and the two-thousand-ton cutter *Champlain* had been sent to Greenland to ferry Mrs. Ruth Bryan Owen, American minister to Denmark, back to New York.

The Coast Guard air station, eighty-eight miles southwest of the *Morro Castle*, had seven aircraft—but only one of them was considered "suitable for rescue or observation work offshore"—and two pilots. Hours passed before they became airborne.

Commercial ships reacted rather more practically to the crisis. The freighter *Luckenbach* was picking up survivors by 4.00 a.m. The British liner *Monarch of Bermuda* turned around and raced to the *Morro Castle*. The *City of Savannah* and the *President Cleveland* also changed course to assist.

In the end, though, it was a Coast Guard surfboat from Sea Girt that was first on the scene. Its captain had put to sea simply to investigate "the ball of flame" he had seen. Aboard was a crew of five, including Helmsman Warren Moulton.

"We had an awful fight until we were within half a mile of the burning ship," Moulton recalled. "Then we ran into something I never want to see or hear again.

"The ocean was alive with screaming men and women, and when the surfboat stopped, so many grabbed the boat that it nearly capsized. I do not know how many times we stopped . . . but certainly not more than five, and I heard the skipper bellowing at me to go ahead on her. I got under way, and for the next half mile there was a fight on that I will never forget.

"Every sea broke over us, washing us from stem to stern. The crew did all they could to keep others off and prevent our running over someone in the water.

"All round—ahead, on each side, and astern—were men and women, all excited, a few with their hands stretched out towards us, calling for help, and we, already overloaded, unable to help.

"As we reached the *Luckenbach* I looked at our cargo for the first time: women back in the stern piled three deep, men and women over the engine box, cordwood-fashion. Just how many there were I didn't know, but we had our hands full to get them aboard the ship and keep our boat from being smashed alongside."

AT 4.00 A.M., radio stations on the east coast interrupted their programmes with news of the disaster, but a New Jersey station announced that everybody on board had been rescued. So fishermen all along the coast decided to wait for daybreak before investigating.

The news flash puzzled James Bogen. At the age of twenty-six he was skipper of the thirty-ton *Paramount*—one of the youngest captains on the coast, with a reputation for boldness and flair. From the wharf at Manasquan Inlet he watched the fireball on the horizon and wondered how anyone could know for certain that everybody had been rescued. He telephoned the local Coast Guard station, and was urged to "go on out there as fast as you can."

Swiftly he mustered a crew made up entirely of fishing-boat captains. At 4.40 a.m. the *Paramount* surged out to sea, followed soon by a small armada of smacks.

That incorrect radio announcement had cost forty valuable minutes. Time enough for the sea and the *Morro Castle* to claim further victims. Some of the fishermen believed nearly seventy more could have been saved if they had put to sea earlier.

"Long before we reached the *Morro Castle* we were picking up survivors," said Jimmy Bogen. "We didn't bother with the bodies.

A lifeboat comes ashore. Of the Morro Castle*'s twelve lifeboats, sufficient for 816 people, only half were launched with a mere handful of survivors in each—nearly all of them members of the crew.*

The Rescue Armada: when the SOS was finally sent, commercial ships, Coast Guard vessels, and fishing-boats raced to the rescue. But for 134 of the passengers and crew it was too late.

We only picked up the live ones. They were all over. If they had on life preservers we got them with grappling hooks." One of these was Headwaiter Carl Wright.

Bogen's foresight in picking the most experienced crew available paid off: "It was a ticklish business running the boat close enough to a person, or a group of three or four, in that rough water, without bumping one of them, and yet getting close enough for a crewman to throw a line with certainty, or even—in the case of weaker swimmers—to reach out and seize them."

ON C DECK, Dr. Joe Bregstein still hesitated. The flames were a few feet away. Gladys and Ethel Knight of the Concordia Singing Society were beside him. The dentist looked at his son. The child looked solemnly at his father.

Joe Bregstein was close to tears. "I can't swim very well," he began.

"He'll be all right with us," urged Ethel Knight. "We're good swimmers. We can make it, sure we can."

From the deck came a dull roar as part of the superstructure caved in.

"Dr. Bregstein—"

"O.K., young ladies. Take good care of my boy." He bent and kissed Mervin on the cheek. "You'll be O.K. son."

The child nodded. Supported by the girls, Mervin Bregstein plunged over the side.

Tears streaming down his face, Joe Bregstein reached the rail, the impulse to be with his son overcoming all else. Then he climbed over backward, hanging from deck level over the side. He felt a sudden, insistent tugging at his ankles. Bregstein let go. For one awful moment he thought he was falling into a void. Then strong hands swept him onto D deck.

He clutched the rail. A passenger restrained him. "The rescue boats are coming. They'll get us off."

Dr. Bregstein looked across the water. Small boats were moving towards the *Morro Castle*. "They're bound to pick up Mervin and the girls," he shouted.

But the rescue flotilla missed the trio drifting towards the shore.

After hours of swimming, the girls lapsed into a stupor. They were unaware when the sea snatched Mervin Bregstein away from them. They finally reached shore, suffering from exhaustion and exposure, but Mervin's body was never found.

RADIO OPERATOR CHARLES MAKI, a powerful swimmer, was in the water for an hour before he reached a lifeboat. At its helm was Seaman Joe Spilgins. Spilgins had behaved with remarkable coolness during the crisis on board. He had marshalled passengers and crew into the boat, telling everybody, "You're under my command." He resisted demands until the last moment to lower the boat. Then, with perhaps a dozen half-dressed passengers, helped by a couple of stewards and Assistant Engineer Antonio Bujia, he manoeuvred the boat down to the water level. It was the last lifeboat to leave the *Morro Castle*.

As it drifted clear of the burning hull, another dozen swimmers scrambled aboard. Among them were several members of the Concordia Singing Society, Rafael Mestre, Charles and Annie Menken, and Father Egan, who hauled three corpses aboard.

The arrival of Radioman Maki encouraged those in the wallowing boat. He picked up an oar and urged the other men in broken English to help row towards shore. After a while, at the suggestion of Father Egan, the others sang to encourage the oarsmen. Uneven voices blended into a chorus whose repertoire ranged from a hymn to "Tea for Two". They were still singing when the boat beached, hours later.

FOR WHAT SEEMED like hours, Dr. Giro had stubbornly clung to the corpse. Once a lifeboat came close. "It seemed to be manned by some of the ship's crew. There were people all round in the water, including some children. But the boat didn't stop to pick up anybody, and there seemed to be only a few people in the boat."

Dr. Giro somehow managed to keep his wits and stamina, believing it would not be long before rescue came. In the meantime the issue was clinically simple: could he stay alive until then? He knew how easily the icy water broke a man's resistance. He had seen it happen several times in the past few hours.

NOBODY REALLY knew what happened to many of the people on the *Morro Castle*. Dr. Van Zile, the ship's surgeon, was the subject of a number of legends, all heroic, but none verified. One account placed him in the ship's surgery waiting for casualties that never came. Another had him on the bridge, passing around a flask of rum before perishing in the flames. In a third version he went over the side, took off his life jacket in the water and strapped it on a child—an extraordinary feat for even the fittest man.

Incredible stories were told of others. The ship's manicurist, Ella Jacoby, died in the flames, witnesses swore, after freeing the liner's parrot from its cage on the veranda café. A ship's musician would be immortalized for playing ragtime jazz through the corridor on B deck—long after the area was a solid mass of flame.

DURING THE FIRST MINUTES of daylight, there was no time for storytelling among the hundreds of people scattered over a couple of square miles of turbulent sea around the *Morro Castle*.

Mrs. Hiram Hulse, wife of a missionary bishop to Cuba, struggled feebly in her life jacket and puzzled over a deep rumbling that seemed to come from beneath the waves. As she and her husband had jumped from the ship, the impact had knocked her unconscious; when she awoke, there was no sign of the bishop.

Nearby, Cruise Director Smith, who had spent several hours keeping a woman passenger afloat, identified the sound as the engines of a large ship. He shouted encouragement to Mrs. Hulse.

She mumbled: "Go away. My husband's dead. He's drowned. It's the Lord's way . . . ."

A FEW HUNDRED YARDS from her, the Right Reverend Hiram Hulse looked around him, and muttered, "Plucked from the valley of death into the arms of safety."

The seaman looked at the old man kindly. In a broad Cockney accent he asked: "Like a cuppa, sir?"

Hiram Hulse was the first passenger to be picked up by the *Monarch of Bermuda*.

On the bridge of the British liner, Captain Albert R. Francis gently nudged the Furness Line cruise ship to within two hundred feet of the *Morro Castle*. In the grey light of dawn the extent of the disaster silenced the passengers and crew lining the rails of the *Monarch of Bermuda*.

Captain Francis recalled that the *Morro Castle* "was anchored, bow into the wind, keeping the flames from the forepeak where a small group of people stood. The rest of the ship was in flames. But you could still hear the screams and cries of the passengers. It was horrible . . . ."

Hours earlier, when the duty operator had awakened Captain Francis with the SOS message, he had bolted to the bridge in pyjamas, ordered the ship around, and then worked out the fastest course to the *Morro Castle*. While he plotted, he fired off a volley of orders: the engine room was to cram on every ounce of steam; the first officer was to prepare lifeboats for lowering.

Others were given specific tasks: to open all gangway doors; to pile blankets on deck; to rig chair slings for the injured, canvas slings for hauling up children, cargo nets for the more agile. The ship's doctor and nurse were ordered to set up a casualty clearing station in the first-class lounge; the purser to man all gangways and channel survivors to the lounge for medical checks; the galley staffs to prepare urns of coffee, tea, and soup; the chief steward to have brandy and whisky ready; all passengers to provide spare clothes for the victims.

The crew responded swiftly, and the engine room crammed on enough speed to send the liner slicing through the water at 20 knots. Up on the bridge, Captain Francis, now fully dressed, waited. "That was the hardest part," he remembered. "We all just stared and strained ahead for the first sight of the ship."

At 7.00 a.m. they saw the glow. Twenty minutes later the Right Reverend Hiram Hulse was hauled aboard and wrapped in a blanket. He received a medical check, was put to bed, and was given coffee laced with rum.

ON THE *MORRO CASTLE*, Acting Captain Warms and the others grouped around him watched the five lifeboats bobbing towards them from the *Monarch of Bermuda*. Clarence Hackney and George Alagna both recalled the excellent seamanship of the lifeboat crews, who had a "calmness and control you only get in a good British ship".

Warms looked at Dr. and Mrs. Vosseler, the only passengers to have reached the forepeak. "Time for you to go," he said.

The couple nodded and shook the hands of those remaining on board. Then they made the difficult descent down a Jacob's ladder to a lifeboat.

"Anybody else?" called a voice from below.

"No. We are staying," said Warms steadily.

"We are all staying," echoed George White Rogers.

In the time the chief radio officer had been on the forepeak, he had laid the foundation of a legend that would survive his lifetime. There had been two theatrical gestures to find a way through the wall of flame stretching back to the stern. The heat had beaten him back. Next had come an attempt to rescue a woman passenger trapped in a porthole just forward of the bridge. First he swung himself out over the side, where he dangled for a while like a monstrous jellyfish. Then he was hauled back aboard. Next he prepared to swing on a rope, Tarzan fashion, down the side of the ship, to rescue the woman. When it came to the final leap, Rogers decided the rope was not strong enough to support him.

While he thought out a new way to reach the screaming woman, she freed herself, fell into the sea, and drowned.

Unabashed, Rogers busied himself with the signal lamp.

"He was so cool," First Officer Freeman remembered.

"He had a limitless supply of advice," Hackney recalled.

It seemed to Night Watchman Pender and Storekeeper O'Sullivan that the chief radio officer was "working at top speed and keeping up our spirits". But George Alagna wondered uneasily why Rogers seemed to be positively enjoying the tragedy all around him.

The *Monarch of Bermuda*'s lifeboats fanned out around the *Morro Castle*'s stern. Through a megaphone an officer urged those remaining on board to jump: "We'll get to you. Have no fear."

Joe Bregstein, standing on D deck, felt reassured at the sound of that voice. "It was so English, so calm, so authoritative." He didn't hesitate. Dropping over the side, he floundered in the water for moments until strong hands pulled him into a lifeboat.

Stewardess Lena Schwartz leaped over the side and surfaced beside another lifeboat. As soon as she was aboard, she began to concern herself with the rescued passengers. When the officer in charge gently suggested she should rest, Mrs. Schwartz replied, almost fiercely, "I still have a job to do."

CHIEF ENGINEER ABBOTT spoke to no one; he seemed oblivious to the cold, the rain, and the pounding of the seas. Around him the other occupants of the lifeboat shivered. There were now twenty-nine of them. Only three were passengers.

The crew found the lifeboat difficult to handle. "Why don't you take an oar and row, instead of sitting there," a seaman shouted at Abbott as the lifeboat bobbed helplessly in the sea.

"I can't. I cut my hand." Eban Abbott held up his left hand to show the rest of the boat's passengers. There was no cut. He held up his right hand. Again, there was no mark.

They eyed the chief engineer curiously. Abbott's only response was to look away.

Then suddenly the sound of breaking surf awoke new fears in him. "Row away from here!" he cried. "It's too dark to go ashore!"

Dr. Charles Cochrane, one of the three passengers in the lifeboat, himself deeply shocked at the loss of his sister, felt sorry for the ship's officer. "In the darkness I had heard him mutter that he would be jailed for his behaviour."

Abbott was still urging the oarsmen to put out to sea when the lifeboat was caught by the crest of a wave and sent scooting onto the beach. A group of fishermen pulled it up on the sand.

Abbott, in full dress uniform, was the first man ashore. Turning to the lifeboat's complement he said, "Remember. None of you should talk to newspapermen. They would never understand." Then he walked up the beach, tears streaming down his face.

BY 8.00 A.M., lifeboats from the *Monarch of Bermuda* had picked up over fifty passengers—the final count was seventy-one rescued by the British liner.

As boatload after boatload came alongside, the survivors already on board peered down, seeking familiar faces. For some the agonizing wait was mercifully brief, the reunions little short of miraculous.

Mrs. Hiram Hulse appeared to Stewardess Lena Schwartz to be "on the point of death when they got her on board", but she recovered quickly when she found her husband; she and the bishop wept openly.

Cruise Director Smith and the woman passenger he had supported for hours in the water also burst into tears when they stepped aboard the *Monarch of Bermuda.*

"The rescue operation performed by the Furness Line ship and its crew," a later commendation stated, "was in the highest traditions of the sea."

So, too, was the work of the crews of the *Andrea S. Luckenbach*, which had twenty-six survivors aboard, and the liner *City of Savannah*, whose lifeboats rescued sixty-five.

BY BREAKFAST TIME thousands of people were moving along the New Jersey shore, keeping pace with the pall of smoke that drifted about five miles off the beach.

There was an almost carnival atmosphere among the onlookers. Restaurants, cafés, and coffee shops had an end-of-season boom. Few of the watchers actually saw a survivor, or a victim. If they did it was only a brief glimpse. But so dense was the crush along the shore that the local American Legion was called out to help the police with traffic control.

After a slow start, the rescue operation had become a massive and coordinated effort between the Coast Guard, civilian and military spotter-planes, police, fishermen, National Guard, local hospitals, and mortuaries.

At Sea Girt, a CBS reporter described the scene:

"Since daybreak, Coast Guard boats have pitched and tossed through the whitecaps, making tortuous progress towards that dreadful pall on the horizon.

"Sometimes you can see the flames, but generally they are shut out altogether by the squalls of rain that must be making it hell for everybody out there. Survivors and bodies are coming ashore along a wide stretch of coastline, but nobody knows yet how many have lived—and how many have died. It will be some hours, perhaps even days, before the final toll becomes known."

While radio relayed a constant stream of instant information, scores of newspaper reporters were also piecing together a first impression of the calamity. A *New York Herald Tribune* reporter had found an immediate angle at Spring Lake, New Jersey:

"Soon after dawn this morning the first boatloads of survivors from the flaming *Morro Castle* drew up on the sandy beach in front of the southern bathing pavilion of this seaside resort, and through the surf from time to time emerged exhausted swimmers, singly, in pairs and in groups, clinging to logs, rafts and life preservers. Private homes all along the shore took in the sea-battered survivors, put them to bed, and furnished warming drinks until medical aid could arrive."

THE OPEN-COCKPIT military two-seater banked and skimmed over the sea. From the rear seat the fifty-five-year-old Governor of New Jersey, Harry Moore, waved a red flag to guide rescue ships towards people in the water. It was a flight that Moore would never forget: "The waves were extremely high and the boats had difficulty in sighting those in the water . . . . When I spotted a swimmer, the pilot would drop a smoke-bomb nearby." The Governor waved at one man who was "struggling feebly, partly submerged".

Dr. Emilio Giro did not return the wave. He had spent many hours in the water, clinging to a corpse. But the will to stay alive had been steadily drained by the cold, the salt water, and his constant seasickness and vomiting. He sensed rather than heard the aircraft; moments later an acrid cloud drifted over him as a smoke-bomb plopped into the sea.

Captain Bogen of the *Paramount* had spent an hour chasing from one bomb burst to another; frequently the result was a corpse to be hooked and dragged aboard. This time he was luckier. Dr. Giro was alive, though barely, when James Bogen pulled him out of the water.

Beached

The *Morro Castle* drifted northward, dragging her anchor. With the rudder inoperative, the hulk from time to time canted to port or starboard with sickening force.

The men on the forepeak stood staring at the pall of smoke.

"How come it got a hold so quick?" asked Rogers.

"It was set! I'm positive," Hackney declared.

His accusation got a chorus of agreement.

Arthur Pender thought it looked like a chemical fire because the flames in the writing room were blue-white.

When Rogers was asked his opinion, he shrugged. "Guess I was too busy getting out the SOS to notice the colour of the flames."

Warms killed further speculation: "If it was set, I guess I know why." He glanced at Alagna. Baffled and still unaware of Warm's suspicions about him, the junior operator looked uneasy.

Warms, morosely, peered out to port. The command he had longed for—master of a luxury cruise ship—had been the shortest in maritime history, barely seven hours. He reviewed every order, every course change, every step he had taken, "and I knew I had done everything correctly."

His seamanship had indeed been technically excellent. His failure had been in not anticipating that the fire could spread so quickly. Such anticipation would have caused him to order all the fire doors on board closed and to ask for outside help sooner.

Warms watched as yet another boat approached. It was the 1800-ton Coast Guard cutter *Tampa*, with a crew of 100 under the command of Lieutenant Commander Earl G. Rose.

"Do you want a tow?" The magnified voice boomed out from the *Tampa*.

"Yes," bellowed Warms.

"All right. We will put a twelve-inch hawser on board you and tow you to New York."

The arrival of the *Tampa* galvanized Rogers. As he watched the *Tampa* lower a surfboat he kept up an elated chant: "They're coming, they're coming, they're coming . . . ."

"*She's here. The* Morro Castle*'s coming straight towards the studio.*"
Radio Station WCAP, *the voice of Asbury Park, 1934.*

The debris of disaster: shoes and clothing discarded by passengers before they jumped from the burning ship.

The surfboat was rowed across to the *Morro Castle*'s bow. A heaving line was thrown down to haul up the hawser. Then the handful of men on the forepeak began doing a job usually performed by powerful winches. They went at it like a tug-of-war team, with Rogers as the anchor man. Inch by inch, foot by foot, yard by yard, almost fifty fathoms of hawser were pulled up and made fast first around the bitts, and then the mast.

It took two hours.

The weather had worsened. The rescue flotilla withdrew towards shore. Only the *Tampa* and a New York harbour tug remained.

"Now slip the anchor chain." The voice from the *Tampa* brought the men on the forepeak staggering to their feet.

The order was unintentionally ironic. The forepeak crew had no mechanical power either to raise the anchor or to "slip" it into the sea. The only way was to cut it.

Rogers hurried to the carpenter shop beneath the forecastle and reappeared triumphantly, holding a hacksaw. He insisted on taking the first turn at cutting through the forged steel link. Soon, he tired of the task and handed the saw to a seaman. Then he wandered off, whistling to himself.

When at last the steel link snapped, five hours had passed since the *Tampa* first offered help. Taking the strain on the hawser, the cutter moved ahead of the hulk; astern, the tugboat, hooked onto one of the ropes trailing over the side, acted as a jury rudder.

Alongside the bow of the *Morro Castle*, one of the *Tampa*'s lifeboats waited to lift off the last of the liner's crew. One after the other, they scrambled over the side. When it was Rogers's turn, he suddenly saw something that terrified him. The lifeboat had picked up three bodies. They lay, bloodied from being smashed against the side of the *Morro Castle*, in the bottom of the lifeboat.

"Jump! God damn you! Jump!" The command from the lifeboat's officer broke Rogers's hold on the Jacob's ladder.

He fell into the boat across the bodies, shrieked and fainted.

IN MANHATTAN, thousands of people lined the waterfront, looking expectantly to the mouth of the harbour. Ward Line offices on Wall Street were besieged by newsmen, relatives, and friends.

At midday the first list of known dead was posted by the Line—eight men and five women. Thirty minutes later the number rose to forty. By nightfall, the list would grow to one hundred and thirty—four short of the final toll. In proportion to their numbers, twice as many passengers as crew died.

Then NBC broke the story that Martin Conboy, U.S. Attorney for the Southern District of New York, had announced he would investigate whether there was any criminal angle to the disaster.

This announcement followed reports from Havana that Captain Oscar Hernandez and his agents were about to unmask the Communist plotters who had not only sabotaged the *Morro Castle*, but were planning similar destruction of other American ships. Captain Hernandez never caught his plotters. After a week of headlines around the world he faded back into obscurity. But by then the damage was done. The investigators in New York were convinced that all they had to do was prove a member of the crew was a Communist and the case would be solved.

Some of the newspapers covering the story were not unduly concerned with accurate reporting. When the *City of Savannah* docked, two women were photographed with two children they were said to have "rescued from the fire". The children had never been on the *Morro Castle*. Other legends obscured the picture even more. From Sea Girt a reporter filed a report of a body washed ashore with a bullet hole in its forehead. There is no official record of that body, but the story persists that a sailor was shot for looting when the fire broke out. Four survivors were credited with swimming ashore, running temperatures of 104°; a Cuban mess-boy was hailed for a nine-mile swim without a lifebelt.

There was no limit to speculation. The feature writers began apportioning blame for the calamity. One criticized government economies that had "struck the Coast Guard a hard blow", while the Associated Press reported a "mounting storm" over the delay in getting Coast Guard spotter planes into the air. Meanwhile, late-afternoon headlines passed on to the public the accusations against crew members:

FIRE ALARM LATE SURVIVOR ASSERTS
FIREMAN HOLDS CREW IGNORANT OF FIRE FIGHTING

DURING THE AFTERNOON, William Warms, dressed in borrowed oilskins, spent most of the time alone at the *Tampa*'s stern, watching the burning *Morro Castle* being towed a few cable-lengths behind. George White Rogers slept the whole afternoon. He was suffering from acute nervous exhaustion and smoke inhalation, and had been put to bed. The other survivors sat silently, shrugging off questions from the Coast Guard men.

At 6.00 p.m., the *Tampa* and *Morro Castle* were abeam of Asbury Park. A few hundred yards to port lay the resort's brightly lit Convention Hall surrounded by hotels. At that moment the tugboat's hold on the liner's stern was suddenly severed and the *Morro Castle* came around broadside to the gale.

For seven minutes the *Tampa* struggled to turn the *Morro Castle*. Suddenly there was a loud crack—and the *Tampa*'s engines died. The hawser had snapped and coiled around the cutter's propeller shaft. Commander Rose dropped anchor and summoned urgent tow by radio.

In the cutter's stern, Warms watched the *Morro Castle* shudder at its new-found freedom. Then, trailing smoke and flame, it seemed to gather speed and head directly for the Convention Hall at Asbury Park.

It was 6.23 p.m.

THE STAFF of Radio Station WCAP, which broadcast from the Convention Hall, had an excellent view of the sea. At 7.30 p.m. announcer Tom Burley was about to give a station identification when he glanced out into the night. "She's here!" he shouted. "The *Morro Castle*'s coming right towards the studio!"

The *Morro Castle* ran aground less than three hundred feet from where Burley sat. In the throng watching on the seafront, the resort's civic leaders stared in amazement. "Carl," someone said to Mayor Bischoff, "she's in our front yard. This is the biggest thing's ever happened to us. Raise a city flag on her to stake our claim!"

BY MIDDAY on Sunday, September 9, 1934, Asbury Park was experiencing an unprecedented boom. The mild sunny weather helped to draw an estimated twenty-five thousand people to the resort. Roads leading into the town were posted with signs reading: "Asbury Park—the Home of the *Morro Castle*"

The approaches to Convention Hall were lined with frozen-custard and hot-dog stands, bingo stalls and shooting galleries. Householders rented their rooms, their lawns, their garages. Over Convention Hall a banner flapped in the breeze:

22 CENTS TO SEE THE S.S. MORRO CASTLE
BENEFIT OF THE FAMILIES OF THE DEAD

By lunchtime ten thousand people had paid for a closer view of the liner. There was little to see besides the blackened hull and the burned-out superstructure: a mass of twisted steel, buckled plates, and charred, rusted framework. The fire was out.

Newsmen paid five dollars to use the breeches buoy rigged between the ship's stern and Convention Hall. A gas mask cost another five dollars; a flashlight, one dollar. A reporter who slipped past Ward Line officials and local policemen to go below, described a "long dark passageway, clogged with ashes, broken bits of steel, the walls bent and the floor ripples of warped steel. Thousands of rivets protruding from distorted decks, forced out by the heat . . . . Girders supporting the superstructure and the floor below sagged terribly." He descended a metal stairway—"all of the wooden ones have disappeared completely"—and arrived on C deck. "Once there were staterooms here. Piles of black ashes are all there is left; even the iron walls have melted." On the boat deck he found that "Five lifeboats still hang from their davits, unused, unwanted now."

Sickened, the reporter left the ship.

Forward, men continued their search for the body of Robert Wilmott. Two days passed before a handful of bones were sifted from the ashes and declared to be those of the dead captain.

WHEN THE *Tampa* finally reached New York, William Warms refused to talk to reporters. George White Rogers, the last to leave, was carried off the cutter on a stretcher to a waiting ambulance.

Newsmen demanded: "Who's he?"

"That's the hero of the day," replied Clarence Hackney.

In a convoy of cars the reporters chased after the ambulance. At the Marine Hospital, Rogers, installed in a private room with a nurse at his side, posed in bed for photographers, and made a brief statement that he only "did what anyone else would have done".

Warms and other officers of the *Morro Castle* spent Sunday closeted with lawyers of the Ward Line. Company attorneys also visited Rogers in the hospital and Abbott at his home. What happened at those meetings is not known, although Abbott's widow, Ada, reported that the lawyers ordered her husband to "button up", and presumably similar instructions were given to the others.

By early afternoon, the lawyers had put together a series of statements to show that the fire had not been caused by any inefficiency on the part of the Line or the crew, and that once the fire had been discovered, every officer and crew member behaved in an exemplary manner. Warms's own statement contained the remarkable information that he "ordered" his chief engineer into a lifeboat when Abbott "collapsed from the effects of the smoke".

Rogers emerged as the hero, lauded by his colleagues as a perfect example of how the liner's officers and crew behaved.

Ward Line officials visited the Seamen's Institute in downtown New York, where most of the crew were recuperating. There they offered free clothing and money to all crew members who signed statements confirming their good impression of the officers.

The one flaw was an interview that George Alagna had given to journalist Damon Runyon of the New York *American*.

SHIP'S CHIEFS IRRESOLUTE, CREW IDLE, AIDE CHARGES
Wireless Operator Declares Captain Failed to Command

The story under the headlines ran counter to almost everything in the sworn affidavits.

Understandably, the story produced consternation in the offices of Burlingham, Veeder, Clark & Hupper, attorneys for the Ward Line. Chauncey Clark, an experienced trial lawyer, saw that Alagna's allegations, apart from the damage they could do to the Line's image, could invite countless damage suits. The Line would, of course, maintain that Alagna's allegations were totally untrue and they would be contested at any hearing. Yet, why had he made them?

Clark discounted financial gain. His inquiries showed the *American* made only a token payment for the interview.

That afternoon the Ward Line lawyers interviewed Warms, Rogers, and Hackney again. By early evening Clark had a new picture of Alagna's behaviour since he had joined the *Morro Castle*.

Rogers filled in the finer details: "Ever since he tried to call that strike, Alagna was looked upon as an agitator and a vengeful person." The words "radical", "troublemaker", and "difficult" appeared repeatedly in the chief radio officer's statement.

Clark advised Rogers that it was his duty to repeat the allegations to District Attorney Conboy. On Sunday evening, Rogers made a statement. So did Warms. The move to discredit Alagna had begun.

THE OFFICIAL INVESTIGATION into the disaster by a board appointed by the U.S. Department of Commerce opened at the Customs House in New York, on Monday, September 10, 1934.

Acting Captain Warms was the first witness. He told the board he believed "some unidentified person wilfully started the fire that destroyed the ship and cost so many lives". Supporting evidence was provided by Clarence Hackney and Ivan Freeman. Then George White Rogers took the stand and presented a picture of George Alagna as a dangerous agitator. Alagna was arrested next day as a material witness and lodged in the House of Detention in New York.

The hearings dragged on for weeks. Warms and Abbott, barred from going to sea until the investigations were concluded, received full salary from the Ward Line. The other deck officers and some crew members whose testimony the Ward Line regarded as crucial also received payments.

By the end of September, the *New York Herald Tribune* told its readers: "A clearer picture of what happened aboard the *Morro Castle* is beginning to emerge. Officers of the Ward Line felt for the first time the sting of official criticism and were subjected to a biting cross-examination."

A great deal came to light: the cargoes of arms; the lack of boat and fire drills; Warms's previous suspension; Abbott's removing his insignia. Evidence was given that inflammable polish was carried on the ship, and the stewards' department was subjected to rigorous questioning. The board strained to show that the polish had caused the fire—a conclusion that would have neatly tied up loose ends. But the theory could not be substantiated.

Other avenues were explored. Passengers were suspected. There was talk of "wild parties" and "sex orgies". But it was soon clear that passengers had not started the fire, either.

Balked, the board turned to the possibility of an "explosion in the engine room".

Seaman Charles Angelo, who mentioned it as a casual afterthought near the end of his examination, was grilled for hours. He failed to come up with anything to support the story, and after several days the "explosion" was forgotten.

Rogers now caused a sensation when he was re-examined and testified that the SOS "should have been ordered forty-five minutes earlier."

What prompted this statement is not clear. Possibly it was because the Ward Line refused to treat him the way he felt a public hero should be treated (the Line had refused his request for a new wardrobe of clothes and a bonus for his heroism). However, Rogers's testimony had one good effect, the release of Alagna from custody. Rogers now testified that his assistant had repeatedly gone to the bridge. "I want it to be known that the earlier testimony at this hearing was given with great reluctance on my part and had no bearing whatsoever upon George Alagna's conduct or his responsibility to me." Rogers had been proud to have Alagna as his first assistant and while Alagna might not have been tactful in dealing with members and officers of the ship's crew, his character was irreproachable.

A reporter wrote: "It is good to know that America can still produce heroes like George White Rogers."

Consequently, the Board of Inquiry found that negligence on the part of Warms and Abbott had caused the ship's destruction. The board dismissed the possibility of arson.

A WHOLE NEW LIFE had now opened up for the chief radio officer. The Radiomarine Corporation of America withdrew his dismissal notice, and the Veteran Wireless Operators Association gave him a medal for heroism.

Rogers politely declined a dozen offers of employment with shipping lines, and stated that his wife preferred to have him at home. Yet most of his time was occupied with making public appearances.

At a lavish official reception given by the Mayor of Bayonne, New Jersey, Rogers found himself surrounded by dignitaries from all walks of life. Among them was Bayonne Police Officer Vincent Doyle, a former ship's radio operator who had established an international reputation by designing the first two-way radio system in the world in the Bayonne Police Department.

Doyle, usually modest and soft-spoken, had a reputation for blunt speaking when aroused. Instinctively, he felt suspicious of Rogers—and he challenged Rogers's statement, quoted in the newspapers, that he had been dragged out of the radio room aboard the *Morro Castle* when it was so hot that the solder had melted out of the terminals of the transmitter panel. According to Doyle's recollection later, Rogers refused to answer, and Doyle asked if he knew how hot an iron had to get to melt solder.

"You have had a trying experience," Doyle told Rogers. "My conscience, however, will not allow me to call you a hero. A hero, in my humble opinion, should be modest and truthful. You are neither and I feel sorry for you. Good night." He then apologized to the guests and left.

A few days later, wearing a spanking-new, white, officer's uniform, Rogers made his stage debut at the Rialto Theatre. He split his thousand-dollar-a-week salary with a theatrical agent. Outside the Rialto, posters announced:

IN PERSON RADIO HERO ROGERS
TELLS INSIDE STORY OF MORRO CASTLE DISASTER

Standing in the footlights, Rogers told his audiences: "You people have made a hero of me . . . ." After a week, interest waned. Plans for Rogers to tour America were abandoned.

IN NEW YORK, a federal grand jury investigating the tragedy now spent months listening to testimony similar to that given before the Department of Commerce Board.

On December 3, 1934, they handed out indictments. Accused of wilful negligence were the two senior deck officers, Acting Captain Warms, and Chief Engineer Abbott.

Prosecuting Attorney Francis W. H. Adams told the court that both men "are accused of a crime of the most serious nature—conduct which caused the loss of life of upward of fifty persons"—a curious figure in view of the final death toll of 134.

Ward Line lawyers posted bail bonds of $2,500 for each man.

The rift between Warms and Abbott had grown to active hatred. All that bound them was the continued pressure from the Line to maintain a united front and the knowledge that any division would be exploited by the prosecution.

BY CHRISTMAS 1934, over three hundred claims totalling $1,250,000 had been filed against the Ward Line by survivors and relatives of the dead.

A game of legal bluff began. Lawyers for the survivors created the impression that they could positively prove unseaworthiness and inadequacy. The Ward Line flinched at the prospect of another public hearing, and made an offer of $500,000, which the survivors' lawyers rejected.

From London came another, more subtle, pressure. Lloyd's of London, the principal British underwriters of the *Morro Castle*, raised their eyebrows at reports reaching them of the Ward Line's attitude.

Seventy-one insurance companies, a third of them British, had insured the *Morro Castle* for $4,200,000. As the word spread that the Ward Line was in a protracted battle with the survivors and relatives of the dead, more than one underwriter must have wondered whether there was something shady about the whole episode. Word reached the Ward Line that it could be assailed soon from all sides and that it might be years before the Line could collect the $4,200,000 insurance.

It suddenly increased its offer to the claimants to $890,000. This was accepted. In the end the Line collected $4,188,999 in insurance.

The Ward Line sold the *Morro Castle* to Union Shipbuilding of Baltimore for $33,605 as scrap iron.

Verdict

On the day the hulk was towed away from Asbury Park, Rogers opened a radio-repair shop in Bayonne. Customers found him a bombastic shopkeeper, fond of telling them how lucky they were to have their radio sets mended by him. His business dropped off.

One day in February 1935, Rogers left the shop "to get a breath of air". Shortly afterwards, it caught fire. Bayonne police files reveal: "An inventory made by Rogers disclosed equipment had suffered damage to the extent of $1,200. Arson was suspected. But no proof existed to warrant an arrest. He collected from the insurance company."

The police inquiries had been perfunctory; serious probing into Rogers's background would have uncovered his implication in the fire at the Egert Company in 1929. Just why the police failed to make those inquiries is a matter for speculation.

Increasingly, Rogers seemed to live in a world of his own. Dominated by his impulses, and with such a deficiency in his sense of reality, he was capable of the most bizarre or dangerous acts. After his return to Bayonne, he showed no signs of wanting either the company or the friendship of others. The destruction of the *Morro Castle* and the ensuing world-wide headlines had made Rogers feel that he was tough, important. But when the headlines faded, his feeling of inferiority remained as strong as before.

After the Bayonne police completed their inquiries into the fire at his repair shop, Rogers dropped out of public sight. Early in 1936, he reappeared in the headlines when he gave evidence at the trial of Warms and Abbott, which had been delayed until then by a series of legal moves.

At the trial, reporters noted that Rogers had aged considerably; he was fatter, his hair thinner, his dress shabbier. Only his voice remained the same—oddly feminine and gentle. He told the now familiar story of the delay in sending out the SOS and how he stayed at his post. After completing his evidence Rogers brushed aside questions about what he was doing with his life.

The verdicts caused a new sensation. Warms was sentenced to two years imprisonment; Abbott received four.

The Ward Line filed an immediate appeal, and Warms told newsmen: "Having no knowledge or experience of the way of the sea, the jury probably didn't comprehend what it means to suddenly battle against a raging sea, the worst storm for years along the Atlantic Coast, and a fire which was sweeping the vessel."

Abbott declined to make any statement.

Some time after the trial Rogers had a chance encounter with a Bayonne businessman who had been present at the reception at which Police Officer Vincent Doyle had called Rogers a liar. The man told Rogers he thought Doyle's behaviour had been uncalled for, and offered to help Rogers get a new start in life—as a patrolman with the Bayonne Police Department.

In June 1936, thanks to this extraordinary turn of events, Rogers joined the Bayonne police force. He was assigned as assistant to Vincent Doyle in the radio department. How he came to be taken on is now impossible to ascertain. The likeliest explanation is that Rogers's businessman friend had sufficient influence to "bulldoze" him onto the force.

Rogers was not subjected to any physical examination before being accepted, though nobody can now say positively why. Nor—and this is more incredible—was any account taken of his record. On more than one occasion he had come under grave suspicion as an arsonist. But all this seemed to have been forgotten.

If Doyle was amazed to see Rogers report for duty, he hid it well. His clash with Rogers almost two years before might never have happened. Doyle was a warm, outgoing man; Rogers was unable to form relationships with anybody. Gradually, though, Vincent Doyle managed to establish contact with his assistant; they found common ground in their seagoing experiences and an interest in things electrical.

Criminal or hero? This press photograph appeared in November 1938 with the following caption: "George W. Rogers, hero of the S.S. Morro Castle *fire in 1934, is shown in Jersey City Courthouse, before the opening of his trial for attempted murder in a bomb explosion which seriously injured his best friend and superior officer, Police Lt. Vincent J. Doyle."*

As the barriers came down, Doyle became aware of Rogers's arrogance. "He just couldn't stop telling me how clever he was." Doyle also detected Rogers's recurring preoccupation with exploding devices. Doyle was both fascinated and worried as Rogers explained how explosions could be triggered by timing devices to go off at an exact moment.

"George, is that how it was on the *Morro Castle*?" Doyle asked at the end of one lengthy explanation.

Rogers looked at Doyle and smiled.

IN APRIL 1937, the U.S. Circuit Court of Appeals set aside the conviction of Warms and Abbott. "Warms," said the Appeals Court, "maintained the best tradition of the sea by remaining on his vessel until the bridge burned under him and all others had left." The court held that Abbott's behaviour was "caused by suffering from smoke, and therefore he was not responsible."

NEWS OF THE VERDICTS brought a marked change in Rogers. He became almost obsessive in his desire to discuss the *Morro Castle*. Increasingly, he dwelt on how the blaze had been set, and Doyle in his turn questioned Rogers on every aspect of the disaster.

The strange cat-and-mouse questioning went on until, on March 3, 1938, Rogers told Doyle that he had set the fire himself. "He told me how to construct an incendiary fountain pen," wrote Doyle, "how it had been placed in the inside breast pocket of a waiter's jacket which was hung in the locker there in the writing room where the fire started. When I asked him why he did it, all he would say to me was : "The Ward Line stinks and the skipper was lousy.""

There is strong circumstantial evidence that Rogers did just as he said.

Just before midnight on that September 7, 1934, he had handed over his watch to Charles Maki, saying that "he would take a breath of air." He returned twenty minutes later.

With Rogers's knowledge of explosive devices, twenty minutes was ample time for fashioning a bomb of the fountain-pen type. He would have had no trouble hiding all the raw materials he needed in the chartroom beforehand. The bottles of acid were unlabelled, while the other parts would look equally innocent: a fountain pen, a strip of copper wire.

The locker containing the spare jackets was a perfect site for a bomb, and Rogers would know that the only person who was likely to pass through the writing room around midnight was the night watchman. It would be a simple matter to calculate his movements to avoid detection there.

Of course, it is difficult to understand Rogers's action, unless it is taken in context.

Rogers looked on the *Morro Castle* as a haven from persecution ashore. Yet while on this "haven", petty crime had cost him his job: the Radiomarine Corporation had dismissed him for stealing.

The need for revenge haunted him. The dismissal notice came at a time when Rogers was disturbed to such an extent that he was capable of anything.

Coupled with thoughts of vengeance was the need to preserve his job. At some stage Rogers's mind probably fused both needs into one: when the bomb exploded he would be the key man in the ensuing emergency.

He often contended that "heroes are never sacked."

DOYLE WONDERED how best to present his sensational evidence to his superiors. He was still worrying over it next afternoon when he met Rogers outside the police radio department. Rogers seemed pensive and withdrawn.

"There's a package for you," said Rogers.

Doyle nodded and went into the department. Rogers remained just outside the doorway.

On the workbench was a package. Doyle unwrapped it and found a heater for a fish tank. There was nothing unusual in that; from time to time Doyle used the department's facilities to repair electrical equipment for his colleagues.

Attached to the heater was a typed label: "This is a fish-tank heater. Please install the switch in the line cord and see if the unit will work. It should get slightly warm."

Doyle was puzzled by the instructions and by the fact that they carried no signature. He turned towards the door to ask Rogers for a comment, but Rogers had disappeared.

For a moment Doyle toyed with the heater, then plugged it into the workbench's double-outlet plug, and flicked the switch.

The resulting explosion shook the main police headquarters building over two hundred feet away.

It was a miracle that Doyle escaped death. His left hand, left leg, and right foot were smashed. His left eardrum was fractured. He was rushed to hospital, where he underwent surgery.

The next day Rogers visited Doyle in the hospital, and asked through his tears: "How can I get the guy who did this to you?"

Two weeks later Rogers was charged with attempted murder.

After eighteen weeks in the hospital, Doyle began to assemble a formidable dossier on Rogers's criminal record. He now learned that Rogers, while being questioned on the attempt on Doyle's life, had admitted to Bayonne's chief of detectives, Tom Masterton, that the bomb on the *Morro Castle* had been a "simple" matter to arrange. The local district attorney's office decided that though the circumstantial evidence on the *Morro Castle* case was strong, it might confuse the charge for which Rogers was then being tried. The prosecution decided to exclude the report, and concentrate solely on the attempt on Doyle's life—a curious decision that caused considerable bitterness among Doyle and his colleagues.

As for the psychiatrist's report on Rogers, the prosecution's attitude is best summed up by a note attached to the bulky police files on the case: "Don't need a fancy doctor's report to tell us that R. is a nut." The note was unsigned. Since the defence was not entering a plea of insanity, it agreed that the medical evidence should remain largely confidential.

Yet this document indicated that to some extent Rogers's repressed sexual wishes probably caused his criminal behaviour. Just as a man who is otherwise impotent can achieve an orgasm by violence, so Rogers could have found relief in such acts as that of sending the fish-tank exploding device.

How much notice the judge took of this medical opinion is not known. By any accounts, he was an unusual judge. At the end of the trial he summoned Doyle to his chambers. "As the victim of the crime, he asked my opinion on a just punishment for Rogers," Doyle recalled. "I did not hesitate to suggest that he be given the maximum sentence allowed by law."

On December 15, 1938, the judge passed sentence: "Your crime is one of the most diabolical nature and it fell short of murder only by the intervention of Divine Providence. It is the type of crime executed only by the mind of a fiend. I hereby sentence you to serve from twelve to twenty years in the State Prison."

Yet, on November 24, 1942, Rogers was released from Trenton State Prison after serving less than four years. The New Jersey State Court of Pardons had granted him parole to "join the armed services". The announcement caused a storm of protest.

The U.S. Navy refused to accept him. But once again his friend who had helped get him onto the Bayonne police force came to his aid. "He still believed in Rogers," Vincent Doyle stated. "Why, I don't know—nor will anybody else. But the day Rogers was released, this man took him to New York."

Next day the Federal Communications Commission gave him a ninety-day permit to operate as a radio officer at sea. The Radiomarine Corporation of America assigned him to a ship sailing from San Francisco to Australia.

The voyage ended with Rogers's arrest in Darwin, Australia. His exact crime was not made clear. There is a veiled reference to "enemy alien activity" in the files of Vincent Doyle. But the FBI, which would undoubtedly have been involved in such a charge, emphatically denied any involvement.

Rogers then worked in a war plant in Jersey City, from which he was dismissed on suspicion of stealing. He was hired by another war plant in Brooklyn, and soon afterwards a number of employees showed signs of poisoning after drinking from a water cooler near where Rogers worked.

Once more he found himself unemployed.

He again opened a radio-repair shop in Bayonne. In May 1952, he was finally discharged from parole. By then his business was in financial difficulties.

Shortly thereafter, he formed a relationship with William

Hummel, an eighty-three-year-old retired printer, and his unmarried daughter, Edith. Hummel shared his interest in electrical gadgets.

Over the months Rogers became a regular caller at the Hummels'. He found William Hummel sympathetic to a new preoccupation Rogers had developed—that he had been framed by the Bayonne Police Department all those years before because they were jealous of having a genuine hero among them.

In all probability the Hummels unwittingly encouraged him in this fantasy; they spent many hours together going through the Bible looking for "proof" (as Rogers later put it) that the change in his life situation could be traced back to the police.

Rogers received not only emotional, but also financial, support from the Hummels. When he told them the police were "keeping customers away from the shop," Hummel offered to subsidize the loss. By June 1953, he had loaned Rogers $7,500.

Then the relationship between the two men underwent a change. In his diary Hummel wrote: "Must collect loan from G." On July 1, 1953, acting on a tipoff, the police broke into Hummel's home. They found father and daughter savagely bludgeoned to death. Suspicion quickly fell on Rogers. After painstaking police investigation, Rogers was arrested, found guilty of murder in the first degree and sentenced to life imprisonment. Police Captain Vincent Doyle, still bearing the marks of Rogers's murder attempt, was in court to hear sentence passed.

On March 4, 1955—seventeen years to the day since he had tried to murder Vincent Doyle—Rogers appealed against the sentence. The appeal was swiftly denied.

At 6.00 a.m. on January 10, 1958, George White Rogers died in prison of a brain haemorrhage.

Authors' note

This book is the result of almost three years' work. From the very beginning our most difficult task was to establish the facts. This involved some hundred thousand miles of travel across America and Western Europe. It soon became clear that the official records did not tell the whole truth—nor did some of the people who testified at the public hearings. In the end literally hundreds of men and women gave us assistance, glad that at last the full story should be told. Some—like Mrs. Ada Abbott and the family of William Warms—had lived a large part of their lives with the recollection of what the disaster had done to their loved ones.

At the outset we had suspected that Rogers was mad: expert medical witness amply confirmed our suspicion. Lawyers we consulted believed that some of the testimony against Rogers, properly presented by the prosecution, would have been unassailable. In that sense justice was not done to Rogers. Had he been tried and found guilty we believe there is a real possibility that he would have been sent to an insane asylum.

We have tried to present an accurate and honest picture of what really did happen on the *Morro Castle*. If we have succeeded in nothing else but that, then we have achieved what we set out to do.

Gordon Thomas and Max Morgan-Witts are co-authors of two best-sellers—*The Day Their World Ended*, and *Earthquake*. Their books have been published in eleven countries. *The Strange Fate of the Morro Castle* is their third joint venture.

A DAY NO PIGS WOULD DIE

Robert Newton Peck

A Day No Pigs Would Die

a condensation of the book by

ROBERT NEWTON PECK

ILLUSTRATED BY THOMAS BEECHAM

Published by Hutchinson, London

The Good Old Days . . . . Were they really so good? Robert Newton Peck looks back to his own childhood and believes that they were. He grew up in a plain-living, rural American village, a community deeply committed to a simple life and to simple ways of worship. By today's standards his family was desperately poor. But they were rich also: in contentment, in humour, in self-respect, in mutual love.

His father had the most uncompromising of professions—illiterate, he earned his family's keep by slaughtering the village livestock. But he was a gentle, compassionate, joyful man for all that. And he brought up his son to reverence all living things, to deal honestly with his neighbour and with God, and to accept gladly the hard, rewarding responsibilities of manhood.

This is a tender story, one that runs deep. The people in it do not talk about love, they act it out. And they know how to laugh. It is a story that must remind all of us that, however much we may have gained over the years, there are also qualities in our lives that we are in danger of losing.

ONE

I SHOULD of been in school that April day. But instead I was up on the ridge near the old spar mine above our farm, whipping the gray trunk of a rock maple with a dead stick and hating Edward Thatcher. During recess he'd pointed at my clothes and made sport of them. Instead of tying into him, I'd turned tail and run off. And when Miss Malcolm rang the bell to call us back inside, I was halfway home.

Picking up a stone, I threw it into some bracken ferns, hard as I could. Someday that was how hard I was going to light into Edward Thatcher and make him bleed like a stuck pig. I'd kick him from one end of Vermont to the other and sorry him good. I'd teach him not to make fun of Shaker Ways. He'd never show his face in the town of Learning ever again. No, sir.

A painful noise made me whip my head around and jump at the same time. When I saw the big Holstein, I knew she was in bad trouble. She was one of many that belonged to our near neighbor, Mr. Tanner. He called this one Apron because she was mostly black, except for the white along her belly, which went up her front and around her neck like a big clean apron. Mr. Tanner told Papa she was his best milker and he was fixing up to take her to Rutland Fair, come summer.

She made her dreadful noise again, and when I got close up, I saw why. Her big body was pumping up and down, trying to have her calf. She'd fell down and there was blood on her foreleg, and her mouth was all thick and foamy with yellow-green spit. I tried to reach my hand out and pat her; but she was wild-eyed mean, and making this breezy noise with almost every breath.

Her tail was up and arched high, whipping through the air with every heave of her back. Sticking out was the head and one hoof of her calf. He was so covered with blood and birth sop that I had no way telling he was alive or dead. Until I heard him bawl.

Apron went crashing through the puckerbush, me right behind. Because she had to stop and strain, I got to the calf's head and got a purchase on him. But he was so slimy, and Apron was so wandering, there was no holding to it. Besides, being just twelve years old, I weighed a bit over a hundred pounds. Apron was comfortable over a thousand, and it wasn't much of a tug for her. As I went down, her hoof caught my shinbone and it really smarted. But the calf bawled again, and that made me get up and give the whole idea another go.

I'd just wound up running away from Edward Thatcher and running away from the schoolhouse. I was feathered if I was going to run away from one darn more thing.

I needed a rope. But there wasn't any, so I had to make one. It didn't have to be long, just strong.

Chasing old Apron through the next patch of prickers sure took some fun out of the whole business. I made my mistake of trying to take my trousers off as I ran. No good. So I sat down in the prickers, yanked 'em off over my boots, and caught up to Apron. After a few bad tries, I got one pant leg around her calf's head and knotted it snug.

"Calf," I said to him, "you stay up inside your ma and you're about to choke. So you might as well choke getting yourself born."

Whatever old Apron decided that I was doing to her back yonder, she didn't take kindly to it. So she started off again with me in the rear, hanging on to wait Christmas, and my own bare butt catching a thorn with every step. That calf never came one inch closer to coming out. But when Apron stopped to heave again,

I got the other pant leg around a dogwood tree that was about thick as a fence post.

Now only three things could happen. My trousers would rip. Apron would just uproot the tree. The calf would slide out.

But nothing happened. Apron just stood shaking and straining and never moved forward a step. I didn't know what to do next. The calf bawled once more, weaker than before. But all old Apron did was heave in that one place.

"You old bitch!" I yelled at her, grabbing a dead blackberry cane that was as long as a bullwhip and big around as a broom handle. "You move, you hear?"

I never hit anybody, boy or beast, as I hit that cow. I beat her so hard I was crying. Where I held the big cane, the thorns were chewing up my hands real bad. But it only got me madder.

I kicked her. And stoned her. I kicked her again, one last time, so hard in the udder that I thought I heard her grunt. Both her hindquarters sort of hunkered down in the brush. Then at last she started forward. My trousers went tight; I heard a rip and a calf bawl. And a big hunk of hot smelly stuff went all over me. As I went down under the force of it, I figured something either got dead or got born.

I brushed some of the slop away from my eyes and looked up. There was Apron, her big black head and her big black mouth licking first me and then her calf.

But she was far from all right. Her mouth was open and she was gasping for air. She stumbled once. I thought for sure I was going to wind up under one very heavy cow. The noise in her throat came at me again, and her tongue lashed to and fro like the tail of a clock. It looked to me as if there was something in her mouth. She would start to breathe and then, like a cork in a bottle, some darn thing in there would cut it off.

Her big body swayed like she was dizzy or sick. She fell to her knees and her head hit my chest as I lay on the ground, her nose almost touching my chin. She had stopped breathing!

Her jaw was locked open, so I put my hand into her mouth, but felt only her swollen tongue. I stretched my fingers down into her throat—and there it was! A hard ball, about apple-size. It was stuck in her windpipe or her gullet. I didn't know which and didn't care. I just shut my eyes, grabbed it, and yanked.

Somebody told me once that a cow won't bite. That somebody is as wrong as sin on Sunday. I thought my arm had got sawed off partway between elbow and shoulder. She bit and bit and never let go. She got to her feet and kept on biting. That devil cow ran down off that ridge, with my arm in her mouth, dragging me half naked with her. What she didn't do to me with her teeth she did with her front hoofs.

It should have been broad daylight, but it was night. Black night. As black and as bloody and as bad as getting hurt again and again could ever be.

It just went on and on. It didn't quit.

"Haven Peck."

Somebody was yelling out Papa's name, but I couldn't see anything. And it was real strange, because my eyes were open. I blinked, but the fog was still there. There was a wool blanket around me. I could feel the wool rub against the raw place on my arm, but the hurt of it seemed to keep me awake. And keep me alive.

There were more voices now. I heard Papa answer, and the man who was carrying me asked, "Is this your boy? There's so much blood and dirt and Satan on him, I can't tell for sure."

"Yes," said Papa. "That's our Robert."

And then I heard Mama's voice, soft and sweet like music; and I could feel her hands on my head and my hair. Aunt Carrie was there, too. She was Mama's oldest sister, who lived with us.

Strong hands were touching my legs now, and then my ribs. I tried to say something. Somebody washed my face with warm lilac water. It smelled right restful.

"We're beholding to you, Benjamin Tanner," said Papa, "for fetching him home. Whatever he done, I'll make it right."

"Better look to his arm. It got tore up worse than proper. May be broke."

"Haven," I heard Mama say, "the boy's holding something in his hand. Can't make it out."

I felt them taking something from my right hand. I didn't want to render it up, but they took it.

"I never see the like of it," Mama said. "Like it's near to be alive."

I could hear Mr. Tanner's rough voice over the others. "I know what that is. It's a goiter."

"Where'd he get it?" Mama asked.

"It's an evil thing," Papa said. "But for now let's tend his arm. Mr. Tanner, we may got to cut away part of your blanket."

"Ain't mine. Belongs to my horse. So cut all you're a mind to."

I felt Papa pulling the blanket down off my right shoulder, until it got caught in the clotted blood. I heard his jackknife click open and cut away part of the wool.

"I tied my bandanna on his arm," said Mr. Tanner, "so he wouldn't bleed dry." When Papa loosened it up, Mr. Tanner said, "He'll bleed again with it loose, Haven."

"He will," said Papa, "and that'll be a good thing for his arm. Let it open up and holler out all the dirt. Only way to treat a wound is to bleed it till it's clean as a cat's mouth."

"True."

"Lucy"—Papa spoke soft to Mama—"better get a needle threaded. He'll want sewing."

He picked me up in his arms and carried me into the house. He laid me flat on the long kitchen table, face up. Mama put something soft under my head, and Aunt Carrie kept washing me off with the lilac water while Papa cut my shirt loose and took off my boots.

"The poor lamb," said Mama.

Somebody put a hand on my forehead to see if I was cool. It was followed by a cold wet cloth, and it felt real good. Funny, but it was the only thing on my entire body that I could feel. Then I felt the first of Mama's stitches going into the meat of my arm. I wanted to yell out, but didn't have the will for it. Instead I just lay there on that old kitchen table and let Mama sew me back together. It hurt. My eyes filled up with crying and the water ran in rivers to my ears, but I never let out a whimper.

When I had took all the sewing to be took (and by this time I must of been more thread than boy), Papa burdened me upstairs to my room. I could smell Mama, crisp and starched, plumping my pillow, and the cool muslin pillowcase touched both my ears as the back of my head sank into all those feathers.

"Tell Mr. Tanner," I said, "that were he to look up on the ridge, he'll find a calf. I helped get it born. Afterward old Apron was still choking, so I had to rip the ball out of her throat. And I didn't mean to skip school."

"I'll be," said Papa.

"Where are your trousers, Rob?" Mama said.

"Up on the ridge. When I tied 'em round a tree, they got busted some. I'm sorry, Mama. You'll just have to cut me out another pair."

Mama put her face right down close to mine and I could smell her goodness. "I'm preferenced to mend busted pants than a busted boy," she said.

"I . . . I can't feel nothing in my right hand."

"That's 'cause it's resting," said Mama. "It wants to get well, and so do you. So right about now your pa and I are going to tip-toe out of here and let you get some rest. You earned it."

I closed my eyes and went right off. Later I woke up when Mama brought me a dish of hot succotash and a warm glass of milking fresh from the evening pail. The bubbles were still on it.

"That's real good," I said.

At bedtime Papa brought me one of the last of the winter apples from the cellar. He pulled up a chair close to my bed and looked at me for a long time while I ate the apple with my left hand.

"You mending?"

"Yes, Papa."

"I ought to lick you proper for leaving the schoolhouse."

"Yes, Papa. You ought."

"Someday you want to walk into the bank in Learning and write down your name, don't you?"

"Yes, sir."

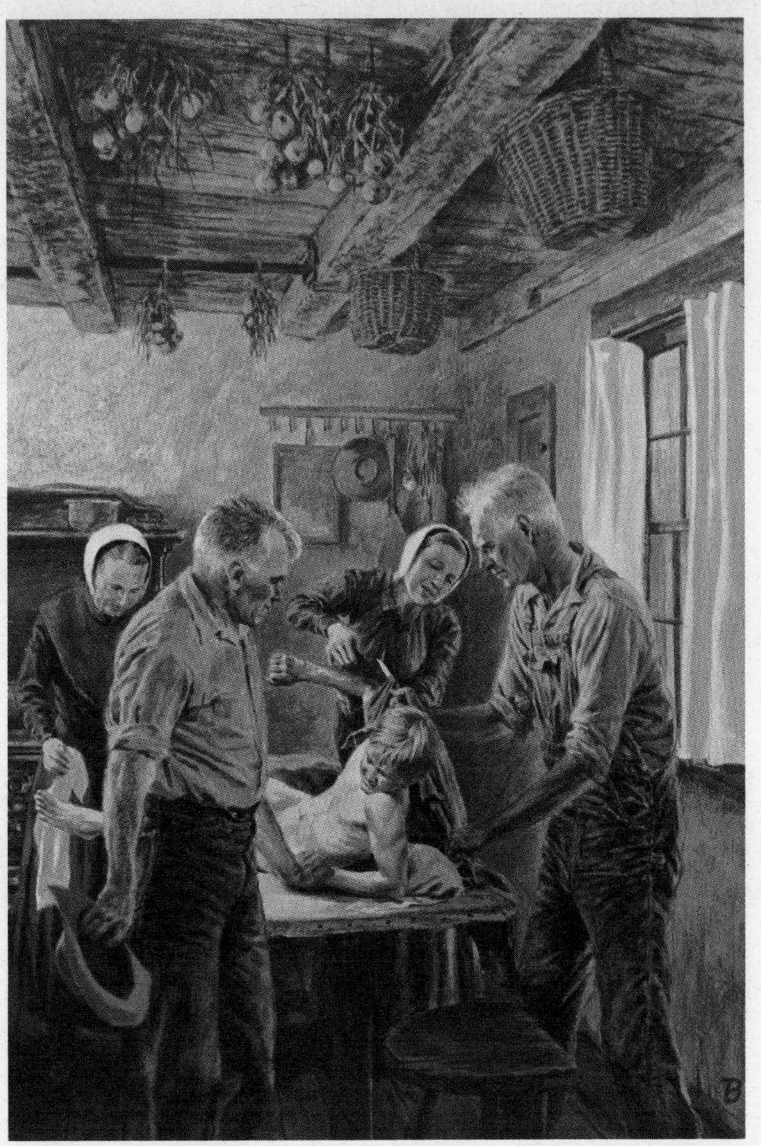

"I don't cotton to raise a fool."

"No, Papa."

I tried to move my right arm, but it made me wince up. I couldn't help but make a noise about it.

"She bit you up fair, that cow. Clear to bone."

"Sure did. I always thought cows don't bite."

"Anything'll bite, be it provoked. You tore out that goiter?"

"Yes, sir. Her calf was hung up, too. So I tore him out. Tore my pants and tore myself. Between me and the calf and Apron, we tore up a good part of Vermont as well as each other."

"How do you feel?"

"Like if I die, at least I'll stop hurting."

"Best you don't complain, a boy who skips school and don't get no stick put on him."

"No, sir. I won't complain. Except when I move it sudden, my arm is real numb. It's the rest of me that's in misery. I'm stuck so full of prickers, it makes me smart just to think on it. Every damn—"

"What'd I hear?"

"Every darn pricker in Vermont must be in me, working their way through and coming out the yonder side. It's enough to sell your soul."

"Well, if your soul looks as poorly as your carcass, I don't guess it'll bring much." Papa fished around in his pocket. "Here's two beads of spruce gum. One's for me. But I don't mention you'd want one, too."

"Yes, I sure would. Please."

"Here, then. Might help you forget where those prickers are nested."

"It's helping already. Thanks, Papa."

Spruce gum is hard and grainy at first. Then the heat of your mouth begins to melt it down so that it's worth the chewing. The bit that Papa gave me was rich and full of sappy juices. Except that every so often you have to spit out a flick of the bark.

"I saw sumac today, boy."

"Is it ripe yet?"

Out of his pocket Papa pulled a twig of sumac that was finger thick and four inch long. He cracked out his knife, ringed the bark, and set a good notch at one end. All there was left to do now was to bucket soak it overnight, just enough to slip the bark sleeve. And boil it to kill the poison.

"That'll be some whistle, Robert. A boy with a whistle as fine as this won't have no earthy reason to skip school. You of a mind to agree?"

"I agree, Papa."

He stood up, big and tall, with his head not quite bumping the roof. "Don't be going to sleep with spruce gum in your mouth."

"I won't, Papa."

He bent down and pulled the crazy quilt up around my throat. I could tell by the smell of his hand that he'd killed pigs today. The smell was like stale death. It was always on him, morning and night. Until Saturday, when he'd strip down to the white and stand in the kitchen washtub and wash himself clean of the pigs and the killing. On Sunday morning, when I sat next to him at Shaker Meeting, he smelled just like the big brown bar of soap he used, and sometimes there was some store-bought pomade on his hair. But when you kill pigs for a living, you can't always smell like Sunday morning. You just smell like hard work.

TWO

I WAS abed for almost a week. My first day up was Saturday. I planned it that way so I'd have me two days out of bed and out of doors, without a mind for schooling.

"Good," said Papa when he saw me hobble down to breakfast. "I can use a hand, and you look ready as rain."

I limped a bit more than need be, but it didn't do a lick of good. An hour after, we were resetting a post in the fence that set Mr. Tanner's land apart from ours.

"Fences sure are funny, aren't they, Papa?"

"How so?"

"Well, you be friends with Mr. Tanner. Neighbors and all. But we keep this fence up like it was war. I guess humans are the only things on earth that take everything they own and fence it off."

"Not true," Papa said.

"Animals don't put up fences."

"Yes, they do. In the spring a female robin won't fly to a male until he owns a piece of the woods. He's got to fence it off."

"I didn't know that."

"Lots of times when you hear that old robin sing, what he's singing about is 'Keep off my tree.' That whistle you hear is his fence. Now a fox walks around his land every day and wets on a tree here and on a rock there. That's his fence. My guess would be that all living things put up a fence, one way or another. Like a tree do with its roots."

"Then it isn't like war."

"It's a peaceable war. If I know Benjamin Franklin Tanner, he'd fret more than me if his cows found my corn. A fence sets men together, not apart."

As we were talking, I looked up from my work and Papa from his. What we saw was the oddest parade in the county coming down the ridge. It was Ben Tanner and his cow Apron. She was looking clean as clergy. Kicking along under her belly and trying to get hold of a teat was not one calf, but two! And Mr. Tanner was carrying something.

"Morning, Haven."

"A day to you, Benjamin."

"Morning, young Rob."

"Morning, Mr. Tanner." But I wasn't looking at him. What caught my eye was the finest pair of bull calves you could ever try to see. They were blacker than Apron, but with a patch of clean white up the front, like a chin napkin.

"Bob and Bib," said Mr. Tanner. "And the Bob of it is after you, Robert."

"Well now," said Papa.

"A matched pair, they be. Always wanted a yoke of matched Holstein oxen to take to Rutland. Now, Haven, thanks to your stout son, I got me the finest pair in the county. Come fair time, they'll do Learning proud."

"Apron had *two?*" It was all I could say.

"Two. Robert, I thank you again. Here's a pig for your trouble."

From under his coat Mr. Tanner fetched out a small white ball of piglet. She had a pink nose and pink ears, and there was even a wisp of pink in the fork of her toes.

"You mean this pig is going to be *mine?*"

"Yours, my boy. Little enough for what you did."

"Gosh'em moses. Thanks, Mr. Tanner."

Mr. Tanner handed me the pig and I took it. She kicked and squealed a bit, but once I held her close up to my chest with both arms, she settled down and licked my face. Her spit was a sad smell, but I didn't care. She was *mine.*

"We thank you, Brother Tanner," said Papa. "But it's not the Shaker Way to take frills for being neighborly. All that Robert done was what any farmer would do for another. It don't add up to payment or due."

I felt sick. Real sick.

"Haven, when is the boy born?"

"February," I said, before Papa could answer.

"Plum forgot," said Mr. Tanner. "In that case, I owe you a sorry to be so late remembering. She's your pig, Robert. And if I catch her on my land again, she'll be bacon."

Papa shook his head. "It's not right."

"Haven," said Mr. Tanner, "what I really come here for is to ask you to help me yoke these two demons come fall. Will you?"

"Yes," said Papa.

"Good, good. That being the case, and not wanting the cloud of debt hanging over me, favor me by taking payment for your help as of now in the form of one newborn pig, just weaned, in pink of prime."

"Done," said Papa.

"Done," I said.

At that the pig and I both gave a squeal. She was mine, mine, mine, mine, mine, mine, *mine!*

Looking at her again, I could now see how beautiful she was. My pig. She was prettier than Apron or either one of her calves.

She was prettier than Solomon, our ox. Prettier than Daisy, our milk cow. Prettier than any dog or cat or chicken or fish in the whole township of Learning, Vermont. She was clean white all over, with just enough pink to be sweet as candy.

"Pinky," I said.

"Fine name," said Mr. Tanner.

"Thank you, sir," I said. Papa's sharp nudge in my ribs with his mattock handle helped my being so prompt and grateful.

Watching our neighbor walk away, taking his cow and twin calves with him, I held Pinky close in my arms. She was the first thing I had ever really wanted and owned. At least the first thing of value. The only other thing I'd wanted was a bicycle, but I knew we couldn't afford it, so there was no sense in asking. Besides, both Mama and Papa would have looked at a bicycle as a work of the Devil. A frill. And in a Shaker household there wasn't anything as evil as a frill. Seemed to me the world was full of them. But anything that Mama wanted and didn't have the money to buy, or the goods to trade for, was a frill to her.

Well, nobody who had half an eye could call Pinky a frill. What a brood sow she'd make. I counted the teat buds on her belly. Twelve. In a year or so she'd be lying in her crib with a dozen pigs sucking away for glory be.

"You'll have to tend care of her," Papa said. "Caretaking of a pig can keep a body as nervous as a longtail cat in a room full of rocking chairs. She'll need a pen and some straw."

"A pen?"

"Course a pen. Where'd you think she'll sleep? Under your pillow?"

"No. But I thought she could bed up with Solomon and Daisy."

"Can't keep swine and kine under the same roof. Says so in the Book of Shaker. That means that you, Robert, are going to make her a place."

"Well, it won't have to be very big."

"Not today, it won't. But do you idea how big she'll get? Before you know it, she'll weigh twenty stone."

"Twenty stone. That's a lot!"

"Durn right. She'll go most three hundred pound. So best you put that pig down to earth, set that fence post, and pen her up for night. Away from Daisy."

"Why that?"

"Close pork will curdle milk, boy. That's plain common."

"I wonder why that is."

"It goes back when Daisy and Pinky were wild. Daisy knows that Pinky and her kind have teeth. Tusk. And pigs are meat eaters, cows ain't. The reason Brother Tanner give you that pig is maybe its mother ate all the rest of the litter. A sow will do that. Daisy won't. Apron won't. It's like Shaker Law. It all goes way back."

"Way back to what?"

"Back to reason. Something that modern townfolk don't care a lick for. They don't understand it, so they think it to be tomfool. It's earthy reason. Solomon's got it at sundown, and that's the only time of day that big ox is ornery. Because once, long long ago, the wolves came at sundown. Even though Solomon never seen a wolf, he knows. He knows that workaday is over and that he wants shelter. He wants a wall at his side so he can blanket one flank and look the other."

"And that's why Daisy won't want Pinky near on?"

"That's why. Because pigs are wild things. Were you to turn Pinky loose, she'd live in the hills. And she'd be wild. She'd even tusk, and they'd be long and mean and sharp. And old Daisy knows it and frets on it."

"Papa, if Daisy run off, would she be a wild cow?"

"Not old Daisy. If we left her, she'd head for another farm and another herd. She'd wait for night and then head for a lighted house. The Tanner's place maybe. The orange window of home and hearth."

"You sure?"

"Well, you remember when we went camping out all night, all the way up on top of Lead Hill? What animal come to us in the night, just to share our bonfire flame, and you thought it was a bear?"

"A *cow*. Papa, you recall what we did when that old cow stayed next to us all night?"

"Come first light, we milked a bit of her. So you could have a cup of fresh warm milk for breakfast. And I could have a spoonful for my coffee."

"Was that stealing, Papa?"

"Not hardly. Were it my cow, I'd share with others. And we didn't take but a glass. It weren't as though we stripped her dry."

"Do you think the Lord will forgive us?"

"I think so. Somehow, the good Lord don't want to see no man start a cold morning with just black coffee."

PINKY sure got to be my pig in a heck of a hurry.

Papa and I had to finish our job that we started that Saturday morning, which was to reset the east fence. All the time I was working, Pinky was smelling around near my heels, keeping her little pink nose to the ground as all pigs do. And when we quit at church bell for the noon meal, she followed us all the way across the east meadow to the house. I was going to bring her into the kitchen, but Mama put her foot down on that idea, though both Mama and Aunt Carrie confessed that Pinky was just about the prettiest pig they ever saw.

Before we ate, I mixed a bowl of milk and meal for Pinky to eat. I didn't think she was going to take it at first. But after I dipped my finger in it and let her suck away on that, she went for the bowl. I made sure that the bowl I used was the cracked one, or I'd a got skinned.

After meal Papa headed out toward the barn with Pinky and me trailing along behind. He walked round the barn a yoke of times and come to a final rest on the south side of it. He put his foot on a stump, elbow to his knee, and looked real hard at our old corn cratch.

"What you got a mind to, Papa?"

"Rob, that there corncrib would make a good house for your pig. 'Cept it's a might too close to the cow barn."

"Close? It's touching it, butt on."

"Lucky it's on skids. We can drag her."

"Papa, we can't drag that. We only got one ox."

"Solomon can do it. We're going to let him use a capstan—a great big crank."

"Like you use at Cousin Matty's to wind up the well water?"

"Like that. Go get Solomon, and mind his hoofs."

I was bringing Solomon over to the barn, leading him with just my hand on his horn and taking two steps to his one. Then I went round to the tack room to get his yoke and stays. The yoke was solid hickory and it weighed near as much as me. I had to lug it back in two trips, going the second time for the oxbow and cotter. Papa showed up with two long poles, a chain, and a post-hole digger.

With the digger he made a hole in the ground, down the meadow a ways from the corncrib. Using a pebble on a horsehair string, he dropped it deep in the hole and let it hang to see if the hole was plumb to the earth. Then deep into the hole he sunk one of the stout poles. So stout it was nigh to be a log. Papa said the post was about three hands around. This was the capstan's axle.

Next Papa fit the handle pole into a hole, just up from ground flush, in the axle.

"Solomon ready?"

"I need help, Papa. I can't put the yoke up on his shoulders by myself."

When Solomon was yoked and coupled to the capstan crank, and one end of the chain was made fast to the crib and the other to the axle, we were ready.

"So," said Papa, "you don't guess one ox can pull that there crib?"

"No," I said. "It's too blundersome. Not even Mr. Tanner's bay Belgian team could move it, if you want my study of it."

Papa clucked to Solomon and the ox leaned into yoke. The crank began to turn. Around and around Solomon walked in a circle, and the chain drawed up real snug. When it was tight, it snapped up off the ground, but old Solomon never stopped walking. After just once around, Papa made a trench for the chain so Solomon wouldn't have to step over it with every circle. The big ox needed no prodding. He walked the circle on his own, and the crib inched toward the axle post.

"Look, Papa. Solomon does it alone."

"He does for sure. Solomon told me he don't want no pig having sleeping quarters near his. He says he abides in Shaker Law."

"Papa, do you believe all the Shaker Law?"

"Most. I'm glad it's all writ down in the Book of Shaker."

"How do you know it's all writ down, Papa? You can't read."

Papa looked at me before he spoke. "No, I cannot read. But our Law has been read to me. And because I could not read, I knew to listen with a full heart. It might be the last and only time I'd learn its meaning."

"I don't cotton to all those Shaker Laws. Especially the one that says we can't go to the baseball game on Sunday. Jacob Henry and his father always go. And I want to see the Greemobys play."

"What's a Greemoby?"

"It's short for Green Mountain Boy. It got something to do with somebody called Ethan Allen. I guessed he was once the captain. Our school library has this book on the history of baseball. There was a lot in it about Abner Doubleday, but it sure was skimpy on Ethan Allen."

"I wouldn't know one of them baseballers from the other."

"Well," I said, "this book I read sure leads a body to believe that Ethan Allen wasn't anyone at all. And that Abner Doubleday did everything there was to be did. But that's where I went sour on the history test that Miss Malcolm give us."

"You told your ma and me you got the highest in that test. Were you falsing a witness, Rob?"

"No, sir. I did get the highest mark. I got a ninety-nine. There was a hundred questions and I only missed one. It was something about which Vermonter *played* a key part in our history. Since I read that book, I just put down the name of Abner Doubleday."

" 'Stead of Ethan Allen."

"That's right, Pa. I sure was wrong. But one thing certain—of the two men, Miss Malcolm tends to favor Ethan Allen. She says that seeing we live in a free country like Vermont, we all better be proud as pie over Ethan Allen and his Green Mountain Boys. She says we have to be proud of our yesterday just like today."

"What's that mean?"

"I think it means to be proud to live in Vermont and proud of Ethan Allen. As well as Calvin Coolidge. We have to pride him, too."

"Say we do. He's our President."

Solomon was walking his circle, pulling the corn cratch closer to the capstan post with every turn. That old ox sure could pull aplenty. He wound up that big chain just like you'd wind a kite string around a spool.

"Miss Malcolm said she voted for Calvin Coolidge, which is why he's a President. Did you vote for Calvin Coolidge, Papa?"

"No. I'm not allowed to vote."

"Me either. You have to be twenty-one to vote. I'm only twelve."

"Reckon I'm soon looking at sixty."

"Then why can't you vote? Is it because you're a Shaker?"

"No. It's account of I can't read or write. When a man cannot do those things, people think his head is weak."

"Who decides?"

"Men who look at me and do not take me for what I be. Men who only see me make my mark, my X, when I can't sign my name. They can't see how I true a beam to build our barn, or see that the rows of corn in my field are straight as fences. They just see me walk the street in Learning in clothes made me by my own woman. They do not care that my coat is sturdy and keeps me warm. They'll not care that I owe no debt and that I am beholding to no man."

"Is that why you can't vote, Papa?"

"Yes, boy. That's the reason."

"Doesn't it make you heartsick?"

"No. I take what I am. We are Plain People, your mother and aunt, and your sisters, you and me. And we suffer the less for not paining with worldly wants and wishes. I am not heartsick, because I am rich and they are poor."

"*We're* not rich, Papa. We're—"

"Yes, we are, boy. We have one another to tend to, and this land to tend. And one day we'll own it outright. We have Solomon here to wind up a capstan and help us haul our burdens. We have Daisy's hot milk. We got rain to wash up with, to get the grime off us. We can look at sundown and see it all, so that it wets the eye and hastens the heart. We hear all the music that's in the wind, so much music that it itches my foot to start tapping. Just like a fiddle."

"Maybe so, Papa. But it seems to me what we have most is dirt and work."

"True enough. But it be *our* dirt, Rob. This land will be ours in just a few more years. As to the work, what matters is that we have the back to do it. Some days I get the notion that I can't knife even one more of Clay Sander's pigs. Yet I always do, 'cause it's got to be done. It's my mission."

"Papa, is that the mission they preach on at Meeting?"

"It is. And every man must face his own mission. Mine is pigs. And I be thankful to be in the picture."

"What picture?"

"The picture of Vermont, boy. Do you know what makes Vermont a good state?"

"No."

"It's simple as beans. Here in this state we know to turn grass into milk and corn into hogs."

"I guess that's as true as a taproot."

"Truer."

Walking his circle, Solomon snorted as if to say he blessed the whole business.

"They sure is a passel of corn and meadowland in these parts," I said. "If'n we turn all that to milk and hogs, blessed if we'd ever keep up with it. Or just keep it in sight."

"Probably wouldn't, be we all dreamers like you. Now old Solomon's a dreamer, too. But yet he walks his circle. And just look how he's drug that corncrib. Plenty far."

I couldn't believe it. Just while Papa and me were talking, Solomon drug that old corn cratch a ways that was twice as long as Papa was tall.

Now Papa began to add some fresh-cut timbers to winter-tight the crib for Pinky.

"Papa, don't the wood got to season before you build with it?"

"Indoors, yes. But you can wood up a wall to stand outdoors and fresh wood will season itself."

With a hand turn Papa sunk holes into both ends of the fresh planks and into the old wood beyond. In each hole he used a mallet to pound in a trunnel peg of white oak that he had soaking in linseed oil. And the sty was done.

Pinky slept in it her first night with us. So did I, because the way I figured it, she'd be lonesome in a new place and away from her big fat old ma. So together we nestled down into all the clean straw, under what was left of Mr. Tanner's old horse blanket.

With Pinky next to me that night, I guess I must have been the luckiest boy in Learning.

THREE

THE NEXT day was Sunday. The four of us—me and Mama and Papa and Aunt Carrie—went to Shaker Meeting. We were all that was left at home. All my four sisters were wedded and bedded.

Solomon pulled the wagon all the way to Learning and all the way home. It was a real good sunny Sunday, perfect all around. And the best part was, I sat in Meeting where I could see Becky Tate and she couldn't see me.

That afternoon Pinky and I went for a walk up on the ridge that parts our land from Mr. Tanner's. We didn't go too near the spot where old Apron and I met up. I didn't hanker to ever see that place right away quick.

Pinky rooted around in the leaves and found her very first butternut, left over from fall. She sniffed it awhile with her little pink nose, and then she tried to crack it with her teeth. She couldn't do it, but it sure wasn't from lack of trying. So I put the butternut on a flat rock and smashed it with another stone. I fed the meat of the butternut to Pinky, and we found a few more. Pinky seemed to take to them, and each time I'd stop to crack one, she'd almost always have her nose in the way of the rock.

One nice thing about April, there were little rivers about everywhere. Where the spruce cover was thick you could still see a patch of snow here or there, but most of the land lay open to sun, and it was soft and brown, ready to be mated with seed. One of the tiny rivers was only about as wide as my hand, but the current was swift. It was a perfect spot to build what I liked to build every spring.

"Pinky," I said, "you ever see a flutter wheel? Well, I'm going to make one, so you watch real close."

I found two tiny fork sticks, which I pushed into the mud, fork up, on both sides of the stream. Then I put a basswood axle from one fork to the other, with a dab of mud in the crotch of both forks to grease its turning. All that was needed then was to whittle three or four paddles and stick them into the axle. I pushed the two fork sticks deeper into the mud until the water touched the paddle blades and the strong current of the tiny creek kept it turning round and round. Pinky watched it for a moment or two, but didn't find it near as comely as butternuts.

As I lay on the ground on a brown carpet of spruce needles, she would wander off by herself. But never very far. One time she went a little farther, and a big black crow over her head in a hickory tree let out a bark that made her jump and squeal like she'd been stuck. She come running to me like the Fallen Angel was after her and never stopped squealing until she was in my arms, with her slobber all over me. I let her feel the warm of my shirt next to her. She sure was my pig.

Only minutes after the crow spooked her she was wading in the water. She came close to stepping on a frog. And when it jumped, so did she. All the frog took was just one jump, and set there. Like he was waiting for her.

He didn't wait long. Pinky got her gumption up in no time and went close enough to smell him. This time when he jumped she didn't spook. Not Pinky. I guess she knew he wasn't anything to run from. She kept right on chasing him, and he kept right on leaping. It was fair to see.

Funny thing about frogs. I was cleaning a mess of 'em one time, with Papa. I said, "Papa, ain't it a caution that we can only eat two legs off a frog, 'stead of four."

And he said, "Rob, here's what you do. You catch a real big bullfrog and make friends with him. And teach him to jump backward. That'll build up his front legs big as the hind."

You know, I actually tried it. I went to the sump the next day and caught me a bullfrog and spent the better part of a morning trying to learn him to jump backward. But you think he'd do it? Not even once. Papa wasn't one to smile every year, but he sure did then.

Before I knew it, there I was, telling that frog story to Pinky. "Pink," I said, "how about it? You want a frog for supper?"

She just looked at me with her funny little eyes, which could of meant yes. So we left the flutter wheel turning and come down off the ridge, heading for the sump. We got there okay and started to wade around in the marsh grass and turn over a few rocks, looking for frogs. But there just didn't seem to be many. Or any. So Pinky thought she'd try her luck. Poking her little pink snout down between two stones at water's edge, she found something on the very first try. It was somebody who could jump backward all right, but it weren't no frog.

Pinky squealed! 'Cause clinging to her nose was one powerful-looking crawdad. I pulled it off and threw it back in the pond. But she kept squealing.

FROM high on the ridge Pinky and I could look down and see Mr. Tanner's farm. It sure looked prosperous next to ours. The barn was long and white-painted, and there were white fences along the lanes.

On the near side of the big white house was a small meadow. That was where we could see Apron and her two bull calves. Just a look at that big Holstein made my arm hurt. The stitches were still in it, and I guessed they'd be there until Hell froze and got hauled to the icehouse. If Mama had any plan to remove her sewing, she sure hadn't told it unto me. I didn't bring it up and wasn't going to. I couldn't say for sure just how you took thread out of somebody's arm, but it would probably mean some cutting. And I wasn't about to step forward for another dose of that.

It was good to look down from the high and lonely and see Bob and Bib tagging along after Apron. Bob was the one named after me. My real name was Robert Peck, but lots of times I got called Bob.

"Pinky," I said, "do you know I was named after Major Robert Rogers? He was quite a man with the Indians. There was a time when there wasn't an Iroquois in Vermont or in New York State that didn't hear the name of Major Robert Rogers and start to fearing. Some said he was Shaker bred. Just like me and you. But he didn't wear Shaker clothes. He wore Indian clothes—buckskin shirts and trousers, and no stockings—people said.

"Major Robert Rogers was a very famous man. So famous that, if you row cross-lake to Ticonderoga, there's a big rockslide named after him. Indians were chasing him along the shoulder that's west of Lake George, and Robert Rogers slid down that slide to escape."

Be it if Pinky was at all brightened to knowing that, she sure hid it good. She just kept rooting around in the ferns and not finding a thing. So I just kept saying to her about Robert Rogers. "Course from everything I've read in history books, he didn't have to run from the Indians at all. He could of turned and fought 'em off one by one. He could of pushed every last one of them right down Rogers Rock."

When my grandfather was still alive, I told him about how Major Robert Rogers hated Indians. And that's when Grampa said the major didn't hate them all. Because a number of Indian women in these parts had children that looked like they was sired by Robert Rogers.

Anyhow, he sure seemed to be an all-around guy. So I was real proud to carry his name.

"Come on, Pinky," I said. "It's getting close to chore time. I got to feed you and Daisy and Solomon. And if'n I'm not to home come chore time, Papa gets mighty stirred up. Right he should. Chores are my mission, not his."

I ran down off the ridge as fast as I could, just to see if my pig could keep up with me. She could. I ran clear to the crick. And even there I didn't stop. I just jumped it. Sailed through the air and landed yonder. Pinky didn't jump. But she sure waded it fast as fury. Splashed right through and made all the silver jump up around her hoofs.

"Come quick," said Mama, who was standing at the barn door. Just inside was a nest in the hay, right next to the warm wall near Daisy. Down in the hay was our calico barn cat, Miss Sarah, and three of the prettiest kittens you'd see anywhere. They were a trio to behold.

"Look, Pinky," I said, lifting her up so she could see Miss Sarah and her litter.

"No matter how many times a barn cat has her kits," Mama said, "it's always a wondrous thing to see."

June come. I sure was happy the last day of school. It was hot that afternoon. The weather was dry as dust, and I was glad to be walking home across pasture on the soft green instead of kicking rocks the long way round, which was by the dirt road. Way off to my right side a wagon was coming down the long hill, headed for town. As the wagon moved along, it blowed up clouds of dust that hung in the air behind it like the wagon was chased by a long gray snake. The driver had his coat took off, riding in his shirt with his sleeves rolled up.

I watched the wagon until it went out of sight around a road bend. And soon the snake had gone, too. It was like the wagon hadn't passed by at all.

From a quarter mile away I could see the corncrib; closer, I could see Pinky moving about, chasing one of the chickens. When I was nearer, I called to Pinky and she come to meet me. Boy! She was growing. I'd had her just ten weeks and already she was about my size. I lay on my back on the grass so she could come up to me and I could see her face. It always looked to me like she was smiling. In fact, I know she was. Lots of things smile, like a flower to the sun. And one thing sure. I knew that just like I could smile to see Pinky, she sure could smile to see me.

I got up, running toward the house. Pinky followed, but not as fast as when she was tiny. Her weight gain slowed her down some. Just as we got to the fence, I saw Mama on the front stoop. I'd hoped she hadn't took notice of me rolling on the meadow grass in my school clothes.

The grass was high now, so the next day I worked on the hay wagon with Papa. It sure felt good when chores were done and I could lie on my back in the soft grass and do nothing except wait for evening.

Pinky was with me, and she was lying down, too. Even though she hadn't put in a lick of work all day. But there she was, a mound of white pig in a whole field of purple clover and kickweed. Here and there was a stand of red and yellow paintbrush. It didn't seem to want to mix with the clover, and it just kept to its own kind.

In the early sundown the clover looked more purple than I'd ever seen it. Pinky rolled in it, over and back, over and back. It was getting ripe now, and you could take a big red-purple ball of it in your hand and pull out the flower shoots. They were good to suck, and tasted just as sweet as the bee honey that was made from them. Drawing one between my front teeth, I squeezed the sugary nectar into my mouth and spit out the pulp. I'd tried to get Pinky to taste some, but I guess pigs don't cotton to clover none.

Overhead I could see a hawk in the sky. He must of just left his nest on the ridge and was making his first circle of evening flight. He went higher, with little moving of his wings. As he passed over us, I could see the red of his tail—like a torch against the softer colors of his underbody. He went up, up, up. His circles were wider as he drifted south over the open meadowland of our farm. So high that he was only a dark speck with wings. The clouds above him were orange now. Like when Mama poured peach juice on the large curds of white pot cheese. At the westernmost turn of his circle, I almost lost him in the sundown.

But soon he came back. As the tiny speck of him passed over

my head, he stopped. For an instant he appeared to be pasted against a cloud, not moving. Then he got bigger and bigger. I sat up in the clover to watch his dive, and for a minute I thought he was coming down for me. Though I knew it weren't me that hawk was hunting. And down he came; down, down, down. Not moving his wings at all, like they was pegged to his sides and he couldn't brake his fall. He was going to hit the ground for sure, and I jumped on my feet to see it.

Whump! The hawk hit only a few rods from where I was standing in the clover. Just the yonder side of a juniper bush. He hit something as big as he was, pretty near. And whatever it was, it was thrashing about on the ground. Seeing his talons were buried in its fur, the hawk was being whipped through that juniper bush for fair. But all he had to do was hang on and drive his talons into the heart or lungs.

Then I heard the cry. Full of pity it was, and it even made Pinky get to her feet. I'd only heard it once before, a rabbit's death cry, and it don't forget very easy. Like a newborn baby, that's the sort of noise it is. It's the only cry that a rabbit makes its whole life long—just that one death cry and it's all over.

The cottontail had stopped kicking, and the hawk was resting, probably trying to get his breath back. So I didn't move. Pinky either. We both stood stock-still, up to our knees in that clover, like we was hitched. That old hawk saw us, you can wager on that, but it didn't mean spit to him.

I started to move real slow toward the hawk. Took about three steps and that was all. Mr. Hawk snapped those big wings out and off he whipped, that rabbit hanging all loose in his talons. He flew close to the ground till his speed was such as he could climb.

The grass whipped on my legs as I ran after him, but he just plain melted out of sight. I sure would of wanted to see his nest. And to see him tear up that fresh rabbit and feed his little ones. I bet, soon as he landed at his nest with his kill, all his brood had their beaks open, wanting to get some hunks of warm rabbit down their gullet.

Any rabbit we ever shot, Papa always rubbed its belly hair up

the wrong way to see if it was healthy. If he felt bumps on the belly, then he'd bury it because of it being down with rabies. If it was sound, it was pie. It made me hungry just to study on it.

So if those young hawk nestlings went after that rabbit meat, it was only because they got to it ahead of me. I didn't know if Pinky would like rabbit or no. But all pigs are meat eaters. They ought to be with forty-four teeth, Papa said. That was more teeth than I got. So maybe old Pinky would of eat rabbit.

I sure fed Pinky good. Just to make sure she got to grow right, I give her as much corn, wheat, barley, rye, oats, and sorghum as I could work out of Papa or Mr. Tanner. She also got some of Daisy's good fresh milk. Anytime I went fishing, she got fish. And all the soybean meal and alfalfa I could muster. Mama said, "Rob, you feed that pig better'n you feed yourself." I guessed it was true. She was my pig. Mine. And I was going to be dogged if she'd eat improper.

That was just food. She drunk about ten pounds a day of water. And like Solomon and Daisy, she liked her water cold and fresh. I was at Jacob Henry's once, and he was watering the stock. They had a horse and a cow, and only one bucket, so Jacob always had to water the horse first. Because a cow will drink after a horse, but no horse will drink after a cow. And a cow'll drink three pails to one for a horse. But the horse got to drink first.

I kept a record of how much I fed Pinky and wrote it all down up in my bedroom. The way I had it figured, for every three hundred fifty pounds of feed, she ought to weight-gain a hundred. As I was setting there in the clover, chewing on a juniper berry, Pinky come over and rubbed against me. And it was some rub, because she sure was growing.

"Pinky," I said, "you get took good care of. You got shelter and shade, and your crib is well drained. There's always dry straw for you to sleep on, and the sump hole by the brook for mud to roll in. I even wet down the yard for you so the dust don't creep in your nose." She snorted. I knew she wasn't saying thank you or anything, but it sure was fun to pretend so.

"You're welcome, Pink. And I'm going to keep right on taking care of you proper. Because do you know what you aim to be? You ain't going to be pork. No, missy. You're going to be a brood sow and have a very long life. You get to be sized good, and heat up like a sow pig ought to, and we're going to breed you to Mr. Tanner's boar. Just wait until you see Samson. He's about the best breeding boar in Learning, according to Papa. Your first litter ought to be at least eight. And after that, ten."

Pinky didn't seem to take to all this here talk of motherhood. She moved away and snapped at a bee.

"Bee," I said, "you must be the last one out tonight. Better get home to your tree. It's getting dark."

The whole sky was pink as peaches. Just looking up at it made you feel clean, even if you worked all day. I penned Pinky up for the night and gave her an extra big good-night hug. I was walking back toward the house and met Papa coming to the barn. One of the kittens was there, too, and I picked her up and carried her. The tiny claws dug into my shoulder, right through my shirt, until I held her close to make her fret no more of falling.

Papa had been mending a harness trace for Mr. Sander, and I waited while he put his tools away, each to its proper bed on the tack-room wall. Then we went out and sat on a bench, me still holding the kitten, and watched the sun go down. The pink became purple, and the purple turned to what Mama called Shaker gray.

"Papa," I said, "of all the things in the world to see, I reckon the heavens at sundown has got to be my favorite sight. How about you?"

"The sky's a good place to look," he said. "And I got a notion it's a good place to go."

FOUR

I DIDN'T know what time it was, and I sure didn't care. Not in the center of night, and raining as hard as it was. The thunder was crashing, too. Water was coming in my window, so I swung it shut. My window looked to the barn, and through the rain I could see the yellow of a lantern deep inside the shed.

Voices were downstairs. I could hear Mama and Aunt Carrie and another voice. A woman that I didn't know was talking. I was about to get back under the quilt, but decided not. Instead I went to the nook at the stair top and listened. Then I recognized the voice. It was Mrs. Hillman from up the road. She was standing at the front door, carrying a lantern.

Mama and Aunt Carrie were trying to ask her into the house. Something was said about a hot cup of tea, but I didn't hear all of it on account it rained so blessed hard. Mrs. Hillman finally come in, and they got the door shut, which improved the listening.

"He's gone," said Mrs. Hillman. "Sebring's gone. I heard him take the team and go, and don't think I don't know where. Spade and all. I saw him go. He picked a night like this so nobody'd see him rile her grave. I know."

Again there was talk of tea, and I could hear cups against saucers somewhere back in the kitchen.

"That Letty Phelps, your husband's kin. She hired out to us when I was poorly, years back. I know. I could see from out my bedroom glass. See her going to the barn to be with him. And then the trouble, the borning and the dying."

Papa come in from outside. I just got back in bed when I heard him call. "Rob, get yourself up and dressed and hitch up the ox to the long wagon."

I got dressed fast, and I pulled on my boots with no socks and run downstairs and out to the shed.

It was all I could do to get the yoke on Solomon. First time I'd ever done it alone. I wanted to go back to the house to learn what was happening. My stomach felt sort of vacant and I had the shakes. Just as I was about to make a dash for the house, I saw Papa coming in his slicker, with a bigger lantern and the shotgun.

Before I could ask what was astir, he threw me up on the wagon seat and covered me with an old buffalo robe. "Hold the lantern, boy."

He poked the long wand to Solomon's rump and the wagon lurched out into the rain and the pitch black. I kept looking back through the mist toward our house, wanting to be home in bed.

"There's talk about a new county road," Papa yelled to me in the raining, "and they say it's wide enough to cut the corner of the churchyard at the Meetinghouse."

"Is that where we be going, Papa?"

"That's where."

"Why?"

"We don't let Sebring Hillman desecrate what's ours that's buried there."

So we were headed for a graveyard. That much I knew. What Mr. Hillman was fixing to dig up, or why, was beyond wondering. I was cold and wet and wanted to go to sleep.

"Sit close," said Papa. "And mind you don't drop that lantern."

Twice we had to get down and push the wagon through mud. It frosted the wheels like they was cake, and it sucked at your boots. Made you feel you were standing in syrup.

We got to Learning and the town was all asleep. We rounded the corner at the general store and went toward the Meetinghouse. There was no lantern aglow in the churchyard. But we could hear his shovel hitting wood. It sure sounded lonely. Solomon stopped at the cemetery gate, and we went in on foot to where Sebring Hillman was working. The ring of light from our lantern took him in its circle. Looking up from the hole, he was brown with dirt.

"Who's there?" he said.

"Neighbors, Seeb," said Papa. "It's Haven Peck and son Robert. And we come to take you on home."

"Not till this work is done. And the sin and trouble is ended for all to see and all to know."

"She's my kin," said Papa. "And I don't aim to see kin dug up. Best you drop your shovel."

I held the heavy wet buffalo robe around me tight as I could. Papa held the gun in the crook of his arm, muzzle down. Hillman come up out of the hole, covered with mud, but holding the shovel high. His face was wet with raining. He was looking up both the barrel holes of Papa's gun.

"You got a gun," he said, and his voice was an illness.

"It's for varmints," Papa said, "not for neighbors."

"I don't purpose to disturb the box that Letty rests in," he said. "And that's Gospel."

"It's best," Papa said.

Papa took a shovel out of our wagon and the two men poked at the mud. They found a smaller box and lifted it up. They replaced the earth as it was before. The headstone said PHELPS, and that wasn't touched.

"By rights," said Papa, "that child of hers could go in our orchard plot."

This was when Sebring Hillman lifted up the small box and held it close to his chest. He was a big man and he needed no help for it. He just stood there, yelling in the raining.

"She don't have folks. They left town after she drown this child, then hung herself. I can't undo what's already been did. But the little girl is mine. You hear me, Haven? This child is mine, and I claim it soul and sust."

"You'll wake the town," Papa said.

"Yes, and I hope to do just that. I never did step forward back then. But by damn I claim it now!"

"So be it," said Papa. "Let's get our young ones home and rested proper."

We watched as Mr. Hillman carried the small coffin to where his wagon and team stood hid behind the Meetinghouse. We followed close along so as he'd have light to see. He tied the coffin firm with rope and was about to mount the seat. He was wet through.

"You don't have a slicker," Papa said, almost like asking.

"No."

"Tie your team behind our wagon and ride with us," Papa said. "We got a slicker and robe."

"I will."

I was sitting on the wagon bench between Papa and Mr. Hillman. Next to the two of them it was warm and dark, and I could smell the wet, musty smell of the buffalo robe. Mr. Hillman held the lantern. Ahead of us the light showed on Solomon's mighty backside as he moved into the darkness, following the road up from town and back home.

By the time we turned into our own lane and got to the house, the rain had stopped. It was sunup. There was a light in the kitchen, and Papa said, "There's coffee on."

"I want breakfast, Papa."

"So do I, boy," said Sebring Hillman. "I want so much breakfast it'll bust britches and crack floors. I never felt so good in a long time."

"Mr. Hillman?"

"Sure enough."

"Is that really your little girl in the coffin?"

"It is, Robert. And if it's all right with you and your pa, I'm going to bury her in Hillman land. With a Hillman name."

"I guess that's proper," I said.

I went to the house with Mr. Hillman while Papa put Solomon in the barn. We went to the kitchen door because of the mud. Mr. Hillman took off my boots on the porch, and I went inside. He said he was too muddy and wet. Mrs. Hillman was sitting in the kitchen. She looked at her husband, but no word passed. Mama handed Mr. Hillman a mug of hot coffee.

"Thank you, Sister," he said.

Mama took a good look at me, yanked me into the pantry, and stripped me down to my skin. "You look like a potato dug up on a rainy day," she said, as she rubbed me dry with a flour sack until I thought all my hide was coming off. Then she wrapped me up in a blanket that she took out of the warming oven over the stove, and gave me a big spoonful of hot honey.

Going through the kitchen on my way upstairs, I saw Mr. Hillman still standing on the kitchen porch, holding the white mug of coffee in both hands.

"Let's go home, May," he said to his wife. They went outside, untied their team, and headed uproad to home.

Behind them rode a baby's coffin.

I WAS just outside the kitchen window, trying to give Pinky a bath. Not really listening.

But I could hear Aunt Carrie and Mama in the pantry, and they seemed to be het up over something. Aunt Carrie seemed to have most of the ache and distress on her side.

"It's shameful," she said. Then I could hear some pie tins rattle, and I figured it was Aunt Carrie who done it, as a snit. "Shameful. Them two living under the same roof, without benefit of clergy. You know well as I what's going on in that house, right under our very noses."

"Maybe," said Mama, "our noses are where they shouldn't be."

"You heard Matty Plover say it when she was here one day."

"Matty says more than her prayers."

"Right under our noses, all that sin."

"Carrie, you know well as I that the Widow Bascom and her hired man, Ira, ain't living under our noses. They're near a mile downroad."

"Too close for comfort."

"Maybe it's time that Widow Bascom took some comfort, and him, too."

"It's shameful. And to think of Vernal Bascom, not yet cold in his grave. Poor soul."

"Carrie, you know weller than I that Vernal Bascom he's been gone two maybe three year."

"Didn't take *her* long to hire a man."

"Haven says he's a worker. And I say the Bascom place never looked better. She couldn't of done it alone, run that farm. Life ain't easy for a widow woman."

"Easy's the word for her."

"What goes on under a neighbor's quilt is naught to me," said Mama.

"Plenty goes on. He's a big strapper of a man, and I'll wager he's more than a year riper than she be."

"You seen him?"

"No."

"You just hear it from Matty."

"Hume told Matty that he was driving by the Bascom place, late one night last week, and he heard laughing. And there weren't a light burning in the whole house."

"Sometimes that's the way of it," said Mama.
"Way of what?"
"Often there's lots to laugh to in the dark."
"Hume heard it all."
"I bet he slowed his horse to listen."
"Hume's a decent man," said Aunt Carrie.
"Decent and dull. They'd be little to laugh at in the dark with him."
"Shame."
"I say if Hume ever smiled he'd break his legs."
"Hume heard what he heard," said Aunt Carrie. "He told Matty it was such a noise and carrying-on that he wanted to whip his horse all the way to the churchyard and wake up Vernal."
"Vernal Bascom wasn't that much awake when he was standing up. Now that he rests in peace, why don't Hume just let him rest."
"Amen."
"I can see it," said Mama.
"See what?"
"I can just see Hume Plover in the churchyard whispering to Vernal. Hume never spoke to him all the time he was alive. Now he's at rest, and Hume wants to spark up a chat."
"You just go on and on."
"That I do, Miss Carrie. There's little enough to snicker at in this old world. And to see Hume Plover whipping up his horse to talk to the dead is enough to give me the all-overs. I just wish Widow Bascom and her hired hand could see it, too." Mama was laughing.
"Shameful."
As I sat there on the bench outside, trying to rub the clay mud off Pinky, I got to thinking about my own run-in with the Widow Bascom.
It was after Vernal passed on, and she was living alone. Me and Jacob Henry had run through her strawberry patch and across her backyard. She come out with a broom so fast we didn't ever know how she got us cornered. We both got whacked so heavy that neither one of us took a step for a week without weeping. She caught me in the shin so hard it gave me a welt.

I touched the place on my leg where Widow Bascom's broom handle landed. The scar of that welt was still there. Needless to say, Jacob never told his mother about it. I sure never told Mama. Papa either. I'd probably got a second birching. Papa didn't take too kind to trespass.

That was the first time I had do with Mrs. Bascom. The second time was just day before yesterday. I was walking by her place on the dirt road—not through her damn strawberries—and she come out the house and called to me.

"Morning," she said.

"Morning, Mrs. Bascom," I said, but I sure didn't stop to say it.

"These flowerpots are so heavy and all," she said. "I don't reckon you'd help me tug a few."

I looked good and hard for that broom of hers that was ten foot long and made of iron. Didn't see it, so I climbed the stairs and got close. She was smiling.

"Flowerpots full of dirt are such pesky things," she said. "No way to carry one except to tug."

"I can lift one," I said, picking up a big pot.

"My," she said, "you're such a strong boy."

"I can yoke our ox by myself, too," I said. If she wanted to be friendly, I was game. It sure beat a brooming. So I helped her move the flowerpots. In the Book of Shaker it says to do a good turn and neighbor well. Besides, it wasn't chore time yet, and I could spare the work. I never saw so many flowers, all of 'em pretty. Sort of like Mrs. Bascom.

"Thank you," she said to me after we got the pots moved into a sunny spot.

"Welcome," I said.

"Just you wait," she said, and ran into the house. In no time she was back with a glass of buttermilk and a generous plate of gingersnaps as big as moons.

"Here," she said. "I bet you're hungry."

"I'm always hungry," I said. I was drinking the good cool buttermilk and helping myself to more gingersnaps when I looked up at a man.

"This here is Ira," she said. "He's my new hired hand."

"How do," I said, trying not to choke on a gingersnap. He sure was big.

"How do," he said. "I'm Ira Long."

"I'm Robert Peck."

"Haven Peck's boy," said Mrs. Bascom.

We shook hands, and Ira helped himself to a handful of gingersnaps. He ate about five on the first bite.

"Say," he said, "you the boy who helped bring Ben Tanner's cow to calf? And pulled a goiter?"

"Yes."

"That was a thing you done, Rob."

"Thank you, sir." I couldn't think of anything else to say, so I just took another gingersnap and stuffed it into my mouth so's I wouldn't have to talk. Sticking out my cheek, it made a shelf you could of set a dish on. Ira and Mrs. Bascom looked at me and started to laugh, and I got so fussed I just turned around a couple times. Then I started to laugh, too. I still don't know what was so all-fired funny. But it was.

"I hear Ben Tanner's taking them two young oxen to Rutland Fair," said Ira.

The very mention of Rutland Fair made my heart jump. Jacob Henry had gone to Rutland Fair last year, and he told me it just wouldn't be believed. Anything that weren't at Rutland Fair just wasn't worth seeing. To hear Jacob tell it, the fair was some spot.

"You ever been, Rob?"

"No. But I'd sure take a pride in going, with the pig I raised. Her name is Pinky. Guess when I get growed up, I'll go every year. But we can't go now."

"How come?"

"We don't have a horse, and I hear it's quite a ways. All we got is Solomon."

"Who's that?" asked Mrs. Bascom.

"Solomon's our ox. He's slow. But he's big and strong and wise, like King Solomon. Anyway, thank you for the gingersnaps and the buttermilk. Best I be going."

"You're more than welcome, Rob," said Mrs. Bascom. "Anytime you come this way, be sure to stop for a how-do."

"I will. Good-by."

"So long, Rob."

That's what I was remembering as I sat washing up Pinky. That pig sure did get dirty. She'd even got mud in her ears. When I first got her, washing her was no trouble on account of her being so tiny and all. But now! She was getting bigger than August.

Papa come round the kitchen corner, carrying a gear for the hand quern in the milk house, which Mama used to grind up meal. I always turned the crank.

"You'll wash that pig away," Papa said. "Won't be nothing left of Pinky 'cept a lump of lard."

"I'm getting her clean so I can put a ribbon on her neck and pretend I'm taking her to Rutland."

Papa hunkered down on his heels and watched me wash Pinky. She was clean as an archangel.

"Rob, do you think you could keep both your feet out of trouble if you was to go by yourself to Rutland?"

I couldn't talk. I knew he was funning me about going to Rutland. It weren't for real.

"Ben Tanner stopped by. He offered to take you to the fair with him. Seems like Mrs. Bascom told Mrs. Tanner how much you wanted going. Ben asked me. He says he wants to show off them young oxen, and he wants a boy to work 'em in the ring. Said that they was too small just yet for him and that he'd feel foolish."

"Papa, if this is a joke, I don't think I can take it."

"You ain't heard all, boy. Mr. Tanner says he's sending some stock up a day early. He says if you want to show Pinky, she can go, too."

"Papa, please . . ."

"Now then. It's more than a week off, so I don't want to be talked to death about Rutland before you even put a foot on the fairgrounds. Before you go, there's the hen coop that needs cleaning out. Manure's so thick in there, you got to kick a path to get eggs."

"I'll do it, Papa."

"Another thing. They won't be no spending money. Not for nothing. You hear?"

"Yes, Papa."

"Mama will make you a lunch basket that'll be breakfast, dinner, and supper. And you're to do all the Tanners ask of you. And *see* things to be done before they ask."

"Yes, Papa. I'll sure do good."

"If they judge hogs and oxen at the same time, your place is with Tanner's yoke and not your own pig. Promise me, boy."

"I promise, Papa. I'll do proud."

"One more thing. It'd be right warm if you stop off and give Widow Bascom a thank-you. You're beholding to her for putting the bug to Mrs. Tanner's ear."

"I will, Papa. I will. I will."

Mama was happy I was going to Rutland. Aunt Carrie wasn't so sure at first. But later that evening she said she was going to give me ten cents for the fair, providing I didn't lose it and didn't tell about it to Mama or Papa. It was a secret.

I slept out in the corncrib with Pinky that night. She was so clean, Mama said, it would be a shame to waste it. Before going to sleep, I put my arms around Pinky's neck and told her all about her and I on a trip to Rutland. And how she was going to win a blue ribbon. I told her about Widow Bascom and Ira Long. And how they giggled together in the dark.

"Pinky," I said, "it may be sinful. But I say the Widow Bascom is some improved."

FIVE

WE'D learned in school that the city of London, England, is the largest city in the whole wide world. Maybe so. But it couldn't have been much bigger than Rutland.

Early that morning Mama got me up. She packed my food basket so full you'd think that nobody in Vermont had ate for a week, and this was it. Papa had gone to the barn to yoke Solomon, to drive me to the Tanner place. And when Mama wasn't looking,

Aunt Carrie slipped me the ten cents. She had it all knotted up in a clean white hankie, and she wadded it so deep in my hip pocket she halfway pushed my trousers down.

"Don't lose it," she whispered to my ear. Lose it? After all that wrapping I'd be hoped to ever find it. "It's for a ride on the merry-go-round," she said. "And if you don't want to spend it, you can squirrel it away."

To make short of it, I got breakfasted and basketed and packed off to the Tanners'. I never thought we'd get there.

"Papa," I said on the way, "tell me about Rutland."

"I never been."

Neither had I, so there really wasn't much point in talking about it.

When I jumped out of the oxcart, all Papa said to me was one word: "Manners."

It sure wasn't far to Rutland. Not the way those dapple-gray horses of Mr. Tanner's moved that rig. They must have been barned all summer, at the speed they trotted. Ben Tanner drove, and I sat between him and his wife. Tight close. But it was all Mrs. Tanner and I could do just to hold tight.

His grays were called Quaker Lady and Quaker Gent. Boy, could they trot. We passed every other rig on the way to Rutland. Mr. Tanner was as proud of that brace of grays as he was of Bob and Bib. He just cottoned to things in twos. I was about to ask him why he didn't keep a second Mrs. Tanner around somewhere, as a matched pair to take out on Sunday. Or why he didn't just wed twins. But I remembered "manners" and owed up to silence.

"Never miss a chance," Papa had once said, "to keep your mouth shut." And the more I studied on it, the sounder it grew.

We got to Rutland the same time everybody else did. There couldn't of been nobody in Vermont who weren't there, and all dressed for Sabbath. When we pulled up at the fairgrounds, I was feared to blink for missing some of it.

The first thing we did was to go see Bob and Bib. The best part was that Pinky was close by, only one shed away. I jumped into her pen and put my arms around her neck and hugged her tight.

"Pinky," I said, "we're at Rutland. Ain't it grand?"

Right away quick, we got Bob and Bib yoked and bowed. Bob was always left and Bib right. We went across an open show area, where some men were exercising those big horses with hairy hoofs, to find a photographer. We spent the better part of an hour getting our picture took. The man who owned the camera got up under a big black tent. His wife held a funny-looking geegaw up in the air. It looked like some sort of snow shovel to me. But it was the first snow shovel I ever see explode. You never saw such a bang of light on a cloudy day in your life. I almost jumped out of my boots. Bob and Bib didn't take kindly to it either. They backed into me and started fighting the yoke. It was a tribulation to me.

Soon it come time to show the oxen. You should of seen 'em. Mr. Tanner nodded to a yoke of Herefords and said they'd weigh up about a ton each.

"Will Bob and Bib get that big?" I asked.

"Bigger. On account that Bob and Bib are Holstein, and they're the biggest and best."

I sure was proud to hear that. Even prouder when we went to the ox pull. When there was a pause in the contest, the man who was announcing things called out Mr. Tanner's name.

"Exhibition only, and not for sale. From the town of Learning, a perfect yoke of matched yearlings by names of Bob and Bib, owned by Mr. Benjamin Franklin Tanner, and worked in the ring by Mr. Robert Peck."

That was my cue to take Bob and Bib around the ring three times and then out. But I couldn't move until Mr. Tanner gave me a healthy prod in the backside with his goad and said, "Git!"

There I be. Me, at Rutland Fair, marching around a big sawdust ring, with all the people clapping their hands and pointing at Bob and Bib. It made my heart pound so hard I felt it was going to pump out right there in that ring. I was wishing that Mama and Papa and Aunt Carrie could see. Pinky, too. It was sinful, but I wanted the whole town of Learning to see me just this once. If only Edward Thatcher could see. And Jacob Henry and Becky Tate. I could see all the folks I know, sitting there in those big circles of seats. Manners, I said to myself, and walked real tall. It was just like I was somebody.

A man leaned over the fence and asked, "What's their line, boy?"

"Out of Apron, Mr. Tanner's prize milker," I said. "The sire bull was his, too. Name's Beowolf."

After three times around the ring, I touched Bib lightly on his right ear with my wand. The two little oxen made a smart left turn, and out we went through the gate. The people were still clapping and yelling. Some even followed us along, asking questions about Bob and Bib as we walked 'em back to their shed.

In the crowd Bess Tanner was not about. Then I saw her coming at a dead run. I could just see the top of her head and her big floppy hat with all the flowers on it that weren't real.

Between her and us there was a passel of people, and they just seemed to melt out of the way for Mrs. Tanner. She was so short of breath when she got to us, she couldn't talk. "Quick," she said to me between her wheezes. "The Four-H Club men are judging the stock that the children raised up."

"Hogs?" said Mr. Tanner.

"No, they're looking at the calves right now. But the hogs are next. I'll pen up the oxen. You take Rob with you, because I can't run another step."

"Let's get Pinky," said Mr. Tanner, and we were off. Pinky was almost the only pig left in the shed. We threw the bars open on her pen and were just about to drive her out when I noticed that she had a big dung stain on her left shoulder and flank. The rest of her was so clean that the dirty spot stuck out like a mean tongue. I went down on my knees and attacked the dirt with my hands and fingernails. If it looked bad, it stunk worse. The strong smell of its freshness made my eyes sting.

"Boy," said Ben Tanner, "that ain't no way to wash a pig. You find some soap somewhere. I'll fill a bucket and we're in business."

I must have turned Rutland upside down trying to find soap. I finally saw a bar of saddle soap in a tack room and made for it. But a man saw me and said, "Hey!"

"Soap," I said. "I'll buy your soap. My pig's dirty and the Four-H

people are judging and we'll miss out. Here, all I got is ten cents. It's in this hankie and you can have it all."

I put the hankie, with Aunt Carrie's dime inside it, into his hand, grabbed the soap, and ran out the door. The man just couldn't say a word.

There went my ride on the merry-go-round. But I was too rushed to care. Mr. Tanner had a rag, and in no time I got Pinky as clean as Christmas. Most of the water I managed to put on myself, and I was soaked through. And there was so much stink still on my hands, in spite of all the soap and water, that I figured I never would be able to eat a noon meal.

Mr. Tanner said I'd took so long we'd never get there in time. But we did.

The kids were walking around an open ring, and each one had a pig. One boy had a real good-to-look-at Poland China, as white as Pinky but not as big. A girl who was taller than I was had a Spotted Poland, and a boy with red hair and lots of freckles had a fine-looking Hampshire. It was coal black, with a white belt around it at the shoulder. Some of the pigs were acting up a bit—not staying in line, and squealing all the time they was handled by the 4-H judges. The circle was about whole when we got there, and Mr. Tanner almost threw me and Pinky into it just as another man closed up the gate.

My face was wet with the sweat of hurry. It feels worse, Papa always said, than the sweat of work. I didn't have a hankie to use, so, as I stood there, I put my hand up to my brow. And right then I got such a whiff of pig manure I thought I'd pass out. Everything I ever eat went sour and wanted to come up my gullet. The judges were coming my way, but it just didn't matter. All the noise of Rutland Fair, and all the music and dust of the place, seemed to float off in a dim whirly dream. I didn't need no ride on a merry-go-round, as all of Rutland was spinning about my head and taking me with it.

One of my eyes was closed shut. But the one that was part open got a quick look-see at a judge putting something on Pinky. Something blue. But when my whole entire world was green, I couldn't of cared. I couldn't of cared if they'd put a pigsticker into both of us. The judge said something to me, and that's when I did it. I leaned my head over, pointed my face at the little square chips of sawdust, and threw up. Some of it even went on his shoe.

The merry-go-round went a whole lot faster, and I'd a fall off for certain. But some big strong hands reached out and caught me, or over I'd a gone.

"He's my charge," I heard Mr. Tanner say. "I'll take him."

Next thing I knew, we were all back at Pinky's pen. I was lying in fresh straw just outside it. Pinky was inside. Mr. Tanner was standing close by, and Mrs. Tanner was washing my face with a clean towel.

"How could you let him get so dirty?" was all she seemed to say to her husband.

Mr. Tanner bent down and put his hand under my chin. "Rob, how do you feel?"

"Hungry," I said.

"Look," he said, pointing at Pinky's neck. "Will you look here."

It was a blue ribbon! And on it, in gold letters, it said: FIRST PRIZE FOR BEST-BEHAVED PIG.

"It's just about noon," he said. "Let's all put on the feed bag. What say, Bessie?"

Bess Tanner sighed. "Start without me. I don't want to put anything on right now. I just want to take off this cussed corset."

"PINKY won a blue ribbon, Papa."

That was the first thing I said when Ben Tanner shook me awake that night to tell me I was home. I must of slept all the way, because I didn't recall much of the trip back. Soon as it got dark I just went to sleep, sitting there between Mr. and Mrs. Tanner and holding on tight to the blue ribbon.

"Pinky won a blue ribbon. It's for the best-behaved pig," I said.

"And," said Mr. Tanner, "he ought to have a second one for best-behaved boy. He worked my oxen like he was born with a wand in his hand."

"How were his manners?" asked Papa.

"Thank you, Mr. Tanner," I said quickly. "And thank you, Mrs. Tanner. I had a very good time."

"Bless you, Rob," she said.

"The stock'll be here soon as the fair closes," Mr. Tanner said.

"I'll send the boy for his pig," Papa said, "and we're beholding to both you folks, Brother Tanner."

"We to you, Haven. I got offered five hundred for my yearling oxen. Five hundred dollars, and not even half growed. Thanks to your boy, who helped born 'em and work 'em at the fair. But I won't sell them two."

"I'm glad he did you proud," Papa said.

Ben Tanner turned his grays and off they went, Bess holding her hat on with the flat of her hand. I just stood there, watching them go uproad into the dark until I could no longer hear their rig.

"Good neighbors," I said.

"The best a man could have," said Papa. "Benjamin Tanner will stand without hitching."

Mama came running out of the house, holding out her hands. I ran to her and hugged her clean and warm and hard as I could. Aunt Carrie was there, too. I wanted to tell her, as I hugged her, as to how I spent the ten cents that she gave me, but I thought better of it. Ten cents for a used piece of saddle soap was a dear price.

"Mama," I said, "looky here. Pinky's blue ribbon! She won it."

"Of course she won it," Mama said. "She's the prettiest pig in Learning."

"She'll be home in a few days," I said.

"I can't wait," said Papa, and Mama smiled.

"Into the house with you," Mama said. "It's way past your bed-time and you'll never get up for chores." That sort of stopped me.

"Papa? You did all my chores today."

"Sure did. And butchered hogs besides."

"Thank you, Papa. I'm beholding."

"I accept your debt," Papa said, "and come 'morrow, you'll work double."

"That's meet and right," I said. "I already owe you for the sorghum."

"Three bags full," said Papa. "I expect payment after your pig has a first litter."

Mama said, "You menfolk don't know when it's time for bed. How about some pie, Rob?"

"Please," I said.

We all sat around the kitchen table, eating blackberry pie and hearing me talk about Rutland Fair. I told all I could tell and made up the rest.

But I never let on that I lost my breakfast on the judge's shoe. That would only distress Mama.

"Rutland," said Papa. "I never went there, boy or man. And here *you* go, all that way by your lonesome with the neighbors."

"It's not so big," I said. "What sets you back is the noise. It's like a big brass band that can't stop playing. Goes all the while."

"Just like a mouth I know," said Papa, "that's got blackberry all over it."

We all got a good laugh on that. It sure was good to be home, and it was hard to believe that I was gone less than a day. It felt like I'd been to a star.

DURING the night there was noise outside in the hen coop. I heard the hens cackle and scold. I saw a lit lantern in the upstairs hall, and then all was quiet. I tried my holy best to wake up, but I just couldn't.

Right after I shut my eyes, it was chore time. I'd milked Daisy and was pouring the milk for separating (to get the cream off) when I saw Papa leaving the hen coop with a dead hen.

"Weasel," Papa said. "And hardly no mark on her."

"Chicken for supper, Papa?"

"Yup. Say, you want to see something?"

"Sure."

Papa took me into the tack room. Hanging on a peg was a burlap sack that moved around a bit. Quite a bit, the closer we got.

"What you got, Papa?"

"What I got is that weasel. First one I ever could corner and sack. He's really got a mouthful of mean teeth."

"Can I look?"

"Later. When I reason out what to do with him. He's caused me too much grief to kill without a ceremony."

"You aim to let that weasel go free?"

"Not likely."

"Papa, you know Mrs. Bascom's hired man, Ira Long?"

"Heard his name."

"Well, he's got a full-growed bitch terrier. I seen her when I went to thank Mrs. Bascom."

"Run down there, boy, and tell Brother Long that we got a weasel to try his dog on. And he's welcome to it."

"Sure will. I never see a dog get weaseled."

An hour later a horse and rig pulled into our lane. On it was Ira Long and me and his dog, Hussy. She was a sweet little dog, and all the way home, as I was holding her, I wondered how she'd fare against a weasel.

Papa was there to meet us, and he gave Ira his hand.

"Haven Peck," Papa said, introducing himself. "We're glad you could pay us call, Brother."

"Ira Long. I already know your son."

"Most folks do." Both the men laughed. I don't know why, but I laughed, too.

"He's a good un," said Ira.

Papa looked at the small gray-and-white terrier in my arms. "You tried that bitch on weasel yet?"

"No. But I hear you got one."

"A big one," Papa said. "Mean as sin."

"Papa," I said, "why do folks weasel a dog? Is it for the sport of it?"

"No," Papa said, "there's earthy reason. 'Cause once you weasel that dog, that dog'll hate weasels until her last breath. She'll always know when there's one around, and she'll track it to its hole, dig it out, and tear it up. A man who keeps a hen house got to have a good weasel dog."

"That's the truth of it," Ira said. "Every weasel in the country will keep wide of my little Hussy."

When the three of us walked into the tack room, I was still carrying Hussy. Soon as we got there, that burlap jumped around like it was loco. And I could feel Ira's little terrier shaking in my arms. Just like she knew what was going to happen and what she'd got to do to stay alive. She was whining, too. Just loud enough to hear.

"I got an idea she'll make a good weasel dog," Ira said.

"We'll see," said Papa.

He picked the sack off its peg and we went outside, and Ira held his terrier and Papa the burlap bag while I took the top off a good-sized empty apple barrel.

"In you go, Hussy," Ira said, placing his little bitch inside the barrel. "You give him what for."

She sure was shaking, that dog. It made the whole barrel sort of tremble. Papa came forward with the sack.

"Soon's I drop him from the sack," he said to me, "you lid that barrel and keep it lidded, hear?"

"Yes, Papa."

Without more ado, he just poured that weasel right down inside the barrel on top of the dog. I slammed the lid into place. I could hardly hold it on, and Ira come over to help keep the barrel upright. Papa, too.

We heard a lot of scratching and chasing and biting inside the dark of that barrel. To be honest, I thought a fight between a dog and a weasel was going to be a real excitement. But I hated every second of it. From the look on Papa's face I could see that maybe he wasn't enjoying it so much either.

At last all the noise stopped. Papa nodded and I slipped the lid a crack, to let some light in so we could look inside. Then we heard the dog cry. It was a whine that I will always remember, the kind of sound that you never want to hear again.

Ira pulled the lid of the barrel away and looked inside. The weasel was dead. Torn apart into small pieces of fur, bones, and bloody meat. The dog was alive, but not much more. One of her ears was about tore off, and she was wet with blood. And making that sound in her throat that almost begged someone to end her misery.

Ira reached down to lift her out of the barrel. As he picked her up, her teeth bared and she ripped open his hand. He gave out a yell and dropped her on the ground. One of her front paws was chewed up so bad it was nothing but a raw stump.

"Kill her," I said.

"What?" said Ira, his hand bleeding into his shirt cuff.

"She's dying," I said. "If you got any mercy at all in you, Ira Long, you'll do her in. She's crazy with hurt. And if you don't kill her, I will."

"Mind your tongue, Robert," said Ira. "You're talking to your elders."

"The boy's right," Papa said. "I'll get a gun."

Until Papa come back with the rifle, little Hussy just lay there on the ground and whimpered. Papa put a bullet in her, and her whole body jerked to a quivering stillness. Nobody said a word. The three of us just stood there, looking down into the dust at what once was a friendly little pet.

"I swear," Papa said. "I swear by the Book of Shaker and all that's holy, I will never again weasel a dog. Even if I lose every chicken I own."

I got a spade and dug a small hole and buried her near an apple tree. I even got down on my knees and said her a prayer.

"Hussy," I said, "you got more spunk in you than a lot of us menfolk got brains."

SIX

PINKY came home.

I had her blue ribbon pinned up on the wall over my bed, and took it out to show it to her. She sniffed at it and that was about all. I was glad anyway she wasn't getting too filled with herself. A swellheaded pig would be hard to live with. I ran in to put the blue ribbon on my wall again, and when I got back outside,

Papa was home from butchering. His clothes were a real mess.

"Papa," I said, "after a whole day at rendering pork, don't you start to hate your clothes?"

"Like I could burn 'em and bury 'em."

"But you wear a leather apron when you kill pork. How come you still get so dirty?"

"Dying is dirty business. Like getting born."

"I never thought of that. I'm sure glad nobody'll kill Pinky. She's going to be a brood sow, isn't she, Papa?"

He didn't answer. Instead he walked to the fence and swung his legs over the rails and knelt down beside her. He run his hand along her back and looked at her rump real close.

"What's wrong, Papa? Is Pinky ailing?"

"No, not ailing. Just slow. She should of had her first heat by now. Weeks ago. We could a bred her to boar at the third. Maybe she's barren."

"Barren? You mean . . ."

"I don't know for sure, boy. Maybe she's barren."

"And you think she is? Tell me true, Papa."

"Yes, boy. I think she be."

"No," I said. "No! No!" My fists were doubled and I hit the top rail of the fence harder and harder. Until my hands started to hurt.

"Rob, that won't change nothing. You got to face what is."

He walked away to the barn, his tall lean body moving as if it knew more work would be done that day, tired or no.

"Rob!" Mama called from the kitchen, and I left Pinky and ran up to where she was standing, drying her hands on her apron.

"Go get a squirrel," she said, smiling.

Inside the house I took the .22 off the lintel over the fireplace and dropped some cartridges in my pocket. I should of been happy, going squirrel hunting, but I wasn't.

There was a stand of hickory trees up on the west end of the ridge. Now that it was autumn, the nuts would be ripe and eaten. My eyes moved to the tops of the trees, searching for a gray, a big fat one with a full paunch. But there just wasn't a gray squirrel to be had. I walked into the trees, sat on a stump, and looked down across the valley. It was yellow with goldenrod. Like somebody broke eggs all over the hillside.

Then I heard him! He was just over my head, sitting flat on a branch, twitching his long gray brush of a tail. And making that scolding squirrel *chip-chip-chip-chip-chip* sort of a sound. Sassy as salt. A round was already in the chamber. Raising the gun, I put the black bead of the front sight deep in the V notch of the rear sight. The bead was just behind his ear when I slowly squeezed the trigger.

It was like he was yanked off the limb by a rope. He fell, kicking, into the brush, and when I got to him, he was still twisting. Holding his back legs, I swung his body against the trunk of a sweet gum tree. His spine cracked, and he was dead.

Back on the kitchen stoop, I took a knife and cut open his belly. I was right careful not to cut the paunch. Removing the warm wet sack, I brought it into the kitchen and washed it under the sink pump. Mama had a clean white linen hankie ready. I lanced the paunch, and we emptied all the chewed-up nutmeats on it, spreading them out so they'd dry. Then Mama put the hankie up in the warming oven above the stove.

I couldn't see the chocolate cake, but it had to be around somewheres. If there was no cake, Mama wouldn't of wanted a gray. Outside I cut up the rest of the squirrel and threw it to the chickens. They fought over the big hunks, and the larger hens bulled the weaker ones away. The scrawny ones got nothing. I was thinking about that when Papa come up behind me. The matron hens ate, while the runts just watched.

"It isn't fair, is it, Papa?"

"Rob, it ain't a fair world."

"How are the apples doing? You think it's time we picked?"

"Two more days," Papa said. "They ain't good this year, and we can't let any drop. The spanner worms were so heavy last June, they ate up lots of the buds."

"We smoked, Papa."

"That we did. But maybe the mix was wrong. Tell me again, boy, what you did."

"Just like you said, Pa. It was last May when I scraped all the black ash off the inside of the fireplace and the cookstove. I mixed in the quicklime and split it up so's I could put a pile of it under every apple tree in the orchard."

"How many?"

"Eighteen. We lost one to winter."

"You add the water to the mix like I told you?"

"Yes, Papa. I threw about a cup on each pile, and the mix hissed up real good. It really smoked up proper."

"Was it windy?"

"Come to think, it was. Some vapors got blowed away."

"Boy, you got to put ash and lime always windward to the tree. Test the breeze for each tree. Currents are strange in an orchard."

"I did it wrong. That's why the spanners were so numbered."

"You'll do right next spring, Rob. Just take time with things. One chore done good beats two done ragged."

"Yes, sir."

"You can always look to how a farm is tended and know the farmer. Ever see Brother Tanner's place? His fence is straight as virtue. All the critters are clean. Mark how he cuts his hay. Ain't no truer windrow in all of Learning."

"He's a good farmer," I said.

"He'll walk to his barn at six and six. You could set a clock at the first chime of milk that hits the pail."

"Is he a better farmer than you, Papa?"

"Yes. He bests me at it. He wouldn't say to my face. But he knows and I know, and there's not a use in wording it."

"I don't want to grow up to be like Mr. Tanner. I'm going to be just like you, Papa."

"No, boy, you won't. You have your schooling. You'll read and write and cipher. And when you spray that orchard, you'll use the new things."

"Chemicals?"

"True. And you won't have to leave your land to kill another man's hogs, and then ask for the grind meat with your hat in your hand."

"But you're a good butcher, Papa. Even Mr. Tanner said you were the best in the county."

"He say that?"

"Honest, Papa. He said he could look at half a pork and tell it was you that boiled and scraped it. He said you even had your own trademark. When you kill pork and twain it, head to rump, you always do what no other man does. You even divide the tail, and half it right to the end. He said this on the way to Rutland."

"I'm sure glad to be famed for something."

"Supper's on!" Mama called from the kitchen door. "You two menfolk intend to stand all evening and preach to the hens?"

"With only one rooster," Papa yelled up to her, "I doubt they *need* much preaching."

Mama laughed and went inside. We followed, after washing up proper at the pump. Papa put his hand on my shoulder as we walked up to the house.

"Try an' try," he said, "but when it comes day's end, I can't wash the pig off me. And your mother never complains. Not once, in all these years, has she ever said that I smell strong. I said once to her that I was sorry."

"What did Mama say?"

"She said I smelled of honest work and that there was no sorry to be said or heard."

We had a good supper, with hot bisquit and honey. And after, we had chocolate cake. The nutmeats that we'd took out of the squirrel were dry. Aunt Carrie took 'em out the warming oven and sprinkled them on top of the cake. Like little white stars in a big brown heaven. And I got cut a slice of that cake that even Solomon couldn't of moved.

Later, while Mama and Aunt Carrie were talking in the kitchen, Papa and I sat in the parlor near the fireplace. It felt good to have a fire, and it was sure a grand thing to look at while you talked. Now it was dying down. Ready for bed, like people.

Papa said once that wood heats you three times. When you cut it, haul it, and burn it.

"Winter's coming, Papa."

"True enough."

"I think I may need a new winter coat."

"Better speak to your mother to start stitching."

"I want a store coat. I *need one.*"

"So do I. But one thing to learn, Rob, is this. *Need* is a weak word. Has nothing to do with what people get. Ain't what you need that matters. It's what you do. And your mother'll do you a coat."

"Just once," I said. "Just one time I'd hanker for a store-bought coat. A red-and-black buffalo plaid checkerboard coat like Jacob Henry's. Just once I'd like to walk in the general store with money in my pocket and touch all them coats. Every one. Touch 'em all and smell all the *new* in 'em. Like new boots."

"That would be fine. Real fine," Papa said.

"Jacob Henry said that in one store in Learning they let you put on any coat you want and walk around the store in it, even if you don't buy it. But you know what I'd do? I'd buy a red-and-black one like Jacob Henry's. It would be my coat forever, and I'd never wear it out."

"Reckon you'd outgrow it before you outwear it."

"Probably would. But I sure do want a coat like that. Why do we have to be Plain People? Why do we, Papa?"

"Because we are."

"I guess I'll never have a coat like that. Can I?"

"You can. When you earn one. You'll be a man soon."

"Someday," I said.

"It can't be someday, Rob. It's got to be now. This winter. Your sisters are gone; all four are wedded and bedded. Your two brothers are dead. Born dead, and grounded in our orchard. So it's got to be you, Rob."

"Why are you saying this, Papa?"

"Because, son. Because this is my last winter. I got an affection, I know I do."

"You seen Doc Knapp?"

"No need. All things end, and so it goes."

"No, Papa. Don't say that."

"Listen, Rob. Listen, boy. I tell you true. You got to face up to it. You can't be a boy about it."

"Papa, Papa . . ."

"You are not to say this to your mother or to Carrie. But from now on you got to listen how to run this farm. We got five years to go on it, and the land is ours. Lock and stock. And you'll be through school by then."

"I'll quit school and work the farm."

"No you won't. You stay and get schooled. Get all the teaching you can hold."

I got up from the chair I was in so as I could be near him. I touched the sleeve of his shirt and felt his whole body stiffen. He looked away as he spoke.

"It's got to be you, Rob. Your mother and Carrie can't do it alone. Come spring, you aren't the boy of the place. You're the man. A man of thirteen. But no less a man. And whatever has to be done on this land, it's got to be did by you, Rob. Because there'll be nobody else, boy. Just you."

"Papa, no."

"It can't be no longer your mother and Carrie taking care of you. Soon you got to care for them. They're old, too. Years of work's done that. Your ma's not young anymore, and Carrie is near seventy. To short the story, I could be wrong, but I feel like it's over for me soon. Animals know when. And I reckon I'm more beast than man."

I didn't believe it, and I couldn't say anything. I hoped he'd reach out and touch me or kiss me or something. But he just got up from his chair, wrapped a hot rock from the fireplace in a sack for his bed, and went upstairs. Mama and Aunt Carrie had left the kitchen and gone up, too. The parlor was still and dark.

I sat watching the red cinders turn gray. I stayed there until the fire died. So it would not have to die alone.

October came, with colors as pretty as laundry on a line. Then it was November, and on dark mornings on the way to the barn to milk Daisy, I thought the air would snap my lungs.

For weeks Papa had looked at Pinky every day. He even said I should feed her some new food, and to mix some meat scraps into her mash. Enough to turn her wild and make her heat. But there was no sign of Pinky coming to age. I saw Mr. Tanner up on the ridge, gunning for grouse. And so I told him about my pig and asked him if he thought Pinky was barren. He said he'd stop over next morning.

He did. I was hardly through chores when I heard the rattle of an oxcart coming down the road. It was Bob and Bib, and were they ever growed! Behind him as he sat, the wagon sides were slatted up, and I couldn't see what was inside. As he turned in, I ran out to meet him and looked between the cart slats. There he was, the finest boar in the county. Big and mean and all male. No one could of ever eat him. His ham would of been strong as tree bark and full of tack.

"Where's your gilt?" Mr. Tanner asked.

"Around back," I said, pointing to where we kept Pinky.

"Your pa home?"

"No," I said. "He left early. November is a busy time for him."

"No matter," said Ben Tanner. "The reason why of it is this. Perhaps your pig is barren, perhaps no. Sometimes a girl just has to be coaxed and courted. You and I can't get Pinky to heat because, to her eyes, we're not that handsome. But wait until she gets a smell of Samson. He can smell heat when we can't. And if he does, she'll change her tune."

We backed the oxcart to the small box pen and put a ramp up for Samson. Removing the slats with Mr. Tanner, I got my first good look at that boar. He must have weighed four or even five hundred. He was one big Poland. Mr. Tanner gave him a prod and he left the cart, walking down the ramp like a king. In his nose the big brass ring caught the sun and it shined real bright.

"All my sows are farrowed, so he'll be more than happy to help. He's been in a pen by his lonesome longer than a week. And he's due."

I went around back and called Pinky. But she wouldn't come, and she was too darn big to push, so I had to take a small switch to her. I swatted her good and proper all the way to the box pen, and in she went to mix with Samson. As she walked through the gate, Ben slapped a handful of lard on her rump. Under her tail.

Pinky was large. But next to Samson she seemed only about half growed. She just looked at him, her nose close to the ground like always, trying to get a smell that would tell her what he was.

Samson grunted. He walked to her and pushed her with his nose. She let him push her like that once more, then she backed away from him. He walked by her, rubbing his shoulder against hers. He tried to get a good whiff of her, but she bolted, kicking away at him with her hind feet. Several times he tried, but she wasn't holding still for it. Turning on him, she got her teeth onto his ear and tore its edge before Mr. Tanner could whack her a sharp blow with his stick.

"All part of courting," said he. "Samson just got his face slapped. That's all."

The two hogs just stood there looking at each other. That's when Ben Tanner lit his pipe.

"Your father," he said. "How's his health?" He asked the question real easy, like it didn't matter none. But I knew it did. Ben Tanner looked at me, and he wanted an answer.

"Fine," I said. "Papa's so sturdy, he never missed a day slaughtering his entire life."

I had to look away when I said it and had no idea what I could of said next. As I was trying to think of something, Mr. Tanner said, "Son, if Samson breeds your gilt, I expect a stud fee. Fifty dollars or two picks of the litter. You're to choose."

"You can have two of her brood," I said.

"Done."

Now it was real business, and Samson seemed to guess what we expected of him. Butting hard into Pinky's front shoulder with his snout, he half turned her about. Quick as silver, he jumped to her rear, pinning her against the fence, and came down hard upon her. Pinky was squealing like her throat had been cut, and as I watched, I hated Samson. I hated him for being so big and mean and heavy.

"You wait," said Ben Tanner. "There ain't a sow in Vermont that'll deny Samson. He's all boar."

He was, and so he had his way with her. But not even after Samson had enough of her and got down off her did she stop her whining. Not even then.

She was shaking like she couldn't stand, her whole body quivering. I started to swing a leg over the fence so I could pat her a bit and clean her up. But I felt Ben Tanner's strong hand on my shoulder, pulling me back.

"You crazy, boy? You go into that pen now and go near her, and that boar will have you for breakfast. Where's your sense?"

"I guess I don't have any," I said.

"Time you got some. How old be you, Rob?"

"Twelve, sir. I'll be thirteen, come February."

"Good. Twelve's a boy, thirteen a man. Now just take Pinky there. She weren't naught but a maiden before this morning. A big little girl. But from this time on she's a sow. And next time she'll welcome the big boy. Even ram herself through barbwire to be with him and get bred by him. Understand?"

"Yes, sir. I think so."

"Your pa is slaughtering today, is he?"

"Yes."

"Hard work. He ought to take it easy one of these days, now he's got you to man the place."

"Papa works all the time. He don't never rest. And worse than that, he works inside himself. I can see it on his face. Like he's been trying all his life to catch up to something. But whatever it is, it's always ahead of him, and he can't reach it."

"You reason all that out by your lonesome?"

"Yes, sir."

"You're a keen lad, for a Shaker boy. How are your lessons?"

"I get A in everything. Almost."

"Everything?"

"Everything except English. I don't never get an A in that, and darned if I know why. The teacher says I have potential. That I could be more than a farmer."

"More than a farmer!" Ben Tanner looked a bit red. "What better can a man be? There's no higher calling than animal husbandry and making things live and grow. Our lot is to tend all of God's good living things, and I say there's nothing finer."

"That's what Papa says. In just five years we'll own this farm. All of it."

"Glad to hear it. You Pecks are good neighbors."

I laughed. "That's what Papa and I always say about you folks. You're good neighbors."

"I watched all your sisters grow up. Pretty girls, they were. And a real credit to your folks. But now it's you, Robert. And you've got a start. Pinky'll farrow at least ten pigs, spring and fall—if you breed her fresh again just three days after she weans. That's twenty pigs a year. In five years that's a hundred hogs."

"Gee! A hundred hogs."

"It's not the number alone, boy. Pinky ain't just another pig. She comes from a stout meaty line. So does Samson. The sow that bore him would often bear twelve instead of ten. Two extra. That's dollars, boy. Dollars you can pay off this farm with. Good solid Yankee dollars that you can bank."

All this talk of hogs and dollars and meat and banks was rolling around inside my head with no direction. It didn't sound Christian to me, but then everyone in the world didn't all live strict by the Book of Shaker.

"We're Plain People, sir. It may not be right to want for so much."

"Nonsense, boy. Bess and I are fearing Christians, same as you."

"But you aren't a Shaker. Are you?"

"No. I'm a Baptist! Wash-feet and hard-shell Baptist. Born one, and I hope to die one. But not yet."

I almost busted out laughing. There they were, the people who probably loved me more than anyone in the whole world, besides Papa, Mama, and Aunt Carrie—Mr. and Mrs. Tanner. Not Shakers, but good shouting Baptists. It just goes to show how wrong I could feel about some things.

And how foolish.

SEVEN

THE APPLE CROP was bad.

The weather had turned colder, and we were lucky to get a few Baldwins and Jonathans barreled for wintering in the cellar. Papa had been right. The crop was lean. The apples that we did harvest were not large, and many had wormholes. The one tree that had died was our greening tree, one that produced smaller apples that were green and very tart. Pie apples. But this winter they'd be no pies.

Twice Papa had seen a buck and several doe upon the ridge. But each time he got the shotgun and slug shells ready, the deer were gone. Jacob Henry's father got a buck. So did Ira Long. One of the men who farmed for Ben Tanner got a doe. But Papa didn't have a deer rifle, only a shotgun with ball loads. He had to get close for a shot.

He still-hunted early almost every morning, hoping to get a buck deer before it was time to go to work. No luck. Once he even sat for four hours in a cold rain, waiting. He coughed after that, a deep rattling cough that made him hang on to things. But the worst thing was when his lungs got so bad he stopped sleeping with Mama. He slept in the barn. It was warmer there, with Daisy and Solomon both enclosed in a cozy area.

The first snow came. It wasn't very heavy; and when the next day's sun broke through, it all melted away. But much more would follow.

Pinky did not have a litter of pigs. She was bred and she was barren. And she ate too much to keep as a pet. Samson had mounted her twice and there was no litter. She never came to heat, not even once.

It all ended one early morning on a dark December day. It was Saturday and there was no school. After chores Papa and I came in for breakfast. I tried to down a big bowl of hot steaming oatmeal, but it tasted like soap. And the fresh warm milk from Daisy's pail was flat. I couldn't swallow it. Papa just sat at the kitchen table, fingering a pipe that he couldn't smoke and looking at a breakfast he couldn't eat. He finally got up from the table to look through the window. Outside, the dark of the moon was just softening into first light. When he turned round to me, his face was sober.

"Rob, let's get it done."

I didn't ask what. I just knew. And so did Mama and Aunt Carrie, because as Papa and I were getting our coats on to go outside, they both came over and pretended to help bundle me up.

There had been a light snow the night before. Just enough to cover the ground the way Mama would flour her cake board. I followed Papa out to where we kept the tools, and I stood there watching as he sharpened the knives on the wheel. The sticking knife was short and blunt, with a curved blade. The edge he put to it was extra sharp. He pulled on some heavy rubber boots and tied a sheath of leather around his middle for an apron. We were ready.

Toting some of the tools and a spine saw, I went outside with Papa to where old Solomon and the capstan had pulled the corncrib—Pinky's house. Inside it she was lying all curled up in the clean straw. It was a soft warm smell.

"Come on, Pinky," I tried to say in a cheerful way. "It's morning." But my throat seemed to catch and the words just wouldn't come out. I nudged her with my foot, but finally had to take a switch and make her get to her feet. She came to me, nuzzle pointed into my leg.

Her curly tail was moving about like it was glad the day had started. People say pigs don't feel. And that they don't wag their tails. All I know is that Pinky sure knew who I was, and her tail did, too.

While Papa lit a fire to boil the water, I pushed her out of the crib and into a box pen, the same one that she'd been in when bred to Samson. She balked at the gate, and I had to hit her hard with the stick a few times to move her forward. It probably hurt her, but what did it matter now.

We followed her in and closed the gate by sliding the bars across. I got down on my knees in the snow and put my arms around her big white neck, smelling her good solid smell. Pinky, I said to myself, try and understand. If there was any other way. If only Papa had got a deer this fall. Or if I was old enough to earn money. If only . . .

"Help me, boy," said Papa. "It's time."

He put his tools on the ground, keeping only a three-foot crowbar. Neither one of us wore gloves, and I knew how cold that crowbar felt. I'd carried it, and it was colder than death.

"Back away," he said.

"Papa," I said, "I don't think I can."

"That's not the issue, Rob. We have to."

Standing up, I moved away from Pinky as Papa went to her head. She just stood there in the fresh snow, looking at my feet. I saw Papa get a grip on the crowbar and raise it high over his head.

It was then I closed my eyes, and my mouth opened like I wanted to scream for her. I waited. I waited to hear the noise that I finally heard.

It was a strong crushing noise that you only hear when an iron stunner bashes in a pig's skull. I hated Papa that moment. I hated him for killing her, and hated him for every pig he ever killed in his lifetime . . . for hundreds and hundreds of butchered hogs.

"Hurry," he said.

I opened my eyes and went to her. She was down in the snow. Moving, breathing, but down. I helped roll her over on her back, standing astride her and holding her two forelegs straight up in the air. With his left hand Papa pushed her chin down so that the top of her snout touched the ground. His right hand held the blunt knife with the curved blade. He stuck her throat deep and way back, moving the knife back through the neck toward himself, cutting the main neck artery. Her blood gushed and bubbled out on the ground in heaving floods. Some of it went on my boots. I wanted to run and cry and scream. But I just stood there, helping to hold her kicking.

It was all so quiet, like Christmas morning. As Papa continued to draw the pork, I held the feet firm and up. The ground beneath our feet was spotted with hot pig blood pumping out of her and steaming on the cold snow.

Between my ankles I could feel her body quiver in death. I had to look away. So as Papa worked on her, I held fast, staring at the old corn cratch that had once been Pinky's home.

Papa worked quiet and quick. The guts got drawed out and were there on the ground in a hot misty mass. Then we each put a hook in the jaws and dragged the body into boiling water. It was boiled, scraped free of all hair and scurf, and sawed in half.

Papa was breathing the way no man or beast should breathe. I had never seen any man work as fast. I knew his hands must of been just about froze off, but he kept working, with no gloves.

At last he stopped, pushing me away from the pork and turning me around so as my back was to it. He stood close by, facing me, and his whole body was steaming wet with work. I couldn't help it. I started thinking about Pinky. My sweet big clean white Pinky, who followed me all over. She was the only thing I ever really owned. The only thing I could point to and say . . . *mine.* But now there was no Pinky. Just a sopping red lake of slush. So I cried.

"Oh, Papa. My heart's broke."

"So is mine," said Papa. "But I'm happy you're a man."

I broke down, and Papa let me cry it all out. I sobbed and sobbed with my head up toward the sky and my eyes closed, hoping God would hear it.

"That's what being a man is all about, boy. It's just doing what's got to be done."

I felt his big hand touch my face, and it wasn't the hand that killed hogs. It was almost as sweet as Mama's. His hand was rough and cold, and as I opened my eyes to look at it, I could see that his knuckles were dripping with pig blood. It was the hand that just butchered Pinky. He did it. Because he had to. Hated to and had to. And he knew that he'd never have to say to me that he was sorry. His hand against my face, trying to wipe away my tears, said it all. His cruel pigsticking fist with its thick fingers so lightly on my cheek.

I couldn't help it. I took his hand to my mouth and held it against my lips. Pig blood and all. I kissed his hand again and again, with all its stink and fatty slime of dead pork. So he'd understand that I'd forgive him even if he killed me.

I was still holding his hand as he straighted up tall against the gray winter sky. He looked down at me and then he looked away. With his free arm he raked the sleeve of his coat across his eyes. It was the first time I ever seen him do it.

The only time.

EIGHT

Papa lived through the winter. He died in his sleep out in the barn on the third of May.

He was always up before I was. But when I went out to the barn that morning, all was still. He was lying on the straw bed that he rigged for himself, and I knew before I got to him that he was dead.

"Papa." I said his name just once. "It's all right. You can sleep this morning. No cause to rouse yourself. I'll do the chores. You just rest."

I fed and watered Solomon and Daisy. And milked her. Then I threw some grain to the hens, made sure they had water, and collected the eggs. One was still wet from laying. There was only seven eggs: five whites and two brown. I wiped off the specks and carried them up the hill to the cellar.

Then I went into the kitchen, where Mama and Aunt Carrie were already moving about. Now that I was thirteen I was taller than both of them. I put an arm around each one of them and held them close to me.

"Put my meal in a basket," I said. "I'm taking Solomon into town to see Mr. Wilcox. Papa won't be coming up for breakfast. Not this morning, and not ever again. I'll be back in about two hours, but first I'll stop and tell Matty and Hume."

"You go," Mama said. "Carrie and I will make do just fine. There's not time to tell your sisters. And scattered all over Vermont, they couldn't come."

"I'll write letters to them," I said. "Now about the funeral. Does he have any good clothes?"

"Yes," Mama said. "They been ready for some time, up in the camphor chest at the foot of . . . our bed."

"Mama, if you could get them out and be ready when Mr. Wilcox comes, it would be a help."

"They'll be," she said.

I kissed each one of them on the brow and went outside to yoke up the ox. I stopped Solomon at the front gate, went inside and got something (which I never did eat) tied up in a clean checkered napkin, and went into Learning.

I told Mr. Wilcox, who was a good Shaker man and who took care of our dead. After telling Cousin Matty and Hume, I came on home. I made just two more stops. To tell Mrs. Bascom and Ira, and to tell Mr. and Mrs. Tanner.

By the time I got home, Mr. Wilcox was already there. His bay gelding was just outside the barn, hitched to a small rig. Behind the driver's bench was a coffin. It was unpainted wood and there were no handles. It was a gift from the Circle of Shakers in Learning. Somewhere I'd find money to pay Mr. Wilcox. His fee would not be high as he was also the county coroner.

"People will be coming at noon, Mr. Wilcox," I said to him as he was preparing Papa.

"Everything will be ready, Robert."

"Thank you, sir."

I told Aunt Carrie and Mama about the time of the funeral. I knew they'd be ready, in their best and plainest.

"They won't be many coming," I said. "Maybe six and that's all."

"Rob," Mama said, "I'm glad we've got you to handle things. I couldn't of done it alone."

"Yes, you could, Mama. When you're the only one to do something, it always gets done."

I dug a grave in the family plot in our orchard. After that I hunted for a chore, something to do. The day before Papa died, we'd been mending a plowshare in the tack room. Now I worked on it a bit. And just about got it righted when the people come.

Before I walked out of the tack room, I noticed something I'd not took note of previous. Most of Papa's tools were dark with age, and their handles were a deep brown. But where Papa's hands had took a purchase on them, they were lighter in color. Almost a gold. The wear of his labor had made them smooth and shiny. I looked at all the handles of his tools. It was real beautiful the way they was gilded by work.

As I stood there, I had the hanker to reach out and touch them all. To hold them in my hands the same way he did, just to see if my hands were sized enough to take hold.

Under the tools I saw an old cigar box that was gray with dust. Inside was a worn-down pencil stub and a scrap of old paper. Unfolding the paper, I saw where Papa had been trying to write his name. One of the "Haven Pecks" was near to perfect, and he almost had the hang of it.

The paper was dry and brown, as if he had practiced for a long time. Carefully folding the paper back to just the way he had folded it, I rested it in its box and closed the lid.

Then I went inside to change clothes, as it was almost noon. As a young boy I'd had a black suit that Mama made me. But I always felt like a preacher in it. Besides, now it was way too small. And what Papa owned was too spare. So I just put on a new pair of work shoes that were tan, and a pair of Papa's old black trousers, which I turned up inside and stuck with pins. I wore one of his shirts with no necktie. I looked at myself in the mirror, to make sure I had the dignity to lead a family to a grave. I looked more like a clown than a mourner. The shirt didn't fit at all. And the tan work shoes just stuck out like I was almost barefoot. I ripped the shirt off and threw it on the floor. "Hear me, God," I said. "It's hell to be poor."

By noon they'd all come. Just after we got Papa dressed and his coffin into the house.

Cousin Matty and Hume were the first. Mrs. Bascom came with

Ira Long. Only her name was now Mrs. Long, legal and proper. In my mind she always was Mrs. Bascom. Mr. Tanner and his wife came in the black rig, with a pair of black horses. I went out to meet them.

"Thank you for coming, Mr. Tanner."

"Robert, my name is Benjamin Franklin Tanner. All my neighbors call me Ben. I think two men who are good friends ought to front name one another."

"And I'm Bess," his wife said, "from here on."

As the Tanners joined the others in the parlor, I looked up-road. A wagon was coming with May and Sebring Hillman. And from town came Jacob Henry and his folks. Last was Mr. Clay Sander, the man my father slaughtered for. Along with several of the men that Papa worked with. There would be no work on this day. A day no pigs would die.

I was glad they came. Some of them were dressed no better than I. But they came to help us plant Haven Peck into the earth. They'd come because they respected him and honored him. As I looked at all them, standing uneasy in our small parlor, I was happy for Papa. He wasn't rich. But by damn he wasn't poor. He always said he wasn't poor, but I'd figured he was just having fun with himself. He had a lot, Papa did.

The coffin was open and lying on the long table in the kitchen. It was the only place for it to be under our roof. Papa was a tall man. But he was not to be seen from the parlor, where all our friends gathered, and I was just as pleased. A man can't rest when he's looked at.

As eldest son it was my place to say words about my father. I didn't know what I was going to say. What I thought about Papa couldn't of been said. Being his son was like knowing a king. "Haven Peck," I said. "Devoted husband and father, a working farmer, and a good neighbor. Beloved by wife, four daughters, and one living son. We are all grateful to know him. And we ask only that his soul enter the Kingdom Hall, there to abide forever."

Mr. Wilcox had coached me a bit as to proper words, so I guess I did all right. We left the parlor and filed through the kitchen, to look at Papa for one last time. Lots of folks said "Amen" as they passed by.

We nailed down the lid of the raw wood box, then six men raised it up and walked with it out to the grave in the orchard. With lowering ropes they let it down into the ground onto two small cross boards, so that they could pull the two ropes out again. There was something in the Book of Shaker that it was unfit to bury the ropes with a coffin. Probably because rope was so dearly priced. It would be an earthy reason.

I had placed two shovels there at the open grave. As soon as the coffin was down, Ira Long and Sebring Hillman, two of the sturdiest, started to shovel the soil into the hole. The first shovelfuls had some Vermont rock in them, and the stones hit the wood like a drum. But then, as more and more dirt was added, it sounded softer and softer. When all the earth was finally replaced, they packed it down with the flat of their spades. There was no marker, no headstone. Nothing to say who it was or what he had done in his sixty years.

We all walked away then, Aunt Carrie and Mama on either side of me. They both looked and walked so proper, and I was proud to be between them. Mama's sweet face was so plain and so empty. What she missed most was not to be spoken of. We all would long for a different parcel of him.

"Rob," said Ben Tanner, as everyone took leave, "if Bess or me can lend a hand or help in any way, just ask."

"Thank you, Ben," I said. "You're a goodly neighbor."

"The way you said that," Ben said, "you sort of sounded like your father."

"I aim to, Ben."

Then they were gone. Mama and Aunt Carrie were busy in the house, scolding each other to keep from weeping. I changed into my work clothes and scraped a wood shim for the door of the milk house.

Solomon had a cut on his eye (I didn't know from what) and I treated it with boric best I could. I cleaned up the tack room and sharpened a scythe. I cut a fresh sassafras tree and prepared it so as I could boil it into a new bow for Solomon's yoke and bore a hole in both ends for the cotter pins.

At chore time I pailed Daisy. Fed, watered, cleaned, and put down fresh straw. Then I ate supper with Aunt Carrie and Mama. There wasn't much to eat except beans. And we'd lived on those all winter. Beans and pork. And none of it was easy to swallow.

After the supper dishes were washed and dry, I could see how tired Mama looked. Carrie, too. So I sent them upstairs to bed, each with a hot cup of tea.

As I knew I couldn't sleep, I put on my coat and walked outside. I took a look in on Daisy and Solomon, and they were both quiet as vespers. Both of them were getting old, and they liked being in the barn. Even on a nice spring night such as this.

Something brushed against my ankle. It was Miss Sarah, just to say hello. Before she went out on the meadow to hunt moles.

I don't know why I walked out toward the orchard. All the work there was done. But I guess I had to give a good-night to Papa and be alone with him.

The bugs were out, and their singing was all around me. Almost like a choir. I got to the fresh grave, all neatly mounded. Somewhere down under all that Vermont clay was my father, Haven Peck. Buried deep in the land he sweated so hard on and longed to own so much. And now it owned him.

"Good night, Papa," I said. "We had thirteen good years."

That was all I could say, so I just turned and walked away from a patch of grassless land.

Robert Newton Peck

Raised in the Shaker tradition, the author was taught to live and work in the Shaker way that endured even after the vitality of the sect had diminished. Its earthy commonsense was embodied in Haven Peck, who believed that a faith is more blessed when put to use than when put to word: "A man's worship counts for naught, unless his dog and cat are the better for it."

Robert Peck was born just across the lake from the setting of this novel. He knows Vermont well—he learned to love it first as a boy walking the stony farmlands with his father, later as a strapping young man logging the great fir trees.

But even as a boy his imagination craved something more than the austere farming life. He left home at seventeen and served as a machine gunner with the 88th Infantry Division for two years in Europe. After the war he went to college, where he channelled his love of story-telling into creative writing.

In the mid-1950s he started a career in advertising as a space salesman in New York City. A self-taught musician from childhood, he became adept at composing jingles. He has also published a number of songs. In 1962 he published his first book, a satire on the advertising business. His second book, *A Day No Pigs Would Die*, was written out of admiration for his father's teachings and as a tribute to his mother and aunt.

He is married now, and the Pecks live with their two children in rural Connecticut.

FLIGHT INTO DANGER. Original full-length version © Ronald Payne, John Garrod and Arthur Hailey 1958. British condensed version © The Reader's Digest Association Limited 1973.

HALIC: THE STORY OF A GREY SEAL. Original full-length version © Ewan Clarkson 1971. U.S. condensed version © The Reader's Digest Association, Inc. 1971. British condensed version © The Reader's Digest Association Limited 1973.

GREEN DARKNESS. Original full-length version © Anya Seton 1972. U.S. condensed version © The Reader's Digest Association, Inc. 1973. British condensed version © The Reader's Digest Association Limited 1973.

THE STRANGE FATE OF THE MORRO CASTLE. Original full-length version © Gordon Thomas and Max Morgan-Witts 1972. British condensed version © The Reader's Digest Association Limited 1973.

A DAY NO PIGS WOULD DIE. Original full-length version © Robert Newton Peck 1973. U.S. condensed version © The Reader's Digest Association, Inc. 1973. British condensed version © The Reader's Digest Association Limited 1973.

FLIGHT INTO DANGER. Reference material for title page illustration obtained by courtesy of Air Holdings Limited and Marshalls of Cambridge.
Photographs by Malcolm Aird by courtesy of DAN AIR.

THE STRANGE FATE OF THE MORRO CASTLE. Picture credits: Title page, pages 399, 461: UPI; pages 372/373, 380 (photograph), 439: The Mariners Museum; page 449, World Wide Photos.

© The Reader's Digest Association Limited 1973.
© The Reader's Digest Association South Africa (Pty) Limited 1973.

All rights reserved. No part of this publication may be reproduced, stored in a retrieval system, or transmitted in any form or by any means, electronic, mechanical, photocopying, recording or otherwise, without the prior permission of the copyright holders.

®"THE READER'S DIGEST" is a registered trade-mark of The Reader's Digest Association, Inc., of Pleasantville, New York, U.S.A.

SS.76